# The Earthrin Stones

Book 2 of 3

## Trials of Faith

(A novel set in the realm of Dhea Loral)

# Douglas Van Dyke Jr.

**The Earthrin Stones**

**Book 2 of 3**

**Trials of Faith**

©2021 by Douglas Van Dyke



Originally published 2006, 2015
This edition published through Ingram 2021

ISBN: 978-1-949060-08-9
Fiction: Fantasy – Epic, Action & Adventure


PUBLISHED BY Douglas Van Dyke Jr
Please Visit:
http://dhealoral.com
Retail Price: $20.00

I wish to thank all those who have supported my writing habit. I have been pleased to see the wonderful reviews, the pleasant remarks from local critics, the help from local bookstores, and the encouragement of readers. Your words and assistance have emboldened me put more focus into my writing. I must have been blessed to know such wonderful people, and I am grateful!

Like the adventurers in my book, I go forth on this personal quest knowing I have friends backing me up. You give me encouragement that no matter how dark the day is, or how rocky the road has been, or how long the distance to my goals seemed…I have people who are there to believe in me.

When the end of the quest is reached, I need only the personal satisfaction that I have traversed that twisted path and overcame my fears. At the end of that road, the treasure I find is given to others to enjoy. My stories are for you.

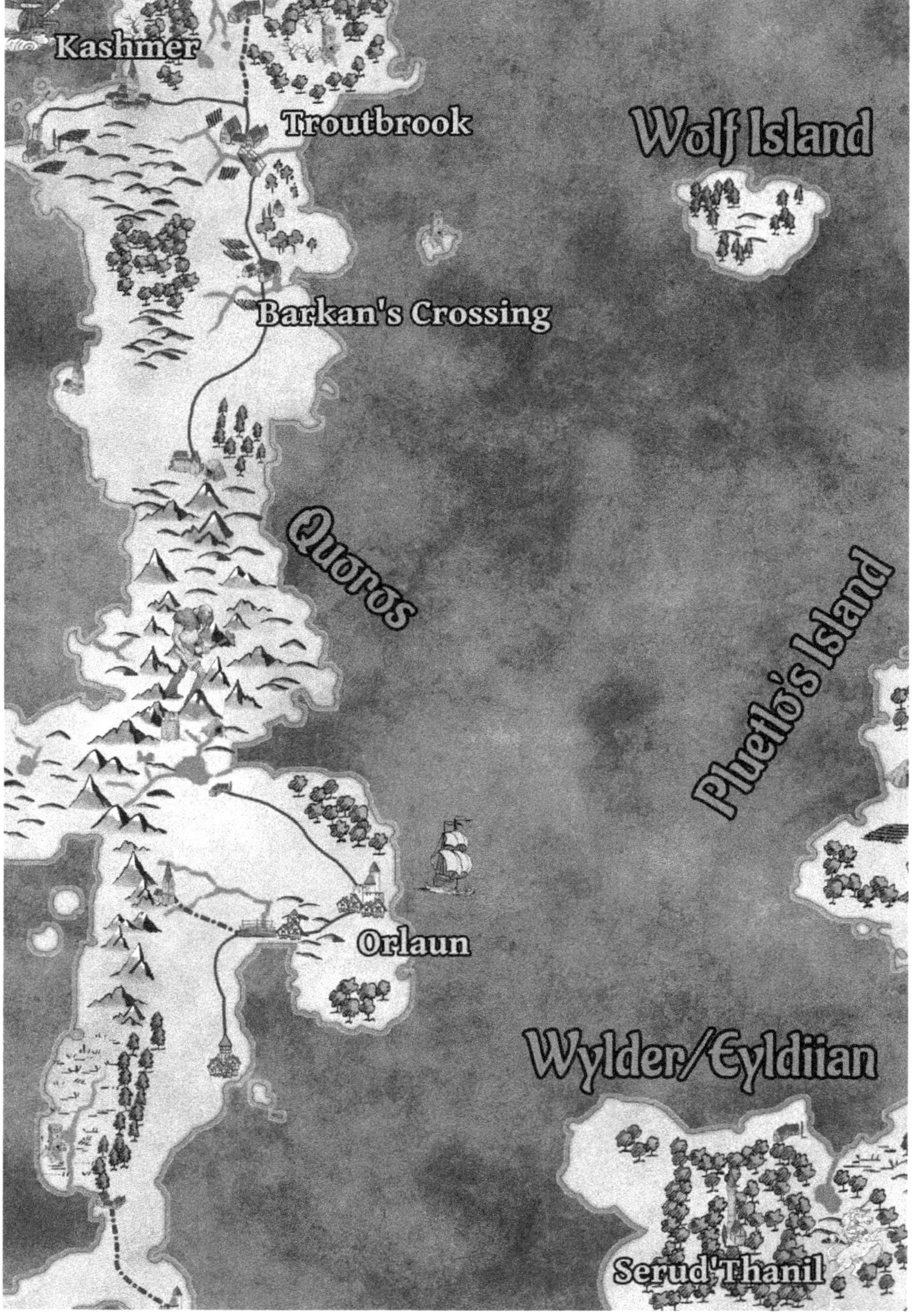

Kashmer
Troutbrook
Wolf Island
Barkan's Crossing
Quoros
Plueilo's Island
Orlaun
Wylder/Eyldiian
Serud'Thanil

## PROLOGUE

Dhea Loral observes a seemingly endless flow of time, as days and centuries are swallowed into the unreachable depths of history. The various cultures of the world set a standard of measurement to mark the time that passes. This standard started marking years upon the creation of the Covenant, for much of history prior to this event is lost or intentionally shrouded. The year is 1254 After Covenant. This represents the years it has taken for much of the civilizations to recover from the slaughter of the Godswars. An age of survival and restoration, spanning over a millennium, serves as a testament to the folly of the gods intervening too closely in mortal affairs. By their own decision, perhaps a bitter admission of their selfish guilt, the gods stepped away from the lands of the living. The Covenant, a binding agreement, bars all the gods from the world of humans, elves, and dwarves. This new arrangement left them with only mortal servants to carry out their will in the realm of Dhea Loral. Through their clerics and paladins, the greater powers work to influence the world on a much smaller scale than prior to the Godswars.

That does not mean all gods have quenched their ambitions, or forgotten old disputes during that conflict. Although one standard calendar marks the passage of time for the mortals of the realm, the rate at which time moves seems different depending on one's perspective.

The passage of the millennium amounted to a short span of time with respect to the patience of the gods. Now that the mortal races are growing and rebuilding their world, it is a time when the gods have started to exert more of their influence back into the realm. Already some are at work testing the boundaries of the Covenant, seeking ways to once again gain a bit of an advantage in their own affairs. Some would even dare to radically change the world if they could, though such events might lead to another cataclysmic Godswars.

Four years ago, an agent of the goddess DeLaris contributed to a theft of three holy relics of unknown origin. The magical stones proved to contain remarkable power, including the ability to summon defenders to protect the wielder. It was even surmised that they may have been weapons during the Godswars. Although the relics were recovered from the thieves, their true worth remains a mystery to most mortals. One relic returned to the small village of Troutbrook, where it continues to yield miracles which benefit the crops and the herds. The other two remain under the watchful eyes of a guild of mages. Unfortunately, the abbess of the Death Goddess and one of her able partners survived the final conflict despite losing possession of their ill-gotten prizes. Though defeated, they were never brought to justice. Their motives remain a mystery, and the threat still lingers.

For humans rebuilding their shattered world, the four intervening years can be a significant chapter in their eyes. In those four years, a young man can learn the lessons which put wisdom behind his eyes and develop maturity in his feelings and ideals. If they so choose, a human could marry and start a family in some quiet corner of the world where nightmares are seldom.

Four years are a small moment to a pair of goddesses whose plans have been set back. It is enough time for DeLaris and her hidden partner to change their tactics, as well as better prepare their followers to accomplish their goals. Their greatest problem is that their bid for power went noticed by other gods. Yestreal and Abriana have had a hand in halting their plot, and now these opponents have mortal followers standing ready to defend the relics. The struggle now intensifies as DeLaris and her ally must recruit a larger following before the others realize the extent of these gods' ambitions. Although careful planning and secrecy have failed, there are always other means to pursue a goal.

The span of four years can pass like a whisper in the day for one of mixed elven heritage. A number of memorable events happen over the course of four years, yet the span of time itself is a short one in the face of their long lives. A half-elf changes little in that time, although they watch as their human friends grow a bit older. If one graced with elven blood happens to love a human, then she has to endure watching the effects of time on the face of her companion. He is maturing now, but gray hair may come too soon. It is said that true love knows no bounds, yet for one of elven heritage the act of loving a human is to ask for the inevitable pain of watching them grow old and die, while her own youth endures. Though the knowledge tortures her heart, she can't resist the allure and pleasantry of his company over the last few years.

Regardless of how intelligent beings perceive the passage of years, the standard of measurement marking the march of time now dawns on Jherad the 2nd, of the year 1254 AC. Warm winds blow across the hills around Kashmer, heralding the summer season. A new chapter opens in the agendas of the gods, though such significance hides from the eyes of most mortals. It is this day that Katressa Bilil has been anxiously awaiting during the past few years. The half-elf woman has enjoyed too-few moments with the human male who lays claim to her heart. Despite their brief respites together, when they could entwine their arms in a loving embrace, he has been a busy young man with lessons to learn. His studies and training have kept him from her for the better part of four long years. Although that isn't generally a long time for the half-elf, it is certainly a sizeable span of time for a human.

Under the morning sun, Katressa rides her horse up the dirt path where the seminary waits. The memories of the first time her and Trestan rode up this path are still fresh in her mind. During that ride. Trestan gifted her the *Taef' Adorina* upon her brow. The elvish tiara sparkled with small charms signifying portions of their first adventure together. Trestan crafted it with the assistance of an elf wizard, and offered it to acknowledge her claim over his heart.

The adventuress normally favored black leathers. However, today her outfit matched the brightness of the radiant tiara. She was dressed in fine, colorful clothes for the special occasion of the day. Long had Trestan and Katressa looked forward to the opportunity to be together again. By every right Cat should have been overjoyed. Despite her other fears about the future of their relationship, this was the date she and Trestan had looked forward to since parting on this same hill four winters ago.

The adventuress crested the top of the seminary's hill. Decorations adorning the large keep, dedicated to worshipping the goddess Abriana, held witness to the significance of the day. Banners and pennants waved from the church spires, and many people gathered about the field outside to cheer on those who would be leaving this day. Among them would be the former smith from Troutbrook. Trestan would be ready to journey forth into the world to do Abriana's will.

Everyone anticipated a joyous occasion, including the half-elf garbed in her most expensive dress. Cat wouldn't have predicted anything casting a pall on this day. Yet, the news she now carried weighed heavily upon her heart. Her emerald green eyes worked hard to fight back any sorrowful tears from marring her beautiful face. In moments she would be with her lover, celebrating his big day alongside him. Sadly, at some point she would have to deliver the news that would shatter his good spirits.

"Trestan, my love, our special day has come," Cat whispered into the warm breeze as it blew through her long, black hair. "And yet, how can I ruin it by telling you of the tragedy at your home village?"

## **CHAPTER 1**      **"Embarking"**


Katressa Bilil urged her horse toward the seminary devoted to the goddess Abriana. A large cathedral bordered by many small buildings formed the holy ground. Although some of these buildings were stables and living quarters, there stood a number of buildings dedicated to meditation and higher learning. The field around the seminary displayed wooden props and roped arenas designed for a number of activities. The chosen followers of the Goddess of Love and Healing gathered about the grounds in a formal observance of this special occasion. All dressed in some of their best clothes, while sacred symbols of the goddess appeared in abundance as jewelry and decorated tabards. Styles of dress differed greatly. Elders sat garbed in robes of office, upon a platform in the center of the proceedings. Several seasoned warriors who championed the goddess wore suits of fine plate armor. A number of priests adorned in the mantles of the clerical faith stood around the field and offered their prayers to the acolytes who would be leaving this day. All about the property, several young men and women wore tabards signifying them as new pupils. Many others, likely cooks, stable boys and other hired hands, watched from various places wearing their own good outfits.

Trestan called this day the "Embarking": the official church name for the ceremonies which marked the graduation of the young disciples. After four long years of study, he would finally be able to leave the seminary and journey the world with her again. Others would be leaving this day as well, and likely they had visitors waiting to take them home.

Cat's elegant outfit outshone many others. Her bright, silvery dress glistened from the sparkle of small gems. The *Taef' Adorina* sat upon her head. The golden tiara, set with charms and woven in elvish patterns, had been a present from Trestan signifying his love. Cat adored this special and rare gift. The half-elf had the sharp facial angles of her elvish heritage. Her long, raven hair, braided through the tiara, bounced about her back like waves of rolling black silk. The pointed tips of her ears peeked out from her tresses. Her emerald green eyes searched the crowds below for the one she loved. Her fine points were in her style and agility. Athletic and slight of build, she rode so smoothly that she appeared to gracefully fly down to the seminary grounds despite the bounce of her horse. Although Cat looked the part of a bejeweled lady of high standing this day, she grew up on the hard road of an adventurer. She wore no visible weapons upon her body, although she always managed to have some hidden about her dress in case an occasion required it. The sun reflected sparkles off the silvery rapier with the cat's-head pommel, strapped to her saddle. For this occasion, Cat rode in style to greet her champion and take him home.

She arrived without much time to spare before the beginning of the ceremony. The promising young acolytes were not yet assembled before their elders. Cat barely had time to hand the care of her horse over to a stable boy before a fanfare of trumpets blared. The half-elf slipped through the crowd until she had a good vantage point from which to observe the platform. At the end of the trumpeted fanfare, the main doors of the cathedral swung open. An assembly of young men and women emerged out from the hallowed silence of the sanctuary. The senior acolytes marched with heads high. They looked ready to leave the seminary and begin their life of service to Abriana. Cat could understand why they called it the "Embarking". The young men and women had trained hard, but now they would venture into the world as missionaries of their goddess. Cat looked over the assembly as it marched closer to the platform. An elder led the student procession, speaking prayers in a loud voice as he walked. Other members of the seminary walked alongside the formation, swinging small pots that gave off the smoke of incense. The students wore red and gold tabards: the colors of Abriana. However, they varied in the rest of their attire depending on their choice of service. Some wore armor, while others who sought to serve the goddess in more peaceful ways had clad themselves in light robes.

Trestan marched along in armor. Cat spotted him among the senior acolytes and smiled with pride. He still seemed the same wonderful person Cat had known from their first adventure years ago, but the four years changed his appearance. He had grown out of any remainder of his adolescence into a mature bearing. Still only a young twenty-three years old, his eyes held new wisdom. Trestan studied and learned much in these past years at the seminary. Even before his arrival at the seminary, he dealt with many pivotal changes in his life: the loss of a dear friend, the full acceptance of a religion to guide his future, a curious wanderlust, and even the selfless sacrifice by which he risked his own life to help others. Even Trestan's dark-brown mustache was no longer the scraggly growth of his teen years. It developed into a thicker, manly fashion, though he still kept his face shaved clean of any beard growth. The years etched only a few, subtle lines on Trestan's face. They showed that his face smiled often, for Trestan had grown happy despite the rigorous training at the seminary. The young man served as a smith, so it was no surprise he still had strong arm muscles. After all the hard work here, the rest of his muscles had caught up. Cat admired his strong legs as one of his finest features. His fingers still had a bit of black soot embedded in them. Trestan's hands bore calluses from hard work. His skin stayed tanned from being out in the sun a lot.

Cat caught Trestan's eye and he bestowed a big, warm smile for her. Ever so briefly, he moved his lips to blow her a kiss even as he marched toward the elders. Cat's eyes drifted over his attire as he moved into position with his fellow graduates. Trestan's armor reflected his calling as a paladin in the service of Abriana. Paladins existed as religious warriors, guided by a higher purpose than the average soldier. While the goddess promoted the ideals of Healing, Love and other peaceful endeavors, she also promoted her followers to protect what they love. Trestan followed in the footsteps of his departed mentor Sir Wilhelm Jareth. The paladin originally taught him the sword as well as opened his eye to other philosophical beliefs. Trestan's armor was not as heavy as the plate pieces that some others wore. The young man devoted time at the forge constructing his own armor. Made mostly of leather and chain, some steel metal plates covered important areas. The only piece not handcrafted by him was the helm he had worn on his first adventure. It still bore a scratch from a scimitar strike which had nearly taken Trestan's eye.

Unlike many paladins, Trestan's method of swordplay accentuated a lot of graceful and agile movements which would be hampered by heavier armor. Upon his back rested the magical elven sword inherited from Sir Wilhelm. The Sword of the Spirit sat in its scabbard, but the hilt still glistened in the reflections of the sun. Trestan carried a spare weapon that had also been created by his hands at the seminary's forge. Probably chosen due to his many years of swinging a hammer at a smithy, he created a warhammer which hung from a loop on his belt. Cat had been amused the first time she'd been able to get a look at it. He had forged the head of the hammer in the shape akin to a bull's head. The significance of it seemed to stem from his narrow victory in defeating a monstrous minotaur, (a half-bull abomination), alone during that adventure years ago.

His faith governed the rest of Trestan's ensemble. His garments, those portions which could be seen despite the armor, displayed the red and gold that Abriana favored. A new symbol adorned his armor. A sigil called the coraross symbolized Abriana's faith. The symbol represented the two sides of her sphere of influence. The first portion resembled a cross, except that the center contained a circular hole in which the perpendicular ends never met. The four limbs represented the elements, (earth, fire, water, air), yet the circular hole in the center identified the fifth element: the spirit. This portion of the coraross identified Abriana's nature of healing the living. Connected to the spiritual cross on one side clung a half-heart shape that symbolized Abriana's love. It was said that after Abriana became the first sentience to feel love, she gave half her heart so that love would flourish in the souls of the mortals. Thus, Trestan and followers of Abriana displayed the coraross on their vestments or jewelry.

Cat watched as the senior acolytes stood before the platform of elders. She could remember a time when Trestan questioned how a person could give up their life in sacrifice by dedicating their years in service to a god. Trestan came to the realization that to follow Abriana was to uphold his own convictions and beliefs. He stood ready to serve a goddess that would in turn serve him in this world.

It was a beautiful day for the Embarking to take place. The only taint was the burden of the news Cat carried from his home. She had ridden from the southern reaches of the Kashmer Protectorate to arrive at the seminary. Along the way, a shock awaited her in Trestan's hometown of Troutbrook. Their joyous occasion would be spoiled when the young man learned of the tragedy on those streets.

One of the elders on the platform stepped forth. He introduced himself as Cardinal Alunetar Gracegiver. Cat noted in the past that several teachers and clerics of the seminary declared last names that seemed self-appointed. As the elder began to give his speech, Cat found it hard focusing on the words. Her mind drifted to the scenery, from the pennants flapping in the breeze, to the colored dress of the attendant worshippers of Abriana, and often to the young man that she loved. Trestan had all of his attention on the speaker.

At some point in the speech, the speaker mentioned something that jerked Cat's attention back to his words. "…those who succeed will immediately leave upon their Embarking to begin your services to Abriana in whatever capacity you choose. Those who fail today's tests will remain for another four months before being tested again. Pray to her for guidance, for there are always those who fail, and must remain behind…"

The words struck worry into the depths of Katressa's heart. Those who fail today's tests? Another four months? Uncertainty began to seep into her mind. Shouldn't this be the day her and her beloved could ride away and finally be together again? If Trestan failed, how would he react when he heard about his hometown? Cat became upset with the notion that Trestan might not be leaving today. Had she misunderstood something he said? Cat listened to the words of the elder, and her fears came to be realized. She began to understand why the field around the seminary seemed to be set up for a number of events. The senior acolytes would have to undergo a number of challenges this day. If they failed, they would be kept in the seminary for another four months of training, only to take the same challenges again during the colder month of Tiquierum.

As Cat pondered, the elder brought his speech to a close. "Go now to your visitors or sit and meditate on the virtues of the goddess. In a few moments, we will start announcing names and having Abriana's young chosen called to the various challenges that await them."

Trestan walked toward Katressa as the acolytes dispersed into the crowd of onlookers. For his sake, she put her fears and worries into the back of her mind. Cat forced a smile, one of her most alluring features, as Trestan came near. It had been a long enough time since they had last met and embraced; both looked forward to the reunion. Trestan came up to her with a formal and respective greeting.

He took her right hand in his, "It is the finest day I could ask for, when both my goddess and my beloved shine their smiles upon me." Trestan bowed and kissed her offered hand.

Now that a formal greeting was finished, Trestan suddenly threw his arms around her in a warm hug. Cat giggled at the attention as they embraced and she found her lips trapped by his. The next minute mixed in a flurry of kisses, hugs, and "I missed you", repeated over and over. Cat didn't know if she could get used to kissing around his mustache, but at the same time she would miss it if it wasn't there. The two remained lost in their own world as they embraced.

In the background, shouts brought Cat back to the purpose of the occasion. The elders read the names of the senior acolytes and assigned them to various areas of the field to face their challenges. The two reunited companions enjoyed their embrace even as Cat tilted her head back to look Trestan in the eyes. His big, brown eyes reflected his joy at seeing her. She wanted to take him away from the seminary, make love to him, and enjoy life together. Cat tried to forget the repercussions of such a union. The half-elf would likely outlive Trestan for many years, and have to endure him growing old before her eyes. The uncertain pace of time worried Cat, but she still loved Trestan. Her worries made every year, month and day even more precious. She hoped she would be taking him away from the seminary, and didn't like the implications that Trestan might have to stay longer.

"My love," Cat spoke. A slight firmness in her tone accompanied her words. "What did the elder say regarding tests and challenges and the price of failing them? Is there a chance you might be called to stay here longer?"

Trestan frowned, realizing he must not have explained all the ceremony in enough detail the last time he saw her. "We have to pass some final challenges in order to graduate and be able to leave the seminary. I wouldn't worry about it much; it's more of a formality. I'm sorry I didn't explain it well before."

Cat inquired, "Just a formality?"

The young man dropped his gaze, "Well, it is possible that they may keep me here longer…if I fail the tests. Actually, I do have a few classmates taking the challenges today because they failed at the last attempt months ago."

Cat's shoulders sagged, her spirits falling at those words. His eyes seemed to take notice. Cat assumed Trestan interpreted it to be her sadness and disappointment that there was a chance they might not actually be together at last. She had waited long enough for him to be free of these walls, only to hear that she might have to wait longer. He could not know there were more pressing things that disturbed her. His father needed him at this time, as there had been much suffering back at his home. Cat wanted to tell Trestan the bad news and get it out in the open. The temptation almost spilled from her tongue…but Cat stopped herself. Much as Trestan needed to return home, the last thing she should do was hit him with that awful news when his focus needed to be on the challenges of the day. If distractions caused Trestan to fail, he would not be allowed to go home honorably. How would Trestan react to her news if he had to stay another four months, into the fringes of the cold weather preceding winter? Cat knew Trestan simply had to win the challenges today.

Trestan ran his fingers lightly through her long hair, offering a gentle, comforting caress. He consoled her, offering words to her unspoken thoughts, "Don't you worry. I will succeed today. I have worked very hard for this day, and would not want to be separated from you any longer."

Cat didn't feel like smiling, but she did. The news from home would have to wait for later, lest Trestan's concentration be shaken. Instead, she donned on a supportive attitude. Her experience as an infiltrator served her in deflecting his thoughts. "Put your faith in your chosen path, Trestan. Be sure to pray for guidance, as that is essential if you are going to become a paladin. I know you can do it, and I'll be with you here as you go through the challenges. Don't be distracted by anything. Keep your mind on the tasks at hand."

A voice called out from the platform. "Senior Acolyte Trestan, report to the riding lane for the rings challenge."

*          *          *          *          *

The students studying Abriana at the seminary pursued different callings. Their final challenges reflected their chosen future in her service. Those who chose roles of clerics and preachers were given challenges that tested their wisdom, intellect and knowledge on various philosophical and arcane issues. Those who were following the path to be paladins, (such as Trestan), were given challenges in combat, discipline and martial prowess, as well as fewer tests of knowledge and wisdom.

Trestan's first test aimed for martial ability. A number of rings hung from bars along the length of a jousting field. There were three rings total, starting large and ending small. Trestan was to gallop past each and skewer them on a long spear. A number of other acolytes and a few ordained paladins stood along the lane to offer encouragement.

Trestan led a horse to the starting end of the field. During his stay at the seminary, he'd had the chance to work with several mounts. A dark, brown warhorse named Belgard served as his favorite steed. Aside from the horse's left rear leg, the rest of the legs were white below the knee. A white stripe ran above its nose, ending in an upward-turned crescent moon shape above the eyes. Tall and muscular, the mount could serve any warrior well. The warhorse stood tall and proud as Trestan double checked the straps and saddle. Trestan had spent many months becoming familiar with this horse's habits. Belgard twitched his ears and listened as its rider spoke soothing words. Both Trestan and his mount readied to face the challenge.

Cat drifted close to the riding lane to watch. As Trestan continued to get ready, the half-elf caught the attention of one of the other senior acolytes nearby. "Excuse me, good sir, my name is Katressa Bilil. Pardon my interruption, but I was hoping you can answer a question."

The senior acolyte turned to her with a smile. She had noticed him eagerly coming up to watch the ring challenge after succeeding at his own task a moment ago. The young man had correctly answered some philosophical question posed by the elders, though his armor indicated his candidacy to becoming a paladin. The young man displayed no beard or mustache, unlike many of the other aspiring paladins. He did have long blonde hair tied into a ponytail behind his head.

He bowed gracefully to her and responded, "It would be an honor to serve, milady. I am Senior Acolyte Leander. How may I be of assistance?"

Cat indicated Trestan as he hoisted himself into the saddle. "I came to watch my beloved, but dismayed to hear about the required challenges. I must ask: how many rings must Trestan take to win this challenge?"

The golden-haired student of Abriana gestured toward the field. "He needs to take only two of the three. I know Trestan, and he would not be satisfied unless he takes all three. With all his practice, it would only be a challenge if they blindfolded him."

Cat watched as Trestan shifted to get comfortable in the saddle. It occurred to her, there was more she should ask while she had the chance. "Even if he passes this one, how many challenges are there? How many does he need to pass in order to go home today?"

Leander replied with a gentlemanly smile, "There are twelve tests, which mix combat prowess with knowledge of scripture and arcanum, as well as the ability to call forth the goddess' miracles. If an acolyte fails two challenges, then their tenure at the seminary is not yet over. They will have to remain and study for several more months."

Cat could not keep a smile on her face at the thought of Trestan not being able to leave. Leander attempted to reassure her. "Fear not. Trestan is very capable, and the goddess shines on him. If for some reason he fails, it is only because she wills it for the greater common goal. Try not to worry much about him; he is a fine student."

Cat could not be inwardly calmed by his words, not when it came to the importance of Trestan finishing his lessons and going home. She stayed silent, along with the rest of the crowd, as Trestan stood still and ready in the saddle on Belgard. He pointed his long spear at the sky in silent salute as he focused on the dirt path before him. Midway down the lane, an ordained paladin held aloft a red and gold banner of Abriana, displaying her coraross. Encouraging words from the onlookers died out as silence reigned. A blanket of quiet settled around the field. One of the elders motioned with his hand, and the paladin with the banner responded by dropping the flag down in a circular motion. At the sight of the falling fabric, the sound of the flag snapping in the air, Trestan put Belgard into motion.

The young man yelled out as he began his first challenge of the day. "For Abriana and those that I love!"

Belgard lowered his head as his tensed muscles sprang into motion. Steel-shod hooves pounded the soft ground as the beast of war lunged forward. As the first ring challenge of the day, Belgard's pounding strides kicked up dirt clods from a freshly raked field. Cat's heart quickened along with the accelerating hoof beats. Trestan had his notched chin visor down, but it did not obstruct the goal from his eyes. Carried along on the back of the powerful warhorse, he gracefully lowered the spear into position. The former apprentice smith of a small village sped at the first ring, dressed in good armor of his own craft and guided by a religion that championed his ideals. His focus narrowed on that first large ring as the sharp tip of the spear lined up for it.

CHING!

The spear pierced through the hole of the ring as Trestan and his mount galloped past it. Cat smiled as the first goal slid down the length of the spear to rest against Trestan's gloved hand. The first large ring trailed ribbons of red and gold as the warrior-in-training continued on to the second ring. Smaller than the first, it would naturally be a harder target on the back of a charging horse. Trestan never took his eyes off of it as every pounding step from Belgard thrust him down the lane.

Trestan stabbed the spear tip at the right moment. The shaft of the weapon penetrated the ring of iron, taking the second necessary ring he needed. The middle ring slid down the length of the shaft to rest beside the first conquered ring. Cat could have yelled out in glee at that moment, but most were holding their silence as Trestan made the effort for the final, smallest ring.

Belgard's hooves threw up a cloud of dust and dirt as it charged down to the end of the lane. Some bystanders were already clapping at Trestan's victory at the challenge. The young warrior paid them no heed as he judged the distance and angle to the final ring. Belgard's strides thundered along, but Trestan glided like a hawk along the wind to his prey.

Cat saw the tip point out at the final ring, but the cloud of dust obscured her vision at the critical moment. For Trestan's sake, she wanted him to come away with all three rings. Out of the blowing dust, Belgard and his rider appeared as they slowed. The senior acolyte wheeled his mount around at the end of the lane and held his spear high. The third ring lay skewered and rested with its brothers on his spear. The crowd cheered at the young warrior. Trestan tilted his head back to the sky, probably voicing another prayer to his goddess at the completion of this first victory.

The elder supervising the test approached Trestan and made a hand sign that was part of a blessing. "Abriana watches over you this day, my brother."

The ritual words were spoken at the successful completion of every test. Trestan handed the spear and rings to others who would set up for the next acolyte's run. Afterward, Cat's chosen champion rode back to her with a smile.

*       *       *       *       *

The next event became decidedly more terrifying for Cat to witness. The half-elf noted an area akin to an arena, surrounded by spectators leaning over a low wall to watch something below. Trestan stood beside Cat, though the young man remained rather silent.

This was understandable, as Trestan had his mind focused on the importance of the tests this day. Cat did her best to relax him with comforting words and soft, gentle massaging touches. In the midst of talking to him, she decided to ask about the partially concealed arena.

"My champion," Cat smiled, "What lies beyond those people there? It seems as if they are looking into a sunken arena of sorts."

Trestan cast a worried glance toward the gathering. He had not yet mentioned this particular challenge to Cat. It was one of the most dangerous challenges that any follower of Abriana faced. Acolytes knew of the seriousness and danger of this test early in their tenure. They accepted it as a necessary trial in order to become one of Abriana's chosen. No acolyte could refuse to undertake this test. They were allowed to fail when attempting it, but not to waive their participation without facing it. This challenge tested the core of their faith. It confronted their ability to channel the miraculous powers of their goddess in the face of danger.

Trestan looked over to Cat's eyes and explained, "It is indeed an arena, sunken into the ground and with high fences around the perimeter. It is part of a challenge that every acolyte must take this day, whether their pursuits are martial or academic, for it tests our faith."

Trestan hesitated. One hand came up as he stroked and smoothed his mustache in silent thought. Cat watched him slide his fingers along his mustache. She knew it was a habit of his whenever he deeply considered something. He caught her gaze, dropped his hand, and tried to give her a reassuring smile.

"Cat, I'll show you what's over there but try to not be afraid. Even as I ask that, I know you will be bound to worry about me."

Now Cat was nervous, more by the fact that Trestan told her not to be afraid than for whatever challenge lay inside that arena. As he guided her to the ring of spectators, he started to explain the challenge. "This is the challenge of the beast. Abriana's love extends not only between the races, but also to the creatures of the lands. Many times, animals of the wilds may attack men, but usually they have their own good reasons. They may be defending their family or property. In this test, a chosen of Abriana must face a wild beast, calm it, and then set it free."

The two of them arrived at the side of the arena fence, allowing Cat to look down into the space below. The arena had an entry on the far side by which the acolytes entered and exited. There was not much room inside the pit itself. Another entry to the arena led from some animal pens nearby. It discomforted Cat to hear the sounds of animal growls and snarls coming from the tunnel to the pens. Several clerics of Abriana circled the top fence, as well as a couple patrolled near the entry points, yet there was little room inside the sunken area for comfort or mobility. Even as Cat and Trestan watched, another senior acolyte entered the arena to begin her test. The woman had short, curly brown hair. She wore some armor made of hardened leather, and yet carried no weapon. It seemed the woman had nothing but faith to protect her from the caged animal that would be introduced into the arena.

"That is Rhijin," Trestan pointed to the young woman. "She is endeavoring to follow the call of a cleric. She bears nay weapons; nor will any of us on this test. It is not about defending yourself with weapons and armor. The challenge is one of faith and channeling of miracles."

Cat shook her head, lips curling in distaste. "I am opposed to this, Trestan. This display actually shocks me. They have enraged animals locked in cages here? And they set them loose in an arena with a lone student? That doesn't sound like the tenets of your goddess to me."

Trestan nodded. "It may sound strange that clerics under such a benevolent goddess would have angry animals in cages. Yet, we did not put them there. They went in on their own."

Cat turned a puzzled look toward the young man. Trestan explained, "Remember that a goddess is at work here. The rationalization is that if one of her faithful were to encounter this situation in the wild lands, would they find out only then whether they could succeed at such a challenge? What value would you put on a cleric if they are unable to channel the will of their patron when it is needed? There may be a life on the line when a faithful has to use this miracle someday, so it becomes one of the challenges here."

She listened as he spoke. The way the young man calmly described it, he seemed different from the days when he swung a hammer at the village smithy. Yet here this same man was now much more knowledgeable about many things. While their earlier years felt like Cat had many things to teach and offer to him, lately he seemed to be showing her a lot of new ideas and concepts.

"Last evening, as they have been doing every evening preceding an 'Embarking' in the hundreds of years this seminary has stood, the instructors left the gates wide open. By morning, as has happened every such morning, the pens were found locked and filled with angry beasts. This was the will of the goddess to test her proclaimed faithful, but not just for us."

The young acolyte Rhijin stood waiting to test her goddess-given miracles on whatever beast awaited her. The elders had selected one, and its growls were heard moving from the pens toward the sunken arena. Trestan caught Rhijin's eye during his explanation to Cat. As he continued to talk to Cat, he offered the acolyte some comfort by performing a motion with his arms. Trestan hugged himself as he bowed his head to her. Among the followers of Abriana, the motion conveyed, "May the goddess keep you in her arms and watch over you." Rhijin smiled in return, and then switched her attention to the gate that would admit the beast.

"As I was saying," Trestan continued, "The creatures enter the pens under the influence of the goddess in the middle of the night. They each have some secret torment that pains and enrages them. They enter the arena below to stand face to face with a senior acolyte who attempts to turn their emotions around. If successful, the beast will not attack. It will be calmed by the acolyte, then led back into the wilds by the same acolyte to run free again. In effect, this display benefits them also. The test cures the pains of the animal."

Cat waited for Trestan to add more. Obviously, Trestan hadn't answered all her questions. She reached out and held one of his hands, "But, the acolytes don't always succeed, do they? What happens when they fail?"

12

As they spoke, Rhijin's chosen animal emerged from the dark tunnel to the pens. It was hard to see it at first, for the hunting cat that appeared was as black as the darkest panther. The creature slowly and cautiously allowed its heavy, muscular frame to appear in the light of the arena. It growled at the young woman. Whatever secret pains haunted its mind, the terrible visions urged a violent release upon the fragile human that stood nearby. Rhijin's eyes went wide and her hands twitched, but she did her best to keep her composure. The wrelcat facing her was no ordinary hunting cat. Although it looked very much like a black panther, wrelcats were known by the pair of long, sharp horns jutting forward from their shoulder blades. The horns extended to a point just beyond the reach of the cat's sharp teeth, and their purpose was to gore an enemy after the cat charged it. Common folk whispered stories of their violent nature and fearsome attacks.

Trestan patted Cat's hand comfortingly as he edged closer to her. "If the acolyte fails, then the creature likely will attack." Trestan felt the half-elf's small hand increase the grip on his hand. "Don't be overly worried, Cat. Look how many priests are standing about the arena. The moment a creature pounces, they use miracles to restrain it and then they take over the acolyte's job of easing the creature's pain. Sometimes the acolyte is wounded, but none have ever been seriously injured. Any injuries are attended right away by one of the other healers present. The clerics of Abriana can completely heal wounds within a short time, so that the acolyte is refreshed enough to continue the rest of their challenges."

It wasn't easy for Katressa to relax at his words. She looked into his brown eyes and saw his hidden thoughts. Trestan tried to cover his own nervousness, and yet he seemed ready and determined to face this challenge. When she looked into his eyes, she remembered how many challenges Trestan overcame during their first adventure together. The young man had been willing to risk his life several times for the good of his friends and his home village. Trestan had even faced off with a minotaur, nearly dying in the struggle but nevertheless willing to endure the punishment it threatened in order to win the day. Trestan put a lot of faith into his path, and usually that was enough for Cat to trust him.

It was hard to keep that trust a moment later, when they heard a loud growl coming from the arena. Rhijin failed to calm the beast, and the wrelcat's response came swiftly. The senior acolyte of Abriana, seeing the creature pounce, screamed as her body attempted to get out of the way. The crowd gave a collective gasp as they witnessed the attack.

**CHAPTER 2**    **"Trestan's Challenges"**


Almost as quickly as the situation erupted, it watchers brought it to a swift end. The clerics around the arena spoke hurried prayers in unison. The wrelcat froze where it landed. One of the elders forced into its mind, calming the beast through a miracle. The creature suddenly lacked all desire or ability to attack its prey. Rhijin lay to the side of the black feline, breathing heavily after her close call. One of the wrelcat's sharp horns hovered inches above, having barely missed her. She trembled slightly as she looked with wide eyes at the muscular beast. Even frozen in place, it held an aggressive posture. Another elder approached and helped her to her feet, leading her away from the arena. Trestan watched the scene as the drama ended, aware that Cat held one hand over her mouth. The half-elf had witnessed grisly scenes before, but her mind's concern was on what might happen to Trestan.

They overheard the elder speaking to Rhijin. The young woman hung her head as he spoke, unwilling to allow others to see the emotions on her face. "You have failed, sister, but this is only your first of the day. Look to Abriana's words and dwell not on this incident until later."

Cat decided it was best to observe some other event while they awaited Trestan's name to be called again. She pulled at his hand. "Come show me anything else, something less worrisome. I have a lot of faith in you, Trestan, but I would rather not think about you facing that kind of situation."

They had not gone far when they heard someone call his name. An elder behind them raised his voice, "Senior Acolyte Trestan, report to the arena for the challenge of the beast."

Trestan let loose a sigh as Cat's worried eyes looked up at his. "My turn."


   *    *    *    *    *


The gate opened, allowing Trestan to stride into the arena appearing more confident than he actually felt. He continued to silently pray to Abriana. From the inside of the pit, he had to admit that the arena looked even smaller than when viewed from the stands. He took up a stance where Rhijin positioned earlier. On the sand floor, he absently noticed the other footprints of previous acolytes, as well as the paw prints of the large wrelcat. The young man stood in that open space without his weapons, though he still wore armor. Across the short pit he stared into the darkness of the beasts' entry. His eyes lingered there only for a moment. He resolved to not lose his gaze in the blackness of that portal. To stare and worry about what animal would come forth would only shake his concentration. Trestan glanced around for another image to strengthen his resolve.

Above the arena, watching over him, he saw his lovely lady. Cat kept the fear from her face, beaming reassurance just by her very presence. The *Taef' Adorina* upon her brow winked sparkles at him in the daylight. Next to her stood Leander, who awaited his own turn at this trial. He had been a friend of Trestan's since the young man started schooling at the seminary. It also comforted Trestan when Rhijin came to stand beside them. The young, curly-haired woman probably still had her ordeal running through her mind. She stood there despite that failure, offering Trestan the same hug and head bow he had offered her.

It conveyed the silent message. "May the goddess keep you in her arms and watch over you."

As much as Trestan wanted to go home with Cat this day, he realized he would lose this or another challenge if his thoughts focused in the outcome rather than his lessons. He had to prove his loyalty and faith in Abriana. In a moment, a beast would come forth that would seem threatening and fierce. Despite the danger, Abriana gave him a task to fulfil. Find the beast's pain, discover the center of its anguish, comfort it, and set it free again. He had to think not for himself, but for the benefit of this fearsome creature. That was the requirements of one who follows the Goddess of Love and Healing.

At this thought, a shape took form out of the dark entry across from him. A menacing growl barely preceded the appearance of a snarling set of sharp teeth. One clawed foot set down inside the arena, soon followed by another as the animal emerged. Its brown snout sniffed at the lone human as it stepped into the arena. Trestan stayed calm despite staring into the eyes of the bear. The ursine form shuffled slowly into the light, casting a shadow that reflected the few hundred pounds difference between it and Trestan. The hefty appearance alone was not enough to unnerve him. The young man had once faced one-on-one against an eight-foot, half-ton minotaur and survived the encounter. The onlookers were more than a bit nervous as the bear let forth another challenging growl.

Trestan delved into his faith. He looked at the bear not as a menace, but as a victim suffering in pain over something. Trestan reached out to the beast with one of the miraculous powers granted to him by Abriana. In his mind, he saw the bear's sadness over a hurtful loss of some kind. The bear slowed its advance as it felt a presence in its mind, seeking its pain. Trestan sifted through a wall of the bear's inner turmoil to sort what type of loss had spurred it to anger.

The image came to Trestan.

The bear was a female, mother of two small cubs. The acolyte of Abriana saw in its mind the images of it herding the two cubs into the cover of the woods. The cubs entered the relative safety of the trees, while the mother bear looked back at its mate. The male bear stood on its back legs and threatened the approach of three humans. The mother also began to move and threaten the small creatures for their presence so near to the cubs, when something frightening and unexplainable happened. One of the humans raised a hand and started speaking. The bear could not understand the nature of its language, but as the words ended, a release of energy came from the hand of that one small creature. It resembled a lightning bolt. The CRACK of light struck her mate in the chest. He let loose a pitiful wail before crashing down. This frightened the female bear beyond the point of reason. It fled into the trees. By the time it emerged later, after leaving the cubs in their den, something else rested in the spot where her mate had been struck. A pile of bone and flesh, and it smelled like her mate, but something was different. His fur had been scraped off and taken by the humans. They left a scent trail, and the female bear followed it with a heart heavy from its loss. Those feelings transferred into anger the more she walked. The bear wanted the blood of the humans on its claws.

For some unexplained reason, the bear felt a calling on a different course. It walked into this arena, and into a cage…trapped there until the sun came up. It was ready to take its rage out on the first target that presented itself. It now stared angrily at Trestan, while at the same time he experienced its tale as if living through the events.

Trestan spoke to the bear, communicating through a mental link granted by his goddess' miracle. The crowd could not hear the conversation. He tried to give comfort to the bear for its loss, turning its attention by reminding it of the cubs left abandoned back at its den. The bear grew worried for its litter. When it responded to Trestan, through emotions conveyed via the miracle, it spoke more from the pain of loss rather than the blindness of anger. Trestan shared with the bear his own memories and loss. He relived the night that his mentor Sir Wilhelm was struck down by the elvish wizard Revwar. The bear offered him a question after it saw the images. The question lacked words or sound, but conveyed through feelings. Trestan understood it all the same. The acolyte answered to the bear that although he lived to see the wizard fall with a terrible wound, that moment never comforted his loss. Trestan's pain eased only when he contributed to the good of his village by rescuing its kidnapped noble, and returning the holy relic which gave life and prosperity back to the village. His efforts followed a constructive path, their fulfillment caused the pain of his loss to subside. Trestan urged the bear to turn its energy to something positive by raising its cubs on its own. He would like to see the cubs grow as big and tall as their father.

Cat, Rhijin, Leander, and the other onlookers looked on with uncertainty when the bear slowly walked over to Trestan. No one could hear or experience the exchange between the paladin-aspirant and the entrapped bear. They saw the surprise results when the bear approached him and nuzzled him gently. It displayed concern for his own loss, letting loose a pitiful moan on behalf of Trestan's past tragedy. The response came completely unexpected to Trestan; however, the bear actually mourned Sir Wilhelm and shared in the pain he felt. Trestan felt the misery of the bear over the loss of its mate, and he mourned for its suffering as well. Trestan threw his arms around the bear in an embrace, as they shared their pain on a level that no one watching them could understand. The onlookers silently watched, amazed, as tears fell from Trestan's eyes over the sharing of loss and the offers of comfort between them.

When some time had passed, Trestan stood and asked for the gates to be opened. The challenge concluded, and Trestan had only to let the animal run free. Cat watched with awe as Trestan walked beside the large bear. Man and beast left the arena headed for the open wilderness. The young man's hand stroked the bear's back as they continued to feel sympathetic toward the pains of the other. When they were far enough away, the bear ran free. Trestan lingered there for some time longer, watching through tears as it went to rejoin its cubs.

The elder who had let them out of the gate spoke to Trestan, even though he would not be heard at that distance. "Abriana watches over you this day, my brother."

Trestan had passed the test. Cat watched him in the distance as his gaze lingered on the bear's departure. This was one of the many things that she loved and admired about him. The test seemed such a little thing compared to the feeling Trestan must enjoy of setting a creature free of its pain. In a world such as Dhea Loral, miracles could be seen fairly commonplace. Yet, for all the times that she witnessed them, Cat had to admire that it was a special thing to see Trestan be able to call such powers forth and do wonderful things.

*         *         *         *         *

Cat and Trestan talked about his excitement over being able to help that bear. They treasured some quiet time sitting together and holding hands before the elders called for his next challenge. This test seemed easy by comparison to the first two. Trestan did not need to show a skill at combat, or risk injury with a wild animal for his third test. The third challenge focused on a set of questions involving the study of arcana. Wizards, conjurors, illusionists, and others all study from a branch of magical sciences they refer to as arcana, which was learned through academic studies. This definition of magic conflicted with miracles, as miracles are a type of energy granted by the gods. While there are other sources of magic available in the land, arcana is the only one besides miracles that the priests could study and achieve some reasonable knowledge of its properties. While paladins aren't required to study any amount of arcana in depth, they are still trained to have knowledge of some basic concepts.

Trestan stood upon a raised platform, his attention focused on one of the elders who had instructed him. Cat stood nearby and listened as the instructor asked Trestan a few arcana-related questions. The elder asked Trestan to define a 'transdimensional bridge', a subject foreign to Cat. Trestan's answer described it as a gate or portal that joined different planes, worlds, or realities, thus allowing individuals to cross between the two. The conversation started to get more in depth and confusing for one such as Cat, who had never studied anything related to arcana. She watched Trestan as he spoke. Katressa perceived that her beloved was struggling to remember the subject correctly. Trestan gave an answer, but to the half-elf his tone sounded unconvincing.

Cat listened with dismay as the elder pronounced the acolyte's answer as incorrect. "You have failed my child, but this is only your first of the day. While others of my brothers may tell you to not look on this event until later, I feel it is my duty to Abriana to reveal the proper answer to you now."

Trestan tried to keep his head up and show no disappointment in his failure as the elder explained the true answers behind his question. "You are correct that in order to open a transdimensional bridge you need efforts on both sides of the portal. Whether by use of a spell, or by the activation of a special device attuned for that purpose, parties in separate worlds must work together to open a rift in the fabric that separates the two worlds. In this way, a bridge is completed between a point in one world and a point in the other.

"Unfortunately, you were incorrect in regards to what happens once it is open. Once the transdimensional bridge exists, you need only one of the two interested parties to continue holding the gate open, thus they can support the portal from only one side. This party would be henceforth called the gatewarden for simplicity and obvious reasons. They may continue to hold the passage open by continuing the proper spell phrases, or by keeping concentration constant on the aforementioned magically focused device. If a foreign interest seeks to close the gate against the wishes of the party that is still supporting it, they must go through extreme efforts. Usually this requires strong spells of the proper type as one method to close the gate peacefully. If nay such spells or power is available, then the gate must be broken by means of destroying the concentration of the gatewarden, by destroying his magical device, or if all other means fails by killing the gatewarden himself. Remember this, Trestan, for it may benefit you some day."

Trestan nodded his thanks as was proper, though he felt heart-struck by failing at such a challenge. The situation shocked Cat to the point of disbelief. It wasn't even a dangerous test! The failure put the worries of the half-elf foremost in her mind again. When Trestan rejoined her, she gave him a warm hug to comfort him and reassure him. Yet, in her mind, she remembered the awful images of his hometown and felt the burden of the undelivered message. She knew Trestan had to be able to go home and bring comfort back to his father...but how could she tell this to Trestan now without disrupting his concentration? She wanted to curse the church for not making it easy for him to go on his way. Trestan had failed one test. He couldn't afford to fail anymore and still be able to leave that day.

With her fears kept hidden, Cat spoke supportively to her beloved. She encouraged him to pray and seek guidance from Abriana, as well as to keep a clear mind in order to focus on the challenges ahead. Trestan attended more tests, and Cat gave him as much encouragement as she could. If anything, Trestan's failure at the arcana challenge did cause him to refocus his thoughts and prayers. The two companions also formed mutual support amongst the other acolytes that Trestan knew from his time at the seminary. Leander and Rhijin often stood nearby. Rhijin stayed quiet and did not speak much, as her own focus had shifted inwards after her failure at the challenge of the beast. Leander often had a serious look about his face as he approached every test, but the young man relaxed in-between tests and answered any questions Cat asked about the challenges.

As the day wore on, Trestan continued to meet every test put before him. One of the martial exercises involved Trestan trading blows with a swordsman. Cat watched with a sincere admiration as the combatants went about several series of strikes and counters. She remembered when they had first met and took to the road to rescue the village's kidnapped noble. She recalled the memories in which she had practiced swordplay with him in order to see how good he was. He wasn't bad with a sword then; today, he performed magnificently. Trestan moved with balance and grace, reacting properly to all the tactics the instructor used on him. Sir Wilhelm initially, and secretly, instructed Trestan's swordsmanship before his death four years ago. It seemed that Trestan's early teaching under that man laid the foundation for some truly remarkable style in the art of the blade.

Another challenge required Trestan to recite prayers and passages from the *Holy Scriptures of Abriana*, some of which lasted fairly long. Trestan not only recited them word by word, he passionately accentuated the meanings to inspire those around. Acolytes applauded his efforts after the elder pronounced the challenge a success. Cat enjoyed all of Trestan's victories...but while she smiled on the outside, her nerves jittered at the thought of Trestan losing one more. Her heart pounded when Trestan was asked to perform another miracle on behalf of the goddess. Her spirits soared when they all bore witness to the miracle and Trestan stood triumphant once again. Test after test Trestan got closer to completing his tenure at the seminary. During all the time Cat watched him, she hid the secret message from back home far behind her lovely green eyes.

Then the elders pronounced a second failure, though not for Trestan. Rhijin stood upon the platform with the elders, her eyes downcast after failing to answer one of their questions properly. The curly-haired cleric-aspirant visibly tried to hold tears back as they pronounced her second fail of the day. Rhijin stood silent as one of the elders spoke to her in regards to her failed question, yet Cat was certain the young woman's mind resided on the hard facts of her failure. She would not be allowed to graduate from the seminary this day. The half-elf held Trestan a little closer, fearing for his own challenges yet to come. Trestan returned a comforting squeeze around her shoulders.

Rhijin walked down from the platform, unable to keep the moisture from her eyes. She started to turn back toward the main housing of the seminary. Trestan excused himself as he slipped out of Cat's grasp. "I have to talk to her. I'll be right back."

Cat watched Trestan run to catch up to the acolyte as she walked away from the rest of the crowd. Leander whispered something to no one in particular, though Cat heard his words. "She is giving up."

"What?"

Leander nodded toward Rhijin, even as Trestan intercepted her course. "Even if an acolyte fails two challenges, they are allowed…even expected…to try and finish the rest of the challenges. They aren't required to finish, but certainly the clergy expect them to continue the rest of the tests for the individual pursuit of their faith. Rhijin is walking back toward the acolytes' housing, away from the remaining tests. She is giving up."

Trestan spoke animatedly to Rhijin, using arm gestures, but the young woman paid more attention to the dirt at their feet. Eventually she tilted her head up and responded to Trestan's words, and the two of them continued eye to eye. As Cat and Leander watched, Trestan turned Rhijin around and guided her back toward the rest of the acolytes.

Leander smiled, "That's good old Trestan. He has a way of inspiring people. It looks like Rhijin is going to finish the rest of her challenges after all."

Cat watched as Rhijin took her place alongside them. The woman still had tears in her eyes, but she stood with her jaw defiantly forward and her head up. Trestan slipped back into Cat's arm without a word. She gave him a tender squeeze around his waist. Cat had another reason to be proud of her man.

 

*   *   *   *   *

 

Trestan faced the last challenge of the day. Though he had lost only one, he still had to succeed in this test in order to leave the seminary. This challenge centered on philosophical beliefs. Trestan stood upon the platform with several elders, facing a row of impassionate stares. He did not return their gazes, choosing instead to close his eyes in silent meditation until they directed their questions at him. Near the platform stood Cat, Leander and Rhijin, each offering their silent support. Leander in particular was in good spirits and full of hope, having just passed his final challenge of the day. The ponytail-blonde warrior looked eager to leave the seminary and begin his new life in the service to the goddess. Cat stood hopeful that Trestan would finish this last task successfully. The half-elf's heart lay with him, and within her heart also lay hidden the images of pain and loss from the small village of his birth. Trestan remained ignorant of his need to be home. The young man stood before his teachers, focused on his goddess, in the near silence of waving banners under the shadow of the chapel.

"Senior Acolyte Trestan," one of the elders addressed him.

Trestan's brown eyes slowly opened, and the depths of those orbs reflected the wisdom gained in four years of teachings. The first elder continued speaking, posing a question to him. "As a paladin, you would fight for the safety of those you love, correct?"

He responded, "Aye, I would. If my loved ones were threatened, I could not stand idly to the side. Mark my words witness: I would be willing to risk my life for that which I love."

Off to the side of the elders sat one who performed a special task. It was one thing for an acolyte to offer words that sounded correct, but it was another thing for them to mean it with all their heart. One or two elders would always be using a miracle that allowed them to judge the sincerity of the acolyte's words during responses. Trestan feared not how the elder would weigh those words, for Trestan had already placed himself in great danger for his friends.

Another of the gray-bearded tutors leaned forward and spoke. "How do you feel when you strike out at your enemies? Please explain it in great detail when you answer."

Trestan's mind conjured up an image as he considered his reply. Words from Sir Wilhelm in days gone by came to him alongside the memory of a one-eyed man who lay bleeding to death from Trestan's sword. "I feel sorrow for them."

Cat watched Trestan answer, aware of the many other people observing nearby. There were younger acolytes listening, as well as the families of the senior acolytes. To some of these people the concepts and faith of Abriana were foreign, maybe even misunderstood. Not even Cat could claim any advanced knowledge of the goddess other than what she saw in Trestan. When acolytes answered philosophical challenges, the words often made anyone stop to think on the goddess' virtues.

Trestan continued his answer. "I try not to let hate ever guide my blade; such emotion is defeating toward love. Many times a loved one may be threatened by another for reasons one cannot understand. If they are an enemy of love, and their ways are evil, it is a choice in their life that I may not be able to alter. I may have to kill them to protect my loved ones, but even as I do, I will feel sorry they chose to end their life that way."

The same tutor spoke again, "And what do you do when such an enemy lies bleeding and helpless at your feet?"

"I experienced such a situation," Trestan honestly replied. His memories recalled the blood on his hands as he tried to hold back the bleeding from the one-eyed man. "When the threat was over, I tried to save him. I wasn't sure what type of man he was, there was even the chance that he had raped or mistreated someone dear to me at the time. That didn't matter to me when I saw him bleeding to death on the ground. I felt compassion, and I tried to keep him alive. In the end, he mentioned some woman waiting for him in some far away port. She probably knows by now, he is never coming back home."

Cat remembered the day of the battle on the bluff as well. Never had she seen anyone display the compassion for an enemy that Trestan carried. Yet, if called to battle, he would fiercely defend those he loved.

The first elder who had spoken offered up the next question. The rest of the tutors and clerics of Abriana looked on and waited to judge Trestan's forthcoming answer as the question was offered. "You will defend your friends, but what about the special holy days of Abriana?"

Trestan visibly paled at this question. Cat brow knitted, unsure of the significance of the days. Something in the question pained Trestan greatly. The elder continued, "On the first day of every month, we are forbidden from using arms or taking aggressive actions against a foe. This sacred edict from the goddess can never be broken or we lose her faith. How will you fare on these holy days when your loved ones are in danger?"

Trestan glanced at Cat out of the side of his eyes, and the movement was not lost on Cat, or on some of the elders. A few of them looked toward the richly garbed, attractive beauty who lingered by Trestan's side all day. Cat began to understand the weight of the question, if not the reasons for it. Trestan was being asked if he would be able restrain from using his sword, effectively ceasing to protect his loved ones if their lives were threatened, on the first day of every month. The idea sounded so odd to Cat, and yet it was apparently a mandate of the goddess whom Trestan hoped to serve. The correct answer would be for Trestan to say that he would not draw his sword to defend Cat's life. Could Trestan truthfully answer such? Could he refrain from using his sword just because of a date on a calendar, despite any kind of mortal danger looming over his love? Another elder still held his concentration on Trestan, and would know by use of a miracle whether Trestan could sincerely speak the truth. From the glances Trestan snuck toward Cat, she knew where his heart lie.

If he couldn't speak sincerely about restraining his sword use during a threat to loved ones, then the challenge would be lost. Trestan would not be joining Cat that night. The unspoken message from home might tear at everything Trestan had built through faith when he found out what had transpired in his village. Cat looked on with near helplessness as Trestan seemed about to fail his second challenge. She knew he could not honestly answer in the way expected of him.

Cat's roguish heart didn't care if her upcoming interruption broke protocol. She had one chance to help Trestan succeed and take him from the seminary with the blessings of his goddess. Her green eyes burning fierce, she stared at Trestan's eyes as he glanced at her and then Cat yelled at him with hard words. Cat spoke in a stern tone that admonished him for his lack of faith.

"Trestan Karok! You put your trust in your goddess once; you must do so again! She puts her faith in you, and you must do the same for her."

Murmurs and words whispered about this outburst, but Cat just crossed her arms defiantly over her chest. Trestan gazed at Cat, digesting the message she had given him. Trestan reflected on the meanings of her words for a few tense moments. The elders glanced from Cat to Trestan but patiently awaited his answer.

Trestan came to a realization, nodding to Cat as the weight of uncertainty lifted from his shoulders. He turned to address his elders. "I once feared putting my faith so deeply into following a god or goddess. When Cat lie dying in my arms, I found my faith. I put my trust in Abriana and she granted the healing Cat needed. I must do so again. This is not unlike the challenge of the beast. We enter a dangerous situation armed only with our faith and reliance upon miracles. If my love is threatened on holy days, I will keep my sword in its scabbard and trust in Abriana."

The other elders looked to the one who weighed Trestan's sincerity and truthfulness. That elder affirmed Trestan spoke from his heart. In return, one of the other elders came to stand in front of Trestan.

"Abriana watches over you this day, my brother."

Trestan smiled from ear to ear. It didn't take Leander's confirmation for Cat to know that Trestan had graduated and could leave the seminary this day.

The elder continued to speak, "Be sure to see the proper instructor before leaving to perform Abriana's service in the world. May she watch and protect you, *Squire* Trestan!"

The newly proclaimed squire bowed to his elders, then rushed down the stairs of the platform to embrace the woman he loved. Cat didn't care that her dress came under attack from a fierce hug, instead she joyfully buried her face against his shoulder has he held her close. She felt the thumping vibrations as other acolytes, including Rhijin and Leander, slapped Trestan on his back in congratulations.

Joy filled Cat's heart knowing that the long period of learning was over for Trestan. He could now travel where he wanted. The world opened before them, and they would travel together and enjoy their time. They would have a romantic night here and then have to visit his home…

…his blackened, damaged home.

She kept her face buried in Trestan's arms. She loved the look of pure joy on his face. He seemed so vibrant and energetic at that moment, like he was in control of his destiny. She was only afraid that when he looked at her face, he would see the sadness hidden within her eyes. Cat could have told him everything then. Yet in his warm arms, and feeling the joyous emotions in his voice, Cat could not bring herself to tell him the news.

Later, Cat thought to herself, she can tell him later…

*    *    *    *    *

"You called for me, Cardinal?" Trestan asked, from beyond the open door.

Cardinal Alunetar Gracegiver stared out one of the open windows in his office, but he motioned for the young squire to enter. "Indeed, come in. I'm here to give you one last item before you are on your way into the world."

Trestan stepped into the office of the seminary's highest ranking official. In truth, Cardinal Gracegiver presided over much of the domain of Kashmer's Protectorate, but he set his office in this holy seminary. Only a lucky few students were greeted by the cardinal as they went into the world. Before this moment, Trestan never even glanced inside his office. As the young squire looked around the room and its contents, he noticed the few luxuries the official enjoyed: including a large library of books and a comfortable chair in which to read them. Symbols of Abriana appeared in abundance, of course, but few other luxurious trappings of any kind. In contrast, the cardinal was dressed in his finest robes in honor of the graduating acolytes. Gracegiver showed the facial lines and white hairs from many years of service to the church and his goddess. Rumor circulated that the aging man had once been a warrior of some repute, but many stories surrounded such a figure of note. A man of such great power and yet soft words often motivated people to stir up fables.

Trestan closed the door behind him and moved into the office, unsure where to stand, how to act, and whether or not to even smile. At seeing his uncertainties, the cardinal responded with a warm smile. It helped to set things in a lighter mood. Alunetar Gracegiver met Trestan in the middle of the office. Trestan could tell the elder had something hidden in one closed hand.

The prominent priest spoke, "The day you have been waiting for is here at last. Despite your completion of this tenure, it is far from the end of your journey. How did you feel about the tests today?"

The question caught Trestan by surprise, "I was…proud and nervous. It is one thing to train for them, and yet quite another thing when the day comes and you face them."

The elder nodded with a grin, "All the training in schools and lessons of books can rarely offer adequate readiness for the trials of the world. That subject brings us to this next part." The older man glanced down at his closed hand, and the concealed item still hidden within that grasp. Alunetar Gracegiver paused and looked into Trestan's eyes once again. "But before we continue, did you have any questions regarding today's challenges?"

Trestan nodded, "I witnessed several responses to the philosophical questions today…some contradictory to one another. In regards to the acolytes that passed, I still noticed sometimes that one or more elders witnessing the answers frowned. It seemed that some disagreed, yet despite the disagreeing looks from the elders, the person would pass the test. Some of the answers that the acolytes gave, well, they would have differed a bit from my own opinions."

The cardinal nodded in agreement, "That is because sometimes there is more than one answer, depending on the view you take of Abriana. You carry the sword of a paladin, which represents a portion of her belief that we must defend that which we love, correct?" At Trestan's nod, the elder continued. "There are others in our order that will never raise arms against others. On your final question, the issue was raised about not using a weapon on holy days at the start of each month. Well, some believe that regardless of the day, we should never raise arms up. After all, she is the Goddess of Love and Healing, which by her very description might hint that she doesn't exactly have much sympathy for swords and what they can do to love or health. Consider another event which you witnessed firsthand. You know that after passing the challenge of the beast, many in our order become vegetarians, but not all. I'm sure that I am only confirming what you have already seen in the seminary here: some people hold rather varied views on our faith and how to follow it."

"Aye," Trestan responded, "It can be…confusing."

The elder shrugged, "Yet all of us who graduate here can cast miracles and preach the words of our faith. If we can do that, it means the goddess is with us. So, it would just seem there is some flexibility in her system, and we all play our part according to our gifts. Some tenets remain unbreakable if we are to remain in her faith. Others merely lend variety. Let this forever be a lesson when dealing with others outside our faith. When you come across a soul, regardless of actions they take or what situation you find them in, be aware that you are not their judge. As missionaries we can try to guide others down the path we call 'good'; however, each person deals with their beliefs in a strictly private manner…between themselves and their chosen deity."

The cardinal held out his hand. "Are you ready to accept this now, and journey into the world?"

Trestan looked down at the cardinal's open palm. A dull, brown ring rested there. The metal was not very shiny, nor did it look well-crafted. It appeared to be carved clumsily from brown rock. One thing special about it included a series of markings and glyphs running around the outside surface of the ring. Trestan had seen them before on the hands of acolytes leaving the seminary after their Embarkings. They called it Faithful's Companion, and there were many constructed like it.

Trestan held out his right hand, with the fingers extended to receive the item. The cardinal took his hand, and held the ring near the end of one finger. "This you have seen before. It is called Faithful's Companion, for this is your only tutor for the next part of your journey. It will go with you and be a link between you and the goddess. The various symbols marked here represent challenges you must pass in her eyes in order to become a full-fledged paladin. Once you have passed these trials, you may come back here and return the ring, and take your surname in the witness of the church and Abriana."

Trestan nodded, as he stared at the ring poised beyond his finger. The elder continued, "It is possible you have already performed some of the needed tasks represented by the symbols on the ring. As each task or challenge is passed, the symbols will disappear, and the ring becomes more lustrous. It will shine with a bright light, appearing as smooth gold, without markings. Once that comes to pass, it will be time to return here and be declared as a full paladin."

With those words, Cardinal Alunetar Gracegiver pushed the ring firmly onto Trestan's finger. The ring, magical in craft, changed its size to accommodate a proper fit. Immediately it underwent another change as both men looked upon it. Some of the symbols started to fade away. The scratches which made up the markings filled from within, smoothing out that portion of the ring. The ring started to brighten from its dull pallor, slowly taking on a golden shine. The cardinal watched with inquisitive eyes as more symbols started to fade. Trestan endured a terrifying adventure four years ago, testing his resolve and willingness to defend his ideals. It seemed as if he had already done several things to fulfill Abriana's requirements. Alunetar Gracegiver's eyes widened as he watched more markings fill in and become polished metal. Rough, brown edges smoothed into a golden glow. The ring took on a shiny quality, to the amazement of Trestan as well.

Finally, the transformation stopped. The cardinal looked the squire in the eyes. "That was impressive! Never once have I ever had a student turn the ring all the way the moment it hit his finger, but you came amazingly close. I still see a few markings here and there, so it seems you have a few unfulfilled tasks yet ahead of you."

Trestan nodded, withdrawing his hand as the elder let it go. The young squire spoke, "I hope to please the goddess quickly. I am also surprised that it changed so much. I'm grateful of my decision those years ago to follow the path Abriana placed before me. If only Sir Wilhelm could see me now."

The cardinal smiled at Trestan. "Go now into the world, Squire Trestan. Find your path. May the goddess guide you safely."

**CHAPTER 3**     **"Cat Brings Sorrowful Tidings"**


As the day waned, the sun put on a colorful display of light hues reflected across the waters of Kashmer's bay. The town circled the harbor, and the harbor faced westward into the setting sun. Many buildings and food establishments took advantage of the view if not obstructed by other structures. Many who had the time to do so paused in silent reflection as they allowed their gaze to be lost in the sparkling lights out on the water. The sun inevitably surrendered the day to the stars and the three moons. Aburis and Nirahha ascended their path in the night sky, while the third moon, Liijay, hid over the horizon. Furled-mast ships crowded the harbor, manned only by those unlucky enough to miss sharing drinks at the many bars on the docks. On a hill near the city, the seminary dedicated to Abriana lie wrapped in its own silence compared to the festivities of the "Embarking" earlier in the day. With night beginning to blanket the land, the activities of the working people shifted accordingly. For several citizens of Kashmer, it was a time for sharing a pipe over the remnants of a feast, or for others a time to go about the streets and bars for the drinking and companionship.

If one wanted to find entertainment in Kashmer, the various taverns suited every taste. Many sailors chose to frequent Yetrayal's Hold, a bar and gambling house settled amongst the docks. There were seafood meals and foreign dishes served there, as well as female or male 'companionship' for the right price. Those less fortunate with cash stayed in the common room at the Lowered Mast, which did not boast any menu except for a list of alcoholic beverages. Other places of entertainment included Ye Sword's Sheathe, which boasted hearty meals and entertainment. Unfortunately, this establishment only offered a room for the night for members of the Sword & Sail adventurer's guild, catering to Kashmer privateers and other adventuring sorts. There were places like Ye Olde Staff which accommodated travelers and trading caravans in the merchant district, as well as the expensive Gold Shield with its nightly performance of minstrels. If a person had the currency, and chose to be treated extravagantly, they could buy a suite at the luxurious Rose Garden. Everything there reflected lavish style, from delicacies to performances by the most reputable entertainers around.

On this night, the reputable entertainment in the dining room of the Rose Garden was inconsequential to a couple who reserved one of the larger suites. The suite boasted several bedrooms and open space to accommodate a group of visitors. Ideally, a minor lord and his family or servants could share the space comfortably. Many times, a wealthy merchant rented it to impress business associates. Aside from the amenities of space and plush furnishings, the room had many other stylish touches.

Large, shuttered windows faced the harbor full of ships. One of the shutters remained partly open; a sure sign that the occupants enjoyed watching the sun as it disappeared under the glimmering harbor waves. A wine glass sat on a table beside the window. A trace of remnant sweet liquid settled on the bottom confirmed that someone indulged beside the scenic view. A companion to the first wine glass sat half full next to a large, oversize tub in an adjoining room with a private bath. The establishment set its outrageous prices due to small perks such as that found in the bath. Instead of a servant carrying up warm water, the occupants of the room could pull a chain. The pull sent a signal; a servant in the room above could pour warm water down a pipe which emptied into the bath. A scattered pile of clothes and wet towels clumped next to the tub, more evidence of someone enjoying all the pleasures the room offered. Despite all the people that the suite could hold, the clothes and wine glasses lent evidence that only two shared the accommodations this night.

There was not much illumination in the suite at all during this hour. The lit candles were located inside the only occupied bedroom. The candles themselves were some of the nicest that the inn could offer. They were locally made; however, the mixture of ingredients which gave life to the bouquet of fragrances was imported from faraway places such as Orlaun. Between the scented candles, luxurious bath soaps, and silk sheets imported from the distant Republic of Lar, a person could relax in comfortable splendor.

Katressa Bilil rested on her belly on those smooth, silk sheets. The half-elf lay mostly exposed to the eyes of her beloved. A section of the sheets drawn over her slim bottom offered some modesty. Other than that thin cover, her dexterous arms, smooth back, and bare legs were exposed to receive the lotion Trestan Karok warmed between his strong hands. Many people boasted the healing effects of massage oils and lotions from Tariyka, but few outside of that country truly were able to afford the enjoyment of it.

Altogether a costly evening, but Katressa would have settled for no less. She planned this day for a very long time. In her work as a privateer for the Kashmer government, they paid her little in coin even though she served the government by tracking and stopping the various thieves and pirates bent on harming the economy. On the other hand, the rules allowed her to keep many of the valuables found on the rogues she helped bring down, as well as receive rewards on any truly notable suspects. Cat proved very good at her job. Her charisma, cunning, gracefulness, stealth and ability with weapons won a lot of victories.

With victories came coins, which also led to a means to afford some of the more valuable things in the biggest merchant center of the known world. Although she wasn't sure if she could truly have a lasting relationship with Trestan due to some of their differences, she loved him and cherished the kind of man he had become. When this day approached, she wanted the best room, the finest luxuries, the best wine…all the best comforts she could buy for a truly romantic evening together. Although her elvish side could have also been just as happy camping in some private lagoon out in the woods, her human half found the inn to be quite relaxing. After a lot of money changed hands, the foundation had been laid for a wonderful evening together. Cat had planned out everything nicely…

…except for the burden of the knowledge of events in Trestan's home village. The bad news left unspoken was an irritation she could never totally ignore. All night she tried to push those thoughts behind her. She hoped to have their special time together, as it was Trestan's first true taste of freedom with her since he had started his learning four years ago. Yet, the images and words in her head would not force themselves to lie at rest. It dug like a thorn in her mind, affecting her smile and her enjoyment of the evening.

Trestan started to rub the lotion over Cat's feet and legs. He also lacked modesty, wearing only an oversized towel wrapped around his waist. A necklace he wore bore the coraross symbol of Abriana. Trestan was well-muscled from his early years as a blacksmith, and his more recent training to become a paladin. His firm strokes pushed the tension away from Cat's limbs. She would have been almost content, save for the demon lurking in the back of her mind.

"*Faunlessa,*" Trestan called her, using the elvish word that translated as 'cherished lover'. As he spoke, his hands continued to massage the road-weary joints of the half-elf. "I realize we have had few quality moments together since I came here to the seminary. In fact, for most of our relationship I've housed within those walls. I want to say, although I kept focused on my studies, I have always longed to be with you and enjoy more time together. There were nights I could not concentrate on the scriptures…nights when I looked up at the night sky and thought of your raven hair, with the stars above shining like the charms on the *Taef' Adorina.* My heart has always yearned for your closeness."

Cat relaxed and let the words sink in with the rest of her pleasure. Trestan continued speaking, "Everything about tonight you set up perfect. It seems like the best evening I could have asked to spend with you, and yet…"

As Trestan trailed off, uncertain how to word his message, Cat stiffened at the realization that he knew something was wrong. Trestan could not miss the renewed tension in her muscles. She listened to his next words, already knowing the point he would make.

"Something is wrong." Trestan stated it as fact. "You have been tense, even edgy, and I do not know why. I'm afraid to ask, lest I spoil the evening. Yet, I do not believe that it would go well for us to hide your feelings, Cat."

Her green eyes were hidden from his gaze, staring off into the pattern of the wood grain on the headboard. "You are perceptive. There is something on my mind, but I have nay wish to talk about it now. I want us to have this night in perfect splendor."

She felt his hands relax their movements as the muscles in his shoulders sighed. With Cat resting on her belly, staring away, and Trestan sitting behind her giving the massage, neither of them made any eye contact. Trestan tried to rub his hands along her muscles again, but he did so with less enthusiasm. The young man remained distracted by his own thoughts and fears.

His deep voice spoke again. "You know I respect you, and I hate to push the matter. How are we truly enjoying the night when our minds are clouded with worry and doubt? I know something is wrong, and yet I am asked just to accept it and simply ignore it?"

Cat closed her eyes, "It's a matter we cannot change. I wish I could just tell you not to worry about it, that you can trust me to tell you later."

Trestan thought about her words, particularly the phrase, 'a matter we cannot change', and it occurred to him what the problem might be. "This is about our lifespan again, isn't it? You are once again looking into the future to see how I might age and wither before your eyes."

The difference in aging between their respective races had always been something hard to discuss. Trestan, a full-blood human, had reached twenty-three years old. Katressa witnessed forty-one winters. However, while her mother had been human, her father had been an elf. Cat looked about the same age as Trestan, if not younger. Due to her elven heritage, she would likely outlive Trestan by more than a hundred years.

Cat shook her head, "Nay, that's not it. I'd rather not discuss that subject. I know that's something I can't change either, but I don't know how to face that fact. I do love you, *faunlessa*, don't you doubt that!"

Trestan stopped massaging her legs. She could feel the movement of the bed as his weight lifted off of it. Her sensitive ears listened as Trestan paced the room. He didn't say anything; he simply paced quietly.

Trestan felt confused and upset, without knowing what issue separated him from his beloved. Indeed, that summed up how Trestan felt: separated. He felt he was being held from her deepest feelings by some intangible but unbreakable barrier between them.

Cat wanted to cry. She had held in the secret for too long, and no additional delay could be justified. Their one night together, anticipated for so long, had started good yet become soured by events beyond her control. The woman worried about how angry he would be at her for holding it in for so long.

Cat grabbed the silk sheets and rolled over to face Trestan. She covered up her womanly attributes as she sat up so they could have an honest conversation without distractions. Trestan looked into Cat's mesmerizing green eyes and saw hurt and pain there. He calmed himself to listen to what she had to say, taking a seat on the bed next to her.

"First of all," Cat had to swallow to get any more words out, "I apologize for not telling you earlier."

Trestan felt nervous, but he valued her honesty and willingness to put things into the open. He reached out a hand for her, and she met it halfway with her own. They sat facing each other, holding hands, as she continued to speak.

"At first I had good reasons. I carry some bad news from your home, and I didn't want to tell you this morning. I wouldn't distract your concentration in the challenges. I think you would have failed and been stuck there at the seminary had you known."

Trestan showed little reaction in his face as she spoke into his inquisitive, brown eyes. He did support her to speak more, by gently rubbing his fingers on her embraced hand. Cat continued despite a tear rolling from one eye. "Then, I guess it was more selfishness that I held it back. We had planned for this day for…Trestan, I waited so long for you. I didn't want anything to disturb our night together, for what happened is already in the past and can't be changed. Either way, we would ride to your village first thing in the morning."

"Cat, my love, just tell me," Trestan said.

She took a deep breath, and brought her other arm forward around Trestan's shoulders. "Forgive me for not saying it earlier. Trestan, your village was attacked almost a week ago."

Trestan felt his jaw drop, even as it seemed as if the floor fell out from under him. Cat used her hands to steady and comfort him. "It was Revwar and Savannah, returning to take the holy relic. They killed a lot of the temple priests and some villagers, burned the church, then set fire to other buildings as well."

Trestan's muscles tensed. He did not say anything immediately, but Cat saw his other hand angrily clench into a fist. Trestan closed his eyes, as if that would shut away all the worries assaulting his mind at that moment. Katressa knew this was hurtful, but he deserved to know. He needed to be told everything. "Your father was…wounded."

*        *        *        *        *

*Village of Troutbrook, 33<sup>rd</sup> day of Florum, nine days before the "Embarking"...*

Hebden Karok set down his smith's hammer for the day. Evening approached, and he decided work was slow enough he could close shop early. The blacksmith of Troutbrook dipped his sooty hands into a bucket of water and splashed his face clean. After such a hot, sunny day, Hebden anticipated washing up a bit and relaxing with a drink. Next to him, his teenage apprentice looked at him questionably.

The village smith spoke to him, "Mikhael, I think it's a good day to finish early. Wouldn't you say?"

The younger man, son of the local general store owner, nodded and smiled. "I would like that very much. My mother is cooking a rare treat tonight, and I'd like to be properly cleaned up before I sit at the table."

Hebden and Mikhael set about storing their tools and closing up shop. Hebden admired his capable apprentice. Although Mikhael grew to become a hard worker, the older smith found that sometimes he missed his son. It had been four years since the younger smith had gone off to the seminary at Kashmer, though with good fortune, Trestan would be returning shortly. Although Hebden's son did not follow in the footsteps of his father, it turned out that Mikhael had an aptitude for the hammer and anvil. It was a good thing that the general store owner had three other children from which to learn the family business, for Mikhael was on his way to becoming Troutbrook's next smith.

"Pardon me for a moment," requested Hebden, "I'm going to refill my water."

Hebden took a second bucket, one kept cleaner for drinking and cooking, and made his way across the main street of the village to the well. The old smith passed several children playing out in the street, enjoying the bright day. The children jumped from spot to spot in the street, as defined by an arrangement of several sticks placed for their game.

The marble well stood in front of the Church of the Sacred Harvest. Dedicated to Yestreal, the God of Sun and Weather, it was the main point of worship for this village of farmers and herders. Hebden drew water from the well, sparing a glance at the item displayed prominently on the rim. A green stone, shaped much like an egg, perched in its age-old place of honor. It was unremarkable except for several white markings on its surface.

Long had it sat there and somehow blessed the village with good crops and soil. Even the villagers discounted it as nothing special, until a day four years ago when a band of adventurers came to the village and stole it. Crops and herds alike became diseased and withered from infestations. Thanks to the efforts of some helpful adventurers and two village boys, (Trestan and his friend Petrow), the holy relic was recovered and returned to its rightful place. Since then, the local church and a wizard from Orlaun named Korrelothar worked together to safeguard the stone by means of spells woven around it. Although it looked vulnerable to a thief, a tight weave of magic safeguarded it. In the years since the return from its abduction, the relic continued to give prosperity and fertility to the lands of the village.

Hebden took the full bucket in hand, offering the relic one last glance before returning home. As he looked into its smooth surface, he heard the sounds of several horses. Hebden looked up from the well, casting his eyes down the village's main street to the south.

His eyes took in an odd sight. A stone bridge spanned the brook which lent its name to the village. A large group of armed men slowly rode over the bridge. They wore no standard uniform nor bore any pennants of heraldry. Most wore leather armor, and the foremost riders carried either bows or crossbows. Once over the bridge, several of the riders fanned out to form a line along the banks of the water.

Hebden stood immobile, perplexed at the appearance of so many armed men. The spectacle held other villagers in a trance as the scene unfolded before them. Several merchants had carts of wares at the south end of the street. Many fishermen stood along the banks as the armed riders took up positions near them. Uncertain silence reigned for many seconds as the horsemen and the villagers faced each other.

A command bellowed out from a rider on the stone bridge. Those riders with crossbows started to cock back the bowstrings in order to load them. Those with bows reached into quivers and proceeded to notch their missiles into place. The riders on either end of the line drew steel from their scabbards as they wheeled their horses toward the defenseless fishermen. People started to panic and cry out in confusion. The commanding horseman atop the stone bridge waved an arm forward, yelling a command to fire. The peaceful day became a bloody nightmare. Bows and crossbows alike loosed a volley, striking several villagers. Screams came from the throats of those stricken, and for many it became their last sound. Villagers surviving the initial attack scrambled in seemingly random directions to escape any additional harm. Carts of candy and fruits toppled their loads as merchants bumped past or dove to the ground next to them. Wounded people cried out for mercy as fleeing neighbors tripped over them. The horsemen went about calmly reloading their bows as if observing nothing more than a game hunt. Hebden watched in horror as the riders who drew swords charged down the fishermen. Men ineffectively tried to use their fishing poles to block razor-edged steel. A few tried pleading for their lives, before losing their blood in the current of the stream.

Hebden stood frozen in panic next to the well. He watched the bloodshed on the south end of the village continue unabated, spreading into madness. It was only a voice from behind that jolted him into action.

"Get to your homes and shops! Get inside and bar the doors!"

The speaker was one of the bodyguards of the local lord. The same force doubled as the law enforcement in the area. Wearing his light blue livery, the speaker and another similar-dressed guard stood out from among the rest of the villagers. Although both village guards carried weapons and wore mail, they were not accustomed to any threat such as what the village faced now. Most of the village's sworn soldiers were more involved in guarding the manor of the lord rather than policing the village itself. The two men attempted their duty to get villagers out of harm's way, but by themselves they were no match for the band of invaders. The two guards looked about as scared as the people they tried to herd to safety.

At their words, Hebden Karok left behind the water bucket and sprinted across the street. As he dashed for the smithy, he saw Mikhael similarly distracted by the murderous actions nearby. Hebden ignored the temptation to look south again. He kept focused on getting to his home, though his ears heard the screams coming from his neighbors. When he got to his shop, he reached out a hand and shook Mikhael's shoulder.

"Don't look. We have to get inside the house."

The home of Hebden and Trestan Karok sat just behind the smithy. A small home with only three rooms, the other side of the house faced opposite to a parallel street. Beyond the street was little cover, for few buildings stood on the other side of it. Mostly farmland stretched from there to a nearby ridge and beyond that lay woods. This was not a large city with many alleys and tall buildings. Troutbrook was a small settlement, with few places of refuge except one's home. The house offered little more than a hiding spot, yet at the moment it was safer than the streets filling with bloodthirsty horsemen.

Mikhael started to move with him, but other sounds nearby reminded the youth of others who needed help. "The children! What about them?"

Hebden gazed into the street. Several children still stood around the area in which they had been playing fun games just moments earlier. Tears blurred their vision, as the slaughter on the southern edge of town froze them with terror. As riders worked their way up the street, the children stood immobile in the path of danger.

Hebden didn't bother to look back as he spoke to Mikhael, "We have to help them. Be swift and wary."

The two men ran into the street and started to get the children's attention. They had to move between the murderous men and those whose eyes despaired of broken innocence. Hebden and Mikhael shouted and grabbed a few in order to push them toward the smithy. Their repeated attempts broke the mesmerizing effect binding the children. A few of the kids dropped rocks, sticks, or other play items from their hands as they ran for safety. Mikhael guided them past the various tools of the smithy as Hebden drove them from behind. Once off the street, Mikhael brought them across the small, alley-like yard behind the smithy, ultimately leading them to the back door of Hebden's house.

Hebden lingered around the smithy for a moment, looking back to the street. The older man looked northward long enough to discern a familiar figure exiting the inn's common room. One of Troutbrook's local heroes made his appearance just when he was needed. Petrow stood out in front of the inn as he took in the scene to the south. The young handyman was carrying his wood axe as he often did. Although a simple tool used for simple chores, Petrow had once carried it on his adventure with Trestan Karok. The two youths had saved the holy relic and brought it back to the village, and ever since had been Troutbrook's heroes. In the interim, Petrow had settled down again and started a family. Yet on many days Petrow had often been seen twirling his axe like a weapon, impressing the country folk with his skill as a warrior, as he retold the same stories from his adventure.

A spark of hope ignited in Hebden's heart as he saw Petrow with his simple axe. Petrow, however, looked down the street with the same fear as anyone else. He backed up a few cautious steps. Finally he turned away from the carnage and ran. His steps carried him at a fast pace toward the north parts of the village. Hebden despaired to see the young handyman-turned-warrior-turned-farmer run away from the other villagers in their time of need. Even as he considered the young man's apparent cowardice, Hebden asked himself what he truly expected Petrow to accomplish against the band of armed men. Petrow was the village hero, along with Trestan, yet what would either young man be able to do alone against this threat?

Hebden once again looked upon the chaos to the south. People fled into buildings or ran straight up the street. Many had tears on their cheeks from both fear and the pain of watching old friends die in such a sudden manner. The riders followed in pursuit, firing bows into the backs of the fleeing peasants. Some riders threw fiery brands onto roofs or through open windows. Shops and homes began to blaze. Hebden knew it was dangerous to linger in the open, yet he could not take his eyes away from the horrible vision.

Beyond the first wave of riders he saw others on horseback crossing over the stone bridge. Those newcomers were not dressed in leather nor did they look as battle-hungry as the other invaders. Hebden could make out three odd riders that appeared different from the rest. When he did, he gasped in recognition of two of them. Although Hebden had only seen the elf wizard briefly, years before, the figure was immediately recognizable. It wasn't just the presence of the yellow-eyed elf alone that led to the recognition. Beside the elf sat a dark feminine figure wearing black plate; a skull helm blocked the view of her facial features. The dark armor bore the markings of the Goddess of Death. Even though Hebden had never seen the abbess who served DeLaris, the pair had been described enough in Petrow and Trestan's stories. The wizard Revwar and the cleric Savannah had returned for the relic, but this time they had brought a small army of thugs. A well-dressed human of middle years rode beside them, though Hebden had no idea who that person could be.

Hebden was shaken from his observations as the action approached closer to his home. The two Troutbrook guards ran for the entrance to the Church of the Sacred Harvest. Both men found themselves faced by a group of attackers. Several invaders dismounted their horses, still carrying loaded missile weapons. An acolyte from within the church, confused by all the excitement outside, wandered out of the doorway at the wrong moment. A wave of arrows launched toward the three villagers. The guards and the acolyte went down from the barrage of death even as the raiders drew swords and charged the church door.

The blacksmith could stay in the open no longer. Hebden ran through the yard behind the smithy and into his house. As he went, he grabbed one of his smith hammers from a table. Once inside the small house, he found Mikhael trying his best to calm the gathering of children. Hebden turned to regard the back entrance to his home. The smith considered the door to the alley yard as being the back door, though it was the one most commonly used. He had nothing to bar the door, but he was able to find a piece of rope and make a use out of it. Trying one portion to the inside iron handle, he looped the other end around a coat hook that had been nailed into the hallway wall. Once he was done, the rope was taught enough to hinder anyone trying to throw open that door.

It was hard to see the emotions on Mikhael's eyes, for the common room was dark except where light crept around the edges of shutters. Hebden could tell that Mikhael looked to him for guidance or reassurances. Hebden could not tell him of what was happening outside for fear of panicking the children even further. The smith remained unsure of what actions to take, but he considered a few as he clenched and unclenched the hammer in his hand.

Before long, the smith considered a dangerous course which might see the children to safety. "We can try for the woods over the ridge."

He could almost hear Mikhael trying hard to swallow in the light of that suggestion. Hebden shrugged, "It's dangerous to remain in town, but if we can get across the fields we should be relatively safe."

Mikhael replied with a very dry voice, "Alright, I'm up for trying."

Hebden went to the door of his house that faced westward. It opened into an outer street of the village, but with little in the way of buildings on the far side of it. It faced a ridge beyond which lay an ample wood to hide in, but to get there one had to cross an open field. The smith had his hammer in hand as he opened the doorway. Hebden even ventured one foot outside, but stopped as he viewed the scene before him.

More than one villager had already considered that escape route. The field to the west was already being used by a score of villagers as their path to safety. Even as those folks ran for a spot to hide, the riders literally cut across the field as well. A few horsemen rode down some of the villagers. They used scimitars and other weapons as they butchered those seeking only refuge from the nightmare. The cropland proved to be a deadly field to those trying to cross. It was scant comfort that the smith noticed one thing unusual about the horsemen's actions. If a rider missed his target, he tended to continue riding north. For some reason, this group had business on the north end of town that prevented the urge to turn and finish their targets. Most did not miss their victims, using weapons or the hooves of their horses to drive the common folk to the ground.

A rider came up the street as Hebden gaped at the field of slaughter. His crossbow leveled at the smith, but Hebden did not notice until the man was almost upon him. Hebden flinched inward as the bolt sailed at him. Pain shot through the smith as he felt the bolt pierce the side of his hip. He fell against the door as Mikhael and the children screamed. The first rider went by, reloading his crossbow as he continued to ride north.

A second rider bore down at the same target. Hebden fought past his agony to spot this new rider armed with a scimitar aiming for him. Gritting against the pain caused by the effort, the smith grabbed the door handle and heaved his body back inside. The door swung closed, though not without taking a parting shot. The sword nicked its edge as the second rider galloped past. Hebden dropped to the floor, showered by a few splinters of wood caused by the hit of the blade.

Mikhael and the children froze in a state of fright at seeing the bolt which bloodied Hebden's side. Hebden winced with every heavy breath he took. The older smith wanted to calm the children and offer them some hope. There was little hope to be found for them as they stared at the bolt sticking out of his right hip.

*       *       *       *       *

Fires burned unchecked amongst several village shops and dwellings. The pall of smoke hanging over the village darkened the nearly abandoned streets. The wind carried embers to nearby rooftops, but none of the surviving villagers could fight the fires. Families and acquaintances huddled in the dark recesses of whatever homes they had found shelter. No candles or hearth fires burned. Crying children were hushed behind barricaded doors. Beyond the walls of their dwellings, they could hear the invaders moving about the streets.

With the threat of death lingering so near, all the villagers nervously hid in silence and shadows, clutching their loved ones or makeshift weapons.

The armed raiders walked unopposed in the streets, illuminated by red fires against the dark backdrop of smoke. Some patrolled the alleys in small bands. These bands did not seek out the hiding villagers for slaughter, but they often banged weapons against walls and doors. It was more of a scare tactic than anything else. Most of the strangers concentrated around the main street of Troutbrook. Their attention focused around the Church of the Sacred Harvest. Blades and bows encircled the building. The swordsmen did not approach the entry, though the door had already been torn from its hinges. They showed little emotion over several bodies near the door of the church. The dead included many church acolytes and young priests. The riders were not a particularly disciplined lot, yet they had performed well at the slaughter for which they had been paid. Whispers exchanged as they waited and watched the church entry. The words passing between them spoke of how they would spend their blood money, or offered cruel jokes at the expense of the recently departed.

A hush settled over the circle of swordsmen when figures emerged from the doorway of the church. The first to exit wore armor decorated to befit a priestess. Her holy symbols and representations of her deity were etched into the surfaces of the battle-ready metal. An abbess of the Goddess of Death exited Yestreal's holy ground. The contoured armor showed her feminine features, yet many would have been too frightened by the dark symbols of the visions of death adorning the outfit. Her cold, blue eyes swept the street from behind the hollow sockets of her skull helm. Short, blonde hair peeked out from under the edges of the helm. At her side, she carried her flail. The weapon had been enchanted by one of her miracles, casting a glow of darkness around the spiked ball on the end. Hebden had already recognized her earlier in the day. Savannah served DeLaris, and her presence in Troutbrook would be unwelcome even if not joined by swordsmen.

Four years ago, she arrived in the village with friends and together they stole the holy relic of the church. When Trestan, Cat and their companions were able to recapture the relic and two other similar relics, Savannah and her accomplice Revwar had last been seen on an island out at sea. The companions from Troutbrook escaped the island by taking the only ship anchored there, so it was thought that Savannah and her party were marooned on the island.

Savannah strode confidently out into the street in front of the church, heedless of the wind-blown embers. One of her previous accomplices followed her out of the ruined door of the church. The wizard Revwar had changed little in the intervening years. His silver hair grew long and braided, while his piercing yellow eyes took in every detail as he walked. His long, angular elvish face remained impassive as he stepped over a body near the door. He wore lengthy, dark robes, filled with many hidden pockets and arcane surprises. The elf's wardrobe had been made from the finest materials. In his right hand he carried a new staff. Like his old one, it had many runes carved into its side, allowing him to access many powers stored within the magical vessel. A long, thin dagger adorned his belt, yet Revwar rarely resorted to such desperate means of defending himself.

While Revwar and Savannah shared masks of cold indifference as they participated in the raid, something in Savannah's eyes existed atypical of her nature. Though the concentration of everyone else focused on the church, her eyes often scanned up and down the abandoned street. Her glances revealed some urgent need; an unsatisfied call lurking in the depths of her mind. She sought a resolution for that hunger somewhere among the buildings of the town. Whatever it was she tried to find, it did not manifest for her convenience.

Two more figures emerged from the church entrance behind Revwar and Savannah. The first of the two was well known on the streets of Troutbrook. Head Priest Gerlach ranked highest in Yestreal's sanctuary. He represented a father figure to the community, offering comfort while wearing the mantle of his office. This evening found him disheveled and dazed. His eyes glazed over under the effects of some enchantment. He stumbled outside, heedless of the bodies of his brothers. In every step he took, one could sense the chains of some entrapping spell held his will prisoner. He moved toward the well in front of the Church of the Sacred Harvest. With every heavy footfall, his outstretched hands moved closer to the green relic stone which stood perched upon that well. The stone stood protected from theft by numerous energies woven around it; a mixture of magic and miracles set forth by the priest and by the elf wizard, Korrelothar. High Priest Gerlach moved in a direct line toward the magical stone, mumbling words as he went.

"Yestreal, my lord, I am coming."

The second figure followed Gerlach closely. While the priest's garb was in disarray, the human male following him wore fine clothes. The man's attire mirrored the fashions of the great city Orlaun. It consisted of many layers of clothing, some parts frilly with lace and featuring puffed out, bloused sleeves. Jentan Mollamos looked to be middle-aged, yet handsome, and he wore his age well. His charming looks and distinguished dress contrasted the armed warriors watching the spectacle. Jentan had thick, black hair, peppered with gray around the sideburns and near his brow. He had full dark eyebrows, once again mixed with gray, overshadowing his intelligent, brown eyes. Upon his face he had a small mustache, thinly trimmed, as well as a small, pointed goatee.

An observer might be unnerved to see the constant grin on his face, almost as if it had been set that way from years of using his smiles and wit. Jentan was ever a charmer more than a fighter. As a mentalist, he had studied exclusively in the branch of magic dealing with the powers of the mind. To him, true power involved being able to affect, alter, and control the minds of others. He carried a wand at his belt for personal defense, but his arcane gift involved the ability to tap the harmonic web from which bards and minstrels drew their magical talents. Using the harmonic web, he could use the sound from his voice in the right inflections and rhythms to hypnotize foes. Those powers extended to affect people's perceptions of their surroundings.

Jentan Mollamos followed the head cleric to the well. During the entire time, the mentalist kept a steady flow of arcane-empowered whispers to distract the priest's mind. High Priest Gerlach responded as if in a dream. More appropriately, the cleric felt submerged in a vision sent by his deity, Yestreal. The effort taxed Jentan heavily, for it was not easy to trick a priest as powerful as this one in such a way.

High Priest Gerlach reached the edge of the well. Once there, the cleric simply stared at the holy relic: the egg-shaped, green stone, covered with strange white markings. Gerlach's hands dropped to his sides as he spoke out loud to his perceived deity. "I am unable touch it my lord, for Korrelothar also wove magical protections about it. I need his help to unravel the bonds."

Jentan replied to Gerlach, casting his voice in an almost musical resonance. The words carried to the cleric's ears on the waves of arcane power. "Korrelothar stands here beside you, ready to assist."

Gerlach's glazed eyes looked to the side where Revwar stood. The elvish wizard did not bear a close resemblance to Korrelothar, but he knew Gerlach saw what Jentan told him to see. Gerlach smiled to the image of Korrelothar. "Hello, my friend. 'Tis good to see you again."

Revwar only nodded, afraid that a spoken reply might shatter Jentan's fragile hold on Gerlach's senses. Jentan whispered more words into the cleric's ears, reinforcing the mental illusion. In doing so, he also reiterated that Yestreal called upon his faithful priest to unlock the relic from its magical bonds.

Gerlach began a prayer designed to undo the god-given miracle holding the relic in place. Revwar waited for his cue to begin casting his own dispel measures. The elf became slightly distracted by the lack of attentiveness from Savannah. The abbess of DeLaris once again searched the streets with her eyes, trying to uncover the specter haunting her dreams. At Jentan's nod, Revwar ignored the woman to begin casting his own spell. Revwar worked to unravel the arcane wards on the relic, while Gerlach removed the miraculous ones. Three disjointed voices worked at once. Revwar stripped away the magic Korrelothar had placed, Gerlach undid his own miracles under the guise of a vision, and Jentan kept whispering spells in Gerlach's ear to reinforce the illusion. The air around the stone shimmered. Particles and streamers of light peeled off of the surface of the stone before fading into nothing.

High Priest Gerlach's hands dropped to his sides, "It is as you have asked. The stone has been freed."

Revwar enjoyed a genuine smile as the wards disappeared. The smile did not last long before Savannah walked closer, and the elf wizard could foresee what would happen next. Would the woman disrupt their plans?

"Ask him," Savannah glared at Jentan, "I have to know."

Jentan ever so slightly shook his head, as his deceiving words still held the priest of Yestreal in limbo. Revwar responded on his behalf, speaking in a whisper to Savannah. "It is difficult for Jentan to keep the charade up for long. It is better that we spend our time having the high priest recite what he knows of the stone from their records."

Savannah scoffed at that, "It was clear the last time we took it that we know a lot more about its properties than anyone here. I have business here other than the relic. Since we are here, I would see both edicts of my goddess fulfilled."

"One is a lot more important than the other," Revwar reminded her.

Savannah's cold, blue eyes returned an icy stare at the elf's impassionate gold orbs. The abbess turned to face Gerlach, despite a warning motion from Jentan. Savannah stood before the priest, unworried that he would perceive her decorated armor. Jentan's whisperings became more urgent, as the priest of Yestreal tried to make out who stood before him.

"Where is Petrow? Tell me where he lives!" The servant of DeLaris demanded.

Yestreal's faithful disciple puzzled at the request. He tilted his head to regard the undefined figure before him. "Petrow? Well…he lives not far from here. Why…who asks?"

Jentan struggled to keep his harmonic spell around the head priest. Revwar saw something uncommon from the abbess: seething anger to the point she was losing her self control. Savannah promptly spoiled the illusionary spell in her anger. Forgetting herself, she reached out with her left hand and grabbed a fistful of the cleric's robe. "Where might I find Petrow?"

Gerlach's eyes lost their glaze as his vision opened before him. The mesmerizing spell shattered in an instant. Gerlach saw the armed riders, the flames, the dark design of Savannah's armor, and the blood of the villagers on the ground. He remembered the cries and screams of his brethren, as well as undoing the miracle which held the holy relic safe.

The head priest tried to react quickly to defend himself. Taking a quick step back, but still held by the abbess, he began to utter the words of a miracle. "Yestreal, grant me the means…"

Jentan stepped back as well. The mentalist tried to speak another spell to disillusion Gerlach.

Savannah's response proved quicker and more lethal. The flail trailed a streamer of dark shadow as its enchanted head swung about. The abbess of the Death Goddess screamed her rage as the spiked ball came down on the head of Yestreal's servant. Gerlach's skull shattered under the empowered weapon. Bits of bone and blood splattered the handsome face of Jentan Mollamos, causing him to recoil.

The body of the priest dropped beside the well.

Revwar's face took on his normal, impassive mask. Stepping over the fallen corpse, the elf reached out and took the holy relic from its resting place. He did not waste any glances in Savannah's direction; however, the wizard's words directed at her, "It is time that we left. We have business that can't be delayed."

The abbess breathed heavily, though Revwar did not understand what taxed the woman's strength. She stared at him from behind her skull helm. "We won't leave yet. We will use the swordsmen if we must, but we will find out where he is hiding."

Revwar spared a puzzled glance toward her at those words. "Bust down every door, tear down every shutter in the village and the outlying farms searching for someone who may not be here? We did not hire enough swords to flush out every villager in a timely manner looking for one man."

Savannah replied. "I claimed his life once for my goddess. As long as he lives, it haunts me. Petrow must die."

Revwar understood what Savannah said, but could not fathom the depth of it. He could not understand why it vexed her so much. He knew that clerics of the Death Goddess claimed a certain control over death itself, and they accentuated this point on a battlefield. When an enemy lay helpless before such a cleric, they would often announce whether they claim or spare the life of the person. Even when a life was spared, it wasn't for pity or benevolence. The whole point of the event stressed the control their goddess had over life and death. Revwar knew that during their last battle, Savannah had claimed to take Petrow's life for her goddess and she proceeded to strangle the life from him. Instead, Savannah failed to finish the kill, and Petrow escaped death.

It was of little consequence as far as Revwar was concerned. The elf came up close to Savannah's angry glare for his reply. "He will die, but not today."

Savannah stood silent before the elf as he spoke close to her fearsome skull helm. "This task is done on behalf of your goddess, as well as another goddess. Its importance weighs more heavily upon us than fulfilling a vow to claim the life of one insignificant man."

To one side, Jentan took a cloth and daintily dabbed at his face to remove the remains of the head cleric of Yestreal. Revwar bent even closer to Savannah, whispering words so that the nearby raiders would not hear. "You know these men accompanying us are already dead. That was part of the plan after all. The ones who rode north are more than a match for anyone Lord Verantir sends to help the village, if he will bother to send anyone. However, Kashmer will not tolerate such a vile attack within its borders. These men will never live to spend their gold, but by that time we will slip away as planned. With strength we take the relic, but we have little time to spare if we intend to get to the south and separate from these thugs before Kashmer privateers or militia kill the men they will hold responsible for the attack. Time is our enemy, Savannah."

Revwar patted the bag which now held Troutbrook's stolen relic. "We will again be pursued for this. Last time our plans were destroyed by a band of inexperienced children. Petrow is nothing, yet this relic is everything. This binds you to a higher duty than your claim to kill one man."

Savannah said nothing. The woman remained still, though she had calmed her breathing. Yet, the abbess did not show signs of backing down. Revwar decided to play one more hunch. "You suffer from nightmares?"

Revwar saw something he thought he would never see in his companion. Savannah actually flinched, and her eyes widened slightly out of fear. The elf wizard knew he had hit a vulnerable spot. "What do you think the nightmares will be like if you fail this task?"

Savannah could not hide the fear in her eyes. Revwar did not know why the woman acted as she did, why Petrow consumed her thoughts, and how she could be unnerved by nightmares. Truthfully, it did not concern him. What mattered most was that they had this relic in their possession again, and plans already set into motion. Savannah could no longer meet Revwar's eyes. The blonde abbess consented to his point of view by shying away and walking to her horse. Jentan also took her cue and moved to his own mount.

Satisfied that Savannah would continue with the original plan, Revwar turned to face the other riders. "We have the item for which we came. It is time to depart, and swiftly."

Revwar, Savannah and Jentan Mollamos rode south out of the town with the horde of armed riders. They left behind burning buildings, shattered families, a slaughtered church clergy, and a wounded smith who was the father of paladin-aspirant Trestan Karok.

### CHAPTER 4               "Homecoming"


It was not the homecoming Trestan had expected.

Though Trestan appreciated having Cat by his side once again, the ride south proved more devoid of conversation than either would have preferred. With the worries over Trestan's father and the knowledge of the damage to Troutbrook, not enough magic existed in the air to conjure smiles or jests. Despite the silent moments, his lover bolstered Trestan's spirit. Cat's presence became a pillar of support even without words. The half-elf's companionship gave him a solid foundation to cling to as his heart dealt with this tragedy.

On Jherad the 5$^{th}$, the third day after the Embarking, Trestan rode into the outskirts of his village. A drizzle of rain wet the clothes to match the dampened spirits. Trestan and Cat rode with cloaks to protect them from the outward chill, but had little protection from the inward chills except the bond between them. Under his cloak, Trestan wore his armor. The breastplate and other portions of it proudly displayed his symbols of Abriana. He wore the coraross symbol necklace openly. He thought it fitting that on his ride home he should dress in the style earned through his years of training at the seminary. With the magical elvish sword strapped to his back, and the forged warhammer at his side, Trestan's appearance differed from the smith who once left this small village.

Cat wore her usual black traveling leathers. At her side rested her preferred blade: the silver rapier with the cat's-head pommel. Two crossbows, her favorite choice of arms, hung from the saddle. Cat wore her old helm instead of the *Taef' Adorina*. While on the road, she wanted to be properly protected and armored against the hazards of the wilds. Her long, black hair cascaded from beneath the helm, too sodden to playfully whip about in the wind.

As Trestan and Cat rode through the outlying farms, the surroundings seemed out of place. At first, it seemed hard to put a finger on anything particular. Trestan wondered if it was simply a matter of his own perspective, knowing what lay ahead. The buildings and countryside appeared just as he had left them four years ago. Despite the peaceful appearance of the farms, there lurked an intangible, sorrowful presence in the land. The two companions could feel the depth of it more clearly whenever they saw some of the village folk in the fields. Mothers kept a closer eye on their children. Everyone looked up when Trestan and Cat passed by, faces tinged with fear for what unknown dangers might wander the road to their settlement. Some moved out of sight at the first glance of Trestan's armor or Cat's rapier. It pained Trestan to see his friends and acquaintances casting such fearful glances at travelers. He could remember how he and Petrow had anticipated travelers passing through the village. The two youths had heard stories of distant lands, snickered at foreign styles of dress, or looked forward to anything exciting compared to the boring tedium typical of small village life.

The eyes of those people gave Trestan the first hint of changes. As he rode onward more differences became apparent. Trestan saw a young lad working a field with his sisters. The dirty trio of siblings paused to regard the strangers with sad eyes. A wooden board at the end of the field marked a mound of dark dirt covering a newly dug grave…large enough for a beloved father to be put to rest. Trestan offered up a silent prayer to Abriana for the children.

The two companions passed by the keep of Lord Verantir. They noted several workers constructing new defensive fortifications along the ground and the walls. Word had been relayed to Cat that the noble did not send any troops to the defense of the village; instead, he positioned the guards on his own walls for fear that he would be attacked. A number of invading riders actually did ride within sight of his keep, but their appearance seemed little more than an intimidation tactic to keep the lord hiding within his walls. Now the noble family took measures to better protect their own home if any marauders ever returned.

When the village came into view, the same palpable sadness and fear emanated from the streets. Villagers lacked jovial chatter and smiles. People continued picking up the pieces of their broken lives. Trestan became aghast when he saw the damage done to his hometown. Many structures stood as blackened wooden frames or worse. The north part of the street endured well, but the southern portion of the village suffered. The inn and several other large structures showed at least partial damage from flames. The stone walls of the Church of the Sacred Harvest stood strong, but the roof and interior had been gutted by fire. The structure did not look livable except for linen sheets covering parts of the inside as makeshift tent rooms. Farther down the street, Trestan saw a sight that immediately brought wetness to his eyes. The home of his mentor, Sir Wilhelm Jareth, had completely burned to the ground. Once the largest private home on the streets of the village, now it was a pile of grayish-black ashes. Even the dirt street became a dark, blackened coloring from the fires and soot.

Trestan worried about the condition he would find the smithy and his home. The smithy stood across the street from the stables, and not far from the church. Trestan noted with some initial relief that the shop stood, as well as the buildings on both sides of it. The carpenter's shop to the south had come close to becoming a bonfire, but the efforts of the villagers quenched the flames just before it could ignite the wood supplies within. As they rode closer, Trestan welcomed the sound of a hammer ringing on metal. The small, thankful smile ended when he realized the situation. The person who worked the forge lacked his father's appearance. The chosen of Abriana barely recognized Mikhael, for the boy had grown since they had last seen each other. Cat had told Trestan that his father had been too weak to lay hand to hammer. It had been over half a week, more than five days, since Cat had last seen the aging smith. Trestan could only hope that his father was on the mend.

Mikhael looked up as the pair of riders dismounted before the shop. He recognized Cat right away, due to her recent visit, but his gaze lingered on Trestan. The smith's son had changed in many ways since his departure to the seminary. The superficial aspects distracted old friends: the large warhorse Belgard, the thicker mustache, the suit of armor featuring religious designs, the confident stride, and the good cloth garments from Kashmer. Trestan stood quietly before Mikhael's inquisitive inspection. The youth smiled with recognition, and some amazement, at the perceived changes in Trestan's garments, gait, and facial expressions. Mikhael set aside the hammer and quickly took to washing his hands for a formal greeting.

"Trestan, is it? Must be! It's been so long, and the seasons have brought changes to you."

The two shook hands as Cat finished hitching her horse to the rail. Trestan asked the youth, "It's good to be home, despite the scenes of sorrow and loss appearing before my eyes. How have the years treated you, Mikhael?"

The younger man put on a brief smile. "I learn much here. Your father treats me well. He gives good instruction without being too angry at me when I spoil something expensive."

Trestan asked, "Your parents do not mind your absence at the store?"

The youth shrugged, "I have two sisters and another brother to help them out. They do not miss me that much, and I love the work here."

Mikhael's gaze drifted beyond Trestan. "It was a good life here until the raiders came. Now…well…there is much grief lingering on everyone. Many souls yet to consecrate and rebuilding to be done. I have been putting out a constant supply of nails, hinges, and any number of tools for reconstruction."

As Cat stood quietly nearby, Trestan picked up on something Mikhael had said. "Alone? What about my father?"

Mikhael could see a whirlpool of doubts and fears in Trestan's eyes. "Oh, your father is resting inside. He is holding himself steady as best he can, but work at the forge is far too taxing on him. There hasn't been enough healing to go around for the survivors, since most of the church clerics were killed. They removed the crossbow bolt that wounded your father, but the wound itself has not fully healed. We should get you inside right away; he will feel better seeing you again!"

*     *     *     *     *

Hebden Karok was resting on his bed until Trestan entered. The return of his son lifted the older man's spirits and put strength back into his tired muscles. Despite the concerns of the others, the injured smith got out of his bed and insisted on sitting up in the common room with his son while they talked over drinks. Trestan assisted his limping father to the common table, while Mikhael and Cat cooked up two pots. His guests enjoyed the finest tea locally grown. Hebden drank an herbal broth set forth by one of the surviving clergy of the village.

Father and son savored the first visual contact with each other since Trestan had left four years ago. Abriana's champion noted the added lines of worry on his father's face. Trestan looked on with concern as Hebden made every attempt to appear stronger than he actually felt. Hebden saw the worry in his son's eyes, and felt embarrassed that his only offspring had reason to look at him in that way. For his part, Hebden admired everything about the younger man. His son had grown strong, with new wisdom apparent in those eyes. Hebden remembered a time when Trestan wore dirty shirts and a rope belt; now the young man dressed in a way more befitting one chosen to champion a god.

Trestan respectfully left the opening of the conversation to his father. As much as thoughts and worries assailed his mind, it would not do to begin the reunion with heavy concerns. Apparently, Hebden shared that sentiment. When the older smith started talking, he began by asking Trestan questions about the seminary, Kashmer and his training. Trestan described life at the seminary, highlighting the conversation with tasks he performed and miracles witnessed. Together, Cat and Trestan talked about the day of the Embarking. They told Hebden how Kashmer had changed in the years since the older man last visited. Though the mood surrounding the village had been so poor of late, the conversation in the tiny home produced smiles and laughter. For a time, they easily forgot the worries of the world, as father and son shared a warm homecoming.

The conversation eventually turned to the gloomy present. Hebden talked of the scourge of riders. "It was a massacre. Bloodlust! I saw the two from your stories, Revwar and Savannah, as they rode into town. Another rode with them; his nature seemed above the rest of the other rabble sacking the town. They came and took the relic while the rest of us hid in our homes."

Trestan stroked his thick mustache as he listened. As Hebden paused to sip broth, the young paladin spoke up. "Were they met with any resistance?"

Hebden shook his head and scowled, "Lord Verantir seemed just as scared. He sent nay men to help, and those unfortunate to be in town at the time died quickly. The lord hid behind his own walls and withheld the warriors fealty-sworn to protect the area."

Trestan nodded, knowing as much from Cat's words. However, the young man felt that Hebden had missed the true meaning of his question.

"I didn't mean from the guards," he spoke, "I was referring to the villagers. We saw many new graves on fields outside of the village. I wondered if there had been townsfolk resisting them."

Hebden looked at Trestan over the rim of his cup. The old smith recalled that night many years ago when the other party of adventurers arrived to steal the relic the first time. Many villagers, Hebden included, holed up in their homes in the hope of not getting involved. Trestan, Petrow and the late Sir Wilhelm were among the few that openly tried to stop the other band. Hebden mused that perhaps Trestan expected an outcome closer to how a paladin would have reacted.

"Trestan, we are simple folk. You had the courage to stand and face adversaries when called to do so, but most here are not up to that danger. There was little we could do. They rode right up to the southern merchant carts and attacked defenseless people in force. We could only run or hide."

Trestan lowered his head, "If only I'd been able to help somehow." A thought came to Trestan and his head raised back up. "What about Petrow? Surely he showed a few of them his axe!"

A sad look crossed Hebden's eyes. The older smith remembered the moment his own hopes lifted upon seeing Petrow that day, only to be smashed again when the handyman turned and ran. Hebden spoke rather hesitantly when he found his voice, trying to speak the truth without judging Petrow too harshly.

"Trestan…he has a family to watch over now. Petrow's first thought when the riders came was to look after them."

Trestan's visage changed to one of introspection. Hebden thought to say more but didn't, allowing the young paladin to interpret the words on his own.

Mikhael and Cat said little since the conversation had turned more solemn, although they continued to sip their drinks next to father and son. At that uneasy silence, Cat decided to turn the conversation toward a subject she knew troubled Trestan's heart. It had been obvious during the whole conversation Hebden's injury still distressed him.

The half-elf indicated Hebden's hip, "Your wound is now a week-and-a-half old, and the clerics have not fully healed you?"

Hebden absently massaged his wounded side as he replied, "There are many still in need of healing. Only two of the clergy survived the attack, and their miraculous healing skills are little at best. They sent for more help. In the meantime, there are many like me: slowly recovering from our wounds with broth and older, natural medicines."

Trestan looked to his father with imploring eyes, "Allow me to help, father. I have my own healing miracles at my command now."

Hebden seemed a little startled; as if in the mood of the occasion he had forgotten his son had schooled for four years to serve a goddess. The older smith nodded, shedding some fatherly pride in admitting his pain to his son. At once, Trestan got up and circled the table to be beside his father. The young worshipper of Abriana tenderly placed his hands on Hebden's side.

"He truly is blessed," Cat said, "You would have been so proud of him at the Embarking."

Hebden looked to his son as the young man tenderly touched the wounded area. Trestan prayed quietly, "Abriana, heed the call of your faithful. Heal this person whom I love."

The warmth and love of his goddess flowed through Trestan. The young paladin-aspirant used his body as a conduit to channel the miracle. Love filled Trestan and buoyed his spirit as he let the healing energies course through him. His mind saw a dark scar on Hebden representing the injury. Through the power of faith Trestan guided healing energies around the wound. The darkness shriveled away from the power of the miracle. It faded to a shade, and then disappeared entirely. Trestan ended the flow of healing. The effort drained Trestan a bit, even though the young man wore a smile from the power of love.

Cat smiled and asked Hebden, "How do you feel now?"

Hebden's eyes opened wide with wonder. The smith started to stretch out his legs and twist his torso. The man gave a hearty laugh and patted Trestan on the back. His other hand held the cup of broth, but that hand set the cup down and pushed it away from him.

"Why, I feel good enough to dump this foul-tasting broth and get some good meat in my stomach!"

Hebden smiled to his son, looking him in the eyes. "You have a special gift, my boy. I feel you are truly destined for some higher purpose."

*         *         *         *         *

There were few places Trestan and Cat considered going after meeting his father, but Trestan felt drawn to one of spiritual significance. The two companions tread up the path westward along the river, into the small wood outside of the village. In a secluded clearing, they came upon the shrine built to honor Abriana. Wooden benches bordered a tiered garden of flowers. People could sit for hours while losing their thoughts in the simple beauty of the shrine. Next to the garden, two magically lit gems cast a constant glow over a stone marker.

"Sir Wilhelm Jareth. Champion of Abriana. A good friend and second father to many."

Trestan kneeled before the grave and offered a silent prayer, while Katressa stood back with her head down in deference to the man who rested there. Sir Wilhelm Jareth first taught Trestan how to defend himself with a sword. The paladin of Abriana, a reputable man in Troutbrook, touched many lives with wisdom and compassion. Upon his death at the hands of the elf wizard Revwar, his magical elvish blade passed to Trestan. The young paladin still wore the sword on his back. Trestan had not known it at the time of Jareth's death, but the aging mentor had already instilled in him the values which would lead him to follow the man's footsteps. Now Trestan adopted service to Abriana, albeit still a paladin-in-training according to the seminary doctrines. The ring known as Faithful's Companion adorned a finger on his right hand, displaying a few runes representing unresolved tests facing him. If Sir Wilhelm could see the young man who prayed before his grave, the old warrior would surely smile.

When Trestan's prayer ended, he took a seat with Cat among one of the many benches. The wind playfully rustled the flowers of the garden as the lovers sat in quiet observance. His dark brown eyes sought out her bright emerald orbs, sharing a loving gaze for some time.

Trestan said, "I'm sorry if you feel I have ignored you in any way, *faunlessa*. For so long I looked forward to being with you, free of the bounds of the seminary. I'm glad for the private time we cherish, yet my heart feels burdened by the plight of my friends and father."

Katressa leaned forward and gently kissed him, offering a comforting smile. "I know your heart troubles you. I am from a patient race; I would stand beside you for whatever time you need."

The paladin welcomed Cat's support, though he disagreed with her perception of time. "Cat, I will love you forever if you would have me for that long."

Cat, born from long-lived elvish heritage, could only offer a sad smile, "I can only wish that we have that time, my love."

Trestan turned to silently regard the flowers once more. Cat inquired about his musings. "*Faunlessa*, you have seen your father and helped him. You have seen the damage to your home village. I would know your thoughts."

Trestan groped for the proper words, "I feel...my spirit is restless. It is daunting to know what we faced those years ago...and succeeded...only to see the violent results and know that the relic has once again been stolen."

Noise from the trail interrupted their private conversation. Trestan and Cat turned, surprised to see a small number of villagers approaching. Some of the villagers limped; others displayed distress from other injuries.

"Hail, Trestan, hero of Abriana!" One of them welcomed.

Trestan and Cat exchanged confused glances. The greeting offered had been most unexpected. Trestan regarded the speaker. "Only Squire Trestan as of yet, a hopeful to champion Abriana. Your greeting surprises me, what honor have I claimed to be addressed in such a way?"

The man, carrying a child close to the age of four, responded. "We are worshippers of Abriana as well. We tended the shrine in the years since Sir Wilhelm fell and you departed. The word spread that you were back to visit after learning the ways of the goddess. When I heard you were here, I had to bring my daughter and seek your help."

Trestan looked down at the young child in his arms. The little girl hugged her father close as she looked at Trestan with uncertainty and fear. Trestan asked, "What would you ask of me?"

The man unwrapped a small blanket from around the girl. Cat gasped, and Trestan stood stunned, at seeing that the child was missing a leg. A bandage covered the stump.

Her father shed tears as he continued talking, "Her mother and I tried to run from the riders by escaping across the field. The butchers rode us down as we fled. My daughter was fortunate enough only to lose a leg, for the same cut took her mother's life. She needs a miracle and there have been little enough miracles to go around between the two clerics of Yestreal that survived."

Trestan got up the courage to walk closer to the girl. Whispering words of reassurance, he gently examined the bandage around her leg. Cat could not see the wound, but she could tell from the way Trestan took in a sharp pull of breath that he didn't like what he saw.

Putting on a confident look, Trestan told the man, "I can help her."

Cat watched as Trestan prayed once again to Abriana. The child cried and squirmed at first, but as the miracle healed her, she looked with awe. The young paladin had no ability to restore a lost limb, but he removed the gangrenous infection afflicting her. The father showed great relief that the wound had been cleansed. He thanked the young paladin fervently, offering his own prayer to thank Abriana for her champion.

Another wounded person stepped forward. Trestan heard another tale of pain and fear about how the raiders had inflicted this wound. Once again, Trestan drew forth his reserves of energy to tap into the healing power. Trestan served as a fine representative of the Goddess of Love and Healing as he moved to help the ones in need. Unfortunately, no sooner had he healed one person then another stepped forward. All of them had a sad, horrified story to tell. Trestan listened to them as they told him of their hurts, their fears, and their helplessness. He brought forth all the healing energy he could muster to help them with their pains.

These were not strangers whom Trestan helped, for all of them he had known from growing up in this small community. The young warrior listened to stories of neighbors and old friends who had suffered from the raid, as he helped to heal those who had survived. He learned the names of many acquaintances that did not survive the attack, leaving behind grieving families. The events of the attack came together piece by piece, until it seemed that Trestan could see himself in the village that day amidst all the chaos.

Trestan's energy expended, and yet still another person stepped forward with a broken shoulder. Trestan looked upon the young man's injured limb with saddened eyes, strained with the efforts of healing and the weight of sorrow for their pains. He knew his spirit felt too taxed to channel another miracle.

"I can heal you, but be not afraid," Trestan reached back and drew forth his magical elvish blade. "I have to rely on a source of healing that will bring some pain to me, but worry not about my safety!"

Runes inscribed on the blade bore its name in elvish, the Sword of the Spirit. It was a rather long but narrow blade, fitted with a hilt that could accommodate a two-handed grip easily. The elvish patterns etched on the blade had been copied into Katressa's *Taef' Adorina* when Trestan and the wizard Korrelothar constructed it. The elvish bastard sword displayed a remarkable, enchanted cutting power beyond any nonmagical sword. Trestan used it now for another power locked within the design of the blade. The sword could be used as a link, whereby one person could send their life energy to heal another, but the drawback was that the healer would be inflicted with pain and injury themselves. Any person could heal the pains of someone dear, if willing to sacrifice their own health.

With a hand on the young man's wounded arm, Trestan willed forth the healing energies of the sword. Predictably, pain wracked him as some of his life-force transferred to the wounded man. Trestan stopped short of fully healing the arm, collapsing to his knees as his own pain became too great. The young villager moved his arm around with fewer limitations than before. Despite his inner pain, Trestan offered up a weary smile.

"Be easy on that arm, it will still take time before it is fully healed."

While Trestan remained kneeling, the young man stepped back, revealing one last person seeking an ailment to her injury. The maiden cradled a hand blackened by fire. Trestan looked into her face and saw hope fade, for she could see in his eyes he had nothing left to give. The maiden looked down, shedding a tear for her hurts. The champion of Abriana determined then that he would risk serious injury to help her. He grunted in pain as he rose to his feet. Trestan wasn't sure he would even be able to make it back to the village under his own power once done.

A slender, feminine hand stopped him. Cat, who had watched villager after villager healed while she could do nothing, held Trestan back.

"It's my turn now."

Trestan looked up into Cat's crying eyes. The half-elf heard every sad story told by the villagers and had wept with them in what little comfort she had been able to offer. Now, her nimble hand latched onto the handle of the sword, but Trestan did not let go.

"I can't ask you to do this." The champion of Abriana implored.

Cat replied, "You didn't. This is my choice, my chance to help. You should rest now."

When Trestan continued to stubbornly hold onto the sword, Cat leaned in close and whispered privately to him. "When you have rested, you will be able to cure our injuries. I would be willing to endure, for one day, the pain that has tortured this woman for over a week."

Trestan looked into her eyes with love, and released the sword to her grip. Cat carried the sword over to the maiden. The young woman shifted nervously, but she spoke her thanks. Cat laid a gentle hand on the maiden's shoulder.

"Be well again," Cat said, before she opened up the flow of life energy between them.

*         *         *         *         *

After the other villagers left the shrine, Cat and Trestan wearily stumbled down the path back to town. They walked slowly, cringing from the aches their bodies endured using the sword's magic. The sun, low in the sky, finally threw rays through scattered clouds. It had been a long day.

"What now my love?" asked Cat.

Trestan considered it for only a moment. "There is time enough in the day to visit a dear old friend. Let's go see Petrow."

**CHAPTER 5**          **"Petrow's Family"**

"I have only embarked on one great adventure since we returned with the stones," Petrow stated as he hoisted the small boy up to his lap. "The adventure and excitement of always keeping one eye on this little troublemaker."

Petrow proceeded to tickle the three-year-old. The child giggled, the only noise the shy boy uttered during Trestan and Cat's visit. His blue eyes matched those of his father, and he wriggled in Petrow's lap. He tried hard to retain a small wooden carving of a bear in his tiny hands. The tickling brought forth laughter from the other occupants of the dining area as well.

Trestan and Cat leaned against each other on a bench running along one side of the table. Both remained exhausted from their ordeal employing the healing powers of the sword. A stew provided some refreshment for them, though their bodies still craved rest. Nevertheless, they stayed awake and entertained by Petrow and his children. They laughed as the little boy escaped his father's arms and ran around the room. Eventually, the child grabbed a hold of his mother's skirt and hid behind it, with just those pretty blue eyes and light brown hair peeking over the length of it.

Inedra, the farmer's daughter Petrow married right after returning with the holy relics, laughed as her child suddenly took refuge near her legs. Her auburn hair was in a bit of disarray, between running after children and taking care of chores on the farm. The woman's freckled face smiled down on her son, even as her hands cleaned bowls.

Trestan asked Petrow, "And you named him Wilhelm? After Sir Wilhelm?"

Petrow chuckled, "Aye, I wanted to honor the man, Tres. The lad goes by the name Lil' Willy; that's what everyone calls him."

Cat turned to regard a crib in one corner, her gaze drawn to the sleeping child within. "How did Leane get her name?"

Petrow looked over to his second child, a young daughter only a year old. Her little cherubic face peeked out from under a colorful blanket. "Leane was named after Inedra's grandmother, whom I never got to know."

Inedra set down the last bowl and herded Willy back toward the table. "My grandmother was a special person, who gave me so many fond memories. I wanted to honor her name."

Trestan nodded, and then asked, "What about the third child? Any names picked out yet?"

Inedra rubbed her palm over her waist, though it was too early for her to show swelling from her latest pregnancy. She answered, "Not yet, it's still early. Give us a little more time. Closer to the date we'll argue over one." She grinned at Petrow, "And how many times have I asked you not to wear your hat to the dinner table?"

Petrow, looking sheepish, reached up and removed the straw hat that had fast become another of his favorite possessions. Some things about Petrow never changed. He stayed tanned and muscular from all the hard work he did outdoors. His old woodcutter's axe hung on one wall. The blue-eyed man still preferred sandals, even though he had a good pair of boots set near the door. Long hours tilling the soil of his farm left his feet dirty. Inedra and Petrow lived in a small house on land that once belonged to her father. He gave a portion to them and now Petrow grew his own crops.

After setting the hat aside, Petrow looked to Trestan and Cat. "And how about yourselves? Any adventures brewing?" A mischievous smile grew behind Petrow's words.

"Oh, that wasn't a very subtle way of asking! You shouldn't pin them with such an open question like that." Inedra remarked.

Trestan's and Cat's faces looked a little embarrassed by the direct query. Surely the two of them were in love and planned on spending time together, but Cat struggled internally with the question of longevity and their respective ages. Trestan and Cat both tended to live for the moment and not dwell as much on the future. In looking at Petrow and his family, it brought to mind their hesitancies.

Trestan dodged Petrow's question. "We hoped to have some good times together now that I'm not restricted by the walls of the seminary. We planned some journeys. Sadly…to come back home and find this…it's shocking. In such a short time, I have learned of the deaths of so many lifelong acquaintances and friends."

Inedra sat beside Petrow, their eyes grim. Although their family survived unharmed, they lost friends and neighbors. It came as no surprise that Willy stayed quiet and shy, often hiding behind the folds of Inedra's skirt, or clutching at his precious wooden bear. The lad was old enough to feel the change around him, but too young to understand it.

Petrow commented, "It's been a hard, sad time since that day, Tres. Many folk do not know how to move on and get past it. Your visit here has been the only joyful moment since then."

Trestan asked, "Petrow, when the riders came, I'm told none in the village put up any kind of a resistance. Why didn't you fight them?"

Inedra's reaction surprised Trestan. She glared at him for a moment, before holding herself tighter to Petrow's side. Petrow paused as if he had a lump in his throat.

He spoke quietly, "Tres, you have to believe there was nay difference I could have made. A small army rode into the town and my first concern was for my family. I had to see them safe."

Silence descended in the room. Trestan and Petrow both had their eyes downcast, though Petrow kept close to Inedra.

Cat reached across the table and put a soft hand on Petrow's arm. "There would have been naught you could do except leave your children fatherless." She turned to look at Trestan. "It has been a terrible time for all."

Trestan nodded, "I'm sorry if I sounded accusing of anything, Petrow. I feel very helpless. Cat and I had the chance to bring relief to a few of the villagers, but if my prayers found their wish it would be that I could undo what was done."

Inedra looked to Petrow's grim face, "Petrow will always be my hero. I couldn't raise the children without him." She turned to look across the table again. "There are many families suffering. I thank the gods every day that we survived unharmed."

Trestan offered a smile to the couple, "It is a blessing indeed that some whom I hold closest and dearest were not hurt. Abriana watch over you always."

50

He continued talking in a more somber tone, "Maybe I'm being selfish; however, I believe it's more than that. I truly looked forward to riding into the far countryside with Cat. We hoped to visit some scenic places she told me about. Instead, my past comes back to pain me. The very adventures leading us down this road were for naught. Revwar and Savannah once again possess the village's relic and the powers it possesses."

Petrow disagreed. "Not all for naught. Even if they have the one stone, the other two are safe in Orlaun. We served a purpose back then, and it was not all undone."

Trestan's eyes widened, "As far as we know, but what if they are to be stolen next?"

Petrow had no answer to that. The rest of the room fell silent as they all considered the implications.

Trestan began to smooth and stroke his mustache as he sat in quiet contemplation. As his hand moved, he caught a glimpse of something. He held his right hand before his face, staring at the metal band on one finger. Faithful's Companion glinted in the firelight. On its surface remained a few symbols of deeds he needed to complete, before he could return to the seminary as a full-fledged paladin.

"Maybe this is my task"

Petrow asked, "What task?"

Cat put an arm around Trestan, looking into his eyes to see the thoughts stirring within them. Despite the weariness Trestan felt, he somehow sat taller as his resolve formed around a solution. The chosen champion of Abriana spoke, "Despite my plans with Cat, I am away from the seminary for a reason. This ring represents challenges yet before me if I wish to continue to become a paladin in the service of my goddess. The squires leave the seminary at the Embarking, only to search out a quest or adventure by which to finish the requirements of Abriana."

Cat's eyes turned sad with the news she expected, and yet she smiled as Trestan reaffirmed the values she loved about him. Her melodic voice asked, "You plan to go to Orlaun?"

"Aye," Trestan nodded, "One relic is stolen, but there are two more to protect. This is an obligation which I shall not shy away. Korrelothar must be warned of what happened here. The other two stones may still be in jeopardy. We can book passage to Orlaun down in Barkan's Crossing…"

Inedra openly scowled at Petrow. The handyman-turned-hero-turned-farmer seemed to bite his lip with indecisiveness on how to answer Trestan's statement. Trestan continued stating his plans to visit Orlaun until Inedra suddenly and hurriedly excused herself from the table. She scooped up Lil' Willy in her arms and stomped into the bedroom, letting the door slam behind her.

"What was that about?" Trestan asked, shocked.

Petrow took in a deep breath, "I think it was the part about 'we'."

Cat studied Petrow's face carefully as he continued speaking, "I'll…have a talk with her."

Trestan tried to move past the awkward moment, "Well, once we get to Orlaun we'll see what needs to be done there. I wish all of our old friends were together again. Anyone know where Salgor is?"

Cat answered, though her eyes drifted between Petrow and the closed door. "I've seen him a few times, but last I knew he was prospecting for a spot to build his pub. He took a ship out of Kashmer some time ago. I have nay idea how we would know where to contact him."

Trestan frowned, "That is unfortunate. How about Mel?"

Petrow pointed southward, "He went back home, though I've heard little from him. Apparently, his family wasn't too happy to see him back, but you know Mel, he's not bothered by it. He took up residence in his home village in the woods along the road, though I couldn't tell you what mischief he may be up to today."

Trestan grinned at that, "We'll be passing right by his home! I can't wait to see him again."

Cat observed the way Petrow glanced at the bedroom to the side, as Trestan stood and stretched. The young squire of Abriana grabbed his helmet and his sword belt.

Cat rose to her feet as Trestan commented, "I feel so tired, and yet so eager now that I have a path before me. It feels good that I can resolve to do something helpful. We can go see Korrelothar and great city of Orlaun. Yet, while there, we can warn him about guarding those relics closer."

Trestan and Cat grabbed their belongings and approached the door. "Thanks again, Petrow, and thank Inedra for us, for your hospitality and the food. We have to get some rest. It's a long journey before us, and I want to get started early."

Petrow said little, but helped them out the door. Trestan and Cat walked under the starry sky, toward the lights of the village. Petrow's small farmhouse receded into the dark.

During the walk, Cat shook her head and commented, "It amazes me. You can read the mind of a bear and see its pain, yet you can't read the emotions on your best friend's face."

Trestan asked, "What do you mean?"

Cat looked back over her shoulder, though Petrow's farm was unseen in the dark behind them. "You didn't see the looks traded between him and Inedra? You didn't see it in his eyes? He isn't coming with us in the morning."

Before Trestan could argue, Cat turned and stopped him, gently putting her hand on his cheek. She lifted up on her toes to plant a small kiss on his lips, before resuming her course toward the village.

Over her back, Trestan heard her repeat the prediction. "He isn't coming."

*        *        *        *        *

The nightmare struck like it often had during the past few years.

A number of faces surrounded him, cruelly laughing at his predicament. They formed the ugly background of the dream: the hazy jeers of drunk, evil men.

At the forefront, he felt the hot breath of the bull before turning to regard its reddish eyes. One of its long horns, broken, leaked blood out of the shattered end. The bull gave out a roar unlike any a bull would utter, a roar more akin to an angry minotaur. It charged him and sent him sprawling to the ground. He was unable to rise, yet the bull rose up on its hind legs and brought its front hooves crashing down on him.

Petrow looked to his legs when he had the chance. His legs splayed at odd angles. He felt no sensation of pain, yet he could remember what the pain of broken limbs was like. The faces at the edges of his vision danced about and laughed at his misery. The men of the *Silver Trident* howled in entertainment at watching the spectacle.

The bull stomped on him again. Petrow shook as the bull pounded his body. The nightmare did not offer physical pain, but Petrow could remember the pain from that night.

When the bull went away, the men still lingered. They joked at Petrow's pleas for mercy. Someone stepped forward. Petrow saw a blonde woman whom at first glance might be considered beautiful. Petrow knew her and felt fear. The cold, blue eyes of Savannah, abbess to the Death Goddess, stared down at him. Petrow wanted to crawl away, but his arms and legs would no longer heed his mental commands. His body lay broken and helpless. Savannah stepped up beside him, and Petrow remembered she was supposed to heal him like she had before. She was supposed to heal him so the bull could deliver more pain to him.

Savannah did not heal him. Instead, the woman knelt over his chest, reaching her feminine hands up to his neck. With coldness in her eyes, she began to close her hands tightly about his throat. Petrow struggled to find air, but air would not come. The jeering faces in the background faded away, until all Petrow could see of the world were those cold, blue eyes.

Petrow jumped out of bed as he awoke, taking a deep gasp of precious air. The noise of his frantic breathing shocked Inedra, Lil' Willy, and Leane awake. With every exhale, he cried out in wordless terror at the fading images of the dream. Inedra called to him, but Petrow could not answer. His mind reeling from the familiar nightmare, he stumbled out of the house, ignoring the cries of his family.

Inedra found him out in the field sometime later. Lil' Willy and Leane had been soothed back to sleep with no help from their absent father. She cautiously approached him from behind. Inedra noticed he looked out into the darkness with his hands tightly gripped around his old woodcutter's axe, like he had on many nights in the past.

"I feel so angry, and yet so helpless," Inedra called to him. "I love you and I always will. Yet, I can't fight your nightmares away from you. I'm tired of putting our son and daughter to bed after they see you panic in the middle of the night. It makes me mad. Even worse is that I feel there is naught I can do about it. I would wipe those bad memories from your mind if I could."

Petrow turned to her, and she could see the trails that tears had run over his cheeks. He released his axe with one hand, and reached out to pull Inedra to him. They embraced under the stars.

"There is a part of me that wants to follow Trestan and Cat." He felt Inedra's body stiffen as he said it. "To ride out there, confront my fears, and once again make a difference for the village. A part of me wants to ride with them once more."

Petrow turned Inedra's face to look him in the eyes. "But I can't do it. My heart is here. Even if it wasn't, a part of me is too afraid of what new nightmares I might face if I went out again. I just wanted you to know that an honest part of me yearns to go down that trail. I can't do it. My heart is here with you and my children. Believe me, I wish I could get past the bad memories too."

Inedra spoke in her quiet voice, "You can't go with them. You can't leave me alone here."

"I know." Petrow paused. "My home is by your side, I'm not leaving. Someday the nightmares will fade away."

*   *   *   *   *

The nightmare struck like it often had during the past few years.

When she awoke from it, she could not stop screaming in terror from the memory. Her thrashing sent her tumbling from the bed, onto the rolling wooden deck of her cabin. She looked about with wild blue eyes at the surrounding room. No more undead spirits came to torture her. The stench of zombies no longer clogged her nose. The nightmare sent by DeLaris, the Death Goddess, faded into memory.

Savannah sat alone in the cramped ship's cabin, with nothing to threaten her but her own recollection of the familiar nightmare. Only her rapid breathing and scared eyes remained from her nightly torment.

She did not stay alone for long, as someone overhearing the screams thrust open the door. Her eyes shifted back to their cold, distant expression, as Jentan Mollamos appeared at the doorway with wand in hand. The mentalist looked to the cleric, sitting in disarray amongst her scattered blankets on the wooden floor. Then, his eyes searched the remainder of the tiny room, looking for any danger.

Savannah composed what dignity she had, standing up in her nightshift and gathering up her scattered linen. "There is nay threat here, Jentan, and I don't approve of you taking such a close interest in my welfare."

Jentan smiled sweetly and casually tucked away his dangerous wand. Rather than leave, he strode into the cabin and allowed the door to shut behind him. "Alas, I must admit it was only by chance that I presented before your door at this moment. It is my humble honor to relay the news that we approach the harbor of the fabled City of Spires, Your Grace."

Jentan always retained charm and elegance in how he spoke to people. Such charm was lost on Savannah, who cared little for the man other than his participation in their mutual goals. "You've delivered the news, now leave me some privacy."

The abbess of DeLaris moved to the only small porthole the cabin offered. Looking out, Savannah could see parts of a shoreline, but not the harbor itself. The woman paid little attention to the scenery, instead replaying in her mind the nightmare and the events which caused it. Savannah noted that while Jentan nodded his head at her words, the mage made no move to remove himself from her presence. In contradiction, he moved closer.

"Perhaps I could be of additional service to my valued companion?"

Savannah could have laughed at the absurd way in which he tried to charm her, if she felt in any mood to laugh.

"If I may venture," Jentan spoke, "Revwar told me of visions that haunt your sleep in the dark reaches of the night."

Savannah turned a glare at the man, her face expressing that he treaded on dangerous ground. Heedless of her look, he continued, "It does not assist our cause if there are demons which plague your sleep. Forgive me if I am perceptive enough to notice the phantoms which haunt your mornings, Your Grace. There is a strain about your eyes from lack of decent sleep. I could offer you assistance. There is a magic called hypnosis, by which one can…"

Savannah scoffed, noting that Jentan's gaze had fallen from her own eyes and drifted southward toward the womanly curves of her nightshift. "I would nay sooner allow myself under your hypnosis than I would walk naked into a sailor bar!"

Jentan looked offended to be compared with such an environment. Savannah continued, "Nor would your mind tricks be of any help. My nightmares are sent by my goddess in punishment, and rightly so. You can't help me. Leave now"

Jentan hovered at the door a bit longer. He seemed about to say more, but changed his mind and started to leave. After the door closed behind him, Savannah continued to look beyond the shoreline, at images from the past.

Savannah whispered to the memory of the blue-eyed handyman from the small village of Troutbrook. "I should have taken the opportunity when I had the chance, while we had all those armed men in Troutbrook. I was there, and yet I turned to follow the greater quest instead of killing you while I could. An abbess of Death delivers life or death as she will in the service to her goddess. I claimed your life Petrow, and it is an affront to my goddess that you still live. I will find nay relief from the nightmares as long as you still breathe.

"Someday the nightmares will fade away." The abbess stated with resolve, "They will be gone from my life after I go back to kill you."

*      *      *      *      *

Dawn illuminated the village. Despite Trestan's insistence on getting started early, they did not leave his home without sharing a good breakfast with his father. Hebden looked and felt much better than he had the previous day. Trestan lent forth more of his miraculous healing powers to his father. The old smith declared he felt fit as ever to work the forge. Trestan brought forth the healing blessings of his goddess upon Katressa and himself as well; curing the physical injuries incurred by using the elvish sword's healing magic. Both father and son expressed sadness at parting so soon after reuniting. Hebden encouraged Trestan to follow his heart, hiding his own lonely feelings at his son's brief visit. Trestan felt odd to be leaving home so soon after returning from the long years at the seminary, but he felt the need of a quest before him. The young man questioned Cat about her feelings, but the half-elf supported him as well. As long as he had a destiny calling him, she wanted to be there to ride the trail with him.

Trestan Karok and Katressa Bilil mounted their horses and rode toward Petrow's farm. Trestan sat atop Belgard in his traveling attire. His magical sword hung over his back, while he wore the armor that he had forged at the seminary. The symbols and colors of Abriana announced his faith as he began his new quest. Katressa wore her black riding leathers and helm. On her left arm, she wore a strange bracer. Something seemed hidden under a portion of it, but Cat would not give any secrets away as to what surprise lay hidden under a fold of leather and cloth. With sword and armor equipped, they were stopped partway out of town by one of the villagers.

The maiden whose hand had been burnt hailed them to once again thank Trestan and Katressa for the healing miracle. The two companions talked with her briefly. She inquired about their destination. Trestan assured her he sought those who stole the relic, and if the gods blessed it, he would see the relic back in the care of the village. When Trestan and Cat continued riding forth, the woman ran out of sight in a rather excited manner. The two companions did not ponder it at the time.

After a short ride, they arrived at Petrow's farm. They saw Petrow walking about his field wearing his sandals and straw hat. Lil' Willy played near the house. As Trestan and Cat approached, Petrow looked up to greet them with an uncertain visage. Both companions noted Petrow did not appear to be dressed or equipped for any type of journey. Cat recognized the emotions playing underneath the straw hat as Petrow looked to them, sighed, and seemed resigned that he must now let down his friends.

"I'm really sorry if you were still expecting me to leave today," Petrow explained, "Believe me when I tell you I am tempted to go down that road."

Trestan offered a sad frown upon confirming that Petrow was obviously not going, though after Cat's intuitive guess the previous night, the revelation was not unexpected. Even as they talked, Inedra came out of the house holding baby Leane in her arms. Lil' Willy ran over to cling to his mother's side.

Petrow continued, "I have a place here that I can't ignore. I have a loving wife, children, and property to watch over. I can't go."

Trestan nodded, "Katressa knew you wouldn't come. I would have loved to travel and quest again with you Petrow, but I understand the reasons which hold you back."

"I wasn't built for adventuring, Tres." Petrow conceded. "I suppose I thought I was trying to be more of a man or such when we left those years ago. However…I still have some terrible memories of the dangers from that time. It is nay place for me to go again and especially not now that I have a commitment here."

Cat leaned down from her horse and lifted Petrow's straw hat, kissing him gently on the forehead. "*Inue fa mersan quelo pesubla dun tieratir, ulos fa avianir quelo detreblo dun beleamos.*"

Petrow smiled in confusion, "That sounds pretty, but what does it mean?"

To his surprise, Trestan answered, "It means, 'May the trees be your walls against storms, and the birds be your sentries against enemies.' She is blessing your home as we say goodbye."

Petrow smiled warmly to Cat, and then blinked up at Trestan. "You speak Elvish now?"

Trestan laughed, "Oh, just a little."

"But I bet you still don't know how to whistle!"

More laughter erupted as Trestan acknowledged his inability to master the simple art of whistling.

It was a good last laugh for the old Companions of the Relics to share before Trestan and Cat turned their horses southwards again. Petrow stood alongside his wife and children, waving as their friends went away to adventure. Trestan and Cat waved back. Cat saw the wetness in the corners of Trestan's eyes. They talked about it on the dirt road. Trestan admitted his hopes that Petrow would join them. He felt blessed to have Cat by his side, but he would miss the presence of his childhood friend.

By the time the companions arrived at the main street of Troutbrook, an unexpected surprise awaited them.

The maiden they talked to had told other villagers about Trestan's intentions. Those fellow followers of Abriana quickly acted to give a suitable farewell to their champion on his quest. Others inquired about the sudden bustle of activity and the tale spread. Trestan, already a hometown hero for recovering the relic and rescuing the local noble's daughter during the first adventure, would receive an appropriate send off. In Troutbrook, where the shadow of mourning and lost loved ones lingered since the bloody assault, the people had reason to celebrate and feel hope once again.

The two times Trestan left the village during the course of their first adventure, both exits happened secretly under cover of night. Now, Trestan rode out in broad daylight through the village, with several of his old friends and neighbors well aware of his plans. People gathered in streets, many more watched from windows, as their knight in armor and his companion half-elf rode back through the village. Trestan and Cat rode in wide-eyed surprise as villagers crowded along the street to cheer the chosen of Abriana. Businesses halted as everyone came out to see the one who would take up a cause for them. Petals of wild flowers sprinkled the blackened street, scenting the path as if a wild garden. Children and maidens alike threw more blossoms ahead of the two horses. A number of seeds were thrown over them: a blessing of future prosperity from a farming community. Someone from the second floor of the inn threw rice as the two companions rode past. Cat giggled as she shook some from her long, black hair. Belgard reared his head tall and proud as he carried Trestan over a street full of colors.

The villagers' show of support bolstered his confidence. Never had he expected to receive a gathering such as his hometown presented. Trestan sat atop his warhorse as straight and tall as any stonemason could carve into statue. People cheered, prayed, waved or saluted him with tankards in hand. An innocent young boy eagerly banged together a wooden sword and shield in excitement. A surviving priest of Yestreal played a fiddle in front of the burned church; its notes carried on the air in honor of the departing heroes. One of the villagers who had proclaimed himself as a follower to Abriana knelt and prayed as the companions went past. Cat observed the way Trestan's quest had energized the people. Once again they had hope in the future of their world. Their own local lord had shown little regard or concern for the village. Now, riding amongst them and larger than life, was a paladin of a goddess willing to see justice done. The people cheered their savior, as if Trestan was already returning with the relic.

Trestan smiled when he passed the smithy. From beside the anvil, Hebden Karok wore his work apron in preparation for a busy day. The healed smith held up a hammer as he saluted his son. Cat saw the fatherly pride shining in Hebden's eyes.

Trestan and Cat arrived at the other end of the village. Someone had wrapped the stone bridge in colorful ribbons and thread. The crowd fell behind them as the two riders began crossing the bridge. Cat reached the other side, but noticed that Trestan had stopped mid-length and turned to face the crowd of onlookers. Trestan sat tall above Belgard as the people gave another rowdy cheer. Wanting to give them a suitable goodbye, Trestan reached over his shoulder and drew forth the Sword of the Spirit. He started to salute with the sword up high, and then prompted Belgard into a practiced motion. Abriana's champion slowly swung the sword low and to the side as Belgard dipped his head and one of his forward legs. Horse and rider bowed, to the delight of the crowd. The people cheered their hero.

With a flourish, Trestan turned and took to the southern road, Cat by his side. Together the two of them sought out their new adventure.

And the send-off to their adventure gave them pause a few miles down the road, when they stopped to remove the seeds and rice which settled in their boots.

**CHAPTER 6**          **"Lindon, Minstrel of Orlaun"**

An insistent knock during the late afternoon hours brought the old man shuffling along, wondering who could be interrupting his latest musical composition. By the sound of the pounding rain on the roof, the aged inhabitant could only guess what urgency would bring someone in such weather. The occupant wrapped a cloak around his own frame to better dress for a visitor, as well as protect from the chilly weather.

"Who dares face dreary onslaught and risks a soaked wardrobe in order to grace my abode with his presence?" The aged composer asked as he swung open the door.

At first, the man worried he had made a mistake allowing entry to the unknown party outside. It alarmed him to see the man outside his door armed with a smallsword and various other implements of combat. The smallsword design included a loop of leather passing through the circular pommel. A crossbow hung visible, as was a small metal buckler strapped to one forearm. The features of the stranger's face hid under a broad-rimmed hat, decorated by reddish feathers in the hatband which drooped under the weight of rainwater. The older man's fears were slightly offset by the presence of a mandolin case strapped over the stranger's back. The unknown visitor seemed to be a fellow musician, despite knowing how to defend himself.

The composer started to shrink back into the door when at last the visitor lifted his head against the patter of the rain. The red beard shook rain droplets as the voice beneath the hat spoke, "It is a former student, come to visit his favorite mentor after a bit of traveling."

Indeed, the older man smiled as he saw the red-bearded face of a former apprentice. He spoke again, talking in a friendlier tone and offering up a rhyme for his visitor. "Long have been the months since you've been around, is it duty or crown calling you back to town?"

The red-bearded visitor smiled back at his old tutor, accepting the rhyming challenge, "In regards to honor and what kings say, that would be a nay, I have debts of kindness aplenty to repay!"

"Then an unexpected pleasure this is, but good, to find you here in this neck of the wood."

"I'm glad I brought such a smile to a friend, perhaps in a few years I shall drop by again!"

The two men chuckled, and the old tutor invited his unexpected guest to enter his home and spend no more time in the rain.

    *        *        *        *        *

The two men relaxed before a warm fire, drinking an old vintage of wine. The host was an aging, retired teacher of music and composition at one of the local artistic guilds. The younger man graduated from that guild, the Artistic Enlightenment College of Orlaun, and had been absent for over a year doing some traveling and making a name for himself in the world.

"I spent my time well this past year," commented the former student, "I entertained royalty over in the various Counties of Diara! However, I admit that was nay great feat, since all of them claim to be descended from royalty! I thought I'd steal a few songs from the rogues in Archer's Port, though I seemed to have lost some coins instead. I also visited Pluetlo, but my time among the halflings and gnomes was quite short."

The older man chuckled at the parodies of the realms. The red-bearded traveler continued, "And when I learned of a rare event planned here in Orlaun, I had to seek out my old master. You nay longer teach the young at the college? I wonder if you still hold influence among those who head the guild, Master Falerno Giantcharmer?"

The aging master composer, whose exploits in turning aside a raging giant in his youth had earned him the surname, nodded to his visitor. "Indeed, I still hold much sway with the current hierarchy. Now, I wonder what influence you want on my behalf? Before you answer, I would ask a question of you. It is so rare these days that someone calls me by my full title. I am interested if you have found a suitable surname as of yet?"

It was common for entertainers who finished their teachings to choose surnames of their own. Sometimes names were chosen for them. On occasions that a student did not immediately pick one, they went by a more generic name until a suitable surname was found.

The recent traveler shook his head, "Nay. Until I find the right inspiration, I still go by Lindon of Orlaun, minstrel and voyager. Through all my travels I have not come upon a suitable situation or feat befitting a proper surname. That is another way of saying: I haven't charmed a giant yet."

Lindon raised his glass of wine in salute to his mentor and drank. The old composer gracefully nodded as he did likewise.

"You flatter me," Falerno Giantcharmer remarked, "The incident with the giant was so long ago..." The old composer paused for some dramatic effect before adding more insight, "I'm sure he has died of old age by now!"

Lindon and his past mentor shared a laugh. For a while, nothing more was said as each man relaxed and imbibed a healthy amount of spirits. Master Falerno looked over Lindon. He knew the younger man to be around the age of twenty-seven. He noted interesting similarities and differences in the man after his year of world traveling. Lindon trimmed his hair, but left long, red sideburns extending into a small, pointed beard on his chin. The mustache was gone, leaving no hair above the lip. The facial growth framed his face and rounded it out more. Lindon smiled well, displaying a row of perfectly cleaned teeth. The younger man's light blue eyes seemed to sparkle with the harmony in the world. The minstrel's hands presented long, thin fingers, allowing great flexibility. From the moment Lindon hung up his cloak and wide-brimmed red hat, Master Falerno witnessed accentuated flourishes, seeing the grace of movement and flexibility which once delivered Lindon through amazingly tiring dance steps. Little was asked about the smallsword and crossbow Lindon carried, for anyone could appreciate the many concealed dangers in the world. Falerno did not even notice a bulge under Lindon's top vest, hiding a bandolier of throwing daggers. Typical Orlaun fashions included a lot of layers of clothing, some of which had decorative ruffles or were worn loosely. A member of the society could easily conceal small weapons. A mandolin case rested beside Lindon's chair, containing the instrument bought from the college during his instruction.

"Now, back to my other question." Master Falerno asked, "What favor do you require of me?"

"I'm told a rare performance will be held soon, atop a lofty stage. I also know the Artistic Enlightenment College was asked to provide entertainers for the affair." Lindon smiled as recognition dawned in the eyes of his mentor.

Master Falerno nodded, "Indeed, but they were asked to send their best *students*. It is a chance of a lifetime for recognition, considering the people for whom they will be performing; however, you are nay longer a student."

Lindon shrugged in acknowledgement of the fact, "But, would sending students, even their best students, be in the best interest of the college?"

"Indulge me with your reasoning as to that conclusion."

Lindon leaned forward eagerly, "Will mere students entertain royalty accustomed to paying for the best? How nervous will these entertainers be considering the atmosphere of their performance? If they falter a tune or fail to stroke the emotions of their audience, how will that reflect on the guild? I think the college may want to consider adding in some past graduates who have more experience."

The elder composer chuckled, "So, you would pull strings with me so that you may pluck strings for royalty? Trying to use me to make a name for yourself?"

Lindon waved a hand, "Well, I can't deny some underlying intent to make a dream come true, spreading my name among the elite of Orlaun; however, there is a more honorable reason at the heart of this particular performance."

The red-bearded minstrel paused to put a hand in one pocket and retrieve the items within. From his vest, he withdrew two flutes much longer than the pocket from which they came. Either the pocket was tailored in a way deceptive about how deep it was, or the vest possessed some magic. Lindon placed one flute, shiny and metallic, off to one side. The other, a well-crafted bamboo flute, Lindon of Orlaun cradled tenderly.

"The music of this flute has such a grand quality to it," Lindon commented. "It plays notes akin to soft breezes carried along a sylvan wood."

Lindon of Orlaun looked up to his former master. "The person who gave this to me, thus starting me on the path of music, will be there. This flute brought me from the slums of the Highwater district to the heights of musical artistry. That is the debt of kindness which needs to be repaid."

Master Falerno Giantcharmer nodded, offering Lindon a warm smile. "Well, I can exert some influence in the college. You realize there is also an audience with members of the wizard guild? They will judge each applicant the college sends."

Lindon nodded.

"Very well," the old mentor spoke, "I shall see what I can do, though I will wait until the rain clears a bit."

*        *        *        *        *

Later that night, Lindon found shelter from the rain within the comforts of Ye Tipped Flask. The proprietors made the establishment more of a drinking house than an inn; a favorite of locals who enjoyed sharing their brew with known regulars rather than strange visitors from the boats. Situated within the Trade district, the patrons of the pub witnessed and participated in many conversations centered on taxes, weather, foreign currency, prospective deals, and many other mercantile concerns. Being a native of Orlaun, Lindon recognized a few faces in the sparse light of the common drinking room. To the minstrel's dismay, one of the great local attractions of the pub was not performing this night. The local Faizinni jugglers, a group of halfling siblings whose show entertained Orlaun for near to twenty years, were one of the major attractions which brought others into the pub. Substituting in their place, the night's entertainment consisted of some unknown bard with more voice than talent. The entertainer went largely ignored as the patrons consumed their drinks

Lindon stood and observed the stage performer, though out of the corner of his eyes he watched a barmaid making her rounds. The woman moved with her own graceful dance as she weaved among overfed merchants to deliver drinks and food to expand their belt sizes. The barmaid worked hard keeping up with shouted orders and coin exchanges, while at the same time dodging personal questions and male advances. Lindon focused on her as he moved subtly closer to her path.

Lindon spoke beside her shoulder, though she had taken no particular notice of him as yet. "A year of traveling has left my lips lonely for the taste of drink or the warm kiss of a woman, would either be found here?"

Jolynn the barmaid looked up at the face of Lindon. She let out a delighted smile at recognizing the man, and then offered a quick retort, "Well since I seem to have a choice you'll be getting a drink for your lips. If I find a woman who similarly wants the warmth of a man's kiss, I'll point her your way."

Nearby bar patrons chuckled, but Lindon only returned the woman's smile. Lindon and Jolynn looked each other up and down, having been childhood friends. After taking the measure of themselves, Jolynn left to get Lindon a drink, promising a swift return so as to catch up on old times. Lindon found a quieter spot to stand, in the hopes of garnering some conversation before the barmaid was called away. As good as her word, she was back at his side before long, offering him a pint of the local favorite.

"Where have you been this past year?" Jolynn asked as he savored the first sip of the familiar ale.

Lindon smiled as he swallowed, "Too many places it seems. While some sights were carved from an artist's dream, I also had my fair share of leaky boats and cheap inns. I could tell you much of the fashions in other countries or the stories from far lands. I wasn't lying when I said it had been too long since I felt the kiss of a woman. There are few such finely-chiseled jewels in the world as I might find back here at home."

"Came back to find a mate did you?"

Lindon shook his head, "One will find me at the proper time. I came back to revisit old friends and repay a kindness. While we are on the subject," Lindon was examining the barmaid's hand, "Your ring is…"

Jolynn shushed him quickly, before the minstrel could remark any more about her missing ring. Jolynn spoke in hushed tones as she answered his unspoken question, "I do not wear it here, and few know I am wed. He serves on a royal vessel, not expected to be back in home port for a few months yet. It is not good if the drinkers know that a bar wench is married, yet separated from her husband. It would cause attention I do not want. Better for them to think my father is a military man of reputation, one who hopes to marry me to someone of influence. That helps lessen the wrong kinds of advances toward me. It scares away many suitors."

Lindon nodded, "Many a merchant or local trying to impress his hostess or sweep you off your feet?"

"Aye," Jolynn answered, "But they don't know my heart lies elsewhere. I don't mind them trying, but I am faithful to my man. I know if he was here, he'd trade some stories with you."

Lindon remembered the young friend of his who won the heart of this lovely woman. The minstrel had hoped to meet him as well, but there was nothing to prevent him from returning in a few months to be regaled by tales of the sea. More patrons could be heard calling for refills. Jolynn excused herself to attend to the others, making one request that Lindon go to the stage and give a proper performance. Lindon sipped at his ale as he listened to the young performer sing.

Jolynn continued to satisfy her patrons. The barmaid took note of another new person entering the pub. The middle-aged man had thick, dark hair peppered with gray, sporting a small mustache and goatee. The man's good looks and easy smile were not particularly appreciated by the serving woman. Jolynn's mind dwelled on Lindon, and her absent, secret husband. The new arrival favored her with a large, overly friendly smile as she approached him to take his order. Inwardly she sighed, knowing that another indecent proposal was probably forthcoming.

"What might I get for you sir?"

"I have just returned from a lonely sea voyage. There is nay drink you could bring me to satisfy my spirit as much as the simple presence of your company," replied Jentan Mollamos.

Jolynn wasn't about to waste time on a stranger trying to get friendly with her. She gave him a serious glare. "Well then, you are in the wrong place, sir. All we offer on the menu is drink and food. We have nothing else to quench a traveler's appetite."

Jentan kept his easy smile and hid any disappointment at the rebuttal. On the inside, however, Jentan still had his own personal needs to fulfill. The mentalist never went long without some kind of female companionship to satisfy his desires. During the seagoing trip north, there had been no opportunity for such affections. Savannah was a woman who had assets to excite a man, if you didn't get drawn into her cold eyes. Sadly, the abbess wouldn't be charmed by Jentan's words, and he dared not use spells to beguile her. Mentalist Mollamos was a man starving against his own lust. Since he could control minds, he did not take kindly to people turning him down.

The magic-user gathered the flow of power and lent its strength to his voice in a subtle way. "Serve me a vision, milady. Look into my eyes and see my desires."

Jolynn felt compelled in some odd way to gaze deeply into the man's eyes to see his vision. The mentalist's voice subdued the noises inherent to the pub.

"Serve me a vision of two travelers with unfulfilled needs. In their eyes, they hold a promise of companionship and love to sate the barren thirst of the road. Between them, is the promise that through their touch they will repel the loneliness of their souls."

Jentan Mollamos continued to weave his enchanting spell on a level beneath his words. Jolynn lost her will to the depths of his eyes. The pub no longer existed for her except at the bare fringes of realization. Her duties and her patrons became shadows lost at the edge of twilight. In her thoughts, she became a lonely traveler meeting another of like mind. Jentan perceived the feelings beneath her eyes. The mentalist knew nothing of her absent husband, but he could see her craving for that companionship.

He continued to weave his spell around her emotions. "Before I knew you, it was as if cold mist obscured my path. I found nay light and warmth until you appeared. Seeing you is like a beacon from the dark; a ray of sunlight illuminating a field of flowers. Now I bask in your warmth, and I offer you my heart and flesh. Let us both find a place away from the cold darkness."

Jentan's enchantment shrouded Jolynn's will. Lost in a trance, she cared only for the images he put into her mind. Jolynn craved this smooth-talking man as much as she missed the love of her husband. In her mind, this man began to substitute himself in the place of the one she really loved. He could make any request of her and she would move to please him. Jolynn had forgotten herself, lost in the promised companionship of his spell.

"Jolynn," spoke another voice, "Is something wrong?"

Jolynn turned to find the spectral voice, seeing a red-bearded face she could no longer comprehend as a friend. His words grated against her reality, taking her away from the satisfying tapestry of emotions Mollamos wove around her.

Jolynn rebuked the voice, "Go away, whatever spirit you are. I am with my love now."

Jentan's eyes glared at the stranger disturbing his spell. "I believe you're interrupting a private conversation. You heard the woman. Be off with you."

Lindon stood silently watching as Jentan whispered more words to Jolynn. The minstrel thought the actions and words of his lifelong friend had been amiss. Why had she referred to him as an unknown spirit?

The ears of the minstrel detected the faint sound of a tune played on the air. Despite the loud singing from the bard on the stage, Lindon sensed an odd harmony of a type that most people were unaware. Although his mandolin was still strung over his back, inside its case, Lindon could almost hear the strings of the instrument resonating from something in the very air.

The minstrel ignored Jentan and Jolynn at the moment, reaching around to free his instrument from its case. Once in his hands, Lindon gently touched the strings with his fingertips, closing his eyes against any distractions. The more Jentan spoke, the more Lindon felt the waves of magic from the harmonic web sending resonating vibes into the instrument. The echoes of the resounding magic in the air confirmed what Lindon already suspected.

True minstrels of talent could tap a source of magic with their voice or the use of proper notes. They referred to it as the harmonic web, a part of the magic inherent to the world. The magic could only be found by those already gifted. Through the use of their talents with sound and volume, they could tap into magical energies to influence people or sometimes cause other effects such as shattering glass. Another group of magic-users could tap into the harmonic web in a similar way to influence people: mentalists. As Lindon felt the energies of subtle magic echo on a level that most wouldn't be attuned to hear, he knew for certain that the strange man used arcane mind tricks on Jolynn.

Lindon of Orlaun turned back to regard the pair, finding Jolynn still fixing an empty stare upon the middle-aged man. The deft fingers of the minstrel poised over the strings of his mandolin when he spoke. "I am Lindon of Orlaun, from the Highwater district, and a friend of Jolynn from many years gone by." As he spoke, Lindon plucked a few notes on the mandolin to the tune of a dance song he and Jolynn had heard often. The notes accentuated the power of his voice, as Lindon also drew energy from the harmonic web to bring Jolynn back from the charm.

"Lindon? Are you hiding?" Jolynn asked to the air before her. Her head flinched, but her eyes remained trapped toward Jentan. Meanwhile, Jentan's black eyebrows lowered as his eyes glanced aside at the minstrel. The mentalist continued to hold his mouth in a friendly grin, but his glare turned unpleasant as he took in the measure of his challenger.

The mentalist spoke again, "The past is lost and buried. Nay Orlaun, nay Lindon. There is naught but the shelter for two lost travelers."

A vehement wave of power surged through Lindon's mind. The words, 'nay Orlaun, nay Lindon' reverberated in his head. The minstrel winced inwardly as his consciousness swooned for an instant. His hands stubbornly strummed the dance step on the mandolin. It was an automatic response, but it kept an anchor on which Lindon could refocus his thoughts. For a moment, the situation in the pub dimmed to a dreamlike state; however, Lindon's mind followed the sounds of the dance jingle back to awareness.

Lindon saw Jentan attempting to make an exit with Jolynn in tow. The level of psychic attack the mentalist had used surprised Lindon, for it had been nothing like he had ever experienced before. For Lindon to break the charm upon his friend, and further protect himself, he had to weave a magic effect to counter mental intrusions.

Lindon's voice surged as his fingers deftly moved over the chords of the mandolin. He sang about remembrance and about holding on to one's past identity. A few quick rhymes, delivered upon a foundation of magical walls, sought to put up a barrier reflecting mental suggestions for himself and everyone in earshot. Jolynn, listening to the words on the edge of her consciousness, stopped in her tracks to shake her head free of the fog surrounding her perceptions. In her mind, the assault of this familiar voice disrupted the offered shelter and warm company of the stranger.

Jentan also stopped to regard the changes overcoming the woman he had been magically seducing. For the first time, his mouth lost its grin as he struggled to maintain dominance. Rarely had he faced anyone rivaling his influential control as Lindon did. The magic-user uncomfortably realized the spectacle began drawing undue attention to his disreputable actions. The mentalist pulled closer to the barmaid and began to whisper directly in her ear. Lindon could feel the magic of his suggestions as the magic-user sought more control.

Even as the mentalist tried to weave his latest magical deception on the serving woman, Lindon struck back viciously. Anyone not already watching the odd spectacle was affected by the resonant wave of discord erupting from the minstrel's mandolin strings. Lindon set loose a magically powered and amplified shriek of disharmonious noise. Most of the bar patrons yelled something incomprehensible as they dropped anything in their hands to cover their ears. Jentan winced and stumbled back, Jolynn clapped her hands to her head, and in the far end of the bar, the performing bard abruptly ended his song and gritted his teeth.

A deep silence immediately followed the auditory assault. The people in the pub started to look around in a daze, searching for the reason their ears rang. Jolynn reacted first. The barmaid looked from Jentan to Lindon and back again. Mentalist Mollamos stood silent for once, trying to think on his feet of something to say, now that the barmaid was obviously back to her own senses. Jolynn did not give him time to use any more of his words. Slightly shaken, yet more than a bit angered, the barmaid grabbed a full glass of ale from a nearby table. Jolynn splashed the contents across Jentan's handsome face, marking his fashionable clothing with the reek of ale. The laughter of some of the patrons followed her as she turned her back to Mollamos and left the common room via a set of stairs, without so much as a word.

With ale dripping from his nose and his disarrayed goatee, Jentan turned to regard the red-bearded minstrel who had thwarted his sexual desires. Lindon stared back with his own smile, though his fingers remained near the strings of his instrument. The minstrel wondered if the irresponsible mage would try any other kind of trick on him. If it ever came to a physical fight, Lindon felt he could handle the dandy of a mage standing before him.

When the mentalist inhaled and began to speak, Lindon tensed to fend off a psychic assault. Instead, Jentan spoke in a normal tone. "Impressive. Lindon of Orlaun is it?"

Lindon relaxed slightly, responding to his title with a flourish of his feathered hat. "Thank you, and aye, that is my name. You would do well to remember me."

"I will," Jentan commented. "You play exceptionally well…"

The next words spoken by the mentalist carried the weight of a strong magical suggestion behind them.

"…for one who has imbibed way too much alcohol!"

Before Lindon could even react, the effects of the suggestion took root in his mind. Lindon tried to fix his eyes on his opponent, but his vision became blurred. The room began to tilt on him, forcing Lindon to clumsily catch something to support his weight. Lindon could have been vulnerable to another mental attack while he fought the augmented effects of the small amount of alcohol that had been in his system. No such assault came, for Jentan turned toward the door and made a quick exit. Lindon wanted to chase the man and get even, but in his badly coordinated state he simply fell forward. Fighting all the effects of a drunken stupor, Lindon barely heard the bard attempt to begin another song now that the display seemed over. Lindon passed out on the floor of the pub.

*       *       *       *       *

Cool water splashed Lindon awake. As the memory of his last waking moments came back to him, he expected to be suffering from a hangover. The magical suggestion inflaming the alcohol had left without any residual effects, for which the minstrel appreciated. The red-bearded man looked up from a bed, Jolynn's face looked down at him with concern.

"Are you well?" She asked.

Lindon could see the worry in her eyes. He doubted she got much sleep that night, and daylight filtered through the cracks in the window shutter. The minstrel slowly grabbed the hand holding the washcloth, taking it and kissing it gently.

"I'm well. Thank you for taking care of me after I lost consciousness. I'm sorry he got away."

Jolynn grinned, "But he didn't get out the door before I gave him my opinion of his flattery."

Jolynn and Lindon shared some mirth over the memory of ale dripping off of the man's face. The barmaid continued with a more serious expression, "The important thing is that you saved me. I owe you a great debt for that. If he ever comes to this pub again, the bouncers will see to him."

"I'm honored to be in the right place at the right time for an old friend. As for that man, he better hope not to cross my path again."

### CHAPTER 7          "Young Vengeance/A Debt Repaid"


"I don't know which pains me greater," Grandmaster Woshan of the Order of the Mind's Eye lamented as he broke the long silence, "That despite all my training you failed to put Rayka down in one mighty kick, when you blindsided him without provocation, or that the incident itself is the third time I made you suffer punishment for lashing out in anger at another of my students."

The master of the martial arts paced across the large, empty exercise room. During the daylight hours, students practiced their combat forms as well as meditated on this floor. This evening, the room stood empty except for the master and his troublesome protégé. He stepped up to face the student who quietly endured her punishment.

"Now that you have meditated on your actions today, I have a few questions to ask of you. I hope you have achieved the proper enlightenment to answer them honestly. Why did you attack a fellow student, Montanya su Troyeal bara Westonhout?"

The student, trying to keep a calm face despite the drops of sweat running down her face from exertion, flinched slightly at being called by her formal name. It was customary for nobles in Orlaun to adopt a formal name denoting their ancestral lineage. The "su Troyeal" portion represented her father's name as Troyeal. "Bara" came from an older version of the human language which meant "clan". After the word for clan came the surname of her family, "Westonhout". Although her name descended from a noble right, the student preferred to go by only her first name, Montanya.

As Grandmaster Woshan's stern eyes focused on her, Montanya neither resembled nor even felt akin to a noble at that point. Sweat dotted the smooth, soft beauty of her nineteen-year-old face. Montanya's long, red hair, tied back by a piece of torn pink fabric and soaked from perspiration, hung down to the middle of her back. The woman wore loose-fitting tan clothes, designed to allow freedom of movement for the rigors of her training. While the clothes did not attempt to cover much more than what modesty required, they stuck to her contours by her sweat. They revealed a lithe and muscular body, formed from a lifetime of disciplined training. While not overly endowed across the chest, the woman's looks would turn the heads of many men. She was barefoot from practicing her exercises in the training hall. Despite her beautiful attributes, a number of old scars and new bruises covered her arms, legs, and stomach. The student did not smile often. Woshan had commented to her on many occasions that her cheeks were often turned into a scowl even when she didn't realize it.

Despite her directive to assume a serene, meditative state, her face formed one of her customary sneers. Though her body suffered under duress, Montanya's training enabled her to cast her mind into a tranquil state allowing for distant self-examination. Apparently, her concentration could not ignore the two heavy buckets of water she held at arm's length and shoulder height. Despite the taxing burden, she endured supporting her arms while also maintaining her balance on one leg. She lost track of the time standing there and struggling to keep the buckets high. The muscles in her shoulders and legs ached for rest.

There should have been ample quantity of meditative enlightenment for her to lose her emotions and be more introspective. Instead, Montanya could not keep all the venom from her voice as she answered. "I struck him because Rayka is a thief who has not learned his lesson in stealing from me. I'm sorry if I offended you, sensei, but I refuse to tolerate such actions."

Grandmaster Woshan let out a disappointed sigh. "Your behavior shows you have a few things you have failed to learn. You still can't focus inward and weigh your actions from an impartial view. You seek to execute your own judgment of others when you see fit. Your apology is hollow."

The master indicated the buckets Montanya struggled to hold level with her shoulders. "You may set those down and relax your body. Even more important, you need to relax your mind. You can tap the limitless power within your Chi, once able to focus your mind and achieve that inner balance. When you came to us, you wanted to learn the art and the prowess of a warrior who is one with the world around him. However, the true name we choose for ourselves is chiaso, which reflects our connection to our inner spirit. It is more important that we develop our mind and awareness before we attempt to strengthen our bodies."

Montanya groaned in relief as she set down the buckets. She lowered her upraised leg and stood on both feet as Woshan talked. Though she wanted to stretch and relax all of her weary muscles, she stood straight and tall as Woshan continued to address her.

"Rayka stole from you in the past to play a prank, and I punished him for it just as you face discipline now," Grandmaster Woshan lectured. "Why did you not come to me this morning when your locket was missing? Did you think I would not punish him if he was guilty?"

Montanya tried to appear complacent, hiding her emotions, but her insincerity was clear to her teacher. He knew she refused to see the wrong of her actions. "He does not respect me. If I come to you for my problems, why should he earn any respect for me then? I didn't feel I had a choice, I needed to show him the repercussions of his actions."

As the grandmaster fixed a stern eye on the insolent student, she shrunk under his gaze. "And was he deserving of punishment today? Did he commit the crime for which you judged him guilty?"

Montanya had no response forthcoming to such a direct question. Her greenish-blue eyes turned downward, finding no suitable answer that wouldn't get her into more trouble.

Grandmaster Woshan brought one hand up, examining the locket in his palm. "You and I found it together with your belongings, where it was supposed to be, at the bottom of one of your sacks. There was never a theft to justify dealing out any form of punishment."

Montanya took a keen interest in the locket her teacher held, but said nothing as he examined it. Woshan took the locket in both hands and opened it to view the contents hidden inside. There, secreted beneath the gold exterior, lie two locks of hair. One had blonde strands, the other red, entwined together in a circle.

He looked up at his troublesome student, "From your parents, I would assume."

At Montanya's eager nod, he offered the locket for her to take. The young student of chiaso grabbed it with trembling hands and held it to her breast for the duration of a silent prayer. Under the scrutiny of her master, she placed the locket around her neck. It hung against the glistening sheen of her skin, as she faced her master with softer eyes.

"And as to your method of retribution," the master stared into her eyes with scorn, "how is he to earn any respect after how soundly he defeated your surprise attack? I'm told you hit him very hard when he wasn't looking. Despite the surprise he didn't even fall; instead, he proceeded to teach you a lesson instead of receiving one."

Montanya shuffled a bit, as if she suddenly remembered the new bruises forming on her skin. "Sensei, he is very skilled. Forgive me for disrupting the training today."

Grandmaster Woshan took in a softer look as he examined his student. An uncomfortable silence passed as Montanya waited to hear if she would be dismissed without more punishment. As it was, she felt she would not sleep well this night among the other students. No doubt there would be many whispers involving her from the other bunks.

To her disappointment, her teacher cleared his throat and continued. "Montanya, I wish I could forgive you as easily as before and trust in you to learn, but you have shown great anger at times and an inability to control it. This is not the first time you disrupted training by striking a fellow student."

"I'm sorry, sensei," Montanya blurted, "it's hard to control my temper with the way some of the others treat me. I am an orphan, an outcast, and I am constantly reminded of that by others. I try my best to keep my mind focused and to train as you teach me. I work and exercise harder than anyone else. The gods know I want to be chiaso. I wish to master the martial arts."

When he was certain she had finished, Woshan replied. "Let's talk on that subject, shall we? I have seen the amount of exercise and practice you put into your skills. Despite your many hours of work, younger students have passed you in talent and ability. You have the strongest muscles of any other female student, as well as a remarkable endurance for lengthy exercises. Despite your effort, you fail at the tests to move onward to greater levels of instruction."

"I push my body as hard as I can, sensei."

He nodded, "Your body yes, and perhaps your heart, but not your mind."

Montanya blinked, "I don't understand."

"Chi is balance within the soul. Tap into that power, and you can do feats that seem magical compared to any mortal. You can break objects harder than your own flesh, you can sense things you can't see or hear, and you can even move fast enough to catch an arrow out of the air."

Grandmaster Woshan took Montanya's hand and led her to a corner of the training room. A stand against the wall supported a dark, wooden board, bare of ornamentation. "You have seen these before. This training board is from the caleocht trees. The wood is very strong and unyielding, making it the perfect tool to test one's Chi."

Montanya stood uncertainly before the board, "Sensei, I've tried. I can't break this wood."

In response, he offered an iron gaze with an equally iron tone to match. "You will find your Chi. You will use your inner balance to accomplish more than just your muscles would seem to allow. It will take solid concentration, but you can break this. Students who have weaker muscles than you have found the inner balance to shatter such obstacles."

The master stood to one side as Montanya faced the wooden caleocht plank. The red-haired student closed her eyes for a moment, drawing a deep breath. Woshan would have expected her to take the time to properly focus, yet Montanya paused only for that one breath before stepping forward with a frontal kick. She let out a fearsome yell as her foot moved to connect with the board. The impact resounded through the empty hall, but the board remained intact. Despite the piece of pink fabric holding most of her hair back, Montanya's long strands tangled about her shoulders as she stumbled backward a few steps.

Her master's gaze didn't leave the smooth surface of the board as his voice sighed. "You did not even try to focus your thoughts. Your kick had some merit, but it paled in comparison to the fluid grace and balance of a chiaso. I asked you to meditate and focus your thoughts, and you did not."

His voice snapped with firm tone. "Butterfly in the Windmill! Do all the steps, focus on the moves, and then split the board."

Montanya practically jumped into the routine. Despite any pain from her bruises or weariness of her discipline earlier, she went right into the graceful momentum of a martial dance. Grandmaster Woshan watched her movements with a critical eye. Even with all the twirls and circles of the routine, her eyes remained focused on the board as if with deadly intent. Woshan saw that her form lacked perfection. Her routine followed the moves, but she hurried too much, lacking any meditation or relaxation. He told her as much, and she slowed her movements.

"What do you see?" asked Woshan. "Do see the strength of your inner soul? Do you see the board breaking in your mind? Nay, you see something else."

Montanya missed a step, but tried flowing back into the rhythm.

The master knew then that Montanya could dance the step a hundred times that night, and never find the focus needed to break the board. She could imitate the moves, but she wasn't focused on the union of mind and body required for the proper effect. He spoke to her as she unconsciously sped up her momentum. "What do you see when you focus on the board? What is in your mind?"

Her greenish-blue eyes flared in anger, and her lips once again sneered. Her tired voice admitted the truth. "I see their faces. I see the boards of the crate they stuffed me in. I try to break their awful smiles."

Grandmaster Woshan lowered his head, "That is the core of your anger: the men who murdered your parents in that robbery long ago. It clouds your mind."

Montanya breathed heavily as she moved. Fluid grace of movement changed to a stiff, almost wooden dance akin to a puppet's jerky movements.

The teacher looked upon the locket swinging from Montanya's neck. "You hold what little they left behind in such high value, such as the locket you hid from them." As the woman twirled, he took note of the pink fabric holding back her long hair. "And a torn strip of your mother's dress."

Montanya moved much faster than the dance required. She should feel her inner strength and focus with calmness, but her body betrayed the pent-up anger building inside.

"How much did they take from you, Montanya su Troyeal bara Westonhout?"

With a piercing scream of fury, Montanya's momentum built to the point of release. She spun a full circle, releasing the full steam of bottled-up anger. Her bare foot slammed into the caleocht board and rattled it. No crack formed, nor did a spray of splinters result. The board simply vibrated in its holder. Its undamaged surface mocked Montanya's frustrations.

Montanya became a wild, untamed beast. As quickly as she recovered her balance from the strike, she launched another one. Time and again she sent forth kick after kick to no avail. Wailing like the banshees of old, she finally resorted to wildly swinging her fists at the unyielding wood. She vented all the frustration she held inside her own little world. There was no school, no teacher, not even the caleocht board. The wooden plank became the faces of the men who had stolen her childhood on a bloody street.

By the time reason came back to her, she sniffled her own tears while sitting against the unbroken board's support stand. She didn't expect to have any water left in her after all her sweating earlier, yet the tears came. She looked through blurry eyes at her bloody knuckles. When Grandmaster Woshan pushed a cup to her lips, she reflexively drank without question. The divine healing potion not only healed the scars on her knuckles, as well as the bruises on her body, it also healed the broken bones in her hand.

"You lack spiritual balance," the teacher lamented to her. "Your youthful anger has built your life around a shaky foundation. What do you plan to do with your life, Montanya? How can you form a living around a core of hate?"

"I won't be a victim anymore," Montanya croaked through a strained throat. "I will save others that pain as well. I will learn to strengthen my body against the physical harm. I don't hate people, I hate thieves. Others still suffer from the greed of others, but I will stand up to them. I swear on my dead parents, rogues will learn to fear my name."

Grandmaster Woshan rose to his full height. His face reflected his shock at her resolute tone. "This is not the way of chiaso. We spend our lives creating a spiritual temple within our minds and bodies. Despite the rigors of the world, we weather the outside storms by drawing from the calm serenity and focus within us."

Montanya, head bowed in shame, got to her feet. She avoided looking toward the caleocht board. Her master witnessed her shame as she stood uncertainly before him. Montanya's body twitched at its limits. She had cried and exerted herself as much as she could for one night. The woman wanted to go to her bunk and sleep away her embarrassment.

In a sudden movement, Grandmaster Woshan launched a fast kick at the caleocht board. A moment earlier he had been standing very still, hands clasped behind his back. Montanya flinched as his body exploded in lightning motion. A tremendous crack resounded through the large, open room as the board broke. The master nonchalantly resumed his comfortable stance. Montanya could not resist glancing at the split wood.

"You're still a victim, Montanya, because you do not choose to live your life. Pain festers under your conscious thoughts. Thieves took your parents from you during a robbery. You once told me thieves in the guise of nobility and men of gold took your mansion and holdings from you while still a young orphan. I have watched you grow. Throughout your whole life, there have been thieves and rogues willing to take something from you or others."

The chiaso master paced. "I question your ability to distinguish a good man from one whom you would bring about your retaliation. You are full of hate. I offered you the chance to train and calm your soul. Instead, you turn away from the spiritual path I offer. You focus only on the perceived ability to turn your body into a weapon to exact your vengeance. Your justifications are irrelevant. Your thoughts will put you into an eternal war against a foe without a face. You ask for training so you can go into the world as a punisher seeking someone to be punished."

Montanya tired of the lecturing. She apologized again, if only to hurry toward her bunk. "Accept my apologies, sensei. I will try to learn better."

Woshan turned toward her with sorrowful eyes. He emphasized every syllable as he responded. "I cannot teach you."

The red-haired student paused her thinking. How could he not be able to teach her?

Grandmaster Woshan adopted a stern visage. "I'm sorry for failing in my teachings. Apparently, I have not been able to send you down a better path. Perhaps someone else will succeed, but I will nay longer attempt to train someone with such hidden rage waiting to be unleashed."

He held his stern visage even as Montanya finally looked him in the eyes. For once, her customary scowl was replaced with open helplessness. Her mind couldn't digest the fact that her lifetime mentor refused to aid her any more.

"Sensei…"

He interrupted her, "You must leave. I will nay longer train you, nor have you disrupt the other students. Remain here while I grab your belongings from the bunkroom."

The older man didn't give her time for any reply. His back turned to her as he walked out of the room. Montanya stood barefoot on the cold floor. Despite the sweat-soaked clothes clinging to her body, she felt naked and helpless. Alone in silence, she turned her master's words over in her mind.

Montanya found it hard to believe that she would not be going to sleep in her old bunk after all. No longer would she share a meal with those whom she trained alongside since childhood. While she had worried about whispers in the night over her shameful actions, it would be preferable to having a closed door behind her. Montanya's future crashed into uncertainty. Who would take her in? How would she make a living? Where could she go for a place to stay? How could she complete her training and make rogues fear her?

All too soon, her master returned holding a couple small bags and a warm robe. He stood near one exit to the training hall. Beyond that exit lay a hallway leading to the street door. She walked with wooden steps toward him. All of her meager belongings, everything she had left in the world, resided in those two small sacks. She accepted the proffered robe, putting it on to guard against the night's chill. Though she said no words, her lips moved in half-formed pleas that never found substance in the air. Holding her bags, Montanya endured his stern arm ushering her to the door. Grandmaster Woshan said nothing else as he opened the street door and stood to one side.

The street appeared dark and uninviting. Montanya tried to find her voice once again, but held it back as her lips quivered. She hoped he would speak and offer anything more. Montanya needed him to give her another chance. She spent so many years under that roof; she had no comprehension of how to survive alone. Her teacher said nothing. The master stood as a cold statue, holding the door open.

Montanya's knees trembled, but she moved past the door and down the dark steps out front. Behind her, the hinges gave a mournful squeal as the door closed. It clicked shut with a finality that Montanya would never forget.

The red-haired woman felt orphaned again. She stood in the clustered side street of Orlaun feeling small, lonely, and dwarfed by the sprawling towers. No one witnessed her expulsion from the place that had been her home for the last several years. Only the stars of the sky looked down upon her, as unreachable as her old bunk.

It wasn't long before Montanya's thoughts retreated into her hatred once again. Her anger at the injustices of the world lending her assurance that she would survive somehow. Montanya slowly put one foot in front of the other, making her way aimlessly. She left the Order of the Mind's Eye monastery without looking back. Somehow, she knew, she would survive this like every other tragedy in her life. In the end, the result would be the same. Some thief would suffer for what Montanya had lost over the years.

*        *        *        *        *

Master Falerno Giantcharmer succeeded in helping out his former student. The Brotherhood of the Circles planned to host a notable event, entertaining the nobility of the city. Some chosen from the order sat in judgment over the entertainers wishing to perform. In the chambers of their magically-laced guildhall, Lindon of Orlaun and many others offered up music and tales.

In the audience hall's lower level, the judging council sat at one end while the performers staged their act before them. A mixed lot of mages, comprised of humans, elves and gnomes, formed the council. In the upper balconies of the same chamber, numerous other guild members and apprentice mages enjoyed the free show. Around the upper balconies, at the base of the great dome which capped the room, were numerous large arches leading to an outdoor patio. On a good day, the doors would let in fresh air from outside. Today the doors were closed, sealing off the noise of the outside world and maintaining a high degree of acoustic isolation.

The Artistic Enlightenment College sent a mix of representatives, but other performing groups also received invitations. Lindon knew the wizards wanted to see a good number of novice entertainers to encourage youthful talent; however, he also believed many reputable acts would be invited to perform. Lindon presumed the mage guild hoped to gain more influence and social standing with the rulers of the city. It was rumored that King Acer MigTolo might even be in attendance, or at the very least Count MigRelke, the ruler of Orlaun's province. The event offered an unprecedented chance for lesser known performers to gain prestige.

The competition would be fierce among minstrels and bards. Just the act of being selected to perform for the occasion would be room for bragging rights. Already in the second day of performances, the council already observed numerous occasions to applaud or reject candidates. Lindon remained nervous, but he wore a confident smile.

He opened his act by throwing his wide-brimmed hat to the floor. Taking up the metal flute, he played a dance jig that went faster with every chorus. The minstrel positioned his body directly over the hat. His dance turned and twisted, never stepping on his hat. As the notes increased in pace, the entertainer danced to a faster rhythm. Between the fast song and the prowess displayed with the dance, Lindon earned applause right away from the upper balcony.

During his next song, strumming on his mandolin, he faced a challenge. Although Lindon sang with a fine voice, fingers dancing lightly over the chords of his instrument, his ears picked up disrupting noises. The chamber accommodated resonating voices beautifully, but also carried the noise of someone who seemed to be doing his best to distract from the performance. The occasional cough, the sounds of a glass of water tinkling against a table repeatedly, and the crunch of nuts from a snack bowl disrupted the otherwise wonderful musical sounds.

Lindon could not believe his misfortune.

A familiar face sat at the table of guild wizards. The man glared at Lindon through dark brown eyes, and gray-peppered hair. Although Lindon did not know Jentan Mollamos by name, he remembered the mentalist who tried to magically subdue Jolynn into a night of unwanted passion. Now the man sat among the council, judging who would be attending the most prestigious entertainment event to hit the City of Spires in many years.

There would be little gain in trying to accuse one of the wizard council members of dishonest acts in front of such an audience. Likely, Lindon's words would carry little weight. The accusation might cause him to lose this chance. Instead, Lindon retreated into that part of his mind where he could feel perfect harmony. The minstrel worked to achieve the heightened awareness of mind and soul that allowed him to feel the magical harmonic web encompassing the world. The musical protégé ignored disruptions while delivering the essence of emotions upon the vibrations of his mandolin strings. His voice carried sweet notes that sparked images in the minds of the listeners. Minstrels so attuned to their feelings could weave spells through such a link, but he attempted no magic other than the natural gifts of his talent.

When he finished, a moment of absolute silence descended among the listeners. The last lingering note fading into pleasant memory. The moment was broken by one disinterested listener that would do all in his power to deny Lindon's dreams.

"Well, I believe we have heard enough cacophonous passages for one afternoon." Jentan Mollamos stated. The mentalist waved a dismissive hand over the pile of cracked peanut shells on his table. "That is enough for now, you may leave and will receive word just like the others."

Lindon looked to the responses from the man's fellow councilors. As the minstrel guessed, a number of the mages on the council looked confused or frowned at the mentalist's outburst. Clearly, the man placed himself above protocol.

Lindon set aside his instrument but made no move to leave. Quite the opposite of what Jentan intended, Lindon put on an easy smile and decided to put his charm to use. Red hair and beard framed an easy, unworried smile as the minstrel addressed the guildsmen.

"You granted me three songs, two of which have already added warmth to hearts and eased troubled minds. I still have a third song to perform, as promised to me."

A few mages began whispering amongst themselves, glancing in discontent toward Jentan. The middle-aged man would not be intimidated by his associates.

Jentan spoke again, "Two was quite enough I assure you. I am unimpressed by your fancy clothing and lackluster notes."

"Jentan," one of the other mages spoke, loud enough for the audience, "You are out of line."

"I was thoroughly enjoying the performance," revealed a gnome at the council table.

Jentan paid little attention to their words. He shook his head as they spoke, self-righteous in his attempt to oust Lindon from performing. The mentalist prepared to strike back any way he could at Jolynn's rescuer. "This man does not impress me; therefore, he would not be my pick."

Before Jentan could say more, Lindon reached into his vest pocket. "I have one more song to perform, at the behest of not only this council, but of one of your own members many years ago."

Lindon drew forth the bamboo flute from his vest, from a pocket that looked too small to hold the entire length of the instrument. The wooden flute gave a polished shine in the light of the room. Lindon's light-blue eyes sparkled as he cradled the treasured piece in his nimble fingers.

"Are your notes so bad because your ears are so daft?" Jentan asked. "Did you not hear me?"

"Did you not hear me, good sir?" Lindon countered, gingerly tipping the flute closer to his lips. "I was granted one more song to play today. The song is at the request of one of your own, many years ago. A beneficial wizard from this very guild, gave me this flute years past and requested me to play for him someday."

A new voice, not so deep and yet spoken with authority, carried easily across the chamber. "By whose request do you offer up this special song today?"

All the eyes under the dome turned their attention to a figure sitting in one of the dark seats of the upper rows. From the well-lit performance area, it was hard to see the speaker in the dim alcoves around the closed upper doors. Lindon of Orlaun could not make out details of the man; nonetheless, the unknown person gave the minstrel the opening he needed.

Lindon told his tale, "It is because of that kind soul that I stand before you this day, instead of trying to scrape a meager living out of the slums of the Highwater district. I was a man without a name and of nay repute. I was simply another of many beggars tucked into the pits of Orlaun until the day when a stranger came to me and handed me a gift."

Lindon cradled the bamboo flute high for all to see. "Such a simple gift, yet it is as highly treasured as the sum of all the coins I have touched in this life. This flute was my gateway to a finer existence. Through it, I learned to know music, the arts, and to revisit the world in a new light. I owe all my fame and successes to the man who gave this to me on a bleak day in Highwater. Along with this gift he gave me one request: learn it well so I can play it for him."

The minstrel looked up to the concealed stranger in the upper rows. "I came to play this flute at the performance, not for the nobility and royalty, but for the generous elf who gave this to me. I owe a song to Korrelothar Balshav, The Highwater Conjuror."

The figure in the balcony stepped forward into the light from below. Those on the ground floor saw the long length of golden hair, streaked with the silver strands of age. His fashions advertised wealth. Flowing elvish designs embroidered a coat next to jeweled buttons. A rough, stubble of hair grew on his chin. Many elves who reached middle-age found such facial hair a common and yet unsightly trait. This elf did not hide it by the use of spells or a razor. Instead, he left his chin hairs to grow, believing it demanded respect. Although no wrinkles marred his brow, deep lines of wisdom etched into his face. A jeweled earring adorned one ear as a common symbol of elven marriage. The figure smiled down upon the minstrel below.

The elf mage spoke, "Korrelothar stands ready to hear his promised song." The elf turned a glare toward Jentan Mollamos, adding, "And you will remain quiet as the grave."

Lindon fell into a graceful bow, holding it for some duration out of respect. More important than a ship full of royalty, his benefactor stood ready to be entertained. The minstrel born from the poverty-stricken Highwater district assumed his full height and brought the bamboo flute to his lips. He retreated into his inner peace, touching upon the harmonic web with his purity of concentration. He spared no thoughts on the silent, smoldering mentalist glaring at his back. Nor did Lindon of Orlaun give consideration to the councilors at the table who were supposed to be judging his recital…his back met them as he faced the elf on the balcony.

A level of silence previously unattainable by most of the prior performers descended, since everyone present knew Korrelothar and took renewed interest in the display. The first notes sounded as clear to those in the upper balcony as if they stood right next to the performer. The bamboo flute made music exactly as Lindon had described to his mentor: akin to soft breezes in a sylvan wood. The melody invited all ears to relish an unspoken tale of the elves. Though Lindon could not sing words as he played, those in attendance could hear the tone of the tale laid out before them. It was a song Korrelothar heard during his childhood, over a couple centuries ago. The elf respected the fact that Lindon traveled long miles into the heart of elven woods to study this tune.

Few present knew the name of the elf maiden Treajuliane, or understood her gloomy tale. In elf lands, performers sung the sad story in the evening starlight, under the full boughs of giant trees. The elven myth had grown old even before the days of the Godswars. The elf maiden Treajuliane, bereft of her family and home in a tragedy, was forced to live in squalor upon a strange land. Over the years, the despondent elf maiden turned her life for the better, tending to her natural surroundings to make a new home. She planted new trees, rid the soil of rocks and weeds, tended the flowers, and used the natural magic of old to bring life to her barren patch of land.

As Lindon's notes took on a stronger, more uplifting mood, Korrelothar envisioned the brighter portion of the tale. A new forest home developed around the barrens in which the maiden resided. A sanctuary thrived where once there had been naught but a lonely, stranded soul. Lindon's notes came to a happy peak at the portion of the tale where another band of elves happened upon the grove. Homeless as Treajuliane had once been, they bonded with her sanctuary once she welcomed their company. Warmth and happiness entered into the life of the elf maiden who had suffered the loss of her family. Among the new arrivals, the maiden met an elf lord who loved her for the rest of her days. After the elf woman and her lover came to the end of their long, merry lives, they left behind many children. An elven community thrived where once existed inhospitable soil.

Similarly, it seemed, as Lindon lived his life. From the depths of his existence in the slums of the city, he worked hard his entire life to reach something once thought unattainable. Lindon's journey had been made possible by Korrelothar's gift, the same bamboo flute, given to a struggling young boy. The song ended all too soon for those who truly knew the meaning of the tale. There were no dry elven eyes in the room, and the humans looked on in wonder at how their companions could lose such composure. Years after the request of music had been made in the slums of Highwater, Korrelothar's promised song was delivered with the highest skill and regard.

A long moment of silence passed as the magic of the song lingered in the air. Korrelothar's tears satisfied Lindon that he had succeeded in a lifelong personal quest.

Korrelothar spoke, "You weave a superb tale in your tune, Lindon. My ears have not heard such a splendid rendition of that song from my homeland in more years than I can recount."

The elf wizard smiled at the red-bearded minstrel, but he directed his next words toward the council of mages. "Every so often I try to do things for people to give them hope and the ability to realize their potentials. I have a feeling Lindon is destined for great things. I hope you will grant Lindon your acceptance to perform. Regardless, however, he will come along as my personal guest."

Since Korrelothar ranked as one of the founding members of the Brotherhood of the Circles, there would be no question that his endorsement meant that Lindon would perform. While the minstrel looked up at Korrelothar with thankful eyes, he could not see the baleful glare coming at him from Jentan Mollamos.

**CHAPTER 8**     **"Katressa's Elven Side"**


This stretch of greenery proved difficult to navigate, but Katressa reassured Trestan they were going the right direction. Amongst the trees they sought a village of forest gnomes that Mel Bellringer called home. The two companions looked forward to seeing the lively gnome again after so many years. Trestan found it hard to imagine a settlement with lots of families, even of a short race, existing somewhere in this tangle of trees. The young paladin became disoriented in the dense wood. He had a hard time finding the position of the sun most of the day. Cat's elven blood accepted the surroundings. Between her heritage, and her life as a scout and infiltrator, she could make out hidden paths. Although this region of Kashmer's Protectorate featured open valleys and pastures on maps, Trestan witnessed patches of dense forest and steep ripples of land. Although his traveling days were marked by urgency and danger, the journeys through untamed wilds took him to wonderful vistas. Cat lived as much in the wilds as inside a town. The half-elf shared her knowledge of the land, teaching Trestan woodland survival skills.

Trestan found ways to change the conversation. While her knowledge of the woods intrigued him, his thoughts dwelled on his future with Cat. His desires prompted him to cunningly shift the subject. Before long, Trestan questioned Cat about the romantic aspects of elvish cultures.

"So, elf women like receiving flowers just as human women do, but it's done differently?" Trestan asked.

As Katressa responded, she reached out to give a gentle, fingertip caress to a flower in the process of blooming. She passed it by with only the slightest pressure. The fragile flower bobbed slightly from the touch as they led their horses onward.

"As with both races, flowers are welcomed by the appraising female heart. Human males may pick wildflowers for their *faunlessa*, but elvish society has different ideals in regards to the plants of the forest. We must give what we take from nature. Therefore, elf males grow the flowers they gather for their lover. In this way, a balance is assured."

Trestan's eyebrows rose, "Elf males have to be good gardeners if they want to be good at romance?"

"Well, not necessarily," Cat replied, "but it helps. It conveys a message to the female in how and where he acquires the flowers. Sometimes the male went and traded for them. After all, some male elves are not gardeners, and they barter their talents for flowers. However, elves have a long lifespan, which leaves plenty of time for pursuits such as watering plants. The type of bouquet he grows tells us something about the male. It is very impressive to the female if he grows flowers that are especially fragile, or unsafe to handle. While such a bouquet has its thorns, it delivers a message that the male will work hard yet tenderly to make the relationship blossom."

Trestan sighed, "How can I compete with an elf male? I have nay bouquet. I suppose for all those wildflowers I picked for you I should be ashamed I didn't give back to the land."

Cat reached around his shoulders as they led the horses. "I love everything you do for me. You may pick as many flowers as you choose, but keep in mind something must be given back as well. I wouldn't fret over it, my love. I know your good heart and what you are willing to give."

"I hope to fulfill all your desires, Cat." Trestan looked into her eyes with complete sincerity. "It troubles me to learn that one nice act I may have done could be viewed in a bad way, because I didn't follow elvish custom. I want to give you treasured memories without taint."

"Taint?" Cat giggled. "You do a lot to appease my heart, *faunlessa*. Do not focus on separate sides of me; I am one woman, both human and elf joined. I like sharing wine with you under a pink sunset. I like when you compose poetry to me, even though you whisper it in a shy voice."

Trestan wondered if his cheeks revealed a blush at that moment.

Cat continued, rather coyly, "I love your strong hands massaging my back. You send waves through me which soothe my troubles. Most of all, I love men who inquire as to my desires so that they may better know how to treat me…like you are doing now."

The half-elf smiled an infectious grin, leaving both of them striding through the woods in a light mood. Under the green layers, amidst the mating calls of songbirds, they discussed more about their own relationships. Trestan felt he had little to contribute. Although he'd had romantic interests in the village, none ever lasted for any lengthy commitment. The former blacksmith never had a relationship as deep and in such closeness as the one he shared with Cat.

Cat admitted that she felt similar. The rogue claimed she had always felt too busy for romance. Abriana's champion believed Cat only skimmed the surface of the tale when she talked about her lack of previous interests. Although Cat didn't say anything about it, Trestan had a feeling her mix of human and elf blood played some role in distancing her from the young elves of her village. Cat may be young in age for an elf, yet her human half caused her to mature faster than her playmates. The half-elf skipped ahead to talk about her young years training to venture into the wild. She became a scout for the elves at an age when her companions still enjoyed blissful youth. Cat scouted orcs, explored nature, and ventured from her home environment while others her age played games.

Trestan felt uncomfortable when Cat talked about aspects of elvish life that reflected their long lives. Elves generally live for several hundred years. To a human perspective, that offers a lot of time to accomplish goals. The way Katressa described elvish life, it seemed that few elves pursued some endeavors the way humans did. With all the time to enjoy life, many elves tended to procrastinate in their work. Trestan had always heard about how talented elf artisans were at their craft, due to all the years of experience by which they could develop their skills. Indeed, many great things crafted by elves sometimes took decades of work or even centuries. It was an eye opener listening to Cat as she described the lazy facets of elvish lifestyle as well. To the elves, there are always plenty of tomorrows.

Trestan balked at continuing the conversation along that course. If he followed that subject to its end, he and Cat would find themselves faced with their differing life spans again. Trestan brought the conversation back toward relationships and romance.

"Yet, elves still mate for life?" Trestan interjected.

Cat looked ahead to the trail as she answered. "Aye. I know of rare cases when elves try to undergo a separation; there are laws and customs to cover it. Separations are shunned publicly, and elves who try to marry a second time, especially after a separation, may never be free of scandal. So, for the most part, elves do mate for life. They usually have plenty of time to get to know their potential mate. Elvish courting can last decades."

Trestan gulped at that, hoping Cat didn't realize his discomfort with that revelation. "What are the elves' symbols of marriage?" At Cat's questioning gaze, Trestan elaborated. "Korrelothar had an earring to denote his marriage. All the human cultures I know use rings on their finger."

Cat nodded her understanding, "Not all human cultures use finger rings, Trestan. I've known at least one that uses a lip piercing to indicate a partnership."

A giggle erupted from Cat as she noticed Trestan's eyes widen at that news. She resumed, "Elves have nimble fingers for crafts, bows, and such. They generally shun finger decorations like rings, calling them a distraction. The elves that favor wearing rings are usually doing so because of the magical nature of the ring. For marriage, elves like to use a variety of symbols. The symbols themselves offer up to the gods some prayers of virility, fertility, safety, mutual compassion, or long life. They appear on charms, which could be either pinned to clothing or worn as a necklace. Korrelothar wears his as an earring. Elves tend to be attracted to sexy, smoothly pointed ears, and by wearing an earring with a marriage symbol they make it known their heart is claimed."

Trestan appreciated Cat's good mood. She giggled over a thought before sharing it with him, "But unlike those barefoot halflings, elves tend to avoid wearing toe rings to signify marriage!"

As Trestan navigated Belgard through high ferns, he dared to delve deeper into the customs of elvish marriage. "So, after two elves decide to mate, how do they go about it? Is there a proposal?"

Cat laughed, "I don't know if I want to give you ideas."

Trestan blushed, "Oh, I'm just curious. I like to learn more about the world."

"Well, there is a 'proposal' as you would call it." Katressa elaborated, "A human term my mother used for engagements was 'oathbond', by which the one doing the proposal offers hand and heart forever to his lover. Oathbond is the engagement; the spiritbond is more or less what the elf term for marriage means. Let's say the male initiates the oathbond, although with elves it could easily be either sex. He announces his fidelity to the female, proclaims his love for her, and asks that she be oathbond to him. There is some ceremony to the occasion. The offer and promises must be made in the presence of a spiritual guide, such as a cleric, as well as both a male and female friend of the couple. These people bear witness to the vows of the one offering the oathbond, and the response of the recipient. Thus, once he has made the proposal to her, she can accept or reject it. She does not have to give her answer immediately. Even if she accepts the oathbond, custom allows her leeway of a full year in which to decline the proposal or fulfill the spiritbond to the male."

As they rode deeper into the green landscape, Trestan tried to visualize the events. "So, they have a year after the oathbond to either get married, or refuse and possibly go their separate ways. And you're also telling me they can accept the oathbond and yet change their mind later?"

"Aye," the half-elf responded, "Of course, the one doing the proposal could change his mind also, but since he initiated the offer, it would reflect badly on him."

Trestan became absorbed in his own private thoughts over the customs. Now he understood more of elvish marriages if he ever proposed to Cat. He wondered if she ever suspected how much his thoughts centered on her. Trestan often wondered what it would be like to be bonded with Katressa Bilil, but it was hard to foresee the future they would have. He wasn't sure that it felt right to ask her yet. After years of spending so much time in the confines of the seminary, Trestan simply looked forward to having their time together on the road. He tried not to think about the one large obstacle looming in the path of their relationship. If they fulfilled everything they dreamed, and raised a family, Cat would be placing flowers on Trestan's grave a hundred years after he ceased to live.

Trestan shook his head, trying to dislodge the notion. By her admissions, no one had ever been as close to Cat's heart Trestan, and he had never met anyone that consumed his heart and dreams more than her. They were deeply, completely in love. Trestan hoped it would last forever.

Her sensitive ears attuned to a noise in the greenery before Trestan noticed it. Cat put a hand on his arm, nodding toward the side of the unseen trail. "Do you hear that?"

Trestan held his breath as he looked off into the tangle of bushes and low branches. Sure enough, distant laughter floated to his ears. The two of them whispered while keeping an ear on the sounds. The half-elf, who had spent a good part of her youth scouting in forest settings, reasoned they were nearing the fringes of the gnomish village. As they listened to the echoes through the nearby trees, they ventured a guess that it was only two people making the noise.

The two companions followed the fleeting laughter. They saw no obvious traces of a forest gnome village ahead. Though Trestan remained uneasy, Cat moved with confidence. The half-elf finally pointed to a spot in the low growth ahead, indicating a group of leafy plants shaking in response to some hidden movement.

A threatening growl emanated near them in warning. Trestan and Cat stood nearly immobile, though their eyes swept off to the side in order to identify the sudden danger. A very large dog stepped into view. The canine, ears lowered, teeth bared, issued a rumbling growl in response to their presence. The dog wore a saddle on its back, suitable for carrying someone of a small race. Clearly the dog had an owner somewhere about, and was trained for protection.

From ahead, where Cat's pointing finger still lingered in uncertainty, a gnome woman's face popped up from behind bushes. Loose leaves clung to the dark hair which lay in disarray about her head. As far as the two companions could see, her shoulders were bare. Both guessed she might not even have any clothes covering her top portion. Her gaze lacked all friendliness at the sudden interruption. The gnome seemed unconcerned about the large dog or its angry growls, focusing solely on the trespassers.

The woman called out to them in a demanding tone. Neither Trestan nor Cat understood the gnome's native language. Cat spoke out, hoping the gnome could at least understand the more common human tongue. "We didn't mean to invade your privacy. We are friends of Mel Bellringer, and hope to find him out here."

Suddenly, a second head popped up from the bushes. Trestan and Cat were relieved to see their longtime friend, Mel. The little gnomish sorcerer looked at them with gleeful surprise. Mel also had his top half bared; the rest hidden by the foliage.

Mel spoke his companion in his native language. The female gnome whistled and called to the dog, which immediately ceased its growling. After the canine guardian had been called off, Mel returned his attention to his unexpected visitors. "Good day, I'm so surprised to see you! I can't wait to talk about old times and find out what you two have been doing!"

Mel jumped a bit in excitement as he spoke, unashamed or unaware that Trestan and Cat could see more than intended. Mel's bottom was as bare as his top, a sure sign they had interrupted a romantic encounter. Trestan pretended not to notice the nakedness as he returned a meek wave back toward the gnome.

Apparently, more than one of his old friends forged relationships since he had last seen them.

*        *        *        *        *

The next day, Cat rode down the road to Barkan's Crossing alongside Trestan and Belgard, but her mood had turned as sour as the weather. The misty rain didn't dampen Trestan's spirits. Even Belgard strode strong and confident despite the currents of water running down ruts in the road. While Trestan rode resplendent in red-and-gold colors of his faith, shining in his armor despite the sunless day, his companion sulked over her horse in her usual black traveling leathers. Her hooded cloak shrouded most of her form. It seemed at odds from what Trestan knew of his love. Normally, Cat wasn't bothered much by any type of rain. Today she covered up, sheltered in her own private thoughts, and shielded herself from the outside world.

Trestan attempted to talk positively as they followed the muddy road. "I'm really going to miss Mel, but I understand his choice matched Petrow's. Mel was ever unpredictable about many things. I thought he'd love another shot at an adventure, but I understand he has someone to share a new adventure. Maybe I'm just rambling. Anyway, I'm glad for Mel but I'll miss having him around…even though he'd be the one doing all the talking."

Trestan's attempt at humor fell flat on Katressa. The young man hoped it would bring a chuckle, but Cat's face stayed shrouded in the hood of her cloak

Cat appreciated the rain helping to hide her emotions, giving her some sense of isolation as she considered an unpleasant thought in her mind.

Trestan continued to speak. "Maybe it's all for the better. I'll miss the company of our other friends, but I'm fortunate to have you by my side again. I look forward to our time together."

In Cat's mind, Trestan just didn't understand. In another time and place she would have acknowledged her views of enjoying their companionship. With a worrying thought on her mind, the last words she wanted to hear paired at once were 'time together'. Her eyes glanced at the road ahead. She noted familiar farms marking the northern fringes of Barkan's

Crossing residents. She weighed her inner turmoil, knowing she should make her decision soon, already aware of what it would be.

"Trestan," Cat asked, "What are your plans once we enter Barkan's Crossing?"

Trestan stroked his mustache as he considered the question. He concentrated on her query, wondering if he could find something to brighten her mood. "Well, we'll have to arrange a ship to Orlaun. Just you and me, along with our horses. That would be safer, quicker and easier than traversing the mountain passes of the giant races. It might do good to stay at the Eagle's Nest for a night, enjoying the view of the falls together. It's possible we might dig up a clue as to Salgor's whereabouts, unlikely as that seems." A smile came to Trestan's lips, "Although I recall you saying there are some finer inns at which to spend gold. Perhaps we can afford a suite somewhere else."

Cat interrupted any further thoughts Trestan had along those lines. "I don't know how my horse might handle a sea passage. She has been…sick, for a couple days now."

"We could rest her up in Barkan's Crossing for a day or two. I could try my healing miracles to help her."

Beneath Cat's hood, Trestan could see the shake of her head. "Nay, its more than that I'm afraid. She can't make this journey."

Silence followed, an uneasy moment for Trestan as he tried to guess what Cat hinted. "*Faunlessa*, what is wrong?"

He glanced sideways to judge her mood, but the young man could still see nothing of the half-elf's face. She answered, "It is nay sickness or injury. I'm afraid it is more complicated than that," Cat sighed. "I've noticed for some time now, though I wished to deny it, but she is unable to run as tirelessly or swiftly as she used to do."

Trestan stroked his dark mustache again as he spoke, "That doesn't mean she is too sick. You're just worried for her, that's all."

"My horse is old, Trestan," Cat turned to give him a serious look, "I've had her for many years and she has grown old on me."

Cat looked back to the road ahead, while Trestan found himself looking over her horse. He watched the way it splashed through the mud, noting its muscle tone and breathing. He understood why Cat wasn't warming up to him today. Aging was ever a touchy issue.

"Is that why you never name them?" Trestan dared ask. "You're afraid to get too attached?"

"Aye," Cat choked on the word. "It doesn't seem to help. This is probably my third horse that I have ridden for many years and yet all too soon they get old and die on me. They pass like the season, a season which comes too fast."

He replied, "That horse still has a few roads to run. You're letting go of her too early."

Cat's voice nearly broke, but she spat out a reply with more venom than intended. "I'm not counting the weeks as I watch another longtime friend whither and fail. Curse the long years of my elf heritage if I have to watch everything I care about grow old and die."

Trestan watched her fists clench and unclench on the reins. He figured there was little he could say to bring any comfort to her. They rode onward in uneasy silence for several hoof beats.

"I've made up my mind," she spoke. "I'm not going to burden her with a sea voyage. She has already had a few of those, and never liked them. The farms around here have such nice, open pastures. It's a good time to give her a quiet home where she can sleep and eat the rest of her days. Maybe she'll find a mate to keep her company until…well, so she won't be lonely."

As soon as Cat declared her intent, she wanted to act on it before changing her mind. Riding past the outlying farms of Barkan's Crossing, Cat looked over all the fields and pastures. Occasionally she made comments out loud…about the condition of a barn, or the looks of the grass, or any of a number of small things that seemed to indicate the quality of life at those farms. Trestan mostly stayed quiet. He wanted to help her in some way, but he risked treading on deeper feelings.

Cat found a pasture she liked. The half-elf commented about the large field, nearby stream, and presence of a few other horses to keep her horse company. Once they started riding up the branching trail to the farmhouse, Trestan knew there would be no turning back on Cat's decision. This was the final trail she would ride on this horse  Cat and Trestan dismounted at the door. Cat held her horse's reins and kept it close as she knocked. Trestan stood back beside Belgard, absently patting and stroking his neck as they waited.

The man that answered looked surprised to be getting visitors in such weather. He acted nervous around Trestan, glancing at the armor and the sword Trestan carried. When Cat started talking, the man waved her off, like he wasn't interested in buying a horse. After more explaining, Cat made it clear she wasn't selling the horse. The half-elf rogue even offered him enough coins to help feed and take care of the horse for some time. The man's mood changed considerably. He went about inspecting her horse, checking its health.

Trestan observed through a dreamlike quality. He felt like he witnessed something he dearly wanted to change, yet knew he couldn't. This was Cat's decision. By her tone and actions, Trestan knew he would not be able to change her mind, only incite her wrath if he tried to steer her away. It would have been so simple if no one had answered the door or if the old man had refused and ignored them. Instead, the ranch owner appeared amiable to Cat's offer.

Cat handed a bag of coins to the old man, both clasping hands over a done deal. Trestan listened as Cat hesitantly made one last request, hoping she might have a private moment to say goodbye to her horse. The ranch owner consented, telling her she could have some time with the horse next to the pasture fence while he readied a stall for it. In moments the old man and one of his sons headed to their barn to put some straw in a stall, leaving Cat and Trestan alone with the horses.

Trestan watched as Cat undid the buckles of her light saddle. The belongings that Cat didn't carry under her cloak were all part of her saddle and saddlebags. As she worked to loosen the saddle from her unnamed horse, Trestan tried to work in his mind anything that he might say. He didn't think any words would turn her emotions around, but he wanted to be able to support her in some way. The former smith moved forward as the half-elf grunted with the weight of the saddle. After throwing a glower at the muddy ground, she turned and sat the saddle on a hitching post. When Cat started to turn toward her bareback horse, Trestan came up behind her and hefted her saddle up.

Her emerald eyes whipped around as he took the burden. "That's my saddle! I will carry it!"

He denied her protest, "This is heavy, Belgard can carry it for us. Take some time with your horse."

Trestan turned away from her with saddle in hand, leaving no opportunity for her to act or say anything except to his back. Cat watched as Trestan carried her saddle over to Belgard and proceeded to balance it on top of his own. Trestan knew she wouldn't stay angry. It would have been silly for her to try carrying the saddle all the way to Barkan's Crossing.


Cat led her old mount to the pasture on the other side of the ranch building. She opened a gate which allowed her horse to walk into the edge of the field. The latch locked as the gate closed. Cat still held the reins of her horse, from the opposite side of the fence. The half-elf leaned on the wooden fence, staring into the face of a trusting friend. The horse stared back at the rider it had borne for so long, sensing the sadness of its longtime partner without understanding the cause. The horse stepped as close as the fence would allow. The half-elf tried not to cry but she could already feel the emotions welling up. The animal couldn't realize it was time for their long partnership to end.

Her mind at odds with itself, she scratched around the horse's ears while a part of her urged her to just turn around and walk away. She wanted to leave and just put this behind her. She found it hard to face the grief of losing a companion after all their adventures together. Its head nuzzled closer, moving the long nose right up against her tunic. Cat tried to make sense of the inquisitive sniffing, until she recalled a pouch of dried fruit treats in her pocket.

"Oh, so that's the real reason for all this attention is it?" The raven-haired woman reached into her pocket, "You're begging for a treat?"

After a slight hesitation, Cat poured the entire contents of the pouch into her hands. "Nay sense in holding back is there? You might as well have the rest of it."

The horse greedily devoured the dried fruit pieces in her hands. Cat felt her eyes watering as she watched the horse through blurry vision. She had the urge to give the horse one more thorough brushing as well, but chided herself for wanting to extend her own pain.

As tears started down her cheeks she made a futile plea. "Don't make me cry."

She intended it as a harsh whisper. Instead, it was muffled as the horse nudged her hands looking for more treats. She leaned against the fence, petting the horse's neck as it looked at her with big, dark eyes. Cat buried her face against its neck and mane, heedless of the wet fur from the rain.

"I'm sorry I never named you." Cat sobbed in a broken voice. "It hurts to give a name when the years go by so fast. One day I'm teaching you how to get used to a saddle, and before I realize it you've grown too old to carry me everywhere. We covered a lot of ground, didn't we? You carried me around Orlaun and the Counties of Diara. We set foot on the edge of the Tribal Expanse, where you wanted to run free with the wild stallions. You were even stolen from me once…and I found you…got you back…"

Her words choked up as they began to disappear into anguish. The half-elf held on to her horse, though she no longer spoke directly to it. Her next words were for any wandering spirits or servants of the gods that might hear her woeful plea. "It is nay blessing to be gifted with a long life, if everything else ages and withers before my eyes. How did my father deal with it? How did he plan to live after my mother's death?"

Even as she asked her question, she remembered well her father's decision. When Katressa was still young, her aging human mother died in a demon attack on her elvish homeland. It was the most nightmarish thing of her many years. Shortly afterwards, her elf father made the suicidal decision to follow the demons back to their own world in pursuit. He never came back. In Cat's questioning mind, she had to wonder if he willingly went on such a grave mission hoping he might join his beloved in death.

"I hate living like this and seeing these loved ones pass on. My faithful horse companions failing in their service to me only because of their short lifespan. My dear mother, whose hair and skin showed her advanced years by the time I grew old enough to remember her. My love, Trestan…he is so strong and handsome now, but a couple of decades will pass quickly for me. By that time…"

Cat didn't finish the thought out loud, burying the remainder of her lament in the fur of her horse. The animal nestled her between its nose and body, keeping her close as it felt her distress.

Cat's voice lost her strength by the time she choked out, "It's not fair!"

A long, silent moment followed as she worked to stem the flow of tears. Her nimble hands shook as she attempted to dry her eyes with the edges of her wet cloak. She found no point in prolonging her personal agony any more. Her sorrow and anger expressed, Cat told herself it would do no good to dwell here longer. The road called her away.

Cat drew away from her horse, staying close enough to work loose the halter on its head. She stood uncertainly for a moment with the tangle of leather and metal resting in her arms. It was a good thing Trestan put her saddle on his horse; she would not have wanted to carry it all the way to town. Even the halter would be an awkward thing to bear as she walked. She convinced herself it belonged to the horse anyway and left it draped over the fence.

Cat took the horse's head between her hands one last time. She leaned forward, planting one tender kiss on the top of its nose. Her eyes closed, she whispered, "Goodbye."

The black cloak whirled around as she broke contact and walked away from the fence. She spared no more glances over her shoulder at her old companion. Though she didn't look, the recesses of Cat's mind conjured up images of her horse standing there by the fence, awaiting its next treat. The hood covered Cat's grief as she walked around the house, passing Trestan and Belgard without looking up. Her eyes focused on the muddy ground as she forced one foot ahead of the other. She worked hard to control her breathing, swallowing back the emotions welling up inside her throat. Barkan's Crossing called to her from just up the road, and beyond that a ship would take them to Orlaun and Korrelothar's wizard guild. No reason remained to look back.

Trestan walked Belgard a respectable distance behind his lover. As much as he wanted to provide some comfort to her at that time, he knew some of her feelings derived from her fears about what her future with Trestan might bring.

Happy solution didn't come easily when one was part of the reason for the sorrow.

**CHAPTER 9**                    **"The Chase"**


Montanya refused to spend the night in one of the many "copper pens" of the city. Such places offered a roof for the night and a share of soup and bread, asking for only a copper piece if one could pay. People rarely paid, exploiting the church's free charity. Disciples of Ganden, (the God of Honor, Duty and Service), ran those sanctuaries. The selfless clerics of that sect would not leave hungry mouths to sleep on the street. Though Montanya's pride had suffered much over the years, she had enough of it left to refuse taking handouts from anyone. The nineteen-year-old woman rejected stooping to the charity of others when her goal was to help people in her own way. She always saw herself as a victim of many crimes, even of some crimes conjured up in distorted memories. If she begged among strangers for food and a place to rest she would feel as if she prolonged her status as a helpless victim.

On top of everything else, she regarded the churches to be thieving organizations as well.

A full week after being cast out from the monastery, (ten days in the realm of Dhea Loral), Montanya curled up beside a boarded window inside an abandoned shop. The moons climbed into the night sky, throwing soft light between the boards nailed haphazardly over the opening. The red-haired woman hadn't even unrolled her blanket, lingering instead to stare at the nighttime sky. She sighed quietly, hiding in her own private corner of the world.

The young woman wore a loose set of linen clothes, covered in places by hardened leather padding. This had been her training gear in her previous home. A leather breastplate, shaped to fit her womanly curves, had shown its worth in the past at deflecting punches and kicks. Leather armguards and greaves covered her forearms and shins respectively. Soft leather slippers covered her feet, crafted of such thin skin that they allowed her to easily get a feel of the ground. Much of her outfit bore a rather drab tan or brown coloring. She possessed only a dark cloak for warmth, bundled in the rolled-up blanket folded over her left shoulder, the ends tied together beside her right hip. She braided her hair short, using the ribbon of pink cloth torn from her mother's dress. The youth couldn't remember the last time she enjoyed a decent bath or washed her clothes. Dirty and disgusted with the way her clothes stank, she sat in her small hiding spot tormented by her own inner demons.

A pair of figures on the street diverted her attention. The first figure walked the street without any knowledge of the other two sets of eyes on him. Appearing as a human in arcane robes, he had little to fear from the dangers of the streets at night. Although illusionist Wendall of the Brotherhood of the Circles mage guild had mastered the arcane arts, he often found that in a human-dominated city it was good to modify one's appearance. Wendall, a gnome, wore a mask that altered him so that others viewed him as human. The short illusionist always found it a handy item to have, for the larger races rarely offered much respect for gnomes. Knowing that any ruffians would be more intimidated to stay away from a human mage, rather than a mage standing at less than three feet tall, Wendall decided it was prudent to wear the mask during the late hour of this errand. Unbeknownst to the unfortunate gnome, the mask he wore only served to attract trouble this night.

Oblivious to the betrayal set in motion by another mage from his own guild, Wendall went about his errand with no advanced warning of the assailant stalking his footsteps.

Kemora Quickfeet knew about the mask the illusionist carried. An accomplice of Revwar and Savannah, Kemora had a use for that magical trinket. Soon a performance like no other would be viewed by elements of nobility in the presence of the Brotherhood of the Circles. Kemora had to be present, but she faced one slight problem. She was a domid, otherwise known as a halfling by the larger races. Standing only three feet, five inches tall, her lack of height would make her stand out among the tall races. No halflings were on the guest list. The mask would be her key to slip into the prestigious event without raising questions. The domid could use the mask to blend among the humans, and Jentan Mollamos taught her all she needed to know about how to use it. She might even remember to thank him for it, after she robbed his guildmate of that precious item.

Kemora wore tan and gray clothes under a black cloak. Such colors helped her to hide in the dark, or mix into a crowd without calling attention to her. The domid's long, brown hair was tied up into a bun on her head. The woman bore a long face and nose, with a spattering of brown freckles in her cheeks. Light blue eyes watched the pace of Wendall's steps, trying to estimate the true size of her target beyond the covering of the human illusion. Humans often mistook domids as children, and Kemora didn't mind if others underestimated her as such. The woman had an ample bustline and hips, hidden under clothes that allowed her to pass as a portly human child. Kemora Quickfeet wore leather armor under her cloak, and carried weapons by which to carry out her wicked assault. Her effective blades stayed sheathed in favor of a different strategy.

As Wendall unwittingly walked past her position, Kemora parted from the shadows. At her belt hung a gag designed to lessen the threat from the spellcaster. The halfling's first attack would be with the unusual weapon in her right hand. Halflings designed bolos as a means to deal with the larger races. Most often it entangled the legs, tripping the larger creature and bringing it down to the level of a halfling blade. A skillful thrower could send the spinning bolo at an opponent's neck. Bolos could knock a target out, distract it into trying to untangle the wire from around its neck, or strangle the opponent if it could be tightened.

Kemora couldn't determine the height of his neck, but she could guess where to aim for the legs. The halfling woman started to send the bolo spinning. Wendall's 'human' head perked up at hearing the strange noise of something whooshing through the air. Kemora spun the bolo fast, launching it at a horizontal angle on the fourth spin.

From behind the badly boarded window, Montanya stared in brief shock as events unfolded. The young woman couldn't believe she was actually witnessing an assault. Montanya knew about bolo weapons from her martial arts master, though she had never seen one used before. Her greenish-blue eyes witnessed the bolo tangle up the legs of the human mage and send him sprawling to the ground. The halfling rogue wasted no time in jumping on top of her quarry with the gag meant to silence him.

Montanya's heart started beating in a panic. Tense energy overwhelmed her body, urging her to action. She foresaw her moment to save someone from being a victim. She envisioned the rogue in the same light as the ones who had killed her parents.

Her window was on the second floor of the empty building. She ran over to the stairs and proceeded to run down at a fast rate. She nearly slipped at the last few steps but got her feet back under her. Inwardly, the youth cursed herself for her clumsiness. All of her strength and agility would finally be tested and she could ill afford a mistake. A hole through some rotted planks offered the one exit. The student of chiaso scrambled through the narrow opening even though it snagged at her rolled blanket. Once in the alley, she hopped back to her feet and sprinted toward the scene of the attack.

Montanya became confused by what she saw. As she arrived, the halfling woman ran down the side alley from where she had initiated her attack. In place of the human mage she saw a gnome dressed in identical robes squirming around on the ground. The young woman noted the gnome's gag, tied arms, and legs tangled in the bolo's cords. The gnome saw Montanya and began pleading for help through the gag.

Montanya skidded to his side and untied the gag. "Don't worry, I'm here to help you. I'm puzzled, I thought I saw a human attacked by that halfling."

Once the gag dropped away, the exasperated gnome talked fast. "An illusion of mine. My mask makes the wearer appear human. Oh merciful gods, she took it as well as my money pouch."

Montanya no longer heard the halfling's footfalls. She looked to the alley by which the short woman had disappeared. She knew what her heart wanted. The chiaso could feel a smoldering anger within her toward the thief. Every second moved the robber farther away from being caught.

Montanya leapt to her feet and took her first steps down the alley. Wendall's voice rose in pitch. "Wait! Untie the rest of me!"

She barely looked back as she ran. "You'll be fine! I have to be quick to catch that thief!"

The gnome sputtered several more pleas in a panicked whine, but the red-haired youth resolved to bring the rogue to justice. Running down the alley in her thin leather soles, she kept her breathing even in preparation for a long chase. She cast a critical eye at every corner and nook in the buildings. Uneven stone faces, support timbers, and clutters of refuse went by in the dark, and she had to glance into the shadowy recesses of each looking for hiding spots. The halfling probably had several escape options, but where did she disappear? Numerous hiding spots and smaller alleys amidst the shadows of the tall buildings offered hiding nooks. Montanya tried to keep her ears keen to any other noise but it seemed as if her own breathing was the only thing to reach her ears.

Losing faith in her course, Montanya eventually emerged at a backstreet. Other people walked along the narrow avenue, past darkened doorways of shops and homes. A few carried lanterns or candles to illuminate the dark as they went about whatever late night business. The young woman paused a moment to catch her breath as her eyes darted about the shadows. Montanya began to feel hopeless about finding the slippery thief. She glanced at the other people within sight. Her senses fell upon a small figure shuffling through the street. It looked like a human child, walking alone, shadowed in a dark cloak.

Montanya casually followed the child as she examined the form more carefully. The short figure looked very suspicious. The height and the cloak matched the robber. Why would a young child be walking alone in these streets anyway? The black cloak hid some details, but Montanya began to feel confident it was the thief. They walked for some distance as Montanya's human strides slowly gained ground. There were times she thought the rogue glanced over her shoulder, but done so subtly Montanya couldn't be sure. Was it truly the rogue, and did she realize she was being followed? Without warning, the furtive character broke into a run. The thief used her small size to her advantage as she ducked through someone's cluster of junk items, bolting into another alley. Montanya dropped all false pretenses and chased her. The agile human vaulted the assortment of discarded oddities in her pursuit of the short rogue.

Beyond the refuse pile, Montanya encountered a narrow alley. A small trench carved through the ground, likely for carrying off rainwater or even human waste. Wooden slats covered portions of the dirt, offering places to walk which would keep a person's feet elevated over the muck. Back doors offered discrete exits for the owners of the buildings, likely locked and wedged.

The flash of a blade signaled Kemora's choice to strike at her pursuer. The halfling sliced at the human's gut. Montanya's chiaso reflexes took over; her torso contorted enough to avoid the first pass of the steel edge. Feet moved to regain a perfect balance as the momentum of the blade reversed.

Kemora's sword was the perfect size for a domid's arm, even though short by human standards. The sharpened blade extended sixteen inches from the crosspiece. Some humans might have considered it as nothing more than a long dagger. Regardless of its size, the deadly weapon sought Montanya's blood.

Kemora's reverse swing swept at Montanya's long legs, testing the agility of the chiaso student. Montanya sprang up slightly to one side, barely getting her late foot out of the path of the sword in time. Her leading foot found purchase on the base of a bricked window. The foot pushed her even farther up and out of the halfling's reach. Kemora ducked and stabbed upwards as the human leapt over her. The stab only attempted to get in a lucky strike, for the domid mostly tried to avoid any surprises dropping down on her. Montanya's vault sent her over the halfling, with her original trailing foot using the far wall to bring her down easy. Montanya landed behind the rogue, trapping Kemora between her and the refuse-strewn mouth of the alley.

They paused for a moment, measuring each other. Kemora held her small sword before her threateningly. Montanya saw the gnome's mask tucked into the halfling's belt. Both women wore similar armor, each choosing hard leather coverings over their more vulnerable areas. The top bun of the halfling's hair barely rose past Montanya's beltline. Size made little difference to the domid, for there were ways to fight in which one could make use of their smaller size against a tall opponent. Humans weren't a threat if one could take out the legs or get to the large artery in the back of the knee. Kemora actually looked upon her opponent as foolish. The domid had her sword as well as a thin stiletto and other surprises, while her opponent stood weaponless.

Montanya tried to stay calm in the face of a rush of adrenaline and emotions. Chiaso studied fighting unarmed against opponents wielding swords and armor. This would be the first time Montanya's training would face a lethal test. She told herself to treat this with as little fear as when she had faced her fellow students on the training mat. If she gave in to fear, she would be vulnerable. Fear wasn't the only emotion clouding her concentration. Kemora represented a focus for revenge against thieves. She saw in the rogue everything she had grown to hate in her life.

Kemora, feeling little reason to fear her unarmed opponent, went on the offensive. Her short arm pumped forward a couple times as she advanced a few small steps. Montanya backed away as the sword jabbed at her waist. The attacks tested her grace of movement. Kemora swayed back and forth in her steps a bit, gaining confidence. Montanya took the time to study her opponent, studying the turn of the hips and the tensing of the muscles.

When Kemora stepped in fast to deliver a serious cut, Montanya fell into one of her reflexively studied combat maneuvers. The youth actually stepped toward Kemora, cloth pantaloons billowing out, as she swept a foot into a kick. The halfling's sword reach extended too far. Montanya's leather shinguard connected with the wrist holding the sword. The domid cried out in pain, nearly losing her grasp on the weapon. If Montanya's mind and body had been more in balance with the discipline of a true chiaso, she likely would have broken the wrist. Instead, mounting rage clouded her concentration even as it swept aside her fear.

Though Kemora retained her grip on the sword, Montanya finished the move with a strike of her own. A backhanded blow to the head, aimed a little too high, sent Kemora staggering. The domid's brown hair partly fell loose from the neat bun.

Montanya took the offensive, letting loose some of the pent-up rage she had stored for so many years. The human lost proper respect for the sword Kemora carried, acting recklessly to continue the assault. The halfling recovered her shock from the first blows and used her agility to avoid a series of punches and spinning round kicks. There were probably many opportunities for Kemora to slip her sword past Montanya's blurred yet wild movements, but the brazen human's movements intimidated the halfling.

Kemora decided to make another escape rather than waste time fighting this interloper. She needed a distraction. An idea came from a cracked piece of pottery sitting in the muck. Her sword tip stabbed through the open space of the handle, gaining leverage by which to fling the impromptu missile. If Kemora aimed to hit Montanya with it, she would likely miss and waste the effort. Instead, Kemora's sword flipped it at the stone building next to her opponent's head.

Montanya ignored the flying jar since it flew wide, but when the pottery hit the stone building it shattered into several pieces. The human flinched and closed her eyes as a spray of broken clay rebounded off the wall into her face. She stumbled backward defensively until she could refocus on the whereabouts of her quarry.

Kemora scrambled back into the open street through the pile of refuse. Montanya began to continue her pursuit. The chiaso stopped short when her opponent pulled another trick from her repertoire. The domid grabbed a lantern from one of the street shops, thrusting a vial of some sort into it, next to the candle. Montanya was about to leap the garbage pile when Kemora spun and threw the lantern into the pile. The impact shattered the vial of oil placed next to the candle. A bright spray of flames caught the edge of the debris, causing Montanya to lurch to a sudden stop. The halfling rogue disappeared from view as the oil gave a quick source of fuel to the flames and smoke.

*          *          *          *          *

The flames caused Montanya to pause. Her eyes searched the alley in frustration as she felt the rush of heat. The initial fuel of the flames started to die down somewhat, although likely the wood in the pile would soon expand into a bigger fire. Montanya, last survivor of the murdered Westonhout family, held too much anger within her to fear the flames for long. The rogue had mugged a mage, pulled a blade on her, and then started a fire that might consume someone's home. There was no way the rogue would escape as long as Montanya had any strength left to fight.

The chiaso tried to fall into a quick meditation, calming her senses and telling her spirit that the fire wouldn't burn. She tried to draw from her chi, then she took off and ran. The woman vaulted the flames, panic still hitting her as she felt a flash of intense heat. Montanya hit solid ground on the far side, falling into a roll to smother any flames that might have caught her cloth. She coughed out a bit of foul air as she rose back to her feet. She felt singed, as if she had been out in the sun too long, but neither her clothes nor her red hair caught fire.

Montanya scowled as she looked up and down the street. She saw no immediate sign of the small bandit. The chiaso ran to a nearby intersection, figuring the thief sprinted down another street. She quickly turned to look down every exit. She had a relatively good view down all four directions, though the darkness still offered many places to hide from sight. She saw no small figures, despite a few people walking the streets. Even now, some were noticing the fire and starting to call out alarms. Montanya's attention diverted to one couple whose eyes looked toward the sky instead of the street or the flames.

The male told his female companion, "I wonder what that was about."

The female giggled, "I didn't know anyone could climb those things so fast."

Montanya turned to follow their gazes. A portion of Orlaun's great aqueduct system loomed overhead. Since the long years of the Godswars, Orlaun had been able to repair and sustain an existing aqueduct despite damage during the dark years following the Covenant. One of those sections that supplied endless fresh water to the city crossed above the street, supported by an arch. As soon as she looked at it, Montanya noticed this section had iron rungs set into the stone for access to the top. Many sections of the waterway were covered over, yet accessible to city officials or the local praetorians. A series of walkways, often called "birdwalks", ran along the upper edges of the aqueducts.

Montanya started hauling herself hand over hand up the set of rungs. The soft leather soles made the bars uncomfortable on her feet, but she endured it. Montanya reached the walkway at the top and pulled herself up next to the covered basin housing the running water. She could hear the flow rushing along the length of the system. At a few spots along the side of the system were spigots. Montanya had never been on the aqueduct to see them, but she knew they offered access for the purpose of fighting fires. Looking down, she realized her perch stood at least thirty feet up, possibly even forty. Since the people of Orlaun valued the water pressure from the aqueduct system, most buildings weren't built higher than where Montanya perched. There were many exceptions from nobles wanting to build to impressive heights. For the chiaso, her view was high enough for discomfort. Just thinking of what would happen if one lost their footing and slipped over the edge invited a wave of light-headedness.

Casting aside her fears, she looked down the length of the birdwalk to see if her hunch paid off. She spotted the halfling just a short way down the length of the aqueduct, hurrying along. Montanya had trained hard to keep good balance. She got to her feet on the birdwalk and broke into a run. Her angry mood would have matched her red hair; she aimed to claim blood. Kemora looked back as she heard noise. The halfling's jaw dropped as her amazed eyes spotted the resilient human continuing the chase. Soft leather whisked across the masonry as the chiaso moved. Kemora started running as well. Agility and speed benefited both women, but Kemora could not outpace Montanya's long legs.

Kemora pulled to a stop at a point where the roof of a building came relatively close to the level of the aqueduct. A good drop loomed below, but it left an escape option open. Montanya never slowed as she approached the domid. The rogue's sword flashed in the open. Calling upon her martial disciplines, Montanya took advantage of her small opponent by launching into a flying kick. Kemora tried to duck the assault. The kick missed, allowing Kemora to sweep the sword behind her. After Montanya landed, on the far side of the halfling, she followed it with a balanced roll. The chiaso effortlessly hopped to a fighting stance as Kemora came in low. The domid fought in a crouch, trying to sever the human's feet. Montanya moved her legs fast as Kemora's sword scratched the limestone slabs covering the aqueduct. The human warrior saw her opportunity, pivoting one of her legs in a circle away from the sword slash. Her foot came back to connect with Kemora's chin.

The domid staggered and fell backward. She narrowly avoided losing her balance on the birdwalk. Montanya moved to take advantage of the situation. The halfling faced away from her, and she held the sword on the far side of her small body. Montanya thought she had stunned Kemora; instead, the short rogue lulled her into coming close.

When the human reached to take control of Kemora's hands and sword, the halfling reacted. Montanya succeeded in clamping a hand around the rogue's left wrist, but the right arm tried to run her through with the sword. Montanya contorted once again, moving her body to the side while trying to maintain her balance. The initial stab barely missed her. Unfortunately, Montanya put herself in a precarious position. One of her hands still held Kemora's unarmed hand, keeping the halfling up close, but her other hand was in no position to block the blade.

Kemora's sword had extended beyond Montanya's side, but the rogue immediately remedied that. The domid looked up at Montanya in victory as she retracted the sword in a way that sliced just under the leather chest piece. Montanya's rage disappeared in a scream of pain as she felt the blade cutting into her skin. She didn't have time to look down at the cut, yet she saw the stain of her own blood on the edge of the sword.

Montanya's delayed reaction twisted her farther away from the sword without relinquishing her hold on the rogue. Kemora saw a danger coming, as the human teetered beyond the edge of the walkway while still holding a crushing grip to the small wrist. Montanya's desperation, mixed with persevering anger, clouded her reasoning. Instead of trying to save herself from going over the edge, the chiaso swept her left foot upwards. A kick struck with jarring force to Kemora's jaw, disorienting her.

Both women fell from the heights of the aqueduct.

Moments later, their bodies smacked against the roof of a stable. The fall could have been far worse, yet it still knocked the wind out of their lungs. Montanya rolled a bit in one direction, while Kemora thrashed her limbs as she slid toward one edge. The halfling clutched against an eave as she glimpsed how close she had come to falling all the way to the street. Montanya gasped in air despite the pain in her side.

Kemora got her feet under her as she glanced back up to the human. Although the taller woman had not risen, Montanya's face assumed her customary scowl. The pursuer appeared more angry than hurt. The halfling decided not to push the matter. Retrieving her nearby sword, the rogue entered the building through a second story hay loft that was within reach.

Montanya forced in a breath, gritting her teeth against the pain. Her side had a bloody but shallow cut. It drew her gaze with an almost morbid fascination. She felt relief that she wasn't witnessing her intestines spilling out.

Her eyes lingered for only a short time before anger drove her onward. Montanya growled as she got to her feet and approached the same entry the rogue used. Leather soles slapped across the roof slates as she descended to the hay loft. She felt a moment of helpless vulnerability as she swung through the opening. To her relief, Kemora was not there to slice at her upon entry. Montanya worked to steady her breathing as her eyes tried to adjust to the gloomy interior. The chiaso knelt amidst a scattering of hay strands on the wooden loft. She heard a soft noise.

Montanya picked up a pitchfork and moved to the edge of the loft to look upon the stable's ground floor. Her aggravating quarry bolted through an aisle below, headed for an exit. Kemora heard the noise above her just as the pitchfork launched like a spear. With a yelp of surprise the domid dodged off-balance to the side. Kemora fell into an empty horse stall as the pitchfork teetered upright from where it had embedded into the soft floor.

Montanya tried to find her focus amidst the pain. The human jumped off of the loft, catching a beam over the stall with her hands to guide her move. The beam provided enough leverage to send her reverse-somersaulting through the air at the rogue. As impressive a kick as it was, Montanya's old master would have still chided the way that her anger took away from her deepest concentration.

Kemora found her feet just in time for her small body to meet the impact of the flying kick.

It knocked the halfling backward. Her small body rolled under the lowest plank and into the next stall, putting her in a bad position under a confused horse. Kemora started sputtering curses in her domid language. Halflings hated the prospect of being under the legs of a large horse. The rogue got to her feet amidst stomping hooves. The thief tried to envision an escape route when Montanya came up with a new attack. The martial artist wielded the pitchfork. Not only did Kemora have to avoid the stomping hooves, she had to dodge the pitchfork stabbing at her from between planks.

Blood dampened Montanya's tan tunic, yet that failed to slow the viciousness of the woman's attacks. Her loosened hair whipped around her head as she screamed in rage; the torn pink fabric of her mother's dress barely hung on. The sight of the strange magical mask at the halfling's belt only fueled her rage. Montanya's every thought focused on killing the thief and retrieving the stolen item to repay a lifetime of loss. The pitchfork splintered wood inches from horse legs in pursuit of that tiny halfling heart.

Kemora had to make her escape if she wanted to avoid trampling or impalement. She dodged to one end, intentionally drawing Montanya into stabbing that direction. When the pitchfork narrowly missed Kemora, the halfling dove for a board that had been cracked by an earlier thrust. The rogue twisted through the space offered by the weakened board, bending back a splinter as she did. The halfling still yelped as she felt one tine of the fork scratch her hind end.

The new stall stood empty. Kemora enjoyed that small bit of luck in her favor. She heard the human moving about, and correctly assumed the chiaso would run up the row of stalls with the pitchfork in continued pursuit. The simple theft became a deadly threat to the small mugger. It was time for Kemora to use resources she hadn't expected to need.

With little time to spare, the domid drew forth two items. She hastily uncorked a small vial of fluid. She poured a thick, mucosal liquid on the blade groove of the stiletto held in her nimble right hand.

The stall door burst open from the force of a kick. Montanya nearly filled the entryway as she let the pitchfork lead the way. Kemora dropped the bottle as she rolled to the side of the attack. The pitchfork missed, moving Montanya's hands close to the head of the small rogue. Kemora hopped up and bit Montanya's hand. The domid let go after just a short nip. Montanya dropped the pitchfork and retracted her arm. While the chiaso tried to keep track of the rogue, Kemora closed the gap between them quickly. Montanya felt the rogue pushing past her long legs and reached downward.

Montanya screamed as she felt the stabbing pain in the back of her knee, causing it to buckle.

If Kemora's attack had been perfect, the stiletto would have pierced the major vessels flowing just behind the knee. Her attack barely missed them, but the fluid coating the blade still had an entry into Montanya's system. Kemora shouldered past as the taller woman fell forward.

Montanya caught her fall, staring at the empty glass vial rolling on the floor of the stall. She picked it up with one hand, determined to have something to throw at the rogue. She heard the small footsteps running away from her. Her leg, inflamed with pain, nearly buckled after she got back to her feet. Montanya searched for the halfling, only to see the drab colors of the thief exiting the stable. Limping forward, Montanya ran as fast as her strength could manage. Her breath coming in gasps, the injuries and pain to her body could not be blocked out by her disciplines. Montanya stumbled clumsily out the door.

This street was relatively busy with people in this late hour. Her greenish-blue eyes swept the street for signs of the rogue, but she saw no short figures. If she had been more alert, she might have noticed a human-sized figure looking much like the halfling. A seemingly human woman with her brown hair frazzled about a loosened bun, dressed in drab brown and gray colors, discreetly wiped some blood and fluid off a stiletto before replacing it in a sheath. Wearing the stolen magical mask, blending in with the humans on the street, Kemora walked away in disguise.

Meanwhile, Montanya drew stares as she stumbled out of the stable. People gasped upon seeing the blood staining the side of her tunic. They wondered if she wasn't slightly drunk, the way she swayed uncertainly. Her long legs moved unsteadily and with great effort. Her loose pantaloons blossomed wet with blood behind one knee.

A wave of dizziness rolled over the young woman. The people in her sight became blurred. When Montanya's vision sharpened a bit once more, she realized she was kneeling on the ground. Something felt wrong with her body: a sickness spreading inside her. People on the street just stood and stared. Montanya felt ill and hot as her insides tumbled. A wave of nausea spewed forth. Montanya shook as her quivering stomach emptied out onto the street.

When the first wave ended, Montanya saw the reflection of light off the forgotten item in her hand. The glass vial rolled loose from her fingers. Poison!

Mortality replaced anger as paralyzing fear took hold of her mind. She barely whimpered a few words out, beseeching those near. "Help me, please. I've been poisoned."

In the torchlit darkness of the street, her vision blurred by dulled senses, people appeared as shadowy caricatures. None offered hope or a comforting face. If anything, several backed away.

"Help me. Anyone…"

Montanya sagged into the darkness, away from the blurry light and the afterimages of people looking upon her in revulsion. She collapsed in the dirt.

**CHAPTER 10**         **"Sanctuary for Those in Need"**


Two pairs of hands glided over the exposed wounds of the unresponsive human female, working around a modest cover of blankets. The patient's long strands of matted, red hair lay in disarray. The helpful hands, one pair young yet calloused while the other pair showed the wrinkles of age, took turns while uttering prayer chants. In this small room in the back of one of the city's Sanctuaries for Those in Need, (known by some as 'copper pens'), two tired priestesses struggled with ridding this nameless victim of a vicious poison.

A concerned citizen had carried Montanya to the closest form of help he could think to find. With the chiaso hanging so tenuously to the edge of life, her best hope depended on the clerics of the nearby sanctuary. Clerics working at those refuges, devout in their self-imposed servitude, duty to the people and their service to the god Ganden, did not normally receive visitors clinging so precariously to the precipice before death's embrace. The priestesses worked feverishly to save the woman's life, without knowing Montanya's name or the conflict with the halfling rogue. The sweat upon the healers' clothes proved how taxing the struggle had been, as well as other signs: numerous bloody towels, dirty water in the wash basins, a scattering of supplies and bandages strewn across table and floor, emptied and discarded containers of healing poultices. The fumes of incense filled the room.

"She is a fighter. Her soul was almost lost, but she has been pulled back from the brink." The older healer, Mother Evine, whispered to the young disciple of Ganden assisting her. "Ganden's miracles have extracted the poisonous taint from her body. Her breathing is strong and untroubled. We can finish sealing her injuries. Her stamina should return swiftly."

Mother Evine examined the pale flesh of their patient, noting not only the two most serious injuries but also the scars of numerous old wounds. It wasn't an exaggeration calling this one a fighter; Montanya's violent history marred her soft skin. The older healer focused on how her assistant fared with the smaller of the two open wounds. It was only a narrow stiletto puncture, though it had been filled with poison.

The hands of her student circled around the stiletto wound amidst prayers of healing. As the wound healed from the inside out, Mother Evine had time to consider the progress of this young disciple of Ganden.

Acolyte Sondra Oskires, a human maiden, knew twenty-three years of age. The young woman's beauty dimmed under a blanket of low self-esteem and quiet introspectiveness. Sondra had curves that could turn the eyes of any young man, except they lay hidden beneath the layers of clerical vestments. Her soft, blue eyes rarely looked up enough to meet the eyes of those conversing with her. She trimmed her wheat-blonde hair to keep it out of her way as she worked. Clerics of Ganden trained for warfare as well as healing, but one would never suspect the hidden muscles under her clothes capable of wearing armor and dealing blows with a mace. On this day, her shoulders served only to carry the rust-colored leather satchel containing healing supplies and various holy implements. Sondra used oils from that bag to massage warmth into Montanya's leg, whispering words of prayer between perfectly clean and straight teeth. Those teeth rarely appeared, because Sondra seldom smiled. Words rarely passed in plentiful numbers from between her natural, dark-red lips. Words of prayer streamed from her in abundance now, as healing power flowed from her spirit to mend the body of the youth. Sondra's shyness caused her to shrink around others, yet she ranked among the most gifted healers Mother Evine ever trained. Sondra Oskires would be a great tool of her god within the world, able to spread her miraculous healing and words of wisdom to many, if she broke past the self-imposed shell isolating her from others. Sondra's timid nature held her back, when she could have been a full-fledged Sister years ago.

Mother Evine watched the bloody stiletto wound close. It soon became smooth, unbroken skin. The older cleric turned toward her own hands, finishing the prayers which similarly healed the abdomen wound, leaving no visible trace. "That is good work, Acolyte Sondra." She studied the expression on Sondra's face as the younger cleric stepped back from her task. Sondra's face reflected something judgmental in the way she looked at their patient. "I would ask, though, how do you see this woman? What is your opinion of her?"

The young disciple wiped the sweat from her brow. Blood soiled her hands as well as her sleeves, so she settled for finding a somewhat clean towel to dab at her face. Sondra looked over the mostly exposed body on the table before them. Mother Evine in turn studied Sondra's reaction, trying to look past the silent, unemotional barrier her young student often had in place.

"Rough life," Sondra replied. The slightest motion of her chin pointed at the old scars present on Montanya.

Mother Evine nodded, "Aye, she's seen many bad days I fear. I'm more interested in how you feel about her. I asked your opinion of her just now, but you judged her from the moment she came in."

Not unexpectedly, Sondra Oskires ducked her face away from the stare of her mentor. Whenever her elder tried to dig into Sondra's emotions, the young woman avoided eye contact and would distract herself with some menial chore. Mother Evine watched as Sondra hurriedly piled Montanya's soiled and bloody clothes into a basket. Sondra paused as she examined a locket on a chain, before turning around and setting it on the table next to Montanya's foot.

Mother Evine firmly but gently grabbed Sondra's shoulders, turning her face to face. "You aren't avoiding me this time. I mean to have a little talk with you."

The older cleric called over two other acolytes. She asked them to provide new clothes to the injured woman, as well as finish cleaning up the room. The two younger faithful went about their task as Evine led Sondra into a small prayer room.

Mother Evine lit a candle. In its soft light she regarded the downcast face of her apprentice. "Did you try on her shoes?"

Sondra's face revealed her confusion at the question. "Those dirty leather slippers? Why would I put them on my feet?"

Mother Evine cracked a smile, "Because how can you truly know a person unless you have walked in their shoes?"

The young woman rolled her eyes at being caught in the old saying. The older cleric continued, "What did you think her background was like?"

Sondra considered it for a short while. "I am not certain. Her locket had an inscription on it…possibly a name of nobility. Maybe she was someone of importance once, or it was a gift."

Mother Evine stayed silent, urging Sondra to continue. "Her clothes, odd style as they looked, were not poorly made. Yet, she seems to have lived on the street for some time, judging just by the lice and dirt. I'd wager that everything she owned was in that rolled up blanket. I wonder if she ran away from home, or if her home was taken from her."

"I also thought it odd that whoever caused those wounds on her used poison," Mother Evine commented. "Someone must have been awfully desperate. It's rare to see an assailant use poison, especially on a wanderer with nay riches upon her."

The older cleric shook her head, "But, that is not the point. The point is that you judged her the moment she was carried in the door. Your work at healing, skillful as it is, lacked a certain care to it. You loathed something about her, and it showed in your actions."

Sondra winced from the sting of the words. Mother Evine knew Sondra could be sensitive, and any small criticism wounded the young woman. Despite that, the older cleric had to instruct and raise Sondra properly by helping the woman find her own spiritual path.

"It's odd, Acolyte Sondra," Mother Evine whispered, "You serve a god who willfully gives much of his strength to others, yet deep inside I think you have felt tormented by people."

"I told you before," Sondra answered, though her eyes once again turned downward, "I love people despite themselves. I always want to help people, yet I feel they care little for me."

"That is the root of your problem. Now look up child, I am not talking to your hair."

Sondra brought her face up immediately, the edges of her eyes wet. Inwardly, Mother Evine sighed that the young disciple was so sensitive to how others viewed her. "Acolyte Sondra, I have loved you like a daughter, please don't be hurt by what I say. Listen to it…cradle it to you for your own spiritual guidance. You have an inner strength that could well surpass mine someday, but only if you can open your heart."

Sondra nodded, a slight twitch.

Mother Evine put a hand on Sondra's head, running it tenderly down her hair. "I don't know if you know it, but there is a beautiful woman here, physically and spiritually."

Sondra blushed at that.

"I have listened to your words and your unspoken messages down the years. People teased you, made fun of you, and I fear such cruel words can hurt a person as much as any physical punishment." The older cleric continued stroking Sondra's hair comfortingly as she spoke. "But you followed a high calling. You came to the service of Ganden, pledged to serve others, heal their suffering."

Mother Evine smiled, "It is good that you do this. Ease the pain of others because you know what it is like to be hurt. However, in order to be true to your calling you must also heal yourself."

Sondra frowned, but listened quietly.

The older cleric withdrew her hand, but indicated Sondra from head to foot as she spoke. "You lack pride and confidence yourself, you don't view the beauty of your soul as your friends see you. You make very little effort to brighten your own appearance, or offer a smile to others. Inside you are still hurt, Sondra. You hear the words of cruel children still ringing in your ears."

"I don't have many friends," Sondra blurted in response to her mentor's choice of words.

"Yet you do have friends, who say they seldom see you smile or laugh. Though you are eager to heal the hurts of others, you tend to distance your heart from them and hide within yourself."

Sondra, lowered her head just a bit, then nodded. Evine knew it must be a hard admission to acknowledge.

"In order to truly commit yourself selflessly to others," Mother Evine continued, "and to be of true service to others, you must learn to love yourself for who you are. Once you recognize your own self-worth and respect, you can truly be great. Your service to Ganden, and your commitment to helping others, is fundamentally flawed unless you can see your own value."

Sondra sniffled as she nodded again. "I will try to see myself as you do. I honestly try to give as much as I can."

"That is a good thing, but save a little for yourself also. I'm not saying you should be selfish, just see to it you don't overburden yourself. Remember too, that not so long ago you grew up dependent on these houses for food and clothes. Everyone who comes through these doors feels as badly as you did sometimes, like the world is pushing down on them. You can't help them if you are also burdened. Be a beacon in the darkness for them."

The cleric hugged her apprentice, the closest person Mother Evine ever knew like a daughter. Sondra hugged back, truly respecting her mentor and valuing her wisdom.

When they parted, Mother Evine spoke again. "I will tell you some news that will brighten your day immensely."

Sondra's eyebrows rose. The elder continued speaking, "I will bring you along on the voyage with me. You will get to see the vessel firsthand, and learn how we pilot it."

Her words put the brightest smile upon Sondra's face that had been witnessed in some time. Sondra became giddy with excitement. "I really get to go? I can be there to watch the Chosen work?"

Mother Evine nodded, "You can see the Chosen go about their most honorable duty. They will pilot the divine chariot with their prayers, while you may enjoy the journey and the enlightenment of the experience."

Sondra virtually squealed. The older cleric continued, "I hope it also reminds you to develop your skills and develop proper compassion for others. Only the most gifted are Chosen, and there is rigorous training to prepare for this holiest of tasks. Someday, if you focus upon your spiritual path, you may be a Chosen."

"Oh, thank you! I'm honored to see it fly while I'm on board!" Sondra exclaimed.


A short time after their talk ended, Mother Evine and Sondra went different directions to look after their duties caring for the poor. As Sondra rounded one hallway, she heard a commotion from up ahead. Someone shouted as another person tried to calm them, punctuated by noises of objects being thrown around. Sondra hurried ahead to investigate. The noises came from the room where the wounded woman had been healed.

Sondra arrived at the doorway, "What is going on?"

The scarred, red-haired youth, dressed in mismatched garments provided by church disciples while unconscious, stood in a fighting stance. Another acolyte, a younger girl, stood back from the woman with eyes wide and frightful. At Sondra's approach, the look of rage from the patient shifted from the young girl to her.

"Where are my things? Who stole them?" Montanya demanded.

The younger acolyte spoke meekly to Sondra, "She wants her old, bloody clothes back."

Sondra nodded, taking a step into the room. The red-haired woman tensed, ready to attack or bolt. Sondra came to a halt and held her hands up in front of her. "We haven't stolen your things; we just healed you from the brink of death. You should lie down and relax."

Montanya's thin eyebrows lowered. Scowling, she asked, "Where am I?"

Sondra sought to calm the woman, "You are in a Sanctuary for Those in Need, run by…"

"A copper pen!"

Stunned, the young cleric just nodded.

Montanya sneered, "Give me my things back or I start making trouble. I refuse the services of a copper pen! I want my belongings."

Flustered, unsure what to say, Sondra decided to let the woman have her way. "Your things are under this pile."

The young cleric threw aside dirty linen to retrieve the basket holding Montanya's dirty clothes. "These were soiled by blood and not very suitable for wear. The leather pads, cleaner clothes, and your blanket roll of belongings are all folded under that sheet." Sondra nodded her head in that direction.

The street youth tore the basket from Sondra's hands. The disciple of Ganden stood back and scratched her wheat-blonde head as Montanya started recovering her belongings. The youth checked through every pile, making sure she wasn't leaving anything behind. Montanya found her locket, with much relief, and placed it around her neck. Even a small scrap of pink cloth, which Sondra recalled had held the woman's hair back, was retrieved from the floor. Montanya paused temporarily when she considered the bloodstains on her tunic and pantaloons, but then angrily stuffed them into her rolled blanket.

Sondra figured it was time to improve her social graces, before the woman did anything else rash, "I'm sorry I didn't introduce myself sooner. I am Sondra Oskires, disciple of Ganden. You are…?"

"Nay longer your patient!"

Montanya stormed past Sondra, bumping her to the side in order to leave through the doorway. Sondra silently followed Montanya, guiding her to the front entrance rather than let the angry youth wander randomly and cause more trouble. The disciple of Ganden got ahead of the chiaso and opened the exit door for her. The younger woman ignored her, stomping out into the early morning air. Montanya briskly walked away from the building, only to hear Sondra shout from behind.

"You're welcome!"

Montanya paused on the street for a moment. Despite her anger, she knew she owed the clerics her life. However, it also fueled some rage inside her knowing she once again had become the charity of others. Whatever Montanya wanted to do at that moment didn't matter to Sondra. In one of her finer moments of social graces, Sondra slammed the sanctuary door behind the homeless woman.

*         *         *         *         *

Several titles described the great city of Orlaun: Sprawling Towers, City of Spires, and even Gem of the World. All of these names reflected Orlaun's ego of being the biggest and the brightest point of civilization in the world. Visitors from far away Tariyka might scoff at that pompous claim, favoring their capital city of Mai-Chong; however, most human-dominated cultures view Orlaun as a fabled city of riches. While Kashmer to the north could lay claim to the most lucrative trade routes and affluence on markets, Orlaun displayed elegance, housed greater centers of learning, and possessed rich resources. The cataclysms of the Godswars damaged the great city, yet it recovered quickly in the years of rebuilding. Some of the commodities breathing life and abundance into the city included its gem-blessed mines, bountiful supplies of quality building materials, wool, oils, and spices. An extensive aqueduct system, repaired from the cataclysms, utilized clean and endless fresh water for the large population. Centuries of culture fostered artists, inventors, and craftsmen at a time when the rest of the world still struggled. A large library proved to be the biggest collection of knowledge to survive the Godswars and the ensuing dark years. Two influential mage guilds settled near this bastion of knowledge, competing for the favor of local officials as they developed centers of learning for the arcane arts. The harbor grew to be the second largest in the world, surpassed only by Kashmer's mercantile fleets.

The large harbor was the first thing to impress Trestan as their ship arrived. Trestan and Katressa shared a lovers' embrace on the deck as she pointed out the various landmark towers shaping the skyline. From this distance, Trestan could imagine it must be dizzying to look down from their lofty windows. The two companions had some experience guessing what the view must be like, recalling their flight onboard Korrelothar's flying vessel *Dovewing*. The memory pained them with some regret, for their flight aboard the stolen vessel resulted in its destruction. Korrelothar's punishment proved to be merciful compared to his loss. The companions admired the elf wizard so much that they felt a lot of remorse for not being able to compensate him for losing his most prized possession.

As Cat introduced Trestan to the sights of Orlaun, the young paladin inquired about an area on one end of the harbor. It looked as if the ocean swallowed part of Orlaun. The wetted sides of decayed towers glistened in the spray of waves as they stood as silent sentinels of old. The tide broke against them as it thundered past, sometimes traveling another mile before reaching the current shoreline. Another casualty from the ancient Godswars, the decrepit stone guardians rising out of the water marked the gravesite of a bygone era.

"Much of old Orlaun sank into the ocean, conquered by the sea god Krakus, or so it is said. Today, you will still find a floating temple devoted to him within that maze of broken towers, reachable by skiff. The Godswars reshaped so much of the old world." Cat paused as her eyes swept inland from the sunken towers. "The portion of the city closest to this blight is the Highwater district. That area also features old structures from the past, but it is prone to flooding in bad weather, hence the name. That is where the poorest residents of Orlaun reside."

Trestan furrowed his brow as Cat talked, "Korrelothar mentioned his title once. 'The Highwater Conjuror', I think he said. I wonder how he got it."

Curious, the companions asked a nearby seaman about the Highwater district. They didn't specifically ask about Korrelothar. He paused in his work to provide them with a hasty answer.

Deeply tanned hands held a knot of rope as the seafarer spoke. "Fer such a gem o' a city, the conditions in that district are a sad tale. People only live there 'midst the filth and mercy o' Krakus' tides if'n they have nay other choice. But I'm told that every so often a wizard bloke comes through and provides gifts fer the folk. Generous fellar that must be; I wouldn't mosey down thar fer fear of my life or purse."

Trestan and Cat smiled even as they turned to regard the swamped area in the distance. It seemed their local friend had a reputation for being generous to those in need. The deckhand moved away to finish his duties as the two lovers lingered by the rail. Both wore fine attire for their arrival into this renowned city. Although Trestan had not worn his armor much during the voyage, given the lack of necessity for it and the general hindrance it would be should one tip over the rail, he decided to wear it for his grand entrance into Orlaun. While Trestan stared over the railings, he failed to notice his lover's gaze drawn to muscular parts of his anatomy not covered by the steel plate. She reached over and casually allowed a hand to slip down to his firm butt as she spoke to him about the city. Katressa partly dressed in her dark leathers, but left thinner clothing and softer fabrics to cover portions of her curves. Brighter colors adorned her dress and blousy sleeves and the *Taef' Adorina* sparkled upon her head. Cat dressed for Trestan today, her leather tunic opened to reveal the top of her cleavage.

The sad concerns about their differences were far from their minds. Cat lovingly escorted Trestan into one of the most magnificent centers of human culture. She spared no unpleasant thoughts for the extra saddle carried on Trestan's warhorse. Once ashore, Trestan led Belgard from the docks as Cat informed him about the city.

King Acer MigTolo ruled the Kingdom of Gheras, including Orlaun. A castle in the city housed government offices, but Cat told Trestan that it wasn't very notable compared to the ornate towers surrounding it. The companions disembarked in the Upper Port district. From there, Cat pointed out a few notable businesses. She noted The Doyal Moon for revelry and evening entertainment, while coyly hinting that the Silk Sheets Inn was more appropriate for a luxurious night together. Perched on a slight rise, her arm indicated a group of buildings sprawled within a small palisade. Cat identified it as the Crystal Sun Guild. The mage guild competed with Korrelothar's guild for favor among the nobles. Cat's walking tour turned somewhat southwards. The rows of towering buildings opened wide to reveal the largest open marketplace the young man had ever seen.

A plaque at the entry identified it as the Sun Market, and Trestan thought the description fit. Amongst the crowded and towering structures competing for dominance and space, the market offered a wide expanse of open air. Merchants of all kinds lined several makeshift streets in an area larger than the whole village of Troutbrook. Some set up inside tents, others hawked wares from the back of wagons or small carts, and there were those who carried their goods in a bag as they wandered the market lanes in pursuit of potential buyers. Smoke from cookfires brought a variety of salivating scents. Voices and noise filled the bustling market. Many merchants shouted in foreign languages to advertise their goods. Immigrants from far lands brought a mix of cultures and dress styles. Not only did the noise compete, but the colors did as well. A number of dyed cloth banners or extravagant hats pulled at the eyes. Trestan and Cat stuck to the larger avenues, urging the big warhorse Belgard through the throng of people. There seemed to be no order in which things were laid out. Wood craftsmen bartered next to a spice dealer, while a tailor dealt with customers near the gaudy tent of a fortune teller. More than once, small boys and girls crowded Trestan and Cat, trying to get the companions to follow them to their parents' shops. The strange and confusing environment made Trestan laugh just to be in the middle of it all.

As Cat looked around, she commented, "Orlaun once had a large building that housed their market. Can you imagine? They made a good decision by moving into an open space like this."

Trestan cocked his head slightly, "That must have been a huge structure. What happened to it after this market opened?"

"I hear it burned down a few years ago." Cat shrugged, "I think they caught the mage responsible."

The smell from one particular baker drew them in. Trestan saw a board marked with prices, but he didn't recognize the names of the foods. "Do they have chicken or ham? What is this food?"

Cat giggled, "Trestan, this land is home to pastas and spicy, seasoned foods. Have you never enjoyed ravioli or spaghetti?"

Trestan shook his head. He had never heard of such dishes. Cat obliged him with a grin, "Well, it is about time you enjoyed some local flavors. You can get chicken or ham almost anywhere, but if you have never before tried pastas, then this is the place."

Trestan couldn't even remember how Cat pronounced the name, but soon he was enjoying a tasty dish made of some white noodles, spicy red sauce and a mixture of vegetables. He looked at the piece of bread on the side with a bit of confusion. "Do they have anything to put on the bread?"

The half-elf, thoroughly enjoying her meal, smiled. She indicated a bottle of yellowish oil. "They do not use jams or jellies here like the people of Kashmer. Spread this oil over the bun. It will moisten the bread and give it more flavor."

The two companions talked and laughed over the strange dishes for some time before Trestan put a hand to his full stomach. Cat asked him, "Are you ready for a bit of an uphill walk?"

Trestan nodded, trying to hold back a burp as he did so, "Where are we going next?"

"To visit Korrelothar," Cat replied, "From here, you can just see the top towers of his mage guild."

Trestan followed her outstretched hand. "You mean that big castle up there?"

"Aye, that big castle that overlooks the rest of the city."

It impressed Trestan even from that distance.

**CHAPTER 11**          **"Reunion with Korrelothar"**


Trestan and Katressa found it problematic to simply walk into the mage guild and gain an audience with Korrelothar, one of the esteemed founders. It could have been the disposition of the stewards at the entry desk or the timing of their unannounced trip. Since the two companions had never visited before, they wondered if the entry foyer was usually crowded with city officials, nobility, and more than a few entertainers. In the midst of that chaotic sea of variety, two adventurers from a foreign land were not high on the priority list for gaining admittance. They could easily have been turned away at the door, except for intervention from a most unexpected source.

Their ignored pleas were overheard by Floranue Balshav, the wife of Korrelothar Balshav. Although they had never met before, Floranue overheard their anxiety in speaking with the stewards regarding an audience with her husband. The elder elf woman knew much about Korrelothar's trip to Kashmer a few years back, and quickly deduced the identities of the two before formal introductions were finally made. Floranue knew her husband seemed to have a soft spot for them, despite the fact they had stolen and lost his rare and priceless magical flying vessel. Korrelothar had always reasoned that the quest had been noble and succeeded in avoiding a danger to the realms. When the aged elf woman overheard the urgency and insistence in their voices that they must see the mage again, she gladly escorted them past the sentries guarding the inner doors.

While Korrelothar worked among the leadership of the guild, Floranue stayed and worked in the kitchen. As she led Trestan and Katressa into the castle, giving them a tour of things wondrous and mundane, she carried a basket of fruits bought at a market. Floranue certainly had a few centuries of cooking behind her. For a race known for their grace and agility, Floranue was the stoutest elf Cat or Trestan had ever seen. Watching the hefty elf carry her basket, one had to assume there was also plenty of muscle under her surface. She had curly white hair that stopped before her shoulders, likely keeping it from dangling into her cooking. On her left ear, the two companions noted the matrimony earring, symbol of her spiritbond, which matched the one Korrelothar wore. She dressed plainly, unassuming of any grandeur, but wore good quality. As she walked, she talked to Trestan and Cat as if they were old friends. The elf smiled often as she told many stories about the building, and about how different things were from when she and Korrelothar first came to Orlaun a couple centuries ago.

The two companions marveled at the structure of the building as they laughed at their hostess' stories. Even as they admired the golden chandeliers, marble statues, and intricately painted wall designs, Floranue made apologies about the luxuries. Their hostess waved a dismissive hand at some of the artwork, feeling somewhat embarrassed at what she felt was an overly garish décor. She mentioned that her husband pushed the guild more and more toward charitable causes, such as the plight of the poor in Highwater. Apparently, the initial lavishness of the Brotherhood of the Circles guild was to impress the nobility and city officials as the mages competed for favor against the Crystal Sun guild. Floranue noted with a disapproving frown that all it probably ever did was increase the city's imposed levies on both magic schools.

They had gone up several flights of stairs by the time they came to a lone door at the end of a carpeted hall. A sign hanging on the door read: "Do not hassle or intrude! Arcane experiments of an important and delicate nature are being tested in a QUIET environment."

Floranue snorted when she read it, "He always puts that sign up just for some peace and quiet; especially these days, with all the excitement building up around here. Lots of important folks are still shuffling to be present for the event."

Before Trestan or Cat could inquire as to the event in question, she leaned toward the door and rapped her knuckles on the aged wood. A stream of curses could be heard from the other side. The voice neither companion had heard in years protested. "Confound intruders! Dare you risk the safety of these halls and your life ruining precious arcane studies? I could make you a subject for my next test!"

Floranue, unshaken, answered right back. "If it's a test of patience, I'll tell you right now that I've a lot less patience than you. If you don't open this door and receive a couple of nice visitors, you will find your next apple pie will taste like a block of spice."

"One moment my love! Allow me to get the room decent!"

At Korrelothar's more complacent tone, the elf woman whispered to the couple, "Two hundred years in this city and he's never cared much for the spices they put in the food here."

After a minute or so listening to the sounds of rustling papers, drawers being opened and closed and hurried footsteps, the door opened. Korrelothar stood in the doorway, unchanged in the last four years. He still dressed in the multi-layered clothing fashionable in Orlaun. His jewelry advertised the wealth he had accumulated in his tenure as a founding member of the mage guild. Long, blond hair cascaded down his back, streaked with some silver of age. A rough stubble of facial hair sat on his chin, a sign of an elf that had passed middle-age. He was not wearing his usual plush hat and feather nor his short cape. Both his staff and sword lay in the room behind, put aside for whatever business or laziness he had been involved in.

His eyes took in Katressa first, recognizing her easily since half-elves do not change much in four years. Korrelothar did seem surprised to see her unanticipated arrival. He bowed to her and called her by name with a smile.

"An unexpected pleasure this is, Lady Katressa. I am happy to have you visit my home, though I wish I'd known to make preparations for your arrival."

As Korrelothar turned to regard Trestan, the eyes behind his smile had the flash of uncertainty. Was this the young man who had once defeated a towering minotaur by himself? Trestan had changed so much in the past few years. The thick mustache, the armor decorated to honor his goddess Abriana, and the wisdom in his eyes, made the mage wonder if this was indeed the same lad. Korrelothar saw the unmistakable elvish sword slung over his back. That fine, magical sword could cut through objects that would block most ordinary steel edges. When Korrelothar noticed the blade, he glanced at the *Taef' Adorina* upon Cat's brow. The elf mage had helped Trestan craft that precious gift for his love, indulging a bit of elvish magic into the twisted gold shape.

The mage smiled at Trestan as he gave a slight bow, "Didn't you used to work as a blacksmith?"

Trestan bowed in return, resplendent in his armor of leather, chain, and steel plate. This young man portrayed more of a warrior than a smith. "Squire Trestan Karok of Abriana, milord, and it is a pleasure to see you again."

"I haven't forgotten the name!" Korrelothar insisted. "Though you have changed much in the past years. I see a strong man before me in place of the brave lad I once knew."

"You honor me sir."

"Nay, your visit honors me," the elf mage replied. "Please come in and relax your weary legs while I inquire as to what roads you have traveled since we last parted."

Trestan and Cat made themselves at home in Korrelothar's study, sipping tea while enjoying the comfort of soft chairs. Korrelothar took a seat at his study desk, while Floranue bustled about serving the tea and providing everyone comfort. It took some time for Trestan and Cat to get to the point of their visit; Korrelothar started off asking them a few questions unrelated to the relics. The couple took it as a good sign, for if anything had happened here already the elf mage would likely have mentioned it at the start. Korrelothar's academic mind prompted him to ask about Trestan's time at the seminary. The young man enlightened the mage on the training undergone to become a paladin of Abriana. The conversation mixed as he also asked Cat about her adventuring exploits during that time. Korrelothar did not ask about the personal relationship between them, for the body language between the two companions spoke volumes of their closeness. Trestan and Cat spoke of themselves almost as one entity at times, even leading off of each other during the conversation. The elf could hear the loneliness in their voices when they reflected on times they were separated, since the seminary had demanded much of Trestan's time. As the young paladin spoke, the mage's gaze drew to a ring adorning one finger.

"I recognized the coraross on your necklace, but I'm wondering about this other jewelry you display. That ring, it is a part of your schooling? I notice you glancing at it from time to time," inquired Korrelothar.

Trestan held up the ring. A few symbols along the band interrupted the dull brown color. "This is Faithful's Companion. Every acolyte that succeeds in the tests of the Embarking goes into the world with one of these rings. It is a guide that reminds us of our path and goals yet unfulfilled. Through trials on the road the symbols disappear and the ring will shine bright gold. When that moment dawns, I must return to the seminary. I will be dubbed a paladin and given a new surname of my choosing."

"Ahh," the elf mused, "So you are in search of a quest or adventure to give you your final test?"

Trestan and Cat shared a meaningful glance. It was time to reveal the urgency behind their trip to Orlaun. The young paladin-aspirant looked into the mage's eyes. "My quest landed before me, on the steps of my home."

Floranue gasped as they heard the story of the attack on Troutbrook: the brutality of the unwarranted assault and Hebden Karok's close brush with death. Korrelothar became saddened by the news of the death of High Priest Gerlach, for he had become fond of the wise human. They described Revwar and Savannah, as Hebden Karok had seen them, as well as the other unknown individual traveling with them. Trestan relayed the appearance of a middle-aged human, dark hair peppered with gray, thin mustache and goatee beard, dressed in Orlaun fashions. Trestan hoped it would be someone recognizable, but to his dismay, Korrelothar replied that the description too vaguely described many human mages accustomed to the styles and fashions of Orlaun.

The news of the loss of the relic stone, after Gerlach and he had placed so many wards upon it, alarmed the mage. As the two companions despaired over the loss of the item they had recovered, Korrelothar tried to reassure them the stones were not considered very powerful compared to some magical constructs in existence. It did little to dampen the companions' fears. The two travelers had seen firsthand how the relic could crush stone structures and call otherworldly beings to its defense. The mage hid his concerns, since the stone's origins remained a mystery. Korrelothar belittled the power of the relic to assuage their fears. He reminded them the only true power for which the village had used it for many years was blessing crops and warding away diseases of plants and animals.

The elf mage concealed his thoughts that some individuals were going through a lot of trouble for the mysterious green relic stones.

*　　*　　*　　*　　*

"Nevertheless, we are worried and saddened that the stones we recovered are once again vulnerable," Trestan said. "Troutbrook is again going to face troubles with crops and cattle due to the loss of their relic. We have nay idea what mischief is planned by those wishing to abuse the powers of the stones. When we found the relics the first time, Revwar's band was on the verge of summoning some demon from another world? I hope the relics you brought here are still safely guarded?"

The elf mage tried to offer a reassuring grin, "I assure you they are well guarded. The relic that had originally been in our possession was stolen those years ago when it was merely part of a student research collection. Now that we know more about their danger, the two stones we brought back are kept warded and isolated. There are chambers we use for magical works of art that have very restricted access due to their nature."

Floranue added, "You can be assured that if my husband says they are safe, then they are indeed so. I feel very secure in this castle, surrounded by such wizards of high power. It is hard to imagine the tragedy of the attack on your home. I do feel sorry for the losses you and your village suffered. It sounds horrific."

"There is nothing that can be done to change the past, but the people will recover." Cat mentioned as she looked over to Trestan. "I'm so proud of my *faunlessa*; he healed those that were still wounded, and undertaking this quest seemed to ease the burden on those troubled minds. Heavy hearts were lifted enough to cheer him as we rode southwards."

Trestan blushed, "I'm just trying to do what I can for my village."

"The last time you tried to do what you could," Korrelothar intervened, "You risked a wizard's ire by stealing his flying chariot. Then, you defeated a minotaur about four times your weight, while wearing a breastplate that I recall had a big hole in it.. "

Trestan interrupted, "Aye, aye. Unfortunately, this time we have nay clue as to where the other party went with the stolen relic. The best we could hope for was to get here and warn you, lest the other two be stolen as well."

While Floranue collected the empty tea mugs and took them away, Korrelothar spoke. "Well, you are welcome to stay here in the guild. I can find rooms for you as special guests. As far as the relics are concerned, they are defended by wards and the most senior members of my guild. They never leave their sanctum."

There was a moment of silence and quiet contemplations before the elf wizard corrected himself. "Well, except for the show that starts in a few days."

Katressa leaned forward, "Show? What type of performance is it that causes nobility to hound your front lobby?"

The mage rolled his eyes, "Everyone wants to attend. Some are still scrambling to secure their spot. The exhibit will begin in a few days. The nature of it surpasses any spectacle in Orlaun history. We constantly battle a 'war of favor' against a rival mage guild, the Crystal Sun guild. We are offering a grand exhibit of magical devices and oddities, as well as hosting a number of musicians and performers in an extravagant show, on a stage like nay other. The stones are included, but are by nay means the main attraction. In fact, compared to the other displayed items they seem rather mundane. The competition between minstrels and performers was fierce to be able to get the privilege of entertaining such a prestigious gathering. For the nobility and rulers of the city, an invitation to partake is extremely coveted just for the stature perceived in attending."

Korrelothar judged the reactions in the eyes of the two traveling companions. "You mean you haven't heard of it?"

Trestan and Cat shrugged their shoulders. The paladin-aspirant answered, "We just arrived in Orlaun today after sailing from Barkan's Crossing. We haven't heard of any special show."

Floranue and Korrelothar shared a knowing smile about some secret. The elf mage spoke, "Well, the most special thing about this show is that it is being held on an impressive stage…"

He paused for dramatic effect, "It will be aboard the *Doranil Star*, the last known surviving divine chariot that still retains the blessing of flight. Recall that I mentioned her when I spoke about *Dovewing*. Although my vessel was infused with arcana, the *Doranil Star* was built during the Godswars by holy men; the predecessors of today's clerics. She is a vessel that gains her ability of flight through miracles granted by a deity. Though my guild houses the vessel in a sort of dry dock behind the castle, she really belongs to the church of Ganden. Without Ganden's clerics at the helm, she could not fly. The divine vessels, including those who nay longer have the power of flight, are a disappearing breed. So many were lost in the Godswars in great aerial battles, and so many lost in the dark years of recovery. Even a craft based on arcana is an extremely hard undertaking to make. *Dovewing* was only about the size of a horse-drawn carriage, yet she took years of effort and research to build."

Cat shifted uncomfortably in her seat. It had been her idea to steal *Dovewing* in order to pursue the lost relics the first time. During the course of that adventure, the vessel was destroyed in the midst of a stormy landing. The half-elf was embarrassed to ask, but she had to find out. "Would you ever build another one?"

Korrelothar eyed the woman rather sternly. "You know, my tired feet ask of me the same question everyday. My joints feel so old from walking and riding everywhere."

"Oh, hush you!" Floranue admonished her husband. Her next words defused his bluster. "Don't let him load you with any added guilt. You weren't around when he spoke to me of the courageous deeds of you and your friends. He always speaks well of you and respects your daring to do what you did."

"Bah! To answer your query though, I shall make nay more. It was a prideful challenge I undertook in younger years. I am satisfied by the simple fact of accomplishment in building one. I don't need to waste the time and resources to create another. My efforts these past years have shifted away from squandering my wealth on selfish decorations. I have begun to reach out more and more to those less gifted with coins."

The elf mage silently mused on some thoughts for a minute before continuing. "A good example is one young man that will be performing for the exhibit. In my younger days I brought food and drink to those in Highwater, but I sought to also give them a means for a better life. Whenever I met someone with a gifted voice, or dexterous fingers, I would give them a musical instrument in the hopes of developing such talents. One such man, Lindon by name, sought me out and showed me the mastery of music he had attained since I gave him a bamboo flute during his youth. There is nay sense of achievement any magical vessel can give that outshines the ability to help a person in need to realize their dreams."

Trestan and Cat smiled along with him as he spoke, for Korrelothar's smile was infectious.

"But, I seem to be drifting off the original subject. The ship, though calling *Doranil Star* a simple ship seems an insult, will be part of a cruise offered by our guild. Three hundred people will be on board the vessel for most of a week. Part of the journey will be by sea, and the rest by air, for it was made to accommodate both modes of travel. It may seem like a large amount of people, and yet this was a small divine chariot by comparison to others that served in the Godswars."

The elf mage rose and waved them to follow. Trestan and Cat fell in stride behind him as he walked toward one of many glass windows. Glass windows were one of the many luxuries in the guild; however, the quality wasn't good enough to be able to see through them. Once at the window, Korrelothar undid a latch that allowed the glass panel to swing open on hinges. Open air from the sea breeze blew through their hair.

The mage stepped to one side, gesturing with an open hand toward the view. "Describing it in words wouldn't do it justice. Look for yourselves upon the last divine chariot, *Doranil Star*!"

*              *              *              *              *

The hull measured two hundred and sixty feet from bow to stern, resting upon a cradle of stone pillars over dry land. Her strongest parts were made from oak, while the rest was made from white spruce and pine timber. The *Doranil Star* was built from the bottom up. Although the vessel once spent a large amount of time in the sky or at sea, her hull had to be strengthened enough to land with full cargo on dry ground. It was built during a time of war, yet the ship did not settle for a merely practical design. The builders spared no expense in a vessel that carried a god's blessing. The symbols of the church and holy references, even holy scripture, was etched in gold designs throughout the ship. Even the figurehead at the front was a knight holding a shield before him, bearing the crest of Ganden. Everything was built so ornately, the golden plume of the knight's helm ran in grand designs up the bowsprit and around the front guardrails. Every facing of the floating vessel, including the bottom of the hull, had large symbols of the church to identify the patron that held it aloft. It would not have been a far cry to compare the vessel to a floating church.

The holy ship had been designed for war, and it still retained some of its bite. There were a brace of ballistae mounted fore and aft, as well as devices amidships that once launched grappling hooks or other projectiles. The weapons had been repaired or replaced, but were now mostly for show. The great aerial battles between divine chariots were now a part of history, even though one great vessel remained.

Built for sailing as well as flying, the ship sported five large masts to fit its large size. The first three were square-rigged, with the aft two having triangular lateen rigging. As a sailing vessel, its size and design worked against it. The ship maneuvered sluggishly in the open sea unless aided by its crew of clergy.

On its entertainment voyage, the vessel would carry over three hundred souls. The guest list included the most important nobles in all of Orlaun, as well as citizens known for their influence in city politics. A number of entertainers sponsored by the local bardic colleges looked forward to making their names known. The highest ranking wizards of the Brotherhood of the Circles would host, even going so far as inviting some rival members of the Crystal Sun guild. Despite all these visitors, the real heart of maintaining the vessel originated in select representatives from the church of Ganden, as well as a highly trained crew. The crew included sailors who could sail the vessel at sea, and people whose sole responsibilities were devoted to the pleasure of the guests. The clerics of Ganden were a necessity, since their devotion to their deity allowed the vessel to break its earthen bonds and fly. It was said that the god would cradle the flight of the vessel as if he was holding it in his own hands. Without the clerics to channel the god's miraculous energy there would be no flight. The effort exhausted the clergy involved, because a team of devoted pilots would be chanting and praying continuously for any duration that the ship remained aloft.

The inner sanctum, where the clerics would pray for flight, was the holy nexus of the vessel. It sat in the center of the ship, below the helm castle. The helm castle sat in the middle of the sundeck, halfway between the fore castle and stern castle. It was on top of this structure that the navigator, crew captain, and an appointed cleric would guide the ship. The instructions for guiding the vessel were sent from the appointed cleric to the pilots chanting in the inner sanctum. In the days of the Godswars, enemy vessels would try to concentrate fire at the inner sanctum. If an enemy ship was able to disrupt or kill the chanting clerics, the ship would lose its miracle of flight and fall out of the sky. During times in which the vessel was sailing on the seas, the clerics could rest although at the cost maneuverability navigating the ocean waves.

Another feature of the divine chariot was the observation deck interrupting the strong hull two levels below the sundeck. While some archers and mages would fire upon enemy ships from the sundeck, another group could unleash death from the partial cover provided by the hull and the first sub-deck above. In times of war, it had helped bring more firepower against an enemy. In times of peace, it served as another sight-seeing deck for the noble guests. The adjoining rooms of the first sub-deck and the observation deck provided the majority of quarters for the guests of the voyage.

Smaller vessels were lashed in places along the sundeck. As with all seagoing vessels, this divine chariot had lifeboats to ferry passengers to safety. Like the ship itself, the lifeboats had a special design with the flight capabilities in mind. Every lifeboat had a globe at the bow filled with holy water and a blessed item from Ganden. In times of war, the lifeboats could actually be used as boarding vessels. A cleric of the patron deity could use the strength of prayer to guide the vessel through the sky, offering a chance to guide archers or boarders around an enemy ship. If there was no cleric on board, the boats had one safe feature the *Doranil Star* itself lacked: levitation. If for some reason the crew had to abandon the vessel while it was still in the sky, they could board these boats and push away into the open air. The boats would slowly descend to a soft landing even with no priest to guide them.

*Doranil Star* sat perched upon the stone pillars in the courtyard; the last of a dying breed of warships that had once battled for supremacy over the skies. Out of the dark pages of the world's history, from a time of war, came this beauty of miraculous architecture. Even sitting upon land, one could view her and imagine what it would be like to sail the skies again.

*          *          *          *          *

Korrelothar had seen the ship many times and dreamed about flight until the creation of his precious vessel *Dovewing* those many years ago. He watched with amusement as Trestan and Cat stared down upon it with mouths open wide in wonder. The mage recalled what it might be like to be young again, and to see such a vessel ascend into the skies for the first time.

While the two travelers remained trapped in their awe, the elf mage spoke. "Trestan and Katressa, it seems you have been charged by your gods to safeguard those relics from harm. Indeed, you already have recovered them once. I see nay reason to stand in the way of the gods."

He paused, looking down at the vessel. Trestan and Cat seemed to be only half-listening to him, so enthralled were they at the divine chariot. "You view it as your quest to safeguard the relics and the relics will be on board that ship for its flight. Well, I'll just have to make arrangements for someone to reserve a cabin for you, so that you may go along on this voyage."

Trestan and Cat were overjoyed.

**CHAPTER 12**          **"The Launching of *Doranil Star*"**

A beautifully sunlit day welcomed the memorable departure. Honored guests made their way past flowery avenues under a rainbow variety of snapping banners. The impressive *Doranil Star* lay ahead, at the end of a hand-carved staircase. The masts of the ship held no sails this day. Instead, the rigging held up a series of canopies to shade the guests from the bright sun. Many had never seen the vessel this closely before, and the sheer size and extravagance of it caused them to pause in awe.

Korrelothar stood alongside fellow members of his guild as he greeted the boarding royalty. Standing alongside the elf, among other guildmates, was the gnome illusionist Wendall. The gnome longed for the comfort of his missing mask: one that could make him appear human. He felt insulted that all these haughty nobles, the vast majority of which were human and simply born into power, looked down on one who had become powerful in his own right through determination and long hours of arcane study. Korrelothar comforted his friend, assuring the gnome that it was only the heart that mattered. No matter how things developed with the nobility, they all would enjoy the rare treat of floating over the world like the stars of the heavens.

The elf stayed busy with preparations for the journey. He constantly bowed to guests or engaged in the delicate arts of diplomacy. At the same time, he conferred with apprentices and crew to give guidance with every small crisis that seemed to addle those preparing for the journey.

Another of Korrelothar's guildmates scaled the decorated stairs and boarded. Jentan Mollamos carried only his middle-aged frame and layers of Orlaun-style dress, while a minor apprentice carried his baggage. Korrelothar dropped diplomacy and met him with a scowl. The mentalist assumed it was just due to the fact he could magically shrink his belongings and carry them easily within a small pouch, but instead he made a student bear the load. The poor apprentice had the punishment of carrying his bags for Jentan, only to leave the ship to do mundane duties inside the guild while most of the rest went on their journey.

"The gods have truly blessed us with favorable weather by which to depart," the human charmer spoke as he approached the elf. "The day itself seems filled with magic to account for a wonderful journey, yet the real pleasure still beckons before us."

Korrelothar glanced at the apprentice who was struggling under the weight of the bags. "A pity all of us can't enjoy this day. The view from the clouds is one best appreciated by the young."

If Jentan felt insulted by the elf's reference to how he treated his apprentice, he did not show it. The mentalist turned Korrelothar's own words around. "A pity indeed someone must stay behind and watch the guildhall while we are gone. Especially pitiful for those who seem to lack any grasp of some basic magical principles they should have been studying in the time they have been granted." The middle-aged human looked down at his apprentice with cold eyes, though the young lad was busy staring at the wooden planks beneath his feet. "Maybe one who studied harder and didn't misbehave in my class would be entitled to treats such as sailing the stars."

Jentan Mollamos, his charming smile back in place, turned away from the elf mage, "If you will excuse me, I must be off to find if my quarters are adequate for my tastes."

*　　　*　　　*　　　*　　　*

Lindon of Orlaun waited his turn among the crowd in the courtyard. He and many others watched as the nobility filed past first, accorded every honor and accommodation that could be provided. The minstrel stood dressed in fine fashion, though he wore his usual red-feathered hat and cloak. His few belongings sat in a bag beside his feet while his fingers kept busy. Those long, nimble fingers plucked at the strings of his mandolin as he looked over the lines of the impressive vessel. It was for this purpose that he didn't mind the wait. His mind focused on the poetry inherent in the divine chariot, transferring its meaning into music. Lindon believed everything had an appropriate tune to match its qualities. From behind the veil of those light-blue eyes, he sought to capture the musical image of the mighty vessel on the strings of his mandolin.

Two fellow passengers seemed to be listening with interest to his incomplete notes. One dressed in a knightly manner, though his choice of armor discarded plate in favor of chain or leather around areas that would help with his movement. Nevertheless, the man wore the tokens of favor representing Abriana, Goddess of Love and Healing. The coraross symbol featured prominently on his necklace. Beside the young warrior stood a jewel of elven blood. A graceful lady with long, raven hair, whose movements suggested a dexterous quality of her own, stood beside her knight as they silently appraised Lindon's melody. A beautiful dress complimented her curves, yet she wore a silver rapier at her left hip. By the steel in her spirit, and the worn look of her pack, Lindon estimated she was no stranger to adventure.

Lindon focused his thoughts on the ship, but during a lull in his playing the beautiful elf complimented him. "Your music carries to the ears and heart, milord. Dare I presume you might be giving a performance on board? I would very much like to hear more of your enticing music."

The red-bearded minstrel turned to properly address her. He took off his hat and bowed with a flourish as he introduced himself. "Lindon of Orlaun, at your service. I will be performing during this voyage among eagles and I would be most honored to entertain you. My thanks for your compliments Lady...?"

She smiled, "I am nay noblewoman, good sir. My name is Katressa Bilil, though you may call me Cat. Please nay more of this 'lady' nonsense either, I have worked for what I own."

She gestured to her companion, "This is my beloved, Trestan Karok. He champions Abriana, Goddess of Love and Healing."

"A pleasure to meet you, good sir," said Lindon as he and Trestan clasped hands in greeting.

"Oh, I'd say the pleasure was mine," the young knight responded. "You play so well. Might we hear that tune in its entirety?"

Lindon smiled as he hefted his mandolin. "I would love to accommodate you, holy warrior, but as yet I am unable. This song is inspired by the divine instrument before us. While I have a beginning, it doesn't have an ending yet."

*      *      *      *      *

A portion of the crowd parted for a procession of priests. Bystanders, even nobility, bowed in deference to them as the clerics marched past. Although the wizards of the Brotherhood of the Circles hosted the event, these clerics of Ganden were the ones who would bring flight to the divine vessel.

Not all of them would be entrusted with the task of keeping the great ship aloft. Sondra Oskires would serve her fellow priests in minor ways while enjoying this rare event. She paraded alongside her brethren as they wore the ceremonial robes of their faith. The plain, gray robes of Ganden bore the symbols of honor and service. One could tell the relevant rank of the clerics by the trim running down the front clasps of the robes. Sondra's acolyte vestments displayed black trim down the front. Very few acolytes were blessed enough to be selected for this venture. Ordained priests sported a different shade of gray along the front of their robes. Those who had the power to give flight to the vessel wore the white trim robes of bishops. The church called them Chosen, while outsiders referred to them as pilots. In all the known realms, only these select few clerics had access to a divine chariot that could still fly. It was no wonder that the crowd parted to honor their approach.

Sondra walked while swinging a lit censer back and forth. The thurible burned with a sweet scent. Her natural, dark-red lips joined the others in reciting a mantra of service. In the trailing smoke of incense, clerics carried chests bearing their symbols. These religious containers carried holy relics devoted to their god. While the Chosen would commune in prayer to lift the divine chariot into the air, the holy items would help provide a conduit for that flow of power. Sondra's superior, Mother Evine, walked among those charged with bearing the holy items to the ship. Neither Sondra nor her fellow clergy wore any armor, not even helmets. They did have weapons stored among some of the containers for defense; however, it was more of a precaution than any real belief they would see any use. Sondra's own light mace lay stored among those hidden weapons, as well as the rust-colored satchel she used as her healing kit.

The wheat-blonde woman looked up to the *Doranil Star* in amazement. Her voice lowered, losing focus on her mantra as she stared in awe. Every young cleric of Ganden dreamed of being a part of this creation. Sondra had never weighed her own self-worth highly, yet in the face of this magnificent ship she felt part of some great good. The young woman never thought she might have much hope of becoming a Chosen, yet in her dreams she could fly.

She resumed her chant. The censer gave off its sweet smell as she followed her brethren up the walkway to the ship. Sondra's face lit with a rare smile as she stepped aboard.

*      *      *      *      *

On the streets outside the guild, a lone human woman attempted to make the flight on time despite awareness that someone was tailing her. She tried to make as much haste as she could without revealing her awareness of being followed. The woman dressed well, wearing many trinkets denoting her prosperity. Despite the advertisement of wealth, she walked without escort and carried her own light baggage.

The pursuer had spotted her and appeared to see through her deception. Montanya tried to hide herself in the crowds of the street as she followed the woman. The chiaso wore her customary scowl as her thin eyebrows narrowed in the direction of her quarry. The homeless youth had not been idle in the time since she had stormed out of the Sanctuary for Those in Need, (or as she preferred to call it, a "copper pen"). She had a determined interest in the domid who had poisoned her. She had spent a good amount of her days patrolling the streets and searching for clues as to who the rogue had been.

Her soft, leather slippers and raggedy cloak made hardly a sound as she worked to keep her latest target in sight. Montanya wore her hardened leather chest piece and other leather padding over her clothes. She had reluctantly acquiesced and donned the garments given to her by the church of Ganden. Much as she liked her old clothes, they had been bloodied and dirtied by her previous fight with the halfling rogue.

Montanya worried a little about how the next fight would go, for it loomed ahead.

The chiaso had spotted this person carrying bags at a fast pace. From the start, the chiaso noticed a striking the resemblance to the halfling rogue. This human had long brown hair braided up in a similar style to the halfling. The face and nose were long, though it was hard to see her freckles from where Montanya had been. The woman displayed an impassionate poker face when she looked about furtively, just like the halfling. Her strides showed grace and yet something intangible seemed out of place about the way she walked. In all though, she appeared to be a human woman and obviously not someone to be mistaken for a short halfling.

Except…hadn't the halfling stolen a mask that could make her appear human?

Thus, Montanya followed the woman at a discreet distance and sized her up. It finally dawned on the chiaso there was something wrong with the human's legs as she walked. It just did not seem completely natural. The illusion of the mask tried to hide the fact that its wearer had the short strides of a halfling, instead of the long, easy glide of a human.

Kemora Quickfeet, well aware of the familiar red-haired human following from a distance, wanted to curse her luck over the tireless pursuer. She thought the poison had finished that threat. The rogue needed to be on board the *Doranil Star* without delay. It would not do to be slowed by a fight or show up at the guild looking like she had just been in a struggle. Watching the red hair moving among the crowd behind her, Kemora figured she had only two things going for her. The first was that Montanya hadn't made an aggressive move against her yet, and likely wouldn't act too quickly as long as she didn't realize she had been spotted. Second, the chiaso likely didn't know Kemora's destination. As long as the halfling didn't act too suspicious, and made her path next to the wizard guild seem random, it might be possible to get into the guild before Montanya caused a public outburst.

Montanya's intense focus kept her unaware of her proximity to several important landmarks. Her old instructor would have chided her for her blind determination. The chiaso believed she hadn't been spotted as she allowed the halfling to walk a good distance ahead. Montanya knew it might be folly to confront the thief in public. She hoped to follow the rogue to some quieter place where she might take her down by surprise and expose her deception. The youth was still mindful of the poisoned stiletto. While she might have survived the first attack, she had to be ready for a similar trick.

Her narrowed mind barely registered all the people entering the castle of the Brotherhood of the Circles. Kemora looked like she might walk past the impressive structure on the opposite side of the street. Montanya realized her mistake too late, as the halfling in disguise suddenly turned hard and went right for the front door. Montanya took a few jogging steps forward before changing her mind and lurching to a stop. Kemora showed an invitation to the door guard. Anything the chiaso attempted against the rogue would be in a crowded street under the eyes of numerous guards.

The guard waved Kemora past, but the disguised halfling turned and pointed down the street at her pursuer. The guard motioned for a second constable to join him, and they called out for the leather-clad woman to approach for a few questions.

Montanya's greenish-blue eyes abandoned her scowl as they widened in alarm. She wasn't about to stick around and see what they wanted to ask. She could have tried to explain her story, but assumed they wouldn't take her word for it. The chiaso bolted with two guards in chain mail running after her. Fleet of foot as she was, she didn't have to run far before they gave up their chase.

With the pursuit gone, Montanya took a circling route which ended up aiming her back toward the castle. She had time to recall the stories on the streets related to some festivities going on at the guild. Montanya didn't hear all the details, but it dawned on her that the halfling may have grabbed that disguise for just this occasion. What mischief was the little rogue planning? What could happen if Montanya was the only one who knew about her, but did nothing? It was never a priority in Montanya's mind of simply trying to warn anyone; the woman wanted to personally stop the rogue and be a hero in her own eyes.

When she arrived at a back wall of the estate, away from most eyes, she determined to commit to a rash action. There was an oddly built section of wall which offered her a place to climb by squeezing against two nearly opposing surfaces. Montanya put most of her loose belongings into the bedroll tied around her torso. She withdrew a set of leather gloves and slippers used exclusively for grip. She prepared to retie her hair, when she paused to consider the torn pink fabric. The nineteen-year-old silently considered that precious reminder of her parents, murdered so long ago. Pausing to feel the fabric against her face once more, she then resumed her task. She tied her long, red hair into a bun and secured it with the strip from her mother's dress.

She had been trained to scale surfaces with few handholds, yet this wall loomed as her toughest challenge ever. Her mind convinced her body this was just another exercise in a life of physical training. Montanya started crawling up the wall, squeezing herself between the wedge of stone. Lithe and muscular, she grunted as every effort pulled her closer to the top. Her body had very little fat to carry following her life of hard training and her recent days of starvation. Rising out of the shadows, the chiaso appreciated the leather gloves more as she got to a portion of sun-baked stone. The heat of the wall could be felt through the animal skin. She told herself that stopping or falling was not an option. Part of her mind worried that if she fell and survived, she would only fall farther the rest of her life until she died a nameless young woman in some deserted building. She tried to bury all her fears that her life might be destined to come to a bad end. Loose granules of stone stung her eyes and sometimes her hands or feet would slip a bit, but she kept climbing. Montanya gritted her teeth as she pushed herself ever higher. She never looked down. She could never look behind her, this day or any other day in her life.

Montanya gasped for air when her hands caught the top. The young chiaso flipped over the wall and landed on a walkway running along the inside. It was lucky for her that no sentries walked the ramparts. In a wizard guild, they generally didn't worry about intruders scaling the walls as much as those who might fly out of the sky.

The sight of the *Doranil Star*, parked on dry stone pillars far from any body of water, amazed her. The woman was no judge of ships yet she realized the impressive size of the vessel. Upon seeing the crowds of people boarding the ship, she knew the halfling rogue must be headed there as well.

Montanya had to get aboard, but how?

Her means came in the shape of one of a number of ropes hanging down to the ground. While most people boarded the ship from the starboard side, the port side was being used to load last minute provisions and baggage to the observation deck. Most of the people working that side had moved forward, leaving a few aft ropes hanging unattended.

Montanya didn't hesitate, though she faced another tough climb. The woman walked across the yard like she had every reason to be there. She reflected on a saying of her master, that sometimes the most obvious place to hide something is out in the open. Montanya moved like she had a purpose, hoping to blend in with all the ground help. When she thought she could be reasonably sure that no one was looking, she grabbed the nearest rope and hauled herself up.

*     *     *     *     *

With the young apprentice dismissed, Jentan Mollamos stood alone inside his cabin. The mentalist rearranged his bags from where the student had set them. The bags weren't very heavy and the mage often used smaller bags to carry magically shrunken clothes. He could have easily carried his belongings himself, but why should he when there was an apprentice to berate?

Jentan Mollamos cast a look about his quarters, confirming that he was indeed alone. The room had a large wardrobe closet, which seemed a necessity for the number of outfits he carried for occasions. A porthole allowed light from one side of the vessel. Even with the window he had privacy, for there were no walkways outside of the hull at the first sublevel. Above him was the top deck, often called the sundeck, while below his level was the open observation deck.

The well-provisioned room stocked lamp oil and candles for illumination. A solitary bed hid under a deep layer of soft blankets. The bed would have been generous enough for two people; yet unknown to Jentan's guildmates there would be four sharing this room. A small work desk against the wall near the porthole offered inkwells, paper and quills. A wooden carving adorned one wall: in the shape of a shield, with two open, outstretched palms prominent on it. This was one of the holy symbols of Ganden, the God of Honor, Duty, Service…and thus not an unusual decoration.

Jentan idly wondered over the whereabouts of his escort for the journey. He expected Kemora to arrive first, under human guise and with his personal invitation. Instead, he found himself alone in his quarters, except for the two companions he "carried" with him.

From out of a pocket, he withdrew two small figurines, finely detailed though carved from clay. There were arcane methods to cast a spell which locked a living animal into figurine form, whereupon it would rest in stasis, untouched and unaware of the passage of time. The spell woven here was entirely more complex. It took a greater effort and cost to weave arcana in a way which would do the same for beings of higher intelligence.

His hands held two small figurines carved in a very good likeness of Revwar and Savannah…except the resemblance was more than just coincidence. The safest, most reasonable way to sneak the two on board the ship involved locking them in that same stasis, hidden in Jentan's pouches. The mentalist had walked right past Korrelothar with the elder mage having no clue that two highly wanted suspects were helpless and within an arm's reach.

Jentan favored arcana relating to the mind for one reason: he liked to control others. To the middle-aged human, the most appealing aspect of his art was to make others do his bidding. He felt a rush of power just holding the helpless figurines of his cohorts in his hands. While in that state, they could not free themselves of their own will, nor have awareness of anything of their surroundings. If the mentalist so desired, he could spend the rest of his life using the powerful wizard and the cleric of DeLaris as pieces on a chess board. Such feelings intoxicated him.

Although Jentan Mollamos relished those thoughts of control, he stood more to gain by going through with their plans. If their band succeeded, the known world would bow at their feet. Anything left of the races after the new conflict would be forced to obey their commands or die. Two goddesses blessed the endeavor, and would reward him well for his part. He would gain much with the help of these allies.

The human mage paused before undoing the enchantment trapping them in figurine form. His eyes glided over Savannah's curves. The figurine wore her customary holy armor. For all his control over people, he had not yet conquered the woman in bed. There existed no love or any respectful reason for his need to bed the cleric, only a means by which to control a companion. Savannah represented another prize for conquest. The mentalist smiled a cold smile, gently rubbing the tips of his thumb over the clay figurine's ample chest curves. He might be forced to wait a long time before she allowed him to her bed, but at least he had been able to take advantage of this one moment to touch her in a place that would normally bring swift punishment.

With a sad sigh, he placed the figurines a few paces apart on the floor. It was time to end his self-delusion. The words of an arcane mantra rolled forth from his handsome stature, coalescing into a mist that shrouded the two figurines. A burst of wind blew outward as the small objects expanded into human size.

Revwar and Savannah stood there in the flesh, slightly lightheaded from the whole experience. The blonde cleric steadied herself against the wardrobe, while the elf wizard stretched and flexed. The two looked about the cabin to orient themselves.

Mollamos assumed his charming grin. "Welcome to *Doranil Star.* As one of your hosts, I hope you enjoy your stay."

*     *     *     *     *

"Cast off!"

Voices shouted from below. Trestan and Cat had not wanted to rush to their cabin when there was precious little space at the ornate balustrade at the edges. Still carrying their bags, the companions packed against the starboard rail to view the castle they were leaving behind. A mass of people lingered around the docking platform to see them off, watching loved ones and acquaintances ascend to the sky. Members of the wizard guild, old and young, smiled at seeing the vessel's departure. Several clerics and acolytes of the church of Ganden also remained behind, though for the most part their arms and mouths moved in prayer for glory of their god. Many noble family members or servants in their entourage waved brightly colored scarves at their departing lords and ladies.

Color and sound filled the air, yet the quiet, unmoving presence of the divine chariot commanded all the attention. Trestan and Cat waved back at richly dressed people who might normally turn their nose up at them on the streets. In the yard below, ropes dropped or reeled back up to the ship. The boarding stairs slid away from the ship as mages of the Brotherhood of the Circles used spells to guide the action.

Trestan glanced around. He saw Korrelothar standing at the bow of the ship amongst important nobles. Amidships at the helm castle, he saw a cleric talking with members of the wizard guild. That group nodded and smiled, making arm motions that seemed to indicate things would be underway anytime. Trestan held tightly to Cat, sharing a brief kiss over the moment. Lindon wasn't even noticed as the minstrel squeezed past them heading for the stern. The red-bearded musician heard the song of the ship playing across his mind as he carried his mandolin along the railing.

Sondra stood in the holy center of the ship, watching the Chosen. She could not see the excitement from outside, though the shouting could be heard. The Chosen sat in a wide circle around a cauldron of holy water. Sacred holy items that were submerged in the cauldron would help channel the needed power. One cleric sat facing a complex set of instruments on one wall. The instruments connected with the steering wheel and other levers on the helm castle. Near this cleric's head, a pipe carried voice commands to and from the helm. This cleric would be the focus that would combine the efforts of prayer into the necessary actions of flight. The Chosen sat upon comfortable cushions, but the rest of the floor and walls were bare of ornamentation except miracle-etched symbols of Ganden. A few incense candles burned along with gold-gilded oil lamps.

Something on the instrument panel changed and words were spoken through the voice pipe. The word for flight was given.

The Chosen raised their voices in prayer, reciting mantras of their faith in complete unison. The words wrapped around the deck until they became part of it. Sondra could feel the vessel vibrate as if alive. She could not witness movement, but she felt a little heavier as the deck initially rose, just as Mother Evine had told her she would. It ascended slow and smoothly. If Sondra had any doubt that the ship was lifting off of the stone pillars, she had only to listen to the noise outside as people cheered louder.

She ran a hand through her wheat-blonde hair as she smiled. She whispered under her breath, so as not to disrupt the harmony of voices around her. "Praise be to Ganden!"

As the vessel levitated a few feet over its stone supports, people were struck with opposing reactions. Some lost their voices in awe of the large ship taking flight. Most cheered in thunderous volumes out of excitement. People standing blocks away from the castle stopped what they were doing to witness if the craft was finally rising over the city. Many on the streets, who could only see the masts draped with the sunscreen canopy over the ramparts, gasped as they saw movement. The last divine chariot enamored the hearts of the local people. Everything stopped as crowds pointed skyward.

Kemora entered Jentan's suite without warning. The halfling wearing her human disguise held her unconcerned poker face despite the wands and spells that nearly blasted her unexpected entry. Savannah, Jentan, and Revwar relaxed after recognizing their partner, resuming a crowded view through the one small window. Kemora got through the door and shut it quickly, not wanting anyone outside to have a glimpse of the uninvited elf wizard or the armored cleric of DeLaris. The rogue threw her bags down and removed her magical mask, resuming her true form.

"Sorry for the delay," she offered, "That red-haired wench from the streets happened across me again but I lost her."

The other three offered mumbles in reply as they crowded the small window. The rogue asked, "Am I missing anything interesting?"

A chorus of unimpressed "nay" came back at her. Kemora huffed over the mages and cleric feigning disinterest in the rare vessel, despite having their attention glued to the porthole.

Elsewhere, Montanya felt a rush of emotion as she felt the vessel lift upwards, but it was more akin to a sinking despair. The initial lift of the vessel almost sent her toppling as she felt a sudden weakness in the knees. Scared, she cracked open the supply room door where she hid, sneaking a view of the crowd at the observation deck balustrade. Everyone's back faced her as they watched the towering spires of the wizard guild sink below. Montanya gasped as she saw the highest pinnacle banner from the loftiest castle tower drop out of sight. Somehow, this great vessel floated into the sky! What had she gotten herself into?

Trestan hollered in excitement as he watched the world fall away from them. Cat continued waving to the dots on the ground below. The two companions had experienced flight before, but it still exhilarated them. In the back of his mind, Trestan felt mortified at what would happen if the vessel suddenly fell, yet for some reason his body turned that feeling into excited verbal exclamations to prove he was still alive.

Lindon had the best view of the retreating castle as he stood near the stern. The crowd had parted for him as his fingers danced on mandolin strings. The minstrel could see the Highwater district on the horizon. As he played, he recalled how his talent and the gift of Korrelothar's bamboo flute had taken him so far into a new world. He wondered if the other unfortunate residents of Highwater could hear his notes from this lofty perch and know that someone had succeeded in aspiring to a better life. Regardless of his recollections, the minstrel focused on the moment. The music of the divine chariot expressed itself through his tones. The mantras coursing through the decks seemed accentuated with the minstrel as Lindon hummed along their tune. The people felt caught up in the moment, and Lindon helped to give that moment a voice of its own in melody.

Korrelothar made his way through the press of the crowd to the helm castle. He approved their course toward the ocean as they flew low enough that the nobility could make out their individual keeps among the rooftops below. The passengers enjoyed an unobstructed view of Orlaun in its grand entirety. White masts dotted the sea blue harbor. Westward they could see expanses of farmland interrupted by roads and minor holdings. The great aqueduct system could be seen running in a maze around the city, as well as its origins drawing a line into the northern mountains.

The elf wizard chatted with one of the other wizards at the helm. "We'll fly into the eastern sky until the city is out of sight, then set down again in the water to resume the seaborne portion of our journey."

Sondra could not enjoy the view from the inner sanctum. As she felt the craft fly, standing quietly by the chanting clerics, she found herself confined to a private world of hopes and fears. While experiencing the miracle of this flight, the calling of her faith lifted her soul. This ship embodied the high point of her spiritual calling. All of her fears and youthful torment paled in the face of her god's power. Although the clerics of Ganden had every right to look upon this vessel with pride, they acted quite humble around it. Sometimes that realization of meek servitude troubled Sondra, knowing the best she could ever achieve would only surmount to an indentured service to others. As the ship lifted under the force of prayer, Sondra felt the strength of her faith surge. Pride could be found when one didn't look for it. All those who tormented her when young would be ashamed to see Sondra able to wield such powerful miracles as this! The young acolyte realized that she should almost pity those immature doubters.

Sondra looked into the faces of the Chosen and saw the concentration and willpower they exerted. The acolyte felt like she should be more assertive and shield herself from worrying about what others thought of her. It was so hard to please people, but the only ones she should need to please were her god and herself by respecting her calling. She originally adopted her religion to repay a debt of kindness, yet had always felt she would never amount to much in life. There was power and prestige in the Ganden's calling, even if nonbelievers scoffed at the subservient attitude perceived in her church. Sondra needed to reexamine her view of her own faith.

Though the young acolyte didn't realize it, Mother Evine secretly smiled at her. The older cleric saw the emotions on the acolyte's face, and she approved the visible impact the flight had on Sondra.

*Doranil Star* tread the barrier between earth and sun as all of Orlaun watched her pass overhead. The shadow of the great vessel drifted over the largest warships in Orlaun's armada. The mariners and their captains could only look up in silent admiration at the warship from a bygone age. After a time, the divine chariot became a speck among the clouds.

Revwar moved away from the porthole as he mused, "A great event in Orlaun. The last of a dying breed taking to the skies as another status symbol of the Gem of the World."

"Indeed, 'the last of a dying breed', how appropriate." Savannah set her skull helm on the writing desk, before pacing across the short cabin. The armor decorated with the images of death made hardly any noise as she moved. "All things die, so is the will of my goddess. Ganden has been able to hold on to his precious ship long enough, but even it feels the sting of time."

Savannah ran a hand along one of the wooden planks on the wall. "This ship will die too, my goddess wills it."

Revwar revealed a smug grin, "Soon enough, once the remaining stones are in our possession. I was just commenting; I wonder if all those who cheered today will truly remember this day in years to come. Will they look back and remember the day the *Doranil Star* sailed away to the skies, and never returned? We sail on the last voyage of the last divine chariot, before time will finally bring her to ruin."

On the vessel, hidden away from all the noise and mood of the occasion, two green relic stones quietly sat in a protected container. Like the ship that carried them, they were also rare weapons of unimaginable power from an old war.

**CHAPTER 13**          **"The Darkest Day of Her Life"**


As his fingers finished their delicate dance across the length of his metal flute, Lindon flourished into an exaggerated bow. More than one haughty listener on the crowded deck restrained themselves to a mild applause. He noted the same people who showed the most appreciation had also been grudgingly indulgent in moving their legs and bodies to the rhythm, while vainly trying to hold an air of indifference. Most of the nobles and royalty on deck were too engrossed in their own conversations to pay much attention to the minstrel. Many passengers were engrossed in their own political maneuvering despite the entertainment and festivities. As *Doranil Star* sailed over the waves of the sea, the performers seeking quick fame found themselves relegated to a position more akin to a colorful rug in an opulent room. They added to the scenery, but were largely ignored by the crowd they attempted to impress.

Two figures did not restrain their applause or compliments from the minstrel. Lindon met the gazes of Cat and Trestan. He offered them a special, private smile in appreciation. Maybe it was because they came from humble roots such as himself, but he felt a connection to their spirits. When the minstrel smiled his bright smile, or moved in his graceful dance steps, his performances were focused on those who appreciated him most. Trestan and Cat were not ashamed to move their feet and clap in public among such royalty.

When Lindon had to surrender the small stage to the next performer, the couple decided to explore somewhere else. Trestan suggested their next destination, "The exhibit room will be open for us now. I feel the need to go down and see…see them from a closer perspective."

Cat could understand Trestan's reluctance to talk about the stone relics in public. "I'm ready, if you are willing to escort me, my knight."

They giggled together as they went arm in arm past the throngs of important nobles who wore false smiles and spoke insincerities to potential partners or rivals. The companions wore formal clothes, though they were a far cry from being mistaken for nobility. Trestan and Cat both had their swords, as well as some slightly seasoned garments. Their displayed weapons proved to be of little concern to the other passengers. The important representatives had armed bodyguards of their own. Trestan's elvish sword and Cat's silver rapier were flamboyant enough to pass as ornamentation, instead of the deadly weapons that they truly could be.

The two of them descended to the first sublevel, and then down another set of stairs to the open observation deck. They politely skirted around a knot of ostentatious tradesmen to get to the next set of stairs. Signs guided them through narrow passageways. Trestan and Cat found themselves standing in line behind others in order to enter the exhibit room.

The two of them had seen the relics earlier in the voyage, though only from a distance. Despite their chosen role as protectors, they had to respect the limitations set by their hosts. Non-guild members weren't allowed to simply walk into the chamber of treasured mage items at their leisure. It also would not do for Korrelothar's guild to have a couple commoners taking liberties beyond what was offered to the royalty.

When Trestan and Cat finally entered the large exhibit hall, they found it was no easy task to walk straight to the relics' resting place. They were content to take their time indulging in the other presentations. Cat noted the displayed items were chosen in regards to entertainment and mystery. There were few powerful magic items in the room, most of the selection had been based on superficial values. A decorative shaman's mask came with a description of some of the oddities of barbaric tribes. Another stand held a crystal ball emanating eerie sounds. Gold and jewels combined beautifully on a necklace reputed to have once belonged to an immortal. A spear on a wall rack added to the collection of treasures from past heroes. All of the exhibits were roped off, with warnings that spells protected the items from theft.

Eventually, they stood before the exhibit which commanded their interest. Two of the three known stones rested under a thin sheet of glass. Both were a smooth green stone, shaped like an egg, bearing white markings. The marks differentiated the stones somehow, though they were basically the same style. Compared with other exhibits, they seemed like painted rocks amounted to no more than a gaudy decoration. The description accompanying them admitted only that they were made during the Godswars for some unknown purpose, and that a slight magical aura still surrounded them. Trestan and Katressa knew all too well the awesome power the stones could unleash. The stone at Troutbrook had given life to the land as it warded off crop infestations and cattle diseases. Just by that fact alone the stones would be invaluable to a farming community. It wasn't until Revwar took possession of the stones that their darker powers were revealed. A knowledgeable person who controlled the relics could call forth elemental spirits and corpses to defend themself. Katressa witnessed firsthand how magic from the relics had shattered a stone balcony, and brought down a ceiling of stone. The companions weren't sure if anyone except Revwar and his party knew the full potential of the relic stones. It disheartened them to know the elf already had regained possession of one stone; it would be a tragedy if he controlled the powers of all three.

"What's this?" Cat murmured softly. "Tres, look at this leather skin lying with the stones. This was wrapped around one of the stones when we recovered them."

Trestan saw the leathery scroll behind the glass screen. When they had set out four years ago aboard *Dovewing*, it had been to recover two stolen relics: one from Troutbrook and one from the wizards' guild in Orlaun. They had discovered a third stone, wrapped in some old skin with strange markings written on the leathery surface. The companions had given it a brief glance but never really examined it. Instead, they handed it over to Korrelothar's guild for research.

"The letters are Elvish, but it makes nay sense. It's all scrambled." Cat wore a puzzled frown as she examined the graceful style of the writing.

Trestan read the description posted beside the exhibit. He absently rubbed his fingers across the coraross about his neck as he spoke. "It says here, the scroll is in a dialect of Elvish, but written in some kind of code which the mages haven't solved. The only portion that is legible is at the bottom where several names have been signed. It seems to be a list of persons who have sworn to the above heritage and pledged to guard it with their lives."

Cat looked over the bottom of the document with a little more scrutiny. A shocked expression overtook her, she made a desperate grab to hold Trestan's arm. Trestan winced as her knuckles went white while clutching his wrist. Cat stared at the document in stunned silence, eyes wide and mouth moving without words.

Trestan hissed, "You're hurting me, what is it?"

Cat responded with a weak voice, "I recognize two of the names. One is Revwar, the other is Reatheneus Bilil…my father!"

*       *       *       *       *

Korrelothar spoke, "Lay back, Katressa. Relax your mind and body."

Cat set aside the empty vial. "It's hard to relax. This whole notion is scary."

Korrelothar shook his head as she lay down on his bed. "I told you nay harm will come of it. You will relive the memories of the past as if they were happening again, but that is all."

Cat looked past the elf mage to her beloved standing over the bed. She looked pale. "That is scary enough. You're asking me to relive the single worst day of my entire life."

Trestan reached a sympathetic hand out to clasp her own. "My love, know that my heart goes with you. If we can learn anything that may be useful, who knows what evil we may counter?"

Korrelothar blew out most of the remaining candles in his cabin as the female adventurer stretched out on his bed. Cat had only removed her boots before settling down for the spell of recollection. The Highwater Conjurer could honestly boast one of the most comfortable beds on board, yet for the purposes of this experiment Cat felt scant comfort. Her trembling fingers and furtive glances revealed her fear of what she would face. Through a sort of hypnosis conjured by Korrelothar and the potion she had drunk, the half-elf would sift through memories long buried in order to examine them in fresh detail. Trestan held her hand, the only comfort the young paladin could offer. Cat didn't want to relive the terrible images haunting her darkest nightmares. Nevertheless, she closed her eyes and tried to think of an old lullaby from her home village.

Korrelothar allowed her to lay quiet as the potion slowly put her into a trance. The wizard watched as Cat started to speak incoherently. Though her eyes remained closed, she turned her head and squinted as if to see something better. The potion had put her into a deep, dream-filled sleep. Her state of consciousness could be manipulated by a trained arcanist in order to explore things locked deep within the mind.

Korrelothar spoke softly to her. Trestan observed the wizard carefully studying her face as he spoke, while the fingers of one hand drew patterns in the air. Mysterious magic unfolded. "Walk into the past with me, Katressa Bilil. Go back to the day when the demons invaded your home."

Trestan watched as her breathing became quick and irregular. The half-elf gasped for air as she cried a couple words out in pain. Reflections from a younger Katressa despaired as she called for her mother and father.

"Go back to the beginning of the day. Go back to the time just before the attack…"

Trestan continued holding Cat's hand as he watched her breathing change. The woman no longer saw the terrors of the demons, but the release of tears from her eyes reflected that the day had not started well either.

"Let events unfold as they did that day, and remember each moment with clarity. Mark well every word, deed and face. Remember, Katressa, remember…"

Cat's mind descended past layers of repressed memories. Images which had been hidden under the specters of past nightmares crawled into the open. The half-elf fell into the past and relived it with no knowledge of how the future would unfold.

*     *     *     *     *

The light shining through the boughs of the great trees lit the simple pleasures of a young elf maiden's room. The doll her mother made when she was a baby looked blindly back at her through her tear-blurred eyes. The flowers blooming on her open windowsill brought no comfort from the sting of the words of others. The world seemed quiet except for the rustle of leaves in the wind, but the words repeated over and over in her mind. She huddled there on her bed, waiting for one of her parents to come home and comfort her.

She loved her human mother and her elf father but hated her heritage. Elf society offered no place for such an offspring of mixed blood. All she had wanted was to join the other elf children in fun games. After they teased her and laughed over the ingenuity of their own insults little Katressa could stand it no longer. She fled to home with a wounded heart. Not even her few friends could comfort her. Katressa knew they looked at her and saw her mortality. All of her friends would likely outlive her by more than a hundred years, and most acted like young children even as her viewpoints and manners matured. The elder teen years were the hardest for half-elves to endure. Their elf side wanted to linger in childhood, while their human side had already forced the emotional and physical changes from puberty upon them. The differences made her stand out from the other children.

Distracted by her own problems, it took some time before she noticed the sounds of the woods had changed. She heard shouting coming from outside. She couldn't make out the words, but the tones reflected fear and anger. The half-elf quietly listened; her hearing distracted by her own sniffles. After she tried to clear her nose, she detected a new smell in the air. The wind carried the scent of smoke through the open window.

Alarmed, young Katressa grabbed her coat and went to investigate. Her first worry was that a fire had started in the forest. Katressa's home nestled in the branches of the tall trees. When she walked out of her door, she stood on a walkway suspended well above the forest floor. Smoke thickened the air, obscuring much of the ground and nearby trees. She squinted through the smoke to get an idea where the fire might be, but then she heard the voices of elves calling for others to grab weapons. Elves ran on nearby walkways armed with bows and wearing armor. The young maiden realized there was more at hand then a simple fire.

A dark shape shrieked as it flew overhead. Fear overtook the young half-elf as she backed against her house to escape the nameless threat. The elves stopped to notch arrows into their bows. A volley of missiles unleashed into the smoky haze. Even with her keen vision, Katressa hadn't been able to see any detail of the flying creature, nor if the arrows hit.

Like from a dream, Katressa's mother ran out of the smoke. Although her movements reflected the age of her advanced human years, she ran up the suspended path with the fear for her daughter sustaining her pace. Borne from the urgency of panic, the human woman raced to be beside her one and only child. Katressa's short relief turned to fear as she saw a patch of red blood amongst her mother's graying hair. The woman carried her trusted staff, which also had fresh blood running along its length.

"Mother!" Katressa buried her tearful face into her mother's dress as they met.

After a brief hug, the human leaned over and held Katressa's shoulders so they could stare face to face. "Listen to me, Cat. Our home is under attack. Demons from another world have opened a portal to strike our world, but you must not give in to fear."

The girl numbly nodded as her mother continued. "Your father is with others trying to handle the threat, but we must get you to safety. Some of these demons fly, so the walkways aren't safe. We'll have more freedom of movement if we can get you down to the ground."

Katressa followed her mother to a rope used for emergency descents. The human woman hailed a band of warriors below, and those elves took up a position around the bottom of the rope.

"You first, my love." Her mother patted her long, black hair, "I will come down as soon as you touch bottom."

Katressa held the rope tightly. Her mother and an elf on the ground worked the rope around a pulley, quickly lowering the young half-elf. Her feet touched the ground and she backed away hurriedly to allow her mother to use it. When Cat looked up, however, her voice caught as she saw something misshapen on the walkway above. She pointed in terror, but her voice failed her. Another elf saw the danger and cried out to the woman above.

Her mother was good with handling a staff, and she had some small talent with magic. The human threw her arm out toward the demon, followed by a sparkling spray of small detonations. The creature screamed its displeasure but barely shied away from the bursts of flame. Staff and claw met as the alien form towered over its prey. An elf from below managed to put an arrow through the creature's leathery wings.

Suddenly, the forest floor became a battlefield. A pair of muscular beasts, their forms tortuously misshapen, charged into the knot of elves. Katressa fell to the ground and feebly covered herself with her bare arms as chaos erupted around her. Swords and spears stabbed as the elves fought back. Animal grunts filled the air as muscular claws reached out. Orders were shouted in Elvish amidst the demon howls. Dust and leaves kicked up into the already smoky haze. Katressa rolled through a tangle of legs and claws as all semblance of order was lost.

She looked up in time to feel drops of blood rain down: her mother's blood. The demon held the human's body in its grasp as it lunged forward with fangs. Katressa heard bones crunch and saw blood flowing freely from her mother's limp form. The demon seemed content to perch on the walkway and continue feasting on its victim. Katressa stumbled backward as she cried out. The sound of her scream was lost among the battle cries of the elves, the roar of the demons and painful shrieks from those injured.

For uncounted, eternal moments Katressa sat trembling amidst the rolling carnage. The young maiden refused to look up, fearing to witness any more of her mother's fate.

Around her, more elves lost their lives as demons ripped into them and ate some alive. A number of demons fell too, but only after taking many of the forest guardians. The half-elf child stared at a gutted demon corpse, as if it could give her an answer for her pain.

Some need within Katressa prompted her to move from the area. She had to get away and find somewhere to hide. She started moving deeper into the woods, but feared to leave the elf city. Though it meant going back toward the sounds of combat, she turned and went through the old gardens. The girl ran along garden lanes hearing screams in the smoky haze. Through the murk of the forest every sound reflected anger, fear or sorrow. She found other dead as she went, both elves and demons. Once she saw a grisly, wolf-like abomination with six legs struggling to move though mortally wounded. The girl avoided it. In changing course, she found herself in the clearing where the other elf children had been at play. Many of those elves lie dead, the sticks and balls from their game scattered about. Katressa looked upon the once-smug faces of those who had teased her for her human blood. The half-elf felt pity as she saw the looks of death frozen on those faces. She would have been a corpse here as well, had not their scornful remarks sent her away in tears.

She ran and ran through the living nightmare.

Bodies rained from the sky. Demons flew overhead while elven archers proved their deadly accuracy with bows. Sometimes pieces of an elf would fall from the walkways above, another victim who had been partially devoured. A number of other panicked citizens ran in seemingly random directions, seeking safety or loved ones. Katressa passed a group of elves using arcana to put out some flames, while another armed group guarded them.

It occurred to her she was heading deeper into the heart of the elven home. In the distance were some of the larger elven citadels built within the intertwining trunks of the oldest trees. Katressa fixed so intensely on these distant structures, that she was almost run through by a sharp pike.

The jittery elf warrior who had almost stabbed her had been pushed aside by his captain at the critical moment. The young girl froze as she eyed the tip of the pike in the ground next to her. Katressa could see panicked fear in the elf's eyes, but it turned to something more like revulsion as they realized who had appeared in their path.

"Watch your blades! It is just the halfer." The captain didn't offer apologies as he led his men down the lane.

Katressa was too stung by his words to care. 'Halfer' was short for 'half-breed', and thought to be a kinder way of saying it, yet it hurt to hear it all the same. She remembered the revulsion they showed at seeing her, and it made her ponder if they thought no better than the demons.

Moving by instinct, Katressa followed the elven troops. The sight she saw made everything else seem small. Before her, in the city's center, raged a large fight between demons and elves. Many demons flew overhead, dodging barrages of elven arrows. On the ground, a wall of elven shields and pikes tried to push back a mass of animal shapes. Both elves and demons had magic and they used it. Fire and lightning exploded in a terrible light show.

Somehow, she felt that one of the demons she spotted seemed to be a leader. It spoke in another language, guiding the rest in their attack. The demon seemed part earth and part spirit, composed of stone and ghostly mist. It and several other demons poured forth from one of the sacred sanctuary citadels. They made their way to something borne by magic in the center of the demon lines: a portal to their home world. Shaped like a bright disc, its surface rippled like water. A heavy mist hung about it at the edges. The lead demon and several others retreated from the battle through this portal.

With their leader gone, the demon ranks lost organization. Several more sought escape through the open portal, while others attempted to fly into the sky. The elves began slaughtering those that didn't flee, though several still escaped into the surrounding woods with more elven warriors in pursuit.

Katressa stayed at a distance until the battle wound down to small skirmishes. She crept forward through the cover of bushes and burnt trees. Although scared, curiosity drew her closer to the gate between worlds.

She saw a group of elders arguing about the portal. Her attention drew to her father, standing among them. Reatheneus Bilil had taken part in the battle and survived. It brought a smile to her face to see her father well. As the elders talked, demons occasionally attempted to escape through the portal or invade through it from the other side. A ring of swordsmen and archers thwarted every attempt. An elf cleric and a few others ran from the closest citadel to the group of elders with crestfallen looks. A heated discussion took place, though much of it Katressa could not hear from where she hid.

She heard the cleric speaking of holy items stolen from the citadel, some of which were objects of great power. Someone called for answers, saying that the only way a portal could have opened in the middle of the elves' city was if someone there helped the demons open it. They argued back and forth insinuating treason by one of their own. Several elves called upon the others to use miracles to shut the portal. At that notion, Reatheneus stepped forward and decried those who wanted to close it. Katressa listened as her father spoke of sworn oaths to protect the stolen treasures…that an attempt must be made to recover them. Some elders would not relent easily, sharing their fears about leaving such a dangerous portal open in the already weakened city.

Reatheneus spoke loud and clear, "Yestreal's gift was a relic, it should not be abandoned so easily! Nor shall we leave the other magical prizes for demons to wield against us later if a new portal reopens. Who will brave this passage with me?"

Katressa watched from afar as several brave elves stepped forward with their weapons. A few elders stood beside Reatheneus too. Through young eyes the half-elf spotted Revwar among those elders. The yellow-eyed elf wizard wore his silvery hair in a long braid. Trapped in her memories, Katressa did not recognize him for his deeds in later years, nor did she know him by name, but she was able to see her past with remarkable clarity. Revwar had been among those advising against going through the portal, yet when her father called upon them to respect their oaths he joined the attempt.

To her surprise, Katressa's presence had not gone unnoticed by her father. As the warriors prepared to charge through the portal, he looked directly at her across the battlefield of their home. Elders prayed for the safety of those brave few. Reatheneus paid them little heed as he stared lovingly at his distant daughter. She wanted to go to him for comfort. She wanted to tell him mother had died and she needed someone to hold her. Across that distance, he would see the tear streaks on her face.

Reatheneus knew his daughter needed him, but he could only hope she understood the sacrifice he might have to make. He wanted to reassure her but there was no time. His eyes focused on hers as he reached up to touch one ear. A gold unicorn earring, his loving daughter had given him recently, dangled there. He treasured that gift. At least she would see he thought about her always, and that he would bear that token with him into the hellishness of the demons' world.

Reatheneus Bilil, Revwar, and a number of elf warriors stepped into the bright disc of the portal.

Minutes dragged by.

An hour went by, as nervous elders and warriors fought off more demon incursions.

More hours passed by, interrupted by brief demon forays, until the sun hovered low in the sky. No elf had come back from the portal, and no more dared go through.

Katressa sat huddled between some bushes, her knees tucked against her chest and arms wrapped around her legs as she stared at the portal. She watched as the elders near it had another heated discussion. Not far away, a band of elf warriors cut down the latest demon to arrive through the portal. There seemed to be a lot of head shakes and helpless arm gestures coming from the remaining elders, but she couldn't hear the words. She simply watched with an empty heart, staring across a field of wounded elves being attended by clerics.

Several elders took up positions in a half circle around the portal. Katressa raised her head as she curiously studied this change. The elders raised their hands in some type of incantation, as wizard and cleric alike joined in the effort. A loud buzzing noise emanated from the portal as the elf voices rose in pitch. Katressa slowly struggled to get to her feet as worry creased her brow. The young girl considered all the weapons lying abandoned on the field of battle. She wanted to grab a sword or bow and rush to find her father through that shiny disc.

With a rush of air and a thunderous noise, the disc distorted and shrunk to nothing.

The shiny light of the portal was gone. Darkness alone stood where the gate between worlds once existed. There was no way any demons could escape or invade now, but at the same time there was no way for the missing elves to return. Reatheneus Bilil was stranded in the demons' home world, if he still lived at all.

She thought she had cried all of her tears out, but more came. The young half-elf fell to the ground weeping. Amidst all the discarded weapons she could have used to aid her father, amidst smoking ash, amidst the many dead bodies of the fallen, Katressa grieved until her tired body surrendered to a fitful sleep. Nightmares plagued her through the night, and would continue to do so for many weeks after.

The arcane-induced memories of the past did not end with the banishment of the demon portal. Her memories tumbled forth to the next day. She saw herself walking numbly through the lanes of the damaged city. Her weary eyes endured sights of unbelievable loss. There were so many dead, and so much had been ruined in the resulting spell fires. Great trees had fallen, taking homes and walkways with them. Gardens tended by generations were reduced to smoking piles of ashes.

Katressa found her home destroyed. The tree supporting it had fallen, taking with it the walkway and a few other structures. The young girl did not know where her mother's body was, and she didn't care to look and see what was left. She numbly walked along the fallen trunk until she came to the smashed walls of her home. Alone, the young girl dug into the tangle of wood looking for any material possessions that might be salvaged. Katressa sorted through ripped linen, broken furniture, and scattered oddities.

In the carnage of her home, she found an item that her father had been entrusted to protect. Taking a seat on the torn blankets, Katressa stared at the odd piece of stone. It was shaped like a block, small enough to almost be concealed in the hand. There were runes carved into the stone, along with a jumble of elvish letters. She didn't understand what it was or why her father had kept it hidden around their house, but she knew he guarded it for some important reason. She hugged the block to her heart, thinking again of her dead parents and crying at the cruel nature of the world.

She was a half-breed, alone in the world, homeless, with all her belongings strewn across that dark, forest floor.

*       *       *       *       *

"Awake, dear Katressa. Come back to us with the memories of the past," a voice urged.

She opened her eyes to see the rafters on the ceiling of Korrelothar's cabin, aboard *Doranil Star*. Cat's head swam disoriented, as if suddenly awakening from a deep sleep, unsure if she still lingered in the dream. The woman turned her head to see Trestan and the elf wizard staring back at her. For a moment she puzzled at where she was and when.

The perfectly clear memories of the worst day of her life came back to her.

The remembered pain of her emotional loss washed over her and drowned her in its sudden misery. Half of her still felt as if she was back in that day, when all the hurt felt new. Cat wailed in misery until it subsided to bursts of crying sobs. Korrelothar sat back as he considered her emotional pain. Trestan instinctively reached out to hold and comfort her.

Half lost in memories of the demon attack, Cat batted Trestan's arms away without fully realizing what she was doing. She turned away from them and curled into a ball on the bed, sobbing to herself.

"I'm so sorry, *faunlessa*," Trestan whispered after a time, "We shouldn't have made you relive that."

"Cat, listen to me." Korrelothar reached tentatively and put his hand on her shoulder. She flinched, but didn't make a move to remove the hand. "I know it is hard, but you must try to remember what you saw and tell us about it. What connection did Revwar and your father have with the relics?"

The adventuress continued sobbing quietly, shaking, for a few moments after he asked the question. Her voice strained to answer between choking back tears. "They were…sworn protectors of…they swore to protect the treasures of the citadel."

Trestan spoke softly. His heart was heavy at seeing the reactions of how badly his beloved had suffered. "The relic was among the items that the demons stole?"

"I didn't see it," Cat sniffled.

The half-elf wiped her red, swollen eyes before rolling over to face them. Her lips trembled as she spoke. "But I guess, aye. Gods, Trestan, that is where the third relic had been stolen. All those years ago from my village when I was young."

She tried to say more but was caught up by her emotions. Korrelothar handed her a handkerchief as she tried to compose herself. Cat sat up on the edge of the bed, dabbing the cloth at her face. The woman shivered, though not from cold.

Cat recalled her memories, staring into nothing as she spoke. "The demons created a gate to our world somehow, right in the middle of the tree city. The elders argued that a traitor was in their midst, someone who had to have opened the portal from this side."

Her jaw grew firm as she remembered the yellow eyes. "Revwar was there that day. I didn't know all the elders, but he was from my people. When my father…"

Emotion overtook her again, interrupting her retelling of the memories. "My father spoke of Yestreal's relic, mentioning that the demons had stolen terrible magic. He went through the portal with many warriors, determined to get back the stolen treasures. Revwar objected to it, but in the end followed them through."

Cat paused. "None who entered that portal were ever seen again. At least not until…until Revwar showed up in Troutbrook four years ago and tried to steal another of 'Yestreal's relics.' I find that suspicious."

Trestan and Korrelothar quietly contemplated the news. Trestan stroked a hand down his mustache, as he often did when deep in thought. Cat's emotions tore at her too much to continue. She excused herself, walking unsteadily to the door of the cabin. Trestan had to release the handle for her; she couldn't steady her normally-nimble hands. Trestan lingered to say their goodbyes to Korrelothar, while Cat almost broke into a run to get back to her room. She brushed past a few puzzled guests in the halls that politely stepped aside at seeing her distraught look. Somehow, she opened the door of her cabin and collapsed onto the bed fully dressed. Late in the afternoon hours, Cat cried herself to sleep.

Trestan quietly entered the room sometime later, to see Cat sleeping curled-up in the center of their bed, tearstains on the linen. He slowly leaned over and kissed her tenderly on the shoulder. He didn't want to wake her up after the visions she'd been forced to endure.

Trestan fell asleep on the floor of their cabin, his pack serving as a pillow.

## CHAPTER 14  "Cauldron Sabotage/Cat's Key"

The inner sanctum of the *Doranil Star*, (the soul of the vessel when soaring in the air), remained empty while the ship crested the waves of the ocean. The clerics weren't always present in the religious center of the divine chariot, especially when resting for the next flight. The ship had sailed within distant sight of the Wilder continent, named appropriately due to the lack of large cities but an abundance of more primitive civilizations. Few traveled to this continent, due to the unknown dangers and lack of outposts for trade. Tonight's schedule featured a flight far above the forested canopy of this strange land. The crust of Orlaun society would feast as they overlooked this strange place, as well as enjoy a spell show put on by the hosting wizard guild. For now, however, the inner sanctum stood deserted as the divine chariot sailed the tides.

Pairs of sentries employed by the Brotherhood of the Circles guarded both doors to the chamber, fore and aft. These men expected little trouble. Though well-trained and given an important position, they did not seriously expect much mischief to go on during the journey. They gave only a brief notice as another richly dressed couple strode down the hall, especially after they saw the emblem of the mage guild on the middle-aged gentleman escorting the lady. No one besides the guards and this couple were in the hall, but it wasn't a busy area as far as the nobles were concerned. The closed and guarded doors certainly didn't offer any entertainment, yet now and then people still walked this way to avoid the busier passages.

"This is where they keep the ship aloft? By prayer alone?" The human woman asked of her escort. The guards watched her out of the corners of eyes dulled by their unenviable chore. The woman had a long face, long, brown hair braided and tied in a bun at the top of her head, and an ample bust line and hips. "Will they let others take a peek?"

"I'm afraid they won't." The handsome mage answered. Thick, dark hair was peppered with gray at the sides, the colors extended to his thin mustache and small, pointed goatee. Dark eyes almost hid under bushy, dark eyebrows. He grinned to his lady as he spoke. "This is hallowed ground, but we should be honored to get this close. It is an amazing vessel!"

The couple stopped near the guards, as the lady paused to plant a small kiss on the cheek of her escort. The gentleman had one arm around her back as they leaned close. When they broke apart, resuming their walk, a small scarf drifted to the deck. The guards noticed it, but the woman proceeded unaware of her loss.

One of the guards stooped over to pick it up. "Excuse me, milady…"

With alarming speed, the woman whirled around toward the guard's voice. Bending over as he was to retrieve the scarf, he was now within Kemora's reach. The human image, created by the mask she wore, disguised her true height and identity. The domid rogue roped a loop of her bolo over the top of his neck, even as her other hand shoved a piece of cloth over his open mouth.

The second guard barely registered the action when the mage escort turned toward him with piercing, insistent eyes. Jentan Mollamos stared into the sentry as he spoke some words. "Stop and hold silent, and you may hear it."

The mentalist's magical suggestion distracted the second guard. The guard went rigid as his ears strained to listen for whatever might be heard. This left him more susceptible to Jentan's next spell. The mage whispered the words of illusion to weave a false situation in the memory of the guard. Off to the side, he heard muffled protests as the first guard tried to back away from the woman. The sound of the struggle seemed detached and distant.

The first guard instinctively tried to raise his head as the cloth covered his mouth and nose. The loop around his neck would not offer him any leeway. Kemora held on tight, pulling the bolo while forcing the potion-soaked cloth forward. The guard found the whole weight of the halfling hanging onto his neck, though her illusion made it look as if a human woman hung onto him. He fumbled around, trying to pull her hands away, but he was already becoming dazed. A smell simulating strong alcohol overcame the man, making him clumsy.

The guard's eyes became drowsy, while his voice lowered to more of a whimper as he lost his strength. He dropped to the floor of the passageway. Confused limbs slowly jerked about without coordination or clear direction. The domid rogue held the cloth tightly against the man's face until the scent of the potion had pushed him past consciousness.

Jentan Mollamos convinced the other guard of his companion's drunkenness. The descriptive spell painted upon the guard's mind held him still. "He overindulged, and shouldn't have even tried to take watch with all that ale in his system."

The second guard scowled down at the first. Kemora released her bolo from around the unconscious man. Anyone who came close to the downed guard would be able to smell the reek of alcohol on his breath. The standing guard paid little heed to the woman, entranced as he was by Jentan's messages.

"A shame that such a good man should try to guard such a holy place when he is so drunk that he passes out." The mentalist's voice altered slightly as he mixed in arcane words with the visual images. It had a musical quality to it. The suggestions became realities in the mind of the charmed guard. "In such a state, the Holy room could have been vulnerable."

Kemora opened the door to the inner sanctum, slowly and quietly. The rogue glanced in, then nodded to the mage that the chamber was indeed empty. She slipped inside.

"A good thing nay visitors have been here yet. Not a soul has walked the hall or dared trespass into the inner sanctum. You stood your watch vigilantly and let none·pass." The mentalist watched the man nod in agreement, though the sentry stared into nowhere. The guard had already forgotten the couple even before Jentan went past and closed the door behind him.

Kemora slipped off the mask, resuming her true domid appearance. Both rogue and mentalist enjoyed being inside the quiet sanctity of Ganden's chamber like two wolves inside a sheep pasture. They silently appraised the room, wall sconces, wall instruments linked to controls on the helm deck, kneeling cushions, and finally the cauldron of holy water set in the center. The cauldron was worth sneaking a closer peek. Jentan and Kemora glanced into the holy water, spotting the submerged holy items that helped provide the conduit for miraculous flight.

Almost as one, they slowly backed away and peered upward. A chandelier holding incense sticks instead of candles hung directly over the cauldron. One, then the other, glanced between the chandelier, the cauldron, and slowly spun to examine the rest of the chamber.

Jentan indicated the chandelier. "That would be perfect, would it not? The pilots sit in a circle around this point, and it hangs directly over the divine receptacle."

Kemora rolled her eyes toward her companion. "You mean the pot?"

The mentalist kept his charming grin, but spoke condescendingly as he replied. "If you are referring to the spiritual conduit, that divine receptacle which channels such miraculous intentions of flight into the ability to raise the largest vessel known to the races up to the heavens, and which consists of a religious cauldron inscribed with a god's favor, containing blessed holy items in the favor of said god…then aye, I'm talking about the 'pot' sitting before us."

Kemora let slip a look of mischievousness as she grinned and batted her eyelashes at the tall human. Jentan had no doubt it was all for show, Kemora always remained deadly serious even when deceptive. The rogue kept a slight smile toward him as she spoke. "I'd parry words with you, but I have to rely on you for the levitation spell to get me up there and carry out the deed. I'd rather not find myself falling back into the pot."

"Nay swimming in the pool of the gods. The cauldron is too big for you anyways; you'd never be able to swim to the side without drowning."

Kemora returned to her poker face after the mentalist's witticism regarding her smaller size. The domid reached into some pouches at her sides. Her dexterous hands pulled forth a couple items. "Sacred grave dust from DeLaris," she spoke as she hefted a bag in one hand. "Consecrated by our own sweet Savannah, who seems to hold the lustful attention of a certain lip-wiggling mage."

Jentan glowered at the halfling's jovial slandering.

Unconcerned, Kemora held a piece of carved stone in her other hand, "And the scion of Mothrok, Goddess of Earth and Stone."

The notion of why these objects were present brought amusement back to the mentalist. "Hardly necessary for these items if the surprise has the intended effect. I somewhat hope the pilots do survive the initial incident, so that the effects of these religious items in the holy cauldron of Ganden can be felt and feared before the end comes."

The rogue looked up at the incense chandelier, "Your levitation spell, please. It's time for a little sabotage."

*　　　　*　　　　*　　　　*　　　　*

Trestan slowly stirred from his rest. He felt blankets tangling him on the hard floor. The mantra from the clerics could be felt in a hum from the deck on which he rested. The sound of that mantra and the lack of movement from rocking waves meant they were in flight once again. Judging by the light through the shutters of their cabin, it was getting dark outside. Even as the young paladin looked at the shutters, a candlelight cast Cat's shadow against the wall in the act of getting dressed.

Trestan thought of how sad Cat had appeared earlier. The tears rolling down her cheeks and her haunted look made him feel guilty about going along with Korrelothar's idea. He wondered what horrors she had been forced to relive.

Trestan also recalled that the mages of the guild had been planning on a display in the night sky. A magical barrage of fire, light, sound and illusion promised entertainment to everyone on the sun and observation decks as they sailed above the clouds. Korrelothar's guild intended to impress in every way they could. Trestan and Cat had been looking forward to the show. Trestan rolled over to see if Cat was getting ready for it…and surprise promptly replaced worry.

Cat was dressing for the evening, but not in fanciful attire. The half-elf noticed Trestan stir, but paid him little attention as she slid into her dark, leather adventurer's outfit. Trestan had become used to seeing her wear a mix of nice dresses during most of the days since the "Embarking". Katressa relaxed her clothing choices around him, enjoying their time together by dressing the part of his lady. Trestan and Cat had put on their traveling gear for the somber trip to Troutbrook, but after departing Barkan's Crossing in a ship they started to dress up for each other. Although they brought most of their gear with them on board the *Doranil Star*, they clothed themselves to mix in with Orlaun's elite as best they could.

Trestan slowly sat up as he watched Katressa dress as if she anticipated a battle. She buckled or strapped protective pieces into place. Her assortment of daggers, her bracers, and the scabbarded silver rapier lie spread out on the bed. The tools of her infiltrator profession, a mix of instruments used for picking locks, or possibly disabling or setting traps, sat alongside the blades.

As the young man eyed her possessions, she commented on one that was missing, "I shouldn't have let Korrelothar talk me out of bringing the crossbow. He said it would look out of place, and it would, but that's not the point. I should have brought it."

Trestan's hand stroked his mustache as he spoke. He made the statement sound like a question. "I didn't know you planned on going to the spell show dressed that way?"

"I'm not going up to the deck."

Trestan nodded, then changed the subject as he tried to figure her motivations, "Cat, I'm sorry about earlier. I don't think we gained anything, and it seemed to bring you such pain…"

She shook her head and waved off his words before he could finish. "You have nay idea, but I'm not needing comfort. If anything, my vision taught me a few things."

"Like?"

Cat rounded on him, her emerald eyes staring into his soul. Trestan met her stare with compassion in his eyes. He didn't see any anger in her look, but there was a stubborn seriousness in her eyes that could not be ignored.

Cat's voice sounded low but firm. "We have a duty, Trestan. This is your quest, and much more is at stake than the villagers butchered at your home…and the elves at my home."

Trestan's brow puzzled a moment at her amendment. "First of all, Cat, remember to whom you are speaking. You sound like you are pointing some accusation or insinuating neglect at me, and for what I have nay idea. What is wrong, *faunlessa?*"

Cat began to realize how stressed she had been, and how rudely she was treating her beloved. The adventuress closed her eyes and made an effort to relax. Trestan, wearing only his pants from earlier in the day and the coraross necklace, finally got to his feet and stood with her beside the bed.

"I dreamed for so long of having you to myself when you were finished at the seminary." Cat confided. "Since then, we have journeyed to Orlaun, stayed at many fine places along the way, and I was able to show you new food. We got to share cabins and massage all the worries from our bodies under warm candles. Then, of all things, we get to go on an unexpected journey to the clouds. This should be the time of our lives.

"But then I saw the horrors from my own home city long ago, and realized how it ties in with the relics we endeavor to protect."

She held out her hands for Trestan to take in his own, which he did. "Tres, we are here to protect them aren't we? We set out from Troutbrook to warn Korrelothar's guild about a possible theft, and we succeeded. Now what? As much as I want to enjoy the time here, I realized that the relics are our duty, our priority."

Trestan looked down at his hands. Cat's fingers glided across his ring as she spoke. Trestan stared at the symbols still present on Faithful's Companion, and the significance was not lost on Cat.

He spoke, "Aye, my love. This is my chosen quest, and I have been neglecting the stones to indulge in the moment. I don't believe we can offer the relics more security than Korrelothar's guild, and yet we have been totally ignoring our charge. We only went down to look at the relics once since coming on board."

Trestan broke away from her grip slowly, only to retrieve his own belongings. Cat smiled as Trestan began to lay out his armor next to her equipment on the bed. The squire of Abriana pulled forth Sword of the Spirit from its scabbard as if to check for rust, though the blade would never tarnish. The magical elvish edge gleamed as bright as ever. He replaced it in the scabbard.

"Are we just going to stand around and guard the relics while everyone else enjoys the show on deck?" Trestan asked. "Not that I'm complaining, I was curious if you had something in mind."

"I do," she replied, reaching into a pouch.

"The memories also reminded me of this item. It was my father's."

The half-elf woman produced a small block of stone from the pouch. It had several runes and elvish letters carved into it. Trestan took it in his hands when she showed it to him, though of course the jumble of carvings was foreign to him. He handed it back to her.

Cat explained, "I have carried that around for years. First I did so because I remembered my father was its guardian. He kept it hidden away for some unknown reason, but I found it in the remnants of my home. I became its guardian. The years went by and I had nay idea what it was, yet I still couldn't part with it since it was my father's."

Trestan waited for Cat to go on, but she stared distractedly at the surface of the block. "And?"

Cat slyly smiled up at him. "I think I know what it is now."

Her smile proved infectious, though Trestan had no idea why the rune block came into the conversation.

The half-elf grinned mysteriously over her hidden secret. She acquiesced and told him. "The leather skin wrapped around one of the relics…I never took a good look at it until today. My father's name is on that document, and my memories revealed that the third relic must have been stolen from my city. You read the inscription by that exhibit even as I got my first real glance at the scroll. The top portion of it had Elvish lettering jumbled into some kind of code the mage guild couldn't break."

She held up the rune block, beaming with pride. "I believe this is the key to the code. We can go see what the rest of the scroll says."

Trestan gave Cat such a ferocious hug that he lifted her off her feet. The two of them began kissing and hugging as if both had already won some major victory. "The faster we get there, the faster we find out how much this can help us!" Cat playfully scolded him.

Katressa and Trestan went about donning their adventure gear. The young squire equipped all of his armor, and even grabbed a pack of miscellaneous belongings of things that might prove useful. Katressa slid all her daggers into various hiding places. Her silver rapier, with the pommel shaped like the head of a hunting cat, hung by her side. Trestan said a brief prayer as he slung the baldric containing his sword over his back. The young warrior grabbed the warhammer fashioned into the shape of a minotaur's head, and tucked it through a ring on his belt. He even reached for his helm since hers lay nearby as well. The *Taef' Adorina* was tucked away in her pack, which she also planned on grabbing.

Trestan paused when Cat strapped on her bracers. Once again, he took note of the oddity of her left bracer, a bulge on top of it concealed by a sizable piece of cloth. "When are you going to tell me what trick you have hidden in that bracer?"

Katressa turned her back to him. "You may have to find a way to pleasantly torture it out of me."

*      *      *      *      *

Others found themselves missing out on the mages' promised spell show. One of them was Montanya, an uninvited guest that knew nothing of the schedule of entertainment. The woman sat saddened and alone in a dim room, but she abated any weak feelings with thoughts tinged of resentment. She always found it easier to deal with problems behind a veil of anger. The nineteen-year-old student of chiaso was no closer to her goal of vengeance upon thieves, and it looked like she could no longer pursue the one on this vessel.

The human youth perked up at a knocking sound from the end of the hall. Montanya heard the small peephole squeaked open, so the guard could see who wanted entry. A woman's voice spoke past the muffling door. "My superiors sent me to deliver this meal to the stowaway, and inquire as to her disposition."

Montanya would have liked to see who was talking, but the bars of her cell would not allow her a view of the door to the brig. Nevertheless, she heard the guard grunt in acknowledgement as he threw aside the locking latch. The chiaso guessed she would see the unknown visitor soon enough. Her stomach rumbled at the thought of a decent meal. She hoped the server would just give her the food and then leave her to her isolated thoughts. Montanya's mood ran sour enough; being captured and held in the brig for a day didn't help her attitude. By habit, she seemed to accomplish very little toward her goals or even stay out of trouble. The more she tried to accomplish, the more she dug a hole for herself. Now, they labeled her a criminal for her efforts.

Footsteps whisked down the hall, but she cast her glance toward the wall opposite of the bars. Initial curiosity about the visitor melted away into a feeling of avoidance. A narrow slit existed under the bottom of the bars for a meal tray to pass back and forth. Hopefully, the woman would just push it through and leave the discouraged chiaso alone. Montanya kept her attention diverted from the bars as she heard a solitary person approach and stop outside the cell. Montanya could see the woman's boots pause hesitantly outside the bars. Out of her peripheral vision the chiaso watched the robed visitor take a few cautious steps forward. The stowaway got the impression the visitor was leering at her like a sideshow animal. Montanya wanted to offer some witty rebuke, but nothing came to mind. Instead, she ignored the person.

It was hard place the voice, but Montanya recognized a familiar tone when the unknown woman spoke. "This is the second time I've seen you in a mess of trouble."

Montanya glanced up at the bars in puzzlement, though her expression quickly turned to her customary sneer as she saw who provided for her. Sondra Oskires, the young cleric of Ganden who had healed her poison wound, stared back at her in a less-than-complimentary manner. The visitor wore her familiar clerical vestments instead of the ceremonial ones adorned when she had come aboard. Although a similar gray color to her ceremonial garb, her current robe and pantaloons were used on a more practical day-to-day basis. It bore little decoration aside from a symbol of Ganden. Another symbol of Ganden, on her belt buckle formed the image of a shield with two open palms on it. The young cleric seemed to have forgotten the tray of food she carried as she scrutinized the locked-up stowaway.

"Don't expect me to fall to my knees and beg for your guidance," Montanya snapped. "I've known a lot of clerics and they never impress me; least of all one who happens to be the rudest representative of a god that I've ever seen before."

A storm flared in Sondra's eyes. "And you happen to be one of the most spoiled brats ever to have dripped blood across my sanctuary. I do remind you, we only met because you were dying and I helped save your life!"

"Is there a problem?" The guard down the hallway shifted his seat so he could get a better view down the hall.

Montanya called back as she glowered. "Only that they let some haughty slip of a girl, who doesn't know the first thing about manners, bring me a meal." The redhead turned her attention directly at Sondra. "What have you brought me anyway…more gruel from a petty copper pen?"

Sondra didn't know what to be more indignant about. First, the young woman in the cell was obviously a few years younger than her, and yet called the cleric a 'haughty slip of a girl'. The youth had the audacity to call the meals at the sanctuaries 'gruel' even though it was the best they could offer for the meager budget from which those houses operated. The fact that Sondra had put a little extra care and effort into preparing a good meal for the unknown stowaway only to have it blatantly unappreciated did not sit well with her either.

Failing to keep her temper out of her voice, Sondra yelled out to the guard even though her blue eyes glared at the chiaso. "I'm just dealing with an ungrateful street whelp who seeks to keep biting the hands that feed her."

While the two women continued their loathing stares, they were unaware that the guard simply shifted his seat to a position by which he could watch the entertainment better. The man despised being stuck below decks and missing out on the mages' spell show, but at least he would get some entertainment between two sparring women.

Montanya spoke in a huff, "I've had years of clerics trying to shelter me, feed me scraps, and put all sorts of nonsense in my ears about complacent forgiveness for all the cruelties put into my life. I have nay wishes to get help from supposed sanctuaries that legally rob the poor of a copper a day just to get basics like food and shelter."

"You think we charge it just to get rich?" Sondra exclaimed, appalled. "The city does not pay us to keep beggars off the streets. Many is the time we forgo the payment and offer our services for free, so that a poor soul may get what can be obtained by the donations we receive from the common man. We close our doors to none."

"I seem to recall a self-righteous cleric slamming the door behind me when I chose to leave."

Sondra had no immediate comment in the face of Montanya's heated glare. The cleric inwardly calmed herself from all the insults and accusations that were thrown her way. A tumult of anger built up in response to the verbal harassment hurled at her, and yet the cleric felt she had done nothing to deserve such poor treatment. Staring into the greenish-blue eyes scowling from the dark cell, Sondra found the teachings of her mentor restraining any additional unsympathetic words. Mother Evine would have chided Sondra for speaking harshly at the woman, despite the disrespect shown. She served under the tenets of Honor, Duty and Service, which bound her to treat people respectfully even if the attitude was not returned. Sondra took in a deep breath as she softened her glare. It would not be wise to provoke the anger of this youth even more.

Sondra spoke slowly, choosing her words with care. "In retrospect, maybe we both got off on the wrong foot. Though I wish you nay harm, you obviously have some reason to be angered at the church. We serve the people, as best we can, and that is why I came down here to serve you with food I personally prepared. My name is Sondra Oskires, acolyte of Ganden. I don't believe I caught your name last time."

Montanya found Sondra's abrupt change in nature amusing. Though she normally went by just her first name, she introduced herself with a self-important lilt. "I am Montanya su Troyeal bara Westenhout. It is a pleasure to meet your acquaintance."

The last comment dripped with sarcasm and insincerity, but Sondra forced a smile to her dark-red lips anyway. At least they weren't shouting anymore.

*     *     *     *     *

The others crowded around Revwar as he meticulously examined the designs marked on the floor of their shared cabin. Savannah, Jentan and Kemora stood armed and ready for a confrontation. The abbess of DeLaris wore in her religious armor, carrying the flail by her side. She held her skull-helm in her arms, absently caressing its features as she waited for the wizard to finish his examination. Jentan had little with which to arm himself, carrying only his dirk and the wand at his belt. The mentalist relied on his charm and powers of the mind when confronted with problems. Kemora fidgeted with her sword while sitting on the edge of the large bed. The disguise mask peeked over her belt. She wore her brown hair braided up and out of the way for the business yet to come, and though her stiletto remained in its sheath she had already disregarded several temptations to coat it with poison just in case it was needed. All their supplies were either on them or packed next to the circle inscribed on the floor. The three others waited with barely restrained patience as Revwar cast a critical eye over the spell laid out in a pattern of glyphs and runes. The elf wizard would not be rushed, considering that a mistake in scribing the spell circle could very well end up being the death of them.

Finally, the elf mage seemed satisfied the spell was drawn perfectly. He used his staff to rise to a standing position. "The teleportation inscription is complete. Once we have the prizes we can get back here and make our escape."

The other three practically jumped forward in readiness to be on with their task. Revwar held up a restraining finger in warning. "Do not forget! Once we get back, our timing will be critical. In order to expedite our chance of escape, I tied the spell that sets off the surprise in the inner sanctum into my staff. Once we get back here, I will place fingers to the appropriate runes on it and…well, you know how dangerous that will be."

The other three nodded, half-listening to the hum of the mantra running through the ship from the clerics inside the inner sanctum. When Revwar activated his surprise, there would be an abrupt disturbance in that miraculous power.

"We must be on this circle of runes when that happens, and I will combine the first spell with the words of transport that will take us off this vessel."

He didn't have to remind the others of the gravity of their situation, but the elf felt that a little reinforcement never hurt. Savannah donned her skull helm in preparation for their upcoming foray. Her cold, blue eyes stared out from within the hollow sockets of the DeLaris helm.

She spoke, "We have waited long enough to reclaim the holy relics. Let us go forth."

The band of four moved out into the hallway, heading for the chamber that displayed the two powerful stones.

## CHAPTER 15   **"An Unexpected Showdown"**

An almost inaudible click sounded as the lock gave way and the door guarding the entrance of the exhibit chamber swung open. Magical globes lit the chamber, shedding light on the two figures peering in from the hall. One of them, the half-elf infiltrator, bundled up her collection of slim lock picks and tucked them away. The human accompanying her tentatively reached a hand past the doorway, almost expecting a lightning bolt to lash out at them both. Noting that no one else was among the exhibits, the two cautiously entered and slid the door shut behind them.

"I'm surprised we got through that door without a magical trap frying us." Trestan whispered.

Cat shrugged, "We're on a flying vessel, so where would a thief escape with stolen goods? The doors may not have been trapped, but the magical items here will surely be warded."

Cat led the way through the displays of arcane oddities. Trestan followed closely, one hand on the hilt of his sword in case he needed to draw it quickly. A thumping noise caused them to pause, but both relaxed as they heard distant cheers and clapping.

Trestan cocked his head to one side. "Sounds like the show has started. Everyone must be on the decks enjoying it."

Cat flashed a sly smile back at Trestan. "Gives us more privacy. Also allows us to check the scroll without raising eyebrows from bystanders."

The companions navigated past several tables of items before they came to the holy relics. The stones sat undisturbed since the earlier visit, displayed under a case of thin glass. The leather scroll formed a backdrop of the exhibit, unfolded to display its letters to the curiosity of Orlaun's royalty. Trestan stared at the stones as he recalled all the troubles they had faced in recovering them. As he did, Cat reached into a pouch and withdrew the rune block.

Cat kneeled before the glass, keeping a respectful distance from its surface. "I'm sure Korrelothar and his wizards left some powerful magic on the case to prevent tampering. It won't prevent me from reading the writing on the scroll, if that is what this rune block does."

The adventuress went silent as she compared the block to the scroll. Trestan tried to look over her shoulder and read the scroll, but quickly gave up. Cat had taught him a good amount of Elvish, but verbal words only. Trestan wasn't as well-versed in the written language. The young squire began to look around the room as he patiently waited for Cat to say something.

"This works! I'm actually deciphering it!" Cat tried to keep her voice down, but she squealed in delight at solving a decades-old mystery.

Trestan smiled, "I thought that is what you said in our room?"

Cat shrugged, "Aye, but then I was only guessing. Now I know I was right!"

Trestan thought he heard something in the room. His attention drew to the crystal ball emanating eerie noises. The crystal let off eerie howls and whistles, making it hard to

146

discern other sounds. He wanted to blame it on that object, but he believed he heard a slight jingling noise coming from a different direction.

Cat spoke, "I translated the first sentence…"

"Shush." Trestan hissed. "Sorry to interrupt, but I hear something."

Her head turned to follow his gaze and tilted to concentrate on any sounds. Cat's gifted hearing detected the unmistakable clicks of a key entering the lock of one of the doors to the room.

She pointed to a different door than the one they had entered. "Someone is coming in that door."

The door began to open even as she finished speaking. The agile infiltrator dove into a roll behind some exhibit tables, slipping the rune block back into a pouch. Trestan stood in the open, wearing too much armor to dive silently behind anything. The champion of Abriana stood mutely, awaiting the unknown visitor to reveal himself.

The first man in the door wasn't anyone Trestan recognized. The middle-age human dressed in a way befitting a spellcaster, including a wand at his belt. Likely it was one of Korrelothar's guildmates, which would leave the companions with only questions to answer, as long as the man didn't cast first and ask questions later. The wizard's charming face looked up in surprise to see someone already inside the exhibit room. The man paused in mid-motion while putting away the key to the door.

The awkward silent moment did not last long. A small, female, halfling followed the caster into the room. When she spotted Trestan, she dove into a roll behind some tables much the same way Cat had done. Trestan looked back to assure himself Cat was there, but she'd already disappeared.

Trestan felt the yellow eyes of the elf wizard across the room as Revwar walked in the door. The champion of Abriana went weak in the knees at this unexpected arrival. The elf wizard's initial surprised look morphed into the most frighteningly evil of smiles. The first mage who had entered dropped the key where he stood, then side-stepped to give his companions room to enter. If Trestan had been afraid when Revwar had walked in, the appearance of the abbess Savannah in her dreadful black armor and skull helm set Trestan's heart racing.

There were no words of wit or bravery to be found as Trestan's voice remained silent. He had traveled this far following his duty to his goddess and his home, and now he unexpectedly confronted his old enemies while unprepared. He wondered if his training with the sword would be enough to defeat these foes in straight combat. With the possible exception of the halfling sneaking around somewhere in the room, the other three had considerable talent with magic. He assumed the human mage with the guild badge had been a part of the attack at Troutbrook. He matched Hebden's description. Even with Cat close by, he felt sorely outmatched.

Trestan drew forth the Sword of the Spirit. The enchanted metal blade whisked from the scabbard as he lifted it aloft with both hands. Revwar laughed in response, as the human mage closed the door to the hall behind them.

Savannah strode forward a couple paces, carrying her enchanted flail at her side. The weapon emanated shadow. The abbess showed neither amusement nor fear from

Trestan's sword. With urgency in her cold, blue eyes, she demanded, "Where is Petrow? He must be here with you! His life belongs to DeLaris!"

Stunned as he was with the sudden presence of his worst enemies, the unexpected question befuddled Trestan. "He is not here."

"He must be! I want him!"

"I'm sorry, you will not find him here." It occurred to Trestan he probably missed a chance to throw caution in their eyes by trying to make up a fast story. For all they knew, Petrow could be walking down to the exhibit room with a host of armed guards even at that moment, but Trestan was too off guard to concoct a convincing story. Instead, he pointed his sword in a more threatening manner at Savannah. "You will just have to deal with me, or walk out of here peacefully."

The middle-aged human accompanying them didn't seem intimidated at all. He put on a charming smile and stepped forward, coming even with Savannah. His face took on a friendly appearance, but Trestan looked at him more as if he were a coiled snake. The man spoke in a sweet tone, "Young sir, there is nay need for your sword. My guild's exhibits, including the one you seem ready to guard, are already laced with their own protections. Nay harm will come to them, but you should not be down here unescorted."

The mentalist acted as if the presence of all these people in the exhibit room during this hour wasn't unusual. As far as Trestan knew, the man was simply delaying so Revwar's party might deal with him more effectively:

Trestan's magical sword shifted slightly to point at the human mage. "I don't know you."

"Jentan Mollamos at your service." The man gave an impressive bow, cool and calm compared to the tension lingering in the air.

Trestan nodded, and then spoke with as much iron as he could muster. "But I do know them. They are not welcome here. This ship is under Korrelothar's protection and he would not consent to their presence. I have undertaken a quest to protect the stones behind me, and I do not take that obligation lightly."

Even as Trestan spoke, he listened for any sounds close by. He could almost feel the halfling sneaking closer. Even as Trestan faced off against a snake nest, he knew a dangerous viper was stealthily slithering around to surprise him. Even Revwar took a few steps to separate from the rest of his group in preparation for the expected.

"I am asking you once more to leave quietly," Abriana's champion demanded.

Trestan didn't think he stood a chance against them. He knew they would not be intimidated by his bravado. All his training had honed his muscles and his mind, but this loomed as tough of a challenge as he could have envisioned. In that moment, he had to drop the fear from his mind. He concentrated on his sword and the footwork he would need in order to avoid deadly spells. He couldn't linger on the evil of the faces before him…it would be time soon enough to simply react.

Jentan spoke strange syllables, his voice carrying a musical quality. The effect shattered before it began as Savannah elbowed past him, intent on Abriana's chosen. The room's light reflected off the nightmarish poses of death etched on her armor as she moved.

She set her flail into a lazy swing, leaving a visible trail in the air from the black glow on the head of it.

A small dagger tumbled through the air.

Jentan and Savannah had barely time to flinch as the sharp point carved a flight between them. The blade struck a gnomish contraption of unknown use on display. Jentan and Savannah saw the air waver in front of the device. Cat's dagger set off the magical trap guarding the gnomish device.

Lightning exploded in sudden fury from the table, sending sparks cascading across the two intruders. The others saw Jentan and Savannah spasm as they dropped to the floor. The two weren't seriously harmed by the blast, since Korrelothar's guild did not want any serious accidents to happen with so much royalty on board. However, the protective ward would hold immobile, for a time, anyone close when the trap went off. Charges of electricity danced about Jentan and Savannah, restraining their movement. Their eyes looked around wildly as they sought to escape their predicament. They couldn't get their limbs to work coherently. The abbess' flail rolled to one side, losing its magical darkness.

Revwar's few steps to the side probably saved him from getting caught up in the same blast. He flicked his braided silver hair over his shoulder as he twirled his staff. Six feet long, capped with a black marble stone with white swirls in a lightning pattern, the weapon extended taller than the wizard. A few fingers placed on the right carvings along the staff produced a magical light which solidified in front of him. A gesture with his hand, and the light flew amongst the tables where the dagger originated.

His aim proved too good for the half-elf's comfort. Cat took a few running steps from her hiding place and rolled behind another table as the light behind exploded. In the place where she had been, a spray of ice shards peppered the floor and ceiling. A layer of frost formed around that area.

Cat changed her mind about hiding behind the table with the howling crystal ball, thinking Revwar could set off a magical trap the same way she had done. She bounced to her feet with a throwing dagger at the ready, but Revwar was already casting the next spell.

Trestan's mindset wanted to charge down Revwar when the trap went off, but his senses alerted him to be wary of a different attack. Reacting more by instinct than anything else, Trestan sidestepped and spun around with the sword. The blade swept around in a deadly arc which could sever the torso of any attacker. The magical sword could cut through just about anything, thus Trestan felt no resistance as it connected with the halfling.

Although, at her height of three feet, five inches, Trestan only managed to cut through the bun of hair on top of her head.

Kemora Quickfeet only paused ever so briefly in shock as her loosened hair tumbled out of the bun. Many severed strands littered the floor. She moved forward with her domid-sized sword in one hand and the stiletto in the other. She attacked furiously. Trestan, off guard after his initial swipe, pulled his sword close and spun it with both hands to counter the halfling's jabs.

Kemora's sword slipped past Trestan's frantic blade. The breastplate deflected it harmlessly even as Trestan tried bringing his sword across. The halfling's opportunity did not last long. The young paladin could swing his two-handed sword very fast, spinning it in patterns that offered little opening. The defensive spin served him well, but he lacked ability to take initiative as the halfling stayed close and worked two blades at once.

Kemora could not match Trestan's reach. With her small size, she had every advantage if she stayed in so close that he could not effectively get a strong swing at her. With two weapons jabbing repeatedly, she left no opportunity for Trestan to break free and go on the offensive. Trestan, on the other hand, constantly moved back or dodged to one side.

It reminded Trestan of Sir Wilhelm fighting the minotaur back in Troutbrook. The man had stood toe-to-toe with that eight-foot monster, and yet the minotaur could not effectively fight him from so close. The monster's strength and reach lost advantage by the ferocity of the adjacent swordplay. This halfling rogue used similar tactics.

Trestan didn't miss seeing a wet gleam on the blade of the halfling's stiletto. All she needed was a scratch with that weapon and he could be finished.

Cat's arm cocked for a dagger throw, but at the same time Revwar's spell lit up from his hands. Both could well hit each other, as they had years ago, but the spell would likely be a lot more deadly than a thrown dagger. Cat twisted to one side instead, avoiding the same destructive beam that had nearly ended her life four years earlier. The magic blew a small hole into the far wall and two more walls beyond that.

Finding her feet again, Cat snapped the dagger into the air. Revwar watched it with little concern as the wizard dipped a hand into a pouch containing spell components. The dagger struck him in the chest, but the blade did not penetrate the robe. There was a slight 'tink' sound as it bounced away as if from solid rock.

"Like my new robe?" He asked, but gave no time for an answer as he whispered arcane words.

Cat wished she had her crossbow with her. It would be a deadlier ranged weapon than the throwing daggers. Too much distance remained between her and the wizard as she managed to advance several steps. The half-elf stayed ready to avoid the next spell.

Revwar's hands reached out into the air before him. With a magical command, he grabbed the air and began to pull it toward him with effort. Cat hadn't witnessed the spell when Revwar used it to unhorse Lady Shauntay and her guards in Troutbrook years earlier. The adventuress didn't see any obvious threats, but crashing noises started building behind her. Revwar created a magical chain from the air, an invisible band of force sliding toward her. The length of the unseen construct whipped across the floor, snapping the legs of exhibit tables and thus cutting a wide path of destruction as it toppled everything in its path. A tumult of magical energies unleashed as magical traps started going off in succession. Cat saw the danger and charged directly at the wizard. She tried to get to him before the invisible chain caught her.

She wasn't fast enough. The band of force whipped her legs from under her as tables and oddities crashed all around, setting off all their traps at once. Revwar lost sight of her amidst the tumbling debris, and the explosions of lightning, fire and ice.

*            *            *            *            *

The crowd on deck cheered as more thunderous booms were heard from the magical display in the night sky, some of the clamor even seemed to reverberate from the ship itself. The noise and carnage in the exhibit room paled amidst the booms of spells in the night sky. While the royalty enjoyed the show, another display of emotions took place below decks in the brig.

"Well I shouldn't expect a stuck up, holier-than-thou cleric to be interested in my petty concerns unless I put coins in their till, which I can't." Montanya's face was flushed with anger. "But I swear to you now, there is a thief on board this ship and only the fates know what she plans."

"I am not stuck up!" Sondra exclaimed, as the guard down the hall continued to watch and grin at the women's verbal sparring. "I dedicated my life to the service of people who don't care one wit about my own welfare or emotions! I could be enjoying the show of a lifetime on the deck. Instead, I chose to offer an act of kindness to a stranger."

The chiaso shot back, "Your god is the one who proclaims Honor, Duty and Service, so it comes with the territory doesn't it? I tried to be helpful to others and look what it brought me! I'm the one stuck behind bars while the real rogue wanders freely. I didn't ask for anyone's 'gift to the church' in exchange for my goodwill."

Sondra angrily shook her head in frustration at the way this red-haired woman repeated certain points over and over. "What makes you think the church is trying to do anything beyond covering the basic costs it needs to run? If your 'profession' is to wage some war against thieves, how will that support your income? How do you plan to make money in order to feed your stomach, or put a roof over your head? Do you plan to charge people or beg for charity?"

While the chiaso wouldn't want to admit it, the acolyte's observation struck a nerve. Montanya hadn't any idea how she could support herself, she had only focused on fulfilling oaths of revenge from her childhood. The woman did not want the pity of others nor did she like accepting any offerings.

After nothing was offered from the cell but silence, Sondra continued her own tirade. "In listening to your words, I am also wonder about your definition of the word 'thief'. It seems you place the label easily on people for almost any offense. I truly wonder by what standards you judge the term. A person is a thief because they took your parents, another is a thief because of some argument you had on the street, and I am a thief because I am somehow stealing your dignity by delivering you a meal!"

At the mention of the food, Sondra realized she was still standing outside of the cell of a hungry person, holding a meal that was becoming cold. With an awkward, embarrassed grace, she set the tray on the floor and pushed it through a space provided under the bars.

Montanya watched the tray slide to her feet. Her hunger overrode her pride at that moment, and she stooped to pick up the tray. She set it on the cell's bench, eyeing it hungrily but leaving it alone for a bit just to salvage some pride.

Her greenish-blue eyes stared past the bars as her face took on its usual scowl. "I'll eat the food because I have little other choice. Don't think I'll appreciate your church sending someone down here to mock me, even belittle me, while I stand helpless behind bars. For all I am concerned, you all deserve a thief in your ranks. As far as I know it might be another homeless person who won't suffer the indignity of a copper pen."

Sondra threw her arms up in exasperation. Mother Evine would probably agree that Sondra could have left the food and walked away at any time, leaving the stowaway to her own beliefs. "I'm sorry you feel that way. I did not come here to engage in an argument with you…"

The acolyte of Ganden shrieked as a splash of water assaulted her. Montanya watched her with an amused smirk, holding the now-empty cup Sondra had provided with the meal.

Montanya's tone was sarcastic, "And I am truly sorry to have you suffer the opinions of lesser people." She almost smiled as she added, "And hopefully Your Grace will forgive my little outburst there. If it makes you feel any better, it did bring some good feelings back to my heart."

Sondra looked down at the wet spots on her vestments as water dripped from her blonde hair. Her chest rose and fell repeatedly as she took several heated breaths. Her temper came to a boil. "Ganden must have forsaken me, if this is how I am treated when simply trying to serve ungrateful people!"

*       *       *       *       *

Trestan and Kemora tried to recover from the bright flashes and thunderous noises that had rocked the room. The young champion of Abriana looked awestruck at the damage done to the nearby exhibits. At a glance, there was no sign of his beloved among the carnage of broken tables.

He told himself to have faith and keep a warrior's concentration. He needed the courage to serve something greater than his own wants. A glance was all he allowed himself to take, for the halfling would quickly try to regain her close advantage. Kemora had no reason to glance over to see what her magically talented friends had wrought. She was quick to charge the more immediate threat.

She lost her advantage of close combat, since Trestan had the full length of his sword between them. He didn't push the attack in order to utilize one more strategy to counter the use of her two weapons. Although the hilt of Trestan's bastard sword could well accommodate two hands, the blade wasn't overly long or heavy, nor did it require a lot of strength to cut through enemies. Trestan wielded it one-handed, as his left hand dipped to his belt for the weapon still hanging there. He brought up the warhammer he had made in the seminary, on which he had modeled the head to look like that of a bull.

This time, Trestan chased Kemora. Elvish sword sparked against domid sword, while the warhammer kept ready to block any jabs of the stiletto. The human made use of his full reach as the halfling sought an opening.

Revwar kept his staff before him as he surveyed the cluster of broken tables. He finally spotted the half-elf, lying still and quiet amidst the ruin. He couldn't see all of her, just both leather-clad legs sticking out from the mess.

The elf turned his attention to his two helpless comrades. Jentan and Savannah still suffered bursts of electrical charges. The effect wouldn't last long, but the wizard preferred to expedite the process. He wove patterns in the air between both hands as the staff leaned against his shoulder. A web of black electricity enveloped the two subdued people, counteracting the remaining energy of the protective ward. All sparks died away as Jentan and Savannah stopped jerking erratically. The two breathed raggedly, though would soon get up under their own power.

The wizard watched Trestan and Kemora spar across the room, but the halfling would just have to take care of herself a little longer. She had lost her advantage against the tall human, but she kept up enough of a defense to keep away from his magical sword.

Revwar turned to approach the stricken half-elf. His yellow eyes kept a very cautious gaze on her as he moved to a better position. Cat seemed to be at least partially conscious, groaning as she tried to stretch one leg. Her black, leather outfit had a layer of some powder or dust on it. Her face had been blackened by a close call. Cat's left hand lay across her stomach, displaying a serious burn. She looked to have taken a painful beating but Revwar wasn't about to take chances. Her eyes opened slowly as she recalled her surroundings. Cat saw the elf wizard pointing a finger at her.

Revwar started casting a spell. The elf wizard stood several steps away from Cat, and she was near helpless on her back. Her right hand looked for something to grab and she found it. Cat hefted the howling crystal ball and pitched it at the wizard with a grunt. The protective enchantment that had once warded it had already gone off when the table collapsed underneath it.

Revwar's casting came to an abrupt stop as the glass globe hit him in the face. The magical item was not as durable as it had seemed. As it bounced to the floor, the impact cracked its surface. An irritating mist spewed out as the eerie noises left the device forever. Its magic formed a choking, nauseating cloud. For a moment, the elf wizard retched as he breathed in the fumes.

Cat got to her feet as quickly as her damaged body would allow. She kept her burned left hand cradled close to her torso. She realized that trying to run or take cover in any way would not help remedy their situation. In order to succeed, she had to charge the wizard. She drew her silver rapier and took up a stumbling run. Raven hair flying behind her, she gained some momentum after a few stumbling steps.

Revwar swung his staff across, but the agile adventuress ducked under it. She then led with the point of her sword. The tip hit the caster's robe and nearly brought her to an abrupt stop. The magical robe slowed the rapier, but her silver blade had an enchantment of its own. The point slowly drove past the robe and into flesh.

Revwar prepared to slam the woman with his staff. Cat was willing to take the hit in order to sink the blade deeper into the caster. She had forgotten how well the elf wizard enhanced his strength in the past. The staff hit her gut with enough force to send her flying away. She landed hard, losing her grip on her rapier and coughing up blood.

Trestan could not help her. He was at the limits of his fighting abilities against a halfling who was simply buying herself time with her movements. She couldn't get close enough to use the poisoned stiletto, but she could keep tiring Trestan until Jentan or Savannah recovered their feet.

Both of the fallen enemies were picking themselves up off the floor. Savannah crawled to where she could retrieve her flail, while Jentan sat up and glanced around the chamber.

Cat retrieved the rapier and got to her feet as Revwar charged her with his staff. Enough injuries lamed the half-elf that she had a hard time keeping her balance. She knew she couldn't begin to parry the staff with all the strength Revwar commanded. The elf caster whirled the weapon like a master. Cat backed up until she felt the edge of an exhibit table at her back. She barely glanced over her shoulder but recognized what stood behind her.

Revwar thrust the magical staff at her midsection. Cat dropped the rapier as she spun to the side, sucking in her gut at the same time. The adventuress grabbed the magical staff as it jabbed at her, nimble fingers feeling some of the symbols carved into its length. She used what strength she could to help guide it toward a target of her choosing.

The black crystal on the end of the staff struck the glass case holding the relic stones.

Magical energies flared along the shaft of the staff. The symbols under Cat's fingers lit up as a stored spell triggered. The prepared magical spell that Revwar had imbued in the staff went off with dangerous consequences, before the staff itself became consumed by flames. The trap guarding the relic also went off, sending out a force of energy that knocked Revwar and Cat sprawling.

Inside the inner sanctum, the clerics of Ganden focused in their meditations in order to speak the mantra that kept the ship aloft. They hadn't noted the incense chandelier, hanging above the cauldron of holy items, had changed somewhat since the beginning of the voyage. A few decorations had been added that seemed to be a perfectly natural part of the chandelier unless closely inspected. As Revwar's staff hit the relic exhibit, with Cat's fingers placed along certain runes, a destructive spell went off prematurely.

The incense chandelier exploded with terrible force.

As part of the surprise, two objects dropped from the chandelier into the cauldron: grave dust consecrated by an abbess of DeLaris, and a carved stone known as a scion of Mothrok. These items fell into the sacred waters dedicated to Ganden and came to rest alongside other holy items dedicated to the God of Duty.

These items had only been put there as a back-up plan, in case the initial surprise did not knock the vessel out of the sky. As it was, the blast of the chandelier sent wickedly twisted pieces of metal spinning out across the inner sanctum. The priests who had been in union humming the mantra of flight were interrupted as jagged projectiles lanced through several at once. A few immediately dropped dead, while others opened their eyes in surprise to see robes turning red with their own blood. A stunned silence interrupted the prayer.

In the absence of the mantra, *Doranil Star* began to freefall toward the clouds below.

**CHAPTER 16**  "Panic and Chaos Spread"

His light-blue eyes stared, entranced by the spell show dancing in the night sky. Lindon held his hat at his side, not wanting the wide brim to obscure any of the arcane details displayed across the heavens. The long, red sideburns of his beard framed a wide smile. He had seen fiery dragons chasing griffons made of blue ice. Explosions of noise and flame lit the sky to symbolize some great aerial battle. Illusions on a giant scale played out over the heads of Orlaun's nobility. Surely this was a night he would never forget!

Lindon's thoughts turned out to be truer than he would have guessed. Amidst all the laughter and delight came a sudden interruption. The minstrel felt it before anyone else. He had been attuned to the background chanting reverberating through the ship. When the mantra abruptly silenced, Lindon realized its absence a split second before the repercussion manifested.

The ship dropped out from under everyone's feet.

It was an odd sight from the deck, as the deck itself didn't seem to move. Everyone lost their footing as they fell away from the stars and from the flickering remnants of the sky display. Lindon stood near one of the rails at the side of the ship when he felt weightless. He drifted up from the deck a few feet before he could cling to the rope netting running to the masts.

The screams from over a hundred throats joined the rushing noise of the wind. Wisps of clouds swirled about and were lost above them as they plunged. The ship did not fall straight, starting to roll slightly toward one side. Lindon looked upward from the rope work, noticing loose clothing items such as hats, scarves, and cloaks flying ownerless in the sky. It seemed that a great wind had thrown them up from the deck, but the reality of the vessel's fall was not misunderstood by anyone. Orlaun's nobles and rich merchants were helpless as they slid across the deck or tumbled in the air a few feet above it.

Lindon's mind recalled the great aerial battles told about the Godswars. He knew that many such great vessels were knocked from the sky at great altitudes, leaving warriors to fall to their deaths from the clouds. This was what it must have been like to be on such a ship as it was defeated in the air: the rush of wind roaring past, ripping of cloth masts, screams as people panicked. A fate culminating at the moment when the great vessel crashed into foreign lands below it.

Since Lindon was the first to hear the mantra fade, he was also the first to hear a solitary voice resurrect the missing prayer to Ganden. Urgent and strong, that lone voice hummed from the inner sanctum. Another voice, weak but insistent, joined the first. A new mantra ran through the hull of the ship. Lindon felt a third voice join in the chorus. As the mantra began anew, the *Doranil Star* began to halt its fall. The ship leveled out as voices brought its descent under control.

Lindon felt the sensation of weight return as the deck slowed. The minstrel let out a slight whistle as he let go of the ropes. Magic tapped from the harmonic web laced the tune. Lindon levitated gracefully back down to the deck, while others around him dropped to the hard wood in a painful manner. He also used his voice to affect the fall of his plumed hat. With a flourish, he caught the wide red brim and settled it neatly upon his head. Most of the people lie sprawled out across the deck. Some were frozen in a state of shock, while others sought to grab any portion of the vessel that offered a handhold. Only a few others from the hosting mage guild were able to also cast levitation spells to settle gracefully back on the deck.

Not all were so lucky. Lindon did not have the magic in his voice to save some others that missed the deck when it regained its buoyancy. The minstrel watched helplessly as a few flailing people dropped beyond reach of the railings. They tumbled away from the ship, leaving nothing but lingering screams riding the nighttime air. The ship still floated above a layer of clouds that hid the land below, thus Lindon watched those people fall against that gray backdrop until they disappeared into the mist.

The minstrel was thankful that the mantra had resumed and saved them all from a deadly plummet. At the same time, he wondered if this was only a momentary respite from any threat that still lingered. What had caused the vessel to fail, and were they only moments away from a more catastrophic plunge?

*      *      *      *      *

"What was that?" Montanya asked from a sprawled position in the back of her cell. The wide-eyed chiaso absently rubbed a sore spot from when her shoulder hit the ceiling.

Sondra didn't have an immediate answer. The blonde acolyte untangled herself from her own limbs a few feet down the hall. Smoothing her disarrayed vestments, the young woman glanced down the hall toward the guard. The man had collapsed, knocked unconscious from a head injury.

"The mantra was interrupted; I fear something dreadful may have happened." The acolyte spoke absently, thinking out loud more than responding to the stowaway. Sondra attuned her ears to the humming noise coming from the deck. She could hear how weak the new mantra sounded. "Something is wrong with the voices of the Chosen, as if only a few of them are still able to chant the prayers."

As Sondra unsteadily got to her feet, Montanya did the same. The cleric realized that a chain around her neck had slipped above her collar when tossed about. Montanya noticed Sondra tucking away a metal symbol, shaped like a dog's form, but was not interested in asking about it at the time. The chiaso brushed away the remnants of food that had spattered her clothes. Sondra, still dripping water from being splashed by the woman earlier, wasn't in the mood to feel any satisfaction upon seeing the stowaway get what she deserved.

Montanya had a different set to her face than before. While she normally scowled at everyone and everything, her expression had been replaced by abstract terror. The red-haired woman came right up to the bars. "Is that going to happen again? Are we going to fall?"

Sondra shrugged her shoulders, a response that did nothing to assuage the chiaso's fears. The acolyte commented, "I must get to the inner sanctum at once and find out what happened. They may need me."

The faithful of Ganden edged past the cell, staying well out of reach of the woman inside. She was brought up short by a frantic plea from behind.

"Wait!"

Sondra looked back at the frightened woman still locked in her cell. Montanya, who rarely begged or ask for charity from anyone, was terrified enough to throw away her pride.

The imprisoned woman slapped the bars of her cell helplessly. "Let me out of here. I don't want to be trapped in a locked cell if something else happens." With great effort, she added, "Please."

Sondra opened her mouth to reply, but paused. Montanya watched as the acolyte's eyes seemed to focus in concern on something.

Sondra wore a look of confusion when she thought out loud, "Why is there rust on the bars?"

Montanya glanced at the iron bars of the cell, noting a few small patches of rust. She absently ran a fingernail over one such spot. "It's an old ship. Why? What else do I need to be worried about?"

The faithful of Ganden cocked her head to one side as she stared at the bars. "It's well over a thousand years old. All the metal, all the wood, is from another age. However, this is a divine chariot blessed by my god and wrapped in its own magic. It isn't supposed to rust."

Sondra was backing away from the cell, heading back toward the exit when Montanya made one more plea. "Don't leave me here. I beg you!"

The acolyte glanced at the unconscious guard, and then back to the ill-tempered occupant of the cell. "It is beyond me. I'll ask the elders if someone can come back to get you out. I have to go do my duty."

The chiaso heard the words of a healing prayer spoken as Sondra knelt beside the guard. The acolyte healed the head injury, and then headed for the door as the guard stirred.

"Nay!" Montanya shouted, but the cleric already disappeared down the hall. In frustration, the martial arts student stepped back and kicked the unyielding metallic lock. "Curse you, cleric!"

*      *      *      *      *

The exhibit room lie in shambles. The abrupt fall had managed to set off all the remaining traps and wards protecting the exhibits inside the room. Light shed by magical sconces still illuminated the wrecked chamber. Other light sources included tables and cloth set aflame by the explosions. A good part of the ceiling and floor had been blackened. Parts of the floor had splintered and fallen away to the next deck below. Everyone inside the room had been tossed around when the vessel had dropped.

Trestan regained his senses after feeling as if he'd rolled down a hill in a barrel. He kept awareness of the danger to Cat and himself. First, he had to stop his head from spinning. His dizzy eyes finally found focus just in time to react to a threat. A deadly blade swept at him. His right arm, the elvish sword absent, reached out and caught the halfling's arm before the poisoned stiletto could reach him. Kemora lie pinned under him, straining against his strength to force the blade forward. Trestan had no qualms about hitting a smaller woman attempting to stab him with poison. Abriana's champion still held the warhammer in his left hand. He cracked across the side of the domid's head. Kemora's pupils rolled up past her descending eyelids as the stiletto dropped from a limp hand.

Trestan dazedly climbed to his feet. The haze of smoke filled the room. Beyond, he could see shapes as his enemies staggered. Even with the halfling possibly dead or severely injured, the rest were more than he and Cat could handle. Trestan spotted the Sword of the Spirit on the floor, and attempted an uneven run to retrieve it.

Cat's sensitive ears were ringing with the sound of bells as she coughed up more blood. She painfully lifted her head up to spot what was left of the relic table. She saw at least one of the stones rolling around on the floor a good distance away. Nearby, flames flickered on Revwar's broken staff. The half-elf tried to move, but even turning her head required a good effort.

She saw the scroll from the relic case lying within reach on the floor. There was no mistaking the skin it was written on. Katressa's left hand was burned beyond use. Withholding a grunt from the effort, she reached out her right hand and seized the prize. Aware of movement in the smoke around her, her right hand quickly rolled it up and tucked the scroll into her belt.

Cat struggled to rise. She had her eyes on the relic stone several steps away. Though her hearing suffered, she sensed Revwar staggering to his feet off to one side. A glint of silver in a pile of debris caught her attention. She spotted the cat's-head pommel partially visible amidst a pair of broken table legs. A few uneven steps carried her to the rapier. She felt safer when her fingers wrapped around the hilt.

Revwar materialized out of the smoke with one of the relics in his hands. The other hand glowed with the power of a spell as he spoke an incantation. The elf wizard and the half-elf infiltrator were within a few steps of each other. Cat dodged toward the spellcaster.

His hand spewed forth a colorful greenish fire. Cat sidestepped so dramatically that she lost her balance. The effort did not lack retribution, however, as the rapier slashed across the wizard's face. Cat landed hard on her rump, aware of a greenish glow behind her where the spell lit up more debris.

Revwar jerked back reflexively, his cheek bleeding from a thin line. Enraged, the wizard did not pause long. With Cat sitting on the ground next to him, there was no time to properly prepare another spell. He reacted with the physical strength an earlier spell granted him. Using muscles in a way that could only be enhanced by magic, he reached down with his single hand and picked Cat up by her collar. The elf wizard spun in a half circle, flinging her body away from him as if throwing a doll.

Trestan ran through the smoky haze to find his love. He led with his sword, the warhammer tucked into his belt. With the brief opportunity he had, the paladin used a prayer to Abriana to fashion a shield from a miracle. A somewhat translucent, glowing disc moved with his left arm without straps of any kind holding it in place. The prayer shield would not have helped against a blade such as Kemora's; it was designed as a guard against magic. He thought it might prove useful as he sprinted through the gloom. The human saw the green fire highlight where Revwar and Katressa fought.

On the way to aid his beloved, he caught sight of Savannah off to his side. The abbess of DeLaris formed a miracle, harnessing dark energies from the surrounding air. Trestan continued to run past her, but raised his shield as the prayer finished. A ball colored like the darkest night flew at the young warrior. The blackness hit the glowing shield, causing both to vanish suddenly. The shield had served its purpose, deflecting one threatening spell before it lost its form.

Trestan halted as Cat's body tumbled to the deck in front of his feet. His heart nearly caught in his throat when he saw how hurt she looked. Abriana's champion kneeled and patted her shoulder. "Cat? Are you with me? We must get out of here!"

Trestan gave up hope of recovering the relic stones in the face of his remaining foes. He managed to help Cat get to her feet, but she was quite shaken. All that seemed to matter at that moment was escaping with their lives intact. Cat could do nothing to offer any assistance of her own. The half-elf leaned all her weight on his supportive embrace.

Revwar came out of the smoke from one side, holding both relics in one arm, while his other readied another spell. Savannah now stood behind Trestan, swinging her darkly glowing flail while she also started a prayer. From a third direction Jentan appeared out of the smoke with a wand in hand. All three were moving in with an arsenal of magic at their disposal.

At that critical moment, Trestan stepped backward and nearly lost his footing. The floor of the deck had also been damaged with all the spell traps being ignited. Trestan's foot rested on a cracked plank that dipped precariously with his weight. The paladin-aspirant looked at the broken floor and saw light seeping from the deck below him.

Trestan dragged Cat another step onto the weakened floor. The wood groaned in protest under the added weight. With three spells about to be launched from different directions, Trestan held Cat close as he brought his sword high. He then swept the magical blade down at his feet.

The sword did enough to finish the damage that was already wrought. Severed planks gave way, dropping Trestan and Cat down to the next deck. Cat's rapier also fell through the opening, nearly adding to their injuries. He did his best to cushion her fall, and looked up to witness what they had narrowly missed. A light show of magical carnage lit the open space above where they had just been standing.

Aching from his own hurts, Trestan acted quickly. He had no plans to stay underneath the opening in case some fiery spell was launched through it. After sheathing his blade and Cat's sword, he leaned down and picked up Cat again. She made no words, only groaned as he set her over his shoulders and carried her down the new passageway.

*      *      *      *      *

Kemora returned from beyond a wall of deep pain. Warmth spread from her face down into her body. She welcomed the sensation. The domid's consciousness drifted toward that alluring feeling. As she became conscious, weariness returned as well as the bad air of smoke. She coughed as she opened her eyes to the world. The cold, blue eyes of Savannah hovered over her, watching her from behind the skull mask. The cleric held the side of

Kemora's head. The halfling couldn't remember what had hit her, but apparently Savannah had healed the damage.

She sat up on her own and looked around. Savannah moved on to their elf wizard as the domid saw the damage around them. Smoke hung like a heavy drape over the piles of shattered wood.

"Leave it be, it is but a scratch." Revwar gently pushed Savannah's hand away.

Kemora noticed the blood on the elf wizard's face, drawn from a line in his cheek. "Looks like more than a scratch to me."

Revwar turned to regard her with his yellow eyes. "We have nay time to lick our wounds, lest we suffer a worse loss."

Kemora got to her feet. The wizard placed the two green relic stones inside a simple cloth bag. He then tied the bag and tucked it into his belt. It relieved the halfling, that after all that effort and trouble, the stones were finally in their hands. The worst seemed over.

Revwar's voice stopped them all short. "The staff was destroyed, and in the process the surprise went off. We all felt the ship fall." All of them unconsciously turned their ears toward the weak mantra still keeping the ship aloft. Revwar continued speaking, "It is well and good that Ganden's clerics are so adept at recovering after such a catastrophe…but then that's why we included the second surprise."

The eyes of his companions widened one by one as they realized the implications. Revwar continued, "The items Kemora and Jentan placed would have dropped into the cauldron. The corruption of the holy cauldron by sacred items of DeLaris and Mothrok will cause a severe decay of this vessel until there is nothing left to fly. We have to move quickly to get back to our room, and use the teleport spell to abandon this ship."

Revwar looked down at the hole by which Trestan and Cat had dropped through earlier. At the edges of the wood, he could see the early signs of rot already progressing.

*       *       *       *       *

Korrelothar raised his hands to quiet the emotional people blocking the deck. "Stay calm, focus on calm, everyone. The vessel has resumed its normal flight. Permit me to pass and I shall get answers for you, but do not give in to panic."

The elf mage tried to soothe others as best he could while moving through a sea of questions. Some of the nobles were demanding answers he could not give. Several more gripped parts of the ship with pale knuckles, as if holding on to it would save them if it dropped again. Some people were lying on the deck, recovering from injuries sustained after the brief fall. Here and there, they heard the anguished cries from people who saw loved ones fall overboard to their deaths. Through it all, Korrelothar tried to hide his own confusion and fright. The mage insistently cut a path through the crowd to find answers.

Amidst the crowd, one other man forced his own path, using a few bodyguards to assist him. Korrelothar let out a sigh when he saw the man angling directly toward him. This was an official that would not be put aside so easily. Dressed lavishly and surrounded by many guards, all in Orlaun paid homage to this man. Without the king of Gheras attending

160

the flight, citing safety reasons, the most important official on board was the one that ruled the province in which Orlaun resided. Duke MigRelke cut a path straight at Korrelothar.

Imposing himself before the mage, he looked down at the elf, "I want answers."

Korrelothar gave a humble bow. "You will get them as soon as I have them, my lord. I would appreciate if your guards can assist me in getting to the helm castle, where I might hope to find the reason for our plunge, and ascertain our questions of safety."

Behind the brute muscle of the duke's bodyguards, Korrelothar walked quickly to the middle of the ship. He found more confusion and questions once arriving at the helm castle. The first thing frighteningly apparent was the loss of the cleric that manned the helm. The faithful of Ganden that helped guide from the top deck had met with an unfortunate accident during the fall. Of the many weapons that were propped upright around the helm castle to repel anyone trying to wrest control of the ship, one spear had pierced the cleric at the conclusion of the vessel's plunge. Korrelothar noted one of the crew attempting to talk to the inner sanctum using the tube that ran down to the room.

The wizard walked up to the crewman. "What have you learned from the inner sanctum? Are we still in danger?"

The officer stood back helplessly, motioning to the metal tube and offering Korrelothar a try. "None down there have replied. We can hear only a few voices keeping the mantra from fading, but there has been nay answer to our inquiries. We're concerned at how weak and forced their voices sound as they chant."

He did his best to hide his worries from appearing on his expression. Too many people stared at him, and they were on the verge of hysteria. "I must go to the inner sanctum myself and see what has happened." He whispered quietly to the duke, "We may not be safe just yet."

*      *      *      *      *

Warm, healing energies flowed into Cat's battered form. She could feel the love in Trestan's touch as his prayer enveloped her. As a champion of the Goddess of Love and Healing, he had learned to expand his gift of curative powers in the time spent at the seminary. Although he could not hope to do as well as most clerics who focused on such arts, it proved enough to heal Cat's burned hand and restore vitality to her body. The half-elf opened her eyes to see him sag against the far wall. The flow of his goddess' energies left him momentarily weak; nevertheless, Trestan offered a weary smile. He had once told her that healing others helped reinvigorate his own soul, even though it seemed to weaken his muscles temporarily.

Cat's own smile faded as she remembered the end of the battle. "They took the relics, didn't they?"

Trestan nodded. "We're all on a flying ship, so I don't know how they would escape. Then again, I wonder what happened that the whole ship lurched so suddenly?"

"They didn't get everything." Cat patted the rolled-up skin tucked in her belt. "But they got what they most sought after, I guess. As far as the ship dropping, I barely recall it." The half-elf's fine brow lowered as she tried to remember hazy events. "Right before it dropped, I shoved Revwar's staff into the trap protecting the relic stones. The staff lit up terribly and burst into flames, but I was sent reeling from some explosion around the relics. I had the lingering sensation of falling toward the ceiling before hitting the floor again."

Trestan may still have been weak, but he pulled himself upright and stood tall. He reached down and helped Cat to her feet. Cat felt nearly free of pain and injury after his miracle. Trestan scanned the dimly lit hall. Disoriented, they started moving to find their way. The passageways were empty since most everyone had been on deck. Eventually, the sound of someone's running feet were heard from the dimness ahead. A young, blonde woman, wearing the vestments of an acolyte of Ganden, skidded to a halt in front of them.

Trestan held out a hand in her path, not directly blocking it but motioning her to stay. "Honorable of Ganden," he addressed her before she could run past, "What just happened to the ship?"

Sondra's blue eyes studied them intensely for a moment. Her attention lingered on the symbols of Abriana etched into Trestan's self-crafted armor. She almost whispered when she spoke. As often as Sondra tried to help people, she never could express herself well, especially around bold people.

"I don't know. I felt something bad has happened…I'm on my way to the inner sanctum now to find out."

Cat hesitantly decided she should add a warning before the woman ran to the holy center of the ship. "We had a bad encounter with some people who were trying to steal some of the mage guild's treasures from the exhibit room. It's a group of troublemakers we have encountered before." Cat paused slightly to better phrase the next sentence, feeling guilty thinking that whatever she had done to Revwar's staff had helped bring about the ship's momentary plunge. "They may have done something to sabotage the ship, for it dropped just as they were stealing certain magic items from that room."

Sondra's eyes widened. "Some type of sabotage? That might explain the rust and the rot."

"What?" Trestan and Cat said at once.

The acolyte of Ganden bit her lip, realizing she spoke too much out loud. It was too late to deny what she had said. She pointed to a metal bracket in the hall which held a magically burning lamp. "All the metal on the ship has shown signs of rusting, and I saw some rotted planks. This ship exists by will of a divine being; it shouldn't be degrading like this."

Trestan and Cat saw a large amount of rust on the bracket. The young paladin reached up and picked at a splinter in the nearby wood. The soft splinter broke easily.

Cat whispered to Trestan, though it was loud enough for Sondra to hear. "What could they be doing? Aren't they trapped on this vessel, flying high in the skies with us?"

Abriana's champion shook his head. "Their spell went off unexpectedly, remember? They probably have an escape plan, but we likely messed up their timing. I think they intended to bring this divine chariot down to hide their theft, though there could be other reasons. Either way we have two problems: they have the relics, and the vessel is slowly being destroyed."

Sondra gasped. "I must get to the inner sanctum fast and see what I can do."

The acolyte started to rush past them but brought herself up short before she had gone more than a couple steps. She whirled around and put a pleading hand on Trestan's arm. "I just remembered something, maybe you can take care of it."

Sondra pointed past their questioning looks to the hallway from which she had come. "The brig is down there. There is a woman held inside one of the cells, named Montanya. She isn't the nicest person, but she doesn't deserve to be trapped in there in light of the danger. I told her I'd try to get help for her, but I may have my hands full once I get up top."

Trestan and Cat shared a questioning look, holding a private conversation with their eyes. The warrior of Abriana turned and patted Sondra's hand, which was still on his arm. "We'll try to see what we can do for her."

Trestan paused to add, "One more thing. One of the thieves stealing the exhibits is a mage from the Brotherhood of the Circles. His name is Jentan Mollamcs. If you see any other members from his guild, you must warn them about their traitor."

The two companions weren't about to waste time. Trestan and Cat raced down the hallway.

Sondra turned and resumed her path toward the top decks. The cleric found stairwells and jumped them two steps at a time. She winced every time she heard the steps groan in complaint. The woman ran until breathless. The main thought hammering inside her brain was to get alongside her brothers and sisters as fast as possible.

She took one slight detour. She burst into the cabins reserved for her and the rest of the clergy. No one was there. All the priests had been in the inner sanctum or present on the top deck. Sondra rushed to the ornate box sitting beside her bunk. She nearly ripped a nail in the hurry of flipping the latch open.

One of the items inside the box was her rust-colored leather satchel. It held numerous items she needed for the channeling of miracles or the care of wounds. Her healing kits and bandages were all stored in the satchel. After claiming it, her hand reached in once more to get the other personal item she had. She slipped the iron mace into a strap on her belt. For some unknown reason, she also decided to grab her ceremonial attire after a slight pause. The clothes were in a bag, which she simply hung on her back.

The young cleric charged from the room and down the halls. There were other people milling about the passageways, sharing several heated or fearful discussions regarding the fall. She saw one other young cleric of Ganden, but he was busy healing someone's head wound. A few of the nobility spoke derogatory remarks about the mage guild and the whole endeavor. Some wiped tears from their eyes over the tragedy of those who fell overboard. Sondra brushed by all of them, offering brief apologies as she concentrated on getting to her goal.

Few people stood anywhere near the inner sanctum. Sondra approached one of the doors to the chamber in a rush. The young woman heard the mantra being chanted inside. The voices sounded weak, and no more than three of the Chosen still sang. She grabbed the door handle and rushed in.

The wooden door opened most of the way before thudding against a dead body on the floor. Sondra's first step landed in a standing pool of blood. She almost retched at the sight before her. As it was, she brought a hand up to cover her gaping mouth, as she stared into the defiled room with a horrified expression.

**CHAPTER 17**             **"The Sacrifice of the Chosen"**

"The training the Chosen endure to reach their post is long and arduous. They are expected to keep the mantra going despite any distractions or extreme conditions, for the safety of all those on board." Mother Evine said to the elf wizard in the inner sanctum. The cleric swept a hand out to indicate the damage done to the room. "We are fortunate indeed for these selfless followers of Ganden who survived and found the strength to resume the mantra."

Sondra barely heard the words from her teacher, instead focusing on the horror inside the door. Her eyes, no strangers to bloody wounds, looked onward with renewed loss of innocence. The shock of the scene muddled her thoughts. She took a few hesitant steps out of the hall, getting closer to the bodies even though the sights brought revulsion. The door she held pushed against the body of a former teacher. She let go of it, allowing the dead body to limply relax to its original position.

Across the room, near the far exit, Mother Evine addressed Korrelothar and a small audience. They studied the same horrors that disgusted Sondra. The incense chandelier had been reduced to a blackened mark on the ceiling. The chamber, formerly rather bare except for the cauldron and the sitting pillows, was now a mess of blood and corpses. Several Chosen of Ganden died immediately in the explosion. Their bodies lie twisted in disarray near the stained, fine pillows on which they had been kneeling. Sightless faces remained frozen in shock. The gray ceremonial vestments lined with white trim had been torn by the jagged metal fragments and darkened by the flow from the mortal wounds. The vessel's plunge had scattered the wet blood and the bodies of the fallen. Splashes of red marked the walls and the ceiling.

The cauldron of holy water seethed with its own inner turmoil. The surface bubbled as if boiling, though nothing heated it. The water had turned a dark color, tinged with crimson.

Three surviving members of the Chosen still ringed the cauldron, tended by a couple lesser clerics of Ganden. Only one of the Chosen continued chanting while sitting upright, though his garments were stained with his own blood. After his voice had restarted the mantra, saving them all, Mother Evine arrived to heal his injuries. The other two chanting Chosen prayed from supine positions, as a priest and an acolyte fussed over their injuries. The weak mantra emanating from these two underlined the continued seriousness of their situation. Despite all healing efforts, they were dying. Rivers of red ran stained their soaked vestments. The Chosen expended a lot of energy through their prayers to keep the vessel aloft with only their meager voices. The mantra weakened as they did. These clerics of Ganden fought a losing battle to keep the ship alive.

"The *Doranil Star* is still in great danger, I can see that." Korrelothar stated. "We owe our lives to these brave pilots, but the peril persists. We need to get everyone to safety. Maybe we can find a place to guide the divine chariot to a soft landing."

Mother Evine shook her head sadly. "Korrelothar, I'm afraid it would not be a soft landing with the Chosen in the state they are now. Worse yet, something seems to have contaminated the cauldron. I have sensed a…for lack of a better description…a sickness within the vessel."

Sondra murmured, "Mother Evine? If I may?"

The older cleric looked across the room, seeing her frightened pupil for the first time. Mother Evine would know Sondra's shy tendencies, and that she would have something important to say if it interrupted these officials. Sondra's words felt like a quivering whisper that barely carried across the chamber.

"Aye, Acolyte Sondra?"

Sondra had a hard time phrasing her message, especially in the light of the eyes of the elf wizard looking at her. It wasn't that he glared or seemed insulted by her audacity to speak. Instead, he offered a look that inspired her to give her best answer. Korrelothar, a wizard who could rightfully stand well above her station, looked to her as an equal.

Sondra spoke, "Someone appears to have sabotaged the cauldron."

Mother Evine and Korrelothar fixed her with such intensity that the young cleric felt a lump blocking her throat. Her mentor interrupted the silence. "Speak plainly, how do you know this?"

"I ran into two people below decks. They said a group of villains were out to steal something from the mage guild, some exhibit." Sondra could feel Korrelothar's interested eyes staring at her, but she avoided direct eye contact. She couldn't turn her eyes downward, for then her vision took in the stricken poses of former teachers. Her gaze locked onto Mother Evine's vestments. "They fought these villains, but apparently lost. These two people mentioned something akin to, 'They have the relics,' and said that the ship dropped as this other group stole from the exhibit chamber."

The elf wizard interrupted as Sondra paused. "Describe the two people who told you this."

"One was a young warrior, wearing the emblems of Abriana, muscular and with a thick mustache. The other was an elf woman, black hair, wearing dark leathers."

Korrelothar nodded at her description. "Trestan and Katressa, I know them. Anything else?"

Sondra continued. "They said one of your own was a traitor helping the thieves. His name was…let me think. Jentar Mollaman or such?"

"Jentan Mollamos," Korrelothar clarified, even as his fists clenched over the news.

Mother Evine interrupted, "In what way did they sabotage the ship? Other than this…catastrophe?" The older cleric motioned to the damage done to the inner sanctum.

"I don't know specifically, but look at the rust forming on the cauldron itself." Mother Evine gasped at the brown splotches visible on the most holy of receptacles. Sondra continued, "All of the metal on the ship is rusting, and the wood is rotting away at a fast rate. I'm afraid something is decaying the vessel."

The elder cleric put her hands against the wall of the chamber and murmured a prayer. In her hands, she rolled a holy symbol of Ganden between her fingers. Her hand recoiled from the wall as her prayer ended. "I sense the weakness within the vessel spreading. Even if the divine chariot could make it to the ground soon, it would collapse under its own weight."

Korrelothar's pale skin lost a shade of color. "What about the life boats?"

Evine answered, "They are separate entities. They were made as such in case anything happened to the vessel they could still serve in their capacity as escape skiffs. They don't even require a cleric of Ganden. Even without one of faith at the controls, the levitation boats will simply float easily to the ground below."

The elf wizard looked to the dying pilots. "How much time do we have?"

Even as he spoke the words, the most grievously wounded Chosen lost the rhythm of the mantra in a bout of coughing. Mother Evine watched as the other cleric and his acolyte assistant tried to stem the flow from the man's wounds with cloth. All the power behind their miracles had been exhausted. The caregivers proved too weary to channel more miracles. "I can't tell. We fly only by the faith of two. We will not stay aloft long. After over a millennium of service, *Doranil Star* is likely seeing her last hour, before she meets her final fate on the ground below."

Those words ripped at Sondra's heart. She knew her church shouldn't be so prideful about this holiest of creations, yet how could she look upon it with anything other than pride? This vessel had been a sacred source of accomplishment and achievement within her church. The mages may have taken care of it, but the vessel belonged to their god  She had dared to dream of being one of the Chosen directing the ship across the skies. Instead, she would face the shame of being powerless to rescue this glorious creation before it met its end.

Korrelothar turned to the elder cleric. "Such a precious artifact this ship has been. Long had I marveled at it. It's unbearable to think of losing it. My endless thanks for the sacrifice of your brethren in the service of this vessel, though those feelings seem paltry as they continue to shed blood to save us. I must get Orlaun's nobility to abandon the ship before the time runs out."

"We will buy you what time we can to save the others," Mother Evine replied with a resigned look upon her face.

To Sondra, Mother Evine's tone sounded like the acceptance of a death sentence. Korrelothar departed with a low, very respectful, bow. The other high-ranking officers of the ship left alongside the elf mage. The whole time, Sondra could not take her eyes off those of Mother Evine. The acolyte could read the bleak future reflected in those eyes. Evine's fate loomed before her with the pull of a raging river.

The door on the other side of the room fell shut as the last of the officers left, slamming with a clarity that made Sondra's mentor flinch.

The weakest of the remaining three Chosen died. The cleric and acolyte working over the man covered his face with a bloody cloth and moved to assist the other whose health remained perilous. Two voices retained the power of the mantra, but one rasped weakly. Sweat soaked the vestments of the upright Chosen. His mind, fixated on the importance of the mantra, left him unaware of anything else happening in the room. Sondra could only be in awe that his faith had kept them stable for so long.

Mother Evine resolutely walked over to one of the stained cushions and began to kneel on top of it, facing the churning cauldron. "Acolytes please leave  Get to the life boats and continue to serve Ganden well in the years to come."

Sondra froze with denial as she stared at her mentor's sacrifice. The other acolyte also hesitated. The ordained priest in the gray-lined vestments beside her spoke a few comforting words, before gently pushing her away. Younger than Sondra by a few years, she tearfully stumbled out of the chamber by way of the door Korrelothar had used. The older priest resumed tending the stricken Chosen hovering on death's door.

"I don't want to go," Sondra nearly whispered to the floor. "I can help by taking my place by your side. I know the words of the mantra."

"Go my child…my sister in faith," Mother Evine spoke with firm compassion. "I have already been training as a future Chosen, and I know the concentration required. You can't help me in this. It would only lead to your senseless death."

Sondra shook her head as tears spilled down her cheeks. Mother Evine spoke more forcefully. "Go, Acolyte Sondra. You are still young in the service of Ganden. Do not lament what is lost; always look forward to what you can save. You will someday find the beacon of strength that lies in your own heart. You will learn the uninhibited joy of being able to help others, as well as the self-respect that comes with honor. May Ganden serve you well."

"May Ganden serve you well," Sondra replied in the customary fashion.

The wheat-blonde acolyte took a few slow steps backward, into the hall. The two remaining Chosen of Ganden continued singing their prayer mantra for the lives of those on board, even though one tenaciously clung to life. The healing offered by the other ordained priest could not save him. Miracles couldn't replace lost blood. Sondra took one last glimpse of Mother Evine sitting peacefully upon a red-stained cushion beside the cauldron.

When the door had softly closed, she found it hard to turn away. Sondra listened as a female tone rose to join in with the fading mantra. She listened to the words of prayer being chanted by the strong voices from inside. The acolyte felt their power rumble through the length of the great vessel. Mother Evine's voice would be a part of the divine chariot now, until the end came. Sondra idly wondered how often any of the pompous royalty on board ever stopped to simply lend an ear to the rhythm of Ganden. Such beauty rang in its notes that it could not be ignored.

Sondra Oskires hesitated by the closed door for a long time, soaking in the perfect harmony of the mantra. She felt no hurry to go anywhere else.

*          *          *          *          *

The cabin door nearly broke off its hinges as those outside shouldered their way in. Ahead, on the floor, lay the perfect sigils Revwar had drawn to enable them to teleport off the vessel in safety. Originally, Revwar hadn't planned on setting off the trap in the inner sanctum until they were in the process of teleporting away. Disaster nearly befell them all when Cat's actions destroyed the staff and set things into motion prematurely.

Revwar, Savannah, Jentan and Kemora had made their way past degrading corridors to get back to their means of escape. The decay of the vessel proceeded fast, as planned, but that brought a scare considering they hadn't planned on being stuck on the ship. The death of the divine chariot would be a certainty. Ganden's clerics would not be able to remove the taint caused by the consecrated grave dust and the scion of Mothrok falling into the holy water…at least not while riding the winds.

Revwar made one final glance at the magical circle as they crossed the entryway. The design seemed intact, but he observed signs of rot in the floorboards. Jentan ushered the others to move quickly so they could be away. Kemora ran breathlessly to make up for her short strides, and Savannah moved as gracefully as her dark plate armor allowed. Floorboards creaked uncomfortably with every step the band made.

As the foursome stood in place upon the circle, an audible snapping noise came from the floor. Worried eyes passed back and forth. They each felt a twinge of nervousness.

Revwar wasted no more of their limited time. He spoke the words of the spell. At its completion, the group would appear at the circle's twin mark back on the continent of Quoros, a couple hundred miles away. Once that happened, there would be no more concerns over the failing of the divine vessel. Their pursuers would likely be destroyed in the crash of the ship. Even if the paladin and the Kashmer privateer survived the disaster, they would have no means to follow the band or even any clue as to their destination.

The others heard Revwar complete the words of the spell. A few lights flickered near their feet, but made no sound.

Their scenery had not changed; they remained on the ship.

Revwar made them all step back so he could examine the floor markings. To his disgust, a few cracks in the rotting floorboards had severed some of the connections. The teleport marker was spoiled.

Arguments flew back and forth as panic started. Revwar argued he couldn't complete another spell circle before the ship's decomposition would be fatal. Carefully laid plots and years of work became jeopardized in an instant. For the second time, the band's plans approached disastrous ruin just as they had acquired all three relic stones.

Jentan's smooth-talking voice suggested their only alternative. Their last and best means of escape would entail making their way to the sundeck and abandoning the vessel via one of the levitation lifeboats. In going to the top deck, they ran the risk of an open fight with powerful members of the Brotherhood of the Circles. The alternative involved staying hidden beneath deck on the slim chance the vessel would make it to the ground in one piece. That choice seemed suicidal.

Despite their foul mood, the group realized they had to take a chance with the lifeboats. Revwar assured them that once on the ground, and hidden, he would have the time necessary to draw out another teleport to bring them home easily. The four of them exited their room, leaving the damaged teleport circle behind, and crept toward the top deck.

*         *         *         *         *

Shouts for help led Trestan and Cat to the brig. They recalled Sondra mentioning a woman who needed rescuing, but the voice was male. Entering the brig, they found a man dressed in the armor of a guard in a plight. The floorboards he had been standing on had rotted to the point where his weight caused them to fall away. He was holding onto the edges of the hole rather than suffer a sizeable drop into a hold below.

Trestan nervously laid on his belly and stretched out to the man the same way as someone would do for a person who had fallen through thin ice. The man thanked them repeatedly as Trestan and Cat pulled him out of the jagged hole. Mixed in were his comments about the ship falling apart.

"I know, the ship is decomposing." Trestan huffed as he pulled the man's weight. "That's why we're down here, to get everyone out."

They succeeded in pulling him out of the hole. Trestan took a moment to brush himself off as Cat tip-toed past the hole to glance farther into the brig. A female voice came from the hallway before them. "Who is out there? Someone help get me out of here!"

Trestan and Cat both reflexively moved toward the jail cells. Behind them, they heard footsteps running away as the guard abandoned his post out of fear. Trestan whirled around and shouted after him, but the man didn't even slow his pace.

Also hearing the fading footsteps, the prisoner wailed, "Please don't leave me here! I'm trapped!"

Edging around the hole, Trestan started searching for a key amongst the meager table at the guard station. Cat went down the hall to check on the prisoner. The half-elf saw the teenage woman gripping the rusty bars of her cell, her cheeks wetted by tears. Cat also noticed an alcove near the cell but out of sight of its occupant. She assumed the youth's belongings were there. She reached through the bars to take the woman by the hand. Cat offered a light squeeze to reassure the youth she wasn't alone. That simple touch brought the hint of a smile to the distraught prisoner's face. The half-elf surveyed the rest of the hallway, not seeing any obvious keys hanging on hooks or any levers to open the cell door.

"Don't worry," Cat assured the prisoner, "We'll get you out of here. Why did they lock you up?"

Montanya shook her head, "You may not believe my story. I have been pursuing a halfling planning some mischief." It went unnoticed by the chiaso, but Cat's eyebrows lifted inquisitively. "I snuck aboard this vessel to pursue her, and they locked me up as a stowaway."

The young human's face took on her customary scowl, "They didn't believe they were in danger, and now I'm trapped while something terrible is about to happen. Some stuck-up little priestly girl left me in here to face a grim fate."

Cat offered, "Short, blonde hair, human, disciple of Ganden?" At Montanya's nod, Cat continued, "And you are Montanya right?"

Montanya nodded again. The half-elf glanced to the guard's station, noting the racket Trestan made looking for the key. She spoke to the scared prisoner. "She didn't leave you alone. She sent us to help you."

A mix of confusion and relief became apparent on the young human. Cat began considering the type of lock on the cell, anticipating Trestan would not find the key. Cat pushed away any worries about the state of the ship, or thoughts as to what the enemy band might be doing. The two companions held this woman's only lifeline to the world. Without them, she would be trapped in the dark, in a ship rotting apart high in the sky. Cat could imagine the loneliness and desperation of her predicament. Given the state of rust on the bars, and the collapsing floor, there might not be time for anyone else to help. As Cat examined the lock, she could feel the warm touch of Montanya's hand on her own.

Trestan walked down the hall, hands helpless out to the sides. "I can't find a key. The guard must have it on him, and he's long gone somewhere."

Montanya returned to a state of panic. "Don't give up. Don't just leave me here."

Cat had to forcefully extract her hand from the youth's grip while calming her. "We won't leave you. I can take care of this lock, but I need my hand back."

The half-elf infiltrator kneeled by the iron door, staring into the keyhole as she reached into a pouch at her side. Montanya's eyes narrowed as she noticed the half-elf retrieve several long wires and a few odd-looking metal rods. Cat set about inserting the probing wires into the keyhole, testing the lock. Trestan saw Montanya for the first time, noting her contempt of Cat's actions with the lock. Montanya's thin eyebrows lowered over a glare at Katressa's dark, leather outfit. The woman backed away from the bars as if they were made of fire.

"You're a thief?! She sent a thief to get me out!" Montanya's eyes morphed into anger.

Cat paused, returning an angry stare at the young woman. "I am nay thief. I lived in my homeland as a scout and for Kashmer as an infiltrator and privateer. Among other things I explore, sneak around, gather information and I get into places difficult for others to reach. My skills are here now for the sole beneficial purpose of freeing a stranger from a cell since the guard ran off with the keys. I would think some compassion and respect isn't too much to ask."

The response shocked Montanya, but she could not deny that this half-elf risked a lot to assist her. She could not help having an internal struggle over the whole idea. Feelings arising from a lifetime of hate against rogues clashed with the reality of one charitable person picking the lock to free her. She looked to the companion of the half-elf as he appeared at her side. The man appeared to be a warrior, but he displayed the symbols of a beneficial goddess. Montanya recognized the coraross symbol. This knightly figure clashed with her mental picture of the half-elf as a thief.

Cat had returned her attention to the lock. The delicate instruments tried to force the tumblers to give way. The half-elf frowned at some difficulty with her progress. One of the probing wires snapped under the pressure. Letting out an exasperated breath, the adventuress tried to use a little more force with a different instrument.

Her slender fingers pulled back on the lockpick, revealing a warped shaft.

Trestan noticed the twisted piece of metal. As a skilled smith, he offered, "I can probably fix that, or make you a new one."

Shoulders slumped, Cat didn't want to admit defeat. It came out as an apology. "This lock is full of rust. The tumblers are frozen in place. I'm sorry but we need to find another way."

Trestan noted how brown the bars and the lock had become. In places, the bars looked partially eaten away, and yet were strong enough to keep a hold on their prisoner. "I have a way."

Trestan began to walk past Cat, drawing the Sword of the Spirit from its scabbard as he did so. Cat looked up at the magical weapon. "You are going to try the blade on these bars?"

The young paladin gestured beyond Montanya's cell toward the next one down. "The next cell is open. I don't know how well this edge will cut iron bars, even rusty ones." Cat knew from experience his magical blade could cut through a number of things effortlessly. "But I don't have to try it on the metal. There are only a few inches of rotted wood between her and this other open cell. Montanya, stay away from this wall."

Moments later, fragments of wood went flying as Trestan attacked the wooden wall from the adjacent cell. The Sword of the Spirit proved its might. Trestan reflected in wonder where his former mentor, the late Sir Wilhelm, had acquired such a magnificent treasure. The elvish sword sheared through the layers of wood once enchanted as part of the divine vessel. Now, rotted away, they were no match to slow the magical blade. The boards might as well have been twigs being split by a lumberjack's axe. Before long, Montanya could squeeze through the hole in the wall.

Trestan took Montanya by the hand and led her to freedom. The red-haired chiaso had trouble meeting Cat's eyes, but she mumbled an apology. Nevertheless, Cat smiled and made introductions, then helped Montanya retrieve her items from the alcove.

Montanya slipped on her leather armor. As she laced on the shin guards an urge came to her. "We must warn others about the halfling rogue!"

Trestan shook his head, "I'm afraid the damage is done. We need to get to the top deck and see what is going on."

**CHAPTER 18**          **"From Orderly Evacuation to Thwarted Escape"**

Lindon made sure he stood within hearing range when Korrelothar re-emerged on the sundeck. The minstrel approached as close to Duke MigRelke and his bodyguards as would be allowed. Korrelothar looked pale, as if he had just swallowed something which turned his stomach against him. The elf wizard explained to the provincial ruler what occurred in the inner sanctum. The duke listened with visible alarm. Bodyguards kept people a good distance from the hushed conversation, yet Lindon was close enough to catch many snippets of conversation. His sharp sense of hearing served him well enough to overhear of the pilots' plight, and that the cause involved some theft rather than an attack on Orlaun's nobility. Lindon's brow furrowed at the news regarding the rot afflicting the ship.

Korrelothar tried persuading Duke MigRelke that they must all abandon the vessel. The noble argued against it, but the elf wizard displayed his inner strength and held firm. To Lindon, it seemed unthinkable to flee the divine chariot. His mind weighed the implications even as he listened. Wilder continent lay below, aptly named due to its primal nature. There were few cultures in the way of great cities or advanced races. Small trading ports dotted the northern coast, little more than frontier settlements on the edge of the uncivilized world. The geography of the land remained unmapped. Forests and mountain ranges stretched endlessly. Abandoning the questionable safety of the ship meant asking the passengers to brave the dangers of that unexplored wilderness.

Though spectators on deck remained ignorant of the conversation going on near the helm castle, the results soon became apparent. The duke conceded to disembark, at the urging of a few advisors. The other royal passengers did not miss the significance of a few of the levitation lifeboats being readied by the side of the deck. The conversations of everyone shifted to hushed whispers as the duke's entourage began filing toward the first boats. All eyes focused on the most influential member of their society.

Duke MigRelke shared more hushed words with Korrelothar before turning to the gathering crowd. The others silenced as the man addressed them. The speech was probably the shortest and most to-the-point he had ever given in his life. The noble, in his heart, could not simply be the first to step off without saying a word. He warned the rest of the royalty the vessel was in grave danger, and they should all follow the wizards' guidance in evacuating the ship. The duke helped quell panic by reminding them of their duties as royalty. MigRelke asked the lords and protectors of the realm to act like proper gentlemen as they chaperoned the ladies off of the ship. Lindon watched the faces in the crowd for reactions. Some seemed stirred to commit themselves to act with honor, yet for others the fear on their faces made any such words lost.

The duke's entourage of bodyguards and advisors took up two of the large lifeboats. The boats sat outside the railings on retractable planks and rope moorings. When time came to cast off, the crew pushed the levitation boats away with poles while retracting the underside planks. It was with some trepidation they left the relative safety of the larger vessel, since only open air existed below. The levitation boats soon proved their worth after so many years of service. Once free of the ship, the globes of holy water at the bow of each lifeboat emitted a soft glow. The lifeboats settled on their own cushion of air as they slowly sank to the clouds and forests below. The *Doranil Star* continued making headway on a course deeper into the continent, so the smaller vessels drifted behind as they left contact with the ship.

The Brotherhood of the Circles attempted an orderly evacuation as the duke's boats floated into the sky below and behind the ship. Crewmembers dragged the lifeboats to the railings of the vessel. The esteemed passengers appeared hesitant, wanting to linger on board until forced to go. Many people feared the lifeboats more than the danger afflicting the great ship. Some of the nobles formed lines in a way that blocked other escape craft from getting to the sides. A few flaunted their rank in order to get off faster, or tried reserving a large escape boat for only their families.

Standing in view of it all, Lindon began strumming his mandolin. He knew the rush of royalty streaming toward the rails would delay any lowly minstrel from leaving soon. He could do nothing but play. Maybe a few tunes would better soothe anxieties. Lindon recalled the unfinished tune he played to honor *Doranil Star* when it left Orlaun. Listening to the weak mantra driving the ship, as people surrendered the vessel to the night sky, some notes came to him with perfect clarity. He felt it would be an ending worthy of the demise of the last divine chariot. As people filled the boats, Lindon played the strings of his mandolin with a sadness rivaling any mournful tune he had ever learned in his travels.

He observed everything with an unrivaled level of detail. Debris and discarded belongings cluttered a deck which survived war and peace for over a millennium. Splotches of dried blood blemished places where the abrupt plunge resulted in injuries. Banners of Orlaun and Ganden snapped back and forth in the cold air over their heads. Blemishes marred the golden figurehead at the bow. Doors started sticking as hinges became frozen. Masts groaned from the weight of the yardarms as rot took them. The ship had become arthritic and brittle with age. They still had most sails furled for the celebration, reflecting a peacefulness of dying as if the vessel retired at some dock. Misty clouds parted as the bow continued slicing its way through the night. The vapors of the clouds drifting along gave Lindon the feel of a coffin floating through fog, searching its final resting place.

A person, unknown to Lindon, ascended the stairs from the level below. When Lindon caught sight of her, she exemplified the plight of the divine chariot from a personal view such as no other source. Sondra wore the ceremonial robes of the patron god of the ship. He noted her slow, reluctant rise from the inner sanctum. Lindon immediately recognized the symbols on her robes and the relationship they held with the similarly adorned vessel. In her eyes, he saw the emptiness of utter despair and complete loss. His tune shifted to better communicate the personal grief which marred that beautiful face. The woman had lovely soft blue eyes and dark-red lips; both spoiled by the haunted expression she wore.

He played for her, listening to the beat of her broken heart and matching it to the rhythm of the weakened mantra. The song found new life and significance in the robes of one of the faithful. Sondra became the essence of the *Doranil Star* as it sailed aimlessly in a dark sky, not knowing how to face the doom yet to come. The cleric's attention turned to the sounds taking shape from her loss. Sondra looked at Lindon through haggard eyes, and he met her stare as he continued to define the moment in music. The young acolyte of Ganden willingly stood entrapped in the bonds of heartrending harmony.

The music cut the air with the grief of the dying ship. The gold-trimmed relic, descendant of the ancient days when gods walked the lands, left behind a trail of descending lifeboats. *Doranil Star* shed the smaller, oval vessels like tears of mourning before the coming of its final fate. Those who slowly drifted to questionable safety in the night watched the ship pass like a shadow against the stars. Several were moved to tears even without the hauntingly tragic melodies from Lindon's mandolin. Just an hour before, they enjoyed a celebration of achievement and power; however, the sabotage in the night made their prideful vessel seem more like those empty towers stranded in the deep waters off the shores of the Highwater district. The *Doranil Star* drifted toward the heart of Wilder continent, straying into the unreachable bounds of history's glory.

*      *      *      *      *

Peering from the dark recesses of a door, Revwar watched the proceedings on deck. The elf glanced to either side, searching for opportunities along the nearby railings. His finely chiseled elven features, still tarnished by blood from Cat's rapier strike, withdrew when he saw their chance at escape.

He whispered to his fellow band, "Most are down the deck from us. There are a few lifeboats lashed near here. If we can move without notice, we could untie one rather quickly and be over the side."

Jentan moved forward, "Leave that spell to me. I can give us invisibility as long as my concentration is unimpeded. I shall start the tune of the spell, but you will need to lead me along to make any speed. They may see the boat being moved, but they won't see us as long as the illusion continues."

Revwar and Savannah stood on both sides of Jentan as the mentalist invoked his spell. The two of them guided him across the open deck. Kemora trailed slightly behind, holding the simple cloth bag containing the stolen relics. They could see each other only as faint, ghostlike images. They looked around, still feeling very exposed on the crowded deck. The invisibility illusion seemed to hold, since no one spared any glances in their direction. They noted that most of the activity was near the aft where people were evacuating. It made sense to evacuate using the boats in the rear first. The levitation boats fell behind as they cast off, so efforts to disembark starting at the rear of the vessel left less chance for boats to collide or drift over top of each other.

Revwar and Savannah worked fast to unlash the weathered ropes from the craft, Jentan standing nearby. They were impeded by the inability to see their own fingers as other than phantom images. Kemora stood silent, holding the bag while keeping an eye out for danger.

Danger arrived on deck, wearing her red hair in a long braid tied at the bottom by the torn, pink piece of fabric. Kemora's jaw would have hit the wooden deck if it wasn't firmly attached by skin and muscle. The halfling couldn't figure how a pursuer could be that stubborn and resourceful as to somehow show up at every bad opportunity. Even worse,

Montanya had two familiar companions arising from the stairwell. The holy champion of Abriana and the black-clad half-elf ascended into the torchlight of the top deck.

The halfling didn't even realize she was uttering audible syllables until Savannah cuffed her on the side of the head to shush her. Kemora sneered at the barely visible outline of the cleric. The emotional display was wasted, for the human had already returned to undoing the knots.

By the time Montanya and her rescuers reached the deck, many lifeboats had already disembarked. As mesmerizing as the scene was, the chiaso reminded herself to search for the halfling rogue. While Trestan and Katressa mumbled some quiet conversation over the evacuation, the teenage brawler began to scrutinize her surroundings with a keen eye. Unconsciously, she adopted a defensive fighting stance as she scanned the area.

When she looked at the empty parts of the deck closer to the bow, she detected movement. A rope slipped off of a lifeboat. No one stood anywhere close to it. Her thin eyebrows dropped into her customary scowl as she saw parts of the rope continue to wriggle like a snake. Montanya blinked her eyes at what she thought was blurriness coming from her own vision. The distortion was not from her eyes, but rather something almost misty next to the levitation craft. Once she realized she wasn't imagining things, that the ropes actually moved of their own accord across an optically distorted area, Montanya moved into action.

A solution came to her in the form of a bucket of sand sitting by the railing. Even divine chariots sometimes faced the threat of fire on the wooden deck, and the bucket of sand was one means to combat such a disaster.

Montanya took off at a run toward the railing. Trestan and Cat turned around in surprise. They watched as Montanya hardly broke a stride lifting the bucket clear of the deck. The braided hair trailed as she continued a fast jog toward the bow.

Kemora saw the threat coming and had little time to react. Anything the halfling did could reveal the hidden band to other eyes, and yet this stubborn woman charged directly at them. All the halfling could do was close her eyes as Montanya heaved the sand at them.

The thrown sand splashed over the heads of the four. It got into Revwar's silvery braided hair, seeped down the inside of Savannah's dark plate, left streamers pouring down Kemora's shoulders. Worst of all, Jentan got a dose of it right into his mouth. Trestan and Cat saw the sand pouring off of the invisible shapes moments before Jentan's sputtering voice allowed the spell to expire. The two companions looked in disbelief at the sudden unmasking of their quarry. Revwar, Kemora, and Savannah looked at each other and at Montanya in incredulity as Jentan spit out sand. Montanya stood in an equal state of shock, staring back at the formidable opponents.

The young martial artist reacted first, noticing the cloth bag which the rogue held. The chiaso whipped both hands forward in rapid succession. Her left hand grabbed the bag while her right hand followed with a slightly awkward punch to the halfling's cheek. Kemora backed away empty-handed from the blow as the chiaso hopped out of reach. Now Montanya had the two holy relics, though she still stood an unsafe proximity to the thieves.

Kemora drew her sword. Savannah held aloft her flail, deadly enough even without its dark enchantment. Montanya wore no armor except for the leather padding. If a steel flail or sword hit her hard enough, she would be in no position to take the relics from them. Savannah confidently gazed upon the youth's unarmed hands. Kemora had already faced the chiaso in combat, and knew she was a threat with only bare hands. Halfling and abbess both charged after Montanya.

The chiaso tried to immediately retreat back down the deck from which she had ran, but the cleric's fast attacks turned her away from the railing. Montanya jumped and twisted to avoid the two attackers. She nearly lost her footing on the edge of an open hold, too wide to jump across. She could see a pile of supplies on the deck below her. Skirting the edge of the pit with her acrobatics, Montanya was forced farther up the bow by the two attackers. The bag with the relics became ballast to help her balance as her footwork kept her a step ahead of death.

*　　　*　　　*　　　*　　　*

Trestan and Cat moved to assist Montanya, but they were several long running steps from being able to help. The half-elf once again lamented leaving her deadly crossbow in Orlaun. Nimble fingers retrieved the silver rapier as she went forward. Beside her, Trestan reached over his shoulder to where the hilt of his sword projected. The Sword of the Spirit gleamed even in the dim light of the night once pulled free of the scabbard.

"For Abriana and those that I love," Trestan yelled as he charged, "Goddess guide me!"

Yellow, elvish eyes fixed on the two heroes as they approached. Revwar reached into a bag of tricks at his side. As his hands sought a quick solution to the charging couple, his voice called to Jentan. The mentalist was still spitting sand out of his mouth as the wizard spoke.

"You are the one often saying you are more of a lover than a fighter," Revwar sneered. "So, it is your task to get the lifeboat loosened and ready. I will take care of the threats but I can't buy us much time."

With a few words of arcana, Revwar unleashed a summoning spell. A small ball of light whisked from his hand toward the advancing companions. Trestan and Cat almost ran headlong into it before the half-elf cried for Trestan to slow down. Trestan had not seen this spell before, occupied as he had been with the abbess at the time, but Cat remembered it from four years ago. The light exploded in a mass of fur and teeth.

A dog-faced creature that moved with the gracefulness of a predatory cat barred their path. The two companions barely skidded to a halt before they were within range of its snapping maw. Trestan found himself distracted by the abomination that the creature displayed. A crab-like claw appendage rose from its back like the tail of a scorpion. The claw shot forward and snapped close to Trestan's arm, barely missing. The creature seemed to be testing its reach.

Trestan and Cat had to deal with this summoned monstrosity before they could get anywhere near Montanya to assist her.

*　　　*　　　*　　　*　　　*

Korrelothar had been preoccupied with his fellow guildmates as they ushered pompous, stubborn nobles to either board lifeboats or stand back. A commotion from the bow soon turned his head that direction in curiosity.

The alarmed elf noted the abbess and her swinging flail. The blackened armor honoring the Goddess of Death had no place on board this ship. He quickly took note of all the people involved in the scuffle. His eyes went beyond Trestan and Cat to the summoned abomination, then peered more intently to fix on the man stealing one of the lifeboats.

His voice spoke with venomous distaste as he spotted the mentalist. "Jentan Mollamos! Betrayer! How dare you show your face in the open after what you have done?"

The elf wizard pulled aside other members of the Brotherhood of the Circles. He pointed out the mentalist. The other mages voiced their anger at the man as Korrelothar told them about the theft and sabotage. Wizards, conjurors, mentalists, alchemists, diviners, evokers and simple apprentices began to form an angry mob. Some simply did nothing more than slander Jentan's name as they watched him pursue an escape. Most others began to draw forth the mystical reagents needed to bring forth a cataclysm of spells worthy of matching that evening's light show. Hands grabbed wands or twisted in arcane gestures, and voices uttered the syllables of magic. Personal magical shields flared into existence. Anger clouded over the assembled mages like a thunderhead, as the air crackled in advance of the approaching thunderstorm of arcana. Korrelothar had rallied the mages into the mood for a fight.

The nobles still on deck became less hesitant about fleeing the questionable safety of the vessel. None wanted to witness a spell duel. Crewmen had no need for urging the civilians. People rushed to board the levitation boats, which then cast off in rapid succession.

In the midst of the throng stood a young woman with no rush to face the future. She watched with dispassionate eyes as royalty scrambled in panic for the boats. She had no wish to move her feet in that direction. The acolyte of Ganden could not abandon her ship so casually.

Sondra turned around, looking in the direction the mages faced. Her blue eyes, empty with loss, saw the middle-aged man undoing the ropes near the bow. Korrelothar was saying his name again to the others, "Jentan Mollamos."

Sondra recognized the name. She saw the emblem of the Brotherhood of the Circles on his fancy lined coat, a wand of magic tucked into his fine belt. This was the rogue mage who ruined everything. Her lips frowned as a new description reach her ears, echoing through the recesses of her mind, a mind that had been empty to all else except her loss.

*Turncoat...*

Two warriors had fought this man in the insides of the ship. Korrelothar had provided their names, Trestan and Katressa. Even now, the same two companions were fighting a nightmarish creation on the deck. Jentan had allies backing up his treachery. Sondra saw the dark designs of death on Savannah's armor. The woman desecrated the divine chariot simply by her presence. Sondra paid little heed to the halfling or the silver-haired elf caster. Her focus returned to Jentan Mollamos. Nothing distracted her eyes from the evil man from then on. Even the high wind, whipping her wheat-blonde hair around her face, was nothing compared to the gathering storm of fury on the deck.

*Traitor…*

Jentan Mollamos had severed the trust of his own guild. A change came over Sondra's heart as she considered the pain he had caused. This man was the reason that enemies boarded the vessel of her dreams. He made possible the sabotage of Ganden's divine ship. In the planks she stood upon, the acolyte could hear the failing mantra of her mentors. Those clerics who hadn't died yet as a result of this man's dishonor were bravely facing their final hour to save whomever they could. Sondra's future and dreams were falling from the skies this night due to this man.

Sondra wore her rust-colored satchel on her left hip, filled with the healing tools of her devotion during her service to Ganden. This had been her entire life up to this night, in selfless service to heal others. Belted on her right hip was the mace she had been trained to use in order to take lives in defense of herself or others, though she had never needed it.

*Betrayer!*

No longer held on her belt, the mace hung from her right hand as white knuckles gripped the handle. The look of firm resolve appeared on her face as she stared at the man who owed blood for his crimes. Despite the other dangers on the open deck, Sondra marched toward the betrayer.

**CHAPTER 19**         **"A Clash on the Deck of *Doranil Star*"**

Lindon's mandolin rested against his side as he watched the deadly play unfolding at the bow. The chiaso did her best to flip or dance gracefully out of range of both flail and the halfling's sword, but her movements lacked harmony.

Although the minstrel lacked skill in the martial arts, he knew the movements required a perfect blend of body, mind, and soul. The most graceful martial artists as well as the best minstrels derived the beauty of their talent from some peaceful inner core. Anyone could train to punch, or master the notes on any given instrument. Yet, for all the training, it was the heart and mind that drove the subject to truly surpass any common limitations. The tranquil mind could adapt fluidly to unusual situations. A strong sense of heart could expand any talent into a translation that was above basic trained movements or music notes on a piece of paper. Lindon had seen chiaso transform defensive movements into an effortless dance. When the minstrel looked upon Montanya's style, he saw limitations. From his standpoint, he could say: she might be able to play the music, but she could not see past it to make up her own interpretation.

It wasn't hard to spot at least one of the youth's distractions. The human chiaso could likely outrun the armored woman or the short halfling if she put her mind to it. Instead, the unarmed fighter tried to take shots at the halfling as she moved. At any given moment, the chiaso would dance away from both weapons, only to risk closing the gap again just to let loose a kick at the sword wielder. Kemora had begun to allow Savannah to lead the attack. They measured Montanya's rage to see if she would try even riskier attempts to get at the halfling rogue. From a distance, Lindon could see that both attackers had their eyes on their own prize: the bag in Montanya's offhand. It unbalanced the chiaso. In order to keep the bag away from her opponents, it kept one hand behind her back.

The woman needed help but no one was nearby. Passengers were surging aft, intent on escape. Crewmen and mages tried to resolve the mass of confusion near the aft lifeboats. Of everyone else, Lindon was possibly the closest person to offer a chance at affecting the outcome. Even then, there was a large, open hold on the deck which he would have to circle.

The minstrel allowed his mandolin to rest from its sling, while his hand went to his belt. He felt the comforting hilt of his lightweight smallsword at his side. He slid his hand and wrist through the leather loop hanging from its pommel as he drew steel. The fine weapon had many qualities similar to a rapier, but lacked certain ornamentation such as a protective basket or any elaborate designs. It favored skillful thrusts rather than heavy swings. Some called it a gentleman's sword, for it could be smuggled into events disguised as a cane. It was known to be used as such at social occasions when insults led to the surprise appearance of steel, and the splash of blood from a rival.

While Lindon didn't pretend to be a gentleman, he did prefer a light weapon which he could use with deft precision. Blade in right hand, his left hand on the strap of his mandolin, Lindon of Orlaun began to circle the edge of the hold.

*         *         *         *         *

180

Montanya was tempted to extend another kick toward the halfling rogue, instead she wisely danced backward to avoid that heavy flail. The chiaso wished she could finally rid herself of that troublesome rogue, but the cold, blue eyes behind the skull helm sought Montanya's demise. The steel head of the flail came terrifyingly close to ending the orphaned daughter of the Westonhout family. Montanya blocked the flail to get in a strike at the human opponent. She regretted the move immediately. The cloth bag swung until it tangled with the chain of the flail. The metallic head wrapped in a descending arc until it clanged against the hard objects inside.

Though Montanya, Savannah and Kemora winced at the sound of the impact, only Savannah knew she was more likely to damage her flail than nick the divine relics. Montanya never flinched from her intended move despite realizing her error. The knuckles of her right hand rapped on the throat of the abbess, in the only open area between the breastplate and the skull helm. Executed properly, the result would be a broken windpipe.

As Lindon had noted across the deck, Montanya lacked the concentration to execute her moves properly.

The abbess felt the sting of the blow though she had no difficulty breathing afterward. Savannah swept her left gauntlet up to shield her throat as she pulled away. Montanya, having already finished the maneuver, also attempted to disengage and focus on the halfling. Both women found they were still entangled by the flail wrapped around the relic bag. Both stubbornly held on to the items in their hands even as they forcefully tried to push apart.

The cloth bag started to rip as Savannah pulled on the metal flail. Kemora advanced from the side. The halfling led with her sword as opportunity presented. Montanya recalled an agile move from her training. It was her only hope of retaining possession of the bag without wearing a sword through her gut.

Kemora stabbed forward, but Montanya was no longer there. The human reversed momentum. Instead of pulling away from Savannah, she used the abbess' pull combined with the strength of her legs to execute a jump. Two feet clad in soft leather slippers came down hard on Kemora's shoulders, providing the extra lift for the somersault. Kemora fell face-forward on the deck while Montanya flipped over the head of the cleric of DeLaris. Savannah's eyes saw a red braid of hair slap her in the face, before she received a shove from behind.

The bag and the flail untwisted, separating at last.

Montanya's relief was almost literally cut short as Kemora regained her feet and attacked. The halfling was aggravated to the point of recklessness. Her sword chopped back and forth as Montanya sought a proper fighting stance.

Beyond the frantic halfling, the cleric of DeLaris prepared a trick. Tired of the straight fight, she softly called forth a miracle from her goddess. The abbess took a step to one side…and disappeared!

Montanya had no time to contemplate the tactic due to the bloodthirsty halfling pushing her back around the hold. The sword actually nicked the chiaso twice, though both cuts were small. The youth remained on the defensive as she waited for an opening.

Savannah now stood behind the unknowing youth. A hard shove from the cleric sent Montanya pitching forward. The chiaso barely registered the sound of the armored plate grinding behind her at the same time she heard the halfling sword slashing through the wind. A wide gash opened in Montanya's hip as Kemora's blade slid past.

Stunned, Montanya half-turned on her weakened leg to find the cleric standing behind her. She also saw the heavy head of the flail sailing toward her smooth, rosy cheeks. Her view swam with the dizzying spin of bright stars as the crunch of bone rattled her head.

Savannah and Kemora felt a wave of satisfaction that turned quickly to horror. As the muscular body of the chiaso went limp, momentum carried her over the edge of the deck. Montanya tumbled into the open hold, taking the relics with her. The sack rolled into darkness as the young woman crashed atop a stack of supplies.

*　　　*　　　*　　　*　　　*

Claws raked ineffectively at Trestan, sliding across the hard breastplate. The attack pushed the paladin backward, his own swing missing the abomination. Cat scored a hit while the creature was distracted. Her silver rapier lanced into its haunches. The creature bled from a number of small stab wounds caused by the two companions.

The claw on the tail snapped at Cat. The half-elf let out a surprised yelp as it caught the trailing edges of her raven-black tresses. A few strands yanked loose from her scalp as she scrambled backward.

Trestan readied an overhand hack at the claw, but Cat shouted, "Keep your sword low!"

The summoned beast turned to face the adventuress though Trestan forced himself into its path once again. He worried less for his own safety given the protection his armor afforded. He abandoned the overhead slash in favor of more direct thrusts to keep the thing's attention. Trestan threw a questioning glance her way as she sought to sneak around the flanks of the beast again.

She answered his unspoken question quietly, trying to avoid the beast's attention. "I saw how this creature disarmed Salgor." Trestan had been too busy fighting Savannah years ago to notice the dwarf's tussle with this summoned monster. "It waits for you to try an overhead attack, then its rear claw snaps up your weapon and pulls it out of your hands while the front claws rake at you."

Trestan nodded his understanding. After a few more teasing movements with his elvish blade, he shouted to Cat again. "Cat, I can take care of this thing. Someone needs to delay them before they slip away."

Cat noted the enemy band at the bow. Jentan almost had a lifeboat loose, while Revwar cast spells to prepare for the onslaught from the mage guild. The half-elf looked back to Trestan. Her emerald eyes flashed her concern for him.

"Just go, Cat. Slip by this thing while you can." Trestan urged insistently.

Trestan's sword danced with the front claws of the creature, keeping it focused on him. Cat had the chance to try another surprise attack if she chose to do so.

"I love you, *faunlessa*. Go before they get away again." Abriana's champion implored.

Cat nodded grimly. The point of her silver rapier finally turned away from the creature as the infiltrator stealthily made her way up the deck. Trestan faced the summoned enemy, knowing he had to solve this problem on his own. He put away fears and doubts. This was the life he had undertaken. He championed the goddess Abriana. Trestan would have to face this abomination and kill it quickly, without help.

He failed to notice Cat wasn't the only one to sneak by the fight. A young cleric wearing the ceremonial robes of Ganden also slipped by, making her way toward the bow, wielding a deadly mace.

*          *          *          *          ×

Savannah and Kemora stood still a long moment, staring in horror into the blackness of the hold. Revwar's words shook them. The elf pointed down the deck with his slim finger. "I suggest you help me delay those people down there, or we are all dead."

Cleric and rogue looked across the hold to see the gathering throng of angry mages. The guild's spellcasters spread out across the width of the deck, holding wands and staves in a threatening manner, aglow with magical shields. Fire, lightning, ice and other elements would soon be thrown at them, on a scale that none of them could hope to defend.

Savannah and Kemora looked to their own resources. The cleric began to pray fervently to the Goddess of Death. Cold blackness coalesced around her, the tangible expression of death itself. She channeled the darkest nightmares of her goddess into her body. A stench reached the nose of those closest, reeking of a tomb left open to decay in the sun.

Meanwhile, Kemora searched frantically for any mischief she might unleash to slow the advancing horde. The halfling noted a man with a red beard and wide-brimmed, feathered hat skirting the edge of the hold. He carried a slender blade in one arm while cradling a mandolin under the other. Kemora had no time to deal with one man when so many others were becoming a threat.

The halfling rogue saw a stack of alcohol casks lashed on their sides. Several had been handy to be served upon the completion of the magical show. If she were to cut some of the ropes, the pile would roll apart, sending several barrels traveling down the length of the deck. Kemora started hacking at the lines with her sword.

Savannah channeled the energy of Death, forming dark orbs in her hands. The cruel miracle from her goddess conveyed the moment when the sands flee an hourglass, and the nighttime cold arising when the sun sets over the horizon. It was the manifestation of time catching up to even the lengthy existence of a divine chariot.

Savannah aimed high, into the masts of the ship. Some of the mages cowered while many more shifted their spell shields upward to deflect any assaults from above. The dark orbs hit the decaying wooden masts and sent darkness cascading along their lengths. The cracking of timbers heralded the weakening of the masts. The ship had already been decaying from the sabotage of the holy receptacle. Savannah's spells expedited the process for the masts. Timbers split as age overtook them. Yardarms cracked under the weight of their own sails.

As Kemora neared the end of her efforts, a thought came to her. It would make much more of an effect if flaming barrels rolled down the deck. As she continued to consider what chaos that could be, it occurred to her there was a ready source of flame nearby. With the last couple ropes barely holding the weight of the barrels, Kemora asked Revwar for a favor.

"I need a fire! Right here on these casks!"

The elf wizard grinned. The halfling jumped away as the wizard sent a cascade of flame tumbling toward the pile. Kemora ducked under the heat as the flames licked away the last ropes holding the pile in place. Ropes gave way, allowing gravity to do the rest. The fiery barrels rolled down the deck, some crashing into other objects, spreading flames as some of the alcohol escaped the containers. The light from the fires lit up the night.

Nobles fled the rolling barrels as flames spread. People panicked to get to the lifeboats. Mages unleashed blasts of cold frost against the fire. Some cast spells to affect the alcohol itself, including the effect of turning some of it to water. The distraction kept the mages busy.

Lindon found himself in the path of the rolling hazard. The minstrel allowed his smallsword to drop from his fingers. It stayed connected to him by the loop of leather around his wrist. He swept up his mandolin and began playing. Waves of sound deflected the barrels coming directly at him, but he still faced the threat of fire.

*       *       *       *       *

The knots proved challenging to a man who prided himself on his agile fingers and physical condition. Jentan silently admitted that the crewmen probably had a quick way to release the rigging that he hadn't discovered. He likely caused some knots even as he tried to undo the mess of rope. Jentan finally had the whole thing untangled except for a couple knots that wouldn't come free. The mentalist resorted to magic. He severed the remaining strands with puffs of intense, controlled fire, avoiding damage to the lifeboat.

Once free, the levitation boat displayed the reason it had been tightly lashed down. The large boat proved weightless in Jentan's hands. The middle-aged human easily maneuvered it away from the rest of its twin constructs. Jentan could imagine how the levitation boats might float around the deck if the divine chariot performed any hard maneuvers.

A pair of feet on the edge of his vision caused him to pause. The mentalist took half a step back in surprise as he looked up. His eyes scanned over a priestess, standing before him with mace tightly gripped in one hand.

Sondra's blue eyes were full of anger. The dark-red lips formed a frown. The fingers wrapped around the mace handle flexed slightly, as if trying to get the best feel of the weapon before she used it. Jentan's eyes roamed over her vestments, noting the symbols of Ganden. He also noted with interest the general shape of Sondra's body. The mentalist always observed the ample qualities of a woman, but kept his eyes from pausing too long on her chest to deal with the hatred in her expression.

184

Mentalists met their foes with a smile and a friendly demeanor. Jentan turned on his charm. "What saddens such a beautiful lady so? What might a humble man do to ease your troubles?"

The words meant nothing to Sondra. Her lips hissed the one word that summed her emotions for this seemingly harmless man. "Betrayer."

"You think I betrayed someone?" Jentan did the best to play innocent. "What crime do you place upon my unknowing shoulders?"

"I, Sondra Oskires, call you betrayer for turning on your own guild. You took the lives of my teachers. You destroyed the vessel of my god. You crushed my dreams."

Jentan felt he had the hook he could use to sink into her mind. Mental control involved knowing what a person wanted to see. If you gave a person's mind something tantalizing enough, they would forget reality. He added a bit of magic to his voice as he spoke again. He had to distract the woman: one more step and she would be within range to bash him with her mace. The mentalist had a wand tucked on his belt, but he preferred to own minds rather than destroy them.

Jentan said, "You can dream again, Sondra. Look to your vessel and see the beauty of it. See what dreams the *Doranil Star* still holds for you."

The magical weight added to the words overcame Sondra's reluctance to listen to the mentalist. She glanced to the side and had no explanation for the sight that met her eyes.

The divine chariot soared once again, and over the rail Sondra looked down upon Orlaun. Pennants of Ganden rippled in the breeze as a strong mantra gave energy to the ship. Off to the side, the voice of Jentan Mollamos disguised itself into the mantra as he spoke arcane words to further the mental image. The hook of the illusion sunk deeply into Sondra's awareness. Her mind dulled to the fighting on the deck, preferring instead to see the ship as she wanted to see it. Sondra wore the robes of the Chosen. Mother Evine stood there, taking her by the hand to the inner sanctum. Sondra knelt on cushions along with the other Chosen. She intoned the mantra with them. She felt her heart soar as her efforts guided the divine chariot through the skies.

Jentan finally relaxed his voice. He considered the spellbound cleric, as she kneeled on the deck, praying the mantra along with the rhythm coming from the vessel. Her mind wandered an illusion originating from her own wishes, although Jentan had given it a life of its own. There was no way to know how long it would last on its own, or how easily it could be broken. For now, Sondra was no longer a threat.

In another place the mentalist would have spent the time getting to know her on a more personal level. The woman seemed to share a superficial resemblance to another cleric he knew. He had noted the swell of her chest almost reflexively and considered what a treat the feel of it would be beneath his hands. He lacked the time to seriously undertake such indulgences. Jentan had a mission to accomplish if he even hoped to live out the night. Despite the fact that serenity comforted Sondra like a muffling blanket, the ship observed a scene of chaos and hatred.


    *       *       *       *       *

Before the mage guild could punish Jentan, they had to get past the defenses of one of his accomplices. Revwar's magical shields formed a line along the deck; a tactic he learned from a gnome sorcerer four years ago. He could not duplicate the type of crenellated magical field that Mel Bellringer had summoned, but he made his own version from a different type of spell. His robes twirled from glowing shield to shield as he cast from behind the safety of those barriers. Extending a hand through the thin space between shields, he would let loose lancing rays or spew forth fiery blades at the grouped mages.

Unfortunately, Revwar was matched against the might of the Brotherhood of the Circles. For every spell Revwar loosed, several more launched against him. Fireballs slammed against the magical shields with tendrils of flame singing beyond the gaps. Deadly beams of energy lanced forth, though most of those stopped at the shields or melted holes in the deck beyond. Shards of ice exploded to pepper the surrounding area with sharp splinters. Revwar took on a few wounds as spell after spell battered the area. The elf wizard used his only healing draught to help fix the injuries.

One conjurer let loose a toxic mist in an attempt to seep around the shields. The spell backfired as he controlled the wind to direct it toward the target. The wind kicked up the flames still on the deck from the rolling barrels. The caster had to dispel his own magic as those mages fighting the fires chided his shortsighted thinking.

Before long, two threats materialized that promised an end to Revwar's defenses. One by one, Revwar's shields were deconstructed and dismissed by spells designed for such use. The elf wizard began to lose his hiding places as more volatile spells continued. The second threat came as other conjurers from the mage guild summoned in beasts to fight. Three creatures, resembling a mix of animals, took shape and began to charge. Once the unnatural animals arrived, they would easily slip around the gaps in the shields and tear Revwar apart.

*　　*　　*　　*　　*

Kemora chuckled at the effectiveness of her flaming barrels. A strange wind lifted a man clear of the fires. His red, plumed hat stayed on his head despite a breeze that billowed his cape outward. He whistled as he played a tune upon a mandolin. The song sounded unnatural to halfling ears. The minstrel levitated over the burning deck and the open hold using the power of his music.

Kemora had hoped the barrels would have stopped him too, but this man was resourceful.

The halfling brandished her sword, ready to skewer him as he floated close. His song changed at the last moment to a banshee shriek. The rogue staggered backward a step, clapping hands over ears at the painful noise. Lindon landed safely and lightly on the deck. Mandolin dropped to his side as his wrist flicked at the leather loop around it. The smallsword hilt snapped up into his waiting hand as Kemora recovered from the noise. Swords rang as they met.

*　　*　　*　　*　　*

186

Volatile spells screamed overhead and to the sides with Trestan and the abomination caught in the middle. The sharp teeth snapping at him seemed even more sinister in the flashes of spell fires. The creature tried to remain just out of reach. It measured his swings and reflexes, searching for the moment it could sweep past his arms in a powerful lunge. Wielding the blade two-handed as he was, Trestan didn't leave any openings. The narrow elvish blade pivoted around his twisting wrists. Trestan never tried to cock the sword back for a powerful blow. Due to the blade's light weight and magically keen edge, he didn't have to seek any greater momentum than what the slight efforts of his wrists and forearms could produce.

Time did not favor Abriana's champion. The more he delayed, the closer Revwar's party came to escaping. He kept mindful of the qualities of summoned creatures from his teachings at the seminary. Such monsters lacked the instincts of self-preservation a living being possessed. Eventually, it would risk a horrible wound in order to take down its assigned target.

Several other forms rushed past in a blur. The summoned creatures of the mage guild concentrated on Revwar. Not a single one slowed to assist Trestan in his task. There was no time to feel any relief that the evil wizard would be facing three times the threat Trestan had been dealt.

Both Trestan and the abomination heard a sharp crack from above. Savannah's withering spell had finally succeeded in sapping enough strength to topple the giant wooden frames standing above the middle of the ship. The weight of yardarms, rigging, sails, counterweights and pennants were enough to bring much of the three middle masts of the ship crashing down. Trestan evaded a lunge from the dangerous beast before he could look up to see the danger.

Abriana's champion came frighteningly close to being crushed as a split yardarm shattered on the deck before him. Screams came from the direction of the Brotherhood of the Circles as they suffered from falling debris. Fragments rained down on mage and noble alike as Savannah's dark miracle came to fruition. Pieces of wood and tangles of rope knots dropped randomly around Trestan as he kept clear of the larger beams. The top of one mast speared through one of the summoned creatures bearing down on Revwar. The ape-like abomination screamed as its insides splattered the deck. It soon faded to mist as the magical fabric of the world reclaimed the spell energy.

Somehow, the canine creature facing Trestan avoided the worst of the bombardment. It leapt over the fallen yardarm. Claws raked across one of Trestan's shoulders as his sword delivered another cut to the underside of the beast. The creature skidded to a stop beyond the aspiring paladin.

Trestan thought to deliver an overhand attack but he paused, recalling Cat's warning about the creature's ability to disarm using the clawed tail. Bleeding from a few claw marks, it occurred to the young warrior he could use that tactic to his advantage.

He raised his sword high over his head, leaving his intentions clear. The canine beast immediately took a ready stance. It ducked low with its front paws as the crab appendage on its tail poised to strike. The Sword of the Spirit slashed downward even as the tail snapped forward. The crab claw clamped shut on the blade. The creature underestimated the magical qualities of the weapon. Trestan's gamble paid off as he felt the keen edge shear through the claw. The severed half of the claw dropped to the side as the blade continued to cut downward, slicing through the tail and leaving a deep cut across the back.

The first instinct of the summoned beast caused it to hop backward instead of pushing the attack. Trestan fluidly spun into the second swing. Anticipating the canine's movements, the young warrior kept his closeness. The blade came across again, taking the front legs from the creature. The chosen of Abriana didn't delay ending the creature's misery, even though it was made of magic. A third swipe proved fatal to the ferocious antagonist.

Breathing heavily, one hand placing pressure over his new shoulder wound, Trestan glanced across the deck toward his foes. Jentan's voice floated to his ears as the mentalist cried out in glee, "Boat clear! Let us depart."

Resigned to continue the struggle, Trestan turned and jogged behind the remaining pair of summoned beasts. The storm of spells continued to flash past him as the elf wizard and the abbess of the Death Goddess remained stubborn against the onslaught of the mage guild. Scanning the battle, his brown eyes searched in vain for his beloved. Where was Cat?

**CHAPTER 20**            **"An Eye for an Eye, a Throat for a Throat"**


Savannah gathered in the energies of a miracle as she watched the summoned monsters approach. The cleric let loose the power of her goddess in the form of a thin, black bolt which streaked across that short space. The energy ripped a creature from its physical manifestation, dispersing it back into the magical essence of the world.

That left one summoned monster bearing down on Revwar. The elf wizard had nearly expended all his arcane energy. The toll of the spells wore down his mental awareness. He managed to let loose another exploding ice projectile which shredded the final monster. Even as he accomplished that minor victory, the spells of the mage guild took down all but one of his remaining spell shields.

Jentan yelled and motioned for the rest of his band to make their escape. The mentalist had the levitation boat poised at the edge of the deck and ready to drop away from the dying hulk of the divine chariot. He continued to ignore the woman kneeling nearby. Completely oblivious to her true surroundings, Sondra remained lost in her false illusion. The acolyte chanted along with the weakened mantra still supporting the ship.

Savannah prepared to meet Trestan's advance with her dangerous flail, but Revwar waved her back. The elf wizard would not take chances where this human was concerned. Trestan slowed slightly when seeing the elf begin a spell. The young warrior wanted to be ready to evade or deflect any magical attack. Revwar would not leave it as easy as that. Flames danced on the wizard's fingertips as he prepared to blast the entire area in front of him with an inferno.

The elf's voice failed him as the tip of a silver rapier lanced his throat, erupting below his chin. Having been injured by that weapon before, he had no doubts as to the identity of the assailant standing behind him.

She whispered in his ear, "An eye for an eye, a throat for a throat. Now you will know how it feels to choke on your own blood."

Four years previous, Revwar had hurled a deadly ray of energy at Cat. The spell severed her windpipe, slowly killing her as she tried in vain to draw breath. If not for Trestan finding his faith and his ability to heal through Abriana, she would have died amongst helpless friends. Thanks to Trestan's miracle, Cat no longer bore any scars on her neck.

With a sudden jerk, Katressa Bilil pulled the rapier free of his punctured flesh.

A gurgling noise escaped Revwar's throat as the elf wizard brought a hand up to his injury. He staggered a couple steps away from the half-elf, turning with surprise in his yellow eyes. Lips moved as he vainly struggled to utter a spell. Without the ability to speak the arcane syllables of magic, the wizard was no more than a bow without arrows. She moved to finish Revwar. His robe would resist being punctured by her fine weapon, so she stabbed high. Revwar proved to have one trick up his sleeve…more precisely, the sleeve itself. The length of the elf's sleeve draped over his free hand. As Cat lunged, he grabbed the blade, using the protection of the silky, magical robe.

Cat struggled, trying to slash her weapon free of his grip. Revwar's other hand, bloody from holding his wound, reached out for her. The wizard lacked the ability to cast spells, but he still had the enchantment which lent him unnatural strength. Those yellow eyes bulged from the lack of air. Revwar grabbed her black leather tunic in one hand and pulled her closer. Boots skidded on rotted wood as she tried to twist from his iron grip. His left hand released the blade, only to grab her belt.

Cat lost the grip on her rapier as the wizard shook her like a rag doll. His throat made awful wheezing noises during the effort. She could not match his magical strength. Panic was in her own eyes as she tried to think of an escape from his firm grasp. She wanted to reach one of her daggers but her body shook too violently to tell up from down.

Trestan advanced up the deck as fast as he could hurry. Savannah had ignored him to come to Revwar's aid. The cleric had difficulty trying to heal the wizard due to the frantic movements.

Revwar, pale by the light of the fires, angrily raised Cat's body over his head. She weakly slapped at him as the world spun around her vision. They were close to the side rail which bordered the long fall to the clouds below. Trestan shouted protest as he saw the intent. Calling upon his magical endowment, Revwar heaved Cat through the air toward the outer edge of the deck. The effort caused Revwar to collapse. Cat's body desperately flailed for any kind of handhold as momentum carried her toward the boundary between ship and sky.

Trestan winced as his love collided with the side rail. To his horror, the rotted railing splintered as the half-elf's body smacked against it. Part of the railing fell over the edge, while the rest leaned away from the deck under the weight. Deck boards cracked and bent. Cat lie sprawled against the wreckage in a daze. Trestan heard the moan of pain in her voice as her weight sagged against the weakened wood. Planks and supports groaned as their strength faltered.

One of her legs already dangled in the open sky. She moved yet seemed unaware of the danger of her predicament. The broken railing and warped floorboards supporting her weight were ready to snap off at any second. Cat's movement only drew her closer to the precipice. Trestan did not have time to worry about the other band. He turned his sprint toward his beloved. He prayed to Abriana he could get to her side in time, even as he heard the wood cracking beneath her hips.

*      *      *      *      *

Kemora heard Jentan's frantic call to gather at the lifeboat. Two worries preoccupied the halfling. One, included the relics in the hold with the red-haired chiaso. The other concern, foremost on her mind, was the fancy human minstrel threatening her with his smallsword.

The human displayed skill with the weapon. His feet moved gracefully, every thrust measured and nearly effortless. Kemora could not cross the gap and get within her short reach.

A fight with this man would be a prolonged waste of time she could not spare. Kemora kept up a defense with her sword while her other hand reached inside a pouch for another weapon. The halfling spun away from the minstrel's reach. As she did so, she set the bolo into a spinning motion around her body. Lindon pursued slowly, expecting a trap. It gave the halfling a little space to work as she flung the bolo back at him.

The halfling weapon performed true to its design. The weighted balls at the ends of the string entangled Lindon's legs. The minstrel could not keep balance with his legs wrapped up in the cord. He stumbled until falling forward. Lindon feared the halfling would have him now, but she sought escape. Kemora turned to run to the safety that the lifeboat offered.

Lindon refused to let her escape so easily. From the pocket of his vest, he withdrew the long, bamboo flute. Still lying on the rotted wood, Lindon began to draw on the harmonic web through his music. He didn't blow into the flute as one normally would. Using magic, he formed notes on the instrument as he inhaled the song.

A rush of wind slammed headlong into Kemora. The notes of an eerie melody crashed against her with waves of resistance, before being sucked past and into Lindon's flute. Kemora leaned into the wind just to take a few precious steps. The notes of music increased, drowning out all other noise as the wind picked up around the halfling. Any human-sized creature might have made progress through the waves of sound. Kemora's small stature wasn't enough to fight against the gale. The halfling soon crawled on hands and knees.

It wasn't enough. She started to slide backward, clawing the deck for any handholds. She screamed for her cohorts to assist her. It seemed as if the musical force took away her voice. The rush of wind pushed her back toward the waiting human.

*     *     *     *     *

Out of the corner of his vision, Trestan saw Savannah at Revwar's side. Her miraculous prayer could be heard as Revwar's neck began to recuperate. There was no time to worry about it. Trestan rushed the last few steps to Katressa even as the half-elf lifted her head, finally realizing the danger of her predicament. She scrambled to find a firm grip even as soft, rotted wood ripped apart beneath her weight. Part of the deck and more of the railing snapped apart. Cat's lower body dropped over the edge and out of sight as her arms clawed at anything that seemed solid. Boards that had stood firm for several hundred years became soft and crumbly. The shattered railing had enough weight to rip a section of the hull and the deck outwards as it caved under gravity. Shattered boards and tarnished metal fixtures tumbled away.

Cat's boots kicked against the sides of the hull. Anything her hands grabbed peeled away under her weight. The railing dipped until a large section snapped completely off. She got one hand on a deck board which then snapped, dropping her a few inches before she could find another temporary handhold. The top rows of boards forming the rim of the hull began to loosen in sequence.

As pieces of *Doranil Star* tore free, they rode the wind currents until fading into the soft haze of clouds below. The observation deck didn't even have an opening below where she struggled. She desperately searched for anything solid as she slipped below the level of the sundeck.

Trestan hurriedly removed his protective gauntlets as he got close. The deck degenerated into a mess of broken boards forming a gouge in the side of the vessel. Trestan dove to the deck, flattening out his weight over more space. The wooden planks groaned under his weight as he reached out for her.

The top of her head and her frightened, emerald eyes came back into view as she pulled upwards. Trestan called out, "Cat, I'm here. Take my hand!"

She locked her eyes on his offered hand. Trestan stretched out, head and shoulders extended over an open area. With a grunt of effort, Cat used the crumbling boards to make one desperate surge forward. There was the briefest touch of her soft hand against his fingertips before she fell again.

Trestan's hand clamped shut on empty air. She screamed only briefly. Trestan worried he lost her, but she retained a grip on a lower board. Trestan tried to wiggle closer to the precipice, as he watched her slender fingers hold on for life.

*　　　*　　　*　　　*　　　*

Jentan Mollamos had wand in hand as he glanced over the situation, his charming face a mask of calm despite the conflict. His magic could do little against the throng of angry mages scrambling over broken masts. The cleric named Sondra was still wrapped in the illusion inspired by his words. The paladin and half-elf woman were sufficiently distracted. Revwar had suffered a crippling injury, but even now the abbess of Death was healing the wound. One immediate threat existed by the side of the hold, where Kemora was dragged against her will toward the minstrel Jentan loathed.

The best illusions were always mixed with some aspect of realism. Jentan began to allow his words to carry on the night air. Arcane syllables floated along the winds, attracted to the sound funnel that pulled at the halfling. The minstrel saw the halfling's sword being carried along the vortex, sliding across the deck point-first toward his face.

Lindon broke concentration as he rolled to one side. The insubstantial mirage of the sword slid past and disappeared. Kemora skittered away from the man, her real sword sheathed at her hip. Before Lindon could resume his song, he saw the mentalist raising the wand in his direction. Legs still hindered by the bolo cord, Lindon rolled to avoid the first blast of energy.

Jentan redirected his wand even as Lindon put the bamboo flute to his lips. A reverberating tune of high-pitched noise came from the instrument. This time, the streak of magic deflected off of an unseen barrier created by sound, dispersing into the night sky.

Kemora, short legs pumping, ran past the mentalist. "I'm ready, let's go!"

The domid paid no attention to Sondra's form as she vaulted the side of the levitation boat. The smaller craft sat on the edge, moored by one final rope that kept it from drifting away. Kemora's head barely peered over the rim of the escape craft as she watched the approach of Korrelothar and the rest of the wizards.

Savannah scolded the halfling, "How dare you try to leave without the relics? They are the reason for being here."

Kemora whined in displeasure, "But they fell in the hold with that red-haired wench. We barely have time to get out alive."

As if to accentuate the point, Jentan fired another blast from his wand out toward Korrelothar and the approaching mob. The founding member of the Brotherhood of the Circles guild avoided the searing energy at the expense of his aim. Korrelothar's fireball roared over the heads of the band only to scorch the figurehead at the bow.

Revwar was the only one that could act fast enough to make good their escape. His yellow eyes swept over them. "All of you get in the boat. I will get the relics and push us off."

Savannah and Jentan retreated to the boat under a hail of wizard bolts and lightening blasts. The worshipper of DeLaris felt the heat as one spell seared through a portion of her armor. Kemora made room, although the domid cringed at seeing the open sky that was to be their escape route.

Since Savannah and Jentan were the only two offering spells in response to the firestorm of mages, Revwar was left unhindered when approaching the hold. The youth with the red hair could be seen sprawled across a pile of supplies. The woman moved, although her face was a bloody mess from Savannah's flail. Her hands pawed a cloth bag lying with her among the crates. Through a tear in the bag, Revwar could make out a shade of green hidden inside.

The elf wizard recited a spell that bestowed upon him the ability of flight. His robes spread like wings as he floated into the hold. Montanya barely made out a dark shape against a darker sky. One good eye stared at the wizard even as her hands clutched the bag. Any words she might have tried to say were lost in the broken mess of bones in her mouth.

Revwar easily batted her hand away, and tucked the top of the bag into his belt. As an afterthought, he decided to claim a spoil of battle that would help his relations with one of his allies. Looking at the golden locket around her neck, the elf recalled how much domids such as Kemora liked shiny trinkets. His slender fingers, augmented by spells to achieve strength far above his own, reached down and snapped the amulet's chain off Montanya's neck. Montanya's throat could only give a mournful groan in protest as Revwar took to flight once again, taking the precious heirloom.

Revwar soared to the deck just in time. Barrages of spells from the mage guild blasted a false image of the boat Jentan had created their minds. As soon as the explosive energies ripped through the false image, the mistake became apparent. Revwar felt a thrown dagger glance harmlessly off his magical robe. Lindon stood nearby, over the cut strands of the bolo cord.

The elf wizard, ignoring the minstrel, used his gift of flight to skim across the deck to his allies. "Hold on tight!"

The air nearly rushed from all of them as Revwar slammed into the side of the levitation boat with his augmented strength. The impact forced it over the edge. Revwar sprawled across the inside of the boat after rolling over the side. The band of four drifted on currents of magic as the boat slowly began sinking below the level of the deck…

…sinking straight downward from the spot it had left the bow, as the momentum of the divine chariot carried the larger ship past it, bringing the members of the mage guild closer.

…sinking very slowly as wands, staves, and hands wrapped in the flames of evocations pointed at the easy target floating off to the side.

Savannah ignored protests as she crawled her heavy armor across arms and legs to reach the front of the boat. "Hold on or prepare to meet DeLaris! I'm getting us away from that heathen ship."

At the lifeboat's bow hummed the globe of holy water which lent its levitation miracle. The abbess Savannah knew she could block the levitation effect temporarily, although the results could be disastrous. She hooked one leg under a wooden slat meant to serve as a seat as her hands firmly closed around the orb.

Her voice chanted the holy words of the Death Goddess. Immediately, the globe at the fore dimmed. The craft lost its magical cushion, dropping like a rock. Words were lost over the rush of air as they fell. Comets of fire, ice, and lightening ripped apart the air where they had floated a moment before. The Brotherhood of the Circles, as well as the nobles floating along in their own escape craft, noted the freefall of the levitation boat. Savannah, Kemora, Jentan and Revwar gripped the craft with pale knuckles as the clouds rose up to meet them.

As they dropped into the dark mist, Savannah ceased chanting. Theoretically, the holy globe would light and resume the cushion of air that would halt their plummet.

Theoretically…

*       *       *       *       *

Trestan winced as he felt the weakened wood beneath him sag dangerously. He eased himself forward, listening to the groaning complaints offered by the deck. Looking down at Cat, hanging on by her fingers to a solitary strong board, Trestan dared to push himself a little farther.

"Don't chance it, Trestan. I don't want you falling also."

Cat's long, raven hair blew across her face as she looked back up at her love. Behind her, nothing outlined her head except the distant, insubstantial gray clouds. Tenuous as her grip was, she didn't try to find any more toeholds. Only a smooth hull curled away where her legs dangled.

Trestan reached down, barely touching her left knuckles. "Reach for me, Cat. This is as far as I can stretch."

Cat swallowed hard as she looked at his hand dangling above her one good handhold. Faithful's Companion glinted at her from his fingers. She was scared but if she did nothing her arms would give out soon.

With a grunt of effort, she tried to throw her body up enough to catch his hand. Her right fingers held tight to the hull as she felt his hand grab her left. They were joined, hand in hand, in a precarious position on the edge of disaster.

Trestan started to strain with the effort of pulling Cat up. The wood beneath him split and cracked under the effort. For one awful moment, it seemed like the deck was about to give away under the weight of Trestan and his armor.

"Stop, Trestan!" Cat huffed, panting from all the exertion. Trestan did stop, holding steady as he considered his own delicate predicament. For a moment, she looked past him into the night sky, or toward whatever gods watched down on adventurous fools. The half-elf's emerald eyes beseeched his, "Just hold me for a moment. I'm going to shift my weight to that hand, and I'll need you to hold strong."

Trestan nodded, anchoring himself as best that he could. Cat released the hull with her free hand. He expected her to jump up for a better handhold, instead she surprised him. While he held firm to her left hand, her right hand moved to the unusual bracer she had strapped there. All her weight suspended from his grip. Trestan gritted his teeth as he strained to maintain the hold and his position on the deck.

Cat's nimble fingers worked at the buttons holding the fabric over the odd lump on her bracer. She undid the first one. She continued on to the next button, panting in effort, instead of trying to find any better hold on the ship. Soon the second button was free, and her fingers fiddled with the last.

Trestan slowly slid closer to the edge. He felt the end of a board splinter away beneath his shoulder. Blood from his wound trickled down his neck. "Cat, get a grip somewhere, I'm sliding."

"Almost…" she started to say, then a loud crack sounded from beneath the young paladin. The third button came free even as Cat felt Trestan on the verge of going over the edge. She slapped her right hand against a board, barely finding purchase with her fingers. Her eyes widened in fear as she saw the deck crumbling beneath Trestan.

"I'm ok, I'm safe. Let go and help yourself lest you fall."

Trestan had to trust her. He allowed her hand to slip from his fingers as he reached back for a better grip on a board. It came not a moment too soon, before a portion of the deck snapped loose and fell away.

The loose wood came apart under Cat's fingers, taking her last firm hold on the ship. She fell. Trestan's outstretched hand reached in vain even as she dropped out of reach.

His mind screamed denial even as her receding emerald eyes were framed by her trailing raven tresses. Her arms remained outstretched to him, as if she could bring him comfort in that moment when he was losing the most precious thing in the world.

Katressa gave a shout as she fell. "Fifteen!"

Trestan barely had time to puzzle that last word, when he saw the surprise hidden under the bulge in her bracer. A grappling hook unfolded as it launched back toward the ship, trailing a cord of thin rope. The hook went over Trestan's head, entangling itself in a yardarm and rigging. The rope snapped taut almost immediately. The weakened yardarm gave a groan from the sudden weight.

Katressa dangled at the end of that slim lifeline, below the bottom of the hull.

Trestan had almost forgotten his own precarious position until a strong set of arms pulled him back from the edge. Lindon of Orlaun helped Trestan into a sitting position. Under that wide-brimmed hat he wore a look of concern.

Cat's plight did not go unnoticed. Members of the mage guild were still looking over the hull at where Revwar's party had made their hasty escape. Many looked on helplessly, but Korrelothar jumped off of the deck, robes spreading out like wings as Revwar's flight spell had done. The guild elder floated easily on the high winds as he gracefully descended. For the half-elf, an angel came out of the heavens to save her. Cat tearfully accepted his embrace as he took her into his arms, her own arms allowed to relax. Korrelothar bore her back up to the deck with his spell.

The adventuress, normally very sure of her footing, went weak in the knees when Trestan reached her. Lindon, Korrelothar, and the rest of the mages standing nearby busied themselves with the other issues at hand as Trestan and Cat tearfully embraced. The relic thieves were gone, but the crew still had to save the last few people on board from the fate of the dying ship.

**CHAPTER 21**          **"Abandon Ship"**


"So that is what you had hidden…"

Cat quickly hushed Trestan, holding a finger to his lips as she showed him the bracer. Underneath a shroud, now only partially covered by it, sat a gleaming metallic disk the size of a coin. It was mounted on the bracer behind where the grappling hook rested. After Trestan had gotten a good look, Cat silently buttoned the fabric back over the disk, hiding it once again.

"Let me guess," Trestan offered, "That is a small version of the gnomish lifting device."

Cat let loose a mischievous smile. "Ever since we encountered that one back on the island, I had some thoughts toward other uses for it. I found some gnomes who made this version for me."

Trestan knew the dangers associated with the magical disk, which could propel people or objects into the air or across level surfaces using a strong cushion of air. The first use they had seen for one was a lift that could propel people up a shaft to different levels of a keep. The maximum number of gnomish-equivalent floors it could project an item was fifteen…which explained Cat's use of that word as she fell. The disk reacted to the command in her voice, launching the unfolding grappling hook hidden in her bracer up fifteen gnomish-equivalent levels. Petrow had wanted to take the larger version they had discovered years ago, but it was a very dangerous item because one had to avoid saying the wrong words. After Petrow was catapulted several meters when it mistook the word 'to' for 'two', he finally agreed to leave the dangerous item behind.

Trestan asked Cat, "Isn't that a dangerous thing to have strapped to your arm?"

Cat tapped a slender finger against the fabric covering the disk. "That's why I have it covered with this. It's also magic, dampening sound to the point where the disk won't hear commands unless I unbutton and pull back the cover."

"Ingenious." A voice commented.

Korrelothar stood beside them, admiring the design of the bracer. He raised his eyes to encompass both of them, extending his arms out to their shoulders. "I'm told that while we were enjoying in festivities, the two of you were fighting below to save the ship and the relics."

Trestan shrugged sadly as he spoke, "They got away."

"Taking the relics with them." Korrelothar nodded. The elf gave Trestan a reassuring squeeze. "But not from lack of effort on behalf of the two of you. You are indeed the appointed guardians and were more vigilant at it than my guild brothers."

His words seemed little comfort to the couple. They had worked and suffered, only to see their efforts fall short. Korrelothar felt the weakness of the deck beneath them, and urged them to think of the present. "The relics will have to wait for another time. At the moment we are still in a predicament. There is nay assurance that the clerics of Ganden can keep us afloat for much longer. We must get everyone off the vessel. I see you are both bleeding, take these." Korrelothar handed them health concoctions.

Trestan and Cat nodded gratefully. Both were too wounded and winded to turn down the regenerative drinks. Once healed, they moved across the deck to see how they could be of assistance. It occurred to Cat she still had the coded parchment tucked in her belt, but she decided to let that news wait until she had more of a chance to decode it. Others had to be saved from the more impending danger first.

*  *  *  *  *

It wasn't hard for Lindon to ascertain why the young acolyte of Ganden had a foggy look to her eyes as she kneeled on the damaged deck. Sondra repeated her mantra at the spot where Jentan and his party had made their escape. Lindon brought the bamboo flute to his lips. A shrill, discordant note shook the cleric from her illusion.

Sondra glanced around to Lindon, the vessel, and the area where Jentan had been standing. Memory replaced illusion so fast it took a moment for her to adjust, as if waking from a vivid dream that seemed persuasively real. The young woman didn't fight Lindon as he took her by the arm and urged her to stand. She was only dimly aware of the mace hanging from her hand.

She turned to Lindon, displaying confused anger. "Where is Jentan Mollamos? Where is the traitor?"

"Beyond our grasp for now," Lindon motioned toward the edge of the deck. "He made his exit beyond the clouds below. Look not to those scoundrels young priestess, but to the rest of the people on board your divine vessel. We must be away soon after the injured receive care."

Sondra walked with Lindon, exchanging the mace in her hands with her rust-colored leather healing satchel. Their steps carried them past the hold, where Lindon glanced down to see a familiar red-haired youth stirring. Her face was bloody yet she was alive. The torn flesh of one hip had been exposed by a halfling blade. The youth writhed in pain, grasping for things only she could see.

"There is someone who needs our help now," Lindon paused to examine some loose rigging that hung nearby. "If we secure a rope somewhere, I can help get her up here."

Sondra barely glanced at the figure in the hold, not recognizing the battered form. The acolyte of Ganden and the minstrel from Orlaun set about anchoring a length of rope. Frustrated by the rotting wood, Lindon finally suggested they find a few extra hands to manage the rope.

Lindon wrapped the end of the rope around one arm and then took up his flute. Using music to tap into magic, he floated easily down into the hold. He kneeled beside Montanya as soon as his feet touched down gently atop the crates. Lindon recognized the youth that had fought without an inner rhythm. He felt the disharmonious qualities of her soul even more keenly as the woman reacted to hallucinations spurred on by her injuries. She whispered incomplete sentences, incomprehensible due to injury, even as she grasped at something intangible in the space above her. One bloody hand reached for something unseen.

It was impossible for Lindon to arrange the rope around her during those struggling movements. Montanya's raw anger motivated her as she pushed away the helping hands. Lindon turned to music to clear her mind. A few notes tinged with magic lulled the youth. Her muscles relaxed, allowing him to wrap the rope around both of them.

Montanya's mind was brought back to the present, although her surroundings were still hazy. The one feeling dominating her senses was the pain that raged against her skull. Normally she would find comfort in anger, but the minstrel's musical notes had settled around her like a soothing remedy. Montanya watched the world but did not intervene even as she felt the arms around her. Her conscious mind watched events as if from afar.

She felt the rough rope encircle her torso. Her ears dimly recognized voices from above calling out their readiness to pull up the rope. Strong arms encircled her even as a red-rimmed hat blocked out much of the night sky. Mixed in among those scattered images, Montanya noticed loose supplies down lower in the hold. The wreckage of crates mixed with scraps of spilled food. Lying in the middle of it all, glinting at the edges of the moonlight streaming into the hold, were a pair of strange green eggs lying at the mouth of a sack. Montanya had never seen eggs like them. They were marked by white lines scratched across their surface; larger than most eggs she had ever seen.

Lindon gestured for the others to haul the rope. As the people above pulled with their strength, Lindon played a tune on the flute. With one arm wrapped protectively around Montanya, the other provided the notes that gave them levitation. The two were lifted up to the deck with little effort.

Trestan and Katressa were among those providing muscles to haul the rope. They recognized the youth they had saved from the cell. Trestan moved to heal Montanya, but a young cleric elbowed past him on her way to fulfill her duties to Ganden.

Sondra fished an item out of her healing satchel as she approached the rescued youth. When the acolyte looked up and finally recognized her patient, she shook her head in disbelief. Although the face was a bloody mess, Sondra recognized the leather pads strapped around the loose-fitting clothes, as well as the torn pink fabric at the end of the long braid of reddish hair.

Sondra Oskires muttered as she squirted a drop of some curative liquid into Montanya's shattered mouth. "This is my third time trying to help this ungrateful whelp. Am I going to get any thanks for this, or more water splashed in my face?"

The acolyte of Ganden put her hands on both sides of Montanya's injured face and channeled a prayer. The initial shock of pain from the touch diminished as the warmth of the healing miracle spread through the injured youth. Bones popped as they snapped back into place, muscles knit back together where they had been torn, and blood flowed normally. The wet blood on the side of her head began to dry up and fall off in flakes. The swelling around her bad eye went down, yet still left a discolored bruise in its place. The wound on the hip also began to close over and shed its dried blood. Ganden's follower did the best she could do before her own strength drained. Sondra leaned back on her heels when she was done. The look on her face mirrored the look of personal satisfaction mixed with mental drain that Trestan felt when he healed wounds.

Montanya still displayed bruises as if she had been in a fistfight, but the broken bones and all of the major damage had been repaired. The young chiaso sat upright.

Montanya's sudden movement accidentally elbowed the acolyte. Her thoughts surfaced as if from a deep slumber. She tenderly touched at her face, wincing when she still felt a few sore areas. Memories returned with clarity in her mind. Hands went to her neck, then patted down closer to her chest, searching in vain for the locket she realized she wouldn't find.

"They took it." Montanya said it as barely a whisper, though clearly enough for the people around her to hear the words. The youth jumped to her feet. She looked over the deck as angry, restless energy was apparent in her movements. "Where are they? Couldn't anyone stop them? They took my locket."

The chiaso missed the disappointed sigh that escaped Sondra's lips. The wheat-blonde acolyte resigned herself to the notion that Montanya did not know how to express thanks. Montanya continued to rage at the departed band as Lindon, Trestan and Cat watched.

Lindon, his head cocked to one side, sought to voice through the woman's tirade. "Whatever they were after, they are long gone. What is this locket of which you speak?"

The woman's foul curses raised eyebrows on everyone nearby. She finally paused to answer Lindon. "They are thieves and bandits. They took the last reminder I had of my departed parents, who were also killed by thieves. They took a precious locket I held dear. That elf mage came down into the hold just to rip it from my neck."

"Don't mind her," Sondra interrupted with more than a little venom in her own tone. "This is Montanya su Tralala bara Something-or-other. She tends to see thieves everywhere she looks. A short while ago she was locked up in the brig…a fitting place I'd say."

Montanya glared at Sondra. "Where I would still be stuck, on a dying ship, nay thanks to you!"

"I couldn't aid you, but I sent help!" Sondra waved an arm toward Trestan and Cat, both of whom quietly observed the exchange. "It seems they were of some assistance. Did you remember to at least thank them for their services?"

Montanya had no answer and no intention to back down from Sondra. Her anger flared from her loss, and Montanya never had an easy time holding back her rage. Rage was comfort. The youth simply huffed and turned away.

"Be easy on that one," Lindon whispered to Sondra. "Her life lacks balance. When someone lacks a direction in life, it isn't helpful for someone to berate them for it. Montanya's emotions could hurry her to choose a path that is destructive for herself and others around her."

Cat decided to intervene in a way that would take the conversation in a different direction. "Montanya is correct in calling them thieves. Trestan and I originally met them years ago when they stole some important relics for reasons unknown. The relics were recovered and were on this ship, but however they managed it, that band sabotaged the ship and made off with the relics again."

As she spoke, Cat absently put a hand on the rolled piece of leather still tucked into her belt. At least she had been able to retrieve something that might be of value.

They were all startled by a crashing noise. One of the rear masts split apart, coming down to the deck in a shower of broken wood. Korrelothar joined them in moments. "Time is short and we are among the last on board. Get on that levitation boat and prepare to cast off."

Trestan, Cat, Lindon, Sondra and Montanya walked toward a boat that was ready to be released. The deck had become quiet. The distant hum of the mantra was the most prevalent sound as they stepped aboard the smaller craft. Less than two dozen of the crew and mages were left, setting adrift the last remaining escape vessels. Korrelothar directed the launches, making sure every boat had a member of the mage guild in it to better ensure safety for whatever lay below.

The five of them sat in silence, the levitation boat resting on two planks, suspended over the edge of the deck. Trestan and Cat sat hand in hand. They used silent body language and glances to make known their love for each other, after the close call that had nearly taken Cat. On the opposite end of the emotions, Sondra and Montanya sat in a way that put Lindon between them. Neither woman even so much as glanced at the other.

One of the planks supporting the levitation boat gave way, weakened by the rotting of the vessel. The craft tipped precariously on the remaining plank. Trestan and Cat were close to the remaining support. The two of them pushed at it, dislodging the light craft from its uneven perch. The escape boat leveled out as it began its slow fall, soft light emitting from the globe of holy water at the bow. Korrelothar noticed the unintentional, early release too late to do anything about it. The elf wizard apologetically offered up a wave of his hand as the boat descended past the level of the deck. Trestan and Cat shrugged at the situation and merely waved back. The elf wizard could only pause a moment to watch their descent before hurrying the last boats along.

The levitation boat dropped leisurely, slowing its forward flight as it lost the momentum that still carried the *Doranil Star* onward into the night. Sondra reached out a hand to the divine vessel, running her fingers along the old wood. She felt the hum of the mantra. Mother Evine's voice weighed strongly in the tune of the meditation. The broken and torn masts resembled a skeleton, reaching up with broken joints in denial of its passing. The open area of the observation deck floated by, gloomy and foreboding. Once, archers and mages had fought the Godswars from this level, and in more recent times spectators had walked along it in enjoyment of a sky cruise. Now, the deck began decaying into ruin. Parts of the ceiling and floor were collapsing under the weight of the ship. Lamps were dark, some hanging crookedly from nails that no longer found solid purchase in the rot. Somewhere inside the ship, a room full of rare magical wonders was slowly being carried to an unknown resting place. Sondra's fingers trailed across tainted lettering gilded on the side of the ship, proclaiming Ganden's divinity. In the heart of the great vessel, a few chanting disciples of Ganden would see the mighty ship to the end of its last voyage, before joining it alongside their god in the next world. The two-hundred-and-sixty-foot-long divine chariot passed by the small levitation boat bearing the companions. The old oak hull drifted out of reach, slipping away from Sondra's reaching arm. The five of them on the boat watched silently as the hulking shape sailed into the starlit horizon. Their drifting refuge slowly descended among a sky trail of descending escape boats.

Squire Trestan Karok watched the magnificent vessel with heavy heart. He could not help but think of the shattered remains of Korrelothar's *Dovewing*. The demise of that vessel had been sudden and chaotic by comparison. *Doranil Star* met its end quite differently. Watching this ship journeying so peacefully and slowly to its death conjured an image akin to an elderly, honorable knight; a veteran of many campaigns whom had served his lord faithfully for much longer than expected. Reminded of his own service, the young paladin glanced downward at the ring upon his finger. Faithful's Companion had a shiny, reflective surface to it, yet symbols still remained on its surface. The quest he had sought after his Embarking remained unfulfilled.

Katressa Bilil leaned against Trestan for warmth. Something in her elf blood made her feel colder on a night that had seen such evil tidings. Her emerald eyes glistened with wetness at the passing of the great vessel. Her own mortality vexed her mind, a concept few of elf heritage ever paused much to consider. Despite the long centuries she expected to live past that of her beloved, her life had still come dangerously close to ending a few times that night. What had they gained for all their efforts? Cat felt the smooth leather of the rolled scroll at her belt and pondered its value. What would they learn from its secrets? She felt Trestan shift as he glanced at his ring, and she only hugged him tighter. She often worried about his mortality over her own: however, who can know the unforeseen future, the lives that adventure brings, or the plots of desperate wizards?

Sondra Oskires could only stare through tears as her beloved dream passed away from her. She worshipped Ganden, the God of Honor, Duty, and Service…and yet she was asked to leave the vessel. The young woman sensed the pull of her calling, and felt that she was being asked to turn from it by not being there in the inner sanctum with Mother Evine. Sondra knew that to stay was to die; leaving the ship meant living to serve Ganden in selfless devotion another day. The concept didn't balance out in her mind. How could escape have been the calling of Duty? Her honor and her service to her own god should have demanded she stay behind and die if needed. It was a confusing swirl of emotions that left her questioning her every action that night. She mourned the loss of her mentor, the divine chariot, and all her dreams that had centered on it. Sondra wept openly, not caring who witnessed it.

Montanya su Troyeal bara Westonhout silently scoffed at the crying cleric. The youth always hid any feelings of helplessness or hurt, and despised such a show from others. She would choose her anger any day over showing signs of weakness to predators and thieves. Her hands absently felt at her chest, where she would normally feel the comfort of her locket. The hairs of her mother and father intertwined within, close to her heart, was now gone. She viewed the world from the horrors of her own childhood. She saw the ship as something that had now been stolen from the church. The unknown relics Trestan and Cat were guarding…stolen. The lives of the people lost that night…stolen. It was easier for Montanya to conform the world into a narrower, straightforward view. Someday she would be the hero. Someday she would make thieves pay for their crimes. Someday that deed would somehow relieve the pains of her personal losses.

Lindon of Orlaun was not one to let any details escape his notice in that emotional time. As a minstrel, it was important that he note the reactions and faces on his varied companions, even as he watched the great divine chariot sail away from the hands of mortals. He recalled his own thrills at flying high above the despondent streets of the Highwater district, while giving the best performance he had ever given while amongst those clouds. It had been a thrilling high point in his life and his career, only to meet a tragic ending. Yet, he was a man apart from the worst of the disaster.

To understand the true range of emotions, he had to look into the eyes of those with him. In Sondra's eyes he saw the obedient cleric whose faith had been strained by the ordeal. Her emotional loss was on a par that Lindon could not truly grasp. In the angry youth, Montanya, he saw only resignation that crime was a part of how she normally saw the world. As long as she was lost in the past of whatever had slighted her views, she would never reach the inner peace desired to bring balance to her spirit. Trestan and Cat had taken it upon themselves to guard something they felt was as important as the divine chariot itself. Their failure, and their concerns over the consequences of the theft, weighed heavily on their shoulders.

Lindon wondered what roles these people still had to play in the continuing struggles. Only Trestan and Cat seemed to have a bold purpose with which to give them direction, the rest were as helpless to plot their course as the drifting lifeboat. Lindon had no great scheme left other than the pursuit of a proper surname. He assumed whatever course these young people picked, his own path would intertwine in some way.

With the *Doranil Star* sailing away blindly, Lindon of Orlaun set his mandolin on his knee and began to play. The tune was the same as the one that had seen the divine vessel depart Orlaun, and which later had been played with a slower rhythm as the vessel was being abandoned. It was played again to honor the somber, tearful departure. Slowly and with great care, Lindon began to play the ballad of the great ship. His earlier notes became more refined now that he had found his ending. Even as the ship drifted far away, those who could hear Lindon play could hear the droning mantra in the background of his music. His tune carried far across the deepening gloom to those other lifeboats that marked the passage of the vessel. Nobles, crewmembers, and mages alike heard music that gave a fitting eulogy for the great warship of old. They watched as the divine chariot took its final curtain bow before leaving the world of mortals.

The keel of Ganden's vessel descended low enough to touch the line of gray clouds. In moments, feathery wisps curled around the ancient hull as it plowed lower. In the light of Aburis, the largest moon, the ship gracefully and quietly dipped deeper into the sea of haze. The skeletal masts were the last glance of the ship as it slipped into the veil of clouds. Lindon's last notes echoed through the air before fading like the great ship itself.

The levitation boat holding the companions also dropped low enough to be swallowed by the clouds. The shrouding fog billowed up around the craft, leaving them feeling isolated in the gloom.

**CHAPTER 22**         **"Revelations in the Mist"**


The setting might have been reminiscent of tales told around a nighttime campfire in the wilderness, when the light in the darkness isolated listeners so that they might better indulge in the storyteller's tale. Instead of a flickering campfire, they had a steady illumination coming from the glass orb containing the holy water. In place of a dark wood, they were surrounded by the fog of clouds. In that setting, the mists around them and the lack of a true fire conspired to seep the warmth from their bodies. They listened to Trestan and Cat talk about the events four years ago. The Companions of the Relics, as they had been dubbed by the villagers of Troutbrook back then, explained their previous adventures when Revwar and Savannah stole three stone relics of mysterious powers. They described how they had finally taken the relics back from the band and placed them back with the rightful owners. One stone went back to Troutbrook, the second was returned to Korrelothar's guild, and the third stone of unknown origin also went to the wizard guild for study. The others in the boat were told of how Revwar and Savannah recently returned with new allies. Many details were shared regarding how they retrieved the stone from Trestan's village by force.

Sondra listened quietly, greatly distracted by the loss of Ganden's ship. The cleric tried ineffectively to hide her weeping, as she absently twisted a holy symbol around in her fingers. It stayed mostly hidden within her hands, but Trestan could make out that it was in the shape of a dog.

Lindon and Montanya provided some insight into the new allies that had joined Revwar's band. Lindon informed them of his first encounter with Jentan Mollamos; when the man had tried to magically seduce a friend of the minstrel. The performer briefly recanted the troubles with Jentan at the recital prior to performing on the *Doranil Star*.

"He is a mentalist," Lindon spoke at one point, "His domain of study specializes in illusions and other tricks of the mind. He seems very good at it, needing only one small hint of a flaw by which he can use his arcane hooks to fool your mind."

Montanya, for her part, told them of her encounter with Kemora when the rogue had stolen the illusion mask. She left out any part about living on the street or being starved for food. The chiaso revealed she had followed the halfling in human guise to the mage guild, and thus snuck aboard the divine chariot at that point.

"But I consider them all thieves!" Montanya said with conviction. "That elf took my most precious possession: the last reminder I had of both of my parents."

Sondra, still shedding tears, interrupted in a low tone. "You cast that title aloft too generously. By your estimation, all the people of churches are cutthroats."

That remark earned her another scowl from the chiaso. "Are you denying that my heirloom is missing? You remember the gold locket I owned. My memory is a bit fuzzy, but I clearly remember the elf wizard snatching it from my neck."

Sondra did not bother trying to make any replies. She continued to sulk while twisting the dog-shaped pendant hanging from her neck. The others on the lifeboat impassively watched the exchange between the two women.

Montanya continued voicing her strong opinions. "What do you know of the real world anyway? You extract coppers from homeless while telling them to save their souls. It is an easy job because you don't even have to rely on any hard evidence to tell you whether or not their soul is saved. Of course, your intentions are honorable, so you have justified it to yourself…"

"Enough!" Sondra cried, "I am tired of being lectured by someone who doesn't contribute anything to their fellows. You have done nothing but get into fights and cause trouble. I gave up my hopes and dreams in order to give it all to a higher purpose. I bowed to Ganden because I can never repay the kindness that others have shown me! I laid aside all my personal goals and ambitions to kneel down in helpful service to others! How dare you mock my choice and even go so far as to label it ignorant or selfish!"

Sondra missed how her words had drawn Trestan's attention. He listened to her emotional outpour as she claimed the sacrifices she had made. His hand stroked his mustache as he read the deeper meaning between her words.

Cat glared at both of them. "I'd love to let you both go into a private room to discuss your differences, but we're all stuck in the same boat. We have larger concerns at stake than catching thieves or justifying our lives to strangers. Those relics are weapons of unknown power. I don't know how we can get them back, but there can't be many civilized areas on this wild continent where one can purchase a boat ride to Orlaun. We need to focus on the larger issue: recovering those stones."

Lindon was glad to have someone interrupt the squabble. The minstrel already sat between the two women; he shifted so as to get directly between their faces, blocking their eye contact. He queried, "Of unknown power? What is really known about these artifacts?"

Trestan and Cat shrugged. After they shared a look, Cat responded. "From what little history we have pertaining to them, it sounds like two were originally given to caretakers by worshippers of Yestreal. I don't know how the third ended up at a Korrelothar's guild. The stones date so far back that it was likely they could have been made during the Godswars, but we don't really know anything about their origin. What we can verify firsthand, is that they have numerous powers. The most subtle of such is they can promote the welfare of farms and cattle. Crops and livestock growing near the relics tend to be healthier, even more resistant to disease than normal."

Cat paused, "But they can be used in warfare as well. They have the power to shatter stone. An army assaulting a castle with one of them could knock down the stone walls easily. I've seen the power of it gut the inside of a keep. The relics also have the ability to summon guardians to protect the bearer. They can create a squad of undead soldiers, or summon in earth elementals. We don't know how much other influence they command."

Lindon had his mandolin in his hands. He strummed a few notes absently as he listened. "What do these relics look like? You said stone, but how big?"

Cat put her hands out to show their size. "Not large at all. A stone could be hefted easily in one hand. They are an odd shade of green, oval, and polished smoothly. They have white runes across their surface…"

Montanya interrupted the half-elf, "Kind of like large, green eggs…with white chicken-scratch marks?"

Cat nodded, "Aye, you probably saw them on display with the other artifacts. They were in that chamber with all the other arcane oddities."

"She likely didn't see them there." The young disciple of Ganden looked past the minstrel at the chiaso again. "She was hiding until they found her and threw her in the brig."

Montanya suddenly found a few inquisitive eyes glancing her way. Trestan put forth a statement for her to acknowledge or deny. "You saw the relics, but not in the display room."

The youth shifted uncomfortably, realizing now what the strange eggs were that she had seen in the hold. "I…well…" She relived the memory again of what she saw, making sure she hadn't dreamed it. "When I was being lifted out of the hold of the ship, I had a few moments of clarity."

Trestan and Cat suddenly sat on the edge of their seats as she spoke. "I saw an opened bag at the bottom of the hold, with two objects glinting at me from the floor. They looked…like two large, green eggs, with white scratch marks on them."

"A bag just like the cloth one you grabbed from them on the deck?" Lindon asked. "I thought Revwar went down and took the bag back from you."

Montanya had her arms out, palms up helplessly, "I don't know. I can't even recall the blow that sent me into the hold. I remember laying down there in pain. There were a few bags and crates. I reached for one…not really too aware of what I was doing. That wizard took the bag in my hands, but I really don't remember well."

"But you saw the stones that we described still in the hold long after they escaped…when you were pulled out of there?" Cat's emerald eyes were no less intense than Trestan's.

The youth was at a loss for words. She just nodded. Trestan looked over the glowing orb at the front of the descending lifeboat. He searched the mist as if he could still see the *Doranil Star*. Katressa caught his eye. Their faces traded a silent conversation. They had despaired that the relics were all in the possession of the other band. Yet, by Montanya's observation, two of the stones were still on board the ghost ship that had sailed off into the unknown.

Lindon actually chuckled over the situation. "Well, they must have grabbed the wrong bag. I wonder what they nabbed instead?"

*          *          *          *          *

The elf's slender fingers drew an outline in the dirt, pausing only briefly to give careful consideration to the magical runes. Yellow eyes gave critical appraisal of the handiwork, before guiding the fingers into the next complex pattern. Revwar murmured arcane meditations as his mind sought to exactly replicate the circle of teleportation that would whisk them back to Orlaun. Every line and figure had to be drawn exactly as its twin. A small mistake would simply prevent them from teleporting…a large error would mean death. The teleportation circles were one of the best means for traversing many miles to an exact target point instantly, but they had to be created flawlessly. Revwar meticulously worked to recreate another one.

His companions mingled nearby, ever watchful that a party of wizards from the ship might be searching for them. Their levitation boat sat among some dense trees, affording them some seclusion. It had been a frightening descent through a tangle of branches. Between their combined magical abilities, they overcame the treacherous landing. The orb at the bow no longer gave off any illumination. Savannah had used the dark miracles of her goddess to destroy the holy receptacle. She wanted to make sure the light did not give them away in the dark, as well as keep any clerics of Ganden from tracking them by looking for its holy aura. The only meager light came from an enchanted necklace Revwar wore.

Kemora kept her hearing focused on the surrounding woods, though it seemed as if the halfling simply lounged in the grounded vessel. Indeed, the domid was relaxing, though occasionally the sounds of people wandering in the woods perked her ears. No one seemed to come close to finding the band, though there were definitely other lost castaways trying to make their way to some point of civilization.

Savannah tried listening to the night sounds, yet she was the most distracting noise in the clearing. The sounds of her plate armor as she restlessly paced was the loudest distraction her acquaintances had to suffer.

Jentan reappeared from the dark trees surrounding their camp. Savannah was about to admonish his disappearance, yet stopped short when she caught sight of the flower offered to her in his hand. The man always seemed to have women on his mind, and would not give up his pursuit of the only female human in their group.

"Even in Orlaun they recognize and covet this lovely bit of nature's art." He smiled at Savannah, offering her the flower. "The fanteria rose, which only grows in the deep forests of this continent. A rare and exquisite gift, best given to a rare and exceptional lady."

Savannah displayed no emotion, though she held a hand out as he gently handed her the flower. Once placed in her hand, Jentan stayed close to whisper in her ear. From the boat, Kemora glanced their direction. The domid wondered if Jentan was going to be foolhardy enough to attempt his magical charms on the abbess that championed Death, and if the priestess' retaliation would be fatal.

Jentan spoke smoothly, "Look down on me not with scorn because I am a victim of my own emotions. Although I may consider myself the master at controlling others, I find my thoughts enslaved by visions of you. Can you forgive me for such strong feelings? I would be unfaithful to myself if I did not express my fondness. Accept this rare token, and recognize it for the compliment that it offers."

Savannah searched her wits enough to make sure the mentalist wasn't attempting any kind of mental charm. She did not detect any magical intrusion into her mind. If she'd felt any kind of spell being worked on her feelings, she would not have hesitated in tearing the life from the man instantly.

The abbess, staring at him through her cold, blue eyes even as she held the flower, responded. "This flower is the best representation of your love? I see your love as weak and empty. It blooms when you wish it then wilts once your goal has been fulfilled."

Jentan watched as she lifted the flower to his eye level. The abbess trickled the power of death into the rose. The mentalist's smile faded as he watched the flower lose color and wilt. The stem and petals became dry and brittle, falling away to ashes that drifted on a breeze.

"I say your love is meaningless." There was no anger in Savannah's eyes, only the impassionate look of a woman who worshipped death over life. "Your feelings are nothing more than spent ashes…carried into the dark by wind."

Jentan had little to say in the face of such a rejection. He could only turn away angrily as he heard chuckles coming from both Revwar and Kemora.

Kemora Quickfeet reclined back in the boat again, feeling like she could easily doze off despite the possibility of danger in the woods. The domid had trouble trying to settle in comfortably. She started to rearrange a bag by the side of her head. Confusion settled in when she realized it was the cloth bag supposedly containing the relics, yet the pair of objects within felt…odd. She sat up with a start, taking a quick inventory of everything still stored inside the boat. Her race had exceptional ability to see in the dark, so the contents of the craft were plain to her vision.

She confirmed that the bag she had been resting against was the one supposedly containing the stone relics, and yet the rogue could tell the objects within were not made of stone. Kemora had seen the relics inside their protective case on board the *Doranil Star*, and was reasonably confident how they should look and feel.

With growing dread, the domid sat upright and began to paw through the bag. There were definitely two round objects inside, but they didn't feel right. She tilted the bag toward Revwar, making more use of the small light from his necklace, and peered inside. Kemora's halfling eyes got as big and round as they could without swallowing the rest of her face.

The halfling felt her throat constrict to the point where she couldn't swallow. She nervously glanced around at her unaware cohorts. After all the efforts they had gone through, and all the planning that had gone awry, only to think that everything had fallen into place…and now Kemora had to break the bad news to the rest of them.

Kemora tried to swallow the lump in her throat. "Ahh. Umm. How do I say this?"

Her voice was nearly inaudible, but Jentan heard her and welcomed any subject that diverted the others from his failed attempt to flirt with Savannah. "What is it?"

"Revwar?" Kemora prompted in a small voice.

The elf wizard looked annoyed at being distracted from his difficult task. "I'm rather busy right now. I hope it's important?"

The halfling rogue held up the cloth bag. "Is this the bag that had the relics in it? You don't happen to have it by you, do you?"

Revwar shifted with an irritated grunt as he held his necklace toward the halfling. The light slid across the side of the bag as he replied. "I left it in the boat beside you. That's it, the bag you are holding. I can see the green relics through the small hole in this side."

Kemora could also see the color green through the small hole, but her glance inside the bag was enough to tell what the green objects really were. "Uhh, well. Those aren't the relics."

The sound of everyone's breathing seemed to stop. Savannah's armored legs halted their nervous pacing, dropping the volume of noise within the camp. Kemora reached into the bag to show the others the objects she had been referring. The rest of her cohorts nearly stumbled over in shock as Kemora withdrew two green limes. She held them up and upended the bag so that they could see for themselves that nothing remained hidden inside.

208

There was a moment of absolute, shocked silence as their folly was realized.

Savannah's fearful cry banished the silence. "Nay! Goddess forgive me. Spare me more punishment."

It was rare for a follower of the Goddess of Death to show fear at anything, since death itself could not scare them. It unnerved her companions to see Savannah drop prostrate in the ferns and moss, begging for mercy. They began to wonder just how brutal Savannah's nightmares had been over the boy who had escaped her claim from DeLaris.

"Spare me more nightmares," she cried into the night. "Allow me to redeem myself. Give me a chance to correct my failure."

Revwar's reaction, though subtle, nevertheless accentuated the storm of anger that had been released inside him. Without a word, the wizard took one slender hand and angrily brushed through the carefully constructed teleport circle. The arcane creation was reduced to a spoiled pattern that bore no more magic than a ruined sand castle hit by the tide. The elf wizard could not believe that after all their efforts another opportunity had been denied to them. He was about to believe that even Kelor, the God of Luck, was casting chance against them.

Jentan shook his head as Savannah still prostrated herself on the ground. The abbess choked out to her cohorts, "We must find where the ship went down. We have to retrieve the other Earthrin Stones."

The fact that the abbess pleaded, instead of using her usual commanding demeanor, sent shivers down Kemora's spine. The domid realized she still held aloft the useless limes. She dropped the fruit back into the bag and casually discarded it.

Jentan appraised the depth of their mistake. "So, we stole a mask from an illusionist." Kemora and Revwar looked up as he began his tirade. "We revealed my allegiances and thus my treachery to my guild. We insulted a god, in nay less a fashion than the sabotage of his divine chariot. Noble families from the most jeweled city were dropped out of the sky. An impressive amount of coin wasted on arcana and information. We lack supplies to navigate this strange land."

Jentan's fists clenched and relaxed repeatedly. "And all of this…the sum of our efforts…bore nay fruit other than a stolen pair of limes!"

The band remained silent, with the exception of Savannah's sobs. Kemora, with a mischievous grin, decided to bring some levity in light of Jentan's words.

The halfling rogue deadpanned, "Imagine what we would have done to get our hands on a pair of watermelons!"

None of her companions seemed to think it was funny.

*　　　　*　　　　*　　　　*　　　　*

"We have to find and retrieve those relics." Trestan said. "That starts with guiding this lifeboat in the direction *Doranil Star* flew."

Sondra shrank back, comprehending what he was asking of her. "I don't think I can do that. You're asking me for what I can't give."

Trestan responded. "You don't think you have it in you, or you simply don't want to try?"

"I failed Ganden," the acolyte whispered. "I should've gone down with his chariot. I wasn't allowed to stay; I'm not even a Chosen. Duty compels me to go back to my temple and report the loss."

"Duty? You're saying you don't have a duty to recover what you can of his relics before the trail is lost?" Trestan did not sound harsh as he spoke. Cat could tell he was testing the young cleric's rationalizations and feelings.

Sondra Oskires was clearly confused by what she should do. It was plain to see she was having trouble deciding her priorities with the loss of her superiors. It seemed the woman favored running home to Orlaun, possibly seeking redemption for her own guilt.

"I'm just an acolyte." She spread her hands apologetically. "I can't fly, nor should I. I can't go out in this land alone like you ask."

Cat interjected a thought, "In regards to that matter, once we get on the ground, Trestan and I *have* to go search for these relics. There is nay time to go for help. Revwar and Savannah are going to realize they have the wrong bag and will set out immediately. I know it's a strange continent down there. If we go after the relics, and you go back toward Orlaun…we're splitting up in dangerous territory. Not a very safe idea."

Trestan agreed with Cat's thinking, but he worried about the tactics she used. He wanted to make sure Sondra's heart was in it. He said, "I was very much like you. I was afraid to really open myself up to my faith, until my beloved Cat lay dying." Trestan's hand reached over and clasped Cat's hand in a gentle squeeze. "I'm sure you can pilot this boat if you try, and it will save us a lot of walking. It may give us the time we need to beat them to the relics. If we do beat them, lives will be saved."

Sondra stammered a reply that never really formed a full sentence. "But…but…" was mostly all she could say. She finally broke down into tears again. "You can't ask this of me, I'm unimportant. I'm just a healer that cares for the poor."

Trestan smoothed over his mustache again as he pondered the acolyte of Ganden. He noticed the dog-shaped pendant on her neck. "You said something earlier…something about giving up all your hopes, dreams and ambitions for Ganden. Is that how you truly feel?"

Sondra nodded. "In order to fully serve a god, you must be their tool in the world. You give everything over to them. I sacrificed myself willingly for all Ganden did for me when I was young. You wear Abriana's crest, surely you know this?"

Trestan leaned closer to the young cleric, grateful Lindon and Montanya kept their silence as he talked. "I once feared worshipping Abriana, feeling I would be giving up my future as well. I was afraid to give her my dedication for fear that nothing would be left of my desires. I was wrong."

Sondra shook her head slightly, but Trestan continued. "You had a teacher that you admired, correct? What was her name?"

"Mother Evine. She…last I saw she was keeping the ship alive for us all to escape."

"Did she have a hobby?"

Sondra blinked at the unexpected question. "Well, she did needlework in her spare time. She loved to knit things for the poor."

Trestan gestured at Sondra, "Do you have a hobby?"

210

She shrugged, "I read a lot, mostly scriptures." As Trestan continued to stare into her eyes, she blushed as she added, "I've also read tales of romance."

Trestan reached forward with a cloth, drying a moist spot on Sondra's cheek. "And what goals do you set for yourself in the future? Do you look for romance and a husband? Do you plan to create things with needlework?"

Her eyes went wide with shock that he would pry into her affairs, "Nay, none of that. I only hoped to be a Chosen one day and guide the divine chariot. That is lost to me now. It is not for myself that I covet anything, but for Ganden. All my life is reserved for him."

Trestan sighed, "With nothing left for yourself?"

Montanya snickered, "Holier than others, eh? She is blind, except for the one thing that rules her life."

Sondra angrily snapped back, "You would be an expert on such matters! Your life is ruled by vengeance…"

"Stop it. I want silence now." Trestan spoke so firm and with such authority that both women leaned away from him even as they quieted down.

Trestan continued in his normal, softer tone. He faced Sondra, his words for her alone. "I was afraid to give myself to Abriana for just that reason. I feared she would rule my life, and my dreams would be replaced by her desires. I was afraid that I would somehow enslave myself to her."

Sondra didn't disagree, continuing to hang onto his words. Trestan did not pause, "I came to realize Abriana accepted me for who I was already…not some ideal into which she wanted to mold me. Abriana did not want a servant; she wanted a champion who already stood for her ideals. It was only because I already lived a life she approved, which allowed me to ascend higher into her graces. I'm sure Ganden sees you the same way. He loves you for who you are…and what you are includes any of your hopes, dreams, and zeal for life."

Her soft, blue eyes were locked on him as he spoke. She wanted to believe what he told her. The woman had spent her life in service and didn't think there was any way that it would change. In fact, she wanted to continue giving back to others. It was intriguing listening to Trestan explain that she could give as much as she wanted and yet still retain something of her own.

Trestan noticed the way Lindon still cradled his mandolin, and it gave him an idea. "When you tend to the homeless, do you ever play an instrument for them?"

Sondra's jaw dropped, "I don't know how to play music!"

"Ganden doesn't forbid you from playing, does he?" With no immediate answer from the woman, Trestan continued, "I know Ganden appreciates your service, but how can you truly benefit him if you don't see to your own needs?"

"I'm confused." By Sondra's expression, she clearly was having trouble grasping the concept that she was missing something important from her own life.

Trestan continued, "What I'm trying to say is that Ganden does not want your selfless service. He wants someone who can nourish themselves in order to better serve the world around them. I'm sure he wants you to smile over your own children, or play music to motivate the poor into dancing with nay thought of what they lack in life, or knit things of bright color and beauty." Trestan reached out and touched her pendant, "I'm not trying to hurt your feelings Sondra, I'm trying to save them. Ganden wants more than a blindly obedient lapdog."

Sondra frowned and immediately tucked the dog-shaped pendant under her collar. She was about to form a protest, but Trestan didn't give her the chance. He spoke in a firm tone. "Ganden wants someone to realize that, in a way, his ship and those other clerics died trying to safeguard those relics. That nay matter what life throws at us, we need to be ready to adjust and respond to it. We need to get to those relics before Revwar and Savannah or great harm will come to others. We need to do it, all of us here, because none know what we know or could help in time. Don't hide behind your fears and doubts Sondra. You are here because you *are* needed."

Sondra looked down at the floor of the boat in silence. No one said a word. Trestan's last words rang enticingly in her thoughts. She was here, alive, because Ganden needed her. Eventually, she left her bench and made her way past Cat and Trestan to the front of the boat. The young acolyte folded her hands in her lap as she kneeled by the glowing orb at the bow. They could hear her reciting some of the words to the mantra to herself, recalling it as best she could.

Lindon began to strum the rhythm of the mantra on his mandolin. He hoped the tune would embolden the cleric into a proper recital of it. The minstrel did not mind that their course went away from civilization. His purpose in performing for Korrelothar had been fulfilled, and now a new adventure waited. Montanya did not complain about their course either. She vowed to fight thieves, and they were doing just that.

Sondra lifted her voice in the throes of the mantra. If Ganden willed it, she could be a Chosen for this one time. If Ganden denied her, then she would crawl back to her superiors in Orlaun, heartbroken, and inform them off the loss of the last divine chariot.

Lindon's mandolin helped pace her voice. Sondra became lost in the flow of the mantra. The others felt the levitating craft slowly move forward even as it continued to drop lower. They could not see past the dark fog, but the craft was pointed in the direction the *Doranil Star* had drifted. Wisps of clouds parted before the bow as they felt the keel slide through the breeze.

The mantra formed from Sondra's lips wrapped around the small vessel and gave it life. Despite her outer look of concentration, her feelings became joyful. Her faith pushed them toward their destination, flying like a Chosen. Her heart was warmed in a blanket of contentment even as she felt more alive than she ever had.

Over uncharted territory the small craft journeyed, a cast-off child searching through mists for the corpse of its forerunner.

## **CHAPTER 23**         **"Taleweaver"**

"The more this fog clears, the more I'm surprised we descended safely through that tangle of branches." Trestan remarked.

Beside him, standing in a mist lit by the pale morning light, the minstrel from Orlaun nodded in agreement. Lindon was rolling up the cloak he had used as a bedroll. None of them had enjoyed more than a couple hours with shut eyes.

Sondra's mantra had kept them aloft as far as her endurance allowed. The miracle of flight had severely drained her strength. By the time her mantra failed, they were already skimming treetops. The young woman fell asleep even as the boat finished descending gracefully to the ground in the early morning hours. They could never even be sure when they left the clouds due to the amount of fog covering this woodland. It was as good a plan as any to sleep on or around the levitation boat until the sun's light woke them.

Only the illumination of the haze gave clue to the sun trying to burn away the fog. It made the foreign wilderness seem even more unwelcoming. They were in a strange land, looking for that which had been lost, in a fog that forbade them from seeing any farther than a few strides would take them. All they could perceive of their world was a tangle of virgin forest, thick with vegetation that had never felt the sting of a lumberjack's axe.

"I'll be happier when the sun shines down through those branches a bit more." Lindon responded, "This endless fog can play tricks on the mind's perceptions. I could swear I saw something glistening up there. It seemed like branches made entirely of morning dew. The mind sure has a way of playing tricks on itself."

Trestan looked up to the canopy of limbs, smoothing his mustache absently while in thought. "I've had uneasy feelings too. It will be good to get underway. A soul feels better when walking toward a purpose. I feel nervous in these woods. Cat must feel it too, she was insistent about scouting the area."

The half-elf left anything she considered nonessential by the levitation craft. She resumed her role as infiltrator and melted into the fog, looking for any trouble lurking nearby. Trestan remembered her saying that the forest didn't feel receptive, whatever that meant. He trusted her feelings.

The squire looked around, yawning from his own lack of rest as he examined their surroundings. "Where are Sondra and Montanya?"

Lindon motioned over his shoulder. "They should be at the fringes of the fog. They needed some quiet time to straighten some of their differences. Those two women seem to have some strong disagreements, so I urged them to have a civilized discussion about the matter."

Trestan nudged the minstrel. As Lindon looked up, the young paladin was already moving toward some noise at the edge of their vision. Trestan focused on the figures silhouetted by the fog as he spoke. "It looks like your idea isn't working out too well."

Lindon soon realized Trestan's observation was an understatement. Montanya tried to get a point across by ripping apart the gray clerical vestments that Sondra wore. For her part, Sondra accentuated her difference of opinion with a firm tug on Montanya's long, red braid, while using her other hand like a claw near the younger woman's face. The two women rolled to the ground while voicing nonsensical shrieks.

Trestan and Lindon ran to the squabble and each moved to whichever woman was closest. They reached for handholds that would help them pull the women apart and yet still be gentleman about it. Sondra and Montanya fought furiously to get in more shots, dragging Trestan and Lindon into the foliage. The women put up a stronger fight than the men would have given them credit. Finally, Trestan heaved Sondra into some tall grass and held on like an anchor. Lindon tackled Montanya against the base of a tree, and then sat on her as she tried to get back up.

The next several seconds were a confused sparring of words as the women remembered the use of their voices as a means of communicating thoughts. Lindon and Trestan shouted for calm as the other two yelled at their rescuers as well as their opponent. Trestan did his best to calm the raging storm, but they were more interested in shouting rather than listening. Sondra spat words through a busted lip. Montanya's cheek displayed scratches as she yelled.

Another angry voice cut into their conversation as Cat ran out of the mist. The half-elf scooped up her pack by the boat as she ran by it. "Nay shouting and cursing in the presence of the Treemother," she voiced as she ran. "Keep your words respectful, lest you awaken one of her nasty children lurking in the mists."

The rest paused at Cat's words, long enough to hear something inhuman scuttling in the woods from where the half-elf approached. A multi-legged monstrosity stalked into sight. Cat was watching behind her as it came into view. She did not break stride as she ran to the others, though she did reach for a throwing dagger.

"Too late!" Cat stood in front of them as they gaped at the chitinous torso in their camp. "I can't believe I allowed my crossbow to be left in Orlaun. Beware the poison in its mandibles!"

The spider loomed larger than any of them, except Cat, had ever seen. Only in the deep, untamed woods of the world did such monstrosities exist. Giant insects and vermin could be found in abundance in such places that were a far travel from most humanoid lands. Although no taller than Cat, the leg span of the spider stretched over eight feet. It cautiously moved closer as it made chittering noises. The companions could see some excreted fluids dripping from around its mouth.

Cat had a dagger palmed and ready to throw as she whispered to them. "It also has the ability to spray a fluid that will quickly form a sticky mass of strands. If it launches that at us, which it can likely do only once, you may be hampered greatly by the web."

Lindon and Trestan stood to face the arachnid, releasing Montanya and Sondra. As it stood there watching them, they froze in place so as to not provoke it any further. Lindon cast a futile glance at his mandolin, lying close to their adversary. Sondra began praying. Trestan wondered if she was casting a miracle, but it became plain she was simply offering a prayer of mercy.

"Can you kill it with your dagger throw?" Montanya whispered to Cat.

"Unlikely. I think swords would be needed here, but this species is not to be underestimated. Any of us could easily be poisoned. I'm hoping it decides to leave us alone."

Trestan slowly edged past Cat. "I think I can help it to change its mind peacefully."

The half-elf allowed him to pass. "Be careful, whatever you are planning. These spiders can move fast."

Trestan stood in a relaxed manner before the dark eyes of the creature. The spider quieted its chittering noises, though it did focus its attention on him. A few of its multi-jointed legs flexed a bit, testing for a good stance. Trestan reached forward with one hand. The squire's brown eyes fixed on the monster with compassion. The spider froze as Trestan probed its mind.

Cat remembered the test of the beast at the seminary on the day of the Embarking. She recalled how Trestan had soothed the angered bear. The half-elf wanted to whisper to the others to remain still and quiet, but the warning didn't seem necessary. The others held their breath as they stood like statues.

In an instant, the situation changed from a frozen painting to that of action. Cat assumed the contact failed as the spider suddenly charged. The adventuress, with arm still cocked and ready to throw, launched the dagger in a blink. The arachnid stalled just short of Trestan's leg as the dagger took an eye out. Its mandibles were still spread wide as it prepared to inject its venom.

Four years of training had honed Trestan's reflexes with a sword. The Sword of the Spirit normally rested in a scabbard slung over his back. Trestan drew it with his right hand, clearing the scabbard even as Cat's dagger had flipped past him. The magical elvish blade sliced through the air almost faster than it took for Sondra to register that he had even drawn it. Montanya and Lindon were still jumping in reaction to the spider's sudden attack, when Trestan's sword finished its arc. Trestan stood poised at the end of his swing, while two halves of the spider fell apart.

The rest all exhaled at the same time. Trestan took one more swing as spider legs continued to twitch, though it was doubtful any real danger remained from the pieces on the ground. The others were still tense as Trestan checked that the spider was finally dead. He retrieved Cat's dagger from the severed head at his feet. The paladin-aspirant wiped it and his sword clean as he stepped back to the others.

"What were you trying to do before it attacked?" Montanya asked.

Sondra's question came on the heels of the chiaso before Trestan's response. Her swollen lip muffled her words slightly. "Were you trying to calm its mind?"

He nodded, "I tried to reach its mind and distract it from us. I hoped to turn its attention elsewhere." Trestan shrugged as he indicated the corpse. "The mind of an arachnid is too simple. I couldn't comprehend it any more than it could comprehend me."

Sondra pondered her knowledge of such divine miracles for a moment before speaking. "Your tutors must have warned you such a thing would likely fail against those creatures. Yet, you still tried?"

Trestan grinned, a move to shed lightheartedness on his next point even as he spoke it, "Well, I figured if it did attack, I'm the most armored person here. It would have had the worst time trying to find a vulnerable spot for its fangs on me."

Sondra was aghast. For all her sacrifices for the poor, she had never been in a position where she had faced any similar choice to what Trestan just did. He had volunteered himself as a target for a monster in order to protect others.

Lindon hurried over to the mandolin. "There is one thing that still concerns me," he huffed as he retrieved the instrument. "What are we going to do about the rest of them?"

The group heard a symphony of chittering noises in the woods. Montanya backed up as some excreted liquid, similar to the first spider's drool, dropped from somewhere above her and hit the ground. Cat switched her dagger to her left hand as she drew her silver rapier. Sondra brought out her dog-shaped pendant and began to utter a miracle. Trestan invoked a brief protective miracle as he also looked for the origin of the noises.

Sondra's miracle brought forth more light into the gloom of the fog, burning a portion of the mist. Above their heads, they could see the branches made of morning dew that Lindon thought was an illusion of the mind. The illumination revealed the glistening branches as strands of webs. Hanging from those webs were several dead animals, ranging from birds to large bats. Numerous spiders moved in the tree branches. Many were the same size as the one Trestan had killed, but a few were even larger. A number of spiders on the ground closed in toward them as well. It seemed there was too much competition for food in the area. The spiders made aggressive moves against rivals who seemed too interested in claiming these new morsels as their own.

The companions tightened into a circle, grabbing what belongings they could. They abandoned the levitation boat as several legged forms scuttled over it. Trestan invoked another miracle, creating a shield of light on his left forearm as he still held the elvish sword ready. Sondra drew her mace from her belt, even as she found it impossible to regain her voice. Montanya assumed a combat stance, having only her bare hands to defend herself. The chiaso wondered how she could fight such inhuman opponents. Lindon held the mandolin as he considered his smallsword, but that seemed like a useless weapon against so many. Cat glanced in every direction looking for a way they could escape. The large arachnids offered no easy routes out.

With so many spiders closing in, there was the very real threat that they would all be overwhelmed with poison before getting away. As the minstrel considered Trestan's empathic miracle, he came to realize its flaws. It was a spell designed for complex minds, so it could not work on simple ones. However, maybe Lindon could find a way to use a simple effect for simple minds. Even minstrels had ways of using measures of mind control through the harmonic web, in order to charm, break a charm, or simply influence the reactions of listeners.

Lindon spoke out. "Hold very still, until the time comes to slip past them. I may be able to attempt something much like what Trestan tried."

The mandolin would not be sufficient to set the tone in these woods. Instead, Lindon shouldered it with its strap and reached into his deceptively small pocket. He withdrew the bamboo flute, ignoring the metal flute hidden alongside it. Of all his instruments, this one should work the best on creatures of the forest. Taking the flute up to his lips, his face mostly hidden by his wide-brimmed hat, Lindon of Orlaun began playing. The flute chirped along with the spiders' language, causing many of them to pause and listen at the new voice. Lindon had to invent the rhythm as he went along, but the tune seemed to catch their attention.

216

The other companions held very still. Lindon slowly changed the course of the tune. He began to mellow the pace of the music, turning it toward a calming effect. Some spiders stood still and made a few low, chittering noises, but many swayed a bit while staying silent. Lindon didn't rush the effect, nor could he have rushed it without breaking the mood. Although his tune was unlike anything the others had ever heard coming from a flute, it seemed to appeal to the spiders. Lindon played them a lullaby, soothing many into a relaxed, dormant state.

The companions were sweating and aching from holding still for so long in the face of all these hungry monsters. They saw arachnids in all directions, aware that none of the creatures were moving either. Some forms still looked down at the adventurers from the trees, while others stood immobile only a few feet away on the ground.

Finally, Lindon nudged Sondra in the midst of his playing. She looked up to him, wondering what he meant. Under that wide hat, his light blue eyes sparkled at her. Seeing her eyes on him, he threw an intentional glance into the woods. The meaning was clear as he nudged her in that direction. It was time to move.

Lindon continued to lull the spiders as Sondra took a few tentative steps toward the woods. She had to pick her path in order to use routes that were the least choked by those long arachnid legs. Cat quickly followed the woman, keeping her silver rapier lowered but handy. They kept Lindon in the middle, followed by Montanya. Trestan took the position of rear guard. Lindon kept his fingers dancing their slow rhythm on the bamboo as he continued his serenade. They slowly walked past several spiders, concerned that any movement on their part might cause one to strike out with its fangs. They all watched their path carefully, lest they inadvertently step on a spider leg. The creatures remained still as statues as the party, following Sondra's illumination into the mist, tread slowly past them. The half-elf guided Sondra on a course in the direction the bow of the abandoned boat pointed. Soon the lifeboat faded into the mist behind them, along with the spiders that had been standing on it.

Lindon kept playing for a long time after they'd passed the last spider. When the day finally burned through the fog, the companions kept watchful for any other signs of webs. It was hours after the incident that Cat tried to make a jest of the encounter for Trestan.

"I do miss the antics of the other Companions of the Relics," she said. "Though you have to admit, Salgor would have likely charged right into that army of spiders with a zest for battle."

That brought a grin to Trestan as he answered with his opinion, "And he likely would have cleared a wide path through which we could escape."

"And once the rest of us were safe and sound," Cat continued, "He would have turned around and charged once again until he scattered the rest of them."

Trestan couldn't help but laugh at the mental image of Salgor Bandago doing just that.

That evening, Trestan interrupted Sondra as she tried to heal the scrapes and swelling resulting from the women's fight. The paladin forced the priestess to heal Montanya first, after both women were encouraged to apologize. Their apologies didn't sound sincere, but it was enough Sondra healed Montanya and Trestan healed Sondra.

Once the two women walked apart, Sondra glared at Trestan and muttered, "I thought your goddess represented Love."

Trestan sighed. He glanced at her. "Ever hear of tough love?"

*       *       *       *       *

Lindon's memories of the spider incident continued to divert his thoughts over the next two days of wandering in the woods. During a break in their walking, the minstrel indulged in the idea of using the event for his surname, rationalizing the occasion was magnificent enough to commemorate. His tutor, Master Falerno Giantcharmer, would likely agree that it was a feat worthy of taking into name.

Lindon voiced his thoughts to Trestan while the squire rested. "Minstrels often have a basic name when they first set out. I have been Lindon of Orlaun since the college, but I always aspired for a notable event by which I can take a proper surname. Paladins are allowed to take a surname after an occasion of some significance as well, aye?"

"Indeed, we do."

Trestan listened to the minstrel, even though his heart and mind worried over his beloved. He looked up, watching the half-elf as she slowly descended from a tree that towered over two hundred feet high. Katressa moved with all the grace that belonged to elf or cat. It still made Trestan nervous to watch her scaling the tree. He had to remind himself the woods were home to her.

Trestan realized that Lindon was awaiting more of an answer. The aspiring paladin didn't mind indulging the minstrel's interest even though his eyes focused on Cat. "We set out from the seminary after training and begin a journey called the Embarking. It is the beginning of a quest. The quest differs from squire to squire, but we must find our own destiny."

Trestan held up the hand that bore Faithful's Companion. Streamers of sunlight from the forest canopy reflected light off its surface. Lindon examined the ring and its remaining etched symbols as Trestan continued his story.

"This ring is our only spiritual guide on this journey. The markings represent trials that we must pass before we can return to the seminary and be granted the full status of a paladin. When that happens, we may also choose a surname in the eyes of our church."

"Have you given thought to what surname you will pick?" Lindon inquired.

Trestan smoothed a hand down his mustache as he reconsidered the subject. "I've thought of a few and discarded them. I've always considered myself Trestan Karok. Sometimes I wonder if I will accept any other surname."

Lindon nodded, "Out of respect for your father, I would assume. There is nay wrong with that. I, on the other hand, have been eagerly awaiting a chance to pick a suitable name. I don't wish to seem prideful, but I feel that guiding us out of that ring of death with my music abilities grants the right to my surname. I just can't seem to think up one that has a good sound to it."

Montanya, who also stood nearby watching Cat's climbing skills put to the test, added her comments to the conversation. "I didn't know some people held their name in such high esteem. I don't mean to sound insulting, for that is not my intent. Why is the surname so important to you?"

Lindon gave a slight flourish. "In entertainment, a name can mean everything. As a minstrel, my name is the gateway to who I am and what I have done."

Montanya shrugged, "My name was important once. Other families respected it, and it seemed to open doorways. I lost its influence in such an undignified way. My family's estate was torn apart like a feast thrown to the wolves."

The chiaso sensed that she had made the two men uneasy with the way she had turned the conversation. "I don't mean to sound so harsh. I had a good name, but it is nay more. From now on it is simply Montanya. I hope the discovery of a good name brings you more fortune than the ending of my sad tale."

Montanya stepped back from the two men, lost in her own thoughts. Lindon silently mouthed the word 'tale' repetitively, as if Montanya's use of it had given him an idea. Montanya distracted herself with the torn pink fabric at the end of her braided hair. She rolled it in her fingers even as she considered the object holding Sondra's attention.

The blonde cleric of Ganden had knelt in prayer before a shattered wreck of wood and iron. Originally, the companions found it hard to recognize what it had been, given the decomposition of the parts. A ballista from the great vessel lay in pieces on the forest floor, marking its trail. The bulk of it had hit the mud with a sizeable impact, driving parts of it into the ground. Sondra reacted to it as if a portion of her own god's body had been cast to the ground. She allowed herself time to mourn the loss it represented.

"Tale...Talespinner. Or maybe Songspinner? Nay, that isn't right." Lindon mumbled.

"Spinner?" Trestan raised eyebrows at the minstrel.

Lindon looked up, responding with a lot of body language to accentuate his inner thoughts. "Well aye, something that directly ties in with the spiders. I don't think I really want to say 'spiders' as part of my name; that would be more frightening than entertaining. They spin webs, so I thought I might try along those lines."

The minstrel continued to carry on his own conversation until pausing again and asking Trestan: "Is it better to be a spinner or a weaver?"

"Pardon?"

Lindon answered his own question. "Weaver would be better. A spinner sounds too simple, too mundane. A weaver gives the impression of an artistic tapestry being created. The spiders would also probably agree that they weave a web, not just spin silk."

Trestan glanced once more at Cat, "So, you are some type of weaver?"

The minstrel straightened to his full height and swept his hat downward into a bow. "Aye, indeed. Lindon Taleweaver at your service. Or maybe Songweaver? Nay, nay, Taleweaver it is."

Trestan couldn't help but smile. "So, it is better to weave a tale than weave a song?"

"Aye it is!" Lindon nodded as he returned his wide-brimmed hat to his head. "A well-done tale has more character and sustenance than a well-done song."

"A pleasure to be reacquainted with you, Lindon Taleweaver." Trestan gave a formal bow.

"Now, if you will excuse me," Trestan continued in a lower voice, "While Cat is descending, I think I will take this chance to have a bit of a talk with our cleric friend."

Lindon subtly glanced at the young woman kneeling nearby, "You have something on your mind? Perhaps a worry concerning her?"

Trestan nodded slightly, "I'm worried she views her faith from the wrong perspective. Maybe I can enlighten her to something she doesn't realize she's missing."

Lindon overheard the start of the conversation as Trestan began with an odd topic. The champion of Abriana asked Sondra how the blisters on her feet were doing. She looked up with a start, replying that her balms helped, yet they wouldn't totally heal as long as they kept trotting through the wilderness. Trestan revealed that on his first adventure, he and his friend Petrow ended up comparing the blisters on their feet during the first full night of rest.

No sooner had Trestan moved away then Montanya wandered back to Lindon's side. It occurred to the minstrel that Sondra wasn't the only one whose perspective was infringing on her enlightenment. The chiaso felt Lindon's light blue eyes upon her as she approached.

"So," she began. "You are Taleweaver now?"

"Aye, I have found my name. I hope my music has been pleasing to your ears."

The side of Montanya's lip twitched, and there was a slight shrug of her shoulders. "I haven't heard anything other than the tune you played when we descended from the ship…and those odd noises you made with the bamboo pipe at the spiders."

Lindon nodded. "I would call it a flute, not a pipe. I should play more for you. I'm told you missed much of the performances on *Doranil Star*, therefore I should be happy to give you an encore."

Montanya gave the slightest hint of a smile as she looked to the mandolin he carried. "I would love to hear some more, when we have the time."

Lindon looked to the tree once more, watching Cat's progress. "We have time now." Lindon wasn't about to add that he had something in mind that might help the chiaso's focus. "I know just the sort of music you might appreciate to match your skills."

"Skills?"

Lindon waved his hand to indicate her. "Your skills as a martial artist. In the past year, I visited far off Tariyka and walked the grounds of monasteries where chiaso trained. I recall the music that played as they went through their meditative dances."

Lindon only partly told the truth. He had been to Tariyka and paused to watch masters training their warrior students, but he had never heard them move to music. The minstrel had a plan which he hoped would help Montanya focus on combining heart, body and soul to achieve her inner balance. If she got past her preoccupation of rogues, and concentrated on her body and movements, she might realize her potential. Lindon was no martial arts master or student; he would have to improvise with what he did know and observe.

Montanya cocked her head to one side, puzzled that students would listen to music during their exercises, since she never had done such a thing. Lindon prompted her. "I'm sure you have a meditative dance that helps you focus, what is it called?"

"Butterfly in the Windmill," she answered without pause.

Lindon hoisted his mandolin into a position by which he could play it. Rather than play, he nodded to Montanya. The youth stood puzzled for a moment before complying. She paused only to rid herself of extra equipment, taking off the hardened leather pieces to allow for freedom of movement.

Montanya started performing the routine. Even without formal training, Lindon believed her movements were too fast and lacked the precision that was likely required. Her style certainly lacked the discipline he witnessed in Tariyka. His hands plucked only empty air next to the strings as he invented a tune to match the movements.

Lindon spoke out. "Stop a moment, please."

Montanya interrupted her exercise and looked to the minstrel.

Lindon had his fingers ready on the first string. "Listen to the rhythm and match it as you go. It is very slow, forcing you to focus and accentuate every little movement. Tariykan students used it to feel the stretch of every muscle, the tautness of every piece of sinew, and be able to perfectly replicate every movement if asked to do so again."

Lindon began strumming the mandolin. The notes were very akin to music he had heard in Tariyka, and yet paced to match the slow movements he had seen from the students there. Montanya listened to the first couple bars of notes. Images were conjured in her mind of that far off land of warriors. When she began the movements, the pace forced her to execute every stretch with patience. Without rushing the routine as she normally did, she could feel every facet of her body alignment, as well as the tightness in every muscle as each move was executed.

She recalled her early days learning the movements. Her instructor had shouted out pauses to the students, and then gone up and down the line to examine if their bodies were poised exactly right. They would stay frozen at several positions throughout the dance. Grandmaster Woshan would let them linger painfully long in certain stances at times. A strike with a small switch would indicate if their backs weren't straight, or their arm was turned too much, or they lacked the proper extension.

As Montanya performed the moves in the woods, her mind refocused on the smallest aspect of every step. No longer rushing herself or skipping the details, she made sure everything was done perfectly. With Lindon's tune playing in the background, she would slowly rotate a fist to the exact angle required, stretch her arms out to their full length, and pivot her weight around her center of gravity. Her mind flowed free of distractions, which was what Lindon had been trying to achieve. The youth felt power in her arms and legs that she had never paused to consider before. Her concentration allowed her to realize she had been lacking in her discipline. She had only been mimicking movements without really using them properly. It was rare that Montanya felt so deeply conjoined with the power of her mind and body. She was content to linger in the musical trance for some time.

The youth did not notice when Cat finally descended to the forest floor. Trestan finished his own talk with Sondra and moved to rejoin his faunlessa. Together, they shared a conversation away from where Lindon performed for Montanya.

"The trees here grow thick and tall," Cat spoke while catching her breath. "From what I could see, there was nay trace that the ship flew low enough to disturb the canopy. The bulk of it must have still been above the treetops when this ballista fell free."

Trestan shook his head in amazement, "Those priests of Ganden must have been very strong indeed to have kept it afloat in the sky for so many miles. I suppose this has been rough terrain on the ground, so it's taking us longer to cross than a flying vehicle could cover. We saw firsthand how much distance *Dovewing* could cover in a day."

"It would be hard to guess which gave out first, the clerics or the floor they were sitting on. Anyway, I guess it's time to move on if we're to get there before long."

Trestan disagreed, "Not yet, you need time to rest." When Cat looked like she was going to argue the point, Trestan nodded toward the minstrel and the chiaso. "Lindon seems to be up to something so let's give him some time. Get in a bit of rest, my love, and I shall offer you some of those fruits we found. Maybe you can relax with your boots off?"

Cat giggled but acquiesced to Trestan's idea. The half-elf settled down on her cloak as Trestan sat next to her. She gladly nibbled at the fruit he offered. Between bites, she voiced one concern of hers. "One thing worries me, aside from the divine chariot. I've been listening to the tree voices around me, and noticed signs that we may not be alone out here. I think we have passed into territorial lands belonging to the Faer'Seelie."

**CHAPTER 24**       **"Into the Hands of the Faer'Seelie"**


They marched for miles under the thick canopies of the trees. The biggest indication that the divine chariot had passed overhead involved the occasional rusted piece of metal lying on the ground. Each discovery yielded no more than bits and pieces. They wanted to rush to find where the great bulk of the ship finally came to rest, and yet they had to be vigilant in case the relics had fallen somewhere along the trail of debris. Even the nature of the land prevented them from moving at any fast pace. As Cat noted, they were not able to move in a straight line. Steep hills, clumps of thickets and the occasional streams interrupted their path. This was a wild forest, the only trails created by animals.

The companions walked apart, covering more ground as they went. Trestan was one of the trio that made up the middle. He set the pace of their trek. Sondra seemed content to be within the middle of the party as well, walking a few steps out to Trestan's side. Lindon, acting as the gentleman to protect the lady, took stride a few steps beyond her to keep her in the center. With the three of them walking side by side and a little apart, they had a better chance of spotting anything hidden on the ground. Cat moved from one flank to the other, taking a wider course that looked out for danger as well as scanned a broader area. Montanya, wanting to be helpful, tried to match Cat's movements on the opposing side of the rest of the companions. The uneven terrain sometimes forced them into a single line, and other times widened through vulnerable, open areas.

While moving together in a runoff ravine, they heard a noise from the brush on one side. The motion quickly stilled as fast as it had begun. The companions stopped in their tracks, looking up to the raised area of earth beside the runoff in search of its origin. To their surprise, they caught the sound of faint whispers in a language other than the human tongue.

Cat thought she understood something familiar in the words. The half-elf ventured a short, inquisitive greeting in the language of elves.

Three elf youths scrambled from their hiding place. They were dressed in skins and leather; faces and limbs painted to blend in with the forest. Whether or not the elves understood Cat, they weren't sticking around for a conversation. They fled at a disorganized run down the upper edge of the ravine. One slipped on a tangle of branches in his haste. The unfortunate elf snapped something in his ankle as his weight pulled on the trapped extremity. He dropped free of the entanglement only to land in agony within the runoff. His two friends noticed but didn't slow down to help.

Shouts exchanged between the injured elf and his retreating friends. He panicked at his helplessness in the face of strangers. The companions stopped, not wanting to give the wrong impression to the native lad. Even as his friends abandoned him, Cat voiced assurances he was in no danger. Trestan couldn't catch most of the words, but anyone could understand by Cat's body language she did her best to show that the party's intentions were only peaceful. The young elf relaxed a bit, despite tears apparent on his cheeks.

Trestan offered an idea. "As long as he nay longer fears we may do him harm, perhaps we should heal his ankle. He looks unable to put any weight on it."

"Right now, he is most afraid of you and your armor, Tres." Even as Cat said it, Trestan could see the elf watched him from fearful eyes masked under the natural paints. Cat continued, "Maybe someone who looks less intimidating can make the first move."

"Sondra then," Trestan tried to keep a friendly smile and warm demeanor as he spoke. "She can heal him and looks less threatening."

Sondra looked nervous as Cat once again traded conversation with the elf. Trestan spoke softly to her, while keeping eyes on the native. "Smile, Sondra. Let him know you're his friend and that you'd like to help him."

The cleric of Ganden did her best to hide her uncertainty and look friendly. The injured boy sniffled and nodded at Cat as they talked. His eyes judged on the human woman now, weighing his limited options. He absently rubbed his ankle as he talked.

As the others examined the boy, they noted his garments were almost exclusively made from animal hides. He wore some beads and ivory as decorations, and he did have carved wooden buttons. It looked as if everything that he had originated from the forest surroundings. There was no worked metal, nor was he garbed in any linen. The colors painted on his bare skin blended well with the woods. The clothes shared similar color patterns, though stained from hiding in dirty places. His people likely made their home somewhere in these deep woods.

Sondra approached, slowly and cautiously. As she knelt by the boy, her own fear fell aside as she looked over the ankle with critical eyes. He flinched a bit at her touch, gentle as it was. Cat whispered assurances to the elf the whole time.

The lad held still while Sondra began incanting a healing prayer. The miracle warmed the boy's leg even as it made Sondra weary from the effort. The faithful of Ganden soon rested back on her heels, a contented look upon her face, as the elf boy wiggled his ankle. Cat translated as Sondra applied a restorative balm that should help with any lingering pain. Once she was done, the elf stood on his two legs again. He offered a shy smile.

"He wants you to have a gift," Cat explained, as the lad pulled out a fresh-picked flower.

The young elf placed the flower in Sondra's hair. He then giggled and ran off unexpectedly. His run wasn't as strong as it had been earlier, but the ankle supported him. The companions felt no need to chase him, and so they calmly began to regroup and continue their journey.

The companions had barely resumed conversation and walked forty meters before more noises came from the woods. There were no sounds such as armor clanking, or crunching branches. Instead, the approach of the elven scouting band sounded like strong wind passing through the leaves. The companions assumed a defensive posture with backs together as elves poured out of the surrounding trees. Cat spoke fast as she voiced peaceful intentions and tried to greet them in a friendly manner. Elf bows drew back with arrows aimed at hearts.

Trestan had a hand near his sword but didn't draw it forth. Lindon gripped his smallsword yet allowed it to stay in the scabbard. Montanya assumed a fighting stance, though she still carried no weapon.

The elves had them outnumbered and surrounded. Each wore an outfit of leather armor that blended well with the surrounding trees. Several wore or brandished an angled wooden club. Many of these cudgels had sharp rocks attached in key places to give it more of a cutting edge. A few carried the only steel that had been observed on these woodland people. The steel was in the form of a long, curved, sword edge mounted upon bowed, four-foot long, pole handles. Elves carrying the pole-sword stood to the fore of their line. Their faces were painted in shades of green, brown, gray, and black. The leather armor they wore also helped disguise the profile of the wearer with the use of colors and oddly shaped angles. They formed a defensive ring around the invaders of their homeland, ready to slay at the slightest provocation.

Trestan noticed a conversation taking place near the rear of the elven ranks. The young elf boy they healed insisted on speaking with some of the scouts. By the tone of voices and expressions, the boy pleaded on behalf of the companions. Another elf responded to Cat's words. It relieved Trestan slightly to know that they were willing to talk, instead of outright attack.

Cat spoke in Hespal, the human tongue, "They are going to take us to their elders. We will surrender our weapons here or die. I suggest we cooperate and go along with them."

"We can't give up," Montanya hissed. The chiaso stared at an arrow pointed at her chest. She recalled her teacher saying a well-honed chiaso could catch arrows out of the air. It seemed she would be tested this day. "We are in the right…"

Cat reprimanded the youth. "We are in their land and they will kill us easily if we don't comply. We have to be alive to complete our quest."

"If you make the wrong move, we will all die," Trestan added, calmer than he felt. Montanya watched the champion of Abriana slide his baldric off and offer it to their captors. "We will be slaughtered if we resist. They only mean to take us to their elders."

Montanya reluctantly lowered her fists. She scowled at the elves closing in around her.

One elf took Cat's belt and silver rapier. She continued talking with the scouts' leader as she was searched. The elf inspecting her found several hidden daggers in her outfit. Before backing away from her, he scrutinized her looks. His stare studied her angular ears, the lines of her cheeks, and the tilt of her eyes.

He wore a look of revulsion as he proclaimed a judgment to the others. "Agora!"

The elven scout spit in her face.

*      *      *      *      *

The scouting party rounded up their prisoners and escorted them deeper into the forest. They wound their way through thick underbrush and over small streams. They went down trails that only seemed fit to accommodate animals. The path veered from the course of the *Doranil Star*, but Trestan knew it couldn't be helped. Hopefully they would regain the trail…if they lived.

The others did not understand the Faer'Seelie as well as Cat and, as it turned out, Lindon. Both offered whispered conversation to explain to the others as they walked.

These elves considered themselves Faer'Seelie, one of the oldest branches of the elven people in the realm, and the ones who most honored the ways of the woods. Although Faer'Seelie also occupied other lands, this clan made a living in the deep woods of what others called Wilder continent. To them, the land was named Eyldiian. They considered the land itself to be the sacred body of the daughter of the Treemother, Laedelious.

The Faer'Seelie called the forests of this continent their home. They had lived here for longer than any elf could recall. The forest kept its virgin look because these people were very restrictive in how they altered the land. They could shape the trees to grow as they needed, or at times they would shape their livelihood to the needs of the trees. The lack of a civilization, such as what humans built, might allow others to view them as barbaric. The truth was far different. It went against their beliefs to clear large tracts of land for cities and roads. They considered themselves children of Laedelious, Goddess of Forests and Wildlands. As such, their lives grew as a part of nature, not apart from it. They disturbed the forest as little as possible, giving creation to a secret world among the trees.

The ties to forests and nature became apparent from the first glance of their scouts. Their armor came from animal skins. The edges of the garments were frilled or cut unevenly to help disguise their humanoid profile when hiding in the woods. Several different colors were used in every piece of the armor, allowing for brown, tan, green, and other natural variations. Some elves utilized browned animal bones to provide extra protection in places or simply for use as decoration. It wasn't until the companions traveled farther along that they saw stronger types of armor worn by sentries closer to home. Though not as heavy as metal armor, the use of caleocht wood offered more solid protection than leather alone, and without much compromise in weight. The elves used strips of the durable wood, mixed with their druidic magic, and banded it around the torso of the wearer. The caleocht wood offered a hard outer shell that fit comfortably around the person it was made to fit. The druids needed to use their magic only once to fit the armor to the wearer, unless battle damage required repairs.

Their favored weapons were shaped from wood. Shortbows made from yew were in abundance. These were handier in the confined woodland areas than the longbows favored by some elves and humans. Many bows were notched for range and angles, though more commonly they displayed markings dedicated to elven gods. Feathers, fur tails, or beads hanging from the bottom decorated many of them.

Another prized wooden weapon included the kittane. These war clubs were built with a lot of individuality and creativity from their owners. The common theme between each involved a length of wood that featured a bend, or "elbow," about two thirds of the way up its length. Many of these bends were a gentle curve, though some were close to a sharp right angle. The goal in crafting the shape of kittanes involved using edged sides and pointed angles that focused the weight of impact into a small area. A cross section of the club might seem very similar to a double-edged sword since they were thicker in the middle but narrowed down to edges on the sides. Even with the slicing edges, the main injuries caused by the kittane depended on the weight of the weapon and skill of the user. It could bludgeon an opponent's extremities until they were too incapacitated to offer resistance. Pieces of flint, bone, and other sharp objects could line the inside of the bend like a row of

226

teeth, while a spike could be positioned on the outside point of the elbow to allow for a wicked, piercing stab. As with the bows, these war clubs often had individual decorations such as bits of amber, colored strips of leather, and markings favoring certain gods.

The one weapon disconnected with the rest of their culture appeared to be the pole-swords with their steel blades. There seemed to be very few, and they were the only advanced metallic items seen. Although some of the elves wore decorated pieces of gold and copper, the steel-bladed staves appeared beyond their crafts. Most consisted of a three-or-four-foot bowed staff of caleocht wood, topped with a two-foot-long curved blade. In place of a cross guard there would be a wrapping of fur and an attachment of bright feathers. These seemed to offer a distraction for opponents, yet they served the practical purpose of soaking an opponent's blood before it ran down the handle.

Except for Cat, the companions didn't realize when they had passed the boundary marking the edge of the elf city. At some point, they looked up and realized a network of walkways stretched overhead. The city welcomed few visitors from such faraway lands. It was as foreign a place as most of them had ever seen. There were few places a wagon could pass easily, flora abounded along every route. Paths meandered back and forth around the trunks of old trees. Open areas were filled with the most beautiful gardens or harbored pools teaming with colorful fish. Occasional wooden statues paid homage to elven gods and heroes. The forest floor was not even a big portion of the elf city. Much of the ground areas were dedicated to gardens that produced the fruits, herbs, spices and plant products the elves traded to other societies. A few places allowed beams of sunlight through the forest canopy to strike among the twisting gardens. Many druids walked the grounds among plants cultivated to make healing remedies and concoctions. Most structures loomed from the trees above, shaped by the growth of branches. The companions were marched around tree trunks the size of merchant ships, supporting buildings just as large. Curious stares found them from every walkway and balcony as they passed through the elves' paradise.

They marched through gathering crowds to the heart of the city. A column of unbroken sunshine called attention to a central assembly of elves. In the Moonglen, a clearing used for gatherings and bordered by medicinal plants, they faced several members of the ruling council. Many elves stood nearby as armed guards or spectators, but it wasn't hard to pick out the elf leaders. The councilors, all female, walked with an air of confidence and masked all feelings behind impassionate faces. Each wore colorful garlands as necklaces. Among scattered conversations, Katressa overheard a title by which other elves referred to their leaders: Naef'ad, which meant nurturer. The half-elf understood more of this society at a glance than her companions, seeing the Naef'ad as motherly figures in a matriarchal society. Cat identified the religious symbols that each displayed. The community favored the Treemother, Laedelious.

A few members of the scouting party conversed with the councilors. The companions' weapons were laid out before the Naef'ad. Trestan's elvish sword seemed to be of particular interest to them. The elves also had discussions over the rust-colored leather satchel in which Sondra carried her healing supplies and religious items, as well as the mandolin taken from Lindon.

One of the Naef'ad, whose green hair cascaded down to her thighs, initiated a cordial greeting despite eyes betraying her suspicious nature. Cat translated the Elvish words for the others.

"She greets us to the city of Serud'Thanil, and introduces herself as Naef'ad Illwinu Wessail. She holds a position on a ruling council from what I can understand. Naef'ad Illwinu asks our intentions in trespassing on their lands."

Trestan stood at the fore of the companions. He gave a low, respectful bow, aware of the many elven weapons poised to slay him. The bow helped bring attention to the coraross symbol hanging from his necklace. He smiled in hopeful friendship as he spoke. "We mean nay trouble for the hosts of this land. We arrived by means of a flying ship that may have fallen out of the sky near here. We seek that ship to reclaim valuables left on board."

As Cat translated, Trestan watched the eyes of the councilor. There seemed to be a slight reaction as Cat mentioned the flying ship. It was a bare flicker of recognition or understanding in the eyes of the elves' leader, though a moment later it disappeared under feigned ignorance. The elf replied in a cool demeanor as she spoke again.

Cat relayed, "She says we scared some children at the borders of the city, and one was injured."

Trestan believed a more accurate account of events was already relayed to the elder. She was likely testing their reactions. "He injured himself in his own fright, and his sudden appearance put a scare into us as well. We did not treat him unkindly or ask about your lands. We simply offered him our healing services and allowed him to go on."

As Cat translated, Trestan spotted the brief glance the Naef'ad took toward the flower the elf lad had placed in Sondra's hair. The cleric of Ganden shied away from those eyes. Cat was finishing her translation as a runner forced a passage through the crowd. The runner approached Naef'ad Illwinu and whispered in her ear.

The elven councilor's face morphed from blank, diplomatic calm into barely contained rage. Angry murmurs came from others close enough to hear the runner's words. The scout had not yet finished his entire message and yet outraged reactions swept through the crowd.

Lindon observed, "They are very upset about something. We could be in serious trouble. What are they saying?"

Cat tried to listen to several elf voices at once. Her fine skin paled slightly. "There has been a death…a murder at the edge of their domain. Some are calling for us to be punished."

Naef'ad Illwinu Wessail and the other councilors commanded silence even as they debated the news. Some discontented voices continued to suggest courses of action toward her back, after she turned to address the companions.

"You brought weapons into our home with the intent to do harm!" Cat translated from Elvish, making it clear as well that the elf's words were made as a statement rather than a question.

Cat quickly switched from the human tongue to Elvish as Trestan started speaking before the translation finished. The champion of Abriana held his hands out and open to gesture that he lacked hostility. "We came with nay such intent. We happened upon your homeland accidentally in our search, but caused nay harm."

Cat listened to the elf councilor's reply, as a disturbance approached the Moonglen from a different direction. The half-elf and her companions understood the body language when Naef'ad Illwinu indicated the new arrivals. Cat relayed the meaning, "She says our friends attacked some of their people without provocation, and killed a few innocents."

Montanya scowled, "What friends?"

The companions focused on the approaching commotion. As soon as Lindon recognized the prisoners, he said, "Make sure they know we *don't* consider those people our friends."

A large party of elf scouts forcefully dragged a quartet of troublemakers toward the gathering. The companions spotted their adversaries struggling amongst the rough handling of captors. Revwar's silver hair, normally braided, flung around his head in a twisted mess. An elf guard held each arm of the spellcaster as they shoved him. The charming mentalist Jentan suffered a muffling gag tied across his mouth. Savannah limped between another pair of guards. The shaft of an arrow jutted from one leg, yet she was forced to walk on it without the use of her healing abilities. They carried Kemora forth in a most undignified way…arms and legs tied to a pole carried between two elves. A ring of druids accompanied the guards, offering little chance that the band would be able to use magical arts successfully without being made to pay for it.

The crowd erupted in greater tumult as the lead elves displayed the band's weapons. A coat of fresh blood colored the halfling's sword and the head of Savannah's flail.

Another group of elves followed the first. Scouts carried the bodies of those killed, as wounded staggered behind them. The hostility in the air weighed like a palpable thing as those cloak-covered corpses entered the glen.

The encroaching elves marched the trespassing band toward the companions. The elves were lumping all of their perceived enemies together. Cat held Naef'ad Illwinu's attention as she tried to explain that the newcomers were thieves whom they had crossed blades with in the past. Cat accused them of sabotaging the ship into falling out of the sky. Though the elf councilor appeared to listen, it was hard to tell if Cat's words were convincing enough in the drowning shouts of the crowd.

Montanya soon made a statement in her own way. The enemy band came within footsteps of the companions, though both parties were surrounded by many guards. The angry chiaso shoved an elf's spear to the side, not caring about the minor cut she received in the process, as she charged at Revwar. The guards around the wizard put up their guard as they expected the attack to come at them. The youth flew between them as she kicked Revwar hard in the gut.

The youth shouted, "Where is my locket!?"

Her hands grabbed around his collar. She didn't find her necklace around his neck, so she contented herself with flinging him into the path of approaching guards. Revwar might have put up more of a fight if he wasn't still dazed by druid spellcraft. The chiaso bolted from Revwar toward a new target, unaware of the elven arrow that narrowly missed piercing her back. Kemora remained helplessly tied to the pole when the angry youth launched into her. Montanya, Kemora, and the elves holding the pole, all rolled into a heap.

When the initial confusion distracted attention from her, Savannah whispered a prayer to her goddess. Limping on her injured leg, she drew into creation a black orb which hung in the air. Trestan noticed the miracle take shape and reacted. The champion of Abriana went through a hasty prayer of his own. Savannah launched the dark missile at the one voice the companions possessed which allowed communication with the elves. Trestan dove into the path of the projectile, interrupting Naef'ad Illwinu and Cat's words. Trestan's summoned shield absorbed the black energy before it could strike the half-elf. Cat responded with a quick and accurate throw from a hidden dagger that the guards had failed to find. The blade bounced off the cleric's bracer as she raised her arm to protect her face.

A whistling arrow of warning hit the ground by Cat's feet; it was not the only one. For Jentan, Sondra, and Lindon, whom had not participated in the brief struggle, guards simply forced them to their knees. Elves swarmed around Trestan and Cat, roughly taking them to the ground and searching them for any more hidden weapons. Revwar alike was thrown down while a pair of druids assured that he could not cast any spells. Another druid called forth energies from natura, taking the air around Savannah's mouth and rendering it into a solid, yet unseen, force. Her cold, blue eyes bulged as she lost her ability to breathe. A number of warriors wearing crafted caleocht armor subdued her seconds later. Montanya fought wildly to hurt Kemora until a scout with a kittane hit her from behind. The war club popped against her skull, dropping her like a string-cut puppet.

Even as the warriors swarmed the prisoners, an angry crowd of townspeople had to be held back from satisfying a blood vengeance for their own fallen. Cat tried to make sense of the many voices shouting in the Moonglen. She overheard one phrase from Councilor Illwinu Wessail: imprisonment until sentenced by the governess of the people.

**CHAPTER 25**                    **"Interrogations in the Trees"**


Thin eyebrows raised periodically as her greenish-blue eyes examined the wooden barricade in a curious manner. Montanya couldn't help but be curious as she observed the structure. "It is definitely caleocht wood. I don't think I've ever seen so much in one place as we have here. This portion is shaped so well as to be unbelievable. Hardly any cut boards at all…just a living tree grown in such a way as to form a prison."

Montanya allowed her hand to slide along the tough bark. The branches she touched sprouted from the same tree, growing together in an intermingling pattern that formed a cage around the companions. The wooden framework that hemmed them in was still part of a growing tree. In a few select places a section of dead wood blocked the more open spaces. Even the dead wood fused to the tree by means of druidic magic, needing no nails or ropes to bind them together.

The chiaso let her hand drop back to her side as she let out a sigh. The companions were becoming used to her hopeless sighs. "This was a test my sensei put before all his students. We would hone our bodies and minds until we could break a caleocht board. We trained hard to achieve that goal. Few could do it without years of training, and the occasional broken bone."

Lindon Taleweaver sat against one side of their entrapment, studying the interwoven connection of limbs barring them from freedom. The enclosure would have been considered a masterwork of art if displayed in Orlaun. Spaces in the limbs permitted the passage of sunlight and wind, and also allowed fruits and water to be passed through to the occupants. It was comparable to a metal cage for those who had no tools to loosen the tree's grip. Druidic magic reinforced the branches, and often those same druids stood nearby to make sure no other magic could enable an escape before they could respond.

The minstrel pushed back the wide brim of his feathered hat so he could view the long-legged youth better. "Were you able to break a caleocht board?"

A wry smirk stole across her mouth as she shook her head slightly. "Nay, I never could. I spent most of my years training hard to perfect my muscles. I thought I was tough enough. I was certainly stronger than any of the other girls. Yet I saw them do what I could not. I don't know how I couldn't move my muscles to do what my heart wanted. More often than not, I broke a bone while the board mocked me. I cost the master much more in healing draughts than the price of the board."

Lindon nodded. "Only rare people can easily touch a talent the likes of which few learn. I have been blessed with my musical abilities, though I cannot claim I was born with an instrument in hand. I'm sure you will find ways to focus your abilities. To have trained so long, you must be close to your goal of breaking past such a barrier. Hopefully the right inspiration will find you soon."

Montanya looked at Lindon in a way that she rarely looked at anyone. Her customary scowl replaced in favor of respect and adoration. "I am inspired by your music. When you played for me in the woods, and I danced the butterfly movements, I felt like I had found the potential I had been missing."

She sighed again as she leaned her forehead against the entrapping branches. "I wish they hadn't taken your mandolin. I would love to stretch my muscles to your tunes again."

A mischievous smile found its way to the minstrel's face. A sly glint came to his blue eyes as he admitted, "They didn't find all of my instruments."

The other companions watched as the red-bearded minstrel pulled forth the bamboo flute from a pocket that appeared too small to contain it. Montanya found a rare smile upon her face as he settled his nimble fingers in the right places. She spoke, "I'm glad you have it, but what if they take it away? Maybe we should hide it until later."

"As long as I'm simply playing a dance tune, I don't think they'll have reason to complain. Music is best shared among people." Lindon put the flute close to his lips. "As far as timing, they have already kept us locked here for close to three days. We might as well spend the use of our time better."

Lindon began the notes of his song, keeping the pace relaxed enough for Montanya to focus on every step of her movements. The chiaso let the rhythm guide her as she indulged in her routine. She danced the familiar steps of Butterfly in the Windmill as alarmed elves outside the prison took an interest in what transpired. A couple druids conversed regarding the nature of the music before apparently deciding to leave the matter alone. They merely observed as Lindon's music brought Montanya to a better appreciation for her own movements. In that relaxed state, the chiaso came to a better understanding of her abilities and limitations.

Sondra sulked in a corner, unable to let herself enjoy Lindon's music. Her companions noted the increase in her anxiety as each day passed. The human woman had grown increasingly despondent at her situation and the choices made that lead to it. She spoke, quiet words passing her frown and aimed into the floor. "Why have we been here three days with naught more than a few questions directed at us? Why are we still alive?"

Cat had no answer, so the half-elf looked toward Trestan. The paladin-aspirant stroked fingers over his mustache. She knew whenever he did that, he seemed to delve deep in thought.

Trestan was not so distracted that he missed Sondra's question. "I don't think they know the best way to handle us yet, I suppose. They questioned our story about the *Doranil Star*, and they played innocent while we responded. I'm sure that green-haired Naef'ad knows something she isn't telling us about the vessel. They also must presume that we didn't tell them everything…which would be correct. They don't have to be in any hurry to kill any of us. They want to extract the most information from us that they can, before serving the best interests of their people."

Sondra glanced over one shoulder, "Then why are the elves also keeping them alive. They were the ones that drew blood."

The roll of her eyes indicated the identical tree prison holding Revwar and his cohorts. The four members of his band had been healed of their beating by Savannah, though druidic spheres, attached to their cage, dampened much of the effects of arcana and miracles. The same spheres positioned around both prisons to absorb magical energies. They did not totally suppress magic, but they drained much of a spell's energy and depleted the mental reserves of the caster. The result meant that Revwar, Savannah and Jentan were unable to blast through the walls of their prison, at least not without totally exhausting themselves with the effort. Sondra and Trestan felt the drain on their own miracles when they had attempted to heal the wounds suffered by their party in the Moonglen.

Both parties hung suspended a good distance above the forest floor. The ground foliage was easily visible, and yet a fall from such a height would seriously injure anyone. Walkways extended to reach the prisons when the elves wanted to bring food and water. When not actively used, these walkways withdrew to a position that would be an impossible leap for human or elf.

The companions were within easy shouting range of the evil foursome. Few words had been exchanged during their days of captivity. Both Revwar and Savannah had tested the magical dampeners around their cell by firing lethal spells at the companions. In each case, the magical forces were drained before they could span the gap. From time-to-time, Revwar called out to his guards in Elvish. It was hard for the companions to hear his words, but the only response that came from the elves of Serud'Thanil consisted of spitting in his direction. There seemed to be not even the slightest amount of respect between the elf wizard and his captors.

The companions did not receive much better respect. Although the elves provided daily food and water, most attempts of Cat's to communicate resulted in an elf spitting in her direction using the term, "agora."

"I think," Trestan mused, "that the main reason Revwar and Savannah haven't been killed by the elves is due to us."

"How so?" Sondra turned to face him squarely.

Trestan seemed to idly twist Faithful's Companion around his finger as he talked. "I'm guessing, based on what we told them about our search for the divine chariot, that they hope to confirm or contradict any parts of our story through what those others might say. Savannah and that halfling were caught with blood on their weapons and elves were killed around their party. They are guilty as any elf can see, and would likely suffer swift justice. However, I sense that the elves aren't so sure what to do with us. We told them why we are here, and did not cause them any harm. Unfortunately, our best intentions are secondary compared to the goals of their leaders in seeing to their people's welfare. It was probably in their best interests to question our enemies to determine how they should view us."

Sondra groaned when it seemed that Trestan was finished expressing his thoughts. She soon admitted, "I feel so far away from my god and his calling. I'm regretting the paths I took that brought me here."

Trestan gave her a reassuring pat on one arm. Faithful's Companion caught her eye as it glinted in the sunlight. "Our gods are here with us, always, to guide us." Trestan reconsidered his choice of words and added, "For our own interests as well as their own. I've had times when I questioned my course, and often I later find that I am a better person for the paths I have chosen."

Cat noticed that Trestan began to stroke his mustache again. Some new thought had entered his mind. Her beloved looked up into her eyes.

Trestan stated, "Cat, the elves should not be the only ones to take advantage of the helpless presence of our enemies." The half-elf raised her eyebrows inquiringly. Trestan added, "We also have an opportunity to get answers to our questions."

Trestan got to his feet and faced outward from their prison. His eyes sought out the prison holding the others, hoping to spot Savannah. His voice easily carried to the dark cleric. "Savannah, why did you ask if Petrow was with us when you saw us on the ship?"

Several moments of silence passed. No answer seemed to be forthcoming.

"You said he belongs to DeLaris," Trestan yelled, "And that you wanted him. Why?"

Another period of silence ensued. Trestan suspected he would get no answer. Trestan almost turned away when that cold voice answered through the skull helm. "Have Petrow come find me to ask me that question sometime, I do not answer to you. Know this, paladin of Abriana: if you are ever under my flail again, I shall not spare your life like I once did."

Trestan turned away and stroked his mustache as he considered her words. Katressa guessed that Trestan had no more questions for the moment, so she decided to start her own inquiries.

"Revwar! You can hear me very well, can't you?"

The elf wizard was seen moving beyond the lattice of branches hemming him in. In her mind, Cat could envision his probing yellow eyes as she heard his voice answer.

"Unless my ears deceive me," he called out, "I hear the adventuress whelp hired as a meddlesome privateer from Kashmer. You are a far distance from home."

"Farther than you know, and that is what I wanted to ask you about."

Revwar's voice bordered on sarcasm. "Oh? Please, entertain me. This cell is so boring."

Cat licked her lips. In her mind, she could see the demons raiding her childhood home as if it had been yesterday. "Two decades ago, you stole that first relic stone, didn't you? You summoned demons into the middle of an elf city, and they took it back to their home plane of existence."

Revwar seemed hesitant to answer the question in the middle of Serud'Thanil, surrounded by elves. "How came you to believe such a thing?"

"I was there. I remember the demon attack. I remember you being among the elders. You were supposed to be a guardian of those relics from the Godswars. Instead, you decided to take them and use them for your own means."

Cat's hand briefly settled upon the scroll tucked in her belt. The elves had not taken it, yet she was far from decoding it all. Revwar apparently decided there was no harm in responding. He understood that the elves already held a death sentence over his band.

The wizard admitted, "Aye, I helped the demons make an appearance. The display brought far too much attention from certain gods. The next two had to be taken with more subtlety. You must have been very young when that happened."

Cat responded only briefly, "Aye, but I remember it."

"Maybe that elf city was your home?" The wizard got only silence as a response. "You lost someone you cared about? Someone very dear?"

"What happened to Reatheneus Bilil?"

"Who are you, that you would ask such a question?" Revwar was testing her.

Cat stood tall within the cell. "Katressa Bilil, his daughter, demands to know!"

Revwar preferred to give another question rather than an answer. "I don't suppose that human wench he took to his bed survived the assault?"

Cat's silence spoke volumes.

"Well, if it is of any comfort," Revwar continued, smiling at the agony he knew he was inflicting on his pursuer, "He died rather quickly and easily, compared to some of the tortures the others endured in that hellish world."

Cat's knees went weak. She held on to the wooden tangle of branches for support. Revwar continued with words that struck to her soul. "If you ever want to hunt down the coldast demon that killed him, it won't be hard. The creature wears a collection of ears of the people it had killed. I hear Reatheneus' ear had a gold unicorn symbol dangling from it when it was cut off."

Cat dropped to her knees, sobbing against the caleocht wood. Revwar went on talking. "Which is a good judgment upon him if you ask me. For an elf to take a human to his bed is revolting at the least. They might spawn an agora that is better off if they are drowned at birth…"

Trestan noticed the change in Cat's attitude as Revwar said "agora." With tears still falling from her cheeks, the half-elf jumped up against the imprisoning branches in fury. Her face, normally displaying graceful elvish lines and delicate skin, twisted into rage.

Cat shouted. "Hear me now murderer and betrayer! I swear if it's the last thing I do I will hunt you down and end your life! Whatever it takes, if you survive here, I will track you down and put steel through you when you least expect it!"

Cat spouted with all the venom she had ever mustered. Her eyes blazed like green fires. It shocked Trestan to see her anger kindle in such a short period of time. Listening to her vengeful words, Sondra couldn't help but take a side glance at Montanya. The often-scowling youth witnessed a mirror of her own rage as the half-elf vented her anger and promises of death, and she did not know how to respond to what she saw. Montanya understood all too well the anger created by the murder of one's parents; however, in that moment, she saw how others must view her outbursts. Cat's moment of blind rage reflected the youth's own uncontrolled emotions.

Revwar's amused chuckle answered from afar as Cat continued. "For my father, mother, and my people, I will make it my duty to hunt you wherever you might hide. I won't be satisfied until your sightless eyes are pecked out by vultures!

"I will hunt you down and my blade or my crossbow will be the death of you…I swear it!"

*       *       *       *       *

An elf handed more sweet fruits through a small opening in the branches. The companions offered thanks. Lindon and Trestan had both insisted to the others that they treat their captors as hosts, and behave as if they themselves were visiting dignitaries. The two men accepted the food with smiles and polite words, translated by Katressa. In return, the elf smiled as he carried out his duty.

The elf, Cassyli, had been a member of the scouting party that captured them. He acted as spokesman and inquisitor for the elves when Naef'ad Illwinu Wessail wasn't present. He seemed to be their chief contact with the elves, and likely Illwinu's ears among their jailors. In observing his dress style and customs, Trestan had come to learn more about elven heritage. The elf's blondish-green hair was kept in a ponytail by a knot of leather shaped like a flower. Elf males favored wearing flower patterns as a sign of virility. By the looks of his spear and his unique shield, (crafted from a turtle shell), he seemed more a warrior than a diplomat. Nevertheless, his likeable bearing earned some trust from the companions. That trust that didn't conceal the fact he likely passed knowledge of their words and actions to the ruling matriarchs. The companions suspected that he might have a greater grasp of the human tongue than he let on. Since Cat could translate, the elves likely kept secret the numbers of their people that could understand the humans. He lingered at their cell to make pleasant conversation as they ate. They wondered if he eavesdropped on comments made in the human tongue.

Trestan voiced his concerns while tasting the sweet fruits offered. "My friends and I worry about how your people see us and compare us to that other band. Surely you can tell we are not like them. We hold much higher values."

Cassyli answered in Elvish while Cat served as translator. "I trust much of what you tell me." The elf smiled as he spoke. He very much wanted to seem like he was their friend, though they could not know how much of his emotions were genuine. "Many of my people do not mark the distinction between our two groups of visitors. Emotions run strong among my people right now. If I were you, I would not worry much. Our leaders are wise and they have listened to your tale with interest."

The champion of Abriana pounced on that answer. "Then surely they must also trust that our intentions are only good, and that we move to secure magic that threatens their city as well as our homes. Why can we not reclaim our weapons and go on with our quest?"

The elf scout shrugged. "If it were up to me, I might let you do just that."

Even as Cat translated, she doubted that his sincerity carried far. As Cassyli spoke, the elves next to him threw mistrusting glances at all the companions, and scornful looks upon the half-elf translator.

"If you'll excuse me, I may have a talk with someone right now who might be able to bend influence in your direction," Cassyli finished as he waved goodbye.

Trestan brought his departure to a pause with one more question. "Will anyone here admit to seeing if the *Doranil Star* came down nearby, or flew overhead?"

Cassyli offered no answer. The elf resumed walking along the elevated walkways to a dwelling not far distant. The structure, like the rest of Serud'Thanil, shaped itself as part of the great tree supporting it. Loose vines screened the windows. A sweet bouquet arose from the flowers terraced around the porch. He was not the first to arrive at the house of Naef'ad Illwinu Wessail. Cassyli could see that his brother sat upright at the edge of a wicker chair, upright, and wringing his hands. The siblings nodded at each other upon recognition. Before they could exchange pleasantries, the resident mother of the house appeared to greet them both.

Naef'ad Illwinu had shed her official councilor garments for a relaxed, airy evening gown. Green hair swayed down to her hips as she walked up to the brothers. "Welcome my sons, I am glad to see you both."

The two offspring bowed to their mother in respect. Cassyli spoke as soon as he could without seeming impolite. "Mother, what is to become of the half-human and her friends? From what I observe, they seem to have only peace in their hearts in regards to our people."

"Have you not forgotten what their murderous friends did?" Snapped his brother, Foyren. "They killed several of our kin. Some who died were playmates of ours from childhood. How could you so easily forget such spilled blood?"

Cassyli frowned. "From what I have seen, they are enemies of those same murderers…"

With a wave of her hand, Illwinu commanded the attention of her grown children. "Can I not come home from council sessions to relax with my sons in enjoyment of a quiet evening? Must you dive right into the subject that has caused much speeches and arguments within the council chambers these past days? I had hoped to sit on the balcony with you and discuss less stressful events."

Cassyli bowed, "I'm sorry mother."

She shook her head. "Well, the peaceful moment is lost. I might as well satisfy your minds. I assume your thoughts were focused along the same lines, Foyren?"

"They are indeed." Foyren eagerly answered.

Naef'ad Illwinu dropped into a padded couch with a sigh. "The governess, Deylirra, will make the final decision herself regarding the group of five that Cassyli helped capture."

Foyren's mood went as black as a storm cloud. He slapped the arm of his chair in frustration as he expressed his feelings. "I saw blood taken from the bodies of my kinsmen. The halfling and the armored cleric drank greedily from the chaos they'd sowed. The wizard burned two of my best warriors to ash. I overcame my fear and anger to help secure them alive. Why is there any question at all as to their punishment?"

Cassyli glanced across at his brother. It was a rare thing to hear him admit fear. Foyren was one of the best hunters Serud'Thanil had in its service. The ivory and beads decorating the belt supporting his kittane signified the accolades bestowed upon him by his people. Beneath dark hair, dyed a lighter brown in streaks, remained a scar that jaggedly cut through one eyebrow. The elf had been a renowned hunter of the most respected game animals around. A necklace displayed the claws and bones of several large carnivores, including the tips of a wrelcat's horns.

The younger brother interrupted on behalf of those he felt were innocent. "I don't deny the evil of those you fought, but do not impress the same judgment on those who have done us nay harm."

Foyren would not be so easily turned aside. "And what makes you think they hold any less evil in their hearts? Both parties came to us on the same day. It could very well be that the agora and her friends are allied with those others, but were clever enough to act on better behavior."

Cassyli noted a grimace from his mother that gave him some relief that Illwinu did not feel as similarly as Foyren.

The councilor interrupted with her knowledge. "They are not in any way allied with each other. I know not only from my talks with both parties, but also from the divinations cast by our druids that there is more truth in one group than the other."

"What you are saying?" Foyren insinuated. "Will they be set free and allowed to walk freely in our wood?"

Naef'ad Illwinu shrugged. "Truly, I don't know. The council is split on a decision, which is why the governess will eventually intervene."

"I can't believe I am hearing this." Foyren continued to fume, upsetting his mother. He angrily pushed to his feet and stormed over to the cache of gear that had been left in Illwinu's keeping. Not all of the companions' belongings were with the woman, but among the items presently kept there Foyren pointed out a bastard sword with elvish lettering. "Are we seriously considering allowing the human to take this elf-made weapon back to his people?"

"Why the interest in the Talo'Seelie blade, brother?" Cassyli asked. "You were offered the honor of carrying a whieu, and you refused it. From what I understood, you rejected it as not being a weapon native to our culture…and yet you show an interest in the human's blade?"

The pole-swords that Cat and Trestan had noticed as being the only worked steel in the village were known as a whieu. There were few such blades because the native Faer'Seelie did not work with metal in such a way. The swords they possessed had been given to them during the Godswars by a Talo'Seelie tribe. They were made of such high quality, and so few had survived all these centuries, that they had become a weapon of honor given to those who could best take care of them. The council granted Foyren the right to carry one. They were quickly disappointed by their choice. Foyren was such a staunch traditionalist that he refused to use a sword crafted by Talo'Seelie. After all, the Talo'Seelie were tribes of elves that had broken away from some of their traditional ways to merge their culture in with humans, gnomes, and even dwarves. While the Faer'Seelie stayed true to the Treemother and nurtured her forests, the Talo'Seelie adapted to new customs and walked among the human cities of Orlaun and Kashmer. Although the Talo'Seelie often lived in woods and worshipped the Treemother, the Faer'Seelie considered their own ways purer.

"I did not say I would use this blade!" Foyren seemed insulted. "Yet it is elf-make, even though made by Talo'Seelie. It should not return to human lands where someday it may be used against elves."

"Foyren! Have a seat!"

Naef'ad Illwinu's voice commanded attention. Once Foyren and Cassyli were both sitting and facing her in silence, she addressed them. "Such is the division of all our people over this incident that we struggle to pronounce judgment. A sentence has already been passed on the four who caused us such harm. They were serving a purpose, and that purpose is finished. As for the five who healed the boy in the woods, they will likely be let go in some fashion or another. If it was up to me, I would march them to the edge of our lands with what provisions they need, then keep an eye on them until they left our forest. It is, sadly, not up to me."

"March them in the direction of the ship they seek?" Cassyli inquired.

"That would be very bad. Who knows what evil dropped their ship out of the sky and now wanders our forest?" Foyren added.

Illwinu Wessail sighed as she leaned back in her couch. "As far as we can tell, their intentions are noble, even if some of their reasons remain hidden. We would not release them without having eyes follow them. I wouldn't fully trust them from what little contact I have had with them, but I don't feel that they intend any harm upon us. The decision is not up to any of us in this room, so it is a moot point."

Foyren was quiet, but the shadow of angry emotions kept passing across his face. "You said a sentence was passed on the ones I fought? What is to become of them? Share with me some good news."

Naef'ad Illwinu weighed the decision in her head a bit before speaking. "They are to be executed in the morning. This will hopefully appease those still demanding blood, as well as deliver a just punishment that is already overdue."

Foyren seemed satisfied with that answer, and took his leave.

   *    *    *    *    *

During the evening hours following Cassyli's visit, trouble once again stirred between parties. Montanya, still angry over the loss of her locket, instigated her own line of questions.

"I clearly remember your face, wizard, leering down at me as you snatched my family's heirloom. Don't think you will see any mercy from me..."

"Why are you calling me a thief, when it was you that stole from me?" Revwar's voice carried back to her.

"What?! How dare you accuse *me* of theft!"

Montana went livid at the accusation. Her face reddened to her shade of hair color as Revwar explained. "It was you that confronted us on the deck of that foundering ship, while we merely sought safe evacuation. You charged us and threw a bucket of sand into our faces. 'Twas not enough that you did that, but you also snatched a bag from our hands. Therefore, I brand you a thief! Cry to your dead mother if you feel you've been slighted."

The words incited Montanya into a series of angry kicks at the unyielding caleocht wood. Sondra couldn't disguise her irritation as she tried to calm the woman's rage. "Can't you see he is just trying to taunt you into acting stupid? Ignore his words. He's playing with your emotions."

Hateful, greenish-blue eyes scowled back at the cleric of Ganden. "What if you lost the last reminder you had of your dead parents?"

Sondra's back straightened at that. "I did lose everything of value when I lost my parents. I got over it and found a new life where I could try to help others..."

A playful, yet small, voice called out to Montanya. Kemora dangled the locket in the magical, artificial lights the elves had around the wooden cage. It lazily swung over the dreadful distance to the forest floor. The domid's mischievous eyes looked down her long nose and freckled cheeks at the golden heirloom. She held it for Montanya to witness as she spoke in gleeful tones.

"Oh, is that where Revwar got me this shiny little present? It looks so pretty! All sparkly and beautiful, I think I'll try it on...after I see what's inside."

Montanya spit protests as Kemora popped open the small clasp. The halfling mocked the chiaso with her tone. "Oopsie, I think it spilled out. How clumsy!"

Montanya screamed in rage as she glimpsed the locks of hair drop past the elves' lights. In an instant they were gone in the darkness, drifting on the wind to find some unknown resting place on the forest floor.

Kemora smiled in response to the anger stirred up in her pursuer. "Oh well, didn't look like anything important. Maybe it was some lint or old spider web. If you don't mind now, I think I'll try it on."

Montanya raged, "I'll hang you by that locket if I catch you, thief!"

The chiaso slammed her feet repeatedly into the entrapping wooden branches. Sondra tried to intervene. "Stop that! You're just going to break bones, then I'll have to waste all my energy healing them again under these magic-draining elven spheres, and all of that effort will go without even a 'thank you,' just like usual."

Trestan, Lindon and Katressa watched in uneasy silence as Montanya turned upon the soft-spoken cleric. The chiaso youth vented a number of angry curses loud enough that it brought laughter from Kemora and her allies. Sondra tried to back down, but she had already gone too far in upsetting the volatile redhead. The two women continued to shout, though for Sondra it was an attempt to make the younger fighter see reason rather than swing fists. Montanya started to close in on Sondra with hands that continually clenched and relaxed. The worshipper of Ganden backed into a corner, her arms raised protectively. Montanya planned to turn her rage somewhere, and had already picked her sparring target. Cat and Lindon told Montanya to back off.

Finally, even Trestan reached the end of his considerable patience. He jumped to his feet, shouting as he did so. "I've had enough! The two of you can't keep up this constant arguing. It's time you had a better understanding of one another."

The champion of Abriana forced himself between the two women. "Give me your hands, now!"

Sondra, wide-eyed and scared, meekly obeyed without thinking. She offered out an arm and Trestan grabbed her gently but firmly by the wrist. Montanya, on the other hand, assumed a fighting stance as she faced him. She cocked a fist for a swing.

Montanya spat, "Stay out of this. You're just another religious zealot. She's the one who insulted me!"

Trestan glared at her...as serious with anyone as Cat had ever seen. His eyes locked on Montanya with such intensity she almost stepped back in fright as his stern voice spoke. "If your idea of a fight is for an experienced fighter to beat senseless some weaker woman...then by all means swing your fist at me and I'll give you a lesson in how to do it properly."

Montanya's thin eyebrows raised in uncertainty. Was this paladin actually going to raise a fist against her? Was he simply bluffing?

She froze long enough that Trestan simply reached out and snatched a hold of her wrist. With a hand on each of them, he began to pray. "Beloved Abriana, Goddess of Love and Healing, help us to understand our brothers and sisters better..."

In her anger, Montanya tried to pull back her hand. Instead, she felt a pull drawing her to Trestan. It was not a physical tug, but a sensation of her mind falling into a pit. Behind Trestan, Cat and Lindon stood back with uncertainty as they saw both human women go weak in the knees. Montanya heard a scream from Sondra that mirrored her own, before her mind tumbled into darkness.

## **CHAPTER 26**  **"A Little Understanding…"**

Although Trestan still held firmly to the hands of both women, they began to lose all physical sensations. Even the former smith of Troutbrook was so deeply embedded in his miracle that he lost track of the outside world. Montanya and Sondra both endured the sensation of falling. Their conscious minds tumbled through a dizzying jumble of memory fragments, half-remembered conversations, images of places visited long ago…and yet not all were their own. Trestan viewed it all as well, lost in prayer through a similar empathic link as he had used during the challenge of the beast. Within the confines of their link, Sondra and Montanya became less aware of the presence of anyone else, even each other. Their world became a sporadic flash of images, smells, tastes and sounds.

*Montanya recalled one of her oldest memories: waking from a dream as her mother scooped her out of bed. She barely could make out her mother's form between the smoky room and some blonde hair that covered her own sleepy eyes…blonde hair? Hadn't her hair had always been red? And who was this unknown woman she thought of as her mother?*

…her mother tried to offer comfort while her father shouted from somewhere near. "I can't find Joshua. Joshua! Get Sondra to the window, and I'll look for him."

The mother of young Sondra Oskires carried her body to a nearby window. Montanya…or was her name Sondra?...grabbed tightly to her mother's arm as the elder woman lifted her out of the opening to dangle over the street. She seemed terribly high off the ground.

Montanya cried for her mom to stop scaring her. Behind her mother, she could see smoke pouring out of the window and flames lighting the roof. People below her cried out, "We have the blanket ready! We'll catch her!"

"Don't let go of me, momma!" Montanya heard herself cry, but it wasn't her own voice

"You must let go, Sondra. Let go and live! I'll be right down when we find your brother."

Montanya fell, screaming, only to land in a blanket stretched between a few men. Montanya viewed Sondra's memories as strangers ushered her away from the burning building. The inn collapsed in flaming ruin, smothering the screams from inside. Little Sondra was orphaned and alone.

*Sondra relived a memory that was not her own. She enjoyed the lavish lifestyle her sire, Troyeal bara Westonhout, had provided for her…*

…she pulled at her red curls of hair as her parents led her to the ball. Father and mother were always invited into the grandest homes, and this time Sondra…or was her name Montanya?...received an invitation and came along. She even wore her latest gift, a locket containing intertwined strands of hair from both her parents. They could have taken the coach, but her father remarked on the beauty of the evening, so they walked.

The trio did not think it a good decision afterward, when men stepped out of the darkness. The rich family had barely gone to the limits of their estate when several swordsmen reeking of ale accosted them. The thugs demanded money. When they laid hands on her mother, her father drew forth a smallsword from his cane. They killed him before it could make any difference.

During the attack, they decided there would be more valuables in the house. The estate guards simply ran. Sondra watched through Montanya's eyes as men seized her mother. The young girl tried to hold on. A strip of her mother's pink dress ripped off as men pulled her away. Strong arms threw Sondra into a crate in the estate's garbage. The lid slammed down, and something jammed it into place.

She screamed and pounded on the hard wood of the crate. It was too strong; she couldn't break free. She heard her mother scream and the ripping of the dress. Through the open slats, Sondra watched men surround Montanya's mother. Finally, one of the men became so upset at the noise coming from the crate that he stuck a dagger between the boards. She felt the pain in her abdomen. The child almost bled to death, but a priest and several praetorians found her in time. The guards were too late to save her father and mother.

*Montanya's consciousness saw through Sondra's eyes at the Sanctuary for Those in Need...*

...as Sondra stood uncertainly before a woman in long robes. The child was drawn to the smell of good stew, and her neglected stomach rumbled. One tiny hand held forth the lone copper coin she had found partly obscured in the mud. Instead of taking it, the sister of Ganden who worked at the copper pen closed those tiny fingers back over the coin. Without accepting payment, the woman found Sondra a bench, warm stew, and a blanket to ward off any chills. Sondra found a place to cry, sheltered in the arms of this stranger.

Day in and day out, Sister Evine would not allow the little homeless girl to pay for any of her food and lodging. Montanya felt Sondra's hunger pains and loneliness fade, as she spent night after night in the same sanctuary. Sister Evine even used her needlework to craft a pretty cap that would keep her head warm on chilly days.

*Sondra felt Montanya's anger and loss at being turned away from her home...*

...strangers flanked by the local praetorian guard locked the fence after carting away everything valuable. Officials stole her fine jewelry, except the locket which she kept hidden. It was the only tangible thing she had left of her parents. Her red hair grew long and unruly. Instead of cutting it, she used the strip of her mother's dress to tie it out of the way.

Sondra watched from Montanya's eyes as the child walked the streets alone, full of anger at the world. She carried meager belongings in a bag on her back. The sanctuaries would take in the homeless for a copper a night, but she had no coins at all. It was just as well, her father often talked about the false worshippers at the church and how they always demanded money to pay for salvation. The last thing Montanya wanted was to deal with more thieves.

On a summer morning, when many buildings had their doors open to the air, she heard something curious. A single, loud scream preceded the sound of broken wood. Intrigued more than scared, the red-haired child peeked into the open building. Her jaw dropped as she watched many kids executing fighting maneuvers. The older children broke pieces of wood with their bare hands and feet! Montanya remembered the strong crate that had kept her prisoner while her parents were killed. She stared as the other children did something she had failed to accomplish.

An older man took an interest in the child at his door. She looked up at him hopefully. Montanya's voice asked, "Sir, I have nay coin to pay. I have nay home either, but I would like to learn how to be strong like them."

The man smiled and took her in.

*Montanya watched Sondra commit all her hours to the study of her religion and helping out at the sanctuary...*

...other kids invited her to play, but shy Sondra would make excuses. She didn't seem good at any games, so she barely participated. It wasn't that she didn't like the other kids; she just didn't know how to act around them.

Besides, there was always the poor, the hungry and other homeless. Sondra was no longer homeless; she could sleep in a temple dormitory now that she had taken up the teachings of Ganden. She spent most of her time caring for the poor and sick at the sanctuaries. It felt good to help others. Deep down, however, Montanya could feel the core reasons for her service. Sondra felt indebted to the church. She owed them everything she could give, for they kept her safe and alive when she had nothing.

Sondra loved others, but she followed Ganden for the sake of obligation. She didn't develop hobbies, play with other children, or envision a world outside the sanctuaries. Her only luxury seemed to be sneaking peeks at occasional romantic writings that some folks brought into the sanctuary. Within those pages, Sondra dreamed about something she felt was beyond her. Instead of following her dreams, she sunk into studying religion and the arts of healing. Duty demanded for Sondra to be the best healer she could be, and give back as much as the church had given her.

*Sondra watched Montanya shy away from other children...*

...the student of chiaso made herself an outcast of her own choosing. Others her age jested at the world and laughed about things they could not change, but Montanya trained to make a change. Students chided her for her serious mindset. Their pranks gave birth to her customary scowl.

Montanya avoided the city, despite its presence right outside the door. She feared where the thieves might lurk, and if they would pounce on her before she was ready. She stayed indoors around the people with whom she trained. With them, the slightest touch didn't frighten her into a paranoia that a pickpocket was feeling her up. Every sparring match she practiced fighting the men that took away her life. Sondra saw how Montanya lived her life and the similarities with her own existence. Both of them disallowed freedom in favor of some lofty and ultimately endless goal.

In one memory, Sondra rifled through Montanya's pack, looking for her missing heirloom. She couldn't find it, quickly coming to the conclusion that her fellow student Rayka must have taken it again as a prank. She marched down the hall wearing her scowl, with her long, red braid whipping behind her. She found the student with others in the training hall. He had his eyes closed in meditation, standing still and vulnerable to attack. Montanya didn't give him the chance to defend himself. Her jumping kick sent him stumbling backward.

He didn't fall. Though they had similar muscles and training, this young man had a balance of spirit that Montanya's tortured soul never achieved. Sondra saw and felt everything as Rayka responded to the attack with more skill and power than Montanya possessed.

*Montanya witnessed her own scarred and bruised body tended by Sondra…*

…the student of Ganden felt sickness enter her own body as she helped Mother Evine draw out the poison from the knee injury. Montanya's consciousness blended with Sondra's thoughts and actions as the young cleric sweated to save the unknown, homeless youth. A spiritual link between healers and patient allowed them to feel how perilously close to death the chiaso had drifted. With the poison extracted, and Sondra fighting her own nausea from the sensation, they felt Montanya's soul pull closer to the world of the living.

At one point during their toil, Mother Evine asked Sondra's opinion of the scarred woman recovering on the table. "Rough life," Sondra replied.

Montanya watched herself storm out of the copper pen in anger over her salvation at the hands of sanctuary priests. Soon afterward, she relived another phase of Sondra's life involving Montanya.

She heard another acolyte of Ganden ask Sondra if she was going up on deck to watch the spell show. Sondra refused, preferring to prepare a meal for the unknown individual held in the *Doranil Star's* brig. Deep inside, Sondra wanted to watch the show, yet she chided herself for wanting to indulge such luxury when some poor soul sat in the brig, likely hungry. It was always her duty to care for people in bad spots, so she set about preparing a meal from the best food she could find at hand. She even borrowed a flower from a display and set it alongside the cup of water. Little did she know that cup would get splashed in her face by the angry youth in the cell.

*Montanya's deepest fears and insecurities were bared for Sondra…*

…Montanya felt that her whole life had been stolen. Since her parents murder, she refused to embrace anything in life except her need for revenge. Will her life become a failure, or even a lie, if she never catches a single thief? Was there any life she could enjoy without first finding a remedy to her heart's sense of loss? Would the simple aspect of moving on to a different lifestyle belittle the deaths of her parents as nothing? She couldn't branch her needs beyond her hate. Now, there was one thief out there within reach. Maybe if she caught that halfling, Kemora, she might have her answer.

*Montanya saw a similar reflection in Sondra's soul…*

…Sondra's responsibilities to duty and her beliefs in repaying the debt she owed to the church superseded her personal wishes. The needs of others trumped hers. Her dreams smothered under the weight of responsibility borne from the attitude that she owed the church everything.

Sondra hoped that one day someone would thank her in a way that would make her feel as if she had done more than her duty. Deep inside, she wanted freedom from the mantle she had taken upon her shoulders. Time and again her efforts in serving others seemed futile. She had been verbally abused by people seeking refuge in the shelters. Injured patients hit or kicked her as she tried to heal them. Most recently, one particular red-haired chiaso refused to thank her for all the good she attempted to do. For some reason, Sondra wanted more than anything to hear Montanya say 'thank you.' Sondra desperately craved some acknowledgement that she was accomplishing something and not simply living a life of self-imposed servitude.

*The vision abruptly ended...*
Both women suddenly jerked back into their own bodies in the present time, arms held by Trestan. Montanya and Sondra stared deeply into each other's eyes, seeing something entirely beyond the walls they had built up around their feelings. Their eyes revealed fear; fear bared by that most intimate sharing of emotions and feelings between two people who would not have consented to it. Montanya and Sondra were so shocked by the sudden experience that they simply stood there locked in their gazes. Both breathed heavily and shivered in the warm night air.

Neither really noticed how bright the druid's magic-dampening globes had become. Neither mind really registered when Trestan collapsed out of exhaustion.

*   *   *   *   *

Deep into the night, Katressa Bilil held her lover closely in her arms. She worried for his health after using that miracle, but it seemed that all he needed was rest. He got plenty of peace and quiet from inside the prison cage. Montanya and Sondra had backed to opposite corners, without a word to anyone, since the miracle had ended. The two women fell into a fitful sleep after staring out from the bars for a long time. Whatever Trestan had done, it took the fight out of both.

Cat's hands rubbed his muscles as he lay in her embrace. Sometimes she couldn't help but lean over and place a gentle kiss atop his head. No matter how she worried about their future, she knew Trestan was the most important thing in her life.

Their stay at the elves' city reminded Katressa of all that separated her from that race. Neither fully human nor elf, she could not settle into either culture. Her home village tolerated her out of respect for her father. Even after his death, that respect followed his daughter despite how others saw her bloodline. Serud'Thanil elves only saw her human side subverting the fine elf blood. It seemed that among foreign elves she might always be an outcast.

As Cat ran her nimble fingers through Trestan's thick, dark hair, she realized how unfairly she had treated him. At times she put distance between them over her fears about his aging. Yet, among these people, Cat saw her feelings from a different perspective. If an elf lord actually took an interest in her, she would not have to worry about watching him grow old and die. Instead, she might be the one shunned because he would not like to see her grow old and tend a frail woman in her last century. Cat knew that elves, as a race, would not be very cordial to her over her human blood. She would always be an inferior minority.

It brought pain to her knowing others would treat her that way, yet she realized that in subtle ways she may have acted the same around her beloved. He moved closer to her heart than she had dared to dream any man would come…and yet her doubts had formed a wall that kept him from approaching closer.

She felt him stir. Looking down, she saw his eyes open. He looked tired, but his eyes wandered outward from their prison with curiosity. "It is so beautiful out here, Cat."

Cat glanced out of the cell, noting the faerie lights, elevated walkways, and the gardens below. Somewhere, the sweetest music was being played for approving ears to enjoy. Trestan was enjoying the sights and sounds as he continued. "What a paradise they have out here. It must make you feel that you miss home."

Cat's feelings had been nothing of the sort. She sighed as she spoke. "It may be beautiful, but I had not noticed. This is far from any place I would call home, *faunlessa*."

Trestan glanced up into her eyes, seeing a hint of tears. Cat's hair bore many tangles from their experience. He offered a straightforward observation. "You have been treated badly since we came here. I wonder what they said to you that you didn't translate?"

The half-elf shrugged off the question as if it didn't matter. "We have all been treated poorly here. We are prisoners."

She hoped he would pry no more. His eyes were looking up to her, but she preoccupied herself by staring out at the city.

Trestan asked, "What does agora mean?"

He likely felt all her muscles go tense as he spoke the word. She unconsciously bit her lip, offering no immediate response.

"If I offended or hurt you," Trestan whispered, "I am sorry."

"Nay, it's not you." Cat sighed. "Can you do a favor for me, Trestan? Let me never again hear that word from those wonderful lips of yours."

Trestan nodded. After a moment of silence deciding how she should answer, she said, "Agora'Seelie is a name given to those broken from the traditional elf race by being a product of a relationship in which only one parent was an elf. Elves use the short version as an insult to those who are…half-breeds such as myself. It is a very hurtful racial insult. I suppose I'm an adult and shouldn't be bothered by rude names, yet this word has been branded on me since childhood. As if my blood was a betrayal to their race."

Trestan reached up and slid a hand behind her neck. He started massaging her muscles. She could trust Trestan to know where to touch her so that all her cares seemed to melt away. "I will never bring it up again, Cat. If another elf uses that word on you, I can't promise to refrain from knocking them from their feet."

Cat giggled, "Don't make fights for me my love; however, if you do, please win them."

Trestan worried that Cat wasn't getting much sleep while worrying over him. At his urging, they settled into a different position in which they could comfortably fall asleep entwined in an embrace.

At least, it was as comfortable as possible in a cage packed with people who hadn't bathed in days.

*       *       *       *       *

In the morning, the companions were roused in short order by the multitude of conversations or by the hands of their fellow travelers. Several captors, warrior and druid, gathered near their cell in anxious discussions. Many elf citizens lingered on the nearby walkways, raised voices talking over one another. Even with no understanding of the elf language, the companions could feel tension behind the voices. They rubbed sleepy eyes even as a misty morning rain brought a cold chill. On such a dreary morning, they could only guess as to why so many agitated elves lurked around their imprisonment.

They all looked to Cat for an explanation. She turned from native to native. The elves of Serud'Thanil seemed to talk around the adventurers instead of addressing them directly. It took several seconds of uncertainty for Cat to filter out the numerous voices.

The half-elf looked to Trestan, her eyebrows raised in surprise. "Revwar and his band escaped sometime during the night."

"What?"

"Escaped?"

"But they didn't get away, did they?"

The companions began raising as much of an uproar as the elves outside. Cat did her best to explain the details as she overheard them. "Their cage was empty this morning. The door appeared forced-open by magic after the removal of several druid spheres. They were supposed to be executed this day! The elves are searching, they want blood."

More than one companion wore a look of worry at the news of the death sentence. They wondered how their own fate would turn out among this strange culture. As Cat continued to translate pieces of information, Montanya and Lindon observed the cage that had once held their opponents. Elves swarmed the cage and the walkways around it, but they saw no sign of their quarry. Montanya slammed a fist against the unyielding caleocht wood. Once again, despite all her training, a wooden cage had kept her from taking action.

Lindon admonished her, "Don't let your anger blind you. You won't do your hand any good fighting a tree. Focus on the present if we are to get out of here alive."

Beside Cat, Abriana's champion mused out loud, "Now they will be free to pursue the relics, and with a head start, while our fate remains uncertain."

Cat eavesdropped and translated all the clues the elves freely discussed. Citizens showed no concern about being overheard by the half-blood. Cassyli forced his way through the crowded walkways. The spear-wielding scout again wore flowery patterns on his tunic, yet his eyes belied a serious tone.

"Did my brother come by this cell last night?" He asked. At Cat's look of confusion, he added, "Foyren. Dark hair, a scar across one eyebrow, a necklace of animal bones."

Cat recognized the name from the scattered elf conversations. "Nay, but I heard others here talking about him."

Cassyli glanced at his fellow citizens in alarm, "What did they say?"

"A few said that he sent away some of the guards around the other cell last night, before the other party went missing."

The elf scout's first response was to yell at his fellow people that they were discussing escape information within earshot of the half-elf and her friends. Cassyli's outraged shout silenced most of the nearby elves as they found a better hold on their tongues. The scout stressed to his people that any news should not be openly discussed in the presence of other prisoners. Cat couldn't gauge his personal reaction to his brother's actions.

Once the conversations abated around the companions, a new disturbance reached their ears. Shouts originated from the foggy ground. The rainfall and mist hindered their vision, yet they could glimpse shadows moving around. Even the elves around the prison cage paused to listen.

Cat whispered a translation in answer to her companions' unasked questions. "The elf warriors on the ground are shouting at someone, asking them to stop."

"Shouting at whom?" Sondra asked, peering through the interwoven caleocht branches.

Her answer came soon enough. The first sign of the unwanted trespasser came as a steady thump-thump. It could have been mistaken for a drum beat, or a series of boulders landing on the ground. Two great legs stomped footprints into the muddy ground as they steadily moved past the shouting elves. The rain and mist seemed to play tricks on the minds of the companions until they realized there was a massive being moving closer. Branches snapped as the creature shrugged past narrow spaces.

The humanoid giant moved determinedly, guided by some secret desire. An unkempt mass of long hair spilled down the sides of a huge face, forming a dangling beard. Its crusty and thick skin resembled the bark of an old oak. Animal hides covered scarce portions of its bulk, revealing some sense of intelligence and decency. The creature had long arms, one of which dragged a tree trunk as a club. Armed elf warriors flanked the giant's path, unwilling to force a confrontation.

Sondra noticed a number of elves shying away from the monster. "Why aren't they attacking it if it isn't listening to them?"

The half-elf indicated the monstrous figure with a tilt of her angular chin, "That is a firbholg. It's one of the 'gentle giants' of the woods. They tend to be peaceful and live in harmony with the elves and nature. Elves won't attack it unless they have good reason to do so." Cat tilted her head, "But it isn't acting natural."

"What do you mean?" Asked Lindon, as he watched its approach.

Cat pointed at its path. "Trees normally bend around the path of a firbholg. He shouldn't need to break limbs as he passes."

Trestan watched the beast sniff the air. It let out a roaring challenge as it approached. "They may have good reason to defend themselves in a moment. That firbholg looks to crave a fight over something. I can feel its anger, and yet its eyes…there is something not quite right about them."

Everyone on the walkways watched the creature below as it turned its head skyward. The dark orbs, sunk into clefts under thick eyebrows, focused on the prisoners. Some of the elves decided to put some distance between themselves and the giant. For the companions, there was nowhere to go. They had some relief in that the creature could not reach their cage.

Lindon gasped as he met the creature's stare. The minstrel noted the emptiness in those eyes despite the anger that carved the face. The firbholg looked at them through a fog of uncertainty. It wasn't hard for Lindon to recall where he'd seen that look before.

"It's under a hypnotic enchantment." The minstrel explained. "I've seen the same reflection in the eyes of those whom Jentan charmed."

"Impossible!" Sondra exclaimed. Yet as the monster roared up at them she hastily changed her opinion. "Or maybe not. Well, at least it can't reach us up here."

The tree trunk that served the creature as a great club collided with a portion of the caleocht tree. It didn't extend long enough to touch the companions' prison; nevertheless, it rattled the tree. The citizens of Serud'Thanil fled the area in panic. Elf warriors moved to assist others. None of them dared to attack the firbholg as yet, though they continued shouting at it.

Taking a more direct approach, the firbholg dropped its club and grasped mighty arms around the base of the tree. The companions stumbled for balance as the giant attempted to shake the caleocht trunk. Leaves and branches began to snap and walkways shook violently. At least one elf slipped on the wet walkway and tumbled to the forest floor.

When the tree finally stopped shaking, the companions braced themselves against the interwoven branches. Montanya scowled, "He doesn't need to reach us as long as he can bring the tree down to where he is."

"What is he doing now?" Sondra asked from a prone position.

Trestan and Cat both looked down to find the answer to that same question. Without having time to reply, both hastily released their hold on the branches and jumped away. The others saw a large shadow fly at them through the misty rain. It was a boulder large enough that a halfling could have stretched out and lounged on it. The thrown missile blasted through the cell with enough force to turn hardened caleocht branches into splinters.

**CHAPTER 27**        **"The Raging Firbholg"**


Montanya felt the force of the thrown missile send her reeling across the prison. Cracked branches landed on her head as she raised her arms for protection. She stumbled and fell, realizing only too late that the ruined cell had lost much of its wooden lattice. Montanya comprehended that her legs dangled over a ruined edge of the floor. Her arms reached desperately to grasp something solid. She glimpsed Sondra in a precarious position next to the edge. The acolyte of Ganden reached one arm to grab Montanya, though the healer hung on by a slim handhold. Sondra clutched Montanya's tan tunic. For the briefest of moments Montanya thought she was saved. The sudden weight jerked Sondra's other arm more than the woman could handle.

Momentum ripped both women from the remains of the broken cell, tumbling into a long fall to the forest ground. Montanya focused on her training as she turned her body to control her fall. She had never before put her techniques into practice from such a height. At some point, a leafy branch slapped at her. She heard a noise from Sondra as the young cleric encountered the same branch on her way down. Montanya kicked at a second branch, snapping it. She delivered a double-hand-slap to another, slowing her descent even more. The chiaso gained some control of her fall as she kicked and slapped passing branches. Just before the ground met them, Montanya kicked outward from the trunk of the tree. Her aim brought her rolling on a muddy slope, yet the impact rattled her whole body.

Montanya lie still and quiet, her mind trying to absorb the situation. Misty rain fell down on her, filling mud puddles nearby. She was waiting to see if she would black out or be able to take a deep breath. It took time to recover from the shock. Her body had been jarred badly, yet she wasn't unconscious and she could breathe. Her ribs hurt, her legs hurt, and one shoulder burned. She willed herself past the moment, having endured pain most of her life. Montanya rose from the mud and glanced around.

Elves ran in random directions, all ignoring her. Debris still rained down from above. Montanya didn't worry as much about surviving the fall once she realized that she was now within easy reach of the firbholg. The creature roared, though its attention fixed on the broken cell. From here, the giant humanoid appeared ten times as scary. Montanya wanted to use her remaining strength to run, but a nearby groan interrupted her thoughts. Sondra had fared worse in the fall, landing on a bush that caused new injuries even as it lessened her overall impact. Breath rattled from her battered lungs in a wheeze.

Montanya wanted nothing more than to run from the firbholg and pursue the halfling thief while she had the chance. Her legs betrayed her, staggering to Sondra's side instead. The chiaso pulled the woman off of broken branches, eliciting a wail of pain. Montanya hushed her right away, concerned about drawing the firbholg's attention.

"Lie still, that giant is near. I can try and find you some help." Montanya whispered.

She wasn't sure how much Sondra understood her words. Blood matted the blonde hair. Even as Sondra looked around, redness colored one eye.

Sondra spoke quietly, saying only, "Dear Ganden…" though she repeated those words a few times.

Montanya thought Sondra was just speaking for the sake of mercy before she lost consciousness. Sondra surprised the chiaso by uttering a healing prayer. The blood in her hair flaked away as the redness disappeared from her eyes. She visibly improved as the miracle mended her body. The healer was able to take in several deep breaths. She still wore blood and bruises, but appeared visibly stronger.

The chiaso revealed more surprise than the cleric as Sondra sat up without a grunt of pain. "Praise Ganden!" Sondra said. The cleric then turned to Montanya, examining her with a critical eye. "Allow me to take care of you. I can sense your broken ribs."

*     *     *     *     *

Cassyli was caught in a swarm of his fellow citizens as they ran scared from the volatile giant. The elf had his spear in hand, the turtle-shell shield on his other arm, yet he knew they would be only a nuisance to a firbholg. He saw many of the warriors below holding kittanes ready in self-defense, yet those wooden war clubs were also an ineffective weapon. Many elf archers lined the walkways, impeded by the flow of fleeing folk, yet their arrows would need to hit the creature in force to get past the tough skin and hamper it. Cassyli knew that the whieu pole-swords could cut the creature easily, yet there were few of them nearby. The druids might be their only hope of stopping the rampage.

Feeling helpless for his part, it occurred to Cassyli that there was a weapon nearby which he could wield effectively against the firbholg. He started to run with the crowd on the wet walkway. His goal was to get to the home of his mother, Naef'ad Illwinu, and borrow the captives' elvish sword.

*     *     *     *     *

Trestan climbed out of the remains of the cell as the giant roared beneath him. The paladin-aspirant turned to assist Cat and Lindon in escaping the wreckage. A platform against the main trunk of the tree offered questionable refuge, as it had been clipped by the huge stone. They crawled over unstable boards looking for a safer spot. The three companions paused to dwell on their next course. The nearby walkways and platforms formed a maze of fleeing elves. The druids and guards concentrated more on evacuating people and the enraged firbholg, rather than worrying over the prisoners. The trio picked a walkway and ran for safety.

The firbholg followed them with its dulled eyes. The giant rammed its full weight into one of the trees supporting the walkway. The great trunk cracked and split. The firbholg kept shoving the tree until it gave way. When it went over, it snapped several walkways and removed a portion of a treehouse support.

Trestan and Cat shouted to each other as they held on to the ropes connecting a suspended bridge. The ropes and wood stretched and ripped as the other tree fell through the tangle. The two adventurers went swinging through the air on a scary ride, barely retaining their hold as ropes whipped around. Now dangling from a web of criss-crossed ropes and branches, they worked to climb back up to a platform.

252

Lindon was not so lucky. The bearded minstrel fell along with some of the wreckage and a few elves. The resourceful human whistled a tune that levitated him down safely. He landed gracefully among fallen elves who did not endure an easy landing.

Lindon was still dressed in the colorful, multi-layered fashions of Orlaun. It was a look that called for attention amidst the woodland garb of the nearby elves. Lindon's blue eyes looked up from the rim of his red hat to see the firbholg's clouded eyes focused on him. Even if he was not dressed so different, the minstrel reasoned that any being charmed by Jentan might pay particular attention to the man that had foiled the mentalist in the past.

The giant paused for a moment. Inside, its fogged mind probably grappled with the mentalist's commands. The minstrel had no doubt what would happen once the firbholg sorted its thoughts. Lindon moved slow and cautious in the hopes of putting a plan into motion before those giant feet went into motion. His hand slowly reached to his vest pocket. He would have preferred the use of his captured mandolin strings to break the enchantment. The minstrel was forced to settle for the notes from his bamboo flute.

A blast of discordant music flew from the flute and thundered painfully on the ears of those nearby. It was a trick designed to break the shell of most mental intrusions. It had rescued both Jolynn and Sondra from Jentan's imposed delusions.

This time the trick had no effect. The firbholg reached for its tree trunk club. Lindon noticed mud packed into its ears, likely shielded by magic. Jentan and his companions had not left an easy opening by which the charm could be lifted.

There was no time left to do anything but run. The firbholg lumbered forth faster than any giant would seem capable of in this forest city. It swung the oversized club. Lindon had to stay one step ahead as the giant slammed aside small trees and stomped flat a small cart.

*　　　　*　　　　*　　　　*　　　　*

Cassyli ran across the central room and grabbed the handle of Trestan's blade. Illwinu appeared, only partly dressed.

"What do you plan to do with that sword?" Her green hair was in a mess as she shrugged her arms into a robe. "You have never wielded one! Did you even find your brother yet?"

"Foyren disappeared around the same time that the prisoners did last night, after dismissing several of the guards from their stations."

Naef'ad Illwinu's jaw went slack at the news; nevertheless, she moved quickly enough to block her younger son's exit. "You are not going back out there without me by your side!"

Cassyli's mother demanded too much of his respect to blatantly disobey such a request. "Then please hurry, mother. Lives are at stake as we delay."

The scout explained the attack with barely constrained patience as the matron of the Wessail family grabbed a few more possessions. None of her choices included a weapon of any kind. Once garbed, she allowed Cassyli to lead her back into the chaos veiled by the misty rain. She said nothing more of his choice to bring the sword. He was a veteran scout

253

and a fighter in his own right. Illwinu could only hope that his decision to wield the magical blade wouldn't lead to something regretful.

*       *       *       *       *

Trestan and Cat succeeded in clambering atop a platform. The tattered rope bridge swung in the rain below them. Other walkways and wooden bridges led from their perch, but they had to decide where they would go next.

"Did you catch sight of where Lindon fell?" Trestan asked.

Cat's green eyes scanned the forest floor. She watched the firbholg as it concentrated on a runner on the ground. "There he is. The firbholg is chasing after him."

Lindon weaved through trees and supports too narrow for the giant. The firbholg pursued with single-minded determination. The creature shoved aside smaller trees as it swung its club. The club sometimes smashed through a support beam that the human ran past. The damage near the ground began to create even more chaos above. Few elves remained in the area that were not warriors or scouts. Those present found themselves hanging onto swaying walkways or jumping from collapsing platforms.

A Naef'ad on the platforms lowered her head, as she issued a sorrowful order to the line of elves nearby. The group of archers fired the first volley of arrows at the firbholg. The creature yelled in rage as some of the missiles penetrated into the hard skin. The feathered shafts sticking from its hide seemed small annoyances. Cat noticed bows and arrow quivers tied against a walkway nearby.

Cat spoke to Trestan even as she started running to the armaments. "I'm going to get my hands on a weapon and help distract it from Lindon."

Trestan nodded. The seminary trained him for crossbows, but never bows. He scanned around the scene for any situation in which he might be useful. The paladin-aspirant noticed Cassyli and  Naef'ad Illwinu on a platform, noting that the scout held Sword of the Spirit.

Below, the firbholg paused its pursuit as it recalled its magical abilities. The creature tapped into the natura used by shamans and druids. As one, the remaining arrows were expelled from its body. The skin hardened considerably as the firbholg's spell sought better protection. The next volley was completely ineffective. Arrows bounced harmlessly without making any scratches. The archers called out for druids to enchant their arrows with magic.

The archer squad didn't have the chance to fire again. The firbholg put its renewed strength into throwing a statue from a garden below. The stone missile demolished the archers' perch. Even as those elves fell from the destroyed walkway, the remnants of the statue continued upward until impacting a house that had already been weakened by the loss of support beams.

The elven structure fell apart. A steady stream of debris rained down as its weight ripped the boards holding it together. Trestan saw large pieces of the dwelling avalanche down on the platform where the councilor and her son stood. Debris swept Cassyli from the platform without warning. The sword was spared the fall, but it teetered on the edge of the battered perch. Naef'ad Illwinu hastily cast a divine spell to protect her. She succeeded in erecting a half-sphere shield that partially deflected the debris. Despite that effort, Trestan soon lost sight of the elf councilor under the pile of wood that dropped on her.

Cat was busy trying to untie the spare bow from where it was lashed to the platform. Trestan didn't try to shout out his intent at her. The young warrior turned and navigated a path that would take him to his sword and the trapped elf.

*      *      *      *      *

Montanya and Sondra hid from the sight of the dangerous firbholg in some bushes. They each wanted to run, but movement would likely draw attention. Although the giant focused on the minstrel, the action was never far away. Lindon proved to have amazing agility. He sang a verse with a fast tempo that granted unnatural speed to his movements. It was possible that Lindon could give his opponent a hard run race, yet the minstrel did not attempt to flee in a straight line. The man kept the enraged creature confined to one area out of safety for the city. He unknowingly ran circles around where the women were hiding. It was only a delaying tactic until the elves could bring sufficient force to bear on it. Most of the citizens had already run to safety.

Some innocents still remained nearby. The human women observed a trio of elf children hiding at the base of a large tree. Cries came from the fearful faces. Montanya and Sondra would have tried to shush the children if they could, fearful of them attracting the creature. Given the difference in languages and the status of the women as escaped prisoners, neither figured they would improve the situation by making themselves known.

Silently, they sat and observed the interaction between Lindon and the firbholg. They watched as the volleys of arrows struck the giant. When the firbholg picked up the statue and flung it high, the two women gasped as they realized he was aiming directly above the children. Montanya and Sondra looked up so see the walkway tear apart and spill the elf archers.

Sondra started to rise and give aid. Montanya grabbed her arm painfully and whispered, "Don't! They will likely kill you for approaching their kids before they understand your intentions are not harmful."

The cleric of Ganden had to admit Montanya could be right. More dreadful noises sounded from above. Amid cracks, screeches, and tearing wood, another elf fell from the heights. Even more terrifying, they saw pieces of wood, furniture, and other debris dropping from the sky. The elven dwelling was falling apart above them.

Montanya jumped backward, "It's going to fall right on us!"

The chiaso started to run. When she heard Sondra running in different direction, she slowed but did not stop. Montanya looked around, spotting Sondra running toward the cowering children. The children huddled against the tree supporting the bulk of the house. Now, that house slowly disintegrated over their heads.

Montanya shrieked, "Sondra, what are you doing?"

Sondra Oskires didn't answer, too distracted with looking upward as she ran. The cleric of Ganden barely avoided falling objects. Her feet slipped on the wet ground. Sondra changed course to avoid a long, wooden railing that impaled the soft mud.

Montanya paused, though she stayed poised on the verge of bolting away from the area. "Are you crazy? Those are your captors! Perhaps your executioners!"

"They are children!" She yelled back. "They need someone to help them."

The undecided chiaso danced from one foot to the other. She felt exposed and open. Around her, objects fell from the sky amidst injured elves, while a giant roared uncomfortably close. In the middle of all that chaos ran a self-sacrificial cleric who seemed heedless of her safety while helping strangers. Montanya stood anchored in uncertainty as crazy events unfolded around her.

Sondra motioned to the children to follow her. If anything, she only served to scare them further. The children trembled and wept. Mucus ran freely from their noses, while tears glistened on their cheeks. Sondra finally went so far as to reach for an arm and try to pull them from the base of the tree.

A loud crack split the air. Montanya and Sondra looked up and saw a large limb snap apart under the weight of a former wall laying on it. It hung directly over Sondra and the children.

Montanya screamed, "Soonndrraaaa!!!"

The wall crashed down against the base of the tree. The chiaso glimpsed the cleric throwing herself over the children protectively before several hundred pounds of rubble covered them.

*             *             *             *             *

The firbholg roared its anger as it pulled at druidic bonds. The elf practitioners of natura had caused branches and roots to ensnare the giant. The spell struggled to hold the creature at bay. While it offered Lindon a reprieve from running, it seemed that the trick would not be enough. The giant proved tougher than the surrounding plant life. It tore roots from the ground and snapped through reaching vines. Many druids hastily gathered around those lending their concentration to the spell. They tried to formulate new plans to thwart the giant.

They ran out of time. The firbholg got an arm free and tried to reach for its massive club. Unable to stretch far enough, it went with a different idea. Despite the fog of the charm the firbholg could ascertain its biggest enemies. It needed to retaliate against the druids or it would continue to be bogged down. The giant grabbed at a piece of a fallen walkway and slung it around like a sling. The rope bridge still had several boards tied to it, as well as a broken support post on one end. He released it in the direction of the druids.

The impact knocked down several elves. Most who had been controlling the plants lost their concentration. The uninjured druids scattered as the rope bridge landed in their midst.

The firbholg burst free of the remaining plant tendrils. It took up its club and focused its rage at the fallen druids. Footsteps thundered closer as they tried vainly to use tricks to slow it.

Lindon ran into the firbholg's vision like a blur. Using the harmonic web endowed in his music, whistling as he moved, he ran in with inhuman speed and jumped higher than most athletic humans could achieve. He threw out his cloak and waved his wide-rimmed red hat. The firbholg couldn't help but notice one of the primary targets Jentan had imprinted upon his brain. In case the aerial leap failed to catch its attention, Lindon also flung a throwing dagger he had succeeded in smuggling past the elves. The dagger bounced off the creature's jutting eyebrow ridge.

The minstrel hit the ground running. Behind him came the firbholg with upraised club. The druids were spared as Lindon led the beast away on a new chase.

The minstrel had passed close to the firbholg to distract it. Lindon's first priority was to get more room to run. He decided to use an illusionary trick to enact misdirection. Lindon brought the bamboo flute to his lips. Changing songs, and thus changing spells as he did, his pace became treacherously slowed as the firbholg closed the gap. A few, quick notes from the bamboo flute, and then Lindon tossed his red hat one direction while he turned in the opposite direction. To everyone else, it seemed as if the minstrel split into twins and charged two different directions.

In order for the trick to work, one had to hear the music. The firbholg's ears were still thick with mud. The giant never saw the illusionary double, only the real minstrel. The giant kicked at this bothersome bug, sending him flying a short distance. Lindon Taleweaver somersaulted over a wall built of piled stone only to land in someone's garden. Dazed, he nevertheless made an attempt to stagger to his feet and keep running.

He didn't get far. The firbholg's tree club swept into the wall of boulders and sent pieces of it flying across the garden at him. A spray of stones knocked Lindon senseless. The minstrel went down, limp and unmoving, at its feet.

The firbholg raised the club high. Its head and back arched upward as it roared its victory message throughout Serud'Thanil. It poised the club for a great blow.

As its head rose, it saw a row of elf archers atop another platform. In the middle stood one who was not fully of elf blood. The firbholg understood her identity from the enchanted whisperings of Jentan. It knew this person as another important target. The misty rain plastered Katressa Bilil's raven tresses to her head and shoulders. Her green eyes displayed the deadly seriousness of a hunting cat, poised for the kill. The other elves let loose arrows that bounced harmlessly off the thickened skin of the firbholg. When Cat fired her elvish bow, the arrow shot into the open mouth. The roar of the giant ceased abruptly as the arrow skewered its soft tongue. Cat stared with unnerved ferocity into that giant's dark eyes.

The firbholg switched priorities to its newest foe.

**CHAPTER 28**          **"Test of the Butterfly/Challenge of the Beast"**


Trestan arrived at the platform to find Naef'ad Illwinu trapped under the remnants of the fallen dwelling. A pile of boards and mud bricks almost obscured the elf matron. Her divine magic kept a shield enacted above her. It held much of the weight from crushing her, but her visage gave evidence of the ongoing struggle. Injured or not, the shield sapped her strength. Trestan glanced around. He saw no others trapped or close enough to help.

The champion of Abriana walked to where Sword of the Spirit lay fallen near the wreckage. The scabbard was missing, but he could find that later. He listened for a moment to the roars of the firbholg. With no time to delay, he turned to the trapped councilor.

Even as she kept her hands above her, keeping her shield alive, she could see Trestan walking toward her through the entrapping boards. She glared at him in fury, expecting the worst from her former prisoner. Trestan still did not have a good grasp of Elvish. He said a couple words to Illwinu that he did know, asking her to hold still. He then raised his sword for a strike.

Naef'ad Illwinu had only venom in her voice as she replied. She spoke the human language rather well, though with an accent. "Now we see your true nature is like that of the others! I am helpless and you could run, yet instead you seek to finish me. Take my head if you dare, you will be hunted down by my kin."

Trestan lowered the sword and replied in the human tongue. "You have misjudged us again. We never came here with malice toward your people. If you hold still, I can try to free you before the weight of this house crushes your bones."

Naef'ad Illwinu said nothing. She stayed silent while measuring him by his actions. If his intent was to harm her, she had no defense. Trestan leaned closer, inspecting the boards around her. He lined his sword to strike at a thick beam. It surprised the councilor that his weapon could be regarded useful in clearing such heavy debris. She had seen the whieu swords display amazing feats with their keen edges, yet no one had ever attacked a pile of brick and wood with one.

Trestan exhaled in a grunt as his sword sliced across. The blade chopped through wood and hardened clay. The squire of Abriana worked methodically at saving the elf woman, despite his anxieties about the giant facing his friends. He had to choose his strikes carefully to avoid sundering her divine shield. The sword had ruptured Savannah's divine shield in the past. Trestan could not afford to make that mistake and be accused of killing one of the city's influential rulers.

As the blade hacked apart more of the rubble, Illwinu spoke to him in a nonjudgmental voice. "Why do you offer to help me, when you could easily leave me where I lay?"

"I worship Abriana, Goddess of Love and Healing. The emblems etched into my armor declare this true. She is a merciful goddess. I know you did not imprison us out of cruelty. You had a justified concern for the safety of your people, after those others attacked your sentries." Trestan paused and drew breath. A swing of his sword shattered a piece of a table that had fallen across her legs. "We'd not consider ourselves your enemies. Despite the race-charged comments I have heard directed at my friend, we'd prefer to know you as allies in a world encroached upon by true evil. I would be an uncaring guest indeed if I didn't offer my hostess help when she needed it."

The last of the obstructions came away with a final sword swing. Trestan set his sword point on the walkway as he offered an open hand to the councilor. She released the divine shield. Naef'ad Illwinu Wessail took the offered hand and allowed the human to pull her to her feet.

Trestan started to turn toward the sounds of the firbholg's roars, but Illwinu reached out to grab his sword arm. By her stance, it seemed that she only wanted him to speak a bit more before turning away from her.

Illwinu asked, "Are you going after the firbholg?"

Abriana's champion nodded. "My friends are in danger, as are your people. I have to stop it."

Illwinu's eyes narrowed. Trestan found himself under her stern gaze of judgment. She nodded her angular chin toward the noise, keeping her eyes on him as she did.

"That giant is not in its own mind. Some enchantment has it acting strangely. My people are trying to stop it without deadly intent. They may regard you harshly if you bring undue harm to it."

"I know," Trestan nodded, "The mentalist charmed it. If it threatens a human or elf, I can't promise to hold back my blade. Yet it is not my purpose to slay the creature needlessly."

Trestan stepped away from the elf. She allowed her hand to fall back to her side, though her eyes still judged him. Trestan's face reflected sincerity, "I think I can save the firbholg from itself. For the sake of all good creatures, as part of Abriana's love, I have to try to save everyone I can."

Trestan turned and ran down a ramp that would bring him closer to the rampage. Behind him, Illwinu did nothing to stop the escaped prisoner. Pulling some of her long green hair behind her pointed ears, she followed him from a distance.

*        *        *        *        *

Montanya could not command her legs to run from the angry firbholg. It was good that the creature had been too preoccupied by others, for she stood immobile next to the fallen dwelling. She could only manage to stare at the rubble that served as a grave marker for Sondra Oskires, acolyte of Ganden. A day or two ago she could have convinced herself that she wouldn't care if Sondra lived or died on their adventure. Montanya had only viewed the slightly older woman as an enigma who challenged the chiaso's beliefs. That impassionate view faded when they shared memories. Suddenly, Sondra wasn't as incomprehensible as before. Montanya had been given a glimpse of her hurts, her longings, and her few precious dreams.

It appeared that those shared memories were the only imprints Sondra left behind in this world. At least, until Montanya saw a slender hand stick out from the side of the debris and push at one of the broken planks. That hopeful sight jolted the chiaso's legs to move. Her run carried her closer to the dangerous area instead of fleeing to safety.

Montanya called out, "Sondra?"

"Help us!" The voice belonged to Sondra, though it echoed in the elf language by small voices.

Montanya ran to the pile of debris and saw how lucky Sondra and the elves had been. The tree and its roots offered them some protection within a small pocket. The beams of the house leaned against the base of the tree in a jumble, offering a weak brace that kept some of the weight from crushing them. They didn't have much room to breathe. The sagging boards pressed Sondra and the children against the muddy ground.

One thick board, wedged between the tree roots and the rest of the fallen walls, seemed to block their easiest route out from the debris. Sondra pushed at it ineffectively. She only managed to drive herself deeper into the mud. The children cried underneath the acolyte and the rest of the pile.

Montanya braced her feet and tried to pull the board aside. Both women strained and grunted. The chiaso's muscles proved insufficient. Montanya stood back, taking a few breaths, and studied how the board was wedged into the debris.

"If it wasn't for the weight of this pile on the one end, I could pull the board out through those roots. I need something to cut the board."

Sondra nodded at that, until a noise from above alerted them to a new danger. Another large piece of debris broke free, dropping several bricks and a table onto the pile. Montanya jumped aside. Both women looked up and saw remnants of the house hanging above them on branches. Furnishings continued to drop. From the sounds of creaks and snapping noises, they knew the weight of the dwelling was losing its fight against gravity.

Sondra verged on panic. "We can't wait to saw through it. We need this board broken now."

Montanya took a good look at the wood and recoiled. "I can't break it. It is caleocht wood."

Memories came back to Montanya from her old monastery. She remembered the planks of caleocht wood used for testing the students. Time and again she failed, only to see supposedly weaker students break through. She remembered the last night at the training hall, when Grandmaster Woshan had ordered her to split the board. She had ended that attempt with tears and broken bones.

More small sticks rained down upon the fallen structure. The acolyte tried to calm the children, but they couldn't understand her. They wanted to crawl past her to safety, but there was no room.

Sondra implored, "Somehow, you need to break it. Find help. We're being crushed under this weight. We won't be so lucky if more comes down on us."

Montanya quietly stepped back from the board. Sondra's worry was plain in her eyes. The priestess breathed heavily, "You have to help, find a way, please."

The chiaso stared at the wood. "I will try. I need quiet, and I will do my best."

Montanya forced calmness into her own eyes as she stared at the board. The caleocht taunted her, mocked her, as that wooden cage did on the night of her parent's death.

*NO!*

Montanya's thoughts screamed inward. She berated herself for all the anger that had clouded her spirit. The words of Grandmaster Woshan came back to her.

*"You will touch your Chi. You will use your inner balance to accomplish more than just your muscles would seem to allow. It will take solid concentration, but you can break this. Students who have weaker muscles than you have found the inner balance to shatter such obstacles."*

Montanya sought the inner peace that had eluded her ever since the violent death of her parents. She had to look at the board as simply her task. She couldn't cloud her feelings with the past. The chiaso was not allowed to lose her focus with anything that distracted her from the moment.

Butterfly in the Windmill.

She began the movements exactly as she had danced them when Lindon performed for her. His music set the tone in her mind, forcing her to feel the power of movement within her body. She could not be rushed, despite Sondra's worried interruptions. Montanya refrained from accelerating the movements, unlike her past behavior. Though more debris fell and hit the ground nearby, she succumbed to Lindon's rhythm of the dance.

The thieves tried to find her there, but she ignored their faces. The student Rayka tempted her with her stolen locket, and she turned away from him. The firbholg roared in the distance, and Montanya sidestepped the fear. Even Sondra's face taunted her, in the number of ways they differed. The chiaso pushed that image away by chiding herself. Sondra accomplished something with her life that Montanya didn't...she truly gave all her efforts to benefit others.

The butterfly danced in the elven wood. She would not allow herself to be rushed. She could not allow herself to be lost in her past anger. The red braid whipped around like a snake in the process of making its deadly strike. Montanya narrowed her eyes in concentration on the board. This was the spinning fan of the windmill that the butterfly must break to escape the millstone. She isolated all other thoughts from her soul as she stared upon the caleocht grains. The power of her mind, body, and soul focused together before the outmatched simplicity of the dead piece of wood.

Montanya kicked...and the board shattered.

It was that simple, and yet it left Montanya in a state of shock. She actually did it! The caleocht board snapped without leaving her any broken bones.

Montanya jumped into motion, sliding the remainder of the board through the roots with Sondra's help. The acolyte clambered out of the hole, helping the elf children escape. The children ran away in search of their parents.

Sondra stared in amazement at the broken board. "That looked easy! I thought you just said you couldn't do that."

Montanya wore her rarest expression over her face. Instead of her usual scowl, she was grinning from ear to ear. "It was easy. How come I could never allow myself to do that before?"

The creaking of strained weight of the treehouse encouraged them to go someplace safer. Before they went far, however, they noticed a wounded elf watching them. They recognized their captor Cassyli. Hurt from the fall, he witnessed their rescue of the elf children.

Sondra immediately went to his side and started her healing prayers. He stared back at them without any words. As during their whole rescue, he watched but was unable to assist. When he became well enough to sit up, he looked from Sondra to Montanya and spoke brokenly in the human tongue. "You have been brave this day, saving the children and healing me. It shall be remembered and made known among my people."

*      *      *      *      *

The elf archers were too distracted by the giant firbholg to pay attention to the foreigner running the walkways. Trestan navigated toward the menace by the noise of the action. He caught pieces of elf conversations. The archers felt useless due to the enchantment that toughened the skin of the firbholg. They didn't hope to kill it, but they couldn't even distract it with arrows to buy the druids time for another surprise.

Trestan came to a bridge that split into ascending and descending sections. He charged down the lower one, thus closer to the firbholg. Though he could not hear her footsteps, the squire of Abriana knew that Naef'ad Illwinu followed. The councilor was likely as concerned about his actions as those of the giant below.

A chaotic scene opened before him. A semi-circle of druids, on the ground and on walkways, were creating barriers of living plants to try hemming in the giant. Archers continued to fire ineffectively. They aimed at soft areas that would not be lethal, yet no arrows could penetrate its bark-like skin. A contingent of elf warriors armed with whieus, spears, stone axes and kittanes stood ready. Their grim faces betrayed the knowledge that, if ordered to attack, it would be at a great cost of lives. Walkways and rope bridges were torn in places from the creature's fury. Carts, fences, and other ground clutter had been stomped flat. Roars echoed through the forest.

The firbholg cornered its latest target, despite clinging vines trying to slow its movements. Katressa crouched on a wood bridge that was being hammered by the firbholg's club. It slammed the cudgel against one end of the bridge until the whole structure sagged. The half-elf raised up long enough to send one more arrow on an unsteady flight.

The giant reached up and grabbed the broken end of the wooden bridge. It began to pull downward with inhuman strength. Katressa scrambled to grab one railing as the bridge tilted downward. Boards snapped. The bridge would not stay intact for long with the firbholg using its muscles to tear it down.

Trestan ran down the length of a rope bridge above and behind the creature. In his haste, he couldn't recall the Elvish words he needed. "Cat! Tell the archers to stop firing!"

Katressa somehow heard him and responded. She held on for her life as she shouted for the archers to stop. Naef'ad Illwinu also took a chance on the young paladin, calling for her people to cease.

Trestan's nerves were on edge as he looked at the space between him and the creature's head. It was a sizeable drop to the forest floor from this height. If he missed, he would suffer great injury in the fall. No more arrows were in flight, leaving one less hazard to his risky plan. A long gap of air separated the walkway and the hair tendrils on the creature's head. Trestan shifted the grip of the sword in his hand. With Katressa hanging vulnerable, he couldn't afford any delay.

A silent prayer whispered as Abriana's champion leapt from the walkway. Wind rushed past his face as his eyes locked on his landing spot. Elf fighters, druids, and rulers along every nearby walkway watched as the insane human jumped the distance to the monster's neck. It wasn't a graceful landing. Trestan barely caught hold of the creature's hair as his legs hit the firbholg's shoulder. The squire sprawled forward, accidentally hugging the creature's neck. Both his legs dropped to opposite sides of one shoulder, painfully, and by then the sword was already hanging at the right spot.

The firbholg released the bridge as it felt the weight of the man on its shoulder. It reflexively reached up to kill the attacker…until it felt the keen edge of the magical sword press against its neck. The blade dispelled the natura protections woven by the giant, leaving it vulnerable to any attack. It resumed reaching up to its assailant to kill the man. The sword would surely cut deep enough to end its life, but that didn't matter to the charmed monster. Yet, in that one, brief moment of hesitation, it felt a presence invade its mind.

The challenge of the beast. Trestan had the sword in place to kill the creature, but he held back in favor of this one miracle. It was the only way to reach the mind of this creature. Trestan could see the mud packing its ears.

The moment froze in time. Trestan's grip locked on the hair; the other hand held the sword at the creature's throat. The elf archers held their fire, though they stood in rows poised to release. The druids held back their incantations, sharing their wisdom to interpret the unfolding events. Naef'ad Illwinu forgot to breathe for several seconds, so intent was her attention. Katressa held on to the bridge slab. She did not move much for fear of breaking the giant from its contact, yet she did not want to lose her beloved. The half-elf tucked her legs into a position by which she could launch herself at the firbholg if it started to rage again. She had no weapon and knew the attempt could be futile, but she would die for the man who held her heart.

Trestan found layers of rage inside the mind of the firbholg. Its thoughts were tied under Jentan's numerous falsehoods. Trestan worked his way past those layers to lay bare the soul of the creature. In their minds, he and the firbholg had an argument that went beyond words. Jentan had bent the firbholg's mind away from reason; Trestan worked hard to untie the knots. He destroyed exaggerations, exposed half-truths, and shed light on what Jentan tried to keep hidden. Layers of rage peeled away one by one; as the creature remembered what the mentalist wanted it to forget. Reason dawned in its thoughts as it reconsidered the mentalist that seeded the lies. The deceptive logic that drove it into a rage was undone as Trestan removed the pillars supporting the deceits. The gentle giant remembered its softer nature.

An anguished wail released from deep within the heart of the giant. All at once it lost all menace. Trestan lowered his sword from the firbholg's throat. The deep, earthy voice of the creature cried out apologies to the elven people. Tears rolled freely as it recalled all the horrors it had just committed under the mentalist's influence. In broken phrases, it begged forgiveness. The firbholg who had been such an intimidating threat became a gentle giant of the forest once again.

Trestan had brought the beast under control in the presence of the city's garrison and leaders. He wondered if the elves would treat his companions more amiably now, or even give them their freedom. Revwar's band would be making headway out in that wilderness toward the relics while he was delayed here. Yet, in his connection with the firbholg's mind, Trestan had learned one more secret.

Trestan had a picture in his mind of the other band when they had stumbled across the firbholg. Their party had grown by one member since arriving at the elf city. Jentan had charmed another subject into joining them…one who could guide them well through the wilderness.

*       *       *       *       *

The companions rested among a crowd of guards as the people ascertained the full damage to their city. The wounded victims were still being treated, elf runners dispatched, and debris checked for survivors. The elves did not seem to view the companions unkindly anymore. Even their guards stood relaxed. Lindon had been healed by the druids to full strength. Sondra and Montanya actually sat together without arguing about anything. Only Katressa seemed nervous, but Trestan put a hand on hers to calm her. He was rewarded by an appreciative smile in return.

Naef'ad Illwinu stood among the other councilors. The rulers of Serud'Thanil were no doubt discussing the day's events away from the ears of their prisoners. When their heads nodded in some mutual agreement, they turned and approached the foreigners. The guards parted as Naef'ad Illwinu Wessail led the way.

She addressed them formally, and in the human tongue. "As you already know me, it is my honor to act as the mouth and ears of our leader, and our people. I introduce you to our…governess," (Naef'ad Illwinu seemed to struggle over the unfamiliar human word.) "I present to you, Deylirra re fa Thenguinal."

Trestan recalled that "thenguinal" referred to a high seat or throne. Naef'ad Illwinu went on to introduce the companions to the governess in Elvish. The leader either did not master the human language as well as Illwinu, or wasn't ready to admit that she knew any of it. The companions responded properly to this figure of royalty. They each gave a formal, respectful bow as they heard their names mentioned.

Deylirra of the High Seat began to address them in Elvish. This time Councilor Illwinu, not Katressa, translated. "Greetings, travelers from afar. We bid you a proper welcome to our city, and apologize for any transgressions in your stay here. You must understand that after the deaths of people dear to us, we had to detain all until we could ascertain the truth. We know now that you are blameless, and express our apologies for any mistreatment during your imprisonment."

If Katressa was still upset about the repetitious use of the word "agora" over the past few days, she concealed it well. None of the companions interrupted as Deylirra continued her speech. "You have shown an honor today that few would match, saving the lives of our kin as well as saving the firbholg from his own entrapment."

The gentle giant had begun to help the elves move the debris on the forest floor in atonement for his destruction. The firbholg paused while it listened to the Elvish words being spoken. The mud was long gone from its ears.

Ilwinu continued translating. "We shall not delay you any longer. You are free to resume your journeys. Furthermore, if we can offer assistance to help you against this band of murderers, let us know."

The elf governess and the gathering of Naef'ad all stood silent, awaiting a response from the companions. Trestan noticed the companions looked to him to respond. He already knew what he wanted to say. He spoke so diplomatically, it was surprising that he had once been the blacksmith of a small village.

He said, "We thank you for your kind words, and accept your apologies. Your behavior was not unwarranted due to the circumstances. If not for the situation we found ourselves in, we would have loved to better enjoy the beauty of your city. As our quest calls us onward, we should go without delay. We ask for a few things that would help us on our way, if you may be so kind."

Trestan thought a moment before phrasing the next sentences. "First, we were dropped in this forest with precious few possessions and food. We don't seek charity, only that we may have fair access to merchants to buy or barter for what we need.

"Second, we need to figure out a direction by which to proceed. I have asked your people if any saw the flying ship pass overhead, so that we might have a clue as to where our path lies."

Trestan paused as Deylirra and Naef'ad Illwinu had a private conversation. The councilor turned to face them, her long green hair sliding across her fair shoulders as she moved. "We shall be able to help you with supplies. In regards to your second point, our governess has asked me to divulge that information, for I saw what you seek. On the night in question, I saw a falling star unlike any other. It was older than the oldest elf, yet younger than the true stars. It disappeared in the gap between the twin hills southeast of here. The hills are known as Armoosa and Telius. Between them is a traversable pass. They guard the path to your goal."

Trestan nodded in appreciation. "Our thanks to you for giving us the way. I have but a third request to ask, if you will grant it."

"Proceed," the councilor responded. Her countenance stood neutral.

"When I looked into the firbholg's memories, I saw that one of your own has been charmed by their mentalist."

To the side, Cassyli stiffened at Trestan's words. Cat noticed the movement, but said nothing.

The paladin-aspirant continued. "They have an elf guiding them; one of our previous guards. He seems to be taking them in that same direction. When I saw him, he wore that blank look upon his face that indicated the enchantment upon his mind."

Cassyli interrupted the proceedings by calling out to the firbholg in Elvish. The firbholg looked surprised, but answered in its deep voice. There were murmurings in the nearby crowd as Elvish words flew between Cassyli, the firbholg, the governess, and Naef'ad Illwinu.

Cat was forced to translate for her friends as the conversation moved along rapidly. "The firbholg gave a description, and it is someone that Cassyli and Illwinu know."

Naef'ad Ilwinu addressed the companions. Her look had gone a shade paler, "This is a powerful mentalist indeed to have captured the mind of one of our most decorated warriors. We will provide you with a guide."

Cassyli stepped forward. Though his words were Elvish, the tone was clear. Even as Cat translated in whispers, it was apparent the scout was asking the council's permission to be the guide.

Lindon whispered to Cat, "Any idea why he is insistent upon being the one to go?"

Cassyli, with his sharp hearing, turned to respond. "Because they have my brother, Foyren. If possible, I would see him returned safely."

The companions could understand Illwinu's pale countenance better. One of her sons now suffered as a charmed slave to the band of murderers, and her other son was volunteering to track them down. The councilor held her bearing remarkably well before strangers in the face of these developments.

"The council has agreed to let Cassyli be your guide, as he knows these lands well," Naef'ad Illwinu translated. "Run swift, and bring back our warrior safely if at all possible."

The councilor walked up to the scout, taking his hands in hers and holding them briefly. "Laedelious' blessings follow you on your journey through the lands of her daughter, Eyldiian." It was the only contact she allowed herself before stepping back. Her heart had to be in pain, yet she outwardly kept her calm.

Cassyli took a place alongside the companions. Deylirra re fa Thenguinal offered her prayers as well. The proceeding interrupted as the firbholg wandered up and made a request of the elf leaders. He pointed at the companions and made a plea.

"What is happening?" Trestan whispered.

Cat turned with raised eyebrows. "The firbholg's name is complicated, but he is called Humut by the elves. He is offering to help speed our journey through the forest. He seeks to make amends."

Deylirra spoke to the companions through Illwinu. "He is offering to carry you, however he can, and hasten you through the deep woods of our home. This is your decision to make."

"How can he accomplish either?" blurted Montanya.

Cat spoke directly to the firbholg in Elvish. The large creature smiled as it talked through warm eyes. This was a very different being than the monster that had attacked earlier. The half-elf discussed the results with her friends. "He genuinely wants to pay us back. He is ashamed of being used as a weapon and wants to make things right between us. He can carry us by lifting a wagon, or maybe by using some netting stretched over his back. As far as speed goes…trust me, firbholgs have the magic of natura to pass through a forest quickly, despite their size."

Trestan stared into the big eyes of the firbholg. Having touched its mind, he knew that this was a very noble creature. He felt its need to compensate for all the trouble it had caused. Since time was not on their side, Trestan's choice was easy.

"Tell Humut we accept his assistance most graciously. We thank him for his help, and will prepare ourselves for the journey."

The companions were ready to depart Serud'Thanil.

**CHAPTER 29**          **"Final Resting Place of *Doranil Star*"**

Katressa's words proved correct in how fast the giant firbholg could run in the deep forest. The companions rode in the relative safety of a canoe and tarp that were slung over his back with some ropes. They could not see the trail ahead, yet it was interesting that no trail was left behind them either. This was different then when the firbholg rampaged under the hampering effects of the charm. The giant didn't push through the forest, the forest parted before it. The firbholg harnessed the natura magic coming from the plants and animals of this land. As a result, branches swayed out of his path, only to swing back into place once he was beyond them. His footsteps left no trace.

In this way, Humut passed miles of greenery without pause. The giant's stride kept a steady pace despite all barriers. His passage was so soundlessly cloaked by his primal magic that many forest creatures did not realize his presence until he was passing them. The giant took several splashing steps through a stream. The companions saw a herd of deer sipping from the water, tended by a slender humanoid female who was nearly naked except for woven vines across her torso. They had the barest of glances at that odd scene before the passing trees curtained their view once again.

When the sun descended, Humut showed no signs of slowing. The companions called a brief halt to relieve themselves and lay blankets down in the canoe. The firbholg then picked up the load and continued his run. They were amazed at how gently his great strides rocked them to sleep. The companions slept that night on the vessel as he traveled. Daybreak came and he was still running. Miles slid past under the giant's legs. The forest did not seem as dark as before. The nearby trees weren't as densely packed, and not nearly as high as those in the elf city. More than one companion asked how they would be able to find their way back to Serud'Thanil, or anyplace else for that matter. Cassyli began teaching Katressa the elf-signs used in the forest. There were many secret routes throughout Eyldiian, marked by stone piles, twig bundles, or dyes on tree branches.

The firbholg ended his run next to a river, at the base between two hills. He pointed out Armoosa and Telius. They could plainly see the gap between the peaks. Beyond, the land continued to rise toward larger wooded hills. Humut apologized that he could go no farther. He had left a few family obligations unfulfilled in his absence. The companions would have to go on foot, yet they could leave the canoe hidden by the river for an easy return trip to Serud'Thanil.

They bid farewell to their newfound friend and began their uphill walk.

*          *          *          *          *

The party spread out as they ascended to the gap. Though they kept their eyes out for pieces of *Doranil Star* that may have broken off, their main concern was getting to the site of the wreckage in time. They felt safe to assume that the relics were most likely resting in the bulk of the vessel. If the stones had fallen somewhere between the elf city and the final resting place, then they would have a more difficult search. Wherever the stones had fallen, the other band was likely racing to the site of the crash; therefore, the companions had to get there first.

Cat still jogged from one flank to the other, examining the ground for both the relics and tracks. Light of foot as she was, the companions often couldn't hear her movements. They had to look around to see where the black-clad infiltrator was running. The silver rapier glinted in the numerous sunrays piercing the leafy canopy. She had a new ranged weapon to replace the crossbow left in Orlaun. It was a short bow common to the elves of Eyldiian. While the Talo'Seelie might prefer armor-piercing longbows, those were impractical in the tight confines of the deep forest. The bow Katressa purchased in Serud'Thanil was compact enough to be wielded efficiently in thick brush. It bore decorations dedicated to the goddess Laedelious.

Trestan asked her how well she could adjust to using bow after preferring a crossbow for so long. Cat shrugged as if it did not matter. "I learned to master all kinds of bows. My aim will remain true, though I doubt this weapon will prove much harm against Savannah's armored plates."

Lindon helped their strides with a few tunes from his instruments. The mandolin once again hung across his shoulders, when not in use. The minstrel practically danced along their path. The elven healers had restored him to full health. There was no sign of his injuries as he treated them to some elvish songs. They asked if he had spent time with elves before, to which he nodded. The red beard and nimble legs bounced with enthusiasm as he regaled the wonders seen in some elven cities. His knowledge of the language proved better than Trestan's. On top of that, he knew a few elven songs very well.

Sondra walked with Montanya most of the time. The acolyte of Ganden held mace in hand. The leather healing satchel hung beside her hips. The blonde woman was hoping to use a divination once they got close enough to the wreckage. The miracle would reveal the nearby location of any holy items sacred to her deity. While the relic stones weren't something she would sense, she hoped once she found Ganden's holy items from the cauldron that the other treasures would be near.

Montanya wore a new outfit when she left Serud'Thanil: flexible and lightweight like her old fighting clothes. Along with her old padded leather guard pieces, the elf-made fabric would not hinder her movements in combat. The tailor had been one of the parents of the rescued children, who insisted on providing a gift for their child's rescuers. Sondra received a present as well, though it was in the form of a bracelet hidden under her long sleeves. The chiaso also had negotiated for a new weapon. Now armed, she often swung the quarterstaff in lazy circles around her as she walked. It felt better to have a solid weapon, rather than relying on her fists for monsters like giant spiders and firbholgs.

The other companions noted the changes in the interactions between the two human women. Sondra and Montanya had not raised their voices against each other since Trestan's miracle. The two formerly private women chatted about numerous things, without tempers being raised. A little understanding seemed to go a long way toward changing their feelings.

Trestan marched forward in all the glory of a knight on a holy crusade. His armor showed no worse for wear from the events at the elf city. His baldric housed Sir Wilhelm's old sword. The warhammer, shaped like a minotaur head, hung from his belt. The only thing missing from the image was the warhorse resting back in Orlaun. Trestan conversed a bit with Cassyli and Katressa during the march. The conversations were often short, but generally revolved around the land and the elf city. In comparison to the others, the squire of Abriana still mostly kept to himself. When Lindon made a mention of his silence, Trestan responded that he was mostly focused inward. The paladin-aspirant was reliving the fights against Revwar's band. He tried to be mindful of how best to use his talents on their next encounter.

Cassyli allowed few words to cross his lips during the trip. Though he understood a good amount of the human tongue, he was also focused on the encounter lying ahead of them. He led the way up the side of the hills. The companions got ample amount of time to stare at the knot of leather, shaped like a flower, which held back his ponytail. His weapon of choice was a flint-tipped spear, and he carried the turtle shell shield on his left arm. The companions mostly left him with his thoughts. The elf scout was understandably worried about the fate of his brother.

They camped that night in the pass. Some trees still blocked the view of what lay beyond, but they could see enough of nearby hills to know that the divine chariot couldn't have gone much farther once sailing through that gap. They hid their camp well that night, and lit no fire, afraid to alert the other band.

Cat and Cassyli settled down only after they thoroughly scouted the game trails. Cat said, "Can't find any sign of tracks at all. We may have passed them somewhere back in the deeper woods."

Cassyli shrugged, speaking in broken human words, "We can't be certain…my brother is…skilled at hiding tracks."

Cassyli said nothing more as he spread out a blanket. Across from him, the young chiaso and the minstrel were exchanging jests.

Montanya's scowl proclaimed her as an unwilling participant to the minstrel's games. She threw an accusatory glare at Lindon. "Are you belittling me by bantering in such rhyme?"

Lindon returned, "Nay, 'tis all for some glee, a game I choose from time to time."

The youth displayed no hint of amusement. "Can't you find more interesting things to do than match words with what I say?"

Again the minstrel was quick to respond. "It will soon be sleep I will choose, until I resume my game upon the day."

"And what will your words be if I my sentence ends with orange!" Montanya settled back on her meager blanket with a huff, feeling she had cornered the entertainer with a word that has no rhyme.

Lindon did pause a moment, before finding a proper answer. "Then I fear I may erroneously end my own words with apple!"

The minstrel let them linger on his odd choice of an ending. Montanya frowned, trying to decipher the minstrel's response. He then finished, "But that would be wrong, because one should never compare apples to oranges!"

The way Lindon delivered that statement struck Montanya as incongruously funny. Before she could control her normal, stern expression, a pig-like snort of laughter escaped her nose. Mortified by the sound she just made, she couldn't stop shaking at a multitude of giggles that bubbled up next. None of them had ever heard Montanya's laughter before. It was as joyous to hear as it was rare. Lindon said no more, comforted to sleep by the sweet amusement he had drawn from her.

Cat curled up beside Trestan. Aburis, the largest moon, glowed at the full moon stage. The light it reflected across the land made it easy to see details well even for humans. The half-elf noticed him glancing at Faithful's Companion in the moonlight. Cat gasped as she looked upon the ring of Trestan's Embarking. The gold shine looked complete.

"Your ring...the tasks are all finished?"

"Nay, *faunlessa*," Trestan turned the ring so that she could make out one final symbol marking the surface. "There is one more trial ahead of me before I can return."

She lay down beside him, pressing close to his warmth. "Which trial is it?"

He answered only cryptically before resting beside her. "The one that scares me the most."

*      *      *      *      *

During the descent from that gap they set eyes on the resting place of the ship. Below them, spread a vale crossed with tiny streams fed from the hills. Rocky formations that had formed and split left the terrain a little uneven. Parts of the rock had pushed up cliffs overlooking wet ravines. There were few large trees in this region. The plant life which dominated the vale struggled to reach the soil buried within the rocks. While there was still an abundance of small trees, they were mostly stunted and twisted.

From the sloping hill, the companions saw bits of color and shapes that did not blend in with the environment. The *Doranil Star* could no longer be described within a single hull. Remnants of the ship scattered over a half mile of disturbed ground. The many displaced pieces caught the eyes of the adventurers in their multitudes of tints. They saw bits of wooden framework propped up by the low scrub brush. Bright speckles of color came from various clothing and broken furniture that littered the land. Here and there, sunlight glinted off metal bits and jewels. Crates, barrels, and bags lounged on the shores of the streams. A long banner had been caught in one of the trees on the side of a cliff. Its wind-beaten threads lazily moved with the breeze.

All of the companions paused as they looked over the strewn wreckage. Sondra fell to her knees before prostrating herself before the corpse of her divine chariot. She prayed words that few among them heard. They were too distracted by the sight of the fallen marvel. Cassyli remained quiet, though his mind tried to envision the impressive size of the ship.

Montanya broke the silence. "That is a lot of area to search. It will take days to find two small stones amidst all that."

Trestan nodded, "Aye, but likely we can narrow it down a bit. Despite the damage, you can make out patterns in the wreckage. You can roughly tell where the cargo holds were by the position of the crates and barrels. The luxury quarters are marked by the gold trim and brightest colors of sheets. Some of the cloth bits are mere distraction, for the wind has carried them farther away from the vessel itself. The forecastle, the timbers and rigging of the masts, the tarnished gold of the bowsprit...all laying in a certain order. It is in pieces and decomposed, but you can tell a bit about where things landed."

271

"So, how do you wish to proceed?" Lindon asked.

Sondra spoke before Trestan had a chance to respond. The young woman remained kneeling in her clerical vestments. "I can look for the holy relics of my church. I can feel their presence down there. I can trace their power and follow the trail right to them."

"Which would lead you to the remains of the inner sanctum." Trestan interrupted, "But not to where the relic stones landed. You can feel the presence of relics holy to Ganden, but not these."

Cat's eyes widened. "Priests can feel the presence of religious items holy to them?"

At Trestan and Sondra's affirming nods, Cat patted the leather scroll tucked in her belt. "From what I've been able to decipher in this scroll about the history of the relics, they were created by three gods working together. Neither Ganden nor Abriana were among those gods, so I assume you can't sense them through your religions. However, one of the gods that consecrated the stones was DeLaris. So, Savannah should be able to sense exactly where the stones are once she gets here."

Montanya's nose wrinkled as she tried to make sense of religion and miracles. "So wouldn't Savannah have known from the start exactly where to look? They could have come and gone already."

The young acolyte of Ganden got to her feet as she answered. "It's a matter of concentration and distance. You have to expend at least some amount of concentration to use the miracle. Also, you need to be reasonably close to the holy item. I only sensed Ganden's relics just now."

Cassyli had been silent up to that moment. "They now have my brother to guide them. He knows how to find this place as well as I did. Our best hope is that the firbholg got us here first."

Trestan was smoothing over his mustache like he always did when in deep thought. The others chatted over the situation…except for Katressa. She waited to hear Trestan's line of thinking.

The champion of Abriana finally reached a decision after looking over the layout of the land. "Whatever happens, we have to move quickly to secure the relics before Savannah finds them. Even once we do that, we'll be carrying a beacon that will allow them to track us if they are close. Either way, we have to move fast and be prepared for a fight."

Trestan pointed partway across the vale, indicating the tattered banner hanging from the cliff. "I should move up to there. I may not be able to sense the stone relics, but I can attempt to use a miracle to help guide me. It's a miracle by which Abriana may be able to show me the location of something specific. Since I've had the stones in my possession, they are an item of which I am already familiar. From that vantage I can likely get a good view once the miracle is activated."

Trestan turned toward his friends. "The rest of you continue forward on the vale floor. The stone relics were in the forward hold, last we knew. You have to travel through the wreckage until you find refuse that could be from that hold. You will also likely be able to see me easily, I can point you toward anything the miracle reveals to me and rejoin you down there."

"I'd prefer you didn't go off on your own with that other band somewhere out there." Cat looked to Trestan with worry in her emerald eyes.

He kissed her reassuringly, "It is better to have as many sets of eyes on the ground as possible, especially eyes as keen and lovely as yours."

*　　　*　　　*　　　*　　　*

Rocks crunched under his footsteps as Trestan followed the cliff overlooking the debris field. He moved to a promising observation point. The uneven terrain obstructed many areas behind leafy branches and natural swells in the land. It took a moment to find the other companions. They walked spread apart, eyes exploring every shadow and the glints of metal in the sunlight. Cat glanced up and offered a fond wave at seeing him on that rise. They were farther away than he would have preferred, but it was a large area to cover.

The champion of Abriana knelt in the hardy grasses that thrived amidst rock. He readjusted the strap that kept his sword on his back. The former blacksmith spread his arms out toward the sacred resting place of the *Doranil Star*. Words were whispered to his goddess above. His prayer asked for the miracle of guidance. He put the memories of the stones foremost in his thoughts.

The miracle tugged at his senses. His eyes opened and were drawn to his left. He saw the remnants of the helm castle, settled among a grove of trees. The spell drew his vision farther forward, toward the blackened remnants of barrels that had set the deck aflame during the fight. Somewhere near them, in the hollow beyond, Trestan could feel the stones. The guidance spell drew a picture of them in his mind: he saw how they settled on the ground.

At last, Trestan found the stones and they had apparently beaten the other band in getting there.

Elated, he looked for Cat to direct her toward their goal, but the companions were moving on the other side of some trees. Instead, he saw movement in a place where none of the companions were walking. Trestan's mouth went dry as he witnessed the most unwelcome forms sneaking up behind his friends. He could see an elf dressed similar to Cassyli, yet it was not Cassyli, leading others of mixed races along the companions' trail. Revwar, Kemora, and Jentan were moving with weapons bared. The only member of the band conspicuously absent was…

A familiar female voice startled him, "I thought this was a good place to use miracles to spot the locations of the Earthrin Stones. Apparently someone shared my opinion."

Whether it was an unintentional slip of Savannah's tongue or not, this was the first time Trestan heard the name given to the relic stones. There was little he could do with the information at that moment. He could only commit it to memory as he slowly got up and faced the abbess of Death.

Those cold, blue eyes stood several paces away, staring from behind the hideous skull helm. "You are quite surprising, chosen of Abriana. You are not the same boy who once shattered a quarterstaff across my jaw. You have been taken in and trained by a goddess."

Trestan made no move to draw his sword, a fact not lost on Savannah. She made no move to draw her own weapon; her flail plainly hitched on her belt. Savannah, as relatively unguarded as Trestan, moved a few lazy steps closer.

A beautiful, slender hand rose up and removed the skull helm from her head, letting it fall in the hardy grass. She caressed her chin where Trestan had hit her with the staff four years ago. "To think of such a blow I had suffered, one might think to find broken bones there." Her eyes were painted with dark circles to imitate the likeness of a skull missing its orbs, a common practice of worshippers of DeLaris. Savannah's chin seemed perfectly shaped as she softly touched her face. "It healed rather well. You wouldn't know by looking at it how badly you smashed the bones. However, when the nights are cold I still feel the dull ache in my jaw that reminds me of that indignity."

Trestan seemed understandably uneasy standing there, simply watching Savannah slowly saunter closer. His hand twitched nervously, as if it hungered for the handle of a weapon to fill it at that moment. Trestan refused to reach for the sword, even though she made it a perfectly easy temptation. Her guard was down, her head unprotected, and her weapon remained by her side. The champion of Abriana was not fooled so easily. He was certain she had a protective ward in place if he attempted to hit her. The Sword of the Spirit could not penetrate that protection on the first blow, though it would disable it from then onward. After that, it would be a question of whether or not she could react faster than him for a killing blow. He wanted to test her, yet he couldn't.

Trestan worried for Cat and the others. They had no idea they were being followed. The companions had been caught unprepared at the worst possible time.

Trying to hide his unease, he spoke instead. "I can only imagine what evil you may have planned for those stones. If you come with us, I shall treat you fairly, as long as you answer my questions."

Savannah, abbess of Death, laughed. The cold sound lacked any true mirth. "It is a game of questions then? That is exactly what I wanted from you today. I would like to ask the first question…if you wouldn't mind holding this for me?"

Trestan felt the cold handle of a weapon slide into his hand. That evil woman had come so close that he could feel her breath on his face when she exhaled. He glanced down, only to notice that she was trying to make it easy for him. The abbess had given him a dagger. She released her hold on the blade. Her hands moved over his breastplate, and then both her arms lazily rested on his shoulders. She may have looked like a lover leaning on her heart's desire, but for the coldness in her eyes. Meanwhile, Trestan stood there uncertainly, with her dagger held in his hand. The evil woman appeared to be defenseless if he attempted to cut out her throat.

"You won't be insulted if I ask the first question?" She asked, through the type of grin that one would wear as they selected which pig they planned to butcher for their meal.

With hardly a pause, she whispered. "What is today's date?"

With steel in his eyes, Trestan answered. "Your funeral."

Another cold, disheartening laugh left her throat. "You bluff so well, I would hate to gamble at cards with you. If I recall, it is the first day of Doyal. Aren't the first days of the month holy days to the worshippers of Abriana?"

The words of the elder at the Embarking came back to haunt Trestan, and of course he didn't need Savannah to remind him of the significance of this day. *"On the first day of every month, we are forbidden from using arms or taking aggressive actions against a foe. How will you fare on these holy days when your loved ones are in danger?"*

The lone remaining symbol on Faithful's Companion reminded him of the one task yet untested. The same hand which bore Faithful's Companion also held the handle of the cleric's dagger.

Savannah leaned so close, with her arms over his shoulders, that he could see the faint pulsing in her neck where one of her arteries lay vulnerable. She wouldn't be satisfied with just killing him. She wanted him to break his faith with his goddess before trying to end his life.

*      *      *      *      *

Cat lost sight of Trestan due to the trees through which she walked. For some intangible reason, her senses kept drawing her gaze over her shoulder. Maybe her ears detected danger nearby, or perhaps this divine graveyard simply spooked her. She couldn't pin down the source of her unease. The half-elf fell behind the others as she sought an opening in the trees by which she could spot Trestan again.

When she regained a vantage point, Cat saw the abbess in her dark armor stepping close to her beloved on the top of that ridge. Trestan stood motionless…defenseless. Cat strung her bow in preparation for a shot. She fit an arrow onto the string and started to raise it.

She heard a magical command from her side. Suddenly, the sensation of lightning coursing through all her nerves assaulted her. Her body underwent one convulsive spasm before she froze in place. The lingering pain made her want to grit her teeth and curl into a ball, but Cat could not move a muscle. The half-elf toppled to the ground.

"You killed her?"

Cat didn't recognize the female voice, though she suspected it was the halfling accompanying the other band.

The smooth, captivating voice of the mentalist Jentan answered, though he sounded weary from the exertion of his spell. "Nay. I used a paralytic spell. It blocks her brain from controlling most of her nerves, but it will wear off before long."

The female voice spoke again, she had moved closer. "That sounds like a good spell! It holds your enemy defenseless for a killing blow. Why don't you use that more often?"

Revwar's quiet and commanding voice replied, "Because you see how much it drained him…he can barely stand and his face has gone pale."

Cat wanted desperately to move or yell a warning to the others. All her effort resulted in the barest of hisses escaping her lips. She was helpless.

Strong hands grabbed her and rolled her onto her back. Cat could see Revwar, Jentan, Kemora, and Foyren standing over her. The latter elf bore the glazed look in his eyes that signified the mentalist's control over his mind. Cat wondered if her eyes were destined for that same, glazed emptiness.

"We should just finish her off now…" Revwar started to say, but then he paused at seeing something tucked in Cat's belt. "Ah, what is this? It's the leather scroll that was wrapped around one of the stones."

"I thought you said it was useless?" The halfling remarked. Cat noticed that the woman was holding a stiletto covered with poisonous slime.

Jentan answered as Revwar knelt to touch the scroll. "I'm starting to think otherwise. Why is she carrying the scroll now?"

The elf wizard nodded, "We declared it useless because we couldn't break the code to read it. I signed it long ago, but even then, we'd only been given portions of the writing. Most of the meaning lay hidden behind encryption, even before presented to the elves who swore to defend it. The person who held the decoding device was killed when he led us into the demon's home plane years ago, though he did not have the device on his body."

The wizard's yellow eyes lit up with understanding. "This is his daughter! I find myself questioning why Katressa and Trestan were down in that hold examining the stones and scroll while the magic show played out on the deck. Surely, a coded scroll is far less entertainment, but maybe she has a means to read it?"

Cat's face stayed rigidly blank thanks to the paralyzing spell. Her emotions couldn't have given her away even if she had tried. The half-elf struggled to move but she had no control.

"She may yet be useful," Jentan stated.

Revwar and Jentan walked away from Cat and talked in a whispered conversation. Even with her remarkable hearing, the half-elf didn't catch enough words to make sense of what they conspired. The conversation seemed to come to a close when Revwar stopped to examine some debris on the ground.

"What is this treasure?"

Jentan and Kemora watched as the elf wizard picked up a jeweled, golden necklace from the ground. The mentalist spoke in a surprising tone, "That is the Gitouro necklace, one of the artifacts displayed in the exhibit. It was worn by an immortal during the Godswars. A great find!"

Kemora piped up, "What is it worth if we sell it?"

Jentan scowled, "You can't just sell it. That is a rare item of power, a gift of the gods. It is a bonus that will aid us immeasurably."

"A bonus for me," Revwar said, placing the necklace over his head to set alongside the others he wore. "As the phrase goes, 'Find it, own it.' I heard about this item; it will be very useful."

Kemora grumbled a response. They began to separate when Revwar looked to the Jentan. His hand waved out toward Cat's helpless form.

"Proceed." Revwar said as he separated from the mentalist. "Kemora and Foyren, come with me."

"We're leaving her?" The halfling rogue sounded dismayed. She eyed her dagger wistfully.

Cat's attention switched to the mentalist as he kneeled beside her. Her ears caught Revwar's trailing words as the rest were walking away. "The others are just up ahead. We should kill their healer first, then concentrate on the rest…"

Jentan began to weave a spell around Cat. So, they were not going to kill her. They wanted to keep her alive to learn what she knew about the scroll. Suddenly, death would have seemed preferable. She didn't want her mind turned, or her body used against her friends. She tried to resist his words. It was useless, for the mentalist had already discovered a 'hook' that would allow him to play upon Cat's emotions. He had surmised her loving relationship with the human she accompanied. He guessed, rather correctly, that the issue of their different aging would be some worry in her mind.

Cat tried to defy him, but the emotions stoked were too strong. Cat saw the future that she had feared would pass. The half-elf lost all memory of the relics and the current quest. A prison forming from her own emotions trapped her, seeing only what Jentan wanted her to see.

Cat shed tears as she knelt at Trestan's gravesite. Her fear of outliving him had come to pass. Her mind lost itself in the grief and loss of her beloved.

### CHAPTER 30             "We Should Kill Their Healer First..."

Montanya walked beside Sondra through the field of debris. "Doesn't Cassyli seem to be anxious about something? He keeps looking behind us."

The acolyte of Ganden was slow to respond. When she raised her eyes from the debris-filled field, she offered an apology. "I'm sorry, I've been too distracted with this." She waved a hand outward to indicate the wreckage.

Montanya nodded, her normal scowl displaced by genuine sympathy for Sondra's feelings. The red-haired youth again glanced over at Cassyli. The elf was once again scanning the surrounding trees, rather than the scattered remnants of the ship. He seemed to be guarding against some perceived threat. Not far from him, Lindon searched the ground for any sign of the stones. When Montanya turned the other direction, she could not see Cat on the other side. Since the half-elf was so good at blending in with her surroundings, Montanya did not worry.

Sondra spoke, "It is an odd, empty feeling inside of me. I see pieces of what was once the grandest thing I had ever known. I feel like I am walking through the cemetery of lost hopes and dreams."

Montanya knew the depth of Sondra's feelings for the vessel, having seen and felt the emotions of her past through Trestan's miracle. "I think I was once in that place myself."

Sondra glanced up at the younger woman. "What do you mean?"

"Do you remember my memories? After the taxmen and officials took everything, I broke into my home to see or salvage what I could. I walked through empty halls and felt overwhelmed with the loss of my future. I was hurt by my recollections of the past: the bed my parents used to share, my emptied room, a nick on the dining room table from my carelessness with a knife. All my thoughts revolved around how everything I'd come to love was lost. I thought I had cried all my tears at my parents' funeral, but more came when I grieved for the loss represented inside that mansion."

Sondra reached over and briefly squeezed Montanya's shoulder. "That is indeed how I feel. This is the grave of my future-that-should-have-been."

The two walked together through more pieces of debris. The acolyte of Ganden sighed. "I can feel Ganden's holy relics ahead. That is where I will find what remains of the inner sanctum and my former teachers. I do not want to go there and be witness, but I have to. I have to discover what lies there, reclaim the items, and report everything back to the church in Orlaun. I do not envy my duty, but I must fulfill it."

Sondra continued to talk as Montanya raised her head to glance around at their surroundings again. She was surprised to see Cassyli, with spear and shield in hand, running toward them. Montanya, seeking the balance between her mind, body and soul, began to sense a real threat nearby. She drew from the power of her Chi, and let her senses direct her.

There, in the shadows, the cutting edge of an arrowhead poised for a kill.

Montanya was not the target; it aimed at Sondra. The acolyte of Ganden walked unaware that death had prepared an ambush. Montanya had no time to warn the woman. The bowstring released, shooting that sharp edge toward its victim.

278

Her master's words echoed in her mind. *"...you can even move fast enough to catch an arrow out of the air."*

All of Montanya's concentration focused on the path of the arrow. Her eyes followed the point as it approached. Her arm shot upward with a speed she had never before achieved. Her fingers snapped like a crocodile's jaw as it came within reach.

Sondra heard the arrow fletching as it whistled toward her back. There was no time to react before the sound of the arrow thudded into flesh. Dumbfounded, the acolyte stumbled to the side and turned to look behind her.

She saw Montanya standing with one arm raised. The chiaso's eyes were wide with shock. Montanya barely managed to speak in a surprised gasp.

"I caught it."

Sondra spotted the arrow in Montanya's grasp. As soon as the younger woman relaxed her grip, the blood dripping down the shaft made the truth apparent. The arrow had impaled the palm of her hand.

*      *      *      *      *

Action broke out across the field. Foyren stepped from the trees, raising his bow for another shot. Revwar stood up nearby, moving his hands in arcane gestures. Montanya and Sondra sought cover and found few options. The chiaso tucked her wounded hand close to her body. Cassyli backed up yet stayed in the open, hoping to attract his brother's attention. The scout called out in their language, though his words to his sibling proved useless. Lindon was the only one that did not move away from the assailants. The minstrel sang words granting speed to his running as he moved to flank around the enemy.

A ball of fire rushed out from Revwar's hands. Cassyli quick-stepped to the side with his turtle shell shield raised, yet the blast of flames exploded close enough to send him sprawling.

Sondra was diving behind a rock draped with torn fabric when she heard another arrow whistle past. She yelped as she felt a sting across one leg. She realized the archer was targeting her, and it terrified the disciple. Once safe behind the rock, Sondra looked for Montanya.

"Montanya?"

"I'm here!"

The voice came from a muddy depression, several long steps away. Sondra reached into her healing satchel as she called out, "I can't reach you without exposing myself to those arrows. You must remove that arrow yourself, then drink this!"

Sondra withdrew a clay vial firmly sealed by a stopper. She threw it to Montanya. The chiaso had to release her staff from her good hand to catch it.

Once Montanya had it, she ducked back into the depression. The youth considered her injured hand, disturbed by the thought of trying to pull the arrow out. How could she manage the pain? She could not delay, so she propped the arrow shaft against a rock. The first step was to break one end of the arrow, then pull it through the other side. Montanya raised her good hand to strike fast at the shaft.

She howled in pain the moment her strike snapped the sharp end. With tears in her eyes, she grabbed the fletched side firmly. It was done quickly, yet agonizingly. Montanya nearly blacked out while letting a stream of curses forth. With trembling hands, she popped the stopper off the vial and drank the healing potion. The pain ebbed as the miracle warmed her body. Her hand was whole again, though it took longer to stop her limbs from shaking.

While Montanya had been occupied, Sondra had likewise dealt with her own wound. The acolyte of Ganden exerted a minor amount of energy to seal the tear on her calf.

*          *          *          *          *

Trestan wanted to kill Savannah, but he knew he couldn't. The dagger she'd generously slipped into his hands would likely bounce off her protective miracles. Even worse, he would be abandoning the tenets of Abriana forever. Savannah knew it. She sought only to tempt him. His brown eyes locked with her cold, blue orbs in a moment of hesitation. He then acted in the only way he could.

He dropped the dagger, bringing up his other hand to shove Savannah away from their uncomfortable embrace. He could not bring a weapon to bear on her for fear of losing the goddess that guided his life. The best thing to do was make some room for himself.

The former blacksmith was strong, but Savannah grabbed his armor and refused to let go. She seemed to want something else from him that required her to be close. She clung to him, clawing her way up his arm. Trestan tried to squirm free, unsure if he could even risk hitting her with his gauntlets. Savannah barked an arcane command. The magical words triggered a magical item borrowed from the mentalist.

Trestan continued to try shoving the woman away, fearing whatever trick she had planned. In his efforts, he almost didn't sense the presence pushing into his thoughts. She was trying to enter his mind through the use of a spell similar to his empathy miracle. Trestan formed a psychic wall. Savannah's will formed a hot ember that was only partly shut out by the wall.

As their bodies struggled, their minds waged a mental war.

It occurred to Trestan that Savannah could do no real harm to his mind. The faithful of Abriana were well-versed with this mind link, yet this abbess of DeLaris needed to use a magic item to instigate contact. Anything she tried to do to him would drain her will faster than his own. The abbess' spell felt similar to his empathic link. Trestan could tell it was not designed to harm him, but rather gather memories and information. It then occurred to him there were many questions of his own that might have answers inside her memories.

Trestan let Savannah's will intrude. He surprised Savannah by his resourcefulness as he shaped his own will and sped into her mind along the connection. Even as the abbess searched his mind, he began probing hers.

Their bodies froze in struggle, as their eyes locked in a duel of minds.

*          *          *          *          *

Revwar shoved Foyren forward. "Go after that healer. You can't hit her from here."

The elf warrior took a hard look at the wizard for a moment. Revwar was reminded that Jentan's hold could be a fragile thing, especially when the mentalist was not around. The wizard rephrased his request. He recalled Jentan's knowledge of what would appeal to this warrior. "Go get the human priest that defiled this wood! Stop her before she can get to her divine artifacts and threaten the domain of Laedelious!"

Those words struck a chord within Foyren's prejudices. He ran forward with his kittane in one hand and his bow in another, ready to use either.

Revwar prepared to use a spell to finish off the dazed elf scout escorting the companions. Something sharp nicked the base of his neck before bouncing past. It ruined his concentration and sapped the energy of the spell. On reflex, he jumped to the side, avoiding a second thrown dagger.

The wizard changed spells. Grabbing an item from a pouch, he snapped it apart while intoning a few words of the arcane. A stationary shield barrier formed on the ground in the direction of the attack. Revwar turned to find that he had erected it without a moment to spare.

The minstrel from Orlaun had circled behind him. Since Lindon's daggers had not done the trick, the minstrel brought a flute to his lips for a different attack. A wave of music rushed out from the instrument with gale force. Saplings swayed and larger trees' branches bent as the force of the wind hit them. The effect created a wall of storm-tossed debris which hammered the wizard's shield.

Revwar actually smiled at this challenge, since he had a similar spell in his repertoire. The wizard went through another arcane ritual, sending his own wall of wind back at the minstrel. The two forces of nature collided with unbridled fury between them. Branches and discarded junk from the wreckage swirled in a maelstrom. Debris flung outward to rain around the two combatants. Revwar fared better, hidden behind his force wall. The air became choked with particles of dust as a small tornado formed between the winds.

Lindon knew he was on the losing end of this match. As soon as his breath started to falter, he ducked behind a solid oak. Revwar dismissed his casting after the minstrel found cover. The noise of the winds died down into a clattering of objects falling to the ground.

*          *          *          *          *

Montanya flexed her newly healed hand. It felt as strong as ever. The youth grabbed her quarterstaff as she chanced a peek out of the depression.

Her chiaso senses perceived a threat even before the sound of something airborne reached her ears. She snapped the staff around one side out of reflex. Instead of catching an enemy, it blocked the airborne set of bolos aimed for her head. The bolos wrapped around the staff instead.

There was barely time to react as Kemora charged at her. The halfling led her attack with the poisoned stiletto. Montanya arched her body out of the harm's way. The tip barely missed contact with flesh.

Montanya used the staff to shove the halfling away. It had become unwieldy due to the weight of the swinging bolos on one end. The chiaso jumped away from the smaller woman but only got a temporary reprieve. The halfling's sword cut at her, leaving a nick in the staff as she parried.

Montanya spun the staff in what appeared like a defensive pattern. In reality, she was loosening the bolos from their tangle. When Kemora came again, Montanya mimicked a strike to buy more time. When the rogue backed away from the attack, the chiaso finally had the untangled bolos in her hand. She threw them back at Kemora ineffectively.

The rogue wouldn't slow down. Montanya's real swing missed as the halfling ducked impossibly low. Kemora had an unobstructed shot at the tall human's legs. The stiletto shot forward.

Somehow Montanya's legs jumped up out of view. The poisoned tip only struck the end of the staff as Montanya used it to vault away.

The chiaso landed in a guard position, as did the halfling. Following that initial attack, they paused to evaluate their next strategy. The two females, pursuer and pursued, stared at each other in silence. They were hundreds of miles from their first alley fight. Neither would have really cared even if a king's ransom sat between them for the taking. They were focused on each other. Kemora was determined to end the pursuit once and for all. Montanya still sought to find some way of redemption from her life of fearing and hating rogues…and she hoped that in facing this one she would find it.

*      *      *      *      *

Sondra also looked up from her hiding spot in time to see a foe coming after her. The cleric had no armor except her cloth vestments. Her only weapon was a mace in which she had received moderate training, yet had never seen real use.

Foyren Wessail charged her hiding spot. The elf warrior had lost one eyebrow to a jagged scar in his past. His belt bore several beads and carvings as decorations. These were all accolades to his service as a warrior and steward of the forest. The necklace of bones sported specimens from dangerous game animals, including the ferocious wrelcat. Trophies came easily to this hunter. The elf shouldered his strung bow, favoring to meet Sondra in battle with his sharpened kittane.

The acolyte uttered a brief prayer with wide eyes. Foyren saw the air shimmer around her as she used a miracle to place some sort of protection around her body.

His first attack launched straightforward and easy. Sondra moved to block it. Mace collided with war club, and Sondra found herself knocked backward by his strength. He quickened as he switched directions for his next attack. Sondra was forced to block again, and once again proved weaker against his powerful swing.

She got the impression he was measuring her reflexes. The warrior toyed with her until he could get an opening he liked. She tried to take a shot at him, hoping to put him on the defensive. Her mace never connected. His left forearm blocked her weapon arm as he brought his kittane around.

Even with her protective energies, the force of the kittane hitting her side forced the air out of her lungs. On instinct, she barely avoided a follow-up attack as she stumbled away.

She gasped for air as she heard him coming for her relatively unprotected back. Nearly blind with pain, she somehow sidestepped his next swing.

She turned to face him as he cocked back the war club for another blow. Raising her mace before his eyes, she gasped a quick prayer. Light enveloped her weapon, glaring against his vision. He stepped back in caution, weighing this new threat.

It was only a temporary light-inducing miracle. Sondra's trick proved simple and fast enough that she could cast it quickly. It faded as quickly as it appeared, and Sondra turned to run. She had no idea where to go, but her ribs burned as she headed for a clump of trees. The woman had no doubt he would catch her, but she needed room to think of a plan.

Her escape path proved faulty. A small drop-off hid just within those trees. She saw more debris scattered on the field below, but nothing offered a strategy against the elf warrior behind her.

She turned to react to his swing. The kittane smacked the mace out of her hand.

Behind him, she saw the elf scout Cassyli calling out in their native tongue. She could not know his words were calling on his brother to stop. It did not seem to matter, for Cassyli was too far away to block the next swing of the kittane.

The end of the angled club, sharpened to a tip, pierced through Sondra's miracles on the other side of her ribs. She saw the sky as she tumbled backward…then pain swept her into oblivion.

*      *      *      *      *

Cat couldn't deny the gravestone which dominated her vision. The chiseled stone appeared more real to her than the woods beyond. Trestan was gone. With his passing, she lost the light in her heart. In the void of his absence, she saw how much he had meant to her. Her heart and her body endured physical sickness as her emotions threatened to drag her over a cliff.

Time passed unmarked as Cat indulged down a path of recollections. She held close every precious moment spent with him, and replayed them lest those events fade in the march of time. She recalled his strong yet gentle hands massaging her back. She remembered showing him new foreign dishes in the Orlaun marketplace. The warmth felt, when he had healed her from the brink of death, still lingered in every thought. Cat could still feel Trestan entwined within her soul.

It is a terrible thing to lose one's soulmate when one's own years counted so young. Cat wished he could have shared her longevity…she wanted to grow old alongside someone. It had always caused her to hold something back from their relationship. Now he was gone, and everything she should have done for him or said to him were now robbed of opportunity.

A significance dawned on Cat. For all the pain his passing caused, she didn't regret having him as her lover. Part of the pain for his passing was eased by elven beliefs in the natural life and death cycles of all beings. Yet, the pain that remained was in the missed opportunities in life. She mourned the way she had tried to guard her heart against his passing and how it lessened the joys they could have had together. She once held back, and now she regretted it.

She had feared loving him for the inevitable pain it would cause her if she lost him. Now that he was gone, her pain arose from not giving all her heart into their relationship. Time had interceded all too soon as she had feared, and yet she found herself realizing she was blessed for the moments they did share.

Running hands through her hair, she realized she was wearing her helmet for some reason. Frowning, she removed it and dug through her pack for Trestan's greatest gift. Her nimble hands retrieved the *Taef' Adorina* he had given her after their first adventure. The intricately woven, gold designs reflected sunlight across one brief smile on her face. She studied the charms adorning it. Each represented some moment or friend from that first quest. Cat placed the tiara on her head.

She honored his life by recalling their time together. As she kneeled before his grave, head bowed in respect, her mind journeyed. His eyes staring at her when she did her exercise routine that first morning leaving Troutbrook…practicing with swords on the road…the battle of the bluff when he was wounded…his healing touch…the first time they undressed…

Eventually, she hit a block in her memory. Cat had trouble getting past it, as if she had no memories past a certain point. She couldn't recall images, though she started to hear sounds from a battle. Frustration showed clearly on her fine elven features as she tried to resolve the gap in her memory she couldn't cross. She couldn't remember if she and Trestan had ever been joined in spiritbond.

What happened on that continent? After they saw the debris of the *Doranil Star*, did they beat Revwar and Savannah to the relics? A horrible, cold realization came over Katressa as she recalled squirming under the mentalist's words.

Her eyes truly opened to the world around her. She faced a large rock. There was no grave, for Trestan was somewhere up on the ridge and very much alive. The sounds of battle persisted. Weapons clashed along with the unintelligible grunts of bodies exerting themselves.

The half-elf bounced back to her feet, the immobility spell long since faded. She ran with bow in hand. Her will drove her forward in case she was already too late. In her passion to join her companions, Cat forgot her helmet on the ground. She was rushing into battle with the golden *Taef' Adorina* upon her brow.

## CHAPTER 31                "The Charmed Elf Warrior/Images in the Mind"

Cassyli arrived too late to protect the human cleric from Foyren's hit. It shocked him that his brother could fall so completely under the manipulations of foreign mages. It also shamed him that he had been unable to save the kind woman who had healed him after his fall in the village.

He called out for his brother to stop and consider reason. The face that whirled on him held only the empty gaze of one whose mind was enslaved. Cassyli doubted that Foyren could even recognize his own brother. The spell incited the renowned warrior into a blind rage, same as the firbholg. The older elf stared upon his sibling without any flicker of recognition.

Hesitation cost Cassyli the use of his weapon. Foyren's offhand reached out and snagged the spear; grabbing it below the raccoon tail at the base of the head. The kittane dove in fast. Cassyli raised the turtle shell shield in time to ward away the blow. He tried to jerk his weapon free to no avail. More violent swings followed in close quarters as the elves maneuvered. They danced in irregular circles around a moving pivot centered on the disputed spear.

Cassyli couldn't out-muscle his brother. Foyren tried to use those opportunities to wrest it from his grasp. The scout fought at a severe disadvantage without control of the spear. Cassyli was stuck on the defensive as the elven war club chipped pieces from his shield.

Words were unable to reason with the crazed man, yet words were in short supply as the duel continued. Foyren used leverage on the spear to force Cassyli into desperate jumps over uneven terrain. The younger brother had to adjust or lose his grip. He nearly lost the spear, save for a shield-punch to Foyren that allowed him to retain a hold.

The last thing Cassyli wanted was to use a deadly weapon on his older brother. He needed the spear back for his own defense. The younger brother attempted to talk reason again. He tried to reinforce Foyren's identity by reminding him of the nature of the strangers manipulating him. In effect, he merely broadened his brother's confusion. Part of the elf warrior listened, but the rage of battle had his emotions further clouding his logic.

Furious energy drove the kittane to tear parts of the shell away. Cassyli's arm grew pained under the onslaught. Sharpened pieces of flint, from the front edge of the war club, fell aside like broken teeth.

They had moved far from their original clash by the time Foyren switched tactics. He threw all his weight against the spear, trapping it against the rusted metal of a ballista resting among some rocks. The wooden shaft snapped. The effort must have been hard on the warrior's body as well, yet the enchanted rage dulled the pain.

Foyren gripped the club two-handed. Strong blows rained down until the scout fell to the ground. There was nothing Cassyli could do but keep his battered shield above him as the hits came down. He felt sure that his shield arm suffered a cracked bone by the time Foyren delivered an agonizing strike to an unprotected leg.

Cassyli's shield arm flew wide as he cried out, "Brother, forgive me! I couldn't save you."

The intimidating warrior paused with his kittane poised to take life. Foyren truly saw his younger brother through the haze of the spell. Even then, his grip on reason stretched tentative at best. A mix of hatred and confusion plain upon his visage as he looked upon his wounded sibling.

Foyren screamed. "Why do you protect the treasonous heretic of Ganden? How can you not see the games the agora and her human friends play on you? How can you be so blind, brother?"

Cassyli shook his head, "Nay, it is you who has been blinded. Listen to me…"

"Enough!" Foyren stumbled back, unwilling to hear anything Cassyli might say. He shook his head even as he spoke, trying to clear the mentalist's fog. "We will have words between us when this is over…after I've dealt with the invaders who have undermined our city."

Cassyli was no longer a threat to his strong brother. He lie there with a broken leg and arm, breathing heavily from his exertions. Foyren ran away from him, seeking out the human cleric to ensure her death. It was the only destination in the tunnel of his mind.

*      *      *      *      *

It felt as if a tentacle of ice writhed underneath his skull. Savannah snaked through his mind, intent on whatever secrets she sought. Trestan tried his best to ignore the physical pain as he drove his will into the abbess' thoughts. He felt her psyche recoiling from his path. He took some comfort in the fact that his intrusion proved as uncomfortable to her as the feelings of her presence in his awareness.

He saw images from her mind pass across a horizon of memories. Trestan stopped to consider a familiar scene. He gazed upon the keep out in the shallow seas where they had fought and recovered the relics. *Earthrin Stones.* He had discovered their name, but he pushed past those fleeting bits of information to find something more useful.

Among the jumble of thoughts he began to understand the purpose of that keep. Savannah and Revwar had chosen the locale due to its abandonment and seclusion in order to use it as a base. A ring of conquest echoed in Savannah's thoughts, but the memory shifted away in favor of a new one.

The failure of the band four years ago had prompted them to abandon the idea of using that keep. Trestan felt a whisper flash past his consciousness, proclaiming a new location from which they could launch…an invasion? With alarm, Trestan followed the path of this thought. He felt the need to hurry before Savannah found what she wanted and broke contact. The squire continuously felt her icy presence clawing at his own mind for clues.

A new image came before him. He saw a structure much bigger than the small keep. This new place was a mighty castle, sporting several tall towers. It had a large inner courtyard surrounded by a wall, surrounded by outer ramparts. The entire structure sat on a rocky hill, next to a river, overlooking a large expanse of open plains. In fact, the river split and forked around both sides of the keep before tumbling into lowlands. The base of the inner wall and the castle had been carved out of the stony hill itself, before more stones were added on later to extend its lofty towers. The place looked bare of exotic designs, focusing on practical aspects. By the brilliant reflections of the stone walls, it was also rather new. It thrived with people who farmed the nearby grasslands. As Trestan looked upon it, he got the feeling it sat on the very fringes of civilization. The grasslands beyond this place signified the borders of known culture. The castle stood sentinel watching the frontier of the world.

In a flash, Trestan knew its name and location. Trestan realized, ' *This is where the next battle will be fought. The forces mustered under Savannah, Revwar, and their allies will sweep into this castle and use it as their launching point against the rest of the world.* "

He saw Savannah's mind imagining a great evil arising from the wild lands beyond civilization. They heralded the oncoming winter in a storm of death. A horde of angry tribes converged from the wild lands to this place…consuming it…multiplying in number…and springing forth from the bones of the towers to darken the rest of the world. The Earthrin Stones, in the hands of Savannah, would once again be weapons of war that could starve and plague villages…or lay waste to stone walls. He could see the blight of the Death Goddess being cast across the realm.

If that fortress fell, the rest of the world might not be able to contain the evil that would spawn.

There was much that Trestan couldn't understand about the terrible images before him. The goal of DeLaris would give rise to a new Godswars. How had the Covenant failed to protect against this threat?

Trestan felt he had found out enough to be able to warn others about Savannah's plans. The fortress on the edge of civilization had to be defended, or the realm would be submerged in chaos. They still had to recover the relics from the other band in order to keep the scales balanced. Trestan decided it was time to see what was so important that Savannah had felt the need to pry into his mind.

His will flowed back to his own memories. He felt along the icy tendril of Savannah's psyche until he found her. Trestan dove into the memory in which her consciousness lingered.

With surprise, Trestan found himself inside the home of Petrow's family. Before him, set like a play, was a scene from his recent memories. He and Katressa sat with Petrow and his wife, eating the meal before their journey south. Lil' Willy dodged around the table to the safety of his mother's dress. Leane relaxed in her crib. The one stranger to this memory was Savannah. Her image stood and glared at the conversation. She glanced up as Trestan's psyche materialized across the table from her. The memory played on between them as Savannah glared at Abriana's champion.

Trestan demanded answers. "Why are you here Savannah? What possible importance do you see in Petrow and his family?"

Savannah waved her hands across the setting, as if it should be obvious. "He has children! Two…born in the years since I last saw him."

Trestan had no immediate answer. The squire felt a troubling sensation tickle the back of his mind, as if he was missing something obvious. He tried recalling his schooling at the seminary, but the exact lesson escaped him.

As the conversation played out in the memory, Inedra rubbed her belly as she talked about the child within. Savannah lost even more of her composure. "A third child fostered by a dead man!"

"Oh gods," Trestan whispered as the truth hit him. "You claimed his life for DeLaris, didn't you? When you fought at the keep on the sea he was helpless before you. Yet, you failed to kill him afterward."

The abbess' eyes actually revealed a hint of terror. Trestan could only imagine the nightmares her deity had visited upon her. Her subtle nod confirmed her admission. "His life belongs to DeLaris as long as I live. I pronounced him dead, and it is my shame that he lived. I must undo that slight against my goddess."

Trestan tried to put steel in his voice, despite the known futility of his next request. "He is beyond you now, Savannah. He desires only a peaceful life with his family. There is nay reason for a vendetta to hunt him down when he bears nay threat to you anymore."

Savannah narrowed her icy blue eyes at Trestan, "He bore three threats to me. These children were fathered after I claimed his life for death. I won't find rest until I finish my claim."

Savannah reached her hand down like a claw, passing harmlessly into the memory of Leane's body. The abbess clenched an angry fist where the baby's heart would be. "They must die too."

For Trestan, it was time to end this intrusion into his mind.

He called forth blessings of Abriana as he worked to close off his mind. Savannah withdrew easily, having all the information she needed, including the location of Petrow's home. As the two of them returned to control of their physical bodies, Trestan tried to shove the abbess away. She fought with him. It seemed important to her that she remain close to him for one more trick. Finally, Trestan ducked down and rammed her backward with his shoulder.

In order for Petrow and his children to avoid a death sentence, Savannah had to be killed. If Trestan used his sword to attack Savannah on this holy day, he would be banned from Abriana's service forever.

A steel blade hissed free of its leather scabbard.

The abbess forced Trestan's decision. As they separated, Trestan saw the Sword of the Spirit in Savannah's evil hands. Trestan may not have been totally disarmed, yet the warhammer he carried could not destroy her spell-shields like the powers of the elvish blade. Savannah stood out of reach, holding his magical sword with triumph in her eyes.

The abbess began to chant a prayer. Dark energies coalesced around her empty hand as she prepared to destroy the squire from Troutbrook.

*       *       *       *       *

The flute Lindon Taleweaver had used for the wind attack has been returned to his magical pocket. The minstrel decided to change tactics. Lindon finished a complex set of notes on his mandolin, even as a blast of fire engulfed the tree to his back. Any wizard could be a formidable opponent, and the minstrel knew he had picked a fight with a talented enemy. The notes from his latest tune coalesced into a physical manifestation in the air before him. A blending of light and sound created a form akin to a dancing fairy. Its appearance was obviously a magical construct rather than a living creature.

Lindon stepped away as smitten portions of the fiery tree began to rain down. He directed the magical fairy with a few words, sending her darting into the brush. The minstrel hoped he had enough time to put his trick into motion. By stepping away from the tree, he ventured into the direct line of sight of the elf.

Revwar's tongue twisted around the syllables of arcane study as he raised a hand toward Lindon. Lindon attempted to counter the spell with his mandolin. The minstrel's method sought to disrupt the act of spellcasting itself. Waves of sound took on a physical nature, forming an angry force of wind which hammered toward the mouth of the wizard. For Revwar, it was not unlike stepping outside on a frigid winter morning, with the tongue gagging at the feel of cold gale trying to force its way into the throat. The wizard struggled to maintain the effort of the casting. Meanwhile, Lindon also weakened under the concentration required to draw such magic from the harmonic web.

The toll would have likely been too much for the minstrel, yet he only needed to succeed long enough for his trick to work. Revwar almost completed his spell when the fairy composed of multi-colored bits of light jumped into the path. The magical construct exploded into a dazzling brilliance of light and sound.

Revwar's spell trailed off to nothing as the display dazed his senses. Lights danced all around his vision. Nonsensical music notes assaulted his hearing. The attack temporarily robbed him of sight and sound.

Lindon Taleweaver could only hope the effects lasted long enough to give him an opening. The minstrel began to chant a song which lent speed to his movements. His feet pumped forward even as he snapped the smallsword level for a lunge. He crossed the distance easily as the wizard struggled to find words for another spell. The performer from Orlaun went for the heart.

Lindon underestimated the nature of the magic-laden fabric. He hadn't known how resilient it proved to be when stabbed by Cat's rapier. The point of his blade pushed the wizard back a step, bowing the blade slightly in the process. Vulnerable as the cloth seemed, the tip couldn't pierce it.

The minstrel recovered his feet as his chant died out. He lacked time to puzzle whether the resistance came from the garment or a deflective ward. Revwar spit out a frantic spell as Lindon dodged to the side.

The desperate wizard, still effectively blinded by the minstrel's trick, used a short range defense. Lindon barely got out of the way as a brief wall of flames erupted in front of Revwar. The minstrel felt the heat of the spell on his neck as he literally cut across to the elf's side. His sword once again bounced off the fabric over an arm.

Revwar only needed to fear if the smallsword stabbed at his face, hands, or neck. He raised a long-sleeved arm in front of his sparkling vision while blindly pushing a hand out at the human. With his magical strength in place, he succeeded in shoving Lindon to the ground.

The wizard backed up, swinging his ringed hand forward and barking a command. The agile minstrel back-flipped over a beam of light that sliced across the ground. The beam cut apart twigs, leaves and small rocks in its path.

Revwar never paused between spells. He went into his next arcane movements even as he backed away from the vague shape of the minstrel. The entertainer charged again while he had the chance, knowing his spell's effects were ending. The elf threw his arms and sleeves up, suffering a wicked cut to one hand.

Any impediment to the hands was a hazard when one relied on them for spells. Nevertheless, his current incantation succeeded in its completion. Robes swelled and flapped outward like wings, propelling him into the air. Revwar soared out of reach of the sword.

Lindon gave a silent curse as the wizard ascended. He would be an easy target for spells on the ground. He could enact a spell that would allow him to jump great distances, but it was not a flight spell. Once in the air, he could not maneuver except to control a levitating fall. He had little choice. The human from Orlaun sprang into the air with a few plucks from the mandolin.

By this time, Revwar's senses had recovered greatly. The wizard anticipated that the minstrel couldn't diverge from the trajectory of his jump. From his hands, he cast a spell that was an old favorite. Three flaming swords took shape in a triangular formation, slicing down at the human.

Lindon deflected two with quick swings, yet the other cut a line of fire down one leg. The minstrel winced in agony.

The two opponents collided in midair. Revwar's control over his flight, augmented by his arcane-induced physical strength, gave the wizard the edge. They grappled and traded blows before Revwar tossed Lindon away.

Looking at the receding wizard from under his wide-brimmed hat, Lindon knew he lost his advantage. He had missed his chance, and now he was falling away from the spellcaster. He began whistling the song of levitation to guide him safely to the ground.

Revwar did not want to give him the chance to escape. The wizard used another reliable trick of his, with a new twist. An invisible chain of force whipped through the air. This one formed vertical, not horizontal, and it descended with unseen yet deadly intent. Lindon felt something invisible slam into him with jarring force, speeding him to the ground.

The minstrel whistled his levitation song with more urgency. Revwar watched with interest as the human dropped down until the chain of force hammered him into green branches below. The elf lost sight of the minstrel's bright red hat and beard. Cautiously, the flying wizard descended for a better view. He couldn't see the minstrel, only broken branches and loosely falling leaves. Unwilling to take chances, he threw a fire spell into the gloom. It tossed out more debris as it exploded.

Revwar searched from the air for a bit longer, debating whether to blow apart the trees, skim hazardously low to search, or simply abandon the chase. In the end, he decided to leave the human to his fate. Securing the relics was his priority. He went searching for Savannah in order to assist her in claiming the stones.

*       *       *       *       *

Cat moved through the debris field as fast as she dared without opening herself up to surprise attacks. The sounds of fighting reached her ears, but they never came from the same direction. It seemed that the combatants were all spread out in personal duels. The half-elf had an arrow fitted to the bow, ready for any threat.

The first figure she spotted moved silently through trees, tall grass, and wreckage. Once Cat got close enough, she recognized Foyren. He seemed to be tracking someone else. There was fighting ahead as well as behind, but Cat could not see anyone except him. She tried to determine his intentions, but nothing about his back gave a hint on whether he was still charmed or not. Cat had to assume he was a threat until he proved otherwise.

The privateer from Kashmer closed the distance with remarkable stealth. When Foyren crouched to nock an arrow into his bow, Cat's arrow aimed at Faer'Seelie's heart. He had apparently sighted someone worth shooting, but Cat couldn't see the target. It was hard to determine if he was friend or foe. Foyren had been a charmed victim; she couldn't just shoot him in the back.

With her bow aimed to kill, Cat spoke in Elvish, "Hold and do not fire if you be a friend."

The elf warrior spun to face her with his drawn bow. Whether charmed or not, the rage that came to his expression left little doubt of his feelings toward her. Cat released the tension on her bowstring as he did the same.

"Death to agoras!" He shouted, even as the arrows were in flight.

His hasty arrow shot past her harmlessly. Cat's aim was more accurate. The arrow thudded into the thick, leather pauldron protecting his left shoulder. Cat bolted for a better spot. She drew and set another arrow on the run.

Her shot soon proved to be superficial. The arrowhead merely lodged in the protective armor piece, having landed just wide of the skin. Foyren paused and snapped the shaft in order to keep it from interfering in his next bowshot.

He had just set another arrow against the string when Cat's next arrow whistled toward him. The elf deftly dodged the missile and proceeded to close the distance with the half-elf. A few running steps and Foyren fired off a second shot.

Elves and half-elves could load and fire with amazing accuracy on the run. Cat rolled away from the path enough to feel the arrowhead scratch along the side of her leather breastplate.

Each archer used the terrain as best they could, going behind trees and bushes as their opponent was ready to fire. Their right arms moved constantly from quiver to string to release and back. Ever closer they moved, making it harder for their agility to react to the barrage from their opponent. Both elves spun and somersaulted with grace rivaling an acrobatic troupe. A few small trees sprung arrow shafts that failed to strike blood. Arrows that the archers couldn't dodge, barely deflected off their armor.

Both combatants stepped into an uneven pile of ship debris as they loaded once more. They were close enough that a miss for either seemed impossible. Both strings did not even draw back to their full strength before snapping with the release. Cat initiated a flip even as she fired. Foyren's arrow slashed through raven strands to scar her face. Foyren spun his bow immediately after firing. He was lucky that the wood partially deflected the arrow into a stinging hit to his side.

Neither opponent gave time for the other to recover. Both bow staves rapped against each other as they closed into melee. Cat's rapier flashed out, severing the string on the warrior's bow. Foyren likewise drew his kittane and used it. His swing knocked the elegant elvish bow from Cat's left hand.

They passed each other on the run, trading follow-up blows as they did. The kittane missed as Cat rolled under the swing, though her rapier sliced a line of blood from Foyren's leg. As soon as she was upright again, he was on her. The arrow and the rapier strike hadn't slowed down his rage. Her own cheek trickled warmth from his last shot.

Something shifted in her hair, reminding her of another danger. She still wore the *Taef' Adorina* upon her brow instead of her protective helmet. Those relatively flimsy and decorative strands of gold were precious little defense against any kind of blow to her head. To Foyren, it left a vulnerable opening.

She tried to stab with the rapier as he forced her back. Foyren used the inside angle of his kittane to hook the tip and push it away. As he did so, his left hand repeatedly hammered toward her with the bow staff. Cat dodged and rolled, avoiding the worst of his attacks while trying to weave a deadly barrier with her rapier.

Foyren made a desperate move. He threw the bow at her feet even as he changed the direction of his war club assault. Cat hopped back, aware only too late that he forced her into a corner. A thick tangle of trees loomed to one side, while a rotted section of decking leaned across the other. Foyren lifted his kittane with both hands for a powerful blow.

He left himself rather exposed in his haste to finish the half-elf. Cat struck with lightning reflexes. Her magical, silver blade stabbed deep into his chest. Even as blood started to run down the blade, Cat knew she had struck a mortal blow.

Foyren paused, only for a moment. Then, to Cat's surprise, he pushed forward again. Pressing himself farther onto her blade, he gave out a roar of hatred.

Cat could not believe he was still coming at her. Some remnant of the charm pushed him beyond mortal limits, even making him reckless. She had no doubt that the wound to his heart would drop him within a step or two, but he was using the last of that strength to vent his rage. Her emerald eyes followed up from the point of blood…up past the necklace trophy that displayed all the tough monsters he had killed…up past the bulging muscles that framed his enraged glare…up to the sharpened war club as it descended.

The decorative tiara would be no defense against a blow that could likely cave in her skull.

"Oh, Trestan…" She whispered, before the sharpened edge clubbed all her feelings and regrets into empty darkness.

**CHAPTER 32**     **"Ganden's Servant/The Chiaso's Vendetta"**

Awareness lingered at the edge of her unconscious mind, yet every time her spirit rose toward it an onslaught of pain dragged her down. She could not remember why she wanted to ascend back into the waking world, nor why she wanted to face the hurt it inflicted on her spirit. She wanted to escape the torment forever. Something cold offered an escape from the pain. It felt like a hand extending to her, offering to take her into nothingness. She embraced it, hoping that she would find solace in the depths of the darkness.

Her mother's voice shouted from her memories, *"You must let go, Sondra. Let go and live!"*

Her name was Sondra. She had to live. Living meant trying to rise toward the pain.

She struggled to see, to hear, and to breathe. In doing so, she invited a torrent of pain that sought to drown her once again. Mentally, she reached out, this time avoiding the cold hand and latching onto the pain. It was a difficult journey to make. Breathing brought more anguish, yet she struggled to inhale. Sondra forced her eyes open.

The acolyte of Ganden woke under the sunlight, sounds of battle distantly ringing in her ears. Her lungs gurgled with her own blood, as cracked ribs fought every attempt at breath. One painful step at a time, she sought the concentration needed for a healing miracle. Sondra had never felt so weak. She wasn't even sure if she could lend enough strength to her prayers to mend the damage.

Somehow, she brought forth the miracle of her god. Divine energy reshaped her ribs, dispelled the fluid in her lungs, and closed the tears in the tissue. The results left her weary, pale, but alive. She swooned but kept her eyes open. It took several minutes before she even attempted to rise from the ground. Sondra staggered to her feet, cautiously, wincing at the lingering pain. The blonde woman found her mace and her satchel in the tall grass.

She looked around, unsure where to go. Her blue eyes caught sight of something familiar. A section of the deck, mostly a skeletal framework of boards, draped over the branches of some trees. In the light streaming through the wreckage, Sondra saw a familiar round shape on the ground. It was the cauldron that once held the holy relics of her church. The slightest whiff of incense reached her nose, almost overwhelmed by the stench of death. Sondra felt like her heart was in her throat. The woman conjured up the miracle which allowed her to see nearby holy relics of her faith. A moment later, she felt the confirmation of several religious artifacts of Ganden lying amidst the rubble.

She felt something else. Sondra discovered the radiance of several smaller symbols...necklaces, trinkets, pins...remainders of the personal holy items the Chosen carried on them when they died. Sondra slowly walked toward the emanations, aware this ground had been hallowed by the bodies of her mentors.

Sondra explored the scene with solemn reverence. She saw bloodied, threadbare cushions and rusty incense holders. She counted the bodies of the Chosen. It was difficult, due to the involvement of scavengers, but she found all of them present in one form or another. She did not find the body of Mother Evine, only the woman's clothes. The energies called forth to keep the divine chariot in the air for so long had consumed Evine's physical form. Sondra noted that even the cleric's personal holy item was missing, yet a shadow of it had been burned into a piece of wood.

The acolyte of Ganden sighed as she surveyed the loss. Even as she did, a sound reached her ears. Someone was behind her!

"You should have died with them, as was the calling of the God of Duty." Sondra heard the voice of Jentan Mollamos, carrying the power of a magical charm. "You should be on your knees, praying forgiveness that you abandoned your duty in their hour of need."

Acolyte Sondra wanted to refute the traitor, yet his suggestion tugged at the guilt in her heart. She found herself compelled to drop to her knees and shed tears for her teachers. She felt overwhelmed by the need to ask for forgiveness that she had not died with them.

Behind her, the mentalist smiled.

*     *     *     *     *

The personal vendetta raged across grass and rock, between trees and broken ship planks. The rogue spun both sword and poisoned stiletto in distracting patterns. The vigilante chiaso flipped the elven staff from arm to arm as an extension of her body. Sweat soaked their loose clothes. The domid's brown hair had tumbled free of its bun. The human's braided, red hair displayed similar disarray, yet a long tail of it was still tied at the end by a faded pink ribbon from a torn dress. Kemora Quickfeet and Montanya su Troyeal bara Westonhout went about their acrobatic exchange with grunts of exertion. Their feet and arms moved to no song, yet strong, primal urges lent rhythm to their dance. They struck at each other to dominate; to become the top predator. The long legs and staff gave Montanya a good edge, allowing her to go on the offensive. Undaunted, Kemora's stiletto weaved like a snake, looking for the right moment to strike with its poisonous fang.

They carried the struggle over a rotted mast stretched across a runoff. The beam acted as a narrow bridge over a shallow ravine, one that carried water into a muddy morass. The wood expelled splinters as their weight passed over it. Montanya's whirling bludgeon came at the halfling from both sides. It spun wildly as the crazed fighter took advantage of the open space. Kemora, reluctant to surrender the ground, hoped she could use the bridge to get Montanya into tighter confinement.

Kemora took a chance, sacrificing a hit to put her plan into motion. The domid charged, raising one arm and accepting the blow to the side of her breast. Meanwhile, her stiletto darted forward, forcing Montanya to stop short of the full hit. Kemora dropped her raised arm over the staff, hugging it in tight as she threw her weight away from the mast. Montanya realized the halfling's ploy as her small body dropped into the ravine, pulling the staff with her. The chiaso had to lose the weapon or fall into the ravine.

Instinct took over.

Montanya leaped from the log and soared out farther than the halfling's plunge. The rogue landed, expecting the human to come down on top of her. Kemora even attempted another stab with the stiletto under poor balance. The thin blade missed as Montanya used the staff to vault farther down the trench. The chiaso never released her grip on her weapon.

The women continued their fight in the muddy confines of the ravine. Montanya flicked a glob of mud from the end of her staff at Kemora, though it distracted her little. Montanya quickly found herself backing away from the domid's attack. She couldn't use any swings in the tight space. Montanya could only jab repeatedly, but the smaller rogue parried that easily while trying to get within the distance needed for an effective strike.

Kemora pushed Montanya back until the ravine widened. The softness of the mud nullified any relief Montanya may have felt with the increased space. The mud sucked at the human's legs, yet Kemora was light enough to avoid getting mired. Amidst every squelch, Montanya's feet slowed.

The chiaso recalled another of her lessons; one she had not spent nearly enough time contemplating. The students had practiced Skimmer Step on rainy days in the Highwater district. Her mind went back to those days of stepping into the mudflows. As a young girl, she had looked upon the poor and homeless. They had stared back at the odd sight of children trying to walk on the muck oozing past their wet shelters. Young Montanya knew that she would grow to be their protector. She had to bring her will and body together, and it helped to recall Lindon's music. The minstrel had risen from those very same poor alleys in that flooded district to inspire her. To Kemora's surprise, Montanya achieved an enlightened level of balance. The chiaso stepped atop the mud and stayed there. Montanya no longer sank into the ground despite all their fighting maneuvers.

The staff attacked with renewed effectiveness. Montanya forced Kemora out of the mud and into a more wooded area.

Kemora changed tactics so fast that it left Montanya hesitating. One moment the halfling repelled an attack, the next she turned and darted into the brush. The chiaso continued to hold her ground and stand guard, believing the halfling was trying to draw her in. Kemora seemed to blend into the foliage. Montanya caught glimpses of color and sound as the small humanoid sought cover.

Montanya cautiously stepped ahead. She expected Kemora to ambush her, and she was correct.

What she did not expect, was to see Kemora the size of a human  The sword came in high, forcing Montanya to raise her staff for the block. Too late, Montanya realized her mistake, trying to drop her staff low instead. The tall rogue seemed to pass through part of the staff.

Montanya felt the strike of Kemora's fang in her leg. Warrior instincts allowed Montanya to retaliate with a blow to Kemora's head, though it seemed as if the staff passed through her abdomen.

Both women fell back. The illusionary mask which allowed Kemora to appear human had been hit by the staff, and now dangled around her neck. She appeared as a normal halfling once again. The ruse had tricked Montanya into reacting to the illusionary size rather than the reality.

Kemora shook her head as she regained her wits from the staff strike. She looked up to see Montanya stagger away several steps. The chiaso's newly provided elven pantaloons had a hole in one leg. Montanya stared back, aghast, at the sight of her blood on Kemora's poisoned stiletto.

*　　　　*　　　　*　　　　*　　　　*

Trestan could do little against Savannah while she held his magic sword, especially due to his devotion to the tenets of Abriana. As she prepared her deadly miracle, he began to pray for one of his own. He barely brought his shield into existence as a magical darkness raced toward him. The divine spells collided and nullified.

Trestan immediately lunged to reclaim his sword. He believed Abriana wouldn't punish him for reclaiming his property. Savannah retreated while chanting another prayer. Abriana's champion nearly grabbed the hilt before a blast of air sent him flying backward. The force of the prayer nearly pushed him off the edge of the small cliff.

Trestan regained his feet as Savannah enchanted her flail with its dark blessing. With heavy heart, he realized he had no hope of getting his sword back. Savannah was shielded, armed with a blessed weapon, and had every capability to throw a damaging miracle at him from a distance. Only one choice seemed available at that moment.

The squire turned and ran along the edge of the rise. Accelerating footsteps carried him back to his friends.

The abbess of DeLaris wouldn't permit it. She called forth another dark miracle. A wall of red mist formed before Trestan, blocking his retreat. It stretched out over a long distance from side to side, even extending slightly over the drop-off.

Trestan recognized the miracle from a past encounter. A disorienting illusion lurked inside the mist, where the images of past loved ones would attempt to distract him from his path. He looked back to see Savannah slowly advancing toward him. She had retrieved her skull helm and stared at him from within the skull sockets. The Sword of the Spirit hung from her belt.

A plan came to Trestan's mind. The mist had scared him when he was young and inexperienced, but he held no fear that it could stop him now. With a nod to Savannah, he turned and plunged into the mist.

Savannah's mouth widened at seeing him willingly thrust himself into that cloud. The abbess ran parallel to the drop-off, dismissing a portion of the mist so that she might run through and intercept him. When she got to the other side, she couldn't see him. Savannah conjured up another dark miracle and sent it exploding within the mist she had conjured. No scream or noise came from the mist.

A realization came to the faithful of DeLaris. She ran forward to the edge of the drop-off. Down below, she saw Trestan running into the woods. The paladin had found the cliff's edge and descended it while the fog covered the escape.

Savannah descended the small rise in pursuit. Both Trestan and Savannah knew where the relics were hiding. She was determined that the young man would not beat her to the Earthrin Stones.

*　　　　*　　　　*　　　　*　　　　*

Sondra knelt on a blood-soaked cushion, staring across a bubbling cauldron at two others. A sphere of soft light, from no apparent source, illuminated the figures and the area next to the cauldron. Although she could not see the walls, the acolyte knew she was within the inner sanctum of the dying *Doranil Star*. Around her, the room thrummed to the song of Ganden, yet she could not find the source of that song, for there were only the three of them present. The other two did not appear to be singing, though she could not see their faces due to the hoods of their ceremonial vestments.

The one on her right turned partway toward her. She could see the edges of a black and gray goatee and mustache. The figure pointed to her, "Chant the mantra along with us. We must keep the ship floating long enough to save the others."

Sondra started to comply, but found herself unable. In her heart, she knew something was amiss. Sondra glanced to the other robed figure, looking for an affirmation or denial.

The robed figure on the right frowned at this action. Across from the unknown priest, on Sondra's left, she saw the face of Mother Evine appear beneath the cowl. Sondra's mentor stared into the cauldron. "Acolytes please leave. Get to the life boats and continue to serve Ganden well in the years to come."

Sondra found herself at odds with her own feelings. She didn't want to stay and die, yet she wanted to honor the call of her god and follow Evine to the very end. She owed Ganden everything. Her entire livelihood felt indebted.

The robed figure on the right frowned. He whispered something that made Mother Evine's face turn away into the dark depths of the hood. Sondra could no longer peek at the face on the left. The male priest rebuked Sondra in a firm tone. "You serve the God of Honor, and his duty to you is clear. Your wishes are nothing compared to the lives of his guests. Begin the mantra or be gone from his service."

The acolyte of Ganden strained to get a better glimpse of his face. The cowl always seemed to cover too much. She felt the compelling need to do as he said. Duty called to her, putting the needs of others before her own wishes. It had always been this way.

She briefly hesitated, looking once again to the left as Mother Evine's face reappeared. "You will someday find the beacon of strength that lies in your own heart. You will learn the uninhibited joy of being able to help others, as well as the self-respect that comes with honor."

"Why do you hesitate?" snapped the robed priest on the right. "Do you actually care to go out among those people? They teased you as a child, tormenting you for being a homeless orphan. How can you care to join those that don't care for you? How thankful are they?"

Jentan Mollamos concentrated on his mesmerizing chant. He could see images in Sondra's mind as he continued to play out his illusion. Though he could not see specific memories, he could sense her feelings as her mind weighed uncertainties. In the physical realm, the acolyte knelt by the debris of the wreckage. Her eyes viewed only the images Jentan wove from her own feelings. While the mentalist struggled to maintain control of her mind, his eyes wandered over the young woman's curves. Jentan enjoyed the truly magnificent power he possessed that could control the minds of such beautiful ladies.

Sondra could only agonize over the punishing feelings that played upon her heart. She was losing herself under the guilt and pain that lay bared for the mentalist.

He continued to assault her feelings, "It is easy to serve meals and heal the beggars to warm your own soul, but the true test of your honor and devotion is your life for your god. You must chant the mantra or the ship will fall. If you refute his call, we will all die anyway."

The mentalist idly wondered if he could get her to eat one of the magic foods he had in his pockets. The mixture, combined with the proper words, was the means by which Savannah and Revwar had snuck on board the divine vessel. If Sondra could be convinced to eat one, then speak the words, she would be transformed into a clay figure. Jentan could carry her away in a pocket. He could then break her mind at his leisure. Savannah had denied him, yet a younger, more innocent woman awaited his domination.

In the private realm of her mind, Sondra anguished over her decision. The path seemed clear, but why did she feel hesitation? She felt a sense that she had left the sanctum before, and brought great pain onto her heart. Maybe she was required to give up the last of her hopes and dreams in favor of dying in Ganden's service. Hadn't her only hopes been rooted in this divine ship anyway? She cast another look at the robed person on her left. Maybe there was one last comfort they could offer.

This time the hood revealed a different face. The paladin-aspirant, Trestan, looked upon her with inquisitive eyes. "Duty? Are you clear on your duty Sondra?"

Familiar words came back to Sondra. She repeated them, though she couldn't remember when she had spoken them to Trestan before. "I'm just an acolyte! I'm just a healer that cares for the poor!"

Trestan smiled a sad smile, "Did you truly give up all your hopes and dreams in your service to Ganden?"

"In order to truly serve a god in this world, you have to give up everything for them!" Sondra said, or was it the robed man on the right echoing words from her past?

Trestan shook his head. "Ganden doesn't want a servant; he wants a champion. He loves you for who you are, and that includes your hopes, your dreams, your zeal for life."

The priest on the right boiled over in anger. He hissed a few sharp words. The image on the left shattered. Somewhere within Sondra, her feelings brought the image back into being. This time it did not kneel by the cauldron. The mystery figure was walking into the darkness.

"Wait!" Sondra cried out, "I'm confused!"

The departing figure paused and turned. Sondra stared into her own face; a face that scowled back in anger at her kneeling form. The robed figure spoke, "Ganden wants more than an obedient lapdog. Someone has to get the relics and the betrayer. The past is set. Ganden's champion needs to seize the path ahead."

The image turned away, venturing into the darkness. Sondra jumped to her feet in her need to follow this version of herself. "I'm not just a lapdog! I know my duty now!"

Sondra reached into the collar of her vestments. She pulled out the chain upon which hung the dog-shaped pendant. Her fist tore it off the chain and flung it at the robed figure by the cauldron.

The holy item flared in brightness as the nightmare illusion shattered. The emblem landed at Jentan Mollamos' feet. Sondra's eyes focused on her enemy. The veil of confusion fell aside.

"Betrayer!"

Sondra came forward with her mace as Jentan threw up his arms to cast a spell. The heavy iron snapped down on one forearm. The mentalist screamed as he stumbled backward. Sondra advanced again. A few quick words and Jentan set off another spell. He seemed to disappear as a flash of light zoomed several meters to one side. He reappeared there, trying to run away from the angry woman.

Sondra gave chase, only to discover several seconds later that it was only an illusion. She turned to see the mentalist running the other direction, cradling his injured arm. Sondra Oskires called out to Ganden, asking for a prayer to shield her mind as she chased down the enemy whom she held responsible for the death of the *Doranil Star*.

*         *         *         *         *

Montanya felt an odd sensation in the stab wound on her leg. The poison was already seeping into her veins, slithering up her own system to siphon her life. Kemora kept out of reach. The domid's poker face flashed briefly to feigned sorrow. The frown mimicked how she assumed Montanya must be feeling at the end of their long chase.

The chiaso felt cheated. Her anger urged her to continue the attack until unconsciousness claimed her. Montanya felt her lust for vengeance, and yet for the first time she became repulsed by her legacy. Where had her anger driven her? It seemed she never escaped her limitations to fulfill her purposes. She couldn't escape the wooden box to save her parents. Montanya got thrown in the brig on the divine chariot, unable to act. The elves had kept her prisoner in a wooden jail, restraining her yet again.

The young warrior only had one event that went beyond the barrier blocking her goals. She shattered the caleocht wood which had trapped Sondra and the elf children. That had only happened after achieving the control of her mind, body, and soul that her anger had denied her.

The red-haired youth spun her staff up defensively when she noted the halfling sneaking forward. Kemora eyed it warily and stepped back. The smaller female wiped blood from her mouth due to the earlier hit.

While Kemora circled, Montanya attempted to relax. She thought of Lindon's sweet music. The tune of his mandolin strings, wind through his flutes, his melodic voice…they brought serenity to her feelings. She sought to find the center of her inner balance. In her mind, she danced the Butterfly in the Windmill. She felt every stretch of her muscles. Her anger disseminated into physical energy.

She briefly recoiled as she felt the foreign poison snaking its way up her leg. Recalling her lessons and feeling her inner strength, she realized she could slow her breathing and pulse to a more relaxed level. Somehow, the energy of her chi slowed the poison, buying her time. The poison would not be stopped completely by her spirit, but it could be slowed considerably.

When Montanya dropped to a kneeling position, eyes nearly closed, staff touching the ground, Kemora assumed that the poison was finishing her. The rogue lunged forward with one more stab to make sure the toxin could complete the job.

Montanya's greenish-blue eyes snapped open. The chiaso saw everything around her in perfect clarity. In the soft beauty of her face, there was no scowl or angry look. The chiaso's left hand instantly clamped over Kemora's stiletto hand. Montanya's right arm lifted the staff and knocked back the arm with the sword. She surprised the domid with her flexibility when the chiaso launched a kick from the kneeling position. The foot slammed the breath from Kemora's lungs.

Though the youth's other leg was weakened, she performed every maneuver with a level of concentration never witnessed by her former master. The rogue's stiletto arm twisted painfully, even as the kicking foot switched to connect with her sword arm. Kemora tried every dirty trick she could attempt. The trapped rogue spat in Montanya's face even as she tried kicks of her own. The martial artist soon sent the domid's sword flying off to the side. They twisted and wrestled, mixing in short punches and kicks.

Somewhere in that tussle, Montanya discarded her staff. With both hands, the human worked over Kemora's stiletto hand until something snapped. The domid screamed out as her poisoned blade fell into the grass. She retaliated with ferocity, biting Montanya's arm.

When they locked eyes once again, all sense of discipline and inner balance fled Montanya's face. The angry scowl returned. Both women slugged blows powered by desperation. Kemora couldn't escape the strong entanglement of the human.

During the fight, the locket around Kemora's neck slipped free of her tunic. Montanya saw it and angrily ripped it from her.

Montanya attacked with a bestial frenzy. The scrap of pink fabric in her hair came loose, drifting past her vision. The human began to shout things that only prompted confusion from the rogue. Kemora sought escape as fragments of sentences uttered forth in rage.

"Not my mother! You can't have her!" mixed with "Damn thieves, stop stealing my life!"

Montanya willingly drowned in feelings of loss and rage. She completely surrendered to the angry beast within her, pounding Kemora with years of unfulfilled oaths. Ghosts of her past clouded her vision. She could no more see Kemora than she had viewed the caleocht board in the training room of the Order of the Mind's Eye. Montanya spent a long time venting a lifetime of frustration.

Montanya never had a clue as to when Kemora's life faded away…she simply kept swinging as long as anger lent her strength.

When it was over, she sagged against a tree. She could no longer find the strength to fight. The limp body of the thief sprawled among grass blades speckled with red. Victory felt hollow. Though she had defeated the opponent she had chased for miles since the theft of a magical mask, there was little sense of accomplishment to justify a life of vengeance. The Orlaun taxmen did not come out of the trees and return her estate to her possession.

Grandmaster Woshan was not there to offer her any congratulations for being a fine student. Her parents remained long gone, as dead as the beaten halfling lying before her.

Was it really a victory anyway? What heroic purpose had Montanya really given to the world? In her heart she knew it was not any desire for heroism that had pushed her along this path. Heroics were only a glorified excuse to justify her need to hunt thieves and hurt them. It had been an excuse to thrash Kemora bloody until her small heart no longer beat.

This was the ending she sought, yet her life's pursuit seemed empty. Montanya felt envious in regards to Sondra, and that small glance she had into another person's life. At the very least, Sondra had put food in front of starving people, earning a smile from strangers for her selfless work. The other woman continued her task when thanks were not forthcoming. For all her criticism of Sondra, the world would miss Sondra, but it would not miss Montanya. The world may indeed be a better place without a rogue like Kemora Quickfeet, yet Montanya was ashamed to think she had bludgeoned to death someone roughly half her height.

Montanya slid to the base of a tree with a shuddering sigh. The poison within her spread unhindered by her skills. She hardly cared about it. The chiaso allowed the poison run its course.

In her thoughts, the young girl named Montanya su Troyeal bara Westonhout had died the same night as her parents. The heartbroken warrior who had borrowed her body afterward was willing to let the poison return the girl's spirit back to her parents.

**CHAPTER 33**     **"Trestan, Where is Your Sword?"**

Cat discovered, much to her relief, that she was not dead. Maybe she had Trestan to thank for it. He held her as miraculous healing energies flowed into her body.

"Are you feeling well, Cat? We need to move quick if you can manage it." Cat could see the worry filling his lovely brown eyes.

After a slight pause, in which she examined the hurts of her body, she nodded. Cat rose to her feet. Foyren lie dead a few feet away. Her stab had indeed been fatal. One hand went to her head, feeling around the tiara.

"I thought I was dead for sure," she stated as she felt for any remnant wound.

Trestan shrugged, "A god must have been looking out for you. I don't know what hit you but it left a small bump under the *Taef' Adorina*."

"A small bump?" Cat was incredulous, given the nature of the blow she had received. As her fingers felt the thin gold loops in the tiara, she couldn't find any deformities from the hit.

"We have nay time to stop. I know where the relics are, and Savannah knows that I can't really fight this day or I lose my faith. We have to beat her to the relics and run with them."

Cat retrieved her rapier and her bow. Together they ran in the direction Trestan's senses took him. They occasionally heard other noises nearby, but stayed focused on the course that would take them to the relics.

"What if they find us while at the relics? What if they have beaten us there?" Cat asked.

Trestan shook his head helplessly as he ran. "We can only pray for swiftness. I will be useless in any combat with them. We'll have to grab the relics and run."

Squire Trestan could feel the worry in Cat's heart as he spoke. She knew he had to honor his goddess with a peaceful heart this day. In answer to her unspoken concerns, Trestan said, "We need to have faith in Abriana. Just like you told me the day of the Embarking."

That faith seemed misplaced a short time later, when Trestan and Cat abruptly halted within sight of Savannah and Revwar. The two antagonists were picking up cloth sacks amidst a field of spoiled food.

Savannah and Revwar remained unaware of their adversaries at first. The abbess of DeLaris' head jolted up, though not due to perceiving Cat or Trestan. Revwar noticed the shock in her eyes. She turned her skull helm toward him as she explained, "I just felt Kemora die. Already a *Karet-Atriul* is recovering her soul."

Revwar straightened triumphantly, holding a sack. "This is it! Both relics are inside. How do you know about Kemora?"

Savannah replied, "I keep a link on all of you, just enough to let me know if one of my companions decides to leave this world before me. Kemora's link ended with the coldness of death."

"We are not alone," Revwar was saying, before Savannah's sentence finished.

The opposing parties faced each other. A fair stretch of ground lie between them. It was too much wild greenery to run across safely under the assault of either a wizard or archer. As Revwar tucked the bag into his belt, Trestan and Cat realized it was too far a distance to make any attempt at stealing the relics and escaping. Cat had her bow strung and a hand poised to grab an arrow from her quiver. Revwar had his pouches of reagents handy. Savannah's flail still glowed with dark enchantments, though the abbess had a number of ranged miracles at her disposal. Trestan's empty hands flexed nervously. His minotaur-head hammer sat in a ring at his belt, yet he was forbidden to use it. Without his sword, residing on Savannah's belt, Trestan only had defensive prayers available.

The quiet, tense staring match shattered as a pair of figures burst from the bushes on the side. The first figure's respectable Orlaun fashion trailed loosely behind him, having come undone by the chase. Jentan Mollamos ran while out of breath. The blousy, lacy sleeve on one arm was dampened with blood; cradled ineffectively as he moved. Sweat matted the formerly well-groomed hair, while his cheeks were flushed red from exhaustion. Chasing the wizard, Sondra's face was flush as she wielded a mace. Sondra breathed only slightly easier as the gap closed within an arm's reach.

"Help me…help…" Jentan gasped through a dry throat.

He was interrupted as Sondra's free hand finally gripped the back of his outer robe. His upper body jerked back as she raised her mace. Jentan turned as he was caught, raising his uninjured arm to fire the wand in that hand. He shouted a triggering word of power even as Sondra screamed in rage. The powerful bolt missed the woman, striking high into the trees. Her mace clubbed him as they both rolled into tall grass.

Savannah reacted as fast as it took to cast a miracle. Savannah disappeared into thin air as Sondra, on her knees, raised her mace and struck Jentan. Trestan ran forward, knowing the abbess' trick. Revwar sent a bolt hurtling toward the paladin and the infiltrator. Fire ignited the grass and bushes, separating them from the action. The last thing Trestan saw clearly was Savannah approaching Sondra from behind.

Although Abriana's chosen and the half-elf were in no position to see all of the action, Sondra's mace crashed down a third time. Jentan's skull crumpled from the continuous impacts. Sondra would have given him more blows in retaliation for the death of her dreams, but Savannah attacked her from behind. Cat observed Savannah touching the back of the acolyte of Ganden. Sondra's muscles went slack under a paralyzing effect. Trestan and Cat knew from experience that Savannah's miracle was not deadly by itself, but the younger cleric would be unable to move or speak for several minutes.

Between them and their enemy, the smaller greenery had been set ablaze. If Savannah wanted to finish Ganden's faithful, there was nothing they could do in time. The abbess of Death showed more interest in her fallen cohort. Savannah glanced at his crushed skull, but it only confirmed what her earlier miracle link had already told her. Life had fled.

An arrow launched from Cat barely clipped an opening in Savannah's helm. A glance toward the companions compelled Savannah to move on to her main goal with all speed. Savannah ran back to Revwar, shaking her head to indicate Jentan's fate. She muttered, "I am not so strong yet as to bring back the dead on my own, at least as anything more than an unthinking zombie."

The elf wizard had already deduced, from her lack of any attempt at healing, that the mentalist had joined Kemora in the next life. With their two most supporting members gone, and Foyren likely no longer their ally with Jentan dead, the odds were turning against them.

Revwar dipped fingers into the next magic pouch. "Let us be gone from this place while we have the stones. We have nay reason to risk injury in a fight."

The abbess of DeLaris nodded even as one of Cat's arrows bounced off of Revwar's magical robe. The elf wizard finally showed his irritation. "Hold these a moment," he handed her the bag with the relics, "I don't want my departure interrupted by her aim."

Savannah stood partially blocking the companions' view of the wizard. Likewise, Trestan stood to protect Cat as she readied another arrow. There was little more the young man could do.

Revwar released his spell. Trestan and Cat watched as a sphere of ice trailed snow like a comet. The spell fired up into the air, disappearing in the branches above. Unsure why the wizard was aiming into the sky, they looked on in alarm as he lowered his gaze their direction and started casting again. Trestan recognized the spell. The paladin-aspirant prayed to Abriana. In moments a spiritual shield formed once again on his forearm. Revwar's second spell lanced straight at Cat in a narrow, deadly beam. The beam found only the shield of Abriana blocking its path. As always, the shield disappeared after deflecting the magical attack.

The straightforward attack distracted them from realizing the tactics involving the first spell. Even as Trestan's defensive shield evaporated to nothing, the icy comet dropped on them from the canopy above. Cat held her bow ready for a shot when Trestan jumped in the way. He had nothing ready to shield her except his own armored body.

His weight drove Cat to the ground as she heard the ice ball shatter. Dozens of sharp icicles launched in deadly arcs. Her half-elf ears heard shards thumping into the ground, lancing into branches, and a few hitting Trestan's armor with a metallic ring. The young man let out a grunt as he felt the impacts.

Trestan tried to roll off of Cat when he was done, but the effort pained him greatly. Cat slipped out from under him without help. Her heart nearly skipped a beat as she worried about his injuries. She doubted there was a luxury of time to check him before Revwar would be able to throw something deadlier at them.

Revwar had used the time to cast an entirely different type of spell. Cat refitted an arrow to her bow as the wizard's cloak spread out like great, black wings. Savannah hugged his body, ready to be carried away. They were set to make an escape rather than a fight.

For Revwar, the attempt was made not a moment too soon. Another enemy came stumbling out of the trees. Lindon Taleweaver staggered into view. His wide-brimmed hat looked as if someone had sat on it. His clothes were ruffled, scorch-marked, and blood-stained. Whatever injuries had caused the blood seemed to have been partially healed by some means. He still walked with a limp. The minstrel had his smallsword in hand when he first appeared. Upon seeing Revwar and Savannah preparing to take flight, he allowed the sword to dangle from his wrist as he brought the wooden flute to his lips.

Revwar and Savannah soared from the ground, content to escape with the relics. Lindon made a feeble attempt to bring the ferocity of the wind upon them before they were out of reach. If anything, he only succeeded in bringing down Cat's arrow.

The silver-haired wizard and his darkly armored accomplice flew out of range, quickly removing them from sight.

*      *      *      *      *

Lindon arrived close enough to Sondra to spot her lying in the grass. The minstrel went to check on her. Cat was fairly sure that the woman was only temporarily paralyzed unless Savannah had learned some new tricks over the years. Cat turned her own concerned eyes toward Trestan.

He was still on the ground. His body sprawled in a way that slightly propped him up from a prone position. From her angle, Cat noticed the extent of his injuries. The young man's metal plates had dents in a few areas. While those plates served to protect him, the areas covered by a mixture of chain and leather fared poorly. One icicle protruded from a shoulder. Another bloodied shard stood embedded in his leg. While there were other puncture wounds visible, those two were leaking a lot of blood. Beyond those shards, Cat had no way of knowing how many might be embedded in wounds.

Cat lost all concern for the relics as her worries shifted to her love. The half-elf dropped to her knees by his side, trying to make eye contact with him. His eyelids drooped past his irises. He barely clung to consciousness. His lips moved as if trying to say something, but Cat's sensitive hearing only picked up gibberish.

"Trestan! Focus on my words! Hear my voice, please." When he didn't respond right away, she dared to gently shake him. He flinched from the pain in his shoulder, but it served to open his eyes more. "Trestan, you have to heal yourself. Pray to Abriana to seal these wounds."

His words were a stuttered whisper, "Cat…spirit…will you?…"

Cat tried to fight back panic while listening to his rambling nonsense. Her normally nimble fingers fumbled drawing out a cloth. Her hands pressed it against one of his wounds.

She looked up to see Lindon running across smoldering grass toward her. She yelled, "Sondra is paralyzed, isn't she?"

Lindon nodded, "Seems so, her eyes followed me…and her fingers twitched…she's breathing, but she can't seem to do more than that. Her clothes appear bloodied from earlier injuries, but those have been healed somehow."

"I need that satchel of hers. We need to find a healing potion." When Lindon turned, Cat fired off another question. "Do you have anything like that on you?"

Lindon held out his arms helplessly, "Nay, I used what I had. Minstrels can regenerate our own wounds to a point, but it only works on the performer."

Cat bandaged Trestan's wounds, but she feared it wasn't enough. Trestan had already lost a lot of blood. Once, she had lain dying in his arms. Now Cat was on the opposite side of the same situation. She felt helpless.

Lindon ran over, carrying the satchel. "There are bandages inside, and medicinal herbs I don't recognize. I'm afraid I don't see any marked as healing potions."

Even as he offered it, she tore it from his hands. Cat upended the contents on the ground. Bloody hands sorted through several vials. All were labeled, and each label added to her frown. Her hopes were sinking fast. "What about Sondra?"

The minstrel shrugged, "She seems quite incapacitated. I doubt she will be able to help for several minutes. She does not bear any outward wounds, only the hindering effects of the paralysis. I don't have any solutions that will grant her a quicker recovery."

The half-elf threw down the latest herb vial with an audible growl, betraying her anger. Lindon put pressure on Trestan's wounds as Cat tried to think up options. The nightmare, instilled by Jentan earlier, was becoming a reality. Trestan's life was slipping from her. If she didn't find a way to heal him, she would be left with a grave. She would also suffer a fair amount of guilt that she had allowed her fears of their aging to interfere with committing all her love to him.

The solution came to her. She recalled the endured pain when using the healing powers of the Sword of the Spirit on the woman in Troutbrook. She would be willing to suffer such pain again if it could stabilize Trestan's injuries. A loan of sustaining life-force was an easy sacrifice to choose. Cat reached for the sword handle, but found an empty scabbard on his back.

Though Trestan could not hear her, a disbelieving Cat could not help but ask of him. "Trestan, where is your sword?"

*      *      *      *      *

The robe gave a final flap of air as Revwar and Savannah safely touched down. They were not far from the debris field of the *Doranil Star*. As they stepped apart, Savannah readjusted the angle of the elf blade tucked in her belt. Revwar patted the bag containing the relic stones once more, as if he needed reassurance that they had indeed obtained their goal.

A teleport circle lie before them, inscribed by Revwar during the night. It was a matching copy of the decayed circle he had created on the ship. Another copy was back in a secret area near Orlaun. The wizard paused to reexamine the circle for accuracy.

Savannah couldn't pass up a comment. "So, what happens, after all this time, if the circle near Orlaun has been tampered somehow?"

Revwar's yellow eyes flashed at her, "Please don't even think about it. I wouldn't envy trying to escape back through Faer'Seelie woods, racing to some friendly outpost, and trying to get to a boat before they track us down."

"And they can't follow us through this?" The blonde abbess indicated the arcane portal.

"Nay," the elf was quick to respond. "The moment we are safe back on Quoros, I will destroy the teleport circle there. Without its twin, a teleport circle is just mere decoration."

After a few more moments of consultation, Revwar announced it was time to proceed. Though they had lost two valuable allies, the goal had been achieved. Revwar and Savannah had captured the weapons which they viewed as stolen. The goddess DeLaris and her undisclosed partner were now in control of all three Earthrin Stones with plans in place for an invasion. Despite gods such as Ganden, Yestreal, and Abriana being aware that fell deeds were being committed, the ambitious goddess and her cohort were playing by the rules of the Covenant. Mortals would now be the sole instruments in this new struggle for power.

Two such mortals, Revwar and Savannah, had played their part admirably. As the wizard cast his spell, the two of them teleported off of the Wilder continent. They reappeared hundreds of miles away an instant later, and promptly removed the teleport circle that could be used to pursue them.

*         *         *         *         *

"Trestan, please come back to me." Cat spoke into his ear.

There was no response. His breathing labored; blood still ran down his body. Cat and Lindon had done all they could to mend the wounds. The ice shards protruding from his flesh, which they dared not remove, started to melt away at a fast rate. Cat's fingers barely felt his pulse. She could hear Sondra trying to speak, but the abbess' paralyzing miracle kept her muscles slack.

Lindon whispered, "We may lose him before she can recover. I have nay talents to help with his injuries."

Cat bowed her head. Tears appeared, running down her smooth cheeks. She felt sorry that she had ever kept any distance between them. She cursed her own hesitancy and age-related fears. At that moment, she wanted nothing more than to be at his side no matter what the future would bring. The half-elf leaned her head on one of her hands for support as she lost her composure.

She felt the golden knots of the *Taef' Adorina* under her fingers. It had been Trestan's most precious gift to her. Forged in secret during their first summer, under the direction of the wizard Korrelothar, and molded in the same pattern as the inscribed elvish weave on his sword.

Cat's head jerked up with a gasp. Lindon noticed Cat's change in expression, as she ran her fingers over the tiara. It surprised him as she leaned forward with renewed zeal, placing her hands over Trestan.

Cat realized she was acting on a hunch, but she had nothing to lose. Just as she had used the sword once, she called upon the tiara to do the same. Cat willed her life energy into Trestan. For a moment, she wasn't sure if it would work. When the sensation of pain traveled down the length of her entire body, she wanted to cry out in joy. It was agonizing yet wonderful, for through her suffering she felt her life feed Trestan's energy. Wounds closed over, sealing the loss of blood. The two largest icicles were pushed out of the skin as those wounds party regenerated. In return for her sacrifice, Cat felt the stabbing sensation of several ice shards.

Lindon watched with interest as Cat contorted in pain, all the while releasing a pained smile. Trestan's wounds stopped bleeding. Color had come back to his face; he began to stir. Yet Cat screamed and writhed as if a brand of hot iron pierced her body. Trestan's eyes opened even as Cat released her connection and fell beside him.

The paladin-aspirant looked at her in alarm, the weariness from his own injuries still lurked in his eyes. She remained conscious, just barely, draping an arm over him. She whispered in a weary tone, "Call upon Abriana. You have to finish the healing for both of us."

Trestan did as she asked without hesitation, soliciting the healing miracle of his goddess. He restored Cat's vitality first. Though she bore no outward physical marks, her insides had suffered damage equivalent to that which had been healed in Trestan. Having used his healing and miracles earlier, it limited what he could accomplish. He still managed to mend most of the damage done to him and his beloved. It left him tired, but only requiring a decent rest.

After Trestan's efforts had been exhausted, Lindon was able to assist Sondra in joining them. The paralysis miracle left Sondra weak in the legs, yet she would recover shortly. The young woman stayed silent, holding her mace in one hand and her healing satchel in another. She looked afraid, as if she would need to use either at any given moment. There was something more in her expression that neither Trestan nor Cat missed. The young woman kept looking at the stains on her mace. She would have to come to grips with the death of a man by her hands.

Trestan looked to Cat with confusion in his eyes. "How did you heal me? I felt you pulling me back from the dark, yet I remain confused as to how you did it."

Cat beamed a weary smile in return. She lifted the golden tiara off her head and offered it to him for inspection. "I was hit on the head hard enough that I should have died, yet the tiara and my scalp came away virtually unscathed."

Trestan looked over the *Taef' Adorina* in his hands. "I'm still…unsure what you mean."

Cat giggled, "You forged this using the patterns and runes carved into your magic sword, under the guidance and assistance of a wizard. It seems Korrelothar put something into this gift that even you didn't know."

By the amazement in Trestan's brown eyes, she knew she was right. He came to the right conclusion, "This tiara acquired the power to heal if offering one's own health in sacrifice, like my sword? And it is enchanted enough to guard your head against a powerful strike?"

Cat nodded. Her smile disappeared just as quickly as she remembered something troubling. "Trestan, where is your sword?"

"Savannah took it."

The words struck Katressa hard. Trestan's valuable weapon, a legacy of his mentor and friend, was in the hands of an evil woman whom had partaken in that man's death.

"I grow concerned," Lindon admitted, "that the elf wizard and the DeLaris cleric have had ample time to get a head start on us. Did they get away with the relics?"

Trestan nodded, "The guidance spell was still active. The Earthrin Stones were in a bag on Revwar's belt when he flew away. I don't sense the stones anymore, so they must be too far away."

Cat raised an eyebrow at Trestan, "How did you know their name? I only translated that from the scroll last night and I didn't mention them yet."

"Savannah told me their name, but that won't be of any help to us at the moment." Trestan released a sigh, "They have gone beyond the reach of my miracle. Likely Revwar and Savannah are running with their prize, trying to reach their goal…otherwise they could have made more of an attempt to finish us."

Trestan unsteadily got to his feet for the first time since his injury. "I think our immediate concerns should be reserved for our missing companions. Cassyli and Montanya are around here somewhere, likely in need of help. Be watchful for that halfling rogue, she could be anywhere."

"And Cassyli's brother?" Lindon looked around the woods.

Cat wasn't able to offer an answer, so Trestan provided his. "He was also a casualty."

**CHAPTER 34**          **"Recovery and Future Plans"**


The companions spread out to search for their missing friends. Eventually, Trestan and Cat found where Cassyli lie injured. Trestan once more called forth his healing powers. By this time, the meager healing he could channel served only to get Cassyli mobile and relieve some of the pain. They informed him of the loss of his brother, without going into details. He appeared to be in the process of grieving for his loss already. The scout lamented that Foyren had been gone the moment the mentalist corrupted his reasoning.

Lindon and Sondra had gone off in different directions looking for their missing friends. They even dared to call out names, preferring to find any wounded companions faster despite the risk of being discovered by any hidden enemies.

Sondra, alone, found Montanya propped against a tree next to the beaten rogue. The silence of the scene, and the lack of movement, disturbed the acolyte. The halfling certainly looked dead. The domid's bloody face and the matching red stains on Montanya's knuckles gave testimony to how brutally she had died.

Montanya looked almost unharmed by comparison, yet gave every outward appearance that death had taken her. Her expression betrayed empty sadness. Her heavy eyelids were almost closed. It sent a chill to Sondra's heart. Maybe it was the shared memories, but Sondra realized she cared for this youth.

Sondra moved her hands slightly, tracing a form in the air as she spoke a prayer. The minor miracle served clerics when searching a battlefield, trying to sort the dying from the dead, and responding to those in the most need of healing. The miracle confirmed the rogue's death. Sondra's hopes lifted when she felt Montanya's life force supporting a heartbeat. The miracle revealed the nature of the poison. Ganden's acolyte had arrived without time to spare, for the young chiaso was surrendering her hold on life.

Sondra's hands went into her leather satchel. She pulled out numerous items to help nullify the poison and give strength to Montanya's body. The young priestess went into a state of prayer, calling for miracles to combat the deadly toxin. It strained her mental exhaustion, but she bore it well. She had rarely healed anyone so close to death, and certainly never without Mother Evine by her side. Even as she went through the healing process, Sondra could feel that her talents had improved. She seemed able to accomplish more with her faith due to the trials of the journey.

Montanya stirred awake. Greenish-blue eyes peered out from the perspiration-soaked red strands clinging to her face. The chiaso watched Sondra's hands floating over her body. Montanya noted a soft glow illuminating those same hands as the healing took place. Sondra's posture showed exhaustion from the toll.

Montanya felt sorry for the effort undertaken on her behalf. "I was ready to die. You could have just left me here."

Sondra peered at Montanya with concerned eyes, but did not lessen her efforts at healing. She weighed the words against the expression in the chiaso's eyes. The follower of Ganden wondered if Montanya felt remorse for her existence, or was rebuking Sondra's heals once again.

Sondra tried to give a simple answer. "If you want to die, there are many ways to do so in this world. Today will not be your day."

Montanya let her eyes slide downward, looking beyond Sondra's healing hands. She spoke with all honesty. "I died a long time ago, Sondra. I died inside and buried my heart. Only my passion for hatred...my desire for some meaningful revenge...kept my spirit alive."

Sondra listened to the words. They held a certain meaning for her as well, after giving so many years for others. The blonde woman expected that Montanya had more to say, so she quietly focused on expelling the poison out of the wound.

Montanya brushed some strands off of her face. Her voice came barely above a whisper. "There is a memory you have, from a festival long ago..."

Sondra started to blush as Montanya talked. She had come so close to this woman once they exchanged memories and began to understand their differences; however, it was a little embarrassing to have someone intimately exposed to her private thoughts and moments.

Montanya continued, "There was a young man, trying to keep warm from the cold. Music played in the sanctuary. He merely requested that you dance with him, and he whisked you around the room before you could refuse."

Sondra remembered the memory clearly. She would have refused the dance, yet once the young man held her close, all the writings from those romantic books she read had sparked a longing within her. It had been a wonderful dance, and it had left an impressionable memory on her.

When Montanya didn't continue, Sondra prompted her for more. "Please go on. Finish what you were trying to say."

Montanya shed a tear. "I've never danced with a boy. I've never been held close like that by anyone since the death of my parents. I've never even dreamed of love."

Sondra had healed to the best of her abilities. She could expend no more effort, yet she continued to look busy as she allowed Montanya to clear her thoughts.

"I feel...empty." Montanya's smooth face, normally distorted by her customary sneer, fell to one of the saddest expressions Sondra had ever seen. "The only motivating passion in my life has driven me to a place worse than any I have ever gone. My quest for vengeance hurt me more than any thief could have. The most precious thing they couldn't directly steal, I gave to them. I robbed myself of my own freedom."

"Sounds like something I could admit to myself as well." Sondra shrugged.

Montanya looked up, "You were free to make a choice, and you made a good one. You have helped people, Sondra, more than I have."

Sondra visibly disagreed, shaking her head. "I made a 'good' choice for the wrong reasons. I really felt like my life was not mine to control. I lost everything when my parents died in that fire. The kids I knew reinforced the message that I would never be anyone of importance. I almost died huddled in cold streets. The only ones to show kindness were the clerics of Ganden."

Sondra paused, unsure how to express her feelings. Montanya waited in silence until the acolyte continued. "We both made mistakes when we were young. We both deluded ourselves under the guise of selflessness."

Montanya's brow furrowed as she tried to make sense of those words. Sondra sat back on her heels as she tried to sort through her meanings. "I didn't go into the priesthood because I wanted it. Quite the opposite, I felt that I was deserting my life. I wanted to repay the church, and my life was all I had to give. I justified it by all the good done by Ganden's clergy. That's what we both did, you and I, justified the easy decisions by proclaiming we were following a great purpose.

"I figured I could be someone to myself, yet let others around me think what they may, even reinforce their view that I never succeeded. Told myself that I didn't try to succeed, therefore I didn't fail. I did accomplish one achievement: helping to feed and clothe people. It was a noble thing, was it not? Yet, I am finding out that my moral path was tread for less-than-noble reasons. I really let go of everything I hoped to be, all for the sake of a debt to others."

Sondra held her hands before her face. "It was always easier to be someone else's hands, rather than have only myself to answer. Easier to live thinking I had sacrificed myself to some greater good. I only isolated myself from enjoying the life around me."

When Sondra turned her eyes to Montanya, and the chiaso could see the hurt hidden under that look, it made the rest easy to understand. The red-haired youth nodded, "As I misled myself. I justified the good I could do ridding the world of thieves, allowing myself a violent way to fuel my anger. My view should have made it easy to walk the path of revenge without feeling regret."

Her greenish-blue eyes looked upon the battered rogue's corpse. "Yet I do have regrets. The world is a better place without Kemora. As for myself, is the world better off with or without me?"

Sondra gently placed a hand on Montanya's outstretched leg. "Do not be hard on yourself. Do not long for death, either. Our souls were hurt, so we buried our hurts under moral superiority, tucking away most of our humanity in the process. I feel that this discovery will make us better and stronger."

"What of your relationship to Ganden?"

Sondra tried a weak smile, "It will change, but for reasons beneficial to us both. I won't turn from the church, for it is my home. What I *will* change, is how I go about the rest of my life and duties."

Sondra stared into Montanya's eyes, "And you?"

Montanya had looked so despondent earlier, and yet the talk with Sondra seemed to lift some weight from her body. The red-haired youth responded, "I don't know what I will do, or where I will be a year from now. All I know is that I need to change a number of things about myself. If I don't, then I might as well have died next to my parents."

Sondra gave her a reassuring squeeze on the healed leg, and then moved to return several belongings to her satchel. Montanya reached out and grabbed her arm gently to get her attention. "I will start with what I owe you."

The acolyte glanced up in surprise. She was about to say that Montanya didn't owe her anything. She stopped short of speaking when she noticed the seriousness in the younger woman's look.

The young noble-turned-warrior said the words that Sondra longed to hear.

"I thank you, over and over again, for all you have done for me. I thank you for bringing me back from death's door more than once. I thank you for every healing prayer you have said over my wounds. I thank you for the effort you put into serving me a meal when I was a strange stowaway locked in a brig. I thank you for finding someone who could get me out of that cell. I thank you for helping me see my mistakes in life. Lastly, I thank you for being my friend."

Sondra didn't know what to say. She opted to lean forward and give Montanya a big hug, which was returned in earnest. Montanya had never been held in any kind of caring hug since the death of her parents. They stayed in that pose for some time, as each had a lot to think over, yet little that needed to be said.

As they parted the embrace, Montanya's nose wrinkled slightly. The chiaso spoke before she considered her words. "It smells like you wet yourself or something."

Sondra went on the defensive immediately. "One of them used a paralysis spell on me. Such spells often have the effect of relaxing the bladder muscles as well."

"You soiled your bottoms?!"

Sondra gave Montanya a hard stare. The chiaso's lips quivered in a visible effort to hold back laughter. The cleric sat back with a sigh as Montanya gave in to a giggling fit.

"I'm sorry," Montanya tried to speak between fits of laughter, "It sounds terrible…it must have been bad…I'm trying not to laugh!"

Sondra blushed as she waited for the younger woman to get over her amusement. She huffed, "Well, when you're ready, we should find our way back to the others."

When the two women rose to leave the spot, Montanya stopped briefly to reclaim her locket. She cradled it close before returning it to her own neck. Montanya also retrieved the stolen illusionary mask from Kemora. She was stepping away when Sondra pointed out the seemingly forgotten pink ribbon, lying on the ground.

Montanya made no move to retrieve it. She spent a moment staring at the cloth as the wind tugged at one end. "That torn piece of fabric only served to help bolster my anger all these years. I have better ways of remembering my mother."

The two went to relocate the others, leaving the pink fabric and Kemora's corpse behind.

*       *       *       *       *

In a sheltered area of the woods, amidst the fallen debris of the ship, a small campfire burned. With the nighttime blanket of stars overhead and no more sign of their adversaries, the companions settled together to rest. Not all of their wounds had been mended. Several bore bruises and scars along with temporary bandages. Those who could heal could do no more without rest. Weariness had burdened them all, yet sleep eluded them.

Sondra Oskires sorted Ganden's religious relics. She reverently laid each on a ripped mast placed on the ground. The holy items of Ganden had been salvaged under the last few rays of sunlight. The blonde woman responded to the conversation at hand even as she cradled a recovered trinket. "I can't say that I've had much experience with such magic. I heard about teleport circles, but I can't say that I've ever seen one."

Trestan nodded, glancing to the side where Cassyli sat. The elf had been silent all day. He sat beside the shrouded body of his brother in quiet mourning. Something about that scene encouraged Trestan to move closer to the half-elf at his side. As he snuggled against her lithe form, he turned his attention over to Lindon.

Trestan asked the minstrel, "So, we're assuming that's what it was? Arcane sciences happened to be my weak subject at the seminary. If it was their escape, where could they be?"

The red-bearded musician was dusting off the wide brim of his hat. Lindon Taleweaver visualized the circular marking they had found on the forest floor after the fight. "I'm very sure that was the design, though I'm nay expert on it either. As far as their escape, they would have gone wherever the circle's twin waited. Likely, a civilized area back on Quoros…but certainly not on this continent."

Wearing the golden tiara atop her head, Cat raised one eyebrow. Her helmet had been reclaimed, yet it sat abandoned to one side. The half-elf doubted she would ever need the helmet again, for the *Taef' Adorina* seemed to offer magical protection that the headgear lacked.

She interrupted, "Why do you presume that? They could have made a similar circle anywhere, correct?"

"Two reasons," Lindon held up two fingers, tapping them with his other hand as he spoke. "First, you need to build one circle as a twin to the other circle. If you build it in the wilderness, then anything, like wild animals, could disturb the older circle and render it useless. Second, I'm guessing the circle was their original escape plan if they meant to abandon the divine chariot as it fell from the skies. If so, then they would have made the other circle in a secure location back in Orlaun."

Cat sighed. She hated the thought that the other band had beaten them to their goal and succeeded in escaping. Her emerald eyes looked around the campfire at her companions. They had all come through intact, so she appreciated that blessing. Some still had unseen injuries. She watched Montanya stare into the fire, saying nothing. The human youth secluded herself in her thoughts, but she occasionally fidgeted with a mask in her lap.

Despite their efforts, the main goal had escaped, and Cat had been forced to slay Foyren in defending herself. Cassyli seemed to hold no blame against her for her actions. He had been severely beaten by Foyren; savagely attacked by one so disillusioned that he hadn't recognized his own brother until it was nearly too late.

Cat sighed, "We failed. They have all three relics and they made their escape to gods know where. Who knows what evil will come of this?"

"All is not lost," Trestan said. "Savannah engaged me in a duel of the minds. I was able to see into her future plans, even as she dug for knowledge in my thoughts."

The champion of Abriana leaned forward, recalling the images glimpsed in his opponent's mind. "I saw a fortress at the edge of civilized lands. I know that it resides on the continent of Shard, and that it is simply called Fortress Stone. I saw the coming of winter heralded by the approach of a horde of angry tribes. That is where they plan to strike next, hoping to use that castle as a base to launch a greater invasion."

Lindon was aghast, "DeLaris means to invade the realm? The lands are only now starting to be fruitful after all the years of peace imposed by the Covenant. I hate to think of the implications another war between gods will bring. Will this start another Godswars?"

Trestan hung his head. "One might think so. However, she's using a mortal emissary to carry out her plans. That may lie within the constraints of the Covenant."

Cat was considering the miles between them and their goal, for she had once seen the castle of which Trestan spoke. "It is a long trip. We will have to find a trading outpost on the coastline, find passage to Orlaun, and voyage from there."

"We have some things that need to be done along the way."

Cat looked to Trestan, "Like?"

Trestan continued. "I have a few stops to make. First, I must get to Petrow and his family. Savannah claimed his life four years ago, but she didn't finish the job. Since then, Petrow has fathered two children and his wife is carrying their third. Savannah entered my mind to find out where Petrow lives, and she found her answers."

Sondra gasped at the news, "A cleric of DeLaris allowed someone to live? The pain on her must be terrible! She will kill the family."

Cat put her hands on Trestan's shoulder, "I care for Petrow and his family, yet the whole realm is at risk, Tres. Are you sure we have the time to go to Troutbrook?"

Trestan nodded, "We have a few months to go before it will get cold. The tribes will come when it is near winter. That will give us the time to visit and then go through Kashmer. We will need help from there, and I must return."

Cat noticed the golden glow of his ring. "Your ring is whole!"

Abriana's champion held up Faithful's Companion for her to see. Not a single symbol marred its surface. "I passed the final test today. I was tempted to bring arms against my enemies…and I very nearly did so had not Savannah disarmed me…yet I held back in honor of this holy day. I held my faith in Abriana, and thus my trials of faith are over. I am ready to go back to Kashmer, become a full paladin, and do what I must. The realm is at stake, we will need to get help to face the threat. The best place to look might be there."

Cat leaned over, hugging and kissing Trestan at his accomplishment.

When they separated, Cat fished a few items from her belt. In one hand she held the leather scroll that had been with the relics. In the other, she held her father's rune block. "I finished translating this, if anyone wants to finally know about the history of the Earthrin Stones."

"The Earthrin Stones?" Lindon tested the name on his tongue, already wondering how the name would fit into verse. "That is what we have been chasing?"

Cat nodded, "Aye. This scroll was a record of their creation and use in the Godswars, as well as information on why they were separated after the war. It also tells us which other deity may be helping DeLaris with her plans for conquest."

Lindon placed his hat back on his head, "Well now, I'm in the mood for a good story."

Sondra reverently set aside the artifacts she had been examining. "I am interested in a good tale, especially if it offers answers as to the loss of Ganden's vessel."

Montanya still said nothing, but her eyes lifted in curiosity.

Trestan assumed a more comfortable sitting position, one in which he could view Cat better. He smiled, "Abriana waits patiently to be enlightened."

Cat seemed to blush, as all the attention focused on her. She spread the scroll out before her eyes, setting the rune block beside it. She paused only to clear her throat.

*"Know ye elves that this be one of the three Earthrin Stones, entrusted to your care in the hopes that they are never again used in war. Yestreal chooses you to safeguard this terrible relic; a source of prosperity to some, and to others a means to destroy enemies. First, ye all should know about the history of these stones.*

*"They were fashioned from an unlikely alliance during the Godswars. Three gods commissioned their creation: Yestreal, DeLaris, and Mothrok..."*

**CHAPTER 35**          **"In the Gardens of Serud'Thanil"**

Katressa Bilil leaned closer to her reflection, though she marveled more at the mirror than her image. The magical creation offered testament to the craftsmanship of the elves of Serud'Thanil. The druids had woven their natura to somehow trap liquid water against a vertical frame. If one blew on it or touched it, ripples would spread across the surface. Once left undisturbed, the water quickly reformed back to a smooth surface. Katressa idly wondered how much it would cost to keep one. Even as she did, she knew the Faer'Seelie would never allow such a wonder to leave their lands.

Returning her thoughts to her own reflection, Cat was critical yet pleased with her appearance. At forty-one years of age, she appeared in the early spring of her life, thanks to her elven heritage. Of course, the down side was that elves would still consider her more as a youth than an adult.

She looked over the strands of her raven hair, approving how it flowed underneath the *Taef' Adorina*. Her hair finally felt vibrant and clean after so much time in the wild and the final fight which had taken place only days ago. She ran her fingers over her cheeks, feeling the softness granted by elven bath soaps. Even as she felt her skin, she approved her newly-trimmed nails.

Cat had gone through a lot of effort to look her best today. Her dress was made locally, purchased from elf merchants willing to overlook her Agora'Seelie ancestry as long as she had valuable goods to trade. Her dress glowed with the warmth of a spring garden, and a perfume gave it a scent to match. The half-elf fidgeted with her top, trying to show the perfect balance of cleavage to tease her lover. She also looked down to judge how much, and how little, the dress covered her legs.

Montanya's voice interrupted her thoughts. "You look lovely; I wouldn't worry about the dress. Still…I don't see why you persist in wearing your sword with your ensemble."

Cat glanced up at the mirror to see Montanya still standing behind her. The red-haired youth also dressed more formal than usual. She still wore clothing similar to the loose-fitting attire of the chiaso, yet she had added a decorative sash and wore her locket in the open. The youth's long hair hung braided again, held in place by an elf-made clasp.

Cat grinned at her, "You probably know more than me. I don't know what Trestan has planned, but he merely suggested that I be dressed for a special dinner. So, I am wearing a very nice dress and my fancy, silver rapier. I am an adventuress first and a lady second."

Montanya smiled, "Is that why you also hid a dagger between your thighs?"

It was unknown when Montanya last displayed any kind of smile, seeing her do so now brightened Cat's evening. The infiltrator laughed, "You saw that as well? It never hurts to be too careful." The thoughts of why she had to be careful sobered her mood slightly. "Trestan and I seem to be part of a secret war between the gods, so it's best to stay prepared for anything."

Montanya snorted at that, "I'm supposed to be your escort and bodyguard for the evening. Let me worry about your safety."

Cat smiled again. She busied herself a few more moments in front of the mirror, unsure what Trestan planned and why the strange requests had been made.

"I suppose I am as ready as I will ever be," Cat arose from the magical mirror with a twirl, allowing her dress to spin fancifully. "Lead me onward, my fair escort."

Montanya took the lead as they exited the room Cat and Trestan reserved in Assiernae. The magnificent structure was built high in the canopy over Serud'Thanil. Only a few honored guests of the city got the invitation to stay within its lovely confines. Cat wasn't sure if they qualified as honored guests, or if this was more to keep them secluded from most of the elf population, but she enjoyed it all the same. The druids and artisans of the city constantly added to the design. Sculptures of living wood surrounded garden terraces. Waterfalls ran down the gardens, dropping into pools, feeding a network of descending waterways. Cat knew from experience that the water came from specially designed leaves fostered by the elves. The leaves would catch much more water than needed by the tree during the rain, and then the branches could direct the runoff to feed the gardens. Indeed, many plants bloomed at this time of year. A myriad of flowers and scents grew as part of Assiernae.

Montanya led Katressa through the elf wonders to a vine-covered gate. This portion of the elevated garden could be, and currently was, cordoned off for private gatherings. Trestan seemed to have found a wonderful place to enjoy the nature of the elves' dwelling yet retain some sense of seclusion. Montanya stepped up to the gate, rang a bell, and with only a small pause opened the way for Katressa to pass.

Trestan stood in the garden, facing them with a smile as they entered. Like Cat, his choice of attire mixed formal and practical. He wore some of his armor, yet left portions uncovered to display an elven tunic and breeches. Cat noticed flowery designs adorning the tunic sleeves. Male elves wore such styles to display fertility and their closeness to nature. Trestan had his dark hair combed back. His necklace, bearing the coraross of Abriana, displayed openly. The only blemish upon his outfit was the empty scabbard he chose to wear.

His eyes greeted her warmly and brought forth a smile to match. He evidently liked what he saw when he looked at her, and her lover appeased Cat's tastes as well. Cat had the urge to take him to an even more secluded room, but he had gone through all this trouble for something important. The garden had been reserved, a variety of drinks offered, and food laid out on a table. Even the fact that Montanya had dressed for the occasion had Cat's interest kindled.

Montanya remained beside the gate as Cat went to greet her man. The half-elf thought to give him a quick kiss since they had company, but once she came close, Trestan enfolded his arms around her and kissed her until she was breathless. They stayed in the embrace, whispering sweet greetings back and forth. They left behind the worries of the road. Their thoughts focused on how little time they had been able to enjoy together since Trestan left the seminary.

When they did pull apart, they did so slowly, hands trailing each other to extend their contact. They sat down together for their meal. Before getting started, Trestan turned to Montanya. "Montanya, could we have a little entertainment please."

318

The chiaso nodded with a smile. Cat found herself nervous and excited as she simply waited to see what Trestan had planned for the evening. Montanya opened the gate to admit Lindon Taleweaver. The minstrel entered with mandolin in hand, strumming the notes of a tune. The gates closed again once he swept in the garden. He didn't go directly toward them, opting instead to idly wander around the terrace as he played some romantic tunes.

Cat giggled as she and Trestan enjoyed the food. They talked more than ate. Lindon switched playing between both of his flutes as well as his mandolin in the background. For Cat, it seemed to be the romantic time they had been deprived of after the Embarking, due to the sad news she had for Trestan about his home.

This was also a time in which they could express their feelings. Trestan said, at one point, "Cat, I know you have worried about the future. As Abriana is my witness, I can see nay other future than spending my life with you if you'll have me."

She paused briefly, deciding how best to respond to such a strong emotional statement. "It took me some time to understand my own heart. I don't mean that my feelings were in doubt, only that I hesitated about where my feelings would lead me. I was reluctant to get too close to you, Trestan, and yet I was already too close. I couldn't go forward or back without risking my heart."

Cat paused again, letting her emerald eyes look toward the greenery of the forest canopy. Trestan patiently waited for her to finish her message. She probably underestimated how much his emotions clung to every word. His heart and his feelings were on the line, but he had to know that Cat had come to a decision about their relationship. He trusted that she would answer in the way he expected, yet the small grains of uncertainty in his mind gave him stress.

She looked back to him, reaching out to squeeze his hand between her own. "Jentan cast that spell on me, one designed to make my worst nightmare come true. I saw your grave, and mourned my loss. If anything, it helped make me see that you are already the most important part of me. I can't turn away from you now, even to save myself pain years down the road. I've come too far with you, and I want to go farther down that road together. Even if it means watching you grow older while I stay young…I want to spend my days with you or I'll only be killing my heart. I love you."

She looked at him, begging for his acceptance of her feelings. Trestan leaned across the table and answered her with another kiss. They remained in that pose, becoming a statue of two lovers, losing themselves in their feelings.

"I love you *faunlessa*, and there is one thing that needs to be done to show you how much." Trestan turned toward Montanya, "Montanya, is there a spiritual guide around here somewhere? Maybe a priest of sorts?"

The youth smiled back, "I think I know where I can find one."

Lindon changed songs to one most often performed when a priest enters an assembly. Montanya opened the door, but then merely stood aside for the new guest. Sondra entered, wearing her official priestly vestments. These were the ceremonial robes she had tucked in her bags during her escape from the *Doranil Star*, though she wore several accouterments that had been stored in her healing satchel. Her look greatly differed from the rugged clothes stained across exploration of this land. As with the others, she responded with Trestan's request to dress her best for a special occasion. Sondra had already guessed at what was coming; the chosen of Ganden was honored to fulfill Trestan's request.

Sondra glided forward, stopping a respectful distance from the feast table. "As I have been summoned, so I stand. I take my place as a representative of Ganden, and as such I place his blessings on all here. Ganden stands as your witness."

"Witness?" Cat repeated, wondering about the use of that word.

Then the meaning of it all hit her. She recalled the questions Trestan had asked of elf relationships. She had told him their customs regarding certain events. Trestan had gone through a lot to arrange a special evening, and it was no longer a mystery to Cat's mind. In fact, her mind and heart fluttered with the realization that this was about to become a very special moment.

Trestan nodded to each of their companions. "Here in Laedelious' homeland, the tradition of the elves will now be honored. We now have a male friend as witness." Lindon continued to play nearby.

Trestan motioned toward the gate, "We also have a female friend as a witness." At his words, Montanya stood straight and tall.

"And now we have a spiritual guide." Trestan gave a slight bow to Sondra.

Cat had trouble figuring whether she was hot or cold. Her heart raced with nervous excitement. She suddenly felt like a little girl, trying to decide whether to smile or cry, where to put her hands, and what, if anything, she should say.

As smoothly as he could, Trestan slid off his bench and went down to one knee before Cat. He reached out, and took one of her smaller hands in his.

"Katressa Bilil, I pledge to remain faithful to you forever if you will have me. You fill my heart of all the longing I could ever want. I dream day and night of the moments we spend together. I ask for your hand in marriage, that we be joined in spiritbond before a year ends."

Trestan withdrew a curved piece of caleocht wood from a pocket. The workmanship on the bracelet was priceless. It detailed several images of Laedelious, Cat's goddess, sprinkled in gold dust. Emerald gems sparkled within the carvings…a gem Cat knew Trestan favored ever since looking into her eyes.

"I know that elves do not give such gifts for the oathbond. Among humans, it is expected to give a piece of jewelry that signifies the engagement. Please wear this if you would be my wife."

Trestan's heart laid bare for all to observe. Cat tried to hold a smile, but her emotions were choking her up. The proposal left the half-elf privateer quivering like a newborn fawn. She opened her mouth a few times, but seemed to have trouble forming words. Some sniffling and quick intakes of breath were the only sounds she could make as her hand rested in Trestan's. She finally grabbed a piece of linen from the table, dabbing her eyes and trying to swallow.

Her voice squeaked out, "Aye…I accept with all my heart, *faunlessa*. I would be yours for all the days if possible."

They rose as one. Lindon's mandolin strummed into an uplifting tune. Cat was still breaking down in tears, but she buried them against Trestan's chest. They embraced tightly, loosening only long enough that Cat could slide the bracelet over her wrist. Trestan helped dry her tears as she looked longingly into his eyes.

Sondra announced, rather quietly, "As Ganden has witnessed the offering of the oathbond and its acceptance, he offers his blessing unto this union. May you never forget your responsibilities to each other, and may your years be happy and prosperous."

With that, Sondra rejoined Montanya over by the garden gate, where they chatted happily in low tones. Cat and Trestan lingered in their embrace for a long time. When Lindon played some happy music, they shared dance after dance.

As Petrow had once told Trestan, "…Life comes on two sides of a coin, Trestan. You can't have the lucky side without the unlucky side, and if the lucky side happens to shine in your favor and brightens one day, you should live that day to the fullest."

For each of them: Cat, Trestan, Lindon, Sondra and Montanya, they had that one day to hold a celebration of life. They smiled together, shared jokes, and lived every moment like they hadn't in a long time. The merriment lasted well into the evening.

If they were worried about the battle that would soon begin, they hid it well. If Trestan and Cat were troubled that they wouldn't live to seal their spiritbond, they kept it shielded deep in their hearts. They hid any fears of the blood and fighting that awaited them down the road.

At least for a time, the newly engaged couple could enjoy the spirit of the moment, under the canopy of the sylvan city…and temporarily bury any fears arising from the plots of gods.

**Bonus material: Lindon Taleweaver's song, "A Tenth"**

A powerful lord with lots of land sat unhappy in his keep,
One day he encountered a gypsy offering him something to foresee,
"For a tenth of your lands, just a tenth!...I'll give you the future in a glance.
You'll see what's destined for you, isn't that worth a chance?"
The lord agreed and saw himself happy on one island out of ten,
And contented himself the vision would serve him well in the end.

The lord hunted his lands often but found the game amiss,
The taxman came on behalf of the king and offered him this,
"For a tenth of your lands, just a tenth!...The courts will offer a way,
We'll use the king's guards and laws to keep the poachers at bay."
The lord loved his hunting, so the acceptance passed his lips,
He issued permission and thus enjoyed his future hunting trips.

The lord had a plain daughter, whom he feared would never marry,
A handsome knight was willing, at the expense of a heavy dowry,
"For a tenth of your lands, just a tenth!...Your daughter I will wed.
As long as she pleases me, I'll keep her unto death."
The lord eagerly took the offer, getting her out of his hair.
He chuckled at his good fortune as he bid farewell to the pair.

The lord looked sadly into a mirror, seeing the aging of time.
An alchemist from afar offered him a potion spiced with thyme,
"For a tenth of your lands, just a tenth!...I'll give you beauty in a vial.
You'll grow old eventually, but not wrinkle in all that while."
The charisma of the lord was worth such a pittance to pay,
He took the potion and nay longer feared the advancing of his days.

The lord pushed away from his table a most unsatisfying meal,
A neighbor baron offered him an appetizing deal,
"For a tenth of your lands, just a tenth!...I'll find you a master chef.
You'll dine in such contentment, on your plate not a thing will be left."
The lord dined well from then on, never better had his stomach felt,
As day after day went by, he was often loosening his belt.

The lord strode in cloth garments as he walked the edge of his stead,
A local armorer stated he needed to protect his heart and head,
"For a tenth of your lands, just a tenth!...I'll make armor of unmatched steel,
Under its silver hue, you'll withstand any blows a foe may deal."
The lord's health was paramount, so he signed up right away,

And he got the finest shiny armor, and not much did it weigh.

The lord's armor was impressive, yet he stood without a sword,
He sent a summons to the city for the best smith to come forward.
"For a tenth of your lands, just a tenth!...I'll craft a blade pure and true,
With my forge's magic, no shield will stop it from passing through."
The lord asked the smith if such a weapon could possibly be made.
When it arrived, the lord spent hours admiring the blade.

The lord felt his humble, old manor was not built too impressive,
The stonemason agreed he should have something built more massive.
"For a tenth of your lands, just a tenth!...I'll build your wall and towers high.
Your peasants will be humbled under banners that scrape the sky."
The lord agreed right away and watched them drag in tons of stone.
In the highest parapet he marveled at the strength of his new home.

The lord's feet were weary from all the stairs and paths he tread,
A traveling merchant caravan offered him an alternative instead.
"For a tenth of your lands, just a tenth!...A champion stallion we'll provide,
Of the finest stock, nay other animal can match his powerful stride."
The lord easily accepted the mount and prepared the stable,
He frequently rode the horse down trails as fast as it was able.

Happy in his new lifestyle, the lord was visited by the clergy,
And for all his lavish means he was made to feel quite dirty.
"For a tenth of your lands, just a tenth!...A tithe gives salvation of the spirit,
It will buy land in the heavenly kingdom, for after death you'll need it."
The lord sighed, "I can't pay my last tenth, I've squandered the rest on whims.
Yet between myself and the gypsy,
The taxman and the knight,
The alchemist and the baron,
The armorer and the smith,
The mason and the caravan,
We'll make a trade with your kingdom's lord, to obtain a tenth of heaven from him!"

If you loved this book, then remember that authors live and prosper by good reviews on Amazon and Goodreads. Follow Trestan and Cat's adventures to a land on the frontier, where the threat of a new Godswars hangs in the balance:

**The Earthrin Stones book 3, Muster of Heroes**

Savannah had nothing but malice in her expression as she hovered above Petrow. "The Covenant didn't stop the Godswars; it just changed the rules."

Now Revwar and Savannah have the relics in their possession, and a secret army assembled from a multitude of misled believers. Together, it seems unlikely that they will be stopped. Trestan and Cat have discovered the nature of these terrible weapons, but they have to find their way out of the endless forests of Eyldiian.

Rallying against the impossible numbers and the weapons from the old war, the original Companions of the Relics reunite to defend their realm. All will suffer and some will die as they race to defend a fortress on the frontiers of civilization. Unbeknownst to its defenders, an army larger than anything that has been gathered in over a millennium marches toward it with fanatic zeal.

Failure could have higher stakes than the razing of that portion of Dhea Loral. The gods may elect to discard the peace-binding Covenant…forcing the realm into a second catastrophic Godswars.

## Appendix A - Reference to Elven nations and Tribes, (1250 AC)


Main Branches of the Elven People

**Faer'Seelie**- These include the elves that make their home in the Wilder continent, (known to them as Eyldiian).  Eyldiian is a heavily forested continent, allowing these elves to preserve their woodland origin and traditions. It is a mistake to call these elves feral or lacking in civilization…their society revolves around nature yet they are not a simple folk. These elves disturb nature as little as possible. They make their homes in trees, either shaping the trees to adapt to their needs, or allowing the trees to reshape their own needs. Their magic tends to favor natura, the natural magic present in the life on the land. They are more adapted to survival and conditions in the deep woods even more than the other tribes. Some clans of Faer'Seelie have ventured into other continents and started new civilizations. These travelers see themselves as pilgrims or missionaries, bringing to other lands the pure concepts that define their relationship with the woods. Their home is always Eyldiian, the continent they feel is a daughter to Laedelious.

**Talo'Seelie**- This general term refers to a bunch of clans that slowly separated from the Faer'Seelie over time. These elves hold many of their old forest traditions, but they also refuse to be hampered by those same customs. The original tribes migrated to other lands many centuries before the Godswars. Although in most cases they clung to forest habitations, many mixed in with other humanoid societies. Today, clans of these elves inhabit human, domid (halfling) and gnome settlements. Even their homes in the woods reflect certain changes adapted from new lands and ideas. While they still have druids who focus on natura magic, they also have intellectual members that study arcana and the harmonic web. These clans recognize and attempt to preserve many old traditions, yet they feel they have advanced more of their understandings and growth through new concepts.

**Duar'Seelie**- The elf clan that was long ago exiled to underground caverns has developed into a race of pale, gray-skinned hunters that have an eternal hatred for their surface cousins. In some ways they maintain the old customs, nurturing underground plant life and building their societies around those deep plants and fungus. They have also embraced the rock and the metal ores within, making them masters of smithing. Although they also have druids who delve into natura, the focus of their craft has shifted to include mystics whose elemental masteries alter the rocks around them. In some ways, their society is more dwarf-like than elf.

**Kruku'Seelie**- This is a marine race of elves who at some point in ages past breached the division between land and sea. They are considered to be far removed from their land-bound relatives, though not shunned as the Duar'Seelie. Their homes are along shallow water bodies, and they prefer salt water. Their skin has adopted a whitish-blue pallor, which does include some fin-like appendages. They are tightly bound with nature like their other cousins. They make homes in coral reefs and large kelp beds. The bones of dead sea animals, some enormous, have also given shape to their dwellings. They may walk uneasily on land for some time, but the water is their natural habitat.

**Agora'Seelie**- This term does not apply to a collective tribe of elves. The definition of this term reflects an individual break with "Seelie" ancestry. It applies to those born from a union that includes only one elf parent, thus they are commonly referred to as half-elves. Regardless of the race of their second parent, the half-elf is secluded into this classification by other elves. At best, it is a means of segregating those who stand out from the rest of elven culture; at worst, it is often used in racist or derogatory connotations. The short version of the name, "agora", is an insult among elf kind. Needless to say, Agora'Seelie do not have a centralized culture. They may try to fit in with their elven homes, or take refuge in the society of their other parent, or they may take isolation from both.


**Appendix B – Deities Commonly Worshipped in Dhea Loral**

This is not a complete list of all the beings that hold governance over the world of Dhea Loral. It is a glance at some of the major powers that exert their influence over the land, people and natural events. The gods make possible all the little things that keep the world from falling into disharmony. They each have agendas carried out by worshippers residing in the world, for the gods themselves are forbidden to tread the realms as they once did. It should be noted that many gods exist under different names across various cultures and languages.

**Abriana** – Goddess of Love and Healing. She is the most loving goddess and a supporter of all that is good and wholesome in the world. She helps instill feelings in mortals of brotherly love, marital commitment, and care of the people. Many of her followers are pacifists and healers. There are others who do take up the call of arms, but only to fight for what they love and protect. Even those that become paladins are restricted from using weapons or incurring fighting on the first day of each month, as these days are sacred to Abriana.

**Boyal** – God of Justice. It is said when the Goddess of Death collects the souls of agnostics, unbelievers, and those who turned traitor to their god, she must bring them before Boyal for sentencing. Once that is done, she is only too happy to carry out the sentence or deliver the wayward soul to its fate. The clerics of this faith often find themselves on city councils, in courtrooms, or even libraries of official records. Boyal proclaims order as a paramount quality of civilization. The concept of law and rights, and how they apply to different people, is carefully studied. Many clerics go on pilgrimages to explore how the cultures of other lands express their laws.

**The Codex** – Book on the Philosophy of Good. Not a god by itself, it nevertheless has inspired a large following. This way of life is based on a literary work that champions a strong belief in the morals and principles that are known as "good". The original Codex was brought into existence with the help of several deities devoted to good causes, and it took a life of its own. People who devote themselves to this following are able to tap into clerical miracles just as if they were praying to a genuine god. There are many that serve to fulfill the moral requirements set forth in the book.

**Daerkfyre** – Dwarven god of Strength, Valor and Courage. Worshipped as one of the dwarven "battle gods", this deity favors strong warriors. Daerkfyre is often referred to with the extension "the Valorous". Often worshippers of this god are as strong and stubborn in the mind as they are with their muscles. Physical strength is a domain honored by dwarven miners and certain craftsmen. Warriors often pray to this god before battle. Weapons blessed by his clerics are exceptionally strong and durable.

**Dalios** – God of War, as well as the humans' God of Strength and Courage. This deity can be wildly unpredictable. At times he sets forth destruction and strife, though sometimes for the benefit of oppressed people. Regardless, this god is a major influence on events that shape the course of the world. His clerics are often eager to go into battle on either side of the lines, and sometimes they do meet across opposing armies. To these clerics, life is met by facing trouble in a straightforward type of manner. The clergy often spends their short lives seeking out glory amidst fighting for a cause. Dalios is believed to look over the world from a huge feasting hall, toasting those who struggle and fight for their beliefs.

**Dawn** – Goddess of Life and Rebirth. Closely related to Abriana, this goddess shares some of the same ideals. However, this deity views life as chaotic, with a bit of mystery. She creates and shapes new life, from babies to new species. Sometimes the new species can be deadly, but that is only to balance out and strengthen other forms of life. This goddess has a special abhorrence of the undead, and her clerics fight to rid the world of their existence. Due to her zeal for all kinds of life, many of her worshippers include people who feel more at home in nature than in civilized areas built upon stone.

**DeLaris** – Goddess of Death. Death can never be anything but frightening. She resides in one of the many Lower Worlds, but travels between them often and freely to carry out her tasks. Her most ardent followers in life may pass into the afterworld to become *Karet-Atriul*, otherwise known as Death Angels. These souls become harbingers and servants of her will, assisting the goddess with the many aspects of her position. She ferries the dead across the other worlds and homes of the gods. Those souls who were unfaithful, traitorous to a god, and untrue in their worship may find an eternity of torture or simply a boring, never-ending imprisonment. Some of her most powerful clerics can raise the dead back to life, but only to prove her power over death. Her clerics are not very strong with social ties, for they serve as a constant reminder to others of the dark fates that might befall them in the next world.

**Foyul** – God of Balance. Foyul works on the principal that too much influence by one side or force tends to imbalance the world. He walks a middle line between anarchy and order, good and evil. His followers come from all walks of life, all serving to sway the balance in their own way when needed. Foyul has few friends among the gods or men, as he tends to fight for all sides in order to not let any single force hold too much sway. His clerics may be evil or good, and may act for any number of good or bad intentions, striving to maintain the balance of the world.

**Ganden** – God of Honor, Duty, Service. This god has followers in many races. Those that feel fulfilled by a calling of decency to their fellow man and sacrifice for the sake of others fit into his followers. Those who break promises, or serve only themselves, fall out of favor to this deity. Ganden serves the other gods in the same way, carrying out honorable edicts and being of service to those that require aid. Often symbols of this god can be found with militias, honor guards, healers, and others who perform even menial services to others.

**Juliustan** – God of Storms and Cataclysms. Many races fear the name of this god, without a full understanding of his focus. On one hand, he strives to balance the natural forces of the world. This can only be done by allowing some of the pressure of the forces of nature to vent their wrath on occasion. He may hold back one storm, while allowing another to rage unchecked. On his other side, he also seeks to ease the suffering of the world's people through such terrible events. This aspect is apparent in his clerics. His followers bring relief to those who have been displaced by storms or cataclysms, and assist in rebuilding. People do not fully understand and tend to fear his name. Many blame him for catastrophes in the first place, and fear that it is somehow anger or wrath. His clerics believe the world would suffer worse destruction than the Godswars if Juliustan relaxed his control.

**Kelor** – God of Luck. Although the other gods maintain that followers must have faith, this god prefers blind chance more openly. He champions games of chance, gambling, and random fate. This god tilts the tables in the direction he prefers, so one never knows how chance will turn up. This god rivals Dalios in unexpectedly bringing down great warriors. Many adventurers worship him, or at least pray for his blessing. Clerics of this god often throw themselves at adventure, or raise funds for the church in gambling houses. This god excels in finding small ways to thwart big plans.

**Krakus** – God of the Sea. The water is home to many creatures, and the oceans and seas have their own unique biology. This god provides a home for some, and can bring down wrath on others with the power of water currents. Sailors pay homage to this god in return for passage over his domain. In time, Krakus can reshape the land with his currents, or smash cities in great waves, (and would do so more often, if not for the interventions of Juliustan). The influence of his domain resulted in several of his churches being built to float out on the water. His clerics have much influence over the element of water and some can walk over its surface.

**Laedelious** – Elven Goddess of Forests and Wildlands. Commonly referred to as the "Treemother", or "Lady of the Green", this goddess has worked through the elves to broaden the protection of nature. Due to her guidance, many elves build their cities within the trees and current topography, rather than cut down the woods. Many elves enjoy a certain harmony with the woodland creatures through their history with Laedelious. Though the race of man shapes the land around his needs, elves have learned to shape their civilizations and homes around the needs of nature. Although this goddess has many cleric followers, there are also a number of mystics that work in her name.

**Mothrok** – Goddess of Earth and Stone. Born of the element of earth, this goddess has a strong connection to earth and stone. She believes in the superiority of everlasting stone, and the plant life that flourishes from the ground. She sees animal life as a type of vermin that infests the planet on which Dhea Loral can be found. Given her perspective, one would think that she would have few followers. In actuality, Mothrok has many worshippers among the underground-dwelling races, and others that work with the land. Even goodly farmers spare prayers to her out of fear for their crops. As part of her control over the land, she has been known to bring forth the corpses buried within the ground and use them as undead abominations.

**Nandorrin** – God of Fire. Worshipped mostly by dwarven smiths, this god is also often seen as a smith. Whenever tales are heard of volcanoes running with lava, it is believed to be Nandorrin reforming part of the world. Many candle makers use his image or symbol on their work. Many wizards praise him for their destructive fire-based arcana. His clerics perform a lot of ceremonies around fire, and to an extent they can shape fire as well.

**Noyugon** – God of Knowledge and Learning. Often known as the "Lorekeeper", this god strives to preserve histories and knowledge, and is said to be a recorder of deeds for the gods themselves. He promotes academies and centers of learning. Needless to say, he does not have many followers outside of educated cultures.

**Scriptum Verash** – A Book on the Philosophies of Evil. Made by several dark gods, and by Foyul for the sake of balance, this tome is the exact opposite of The Codex. It details greed and lust, power and glory, and encourages the strong and cunning to take what they will. It is in every way a document of "evil", yet at the same time it also has a life of its own. These clerics practice in secret, with no room for honor or compassion. In the past they have lead armies filled with hate against enemies for no more reason than the cleric's own selfish needs.

**Taekbol** – God of Underworld. This dwarvish and gnomish god favors those who dwell under the ground, away from the light of the sun. This god also spreads gems and metals under the surface of the world, sometimes in competition with Mothrok's stone empire. Some human miners even claim worship to him.

**Westrealei** – Elven Goddess of Wind and Air. This goddess communicates with her followers by means of various flying creatures. Her own image is painted in the shape of a pegasus, whose head and neck is replaced by the upper half of a beautiful elven female. This elven deity is of the sky, and a force of nature. Elven arrows need to ride her winds to strike true to their targets. In this respect, a windy day is said to be a bad omen for going into battle, as the archers will have a harder time hitting their targets.

**Yestreal** – God of the Sun and Weather. This nature deity, worshipped by many who till the soil, exerts his influence on harvests and crops. Many times, this puts him in direct competition with Mothrok for the success of farmers, but the two gods were once allied during the Godswars. The sunflower is often used as his symbol. His followers often come from agricultural regions, and are generally good at farming. Clerics of this god never condone weddings on rainy days, as they feel their god shuns the marriage. Elves also have numerous followers to this nature god.

**Yurtash** – God of Spirits. It is hard to define what spirits are to the common man, due to superstitions and drunken fireside chats. In short, spirits are creatures neither living nor dead that perform specific tasks in the world. They are the after images of once-living creatures. While the soul may depart to another world, a part of the spirit may remain in the world, trapped, only to be harnessed by magical means. Yurtash seems to store and nurture these lost energies of forgotten souls until they have a use in the world again. Mystics, greenmen and some arcane casters call upon the spirits in spells. Many of this god's clerics share the powers of mystics over these spirits.

### Appendix C – The Calendar of Dhea Loral

The calendar of Dhea Loral is four hundred days long. That reflects the time it takes for one year to pass for the planet of Epos Goth. The calendar is divided into five seasons, with two months in each season, as follows...

Planting season: Primus, then Florum
Summer season: Jherad, then Doyal
Harvest season: Othgar, then Novak
Waning season: Tiquierum, then Norgrad
Winter season: Vientula, then Icethule

Each month is forty days long. Each week is ten days. The civilized societies of the land do tend to observe two-day weekends, however much work is still done on these days. The value of a weekend in Dhea Loral is seen more as a time for socializing and public events, but even on these days many merchants are still doing business. There is also a midweek day by which many government offices in the civilized lands take half of the day off. The evening on these days is usually reserved for balls, feasts, religious observations, or other relaxing endeavors. Note that many people do not observe such luxuries, as the struggle to work and survive has bred a strong work ethic into a number of cultures.

The New Season Day, which commemorates the start of the New Year, is held at the traditional end of winter. Usually, it begins to snow in most of the lands by mid to late Norgrad, and by the first of Primus the snow is melting away.

The calendar is measured by an important date in Dhea Loral history. In a time when war was sweeping the lands, several immortals and demigods were taking sides. Several were trying to attain more power, while some defended the common man. Several gods lent their powers to affect the outcome as well. It was a dark time in the world when great civilizations fell and new governments arose. During the waning season of 1 BC, (Before Covenant), the fury of the demigods and the use and destruction of several artifacts led to the destruction of the last great empires. The winter season that followed was a struggle for survival for many races. Even those living in the vast cave and underground systems of the world, while not affected by the surface winter, were weak and foraging for meager foods. The major powers, those gods who exerted the most influence in the world, stepped in and forced an end to the conflict. On the first of Primus, in the year now called 1 AC, (After Covenant), the gods and demigods signed a pact regarding the involvement of the deities in the future of the world. Although the gods were capable of controlling the world much more directly, restrictions were placed and honored by all. In this way they voluntarily gave up several privileges, and bound their oaths. Even the most chaotic of gods can never break the Covenant.

This was more or less the start of the churches and clerics, at least in their modern-day incarnation. Clerics are the necessary vessels through which the gods move the races, although the gods retain the necessary powers over nature and magic to make the world run smoothly and stay in balance.

**About the Author…**


Douglas was born on Nov 28th, 1971. He got the chance to live in many different places while growing up, courtesy of the assignments the US Army offered to his father. Too quiet and too shy for too long, there were always dreams of other worlds and places…and the desire to write about them. He got into fantasy role-playing games in his mid-teens. To this day he has friends whom he meets in tabletop role-playing games, as well as online adventures. Many of his characters evolved in games, and each developed their own personality.

Having to rely on self-publishing for his first novel, Douglas was surprised at the amount of good reviews and publicity it has received. Since going back to revise the trilogy, and re-release his titles under a new publisher, he has been surprised again at the amount they have sold. *Trials of Faith* continues the story set into motion in *Inheritance of a Sword and a Path*. The work continues on several other stories set in the world of Dhea Loral.

Douglas lives with his wife and two sons in Minnesota. He works in health care, serving people's needs in medical imaging. When most people see him, he is wearing scrubs.


Learn more about the author and the Realm of Dhea Loral at…

**Website – DheaLoral.com**
**Facebook – Dhea Loral**
**Twitter - @ThaminDheaLoral**

Want to experience more of the world of Dhea Loral? Explore the dwarf homelands through the eyes of revolutionary Duli! *The Widow Brigade* opened on Amazon with five critiques praising the story, and each giving it a perfect 5 stars! This story features strong women, in a fantasy setting, rebelling against the traditions of a male-dominated society.

"I felt the plot was well developed, well-paced, and the motivations of the characters really drew me in, caring about what happened as the plot progressed. I felt the main character was not your typical shiny hero, or dastardly anti-hero. She just felt real. I highly recommend this book..." - Tom H

"This book is very well written and as always with his stories, the battle scenes are intense, with details that pull you in and fully immerse yourself in the story. The characters are well developed and allow you to enjoy loving and hating them." – Lockhart

Strangers thrown together, forced into service on a common quest, form a bond of camaraderie. Each seeks to find their focus in the world, amidst their private mysteries.

The half-orc savage, who takes pride in a company he no longer serves. The dusk-skinned archer, carrying a bow from her forgotten homeland. The dwarf who studies the past so he can create a future. The knight who pays fealty to no lord. The elf sorceress seeking knowledge, but what specific question is she trying to answer?

They will band together, seeking separate goals. How far will pilgrims travel to discover who they are?

-Pilgrims with Blades: Pressed into Service- (released Oct 2017)

Facing a crisis and looking for any excuse to strike in force against the orcs occupying the hills to their south, the city-state Kashmer conscripts privateers and adventurers into war. A band of strangers must learn to support and adapt to each other as a daring plan separates them from the main force in hostile territory. Each possess their own mystery, but without cooperation and trust, they will be doomed to failure.

Pressed into Service is the introduction to the bold Pilgrims with Blades series.

The Boxer series features non-chronological adventures in an alternate Earth history. It's a Steampunk Wild-West flavor mixed with the old 1930s adventure serials that inspired Indiana Jones. This short novella, (19,000 words), will take you into a new reality.

Brian "Boxer" DuWold is feeling outdated in a booming industrial age of electricity, magnetism, and stiff competition between steam and fossil fuel engines. The tough conman makes a living off gamblers, using prize-fighting rings or shooting matches. Few realize his livelihood supports his blind sister; unfortunately, the suits of the United Republic Agency use this leverage to their advantage.

The United Republic has seen a lot of technological advances since defeating the southern rebels in its Civil War years ago. Now, the territory of Texico has won its independence from Meztica, and is considering joining the UR. One hitch: the mad scientist who helped win the revolution for Texico is pursuing his own agenda, which includes a train full of chemical explosives steaming straight for the capital! The doctor is rumored to have zombie soldiers, steam war machines, and high-tech weapons at his disposal.

Boxer barely has time to grab his brass knuckles and six-shooter before URA men send him on a mission that one team has already failed. He's loaded into the most advanced biplane of his time and tasked to stop the train. It's time to buckle in for a wild ride of an adventure.

Apprentice Storm Mage begins a new series of YA fantasy in the world of Dhea Loral. Thomena wishes to cast fire spells, but the guild must test her responsibility first. Events in this book precede the Earthrin Stones trilogy.

Thirteen-year-old Thomena is proving to be a talented storm-mage, though she doesn't like the title. Her mastery of wind and water elements allow her to pursue hobbies like foot-tall snowflakes and snowball fights in the oppressive summer heat. Yet, she yearns to study the element of fire at an age younger than guild rules allow.

Her master decides to test her responsibility alongside the tough, vigile fire-fighters of Orlaun. Thomena is tasked to protect these heroes from a safe distance, though they are an intimidating crowd for a young girl to impress.

But no one planned for her to get as close to the fire as events force. No one expected her to be a nearby witness as tragedy strikes. No one thought she would discover evidence that another mage is starting the fires.

Can a coming-of-age girl find the resolve and magical talent to seek justice when facing pressure from every direction to quit?

Book 1 of the Storm-Mage Chronicles opens up a new chapter in the fantasy world of Dhea Loral.

Dhea Loral